# Finding Love

## THE COMPLETE COLLECTION

USA TODAY BESTSELLING AUTHOR
# NIKKI ASH

*You don't find love...*
*It finds you.*

*Finding Love series (My Kind of Love, My Kind of Beautiful, My Kind of Perfect)*

Copyright © 2020 Nikki Ash

Cover design and book formatting by Juliana Cabrera, Jersey Girl Design

Photos by Sara Eirew Photography

Edited by Emily A. Lawrence

All Rights Reserved. This book contains material protected under International and Federal Copyright Laws and Treaties. Any unauthorized reprint or use of this material is prohibited. No part of this book may be reproduced or transmitted in any form or by any means, electronic or mechanical, including photocopying, recording, or by an information and retrieval system without express written permission from the Author/Publisher.

This is a work of fiction. Names, characters, places, and incidents either are the product of the author's imagination or are used fictitiously, and any resemblance to actual persons, living or dead, business establishments, events, or locales is entirely coincidental.

# MY KIND OF *Love*

*A Finding Love Novel*

# NIKKI ASH

*To Michelle, for seeing something in Ryan I didn't even see myself.*

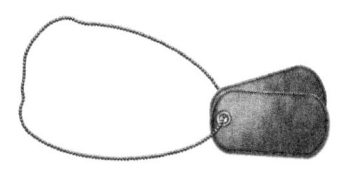

# PROLOGUE

## RYAN

"So, that's it? You're just going to pack up and leave without saying a word?"

I stuff the last of my toiletries into my duffel bag and pull the strings to close it. After taking a calming breath, I set the bag on the ground and give my wife my full attention. "I don't know what you want me to say."

Her brown eyes are filled with tears and her eyes are puffy from crying. I hate that my leaving is hurting her, but it's out of my hands. Being in the military means leaving. She knew this when we married six years ago. When I left on my first deployment fresh out of high school. She knew it the following four times I was deployed after that.

"I guess I don't want you to say anything." Laura sighs, her eyes closing in hurt and frustration. "I want you to stay... I want you to *want* to stay." She's standing in the middle of my bedroom in her aqua-colored work scrubs, her hair pulled back in a ponytail. She's a beautiful, smart, educated woman, and I wish I could feel something more for her than friendship, but I don't. I wish I could give her what she wants, say what she needs me to say, but I've never lied to her, and I'm not about to start now.

When I don't say anything, she opens her eyes and several

tears fall. "I can't do this anymore," she whispers. "I love you so much, Ryan, but you'll never love me back."

"You know I love you," I argue, but the conviction in my voice isn't there because she isn't referring to *that* kind of love. The love I felt for her in high school when I asked her to marry me. We were eighteen and about to graduate. Foster care fucked her over and she was on her own, on the streets. She was getting mixed up with the wrong crowd, and I couldn't let it happen. She was my best friend—still is my best friend—and I refused to let circumstance destroy her. So, I asked her to marry me. Being my wife meant she would be taken care of. She would have a roof over her head, food in her belly, health insurance. She would be able to go to school and be safe.

She said yes, and after signing a prenup—something my dad insisted on—we said our I do's. Three months later, I shipped out on my first deployment.

"I'll always be grateful for what you did for me," she says, taking my hands in hers. "I don't even want to imagine where I would be if you hadn't saved me." She presses a soft kiss to the corner of my mouth, and I will myself to feel something, *anything* for my wife that amounts to more than friendship. But there's nothing more.

"It's because of you I was able to get my degree, be able to provide for myself," she says, her lips upturning into a sad smile.

"You got more than a degree," I joke. "You're a fucking doctor." I'm so damn proud of this woman. She came from a home similar to the one I was born into—drug addicts and neglect—but unlike me, who had Bentley and Kayla there to adopt me, before I was even old enough to understand how shitty life could be, she had no one—except me.

Laura laughs, a single tear sliding down her cheek. "A nurse practitioner," she corrects with an eye roll.

"Same shit." I shrug, wiping the tear from her face. I hate to see her cry. All I want is for her to be happy.

"I thought over time you would love me the way I love you," she says, steering the conversation back on track. "I thought you would come home from being away and miss me and want me." She swallows thickly. "But you never did. You're away more than you're home."

"Tell me how to fix it," I offer. I never set out to be a shitty husband. My intentions were honorable, but I was young and didn't know what I was getting myself into. My dad warned me not to marry her. He said he would allow me to use some of the money from my trust fund to set her up. But throwing money at her felt ungenuine. Marrying her meant giving her a family, only in the end, I guess I never really gave her that either.

"That's just it," she says. "You can't fix it. You didn't do anything wrong. You can't make yourself feel a certain way. And I'm starting to think the reason why you keep volunteering to go on these tours is to stay away from me."

I open my mouth to argue, but she shakes her head. "Ryan, five tours in six years isn't normal. I looked it up. You're choosing to go. Most husbands don't want to go, but you can't wait to."

She's right, but it's not because of her. It's all I know. It's what makes sense to me. Growing up—once I was adopted by my parents—I was raised in a loving household. My parents are married and in love, and are damn good parents. My older sisters, Faith and Chloe, never treated me like the annoying little brother. I went to the best schools and was given everything I could ever want.

But I never felt like I truly fit in. Something deep inside me craved something more. I can't explain it. It was like my body and mind were at war with each other, both on the losing side. I wondered if maybe it was genetic, like my bio parents were broken, so I was too. So, I did the only thing I could think of—I ran—used the military as a way to escape and not have to deal with reality. While serving, I took classes and received my engineering degree. I worked my way up the ranks, proved myself, and eventually became a sergeant in the Special Forces. When I'm at work, I feel like everything just clicks, like I have a purpose.

"When I get back, we can talk," I tell her, unsure what else to say. I have to be at the base in less than twenty minutes. I have men who depend on and need me.

"When you get back, I won't be here." She doesn't say the words with malice, but as a matter-of-fact. We're married, but everything we have is technically mine, and the prenup protects me completely. The cars, the house, the money—everything is mine. She never asked to be on anything, and I always just handled it all.

"You can have the house. It's paid off. I'll have the deed transferred to you." It's only right. She's lived here since we got married and moved to Carson City. She's decorated and furnished it the way she likes, and it's only five minutes from the hospital she works at. "And your car too, of course. You can have that."

She nods once, her lips forming a flat line. "And what about our marriage? I would like to find someone..." she says slowly. "Someone who wants the same things as me. I want to start a family. And I would never cheat on you." I know she wouldn't. Laura is as loyal as they come. She's the perfect wife, and I fucking suck for not being able to love her like she deserves.

"I'll have someone draw up the papers for us to sign." The last thing I want is for her to be stuck with me for another year while I'm gone. She deserves everything life has to offer, and I hate that I can't be the one to give it all to her.

She nods again and then wraps her arms around my neck, hugging me tight. "One day you're going to fall in love and you won't want to run away," she whispers into my ear. "You'll want to be with the woman you love. But first, you have to stop running so you can meet her."

She backs up slightly and grants me a soft smile, then kisses my cheek. "Be safe, Ryan."

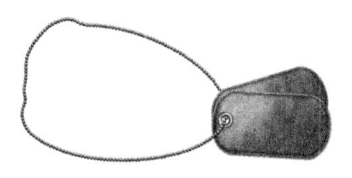

# CHAPTER ONE

## MICAELA

"I can't believe you're graduating tomorrow." Lexi, my best friend and pseudo cousin, takes a hit off the joint she brought with her as a graduation gift and passes it to me.

I take a small hit, since I'm not usually one to get high, and nod. "This will be you next year." I pass the joint to Georgia, my other pseudo cousin and best friend. "Both of you, right?"

"Yep," Lexi says, speaking for her younger sister like she often does. "Georgia took extra classes and we'll be walking across the stage together. We'll both be free from educational hell in twelve months."

Without taking a hit, Georgia passes the joint to Lexi. "I'd hardly call it hell. We go to a private school that costs more a year than most pay for their house." She rolls her eyes playfully. "Our lunch is catered and includes items like sushi and Thai, and we have a Starbucks... an actual Starbucks in the quad."

I laugh at that, but don't argue. She's not wrong. Lexi and Georgia live in Los Angeles and attend one of the most prestigious private schools on the West Coast. Similar to the one I attend here in Las Vegas... well, *did* attend. As of tomorrow at ten o'clock I will officially be a high school graduate. And come August I'll be a freshman at the University of Las Vegas.

"Semantics." Lexi takes another hit. "I can't wait to be done with high school. It's such a waste. I don't need a diploma to do what I want to do."

"You need one to go to college," Georgia points out.

Lexi rolls her eyes. "Maybe I won't go." She shrugs, making Georgia and me laugh. We all know Lexi is all talk. She's a daddy's girl through and through, and Tristan Scott has made it clear a college education is important, which means Lexi Scott will be getting one, whether she likes it or not.

"Go where?" a male voice booms, making us shriek in shock. Lexi tosses the joint off the balcony, and I jump to my feet to make sure my parents aren't down there. When I see the coast is clear, I spin around and fly into Ian's strong arms.

"I can't believe you're here!" I wrap my arms around his neck and he lifts me up, twirling us around. The fresh scent of his cologne has me sighing in contentment. I haven't seen him in person in over five months, since Christmas. Sure, we video chat and message, but nothing is like being in his arms.

I pepper kisses all over his face while he walks us into my room. He sits on my bed, leaning against the headboard, with me straddling his lap. Lexi and Georgia follow us in, but don't sit, instead heading straight for the door.

"You guys don't have to leave on my account," Ian says, his brown eyes never leaving mine.

"Yes, they do," I tell him, making them laugh. My time with Ian is limited, and I can see Lexi and Georgia any time I want.

"Yes, we do," they agree.

"We'll see you tomorrow at the graduation," Lexi adds.

The second they're out of the room and the door is shut, my lips connect with his and butterflies tickle my belly.

"I've missed you," he says once we separate.

"I didn't think you'd be able to make it."

"I made it."

"I can see that." I kiss him again.

Ian pulls me off his lap and moves us down the bed so we're lying on our sides and facing each other. "I couldn't miss your big day." He moves a wayward strand of hair out of my face and tucks it behind my ear. "I put in for it months ago, but I wanted to surprise you."

"I'm surprised."

"Good." He pulls me toward him and kisses my cheek.

"I can't believe you're really here," I say, shocked and excited that Ian was actually able to make it to my graduation. "How long are you here for?"

"I have to be back Sunday night."

Ian was one year ahead of me. We met my freshman year in Algebra II. We hit it off immediately and he asked me out. I knew the first time we kissed, Ian was the one, and four years later, we're still going strong, despite the distance between us. When Ian graduated last year, he signed up to become a Navy SEAL. It's a grueling program that can run anywhere from a year and a half to two years. Most don't even make it through, but he's already made it through boot camp, BUD/S (Basic Underwater Demolition SEALS training), and is in the final stage—SQT (SEAL Qualification Training). If he makes it through SQT, he'll officially be a Navy SEAL, and shortly after, he'll leave for his first deployment. Ian has wanted to become a SEAL his entire life. His father and grandfather were both Navy SEALs.

"Are you staying with your parents?" I ask, running my fingers along his shaved head. Every time I'm around him, I find myself having to touch him in some way, knowing when he leaves it'll be months before I get to touch him again.

"Yeah, Mom asked if you want to come over tonight for dinner since we'll be here tomorrow night for your graduation party."

"Of course." I kiss his cheek then trail more kisses along his jawline and neck. "But right now, I need you inside of me." I reach for the button of his jeans, but he grabs my hand and stops me.

"Your dad is right downstairs."

"So, we've snuck it plenty of times, and in case you forgot, I'm eighteen years old." I roll him onto his back, and when I straddle his hips, something hard pushes against my leg. "Are you happy to see me?" I joke, getting off to see what it is.

Ian laughs and sits up. "I am, but that's not what you felt." He reaches into his pocket and pulls out a small red box.

"Is that... what I think it is?" My heart picks up speed at the thought of Ian proposing.

"Maybe." He smirks playfully. "First, tell me again about our five-year plan."

I want to snatch the box out of his hand and open it, but

instead go along with his little game. "Fine." I huff, making him laugh. "Our five-year plan ends with us married. The end."

Ian chuckles. "Nope, tell me all about it."

"You already know it," I whine. "Let me see what's in the box."

"Once you explain the plan."

I cross my arms over my chest and pout, but he just smiles. "You graduate from high school and spend the next couple years becoming a Navy SEAL. During that time, I finish my senior year of high school and start college at the University of Las Vegas. Once you become a SEAL and are assigned to one of the locations, we'll get engaged and I'll transfer to the college near the base so we can live together. We're hoping it will be in San Diego so I can apply for the internship with Scripps, so I can study marine biology while I finish up my degree. Once I've graduated we'll get married."

Ian's lips, which were curled in a wide grin, turn down. "There's just one problem with that plan."

"What?" I ask, the organ in my chest tightening. We've had this plan since before he graduated from high school. Ian knows how important my plans are to me. Whether it's making a plan for a project or a plan for my future, I need them. Without them, I feel like I'm spiraling out of control. "What's the problem?" I ask, my hands beginning to shake.

Ian opens the box, and nestled inside is a beautiful diamond ring. "The problem is that I don't want to wait until you move to San Diego to get married." He climbs off the bed and gets down on one knee. "Micaela Lizbeth Michaels, will you marry me?"

"But... what about our plan?" I ask stupidly.

Ian laughs. "We can write up a new one. Everything else can stay the same. The only change will be your marital status and last name." He winks, and my belly does a flip-flop.

"Yes!" I squeal. "Yes." I jump from the bed and into his arms, tackling him to the floor. "Yes, I will marry you."

---

"YOU'RE NOT GETTING MARRIED," my dad says. "You're too young. You had a five-year plan. What the hell happened to the five-year plan?" He looks at my mom with wide eyes. "She had a goddamn five-year plan."

"We tweaked it," I tell him calmly. "The plan is still the same, only we'll be married a little sooner. You and Mom got married when she was only a few years older than me." I glance from my dad to my mom, silently begging her to help me out here. She had me when she was only twenty-one, and shortly after, they got married. At least I'm doing things the right way.

"Marco," Mom says to my dad, and his shoulders slump. "We can't stop them from getting married if that's what they want to do."

"No, but I want you to be on board." Technically I don't need either of their permission to get married, but I want their blessing. Their approval means a lot to me. I'm one of the few kids who has a good relationship with my parents. My mom is my best friend, and I'm close with my dad.

"And you can't make it a long engagement?" Dad asks.

"We could," Ian says, "but I love your daughter and would like for her to be my wife. And with her being my wife, she'll be able to visit me on the base."

"And you're still going to stay here and go to college?" Dad confirms.

"Yes, Ian still has to go through SQT, and once he's a SEAL, he'll most likely be shipped out on his first deployment. I already have a year's worth of college credits, so I'll get my associate's and then transfer to a school near him to finish my bachelor's."

"Damn it, Micaela." My dad's gaze meets mine, unshed tears in his eyes. "I want to tell you that you're not thinking rationally, but you're the most responsible, well-thought person I know." He sighs, accepting my decision. "This weekend?"

"We don't know when he'll be able to come back here and we want both our families there."

"All right," Dad says. "If this is really what you want, then we'll support you." He puts his arm around my mom and pulls her into his side. "But no babies until you're thirty."

I roll my eyes and laugh. "Trust me, getting pregnant is *not* part of our five-year plan."

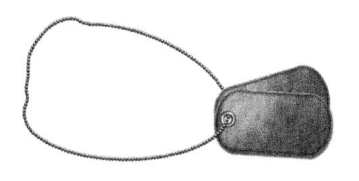

## CHAPTER TWO

### SIX MONTHS LATER

### MICAELA

"We have Chinese or Japanese." Ian holds up two takeout menus and shrugs a shoulder sheepishly.

"So, pretty much only the places that most likely don't celebrate Thanksgiving," I say with humor in my voice. "I guess we should've thought this through." When Ian found out last minute he would be off for Thanksgiving and not have to report back to training until noon on Friday, I booked a hotel room near his base and flew in last night. It would be too much for him to fly over for only one day, but there was no way I was going to let him spend the day alone. Not when I could be here with him.

"Yeah, where are our parents when we need them?" he jokes.

"Apparently at home with all the turkey and mashed potatoes." I laugh, plucking the Japanese menu from his hand. "Sushi or Pad Thai?"

Ian drops the other menu on the counter and pulls me into his arms. "I'm sorry, babe. I should've—"

"Seriously, it's just food." I let the menu go and circle my arms around his neck. "Japanese, Chinese, turkey, pizza... None of it matters but being here with you." I kiss him tenderly, happy to finally be in his arms. Training has been hard on him. It's demanding and taxing on him—physically and mentally—and when he isn't training, he's so exhausted, he spends his time off sleeping or working out. He says it's because the missions he'll have to go on will be life-threatening, and if the men aren't the best, they'll put each other, as well as others, at risk. I Googled Navy SEALs and was shocked to learn just how dangerous it is. Thankfully, Ian is in shape and has been preparing his entire life for this. If anyone can become a SEAL, it's him.

"It's our first Thanksgiving as husband and wife," he says, giving me a kiss. "It should be special. I didn't get off until late, and I completely forgot…"

"It doesn't matter what we eat as long as we're eating together," I insist. "We only have twenty-four hours together, so let's make the most of it. We'll have many more Thanksgivings to eat turkey."

"Okay," he agrees. "How about we order something to eat, and while we wait for the food to get here, I eat you?" He waggles his brows then nips on my chin playfully. "I'm starving."

"That sounds like the perfect way to spend our first Thanksgiving."

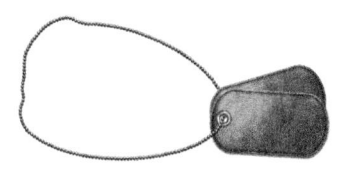

## CHAPTER THREE

### ONE MONTH LATER

### MICAELA

"Hey, babe." Ian's face comes onto the screen of my laptop. "How's it going?"

"Good." I run my finger down the screen, wishing I could actually touch his face, feel his lips. "Wish you were here."

"I wish I were there too." He sighs. "Only a few more months."

"It will fly by," I assure him.

"Getting some skiing in?"

"Of course." My family has a cabin in Breckenridge, a ski resort in Colorado. We come here every year for winter break. My parents have been coming here since they were kids. It's tradition. We spend Christmas and New Year's with everyone, skiing, snowboarding, and having a good time.

"Hopefully next year I'll be there to race you down the slopes."

"I can't wait. Until then, I'll just have to keep whooping Lexi's ass."

"I heard that!" Lexi yells from the other room. Even though our parents all have their own cabins, we always end up hanging out together at one of them. Apparently, this year, it's ours.

"Oh, I forgot to tell you," Ian says. "I spoke to Lieutenant

Gaspar, and he said if all goes well, I should have no problem getting stationed in Coronado."

Coronado is where the Navy SEAL base is, which is only about ten minutes from the University of San Diego, where I'm planning to apply to once I finish my associate's degree in May. It's also near Scripps, which is where I would love to snag an internship. Him being stationed in Coronado will mean both of our dreams will be able to come true.

"That's awesome. Any chance you're going to surprise me for Christmas like you did for my graduation?" I hate that we're spending our first Christmas as a married couple apart. I wanted to fly out to spend some time with him, like I did for Thanksgiving, but he insisted I spend the time with my family since he would be in and out on missions and didn't want me to be alone.

"I wish," he says with a frown. "We're actually heading out on a training mission. We'll be gone for at least a week."

"Where are you going?"

"Arizona." He grants me a boyish grin. "We're going to do some skydiving."

"Sounds like fun."

Someone yells something in the background and Ian yells back that he's coming.

"I gotta go, babe. I might be off the radar, so if I don't talk to you beforehand, I hope you have a good Christmas." He brings two fingers to his lips and then places them against the screen like he always does, and I do the same.

"You too. I love you."

"Love you more."

I wait for him to disconnect the call and then shut my laptop down.

"You ready to hit the slopes?" Lexi asks.

"Yep."

"Let's do this."

---

"MERRY CHRISTMAS!" My mom wraps me up in a hug and then moves on to hug my younger sister, Liza, and then my younger brother, Liam.

# CHAPTER THREE

"Merry Christmas, Mom," I say, sitting on the couch near the Christmas tree. Since my brother is still young enough to believe in Santa, we follow the tradition of Santa coming on Christmas Eve. Even though Liza and I no longer believe, it's still nice to continue the tradition.

"I have coffee for you." My dad hands me a steaming cup of coffee. "And hot chocolate for you." He hands Liza and Liam each a cup of hot chocolate, complete with marshmallows on top.

"I want to open this one first," Liam says, shaking one of the gifts.

"We need to wait for your grandparents to get here," Mom tells him.

My cell phone rings, and I jump up to grab it. It might be Ian. As I hit answer, the front door opens and in walk both sets of my grandparents.

"Hello," I say, not recognizing the number on the caller ID.

"Hello, may I please speak to Micaela Anderson?"

Everyone is saying Merry Christmas and giving each other hugs and kisses, so it's hard to hear. Stepping into the kitchen, where it's quieter, I say, "This is she. Who's this?" I can't help the smile that forms at the sound of Ian's—now my—last name.

"This is Lieutenant Gaspar." Everything that comes after his name is a blur. My brain is fuzzy, and my heart is struggling to beat. Ian was in an accident while skydiving and didn't make it. I knew it was dangerous for him to be a Navy SEAL, but I never imagined he would be at risk before *actually* becoming one. He's so young, and is in shape, I never gave the risks more than a quick thought. I never imagined in my worst nightmares something like this would happen to him.

At some point, my parents find me curled into a ball in the kitchen. My dad takes the phone and finishes the call, and my mom takes me into her arms, holding me close. It's hard to breathe, to see, to hear. My body isn't working right, everything is wrong.

Ian has been in an accident.

My husband has been killed.

I'll never be able to see him, touch him, feel him again.

All of our plans... our promises... our love.

In the blink of an eye, it's all over.

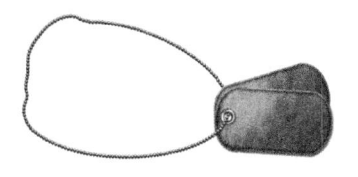

## CHAPTER FOUR

### FIFTEEN MONTHS LATER

### MICAELA

**Dear Ian,**

I STARE at the unfinished letter in my hands, a letter that's pointless to write because Ian is dead and will never get it. He'll never read any of the words I have to say. My dad suggested I write Ian. He said when he was younger and had a problem with drugs, while he was in rehab he wrote my mom every day. Even though he never sent her any of the letters, he found the act of writing to be therapeutic. He wrote eighty letters, and I can't even write one. I've been trying to write this same letter for almost fifteen months and I can't do it. **Dear Ian,** that's all I've managed to write. I have no idea what to do or say. My parents think I need to see a therapist, and I don't disagree, but I'm not ready. My mom thinks I need to go back to college, and, again, I don't disagree, but still, I'm not ready.

"Ewww," a feminine voice says. "It smells like depression in here."

I swing my head around to find Lexi and Georgia standing in my doorway. Lexi is smirking and Georgia is smiling softly. My heart constricts and tears fill my eyes. I can't remember the last time I saw them. Maybe their graduation... Wow, that was... ten months ago?

"What the hell are you waiting for? Get over here and give me a hug," Lexi demands. I stand, but stay frozen in place. If I hug her, I'm going to lose it. It's what I do now—lose it.

"Fine, then we'll come to you." They both cut across the room and wrap me up in a tight group hug. The tears that were clogging my throat fall. One after the next, they flow down my cheeks like a river escaping a dam.

"It's okay," Georgia says, rubbing her hand up and down my back.

"What are you guys doing here?" They—as well as my family and friends—tried to visit several times after Ian died, but I pushed everyone away over and over again, until they finally gave up and let me wallow in my grief alone.

"We've let you have your space, but now we're not going away." Lexi pulls back and places her hand on her hip. It's then I notice her hair.

"You dyed your hair?" I run my fingers through it. "Holy shit, it's blond... like blond-blond."

Lexi laughs and gives me a look of confusion. "I dyed it like a year ago..."

"And I didn't even notice..." Wow, I'm seriously a shitty friend.

"You've had a lot going on," Georgia says, trying to make excuses for me.

*Have I, though? Had a lot going on?* Since Ian died I haven't done anything but mourn his loss. I dropped out of school, stopped working at the recreational center my family helps run. I haven't worked out at the gym. The truth is I haven't had anything going on.

"It's pretty," I tell Lexi. "Suits that sexy surfer vibe you got going on."

Georgia laughs and Lexi rolls her eyes.

"So, what are you doing here?" I ask again.

"It's spring break," Lexi says. "We're heading to Cabo with our parents and thought we could drag you out of this house and get you into the sun for a few days. I'm dying to hit the waves."

I'm already shaking my head before she can finish, and both of them frown. "I appreciate it, but I'm just not ready for all that." The last time I was in Cabo was with Ian during spring break of his senior year.

"Ready for what?" Lexi argues. "Flying on a private plane to Cabo and spending five days lying out by the pool and beach?"

I get what she's saying, but I can't explain it. The idea of having fun there without him makes me sick to my stomach. Every memory we created would be replaced with ones without him. I can't do it. All I have left are my memories. I can't replace them...

"Ian and I went to Cabo together," I choke out.

Both girls frown and nod.

"You can't do this forever," Lexi says.

"But she can have more time," Georgia argues.

Time: Something I thought Ian and I had plenty of. Only it ran out long before it was supposed to, leaving me with only his memory.

"I'm sorry," I tell them. "I can't. I hate that you came all this way..."

"We flew in with our parents. Dad had some business with the gym before we go," Georgia says.

"Next time," I offer, my tone holding no conviction.

"Okay." Lexi sighs, pulling me in for a hug. "I love you."

"I love you too," I tell her, before I give Georgia a hug. "Have fun."

As they're walking out the door, my mom walks in. She gives them each a hug and tells them to have a good time. And then we're alone.

She doesn't say anything at first, just walks over to the balcony where I was sitting and picks up the worn-out paper. "How many of these have you written?" she asks, holding it up.

"None."

Her eyes widen briefly. "But I've seen you..."

"That's all I've written." I nod toward the paper, my throat filling back up with unshed emotion. I hate that all I do is cry. And when I finally get myself composed, I cry again.

"Oh, Micaela." Mom drops the letter on my bed and pulls me into her embrace. "I hate to see you like this, my sweet girl." My face falls against her chest and I let out a choked sob. "I miss you so much," she murmurs while I cry into her shirt. "It's time, sweetie. Time to move forward. You deserve to have a life."

"I don't know how to get past this," I admit. "My heart... It hurts, Mom." Tremors rack my body, and my mom holds me tighter. "I feel like I'm frozen in place to fifteen months ago, on Christmas morning when I found out Ian died. Everything I do or think reminds me of him, of us." I sniffle. "We had plans, and now..." I hiccup. "I don't know what I'm supposed to do. I feel so lost. He was supposed to be my forever."

Mom pulls back slightly and looks into my eyes. "You take it one day at a time. One step a day. It's all you can do. But you have to actually move forward."

"I don't know how."

"Only you can figure that out," she says. "You're the one grieving. But sitting in this room, avoiding life, isn't the answer." She kisses my forehead. "I'm heading to the rec center. Would you like to join me?" My parents help run a recreational center that was created to keep kids off the streets. My grandparents started it because my dad used to be one of those kids.

I shake my head. "I just..."

"I know." She nods, a frown marring her face. "You want to be alone." The way she says the words has my stomach churning. My grieving is not only affecting me, but is also affecting my family. Sure, they give me my space, but they also take turns checking on me every day. Even my aunts and uncles have started to join in the rotation.

My mom gives my arm a squeeze and then walks out. Taking the paper from the bed, I sit on the balcony and stare at it. My mom is right. Only I can move forward, and sitting here in this room day after day, trying to write a letter I can't write isn't helping. What's that saying? *The definition of insanity is doing the same thing over and over again but expecting different results.* I need to try something new. I can't keep living like this. It's breaking my parents' hearts.

But where would I go? Cabo is out of the question. I need to go somewhere I haven't been with Ian. A place I can focus on healing and moving forward. Maybe even make a new plan. My stomach knots. The only plan I want is one that includes Ian. Only that's never going to happen.

*Where can I go?*

And then an idea hits me. I know just the place.

After packing my stuff into a small suitcase, I grab a new piece of paper and write a note to my parents to let them know I had to get away. I need time to myself to move forward. I let them know not to worry, but I don't tell them where I'm going. If I do, they'll send someone to check on me, and right now I just need some time to heal. To figure out a way to move forward.

Since my car is relatively new—given to me by my parents a few years ago for my sixteenth birthday—I decide to make the drive. It's four hours to our beach house in Venice, California, but it will do me some good. The best kind of thinking happens in the car, with the windows rolled down and the music blasting. I stop once for a coffee and again at the grocery store to pick up some groceries, since the place will be empty.

My parents bought the beach house years ago, since they travel to LA often for UFC competitions, as well as to visit my aunt and uncle. Both my parents are retired UFC fighters and own a UFC training facility they took over from my grandpa called Cooper's Fight Club. Since we rarely come here, I've never been here with Ian.

I arrive close to nine o'clock at night. It's the first time I'll be here alone, but it's in a good neighborhood, on the water, and has an alarm system, so I know I'm safe. I park in the driveway and gather my stuff. As I'm walking to the front door, with my luggage in one hand and the bags of groceries in the other, my cell phone rings. I'm sure it's my parents. They're probably now seeing the note I left and wondering where I am. Balancing the bags and luggage, I insert the key into the door and twist it open. With my foot, I kick the door open, preparing to shut the alarm off. Only it doesn't go off.

Hmm... That's weird.

I step into the house and notice a light is on. My heart beats erratically in my chest. Is someone here? I haven't heard my parents mention renting the place out. But then again, I haven't really been paying attention. I'm about to step back outside and call my parents, when a massive shadow makes an appearance. I step backward, preparing to run, when the figure grows larger. A huge muscled man appears and, without thinking, I let out a cringe-worthy shriek. My bags fall from my hands, and my luggage tips over. I twirl around to flee, but the door has closed on its own and I run directly into it, my forehead smashing into the hard wood.

My brain goes fuzzy, stars lighting up behind my lids. I stumble back slightly, my head throbbing in pain. A strong hand grips my wrist, and it's then I remember... there's someone here.

"Let go of me!" I scream, yanking my hand away and preparing, again, to flee.

"Whoa, calm down," the masculine voice says.

Figuring it's best to know what the face of my attacker looks like, I swivel around, only to come face-to-face with Ryan Cruz.

"Ryan? What are you doing here?" I ask, confused as to why he's here, in my family's beach house. The last I heard he was in the military and stationed overseas.

"I'm on vacation," he says, his voice as strong as his grip, which is still holding on to my wrist.

"Here?" As I pull my wrist away, this time successfully releasing myself from his grasp, I take a moment to take him in. He's a good foot taller than my five-foot-two self, dressed in only a pair of camouflage sweatpants, which are hanging low on his hips. Without a shirt on, his entire body is on display. From his hard pecs that are covered in various tattoos, to his chiseled abs, all the way to the well-defined V that disappears into the front of his pants, the man screams sex and—

*What the hell am I thinking?* I shouldn't be thinking of him like that. For one, he's a friend of my family's, and two, Ian...My heart clenches behind my rib cage. He's dead and I'm ogling another man.

"Yes, here," he says, ripping me from my thoughts. He crosses his arms over his chest and I make it a point not to look at how ripped his forearms are. Only it's a huge mistake because when my gaze ascends up to his face, his mesmerizing blue eyes draw me in—like the color of the ocean on a beautiful, cloudless day.

Unable to look at him a second longer, I drop my eyes to the ground. They take in his bare feet. My God, his feet are huge. *I wonder if it's true what they say... big feet means...* Oh my Lord! I close my eyes. Nothing about Ryan is safe to look at. Not even his damn feet! Feet should be ugly, not a turn-on.

"Yes."

I glance back up at him. "Huh?"

"Yes." He tilts his head slightly and grants me a cocky smirk. "You asked if the saying is true... Big feet mean a big dick. Yes." He shrugs, the corners of his lips quirking up into a full-blown two-dimpled grin. "Well, at least in my case. I can't speak of every man with big feet."

Kill. Me. Now. I did not ask that out loud...

"Yes," he says again, with a laugh that somehow sounds masculine and melodic at the same time.

"What?" I say, embarrassed at the way my words are coming out all breathless, and mad at my body for behaving this way.

"You did ask it out loud."

"There has to be some mistake."

"About my dick being big, or you asking about it out loud?"

"About you being here!" I shriek, my face and neck heating up.

Ryan laughs harder. "I can assure you, I am not a squatter. I'm not only allowed to be here, but I was invited."

"By who?"

"Your dad."

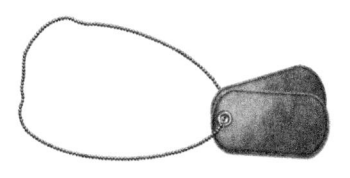

## CHAPTER FIVE

### TWELVE HOURS AGO

### RYAN

"Well, look who the cat dragged in." I'm not even ten feet inside Cooper's Fight Club when Marco, a family friend and part owner of the UFC gym, comes walking over. He grabs my hand and pulls me into a bro-hug. "How you doing?"

"Good." I pat him on his back before I step back.

"I heard you're in town for a couple months. Took you long enough to come by."

"I've been busy. Transferred to the base here and then left for training. I leave to Texas in a couple weeks for another training, and then we ship out to Afghanistan."

"Fuck, man, how many tours have you been on now?"

"This will be my seventh. Mom is pissed. She thought me transferring would mean I'm home for good. Love that woman to death, but she's driving me fucking nuts."

"That's what parents are supposed to do." Marco pats me on the shoulder. "Wanna get some sparring in? I have some time."

"Sure, let me drop my stuff."

After throwing my bag into a locker, I head back out to find Cooper—Marco's father-in-law—and my dad standing near the octagon, gossiping like girls.

"Dad, you following me?" I ask, walking up next to him.

He grins and shakes his head. "If I had to listen to your mom tell me one more time that we need to find you a house to ensure you'd come back, I was going to lose my shit."

The guys all laugh.

"Seriously, though, you made her year coming back home," Dad adds.

"Let's spar," Marco says, jumping in and saving me.

We enter the octagon, and since we aren't really fighting, the only gear we use is a head piece. We circle around for a minute or so and then Marco comes at me with a sideswipe, knocking me onto my ass.

He booms with laugher and I shake my head. "So, it's like that, huh?"

Still laughing, he extends his hand to help me up.

"You back for good?" he asks, bouncing on his toes with his hands up.

"I transferred, so yeah. Wasn't anything left for me in Carson City." I throw a punch to his face and he ducks.

"How have things been since the divorce?"

"Thought you were saving me from the gossiping chicks over there." I nod toward my dad and Cooper.

Marco laughs and throws a punch. It connects to my stomach lightly.

"The divorce?" he prompts.

"I'm all good."

"And how's Laura?"

"She's good, met a guy, started a family..." I come in with a roundhouse kick and it connects with his head. Since we're only fucking around and wearing gear, it doesn't hurt him, and he easily shakes it off.

"You're a good man," he says. "What you did for her was beyond generous."

"It is what it is." I shrug. "She deserves a good life. She didn't have the people I do." I look him in the eyes and he knows I'm not just referring to my parents. Marco is one of the few people I talk to besides my parents. We connected when I was younger. I don't remember it, but over the years he's always been there. Even when I was a teenager, I would come here to work out and we would talk. He's become like a second dad to me, a friend. And no matter how long I'm gone, when I return, he welcomes me with open arms.

"When are you going to start doing for you?" He throws an uppercut, and I block it, immediately coming back at him with a left hook. He bends and grabs my legs, throwing me onto my back. He pulls my arm back into an armbar and I tap out.

"Fuck." I laugh. "Your old ass still has it."

"Always." He grabs my hand and helps me up. "Now answer my question."

"There's nothing to do for me." I walk over to the side and grab a towel, wiping my face and neck.

Marco does the same. "You've spent your adult life doing for Laura and for your country. When are you going to do for *Ryan*?"

"What do you want me to do?" I put my hands on my hips, slowly breathing in and out.

Marco grabs two water bottles and throws one at me. I barely catch it before it hits the ground. "Whatever you want to do. When's the last time you went on a vacation?"

"I was at Breckenridge with my parents for Christmas." Marco and his family didn't go because his daughter Micaela wasn't feeling up to it after losing her husband last year, and they didn't want to leave her during the holidays.

"That wasn't for you. That was for your parents. All these deployments have you traveling, but you never actually do anything for yourself."

He's right, but I've never been good at sitting still. I get antsy and then I find myself needing to get up and do something.

"I'm leaving in a couple weeks. Maybe I'll do something when I get back."

"Hey, Ryan," my dad yells. "Your mom wants to know if you'll be home for dinner tonight."

I let out a groan and Marco laughs. "I need to find my own place. Staying with your parents should never be allowed after you've moved out."

"Agreed." He nods. "Did that shit years ago after I moved back home. My mom babied the shit out of me." He takes a long gulp of his water. "I have a beach house in Venice. Why don't you spend some time there? Some time for you. It's backed up to the Pacific Ocean. Private beach. You can go for a run. Eat on the pier. Go to a club. Pick up a woman. Get laid. Tristan has a gym only twenty minutes from there. Do something for you."

Well, shit, when he puts it like that...

"Ryan," my dad says, walking over. "She wants to know if you want lasagna or chicken marsala."

Marco gives me a small one-shoulder shrug.

"Tell her I won't be home for dinner. I'm heading out on an impromptu vacation."

Dad frowns. "You're leaving for your deployment soon."

"Not for a couple weeks. I'm going to the beach. I'll be back before I leave. Promise."

Marco hands me a key off his key ring. "Fridge needs food, garage is empty, so you can park your truck in there. Alarm code is two-five-four-two. Have fun."

I take the key from him. "Thanks."

After stopping at home to say goodbye to my mom, and assuring her I'll be back to spend time with her and the family before leaving, I pack a bag then take off to Venice.

Four hours later, I arrive and park my truck in the garage so the saltwater doesn't fuck with it. The house isn't huge, but it's nice as hell. Three bedrooms, two bathrooms, and like Marco said, it's literally backed up to the beach. You walk outside and the sand and water are right there.

The first thing I do is take a walk along the beach to the pier to get something to eat. I can't remember the last time I spent time by myself. When I'm deployed I'm in a room with a dozen other guys. At the base, someone is always around. When I lived with Laura and was home, she always wanted to spend time together. She tried so damn hard to make shit work, but it was like trying to fit a square peg into a circle. No matter how hard she tried, we just didn't fit the way she wanted us to.

When I moved back to Vegas, my parents offered to let me stay with them while I searched for a place. It's been a few months and it's definitely time, but since I'll be leaving in a couple weeks and will be gone for a year, I figured it would be best to wait until I get back. I will definitely be getting a place when I get back.

I find a seafood restaurant near the pier, order a beer and a mahi sandwich, and eat outside, watching the sunset. I can already feel myself getting antsy, needing something to do, but I

## CHAPTER FIVE

push it back. Marco was right. I need some time for myself. To just relax and think.

When the sun has completely gone down, I walk back to the house. I jump in my truck and grab some groceries, then spend the next couple hours on the back patio with a beer in my hand, watching the waves crash.

Around nine o'clock, I decide to call it a night. After throwing the empty beer bottle into the recycling bin, I shut the French doors and step inside. I'm almost to the bedroom when I hear a door open. My first instinct is to reach for my gun, but I quickly remember where I am and that my gun is in my truck. I'm in Venice, in some rich as fuck neighborhood.

I step into the foyer and find Micaela screeching in fear. She drops all the shit she has in her hands and then runs into the door. Her forehead must hit the wood hard because the loud bang rings out through the house. She sways from the hit, and I try to help steady her, but she pulls away.

When she finally stops freaking out, realizing it's only me, she does something I wasn't expecting or prepared for. She eye-fucks the hell out of me. Her brown hair is in a disarray, and her matching brown eyes are scanning my body. Her lips, plump and juicy, are being nibbled on by her perfectly straight white teeth. She's dressed casually in a white tank top and cut-off jean shorts. It's been quite a few years since I've seen her, and holy shit has she grown up.

She mumbles some shit about my feet and dick being big, and I crack up laughing. She's not only beautiful but fucking adorable as well.

When she realizes what she said out loud, her entire face turns a light shade of pink. Her eyes, the color of milk chocolate, meet mine, and her lips curl into a shy smile. And in that moment, something strange happens to me. My heart... it calms, like it actually beats a little slower. The racing in my head comes to a standstill, and my dick, it appreciates the view almost as much as I do.

"Kill. Me. Now. I did not ask that out loud..."

"Yes," I tell her with a laugh. I've never met anyone who actually says what they're thinking out loud without meaning to.

"What?" Her eyes go wide, and if it's possible, her cheeks get even pinker.

"You did ask it out loud."

"There has to be some mistake." She shakes her head, looking embarrassed and confused and so fucking cute.

"About my dick being big, or you asking about it out loud?" It's not like me to fuck with a woman like this, but I can't help myself.

Her eyes widen into saucers and her face turns crimson. "About you being here!"

I bark out a laugh at how worked up she is. "I can assure you I am not a squatter. I'm not only allowed to be here, but I was invited."

"By who?"

"Your dad."

Her mouth gapes open and then closed. "Oh." Her features cool as she looks around, her pouty mouth going flat into a frown. "I didn't know."

"It happened today. I got here earlier."

"I guess..." She glances down at her luggage and bags that are laid out all over the floor. "I guess I should go." She bends to pick up her luggage and I step forward. The sadness in her voice pulls at the strings in my heart. She lost her husband. I've heard she's having a rough go at things lately. She must've come here to get away.

"Wait." I gather her bags up for her. "It's your family's home. There are several rooms. I can leave in the morning."

She shakes her head. "You were invited. I... kind of ran away." She shrugs sheepishly.

"You're over eighteen, right?" There's no way I'm keeping her being here a secret from her parents if she's going to be plastered all over the news as missing.

"Yes." She laughs. It's soft and sweet and does shit to my insides. "I'm twenty. I left them a note letting them know I was leaving, but I didn't tell them where I was going. My mom told me I should get away, go somewhere to try to"—she swallows thickly—"deal with everything." Her eyes shut, and she takes a deep breath, calming herself before she reopens them. "Anyway, I just meant I left suddenly. I didn't actually run away."

So, she came here to try to finally deal with her husband's death. Marco mentioned he's been worried about her and not sure what to do about it. I should probably text him that she's here so he doesn't worry, but I don't want to go behind her back. She's over-age and it isn't my place to interfere.

"It's late. Neither of us should be driving back home at this time of night. We can stay here and figure it out tomorrow."

"Okay," she agrees.

We put away her groceries, which consist mostly of ice cream, cookies, and other sweets. She also has a gallon of milk and a bag of chips. The complete opposite to the meats and vegetables I picked up.

"I better answer that," she says when her phone rings. "My mom."

"All right. I took the master, but—"

"No, stay there. You're fine." And with that, she disappears down the hall and into a room, closing the door behind her.

Feeling restless, I stay awake most of the night watching crap TV. Micaela never comes out of her room, but through the walls, I can hear her crying. I find myself wanting to go to her, hold her and tell her it's going to be okay. But I don't. The last person I tried to help, I only ended up hurting when I couldn't be the person she needed me to be.

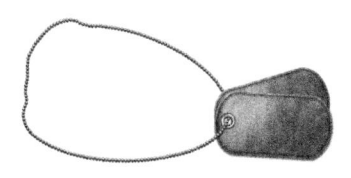

## CHAPTER SIX

### MICAELA

I WAKE in the morning to an empty house. My first thought is Ryan must've left. But when I walk by the master bedroom I spot his duffle bag on the floor next to the dresser, so he must be around here somewhere. I pad out to the kitchen to make a cup of coffee, and while I'm there, make myself a piece of toast. I probably should've bought food to make meals with, but I wasn't thinking. Plus, I don't really know how to cook, so I'm not sure how well that would go over.

With a cup of coffee in one hand and my toast in the other, I head outside. It's March in Venice Beach, so the weather can fluctuate, but today it's warm, so I sit in the chair and watch the waves crash against the shore while I eat my breakfast and drink my coffee. I'm not sure where to go or what to do. I came here to try to move on. A change of scenery. To give my family a break from worrying. But I haven't the slightest clue what the hell I'm supposed to do now, and so far all I've done is spent the night crying in my room.

It doesn't matter whether I'm in Vegas or Venice, my heart still aches. The lump in my throat still remains. Every time I close my eyes I can still picture Ian's lifeless body lying in the casket—my mom warned me not to look, but I had to see for myself he was really gone. In Venice, my plans are still shattered, my heart is still cracked and broken.

I move from the chair to the lounger, so I can lie down and get comfortable. I close my eyes and let the sun beat down on my face. The warmth a reminder that unlike Ian's cold body buried six feet under, I'm still alive.

I spend the morning doing nothing. I try to write my letter to Ian, but, like always, nothing comes to me. I have no words, no thoughts, no feelings I want to write down. Anything I write will make Ian's death a reality. My husband is dead and isn't coming back. The fact is, it's been the reality for the last fifteen months—I just haven't wanted to admit it. Which is why I'm here. Only I seem to be doing the same thing here I was doing at home. Tears prick my lids, but I shut my eyes, forcing them back.

*First step*, I think to myself, *no more crying*. I can't move forward if I keep crying.

Early afternoon, Ryan returns. He's dressed in board shorts and flip-flops with his shirt flung over his shoulder. His short hair is wet, and his skin is bronzed from the sun. His body is ripped, from his strong muscular shoulders, to his chiseled chest, down to his defined six-pack abs. He has several tattoos covering his flesh.

I briefly chastise myself for ogling him, just like I did last night, but then I mentally roll my eyes. It's not like I'm cheating on Ian, since he isn't here. I might be stuck frozen in place, unable to move on, but I haven't completely lost it. I know my husband is gone and isn't coming back. I know eventually I will have to move on. One day, I imagine I'll get married again, have a family. I'm only twenty years old. I have my entire life ahead of me—unlike Ian. But the thought of actually moving on makes my heart hurt. The idea of taking a step forward without Ian by my side is gut-wrenching. I didn't want to have to move forward without him. I was supposed to walk with him, start a family with him. Create a life with him. Like always, my throat clogs with emotion and I have to force the sobs back. I told myself no more crying. I can't move forward if I keep crying.

Instead, I focus on Ryan. He's carrying my dad's surfboard under his arm. He nods once toward me, and I force myself to smile at him. The smile feels foreign but also good. Like in my own way I just took a step forward. I can't even remember the last time I smiled. So, yeah, I'm counting the smile as a step forward.

He steps onto the back patio and sets the board against the side of the house, then goes about rinsing the saltwater off his body using the outdoor shower. When he's done, he grabs a towel and dries off.

He goes inside, and then a few minutes later, comes back out, dressed in a pair of shorts and a T-shirt, the same flip-flops on his feet. I watch as he walks down the beach toward the pier, realizing he never said a single word to me. I wonder if maybe he's afraid to talk to me, like he's scared I might lose it on him. Or maybe he's just trying to give me my space. Even though he's been away overseas, he has to know my situation. His parents are best friends with my grandparents, and despite him always being gone, I know he's close with his, just like I am with mine—or at least was, until Ian died and I pushed everyone away.

A little while later, I head inside to make myself something to eat for lunch. Ryan bought a shit load of food, but I don't want to touch it without asking, so I stick to what I bought: a pint of ice cream and a bag of chips.

After eating enough so I'm no longer starving, I lie down for a nap, but since I haven't really done anything, I'm not tired, so instead I just lie in bed and stare at the ceiling, allowing my mind to wander. When I can't take it anymore, I climb out of bed to grab a book I brought. When I open the luggage, a small box catches my eye. I'm not sure why I packed it. Maybe I was afraid if I left it at home, it would feel like I was leaving Ian there as well. I open it up and sift through it—something I haven't done since I filled it. It's everything from Ian's and my time together. Letters he wrote me, pictures of us, his wedding band. One day when I was having a bad moment, I put everything into the box so I wouldn't have to see it. I told myself out of sight out of mind. Obviously that didn't work.

Clutching a photo of us laughing and smiling to my chest, the tears fall like a waterfall. My heart aches for Ian, but I'm so tired of hurting, of feeling broken.

My eyes flicker to the fireplace, and for a brief second I consider tossing it all into there. Lighting it on fire, so I'm forced to move forward. But then I come to my senses. I would no doubt regret that and there would be no way of getting any of it back.

So, instead, I put the box back into my luggage and, taking the single photo of us, climb back into bed and cry myself to sleep. *Tomorrow,* I tell myself. Tomorrow I will try harder to move on.

---

"I'LL TAKE THAT." Ryan comes out of nowhere and plucks the joint I was bringing to my lips out of my fingers, and flicks it toward the sand. "And I'll replace it with this." He sets a deliciously-smelling plate of food in front of me. A scrambled egg omelet that looks like it's mixed with ham, cheese, mushrooms, and peppers, home fries, perfectly cooked, and sliced mixed fruit.

Ryan disappears, then returns, juggling two glasses of orange juice in one hand and a plate of food for himself in the other. I grab the glasses from him and set them on the table.

"Shit, forgot the utensils," he says, setting his plate down.

He comes back a few seconds later and sits, handing me a fork and knife.

"Wow, a man who can cook. What else can you do?"

"Smoking is not how you deal," he says, ignoring my joke.

"Oh, that's right." My eyes roll upward. "I've heard all about your savior complex." I lean over my plate of food. "But guess what? I don't need to be saved. What happened to the guy from yesterday who let me deal in peace?"

"I was giving you space. The space stopped when you lit a joint."

Not wanting to argue, I stand, and Ryan does as well. "Sit and eat." He gestures toward the food and my stomach, of course, rumbles. His one brow goes up, and I sigh, giving in.

"Fine, but no talk about how to cope or deal or whatever." I grab my fork, pierce a chunk of melon, and point it at him, while hitting him with a hard stare.

"Fine." He shrugs nonchalantly, not fazed in the slightest by my glare. "Since we both know you're not doing either." He pops a potato into his mouth and chews.

"Excuse me?" I fork a piece of omelet and push it into my

mouth. It's fluffy and flavorful. A loud moan escapes, and Ryan laughs.

"Smoking weed is avoiding, not dealing. Not coping. Avoiding."

"I'm trying."

"No, you're not," he argues. "Yesterday you did nothing all day but ate shit food and cried, now today, you're waking up and getting high before the sun is even up." Okay, so apparently, even though he wasn't talking, he was paying attention.

"Whatever." I take another bite of my food, and he chuckles.

"What?" I huff.

"Nothing." He laughs, shaking his head and taking another bite of his food. I try and fail to ignore how strong his jaw is. Like, how can a jaw be strong? But somehow his is... "You're acting your age," he adds, snapping me out of my ogling. "I haven't been around someone your age in a long time, and I'm the youngest in my family."

Really? He's like eight years older than me and he's acting like he's my dad's age. I don't bother responding to his dig, though, not wanting to bury myself deeper.

We eat the rest of our meal in silence. When our plates are empty, he stands and goes to take my dish, but I grab his from his hand instead. "You cooked, I can clean."

He follows me inside. The kitchen is spotless, so he must've cleaned up as he went. I set the dishes next to the sink and pour some soap over them, then grab a sponge and begin washing them. Ryan joins me, leaning against the counter, his arms crossing over his chest.

"How long were you planning to stay here for?"

"I don't know," I say, placing the clean dishes into the strainer. "My mom mentioned it might do me some good to get away, and the next thing I knew I was packing a bag and heading here."

"And they don't know you're here?"

"They know I'm safe. I didn't tell them where I am, but I told them I'm okay and I'll check in so they don't worry. I didn't want them sending anyone over to check on me."

"I have to report to the base for my tour in a couple weeks."

"Tour?"

"Afghanistan."

Oh, yeah. He's in the military. I knew that. I nod, a lump the size of a golf ball blocking my throat. He's going overseas to Afghanistan. Putting his life at risk. The same way Ian would've been, had he not—I shake my head, trying to block out any thoughts of Ian.

"Hey, I got you." Ryan pulls me into his arms, and it's then I realize my cheeks are wet with tears. He picks me up and carries me over to the couch, setting me next to him.

"I'm sorry. You mentioned Afghanistan, and it..."

"Your husband died in training, right?"

I nod. "Fifteen months ago." I swat at my stupid tears and close my eyes, willing them to stop. "I should be over it... moved on by now. That's why I'm here."

"I've never lost anyone close to me the way you have," Ryan says. "But I have lost a few men during deployments, and I considered them family. I'm not sure you ever fully get over it, and there's no set timetable for when you have to move on."

I open my eyes and for the first time in a while, I find myself smiling. "Thank you." When he gives me a confused look, I clarify. "You're the first person not to tell me it's time."

Ryan nods. "You'll move forward when you're ready. You'll never forget, but one day, when you're ready, you'll take a step forward and then another one."

"I want to," I admit, finding it easy to talk to him for some reason. "It's just..." I take a deep breath, trying so hard to block the tears. I'm such an emotional wreck. "We had these plans, and now, every time I think about them..." I take another deep breath in and then slowly release it, trying to fight the anxiety attack I feel coming on. It happens every time I think about Ian's and my future.

Ryan extends his hand and pulls me close to him. His hand rubs up and down my arm, calming me. "Breathe," he murmurs into my ear. "Just breathe."

His voice is commanding yet soothing, and I find myself doing what he's telling me to do. A few minutes later, I glance around and realize, between his touch and his words, I made it through my attack.

"I'm going to take a walk over to the pier. I saw your dad has some poles and chairs in the garage. We could pack a lunch and go fishing. What do you say?"

Without giving it thought, I nod. *One step forward.* "Yeah, sure. That sounds good."

While I get dressed in a pair of leggings, a racerback tank top with a sports bra underneath, and a pair of tennis shoes, Ryan packs a cooler lunch and grabs a couple poles and chairs. He's dressed in a pair of loose khaki cargo shorts and a black T-shirt that stretches across his chest. I take the cooler from him, so he can carry the poles and chairs, and then we set off down the beach. The water is choppy today and I get lost in my thoughts and the sound of the waves crashing. Walking with Ryan is nice. He doesn't try to make forced conversation. He's simply content walking together in silence. And it's not awkward silence either. It's comfortable, and it makes me feel relaxed.

Once we get to the pier, Ryan buys some bait and then we find a spot that isn't too busy to set up our chairs. He puts the bait on both our lines and then casts them into the water, making it all look so effortless, while I sit in my chair and watch. He sticks the poles into the holes and has a seat next to me.

"Do you go fishing often?"

"First time," he says with a laugh. "I looked up how to do all that online." He shoots me a sexy wink and my insides tighten, the air knocking out of me.

"I'm not usually one to sit around," he adds. "But your dad told me I should spend some time doing nothing."

"Wow, my parents are just full of advice." I laugh humorlessly.

"They mean well."

"Yeah," I agree. "So, what do we do now?"

"We wait."

We sit in silence for a few minutes, and then, all of a sudden, the pole he placed in front of me starts to bow. "Oh! I think something is happening!"

We both hop up from our chairs. Ryan grabs my pole and reels in whatever it is that's been hooked. When he brings it over the railing, I spot the fish. A real fish. A cute, innocent, silver fish. And it hits me... We're fishing... for fish! It's wiggling in fear—its tiny mouth open, practically begging to be saved.

"Oh my God!" I shriek. "Help it!"

Ryan's eyes go wide. "What?"

"The hook is in its mouth!" I rush over to the poor little fish who's squirming, most likely in pain. "It's hurt, Ryan! We have to help him." Ryan stares at me like I've lost my mind, but I ignore him, my entire focus on saving this poor little fish. Carefully, I unhook the hook from his mouth. "It's okay, little guy. I got you. You're going to be okay." I quickly toss him back into the water and watch as he lands with a tiny splash, disappearing into the abyss.

I grab the pole that's still in the water and reel it in. "No more fishing." I hand the pole to Ryan, who's looking at me like I'm crazy. "Those poor fish don't deserve to be hooked and reeled in for our entertainment."

A slow smile creeps up on Ryan's face, making his dimples pop out.

"What?" I huff, crossing my arms over my chest.

"Nothing." He shakes his head, his amused grin widening. "You're just... kind of fucking adorable."

*Great, he thinks I'm adorable... like a damn child.*

"What did you think we were doing when I mentioned fishing?" he asks.

"I don't know." I shrug a shoulder. "I wasn't really thinking about it, until you reeled in that poor, helpless fish."

Ryan laughs, and his strong shoulders shake. "Okay. So, no fishing..."

"No fishing. It's not nice." I glance around, eyeing all the people who are fishing on the pier. Those poles aren't just poles, they're weapons, threatening to hurt and kill all of the sea life.

"You can't stop all these people from fishing, so don't even think about it," he says as if reading my mind. "Why don't we go for a walk and sit on the beach."

I shoot the people fishing a stink eye. "Fine, okay."

Ryan takes the chairs and poles, and I grab the cooler. We find a secluded spot, but instead of sitting in the chairs, we opt for sitting in the sand.

After a few minutes of watching the waves come in, I say, "My major was marine biology."

"Was?"

"I had a semester left to get my AS... my associate's in science," I explain.

"I know what that is. I have an engineering degree."

I whip my head around, looking at him with new eyes. "Really?"

"What? I can't have a degree because I'm in the military?"

"No, I just didn't know you went to college. Ian..." At the mention of his name, I stop for a second, but then force myself to continue. "Ian enlisted." He bypassed going to college to enlist directly into the Navy SEALs.

"I did too. But I took online classes. I wanted a degree I could use one day, as well as in the field. I'm a combat engineer." He takes two bottles of water out of the cooler and hands me one. "So, you were majoring in marine biology?"

"Yeah, the plan was for me to apply to the University of San Diego and to Scripps for an internship. I want to study marine life. I find it fascinating."

"What made you want to do that?" He twists the top of the bottle and brings it to his lips. As he swallows the water, his Adam's apple bobs, and I find myself squeezing my thighs together. Why does everything he does have to be so damn masculine and sexy?

"Micaela," he prompts with a smirk, telling me he totally caught me staring at him.

"Umm..." I shake my head slightly to clear the hormones clogging my brain. "We went on a cruise when I was thirteen. We went snorkeling and I was drawn to the marine life. A few years ago, my dad and I got our scuba license and went scuba diving. I became obsessed with learning about everything. I would love to be able to research the mammals, maybe work to help save those that are endangered." I shrug. "I haven't really given a lot of thought to the logistics. The first two years are just the prerequisites. I figured I have plenty of time to figure out exactly what I want to do." *Time*, something I've learned the hard way we never really have enough of.

"And what, now you don't want to do that anymore?"

"No, I do... I just..." I was supposed to move to San Diego to be with Ian. That was part of our plan.

"You just what?" He's not going to let me off the hook. I

already know this about Ryan. He's the kind of person to push you past the point of safe.

"Ian and I had this five-year plan." I open my water and gulp down several sips. "When he died, it was like my life paused, and I don't know how to press play again."

"You will when you're ready."

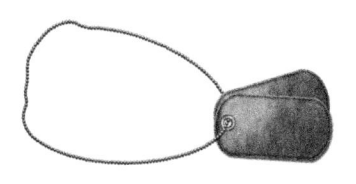

## CHAPTER SEVEN

### RYAN

Micaela is a good eight years younger than me—barely an adult. But her eyes scream maturity. She's experienced the kind of heartbreak that ages you by several years. I've never experienced it myself, but I've seen my men go through it. I've lost men along the way, on a couple of rough deployments. Shit goes wrong. But I've never allowed myself to be close enough to someone to feel the loss the way Micaela feels it.

She should be in college, going to parties, having a good time. Not struggling every day to just simply breathe. I have two older sisters—Faith and Chloe—and even though we aren't as close as they'd like because of me being away more than I'm home, we still talk a lot. They're close with Micaela's family, so I've heard on a few different occasions how Micaela is handling the death of her husband—or not handling it. I don't know what it is about her, but something draws me in and holds me captive. I want to cut her open, learn all of her secrets, her deepest wishes and desires, and then sew her back together and make them all come true. I shouldn't feel this way. I've only been around her for a few hours. She's too young, too jaded, and I'm... well, fuck, I'm just me. I'm—

"If you want to stay at the house I can go home," she says, knocking me from my thoughts. "It doesn't really matter where I am."

"Or we can both stay here," I blurt out, not ready for her to leave. I can't remember the last time I felt this content. And I can't help but think it's because of her presence.

Her eyes go wide, and her mouth opens and closes like the fish she saved earlier. "Umm..."

"We're both already here. There are plenty of rooms. I can cook, you can eat."

Micaela glares adorable daggers my way, and I laugh. "C'mon, you brought weed and ice cream. That's not exactly part of the food pyramid."

"That was my only joint," she argues. "I'm not a junkie. Lexi gave it to me." She shrugs. "It just helps me forget for a little while."

"Maybe it's time to work on accepting and moving forward."

She rolls her eyes. "There you go... doing that whole savior shit again."

"Oh, yeah. I'll show you a savior."

Before she can question what I'm saying, I'm picking her up and throwing her over my shoulder. She shrieks, slamming her fists against my ass and back, as I run us straight into the ocean. It's cold as fuck, but it doesn't deter me. Holding on to her, I dip us both into the saltwater.

When we rise to the surface, her hair is plastered to her face and forehead, and the little bit of makeup she's wearing is running down her eyes.

"I can't believe you just did that," she splutters.

I push the hair from her face and wipe under her eyes. "There are healthier ways to deal with what you're feeling. No more getting high." I give her the look I give my guys when I mean business, and she nods.

"It's hard," she says softly. Because the water is deep, she can't reach, so she wraps her arms around my neck. Our bodies are adjusting to the water, so it's not as cold anymore.

"I can't even imagine how hard, but you're still young and you have your whole life ahead of you. Would you want him to act like this if the roles were reversed?"

She thinks about it for a second then shakes her head. "No, I would..." She visibly gulps. "I would want him to move on. Live his life." Tears prick her eyes and she takes a deep breath. "But it's easier said than done."

"Have you tried? And I'm not talking about moving on with another guy... just moving forward."

"You sound like my mom," she says with a huff.

"Well, if she's anything like mine, she's probably really fucking wise."

"She is."

"We're both here anyway," I say, ignoring how close our bodies are, the way they line up perfectly. She's wrapped her legs around my torso and it's doing weird shit to me. "Why don't we stay and keep each other company. There's a reason why we both came here, right? Plus, I have a little less than two weeks before I have to spend the next year with a bunch of guys crammed into a small as hell base in the fucking desert."

Micaela searches my eyes for several seconds, for what, I'm not sure, but she must find whatever it is she's looking for because she nods once. "Okay, help me forget."

"No," I correct her. "I'm not going to help you forget. You will never forget, and you shouldn't. You love him. He's a part of you and always will be. I'm going to help you move forward."

"And what will I help you do?" she breathes. A million thoughts come to mind, all of them completely inappropriate, so I push them away.

"Relax."

"Relax?"

"Yeah, your dad thinks relaxing will be good for me. Taking time for myself. You can help me do that." She's already doing that and she doesn't even know it.

"Okay," she agrees. "And the first step of relaxing and moving on is..." She raises her body and lets go of my neck. Her hands come up and push on the top of my head. At first I'm confused, but then it hits me... She's trying to dunk me into the water. Silly girl, doesn't she realize who she's messing with?

"That's cute," I taunt. "My turn."

Realizing her efforts are futile, and I'm not going under, she resorts to plan B: run, or in her case, swim. She lets go of my neck and pushes off me, attempting to swim away, but before she can get far, I grab hold of her ankle and pull her back to me. Then, lifting her into the air like a rag doll, I throw her a good three feet away.

"Oh my God!" she shrieks when she comes up, bobbing up and down in the water. "I can't believe you just did that."

"I thought you would want to be released like that fish you saved." I laugh.

"Real funny." She glares. "Just remember paybacks are a bitch."

"Bring it, sweetheart," I yell as I watch her sexy ass swim to shore. And with that thought, it hits me. I just suggested spending several days in a beach house alone with that woman.

A woman I shouldn't find sexy but do.

Who is off-limits, but has me wanting to be near her.

And she agreed.

*What the hell was I thinking?*

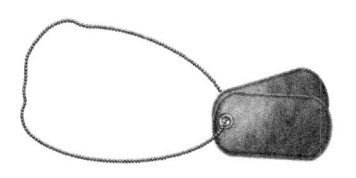

## CHAPTER EIGHT

### MICAELA

"C'mon, slow-poke, you need me to carry you?"

I'm following behind Ryan up the beach, but since my tennis shoes got soaked in the water earlier when he threw me in, I'm barefoot and my feet are sinking into the sand.

"Maybe if you hadn't thrown me in with my shoes…"

"Get on."

I glance up and almost run into Ryan's back. "What?"

"Get on," he repeats. "We have another half-mile to the pier and you're taking too long."

"What are we even going back there for? I'm not fishing again."

Ryan chuckles. "It's a surprise. The first step to you moving forward."

"Fine, but it's technically my second. My first is no more crying." I hop on his back and snake my arms around his neck. "Giddy up." I make a clicking sound and quickly squeeze my thighs together. Ryan laughs and takes off like a horse.

When we get to the pier, I notice it's busier than it was earlier this morning. He drops me on my feet and takes my hand. I think it's only to guide us through the throng of people, but I can't help but focus on how my hand feels in his. The last hand I held was Ian's, and that was years ago when we were both in high school.

His hand was soft and gentle, untouched, the opposite of Ryan's hand, which is rough and strong, callused from years of working with his hands. I don't know what it is about his touch, but it instantly calms me. Makes me feel protected and safe. Like he could easily shield me from anything life throws at me.

When we arrive at the end of the pier, he lets go of my hand, and I want to thread our fingers back together. Something about him, his presence, makes me feel less alone. When he told me he would help me move forward, for the first time I felt like it was actually possible.

"What is this?" I ask, taking in our surroundings. There are several booths and tents set up around the perimeter of the pier. I didn't notice this before because we didn't make it all the way to the end of the pier.

"The Venice Oceanarium. I saw a flyer for it. They call it the museum without walls." Ryan entwines his fingers with mine once again and steers us over to the first booth. "What better way to take your first step forward than to remind yourself why you need to graduate college?" He glances over at me, a confident smile on his face, and my insides turn into mush.

"Hello," a sweet woman, who's wearing a red jacket with a logo that reads Venice Oceanarium, greets us. "Would you like to take a look?" She points to the booth with a microscope and several pieces of marine life placed all over the table. "All of these were found right here in the Pacific Ocean."

I grab a sea urchin and place it under the microscope to examine it. While Ryan and I take turns looking at each sea creature, the woman tells us some fun facts about each one, how we can help the ocean and marine life, and how to donate. It's cool getting to see all this. Because I still have a semester left of my prerequisites, I've yet to have any hands-on classes.

We spend the next few hours going from booth to booth, learning about the ocean and marine life. I even speak to a nice guy who has a degree in biology and is getting his PhD. He works in a lab, studying the effect human activity has on certain marine wildlife. With every booth we stop at, each person we speak to, I feel a little more like my old self. And by the time it's time to go—because they're shutting down—my adrenaline is pumping from excitement.

"That was fun," Ryan says while we eat lunch at a small restaurant on the beach.

"It was." I take a bite of my tuna salad (minus the tuna because I'm still traumatized from earlier). "I forgot how much I love learning about marine biology. The wildlife and water…"

"It's your passion."

"Maybe." I shrug. "I've only taken one course in high school and an elective credit when I was in college."

"I could see it in your eyes. The way they lit up over every detail and fact. When the guy was talking to us about the water, you were practically bouncing in place. Nobody gets that excited over the topic of saltwater unless it's their passion."

"Maybe," I repeat with a laugh. "What's your passion?" I ask, finding myself wanting to know more about Ryan. I've known him my entire life, but with our age difference, he graduated and moved when I was ten—only going to Breckenridge once when we were there. He was with his wife, but I didn't really spend much time with them. Now he's back—and divorced—and I feel like I don't really know much about him.

"Growing up, I enjoyed robotics engineering. Learning the codes, inputting them, and building the robots. When I joined the military, I found I was good at applying those same types of skills to my job, so I got a degree in engineering."

I shake my head in frustration. "I would've already graduated with my associate's and been in San Diego working on my degree. Ian and I—" I cut myself off, refusing to finish my would've, could've. If I'm going to move forward, I have to think about what is, not what could've been.

"You can still do all that," Ryan says, refusing to let me get lost in my thoughts. "You took a little detour, but you can still get back on track. No, it won't be the same plan, but it'll be *your* plan."

We finish eating dinner, and then, after stopping by our spot on the beach and grabbing our stuff, we head back to the house. The walk is filled with comfortable silence, and once we're back, we go our separate ways to shower. When I get out, I notice a missed call from my mom, so I call her back.

"Hey, sweet girl, how are you?"

"I'm good," I tell her, and for the first time in a long time it's the truth. My day out with Ryan has been really good for me. I not only thought of Ian less, but I didn't cry once the entire day.

"What did you do today?"

"Is that your way of trying to find out where I am?"

"I can't help but worry." Mom sighs. "I know you're twenty and free to come and go, but you've been holed up in your room for over a year, and then you disappear with nothing more than a note telling me I was right and needed to get away. What if something happens to you? I wouldn't even know where to look."

The worry in my mom's tone isn't something I like to hear. It's the same tone she's been using since I lost Ian and, in turn, lost myself. I left to give everyone a break from worrying about me, and until she knows I'm safe, she's going to keep worrying.

"I'm at the beach house, but please don't tell Dad. He'll have someone come check on me, and I'm okay. I promise. I went for a walk today to the pier, did a little fishing..."

"You fished?"

"It was horrible. I don't recommend it."

Mom laughs, and I find myself joining in. I've missed talking and laughing with her. "What else did you do?"

"There was a pop-up museum on the pier. An oceanarium. It was really cool. Did you know that less than five percent of the ocean has been explored?"

Mom laughs again, but this time it sounds weird, kind of watery. "I didn't know that," she says with a sniffle.

"Mom, are you crying?"

"Oh, sweet girl, I'm just... You sound happy, and well, that makes me happy. This last year, seeing you hurting. I hated not being able to help you."

"I'm sorry, Mom."

"You have nothing to be sorry about. You lost your husband and you were mourning. And even though you're happy today, there will probably be more bad days. Days when you miss him and feel the pain. But I'm glad today was a good day."

"It was." And it was all because of Ryan. Because he forced me to take a step forward. He distracted me with fishing and swimming and the museum and dinner. It was the first day I didn't focus on Ian and the pain I feel from his death. Instead I focused on myself, on taking one step forward. And it felt good.

Ryan was right. Ian wouldn't want me mourning him for the rest of my life. He would want me to live.

Mom and I talk for a few more minutes about my day, and I make it a point to leave Ryan out of the conversation. Dad mustn't have told her he gave Ryan a key, or she would've mentioned it the moment I told her I was here. With the promise to call her soon, we say good night.

I throw on a pair of leggings and a Cooper's Fight Club hoodie, then head out to find Ryan. He's lying out on a lounge chair on the back patio, staring out at the ocean. I grab a Gatorade and a beer from the fridge and join him.

"Didn't we talk about this?" he asks, when he spots the bottle in my hand.

"It's for you." I hand him the beer and sit next to him. "I thought you could use one." I show him the Gatorade in my other hand. "This is for me."

He grins and his two sexy dimples make an appearance. "That a girl." He pops the top and raises the beer to his mouth. His head goes back slightly, exposing his neck as he swallows a mouthful of the liquid.

"You did good today," he says, setting the bottle between his muscular thighs, which are stretched out in front of him.

"Because of you."

"No, because of you. I just steered you in the right direction." He turns his face toward me, granting me the most gorgeous smile, and a knot forms in my belly. This shouldn't be happening. I'm nowhere near close to being over Ian, but for some reason my body and heart aren't communicating with each other.

I push the feelings aside, refusing to acknowledge them. I need to focus on me, on healing, on moving forward, creating a new plan and life for myself.

Ryan is here to relax before he leaves to go overseas. Why he's here with me, I don't know. I know he's got money. He doesn't act like it, but Bentley and Kayla are loaded and their kids all have trusts in their names. The moment he saw I was here, he could've just rented a hotel room. Is he that good of a guy he would stay here just to help me get through my shit?

His phone rings, momentarily pausing my thoughts. He holds it up and it says Laura—his ex-wife.

"Hey, Laura. Everything okay?" I would expect him to walk away to have some privacy, but he doesn't move. He nods slightly, listening to whatever it is she's saying, and a small smile creeps up on his lips. "Congratulations." He takes a swig of his beer then sets it back down. "That's great, Laura. I'm happy for you."

I try to find a hint of insincerity in his voice, but can't find any. "I love you, too," he says. "Talk to you soon."

He hangs up, and I wait for him to speak, unsure of what happened just now. Did he actually tell his ex-wife he loves her?

"Laura is pregnant," he finally says. "A surprise, but a pleasant one. She and her fiancé are going to move the wedding up so they're married before the baby comes."

"And you're okay with that?"

"Of course."

"And this is Laura... your ex-wife?"

"Yes," he confirms, taking another drink of his beer.

"Why did you two divorce?"

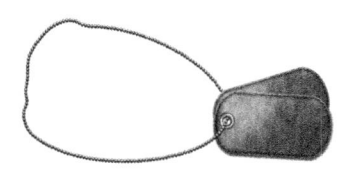

## CHAPTER NINE

### RYAN

"Why did you two divorce?"

I think for a moment how to answer that question. When I told my parents we were getting a divorce and that I was giving her the house, they didn't question me. I think deep down they knew this day would eventually come. It was the reason my dad insisted on a prenup.

"I married my best friend," I tell her honestly, which has her looking at me like I'm crazy. "But unlike most people who say that but really mean they married the love of their life, she really was just my friend. She had needs I couldn't meet." She wanted a life I couldn't envision ever having.

Micaela raises one brow. "Ohhh." She nods slowly, her heart-shaped lips forming a perfect, pouty circle, and my dick takes over my brain as I imagine what it would be like to have those lips wrapped around my shaft.

"Oh, what?" I choke out, trying to shake off the vision.

"You suck in bed," she deadpans. "They have tutorials for everything on YouTube, you know. Including how to meet a woman's needs." She cracks a smile, telling me she's kidding, but my vision of her sucking my dick turns into me taking her to bed and showing her over and over again that I more than know how to meet a woman's needs. Fuck, I can't go there. She's mourning the loss of her husband. She's twenty. A family friend...

I grab the towel from behind me and throw it at her, smacking her in the face. "Not like that, perv." Although, she isn't far off. The sex, when we would actually have it, was similar to our marriage: forced and awkward. I always made sure she was taken care of, but it wasn't enough. She wanted intimacy, to feel cherished and loved...

"What needs then?"

"Marital shit. Like, she wanted to start a family." And I wasn't about to place roots in a failing marriage—hell, if I'm honest, I don't think it was ever succeeding. I grew up in a household with two people who not only were madly in love with each other, but loved being parents. My dad chose to be a stay-at-home dad. I couldn't even stand being home for more than a day before I was itching to leave again.

"You didn't want that?"

"I wasn't capable..."

"You're not helping your case here," she says with a soft giggle that has me wanting to throw her over my shoulder and take her to bed.

"Physically, I'm capable. But mentally..." I clear my throat. "She wanted a real marriage, a relationship, the family, a husband... But the only things I could give her was my last name, a roof over her head, and money to make sure she was living comfortably." I sigh, hating that the most important role a man can take on is the one I sucked at. "I'm good at my job. Fixing things, making them right."

"Saving people."

"I guess..." I take a sip of my beer. "In my job, when there's a problem, you fix it. When we were younger, and Laura was hurting, I fixed it. But she needed more than to just be fixed. She needed a husband, and I wasn't so good at that."

Micaela eyes me for a moment, all joking put aside, and I avert my gaze, hating how vulnerable I feel. I'm not good at this talking shit, but she makes me want to actually talk. I've said more to her today than I've probably said to Laura in all our years of marriage.

"I'm sorry. I shouldn't have—" she begins, but I cut her off. She has nothing to be sorry about.

"No." I wave her off. "It's why I'm here. I'm not good at staying still in one place for long. It's hard to make a marriage work when one of the people in the marriage is never home."

"So, why didn't you stay? Try to make it work?"

"The truth?" I look her dead in the eyes, and she nods. "I didn't want to. I mean, I did... but I didn't. I tried to want it, but deep down, I couldn't. Every time I would return home I was itching to leave again. My skin would literally crawl."

"Leave her, or just leave in general?"

"In a marriage, aren't they one and the same?"

"Maybe... I don't know," she admits softly. "I was only married for seven months, and during that time I only saw him a few times."

"I don't know either. I see what my parents have and I want that, but when I was with Laura, I didn't feel it. I felt restless, and the idea of starting a family... She deserved to have all that. So, I'm happy she finally has it all and with a man who will be by her side."

"Ian and I never discussed kids. It wasn't part of our five-year plan." She stares toward the water, her eyes slightly glossing over. "I don't even know if he wanted kids. Guess it doesn't matter now."

"What do you want?"

She sits up and throws her legs over the side of the lounge chair. "I want to curl up in bed and watch some *YOU* on Netflix." She pats my leg. "I'm off to bed. Thank you for today." She leans over and kisses my cheek. "For what it's worth, I think you would make a great husband. I think you just have to find the woman you're meant to be with."

As she walks away, thoughts of the day Laura asked for a divorce resurface. *"One day you're going to fall in love and you won't want to run away. You'll want to be with the woman you love. But first, you have to stop running so you can meet her."*

I try—and fail—to ignore the fact that today was the first day in years where I didn't feel the need to run.

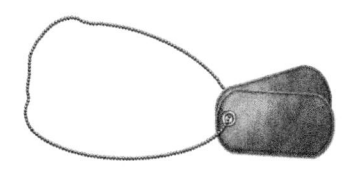

## CHAPTER TEN

### MICAELA

"Up and at 'em," a deep voice says, waking me from my slumber.

I release an annoyed growl and turn over, so the light shining in from the open door disappears, and pull the blanket up to my head to cover my face.

"Time to get up."

"Go away," I groan.

There's a slight tug on my blanket, so I fist it tighter, but Ryan's too strong, and he easily rips the blanket from my body, dragging it off the bed.

"It's cold," I whine.

"That's because you turn the air down to arctic temps before you go to bed."

"Which is why I need my blanket," I argue, my eyes still closed and my hand blindly waving in the air, trying to grab the blanket back. "Please."

"Nope, breakfast is ready. We have plans today."

I open one eye, my interest piqued. "Plans?"

Ryan smirks. "Come eat, so we can get going. We're leaving in twenty minutes."

I crack up laughing. "I thought you were married."

Ryan scratches his head. "I was."

"And your wife ate and got ready in twenty minutes?"

His face twists into confusion. "I..." He scrubs his hand up and down the scruff on the side of his face. "We didn't really..." He sighs. "Look, I wasn't a good husband, and we didn't have a normal marriage. We didn't hang out all that often. I'd been overseas for the majority of our marriage, and when I wasn't over there, I was working."

I nod my understanding. Not about their marriage not being normal, but about him being busy with work. When Ian told me he was going to be a SEAL, I did my research and learned how busy it would keep him. I knew the divorce and cheating rate for couples in the Navy was higher than others, but I was determined to make sure we weren't a statistic. Unfortunately I never considered something as permanent as death would be the reason I wouldn't spend my life with my husband.

"Well, just a word of advice for the future, women take at least an hour to get ready. More if we're expected to look good."

Ryan scans his eyes down my body, and my girly parts tighten in response. It's been a long time since a man has checked me out, and it's obvious he likes what he sees. Too bad nothing can ever happen between us. "You already look good," he says, clearing his throat. "Let's go." He throws the blanket on me and walks out.

"Why are we up at the crack of dawn?" I ask, sitting at the table. I quickly rinsed off and threw on a pair of cut-off jean shorts and a tank, unsure where we're going.

"We have about an hour drive south, and I want to get going before traffic hits."

Ryan made eggs Benedict with hollandaise sauce this morning. I take one bite and release a moan in pleasure. If it's possible to orgasm from eating delicious food, I would be having the orgasm of my life.

"My God, can I keep you?" I take another bite and moan again.

Ryan's eyes bug out in fear and I laugh. "Calm down, I didn't mean literally. You're just such a good cook. I can't cook for shit. Since my siblings and I are older, my parents tend to order in, or on special occasions, my dad will grill. But usually I live off pizza and cereal."

"I like cooking," Ryan says, taking a bite of his food. "My dad taught me how to cook, said a man should know how to take care of himself. If I'm home and have time, I like to cook. It's healthier. I usually include ham, but I wasn't sure your stance on animals after yesterday."

I stab a potato with my fork and pop it into my mouth. "Oh, as much as I love the animals, I can't live without meat. But I think I might have to skip fish for a while, just until I've had time to get over what happened."

Ryan snorts a laugh and takes a sip of his orange juice. "Noted. No fish until you've recovered."

"My mom knows I'm here." Ryan is taking another sip of his OJ when I say this, and he spits it out, his eyes going wide. "Not with you. I don't think my dad mentioned he gave you the key. And I asked her not to tell him where I am."

"He would try to kill me if he knew we were here alone together."

"Nah." I wave him off, taking a bite of my yummy food. "I'm an adult. Plus, I'm mourning. It's been a rough year. He would just be glad I'm finally attempting to move forward."

"I'd rather not find out."

"Well, hopefully my mom doesn't tell him." I pick up our empty plates and bring them to the sink. "So, where are we going?"

"It's a surprise."

"Is it for you to relax or for me to move forward?"

"Both," he says, his voice way too close to me. I look over my shoulder and find Ryan right behind me. He reaches around and places his cup in the sink, and I catch a whiff of his scent. All. Fucking. Man. None of that expensive cologne for him. Just body-wash and all him. I suppress a groan, rinsing the dishes and throwing them into the dishwasher. I seriously need to get a hold of myself. I know it's just my body recognizing there's a hot man in the vicinity, but it's hard to ignore the way I find myself gravitating toward him and wanting to act on these feelings.

Since Ryan's truck is bigger and more comfortable, he insists we take it to wherever it is we're going. In exchange, I call dibs on being in control of the music. He isn't thrilled but agrees. The ride is filled with me singing to my favorite jams while Ryan bitches that I have the worst taste in music known to man. It's a blast.

Since we're up before the rest of California, the drive is smooth sailing, and an hour later, we're parking at the Long Beach ferry terminal.

"Are we taking the ferry to Catalina?"

"Yep."

I clap my hands together. "I've always wanted to go there." I take Ryan's hand in mine. "Let's go."

Once we board the ferry, we grab a couple lattes then make our way to the edge of the boat. A few minutes later, it leaves the terminal. The water is choppy, so the ferry sways. I lose my footing, and Ryan catches me before I fall to the ground.

"Careful there," he murmurs, placing his arms on either side of me.

"Always the savior," I joke.

My back is to his front, and even though it's a tad chilly from the wind, his body blocks most of it, keeping me nice and warm. I allow myself to sag against his chest, reveling in how good he feels.

"Look over there." He points to the left at the dolphins swimming by the ferry. It's beautiful and magical. I reach into my back pocket and pull out my phone, taking a million pictures.

When they're gone, I flip the camera around. "Say cheese." I make sure Ryan and I are both in the picture. He glances down, his eyes searing into mine through the camera. "Smile." I poke his side with my other hand, and a small smile appears. I snap the picture, then take a moment to look at it. I haven't taken any pictures in the last year, the last one being when I was with Ian for Thanksgiving. My face is a tad slimmer from me not eating as much, and I have slight purple rings under my eyes from sleep deprivation, but my smile is real, and my cheeks are pink. For the first time in a long time, I'm genuinely happy.

Once we arrive, we grab a golf cart and take it for a ride to explore the island. Ryan drives with one hand, holding mine with the other. I don't know when it happened, that holding hands became the norm for us, but I like it—his strong hand in mine.

We eat lunch looking out at the marina and afterward, we walk along Crescent Street, window shopping.

"This is so pretty." I point to a beautiful shell necklace. I've never seen anything like it. "The colors are so vibrant. It reminds me of happiness." It reflects how I feel.

"You should get it."

"Eh... Maybe I'll come back." I go to set it down, but Ryan takes it from me and proceeds to the register.

"What are you doing?"

Without answering me, he has the cashier ring him up. Once he's paid, he says, "Turn around."

I do as he says, and he brushes my hair to the side. He puts the necklace on me and clasps it in the back. I find a mirror so I can admire the necklace. When my eyes land on the mirror, my heart skips a beat. The necklace is beautiful, but that's not what has my attention. It's the way Ryan and I look together. His pout to my smile. His roughness to my softness. I'm tiny and he's huge. But somehow I can imagine it—Ryan and me. I swallow thickly and briefly close my eyes, pushing the thought to the side.

"What do you think?" he prompts, forcing me to crack my eyes open.

"It's beautiful."

"It looks perfect on you."

I turn around to face him. "Thank you." On my tiptoes, I kiss his cheek, only he doesn't realize what I'm doing and he moves slightly. My lips land on the corner of his mouth, his light stubble tickling my flesh.

"We better get moving," he says, clearing this throat and backing away.

I want to pull him back to me and kiss him, get lost in him, but I don't. Instead, I plaster on a smile and say, "Where to next?"

After we finish our window shopping, we have an amazing seafood lunch (yes, I gave in to eating the poor fish. I'm a horrible person) and then stop to have some ice cream, before we head back to the ferry.

"Where are we going next?" I ask, once we disembark.

Ryan laughs. "Who said anything is next?"

I tilt my head to the side and plant my hand on my hip, popping it out slightly.

"It's a surprise."

"I'm starting to really love surprises."

An hour later, we're pulling up to the University of San Diego. I've never been here in person. The few times I visited Ian, we stayed at the hotel or he showed me around his base.

The campus is beyond gorgeous and massive, way bigger than my university back home. My heart pounds against my chest at the idea of going here. Of following my dreams. It's one thing to move forward, but to actually see what my future could look like is a whole other story. Which is exactly why I bet Ryan brought me here.

He finds visitor parking and jumps out to pay the meter. I should probably get out, but I'm stuck in my seat. Scared to actually face this dream alone. But then Ryan opens the door, and with a warm smile, extends his hand to help me down, and I take a deep, calming breath. I'm not doing this alone because Ryan is with me. And the thought sends warmth flooding through my body.

I take his proffered hand and jump down. When I land, our bodies collide, chest to chest. He looks into my eyes and I swear there's something in his. A glint of emotion. A flicker of something more. The spark that could easily turn into a forest fire if we were to stoke it. It's enough to make me close my eyes and break the connection. Because whatever it is he sees in me, I'm almost certain I wouldn't have to look hard to see it back. But we can't do that. That's not the purpose of our time together. I'm only just finally moving forward and latching onto another man wouldn't be healthy. Especially a man like Ryan, who admitted he isn't capable of being a husband or creating a family.

His life is the military, and I would rather spend the rest of my life alone than fall in love with another man who has dedicated his life to serving his country. I get people can die at any moment. They can get hit by a car or have a heart attack. But being in the military—or in Ian's case, the Navy—means purposely risking your life, and I can't ever go through what I went through with Ian's death, again. I not only lost him, but I lost myself. And if it wasn't for Ryan bringing me back...

"Micaela," Ryan murmurs, and I realize I'm standing here with my eyes closed. He must think I've lost my mind.

"Thank you," I say, slowly opening my eyes.

He nods once, no doubt understanding that I'm not just talking about him helping me out of the vehicle but everything else he's done for me in the last twenty-four hours.

Wow, is that all it's been? Twenty-four hours. It feels way

longer than that. It's probably because I spent the last year keeping myself secluded. I'm out for one day and it feels like it's been a freaking week.

"What are we doing here?" I ask when he takes my hand in his and walks us toward a huge building.

"You'll see."

We walk down a long sidewalk, and I have no idea where we're going, but Ryan seems to. We step in front of a door that reads: Marine Biology Seminar - Hubbs Hall. Ryan opens the door for me, but I stop in my place, confused.

"We can't go in there."

"Yes, we can, and we're right on time. Go." He nods toward the entrance, so I walk through. There are dozens if not hundreds of people all over, finding their seats. The room must have three hundred seats. An older gentleman steps up to the podium, just as Ryan and I find our seats in the back, and everyone else quickly finds theirs.

"Good morning, and welcome to the seminar on Oceanography," the gentleman begins. As he explains the purpose of the seminar today, my heart picks up speed. This seminar is for seniors who are majoring in biology. He discusses the topic and the organ in my chest swells as I imagine myself a couple years from now sitting here, in this very room. The students raise their hands to answer questions, discussing large marine animals' habitats. Most of what they're saying goes over my head, but it doesn't matter. The topic isn't the point. It's being here. Where I'm supposed to be. Where I want to be. Where, if it wasn't for Ryan pushing me to move forward, I'm not sure I would ever be.

And in this moment, as I watch two students volley back and forth while the professor laughs and prompts them to continue, it hits me. This is my dream. It wasn't Ian's, it wasn't ours. It was —*still is*—mine.

Fat tears fill my lids and, not wanting to draw attention to myself, I quietly excuse myself, quickly walking from the auditorium and out the door we came in from.

Ryan follows me out and, once we're outside and away from people, pulls me into his arms, where I cry harder than I've ever cried. Harder than I cried when I found out Ian died, harder than I did at his funeral. Ryan holds me in his arms while I release every pent-up emotion inside me. When Ian died, I allowed myself to die with him, and this isn't what he would've wanted. He loved me until the day he died, and what happened to him was tragic, but instead of mourning him, I should be living for him—for myself. Because I'm still alive.

But I haven't been living. I've been mourning. I've tried to write him a letter a million times, but I haven't been able to because I have nothing to say. I haven't done anything worth writing about. I was so caught up in the fact that our plans were destroyed that I forgot I'm still alive and can have a life, have a future. It breaks my heart that I won't have Ian by my side, but he would've wanted me to keep living. And that's exactly what I'm going to do. I'm going to live—for him, and more importantly for me.

Once I've calmed down enough to speak, I back up slightly and look into Ryan's azure eyes. "Thank you for this. For showing me what I'm missing, what I could still have. I needed this more than you will ever know. I think I'm finally ready to move forward."

Ryan's lips curl into a beautiful smile. "Already? But I had an entire week of activities. I guess I'll be going boating on my own in Newport." He fake pouts, but I find myself really pouting. I'm not ready to leave Ryan yet. I might be ready to move forward, but I'm not ready to move forward from him yet. I'm enjoying his company. He makes my heart feel full, my head feel less foggy.

"We could still do everything you have planned," I suggest. "I don't have anywhere I need to be."

Ryan glances down at me, and I realize how close we are. Our bodies are molded against each other. His hard, muscular arms wrapped around my backside. My hands planted against his firm chest. He sucks in his bottom lip, then runs his tongue along both lips, wetting them. And I do something I've wanted to do since the first time I saw him in the foyer of my parents' house.

I kiss him.

On my tiptoes, I reach up and press my mouth to his. At first he doesn't reciprocate and I worry I made a big mistake, but then his strong yet soft lips react to mine. Just like he did a moment ago to himself, he sucks my bottom lip into his mouth and then runs his tongue along the seam of my lips. And then he kisses me. His tongue enters my parted lips as my hands glide up his firm chest. His fingers dip into the cheeks of my ass, and he picks me up, carrying me backward until my back hits the hardness of a wall.

Our tongues find one another and move in sync, caressing, stroking... our kiss deepens. Ryan's skilled mouth devours mine. He captures my tongue and sucks on it, and I moan into his mouth. The noise must startle him, because all too quickly, I'm being dropped to the ground and Ryan's backing away like a caged animal.

"That shouldn't have happened," he says, wiping his mouth with the back of his hand. "You're grieving."

"It's been fifteen months."

"Fifteen months you've spent grieving and not moving forward."

"And now I am. I'm ready to move forward."

"With someone your age," he argues.

"You're a whole eight years older." I roll my eyes, immediately regretting it, when he raises a brow.

"You're a family friend," he volleys.

"I'm not asking you to marry me, but let's be honest..." I step forward. Ryan looks like he wants to run, but he stays where he is. "We've both been dancing around the chemistry between us."

"You're right. I am attracted to you. But *that* can't happen again."

I stop in my place and stare at him. He's nibbling on his bottom lip nervously, and even though he isn't physically running, he's still pushing me away. And I get it. There are several reasons why nothing should happen between us, but I don't care about any of them. However, it's clear Ryan does. And these last couple days have been the best days I've had in a long time. And I'm not ready to leave yet. Do I think we have a future? No. He's in the military and heading overseas. I'm going to go home and enroll in college and start living my life again. But right now, the only thing I want to do is spend time with Ryan. Help him relax. Let my heart heal. Continue to put one foot in front of the other. And in order to do that, I'm going to have to ignore the sexual tension between us and focus on being his friend.

"Okay," I reluctantly agree.

"Okay?"

"I'm not sorry for kissing you, but it won't happen again. At least not without you wanting it to." I wink, hoping to lighten the mood. "If it's okay, I would like to keep hanging out."

Ryan groans softly, but loud enough that I can hear him. "Micaela, I'm not sure that's a good idea."

"Please." I step closer to him. "I feel like I'm finally making progress, but I'm not ready to go home yet. When I do, my parents are going to be all over me. I'm going to have to face reality, make a new plan, and I'm excited to do that, but I would really like to spend some more time with you first. Plus, if I leave, you're not going to relax."

The corner of Ryan's lips tugs into a small smirk. "You don't know that."

"Yes, I do. You'll probably follow me back home and then go in search of someone else to save. Now that you've saved me, we can focus on you relaxing."

Ryan groans.

"Please. Just a few more days. Then we can go back to Vegas, and you can spend time with your family before you leave, and I'll be ready to face my family and friends and start living my life."

"Fine," he says, giving in. "But no more kissing."

"Fine."

The drive home is quiet but comfortable, and once we arrive, we lie out under the stars, me with a Gatorade and Ryan with his beer, talking about the seminar and my future until I can barely keep my eyes open and Ryan insists I go to bed since we have a big day planned tomorrow.

And that's how the week continues. Every morning Ryan wakes me up with a delicious breakfast. During the day we explore California. We go to different museums and parks and beaches. We rent bikes and scooters. We even do a day of surfing lessons. The hand holding and flirty touches have stopped, and I miss them, but I would rather have Ryan's company without the touching than not have him at all. Every night ends with us talking under the stars.

With every activity, every conversation, it feels like a weight has been lifted off me and I can finally enjoy myself. Does it mean I'm over Ian? No, a part of me will always remember and love him. He was my first boyfriend, my first lover. I married him with the intent to spend my life with him, and we did just that, until he took his final breath. When he died, I refused to move forward, didn't want to experience life without him, didn't want to create new memories he couldn't be a part of. But now I realize I can still love him and mourn him and miss him while living my life.

Then, one day, I sit down and finally write him a letter. When I'm done, I read over the three pages where I tell him I loved him and how much I miss him but promise to live my life for the both of us. I'm not sure what to do with it, and when I tell Ryan, he suggests I hold onto it for now, and when the time comes, I will know what to do with it.

While I text with my mom, so she knows I'm okay, for the most part I've lost track of the days, absorbed with what we're doing, so I'm shocked when one evening, there's a knock on the door, followed by Lexi yelling, "Micaela Anderson! I know your ass is here!"

My stomach knots at the sound of Ian's last name, but for the first time, I don't lose it. Not a single tear comes. Instead, I find myself smiling. I have his last name. A small piece of him. One day I'll get married and it will change, but for right now I get to have his name. A reminder that we were so in love we got married. I vowed to love him until the end of time, and even though he's gone, I'm going to do just that.

"What are you doing here?" I ask, turning the water from the sink off. I was doing the dishes while Ryan takes a shower. We just finished eating dinner. He grilled steaks and shrimp and zucchini, and I baked a couple potatoes.

"You posted a picture of the sunset on your Insta." She rolls her eyes, and Georgia laughs. "Forgot to turn your location off." Shit, I didn't even think about that. I really have been lost in my own world.

"You look a lot better," Georgia says, wrapping her arms around me for a hug.

"I feel better," I admit.

"You've got a gorgeous little tan going on," Lexi says. "How long have you been hiding out here? You seriously look great."

"Thank you, and who says I'm hiding?"

"Your—"

Lexi's words are cut off when Ryan walks into the kitchen,

completely unaware we have company. He's shirtless, and his hair is freshly wet from the shower. His skin is sun-kissed, and his chest and abs look like they were carved from stone. But more importantly, as he saunters up to me, he looks completely relaxed.

Georgia's mouth drops in shock.

Lexi's mouth forms a perfect O, her gaze swinging from Ryan to me.

I'm trying to think of a way to spin this, but before my brain can muster up an excuse, Lexi lets out the most unladylike snort and says, "So, this is why you look so great." She nods her approval. "Nothing like getting under someone new to get over—"

"That's not what's happening," Ryan says, cutting her off.

"Oh, yeah?" Lexi taunts with a devilish smirk. "Then what *is* happening?"

"We're relaxing," I tell her.

"And moving forward," Ryan adds.

"Uh-huh." Lexi smiles mischievously. "Well, how about you relax and move forward at Club Onyx tonight, and I'm not taking no for an answer. Alec has been promoted to lieutenant, which is a huge freaking deal, so you're joining us to celebrate." Alec is a firefighter in Los Angeles, and Lexi and Georgia's best friend. Their parents are best friends, so they've practically grown up together in LA. I'm friends with him as well from the years of all our parents hanging out and them joining us in Breckenridge for the holidays, but we're not close like the three of them are.

"I'm in," I say as Ryan shakes his head. "And Ryan is too."

He mock-glares at me, and I laugh. "You're in. What better way to relax than with a beer and some good music."

Without giving him a chance to argue, I turn back to Lexi and Georgia. "We're in. We need to get ready, but we'll meet you there."

"Yay!" Lexi bounces over and gives me a hug. "I've missed you so much," she whisper-yells. "We're totally going to get our party on."

And with a wink and a twirl, Lexi grabs Georgia and disappears from the house.

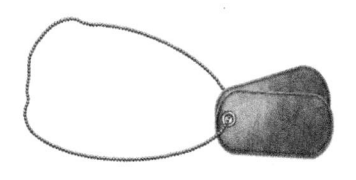

## CHAPTER ELEVEN

### RYAN

I AM COMPLETELY out of my element here. In the grand scheme of things, at twenty-eight, I don't consider myself old. But here at this club, where the median age must be twenty-two and still in college, I feel old as fuck. Since I didn't have any "club clothes," as Micaela put it, when I tried to leave in a pair of jeans and a T-shirt, I borrowed a pair of shoes and button-down shirt from Marco's closet—at Micaela's insistence. When she realized she didn't have anything to wear, she insisted we swing by Lexi's house so she could borrow a dress from her. I waited in the truck while she ran in, and thirty minutes later, when she came sauntering out with a face full of makeup, her hair down in waves, and in a skin-tight dark purple dress matched with a pair of tall-as-hell heels, I damn near lost my shit.

The organ in my chest tightened at the same time my dick swelled. I've seen Micaela in tiny bikinis all week. Her body is fucking banging. She's got tits that would fit perfectly in the palms of my hands, and an ass that's toned and plump. Her stomach is flat, and her hips are wide. A man could grip them and use them to—*fuck*. My point is I knew she was hot, but dressed the way she is tonight, she looks older, more mature. And not only that, but she also looks happy and confident. She's done a complete one-eighty since the first night she showed up at the beach house. She's no longer mourning, but instead choosing to live again. And I'm so damn proud of her.

As I sit here, watching the girls dance, I know without a doubt I'm out of my element here. I don't do clubs. I don't hang out and dance and get drunk. I design weapons and conduct demolition missions. I clear minefields. I don't *hang*.

Yet, here I am at Club Onyx, with a beer in my hand, watching as Micaela shakes her perfect ass on the dance floor. We leave the day after tomorrow and I've almost made it without kissing her or touching her again, but if I have to watch her grind against her friends for another damn minute, there's no telling what I'm going to do. I'd like to think I have a good amount of restraint. I was married for years, was propositioned a million times in several different countries, but I never cheated on my wife once. I never even considered it.

But right now, that restraint is hanging on by a thread. A man can only handle so much taunting and teasing. And I use those words because I know damn well that's what Micaela is doing. It doesn't go over my head when her hypnotizing eyes meet mine, mischief and seduction gleaming in her irises, that she wants me to know exactly what I'm missing out on. She might've agreed to no more kissing or touching, but that hasn't stopped the looks she gives me. And as much as I try to act like the chemistry is one-sided, we both know damn well it's not. I've never wanted anyone the way I want Micaela, and if I don't get away from her soon, I'm going to lose all my restraint and give in to my baser instincts.

"So, Micaela, huh?" Alec nods toward the woman I can't take my eyes off of. I don't know him that well since he's a good five or so years younger than me and lives here in LA, but we've hung out on a couple occasions with our families, and he seems like a good guy. The entire time the women are dancing, he's either been dancing with them, or watching them, making sure they aren't bothered by any assholes.

"We're just friends," I grunt out.

"Yeah, okay." He chuckles. "I don't know what you did this week with her, but she's looking pretty damn close to her old self."

"She did it herself. I was just there."

I feel Alec's gaze on me, but no matter how hard I try, I can't take my eyes off Micaela. I'm transfixed by the way her body moves. My dick doesn't understand that she's off-limits. Hooking up with her would be a huge mistake, not only because she's younger but because she's finally moving forward and deserves more than a one-night stand. And if we got together, that's all it could be.

"Damn, man, you have it bad." Alec pats my shoulder. "I get it, though. Try being in love with a woman for years and knowing all you can ever be is friends."

"Years?" I reluctantly peel my eyes from Micaela to look at Alec.

"Years," he repeats, shaking his head.

I've only been around Micaela for a little over a week. Years of being around her and not being able to be with her would fucking kill me.

"Why haven't you gone after her?"

"First, the timing was off. When I realized that my feelings for her were more than friendly, she was still in high school. My parents were high school sweethearts and grew apart. Ended in divorce."

Makes sense. I'm not the same person I was ten years ago.

"And now?"

"I'm scared shitless." His eyes lock on the women in the corner of the dance floor. We're in VIP, so they've formed their own little private dance party. Micaela's arms are up in the air, her hips swaying to the beat of the music. Lexi's dancing behind her with her hands on Micaela's hips, her ass moving in sync to Micaela's. Georgia is facing Micaela, a huge smile on her face. One of the girls must say something because she throws her head back in a laugh then wraps her arms around Micaela's neck.

"Scared of what?"

"Of not being enough. Of not loving her the way she needs. Of destroying our friendship. She's everything to me and the thought of losing her... *fuck*."

"Does she know?"

"Nah." He laughs humorlessly. "She holds my fucking heart in the palm of her hand and has no damn clue."

With a final shot, he heads over to the girls. Georgia and Lexi both flock to him, but Micaela backs up, her eyes swinging over to me.

She curls her finger, beckoning me over. I shake my head, and she nods. When I don't move, she juts her bottom lip out, reminding me of when I sucked on that same lip. She tasted sweet like sugar, fucking addicting. I've been craving her ever since.

Some asshole notices she's now alone and saddles up behind her, his hand landing on her hip. Her eyes widen in shock, but before she can even turn around to dance with him—or reject him—I'm in front of her, pulling her out of his grip and into my arms.

"So, that's all it takes to get you to touch me?" she yells over the music, snaking her arms around my neck. "Some strange guy wanting to dance with me?" Her body, which is now flush with mine, grinds against my front. Her perky tits rub against my chest, and her warmth hits my cock. And that little bit of resolve I was barely hanging on to, snaps. Gripping her nape, I crash my mouth down onto hers. My tongue pushes past her parted lips, and the taste of vodka overtakes my senses. She moans into my mouth, and I reach down, lifting her up. Her legs snake around my torso and I walk us off the dance floor.

I find a dark hallway and push her up against the wall, my mouth never leaving hers. With passion I've never felt before, I devour her mouth before I move to her neck, sucking and kissing her salty flesh. She moans in pleasure, rubbing her center against my stomach.

"Ryan, please," she slurs. "I want you."

Her words snap me out of my trance, and I let go of her, dropping her to the ground.

She's been drinking all night. She's drunk. And twenty. And deserves more than a drunken hook-up.

"What are you doing?" she whines, stepping forward and pawing at me. "Ryan, please."

"It's late and you're drunk. Let's get you home."

She pouts, but I ignore it, wrapping my arm around her to help her walk out. She congratulates Alec on his promotion, gives Lexi and Georgia a hug and a kiss, and then we head back to the beach house. Since I only had a couple beers I'm good to drive.

Micaela falls asleep on the way home, only waking up once we pull up and I shake her awake. Wordlessly, she disappears into her room, so I assume she's going to pass out.

I change out of my clothes and throw on a pair of sweats and a

T-shirt. I figure I'll give her a little bit and then go check on her to make sure she's okay and in bed.

"Is it hot in here?" she asks, stepping into my room a little while later. Her makeup has been removed, her hair is up in a messy bun, and she's dressed in a pair of tiny pajama bottoms and a thin tank top that shows the outline of her hardened nipples.

Without waiting for me to answer, she floats back out of my room. I follow her to the kitchen, where she grabs a water from the fridge and downs half the bottle. "Ahh, that's better."

Snatching the blanket off the couch, she stumbles out the back door. She lies on the double lounger and glances up at me. "Watch the stars with me?"

When I hesitate for a moment, nervous as hell about being too close to her, she rolls her eyes. "I promise to be on my best behavior."

Unable to tell her no, I join her. She throws the blanket over us and lays her head on my shoulder. Her warm body snuggles into my side, and my heart relaxes like it always does when she touches me.

"Did you have fun tonight?"

She nods into my shoulder. "It felt good to let loose. Felt a little like my old self." She glances up and kisses my cheek. "Thank you, Ryan. I couldn't have done this without you." She lays her head back on my shoulder, and my heart sinks. Her thank you almost sounds like a goodbye, which makes sense since it's already after midnight. Tomorrow we'll be parting ways. She'll go back home to her family and start over, and I'll say bye to mine before shipping off overseas.

"Yes, you could've," I tell her, giving her forehead a kiss. I inhale her sweet, comforting scent, praying that when I'm in the desert with my squad, I'll remember what she smelled like. "But I'm glad I was here for you."

"It's hard," she admits. "Like every second, every minute, I have to remind myself it's okay to move forward."

"But you're still doing it." I glance down and her warm chocolate eyes meet mine. "You're laughing and smiling, and you're talking about your future."

"It took me fifteen months."

"It takes strength to move forward from what happened to

your husband. I've seen men turn to the bottle, to drugs. I've seen them destroy their entire lives over losing someone. So, it took you a year. So what. You still did it. You're doing it, and I'm damn proud of you."

Micaela's eyes glimmer with unshed tears. "Thank you," she chokes out, setting her head back on my shoulder. "It's nice out here," she murmurs lazily. "Maybe... we can... sleep..." She doesn't finish her sentence, her words being replaced with soft snores. Closing my eyes, I inhale her scent one last time before I allow sleep to overtake me as well.

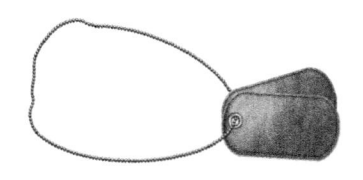

## CHAPTER TWELVE

### RYAN

Micaela peppers kisses all over my face...

Down my neck...

Along my collarbone.

She runs her hand down my torso, and I moan at her touch.

"Ryan," she purrs, but her voice sounds distant.

I reach for her, but she's not there. "Micaela? Don't leave, please." I need her close to me. When she's with me I feel centered. The racing in my head calms.

"I'm right here," she says, but I don't see her. Where is she? Is this a dream? It must be...

"Open your eyes, Ry."

I grin at the nickname. She's never called me that before, but I really like it. I do as she says and her gorgeous face comes back into view. Only it's sharper, more clear.

My hands, of their own accord, move to her hips, only to find her next to me. It's then I realize my dream wasn't really a dream...

"Micaela," I groan, reality hitting me.

"Please." She frames my cheeks with her soft, delicate hands. "I just want to feel you—our connection. I'm not asking for anything more."

*But what if I want more?* I think but don't say out loud.

"I don't want to hurt you."

"I know what this is," she says, her voice strong. "When we leave tomorrow morning, I'm starting my new life with my new plans and I know they can't include you." Her words slam against my ribcage, cracking my heart wide-open.

"It's not that..." Fuck, I want nothing more than to be part of her plans, but it's just not possible...

"I get it." She kneels next to me and presses her mouth to mine. "I know the score, and I respect you even more for resisting because I know you're only doing it to protect me. But I don't want to be protected. I don't *need* to be protected. This built-up sexual tension between us is suffocating the hell out of me, and I..." She swallows thickly, her eyes locking with mine. "I just need to breathe."

Her admission is my undoing.

Gripping her hips, I lift her onto my lap, so she's straddling my thighs, and kiss her hard. She grinds down on my dick through my boxers, moaning when she feels I'm already hard. She wasn't wrong. The sexual tension between us is like a firework, waiting to be lit. You're holding it in your hand and know what it's capable of, but as long as it stays unlit, it's safe.

Frantically, she pulls my boxers down and takes my shaft in her hand, stroking it up and down. Lifting up, she quickly rids herself of her shorts and panties, and then sinks down around me. Her warmth acting as an ignition. Her soaking wet cunt sucks my dick all the way in, and that firework sparks to life.

With her hands resting on my shoulders, she lifts and then drops, taking me in as far as she can go. Fireworks go off, loud and bright and earth-fucking-shattering, as she rides my dick. Briefly, I close my eyes, losing myself to the way I fit inside her so damn perfectly.

My eyes open and I find her face. Her eyelids are hooded over, and her fleshy lips are parted in pleasure. She rolls her hips and moans, finding the perfect spot to set her off. Her pussy walls grip me like a vice and she contracts around my dick. Taking over, I grab hold of her hips, plunging into her from underneath and finding my own release.

It's never felt like this before. This raw and gritty and... *Fuck!* It hits me just seconds before I'm about to let go. *No condom.*

Gripping her sides, I lift her up quickly, my dick popping out of her warmth just in time for me to come all over the outside of her neatly trimmed pussy and my thighs.

"Holy shit," I breathe once I've somewhat caught my breath. "That was..."

"Amazing," she finishes, sighing in contentment. The word I was thinking of was *close*, as in I came damn *close* to filling her with my cum, but amazing works too.

"Yeah, it was," I agree. I glance around and realize we're still outside in the double lounger. She's naked from the waist down, and we're both covered in my cum.

"Let's get inside and shower." Grabbing the blanket, I wrap it around her so she's hidden. Luckily it's still dark outside. We're supposed to be leaving soon to go to Newport Beach for the day.

We separate once we're inside, each taking a shower by ourselves. I'm putting my board shorts on when Micaela appears in the doorway. She's wearing her tiny yellow string bikini and ripped jean shorts. Her hair is wet from the shower and down in messy waves.

"Are you ready to go?" she asks, lifting the tank top over her head and hiding her body. A body I felt against me but didn't get a chance to fully explore. She was in charge, and while it was hot as fuck, it wasn't as satisfying as I was hoping it would be. Yeah, we both got off, but I didn't get to touch all of her perfect curves, taste her juices. I don't know how soft or firm her breasts are. How she would react if I took her nipples into my mouth and sucked on them.

I want to say fuck the day and take her back to bed, explore every inch of her I didn't get a chance to do this morning, but it's our last day together and I want to make the most out of it.

"Yeah," I tell her, throwing my shirt on.

The two-hour drive is filled with Micaela playing deejay. I hold her hand the entire way, unable to keep from touching her, and she lets it happen without question. When we arrive at the harbor, I rent us a boat and then we take off toward Balboa Island.

"Can we anchor out here?" Micaela asks from behind me.

"Right here?" I glance around. We're between Lido and Balboa Island. "Yeah, if you want."

"Please."

I check the scanner to make sure we're in a somewhat shallow spot, then go about dropping the anchor. Growing up, my parents loved to go to Florida for vacation. My mom is from Jupiter Beach and grew up on the ocean. They taught us how to surf, jet ski, and drive a boat, and when we would visit my mom's mom, my sisters and I would take the boat out for hours.

Once I'm done, I walk back over to the helm and move the boat backward a tad to make sure it's anchored good. When I feel the slight tug, I turn the engine off. I'm about to ask Micaela what she wants to do, when her arms wrap around me from behind, her hands running across my naked torso.

One of her hands descends, landing on my dick and squeezing it softly through my shorts.

"Babe," I groan, knowing immediately where this is going.

"Nobody can see us," she says, confusing my tone. The cruiser I rented isn't large by any means, but it has three glass tinted windows shading half the boat, giving us almost complete privacy. I'm not worried about anyone seeing us. I'm worried about what we're about to do—*again*. How deep we're getting only hours before we have to find our way to the surface.

Her hands disappear and then she's crouched in front of me, hidden between me and the helm of the boat. I glance down just in time to see her take my dick into her mouth through the material of my shorts. She teases me like this for a few seconds before she tugs my shorts down and takes my shaft into her mouth as far as she can go. She gags slightly when the head hits the back of her throat, and I come close to losing my shit. I'll be damned if she's going to take charge again.

Backing up slightly, I pull her into a standing position, then lift her into my arms, walking us over to the bench that stretches across the entire area. Laying her across it, I take a moment to drink her in. She's shed her shorts and shirt, leaving her in only that barely scrap of a bathing suit. The triangles of her top showcase her full breasts, and because she's turned on, her nipples are straining behind the fabric. Her bottoms are only held together with thin strings. All it would take is a pull on each side and her perfect cunt would be bared to me.

"Ryan, please," she whines desperately.

"No," I tell her. Her eyes thin, glaring at me, but before she can argue, I explain. "The first time was quick."

"That's not my fault," she sasses, and I bark out a laugh. Fuck, I can't get enough of this woman. What am I going to do when we part ways tomorrow? The thought is sobering, but I push it aside for now, wanting to stay in the moment with Micaela.

"That's not what I meant." I bend down and kiss her soft lips. "It was filled with passion. Like you said, we needed the release, but this time I'm going to take my time and worship every inch of you." Burn every detail of her perfect body into my brain for when she's gone and all I'll have is the memory of her.

Taking her foot in my hands, I place a kiss to the arch then to her delicate ankle.

"Ryan," she moans, impatience in her tone.

"Shh, every inch."

I continue kissing her heated flesh: her toned calf, the inside of her knee, up her thigh. She squirms in place, silently begging me to continue my ascent. But I don't. Instead I start all over again, this time with her other foot, making my way back up her leg. Her skin is silky smooth and smells good. Like what, I have no fucking clue. Something sweet mixed with just her. A scent I hope is engrained in my memory for when I'm gone.

When I get to the apex of her legs, I press the inside of her thighs, pushing them open. I run my nose up the center of her, inhaling her, mentally memorizing every minuscule detail.

"Ryan," she shrieks. "What are you doing?"

I assume she's asking a rhetorical question, but when I move the fabric of her bathing suit to the side and stick my nose between her pussy lips, she grabs the ends of my hair and pulls my face up.

"Ryan." Her eyes are wide in shock, her cheeks tinged pink in embarrassment, I think. "Wh-what are you doing? Get up here and fuck me."

"Every inch," I repeat, separating her lips and licking up her seam. I stop at her swollen clit and nibble on it.

"Oh my God." I glance up and her eyes roll backward. "Do that again," she breathes.

Untying the strings, I rip her bottoms from her body and drop them on the floor. Then, with my hands holding her legs apart, I devour the hell out of her pussy. Micaela's breathy moans spur me on as I work her up into a frenzy. When she's moaning loudly, begging to come, I insert two fingers into her, and she shatters around me.

"Ry..." she breathes. "It... I..." I chuckle softly at her incoherence, loving that I have her so worked up. "Ohmigod... right... there!" she screams, right before she comes all over my tongue and fingers, soaking the hell out of the leather bench. Her legs shake, trying to close of their own accord. If I wasn't holding her down, she would most definitely bow right off the seat. But with my one hand, I keep her on lock, pressing down on her pelvis and licking her straight through her orgasm.

Once her legs stop trembling and her breathing slows, I stand and push my shorts down. As I stroke my already hard as fuck dick, I make eye contact with Micaela. Her eyes are hooded over and the corners of her lips are pulled up slightly in a lazy, satiated smile. If it wouldn't be creepy as fuck, I would grab my phone and snap a picture of her just like this because there's no way my memory will ever do this moment justice.

Grabbing her legs, I pull her toward me, wrapping her legs around my waist. I drop my palms to either side of her head, and with my mouth fused against hers, I enter her in one swift motion —her hot, wet cunt damn near making me come on the spot.

Fully aware I'm only going to last so long, I break our kiss, and with my nose, move her bathing suit top up so I have access to her tits. Taking one rose-budded nipple between my lips, I suck on it, making her squirm in pleasure. Then I release it and give the other one equal attention. I suck and lick her breasts while I continue to fuck her. My pelvis rubs against hers, and she moans into my ear how good it feels.

"Ryan." She takes my face in her hands and locks eyes with me. "I... I feel like I'm going to come again."

"Go ahead, baby. Come again."

"It's right..." She grinds against me once more and her body detonates—like the most beautiful, bright fireworks, she goes off. Her eyes close, her head goes back, and her mouth makes a perfect O as she climaxes. It's the most gorgeous thing I've ever seen in my life. Our bodies are so close we've become one—two broken halves coming together to make one whole.

The sight of her is my undoing. Remembering I'm not using a

condom, I pull out and come all over her flat stomach, some of it shooting onto her tits.

Her eyes open, and the side of her mouth tugs into a satisfied smirk. "That was…"

This time I finish for her. "Fucking amazing."

After we get cleaned up the best we can, we spend the rest of the day boating and exploring the islands. We kiss and touch and make out like two horny teenagers, completely ignoring the reality of what is to come tomorrow when we wake up. We stop for dinner at a delicious seafood restaurant and when we get home, we spend the entire night under the stars talking about nothing of consequence, until Micaela can't keep her eyes open any longer, and she falls asleep in my arms.

When I wake in the morning, I'm still outside on the double lounger, only Micaela isn't here. Her side is empty. My first thought is she left without saying goodbye, and my heart sinks, praying she's not gone yet. I can't let her go. I know I said I have to, but I can't. Maybe if I hadn't felt what it's like to be with her, kiss her, touch her, I could've walked away. But now I know, and I can't do it. I don't care what it takes. We'll make it work. This can't be the end.

I tear the blanket off me and jog inside, hoping she's still here. When I open the door, I find her in the kitchen, cooking at the stove. Her back is to me, her hair up in a messy bun. She's wearing a tiny tank top and shorts, and she's dancing to the silent beat in her earbuds. I inhale a sigh of relief. She's still here. I'm not too late.

As if feeling my stare, she twirls around with the most beautiful smile on her face. "Morning," she says, plucking her earbuds from her ears. "I made us breakfast." She practically bounces over to me, setting a plate of food on the table for me.

"I woke up this morning and didn't want to wake you," she says, sitting in her seat in front of her own food. "Look what I did." She grabs a piece of paper from the other side of the table and hands it to me. I sit across from her and read it:

***Enroll back at ULV***
***Apply to USD***
***Apply to internship at Scripps***

**Ask Mom about job at rec center**

The list goes on, detailing every step of her new plan.

My eyes meet hers, and I swallow my emotions. She came here to heal, to move forward, and she did exactly that. We both got what we came here for, and now we have to walk away. It doesn't matter that I've fallen in love with this woman. I can't ask her to wait for me, to put her life on hold. She's young and happy and carefree, and she deserves to have this fresh start, to look forward to her future again. I would only hold her back, and I won't do that to her.

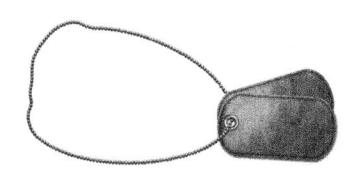

## CHAPTER THIRTEEN

### MICAELA

I finish packing the last of my stuff and glance around my room, double-checking to make sure I'm not leaving anything before I turn the light off. In the dark, I take a deep breath, willing myself to smile, to be happy. In a few minutes, we'll part ways and then I can have a good cry. But right now I need to be strong. I promised him nothing more, and even though I've fallen completely in love with him, I won't put Ryan in that position. It's not fair to him, to me. He helped me heal, move forward, and when I get home I'm going to do just that. I will focus on my future. I can't be with him. He's not the man for me. I just barely moved past the death of my husband. It would be idiotic to even consider being with another man whose job involves risking his life. No, Ryan is not the one for me. He will always hold a special spot in my heart for what he did for me this week, but he's not my future.

I roll my luggage down the hall and find Ryan in the foyer with his. He grants me a small smile, but it doesn't reach his eyes, and I wonder if he's already missing me the way I am him. If he is, though, he doesn't say anything.

We step outside and he locks the door. I want to push it back open, beg him to give us a few more days. I'm not ready to go home yet, ready to leave him.

But I don't. I plaster on a fake smile and wrap my arms around him for a hug, breathing him in, trying to memorize everything about him before we part ways.

"Thank you for everything," I choke out.

Ryan holds me tight against him, and I sink into his touch. "Thank *you*," he murmurs into my ear. "You got this, Micaela. Promise you'll invite me to your college graduation." He laughs, and I join in.

"I will," I vow.

Reluctantly, we separate. He looks at me like he wants to say something, but he doesn't. He bends slightly and kisses the corner of my mouth. "You're going to do amazing things."

"While you're off saving the world," I half-joke.

"Something like that."

I reach up on my tiptoes and kiss his cheek, needing to touch him one last time. "I will never forget this week," I tell him.

"You and me both."

---

FOUR HOURS LATER, I get home and my family is waiting for me. My mom pulls me into a hug and tells me I look great. My dad says he's missed me and is glad I'm home. My brother and sister both hug me and tell me they've missed me.

The following days I keep myself busy. I do exactly what I said I was going to do. I enroll in ULV for the fall semester. I only have one semester left, so I also apply to San Diego for spring semester. I submit my application for the internship at Scripps. I also get my job back at the rec center. It'll not only keep me busy until I start school in August, but will help me put money away for when I make the move to San Diego.

I don't see Ryan again, but my dad mentions he left. Two months in Texas at Fort Bliss for training and then he'll be in Afghanistan for the next year. I send a prayer to God to keep him safe, and then I visit Ian's grave, and for the first time since he died, I talk to him without crying. I read him my letter, and when I'm done, I rip it into pieces and let it go into the wind.

The days turn into weeks. I stay busy with work, my friends, my family. I think about Ryan often, but I don't allow myself to go there. I can't. I'm finally back to my old self. My heart is finally healing. My future is mapped out. And then one day my phone rings with a number I don't recognize, shocking the hell out of me.

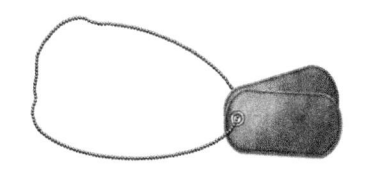

## CHAPTER FOURTEEN

### RYAN

"Hello." Her voice is so sweet over the phone. I want to record it and listen to it over and over again. It's been two months since I've seen her, heard her, touched her, and I miss her so goddamn much.

"Hey," I say dumbly.

"Ryan," she says back, curiosity and maybe hope in her tone.

"I got your number from the receptionist at the Fight Club." I take a deep breath. "I'm in Texas…"

"Fort Bliss." She knows where I am. Does that mean she asked about me? Does she miss me the same way I miss her?

"Yeah. We have a weekend before we leave, and I was wondering…" I clear my throat. "I thought maybe I could get you a ticket and fly you down here for a few days."

"Ryan." This time, the way she says my name has my heart plummeting. I already know what she's going to say, and I don't blame her. This was a bad idea. We said goodbye, went our separate ways.

"I know," I tell her, not needing her to explain. I shouldn't have called, shouldn't have put her in this position. "Everything's okay with you?" I ask, steering the conversation away from rough waters.

"Yeah," she says softly. "You?"

"Yeah." We're both silent for a moment, and I mentally kick myself for calling her. I already know she's doing good. I've asked around, stalked her social media. She's happy, moving forward. "I better go," I finally say. "I just want you to know I'm so proud of you." And before she can say anything back, I hang up.

"Cruz," Antwon Stark, my friend and squad mate says, walking over. "The guys and I are going to head to Trolley's. You down?" Trolley's is a bar near the base where everyone goes to have a drink, get dinner, chill out when we have downtime.

I stare at my phone, wondering if maybe I should've tried harder. Told her how I feel. Begged her to come visit me. As I'm contemplating calling her back, a text comes through from her.

Two words: **I'm sorry**

"Yeah," I say to Stark, "let's go."

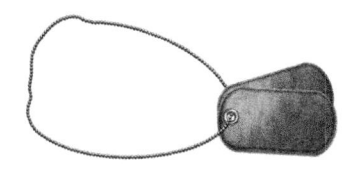

## CHAPTER FIFTEEN

### SEVEN MONTHS LATER

### RYAN

"Oh my God, you're here!" My mom runs across the room and throws her arms around me for a hug. "Let me see you." She backs up, wiping her happy tears from her eyes, and assesses me from head to toe like she does every time I come home. I'm seven months into my tour in Afghanistan and was able to put in for my leave for the last two weeks of December. As soon as I arrived on U.S. soil, I drove home to see my parents. I had assumed they would be in Breckenridge for the holidays, but luckily, instead of surprising both my parents, I told my dad to give him a heads-up, and learned they were staying home this year.

"Welcome home, Son." My dad pulls me into a tight hug.

"Thanks." I glance around the house. "Where are Faith and Chloe?"

"They're at the boutique," Mom says. "It's crazy busy with the holidays. They'll be over later with Cameron and Brad and the kids." Mom hugs me again.

"Is that why you guys aren't in Breckenridge this year?" I ask, bummed they're here while everyone else is there. It's been seven months since I've heard Micaela's voice, almost nine since I've seen her. I considered calling her a million times, but didn't think a satellite call from overseas was the best way to talk about us. I typed up a dozen emails, but nothing I wrote seemed to convey my thoughts correctly. I checked her social media a couple times, but she hasn't posted a single thing. To say I was looking forward to finally seeing her would be an understatement, but it's not like I could go to Breckenridge when my family is here.

"Everybody stayed home this year," Mom says, shaking me from my thoughts.

"What do you mean?" Everybody always goes to Breckenridge for the holidays, every year since I was brought into this family. *Except last year when Micaela's family stayed home because she was mourning the death of her husband...*

Mom frowns. "It's been a weird year. Micaela left for a couple weeks and when she came back..." She clears her throat.

"When she came back, what?" I prompt, starting to freak the hell out. My dad gives me a weird look, but I ignore it, focusing on my mom.

"She found out she was pregnant." All the blood drains downward. "She's due soon and can't travel, so everybody is staying home for the holidays. We're planning to still go up for a couple weeks after the New Year."

"She's pregnant?" I choke out. "How far along?"

"Nine months. She's due in a couple weeks," Dad says, eyeing me curiously. "You okay?"

"Who's the dad?"

Mom shakes her head. "We're not sure. After she found out, Marco and Bella kind of stepped back from everyone. I think they're just trying to be there for their daughter."

"I need to go," I say, already halfway out the door.

"What? Why?" Mom calls out.

"I'll be back!" I yell, slamming the door behind me and jogging to my truck.

The drive to Micaela's house isn't far since they live in the next neighborhood over. I could've walked, but I'm too worked up. There's no way... She can't be... I'm not... I can't even finish a single fucking thought. My fists are clenched around the steering wheel, and I'm dripping in sweat from the adrenaline coursing through my body. There has to be an explanation. Maybe she got home and slept with someone else. The thought of another man inside her only pisses me off further.

I press the code into the call box at their gate, knowing it since

I've been here several times over the years, then pull through, stopping behind Micaela's vehicle. I slam the truck into park, turn the ignition off, and jump out. I bang on the door, and several seconds later, it swings open.

Bella. Her eyes widen knowingly, but I don't ask her shit. I don't want to hear it from her. I want to hear it from Micaela herself.

"I'd like to speak to Micaela, please," I grit out, trying to remain polite.

She nods once. "Come in." I step inside, but before she can call for Micaela, she comes waddling out of the kitchen, her eyes on the slice of pizza she's consuming and her phone in her other hand. She doesn't spot me at first, and I use the moment to take her in. She's strikingly beautiful. Her hair is up in her signature messy bun, exposing her slim neck, the same neck I kissed and sucked on. She's wearing a shirt that says *Mama in the making* and tight leggings that cover her legs. Her feet are bare—the same feet I trailed kisses across.

My eyes go back to the shirt, to what's *under* the shirt. The reason for the saying on the shirt, the reason why she's waddling. There's a large bump—a bump that only comes from a woman being pregnant.

"Is it mine?" I blurt out.

Micaela's gaze shoots up, her eyes turning into saucers. The pizza is hanging out of her mouth, and in shock, she drops her phone. She scrambles to pick it up, but her belly is big and she can't bend easily. Her mom rushes over and picks it up, then takes the pizza and plate from her, setting it on the counter.

"Ryan," Micaela breathes, stunned frozen in place. "Wh-what are you doing here?"

Her question rubs me the wrong way. "I asked you a fucking question." I step toward her. "Is the baby mine?"

Her eyes dart from her mom to me, and then she nods. "Yes," she whispers, at least having the decency to look ashamed.

"Do my parents know?" There's no way they would know she was carrying my baby and keep that from me.

"No," she says, confirming my thoughts. "They just know I'm pregnant."

"Did you know?" I ask Marco, who has just stepped into the

room, joining his wife and daughter. "Did you?" I glance at Bella. "Did you guys know your daughter was pregnant with my fucking baby?"

"You need to calm down," Marco says, stepping toward me. Judging by how calm he is, he either knew, or he's putting on a damn good front pretending not to be shocked.

"Fuck calming down," I boom. "She's pregnant with my fucking kid." I look over at Micaela. "Why don't my parents know?"

Micaela swallows thickly. "Nobody, besides my parents, Lexi, and Georgia, knows you're the dad."

"Were you going to ever tell me?" I ask, my fists clenching at my sides.

"I—" Tears prick her eyes, and normally that would have me trying to comfort her. While we spent time together, I would've done anything to make sure she didn't shed a single tear. But I'm too pissed right now.

"Don't you fucking cry," I bark, stalking up to her.

Marco steps between us. "You need to calm down," he repeats.

I get in his face, towering a good four inches over him. "Don't fucking tell me to calm down. I just found out the woman I slept with is pregnant and didn't even have the decency to tell me."

I step around Marco, so I'm face-to-face with the woman who's been keeping secrets. "Were you going to keep my baby from me?" I don't give her a chance to answer. "Tell him he has no father? Or that his didn't want him?"

She shakes her head, tears coursing down her cheeks.

"Fuck, Micaela. I came from a home where my parents didn't want me. I was adopted because they chose drugs over me. How the fuck could you do this?"

I point my finger at Marco. "You of all people should understand. She"—I jab my finger toward Bella—"kept her"—I point at Micaela—"from you."

"That's enough!" Marco barks. "One, you need to keep my wife the hell out of this. And two, nobody was keeping the baby from you."

"No? Then explain to me why she's standing there nine

fucking months pregnant and I'm only just finding out about it. And only because my mom told me!"

There's a gasp from behind me, and when I turn around, my parents are standing in the doorway. My mom's covering her mouth with her hands, and my dad is glaring at Marco.

"The baby is yours?" Mom asks, walking farther into the room. She directs her next question at Micaela. "That baby is my son's and you weren't going to tell him?" She looks at Bella, confusion and anger in her eyes. "How could you?"

"You knew?" my dad asks, his question directed at Marco.

"It wasn't our place to say," Marco says. "It was Micaela's decision and whether we agreed with it or not, we had to respect it."

"Please," Micaela says softly, her eyes bloodshot, and her cheeks tearstained. "Let me explain."

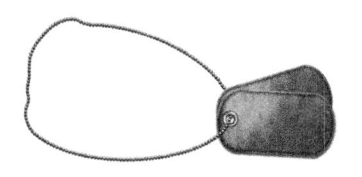

## CHAPTER SIXTEEN

### SEVEN MONTHS AGO

### MICAELA

"Yep, you're pregnant," Lexi says as I flush the toilet after throwing up for the third time. She turns her phone around so I can view the screen. "Throwing up, sore breasts, no period. All signs point to you being knocked up."

I rinse my mouth out with mouthwash then wash my hands. "It could be food poisoning," I say, completely in denial.

"Or the flu," Georgia adds.

Lexi scoffs. "Yeah, sure. Let's go." Lexi swipes her keys off the dresser.

"Where to?" I ask.

"The store to get a test," she says over her shoulder, already walking out the door.

The three of us jump into her jeep and she heads to the store. The entire way my heart thumps against my ribcage as I continue to pretend Lexi is crazy. There's no way I'm pregnant. We only had sex a couple times. Mentally, I roll my eyes, knowing that's all it takes.

"You coming in?" she asks when she pulls into the parking spot in front of the drug store.

"No, you go." I pull my credit card out of my back pocket, but she waves me off.

"Save it, you'll need all the money you can get when you have this baby."

"Lex," Georgia groans.

"What? It's the truth." She shrugs. "And I call dibs on throwing the baby shower."

A few minutes later she gets back in the car and drops the bag into my lap. "I bought a few just in case. Did you know the tests are on the same aisle as the condoms and tampons?" She cackles, and Georgia smacks her arm, glaring. "What?" she says, exasperated. "It's pretty damn ironic. You're going to that aisle for something. If not to get condoms, then to get a pregnancy test. It's like a reminder every time you go to grab condoms. If you don't use these, you'll end up buying those."

If what she was saying wasn't so damn true, I would be laughing right along with her. But the fact is, Ryan and I didn't use protection. He pulled out every time, but everyone knows that isn't foolproof.

We get back to her house and I take all three tests. All of them saying the same damn thing: **PREGNANT**

I'm freaking pregnant.

Lexi was right. All the signs pointed to my being pregnant, but I didn't want to admit it. Now, I have no choice.

"Are you okay?" Lexi asks, her voice unusually serious.

"No, I need to go."

"Go where?" Georgia asks, concerned.

"Home. I need my mom." I'm every bit aware I sound like a child when I say this, but I don't care. I need her now. I need to tell her what I've done. What's to come. I need her to hold me and tell me it's going to be okay. She had me when she was close to my age, so she'll understand.

"I'm not sure you're okay to drive," Lexi points out.

"I'm pregnant, not handicapped."

"And in shock," Georgia says.

"I'll be okay." I throw my clothes into my luggage. I came to visit for the weekend, needing to get away after Ryan had called and asked if I would visit him. I almost said yes, but I couldn't do it. I couldn't allow myself to fall for a man whose job involves risking his life. Not again.

Four hours later I arrive home, and the second I stumble

through the door and find my mom, I throw myself into her arms, letting the tears come.

"Micaela, what's wrong?" she coos, sitting us on the couch and holding me in her arms.

"I messed up," I say through a hiccup. "I'm pregnant."

She stills momentarily, but then rocks me in her arms, allowing me to cry without asking any questions. "Everything is going to change," I say through a sob. "All the plans I made..."

She pats her lap and I lay my head down on it, curling up into a ball. She runs her fingers through the strands of my hair, calming me down as I cry into her lap. "Shh, it's okay, sweet girl, everything is going to be okay."

When I finally get a hold of myself enough to talk, I sit up and she wipes my tears, giving me a soft smile.

"I didn't know you've been with anyone," she says, her voice hurt but not judgmental. My mom and I are close and I usually tell her everything.

"Only one guy," I admit. "When I was away..." She nods. "As you know I went to the beach house, and when I got there, Ryan was there."

Her eyes widen briefly. "Ryan..."

"Cruz." I sniffle. "Dad had given him the key so he could spend some time there before being shipped off to Afghanistan."

"I didn't know that," she says.

"I figured as much when I told you where I was and you didn't mention it."

"Which was why you asked me not to tell your dad where you were." Her lips turn down into a slight frown.

"I'm sorry. I just needed some time and I knew he would send someone to check on me."

"True," she agrees. "He would've."

"I didn't plan on this," I say dumbly. "I finally moved forward... Made all these plans."

"Stop," Mom says, resting her palm against my cheek. "I didn't plan for you, but you were without a doubt the best damn surprise of my life."

"And mine," Dad says, walking into the room. He takes one look at me and stalks over. "Why are you crying?"

His question has the waterworks starting all over again, and I burst into tears. "I'm pregnant."

"What?" Dad gasps, sitting next to me. "Who the fuck knocked you up?"

"Marco," Mom chides. "Calm down, please."

"No," he booms. "I want to know who the fuck knocked up my daughter, and why he's not here with her right now."

"He can't be here," I mutter through my cries.

"He had no problem knocking you up. He should be man enough to come here with you and support you through this."

"He doesn't know," I admit.

This gets Dad's attention. "Who is it, Micaela?" he asks again.

"You can't tell anyone, and you can't freak out, please," I beg.

Dad nods.

"The baby is Ryan's," I murmur.

"Ryan who?" he asks slowly.

"Cruz."

"When the hell did you hook up with him?" He stands, knocking the coffee table back a couple inches.

"Two months ago... at the beach house."

I can see it when he puts the pieces together. He begins pacing the room, murmuring to himself, while Mom and I stay seated, waiting for him to calm down.

"I'm going to kill him," he finally says, stopping in place. "He's dead."

"He's in Afghanistan," I choke out, fresh tears welling in my eyes.

"Fuck." Dad's face softens, and he cuts across the room, pulling me into his arms. He holds me for a few minutes, until I get control of my emotions.

"You have to tell him," he says. "You can't keep it from him." When his eyes meet my mom's, I know exactly what he's thinking. When she was pregnant with me, she kept it from him. It's not something they talk about often, but my mom and I are close and she was honest with me. When I lost Ian and Dad recommended I write him a letter, they told me the story behind my mom's pregnancy and what my dad went through when he was addicted to drugs.

"This isn't the same thing." I stand, needing some space. "He's in another country. He could die over there."

"Honey," Mom says sympathetically.

"How would I even get ahold of him? Email him, send a damn letter. Hey, surprise! I'm pregnant and you're thousands of miles away, fighting for your life in the desert. Congratulations, Baby Daddy!"

"Micaela," my dad starts.

"No, I'm going to tell him. But not now. Not while he's over there. It's not the right time. And I'm asking you not to tell anyone either. *If* he makes it back alive, I'll tell him."

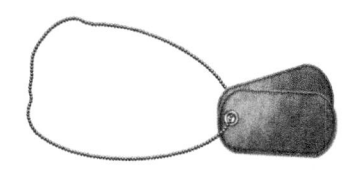

## CHAPTER SEVENTEEN

### PRESENT DAY

### RYAN

"I WAS GOING TO TELL YOU," Micaela says softly. "But I was..." She sucks in sharp breath. "What if you...?" I fill in the blanks, knowing exactly what's going through her mind. She was scared. What if I didn't make it back alive? It doesn't make up for her keeping me in the dark, but on some level, I get it. She lost her husband, and she was scared of losing me. It's why I walked away from her that day. I knew we couldn't be together. I knew she would never be happy being with someone like me, and she deserved to be happy.

"I'm sorry," she says, her hand landing on her protruding belly in a protective manner.

I want to tell her it's okay, but I'm still pissed and hurt as hell. "If I hadn't come here, I would've never known. I would've gone back to Afghanistan none the wiser."

"She can't take back the way she handled it," Marco says. "But I can tell you it's been eating her up."

"That's our grandson as well," my mom says. "We had a right to know. That baby is our family."

"I wanted to tell Ryan first," Micaela says. Her hands tighten around her stomach, and she flinches.

"You okay?" I ask, my concern for her overpowering the anger.

"Yeah. I've been having contractions all day."

"How far apart?" Mom asks. Between her own and my sisters', she's been around for five pregnancies.

"Maybe twenty minutes or so. I still have a couple weeks."

*A couple weeks.* I'm only here for a couple weeks, and then I'm gone again for another four months. During which time she's going to have her baby. *Our baby.* And just like that, my anger is back.

"I could've been here," I say, trying to keep my tone in check. "I could've planned my leave for when the baby comes, but now I'm here and I'll probably be gone when you give birth."

"I'm—"

"Yeah, I heard, you're *sorry.*"

Needing to get away before I say something I might regret, I turn around and walk out the door. My parents call my name, but I ignore them, slamming the door behind me.

I'm about to get in my truck and take off when I hear Micaela call my name.

"I can't do this right now."

"Ryan, please," she begs. "I didn't mean for this to happen."

"What did you think would happen by hiding this from me? You didn't even try to get ahold of me. No letter or email. I have my phone." I pull it out of my pocket. "Not a single text or phone call. So, please, Micaela, tell me... what the hell did you mean to happen?"

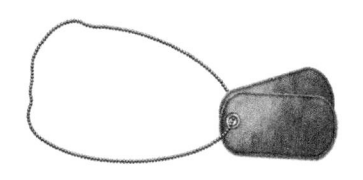

## CHAPTER EIGHTEEN

### MICAELA

Ryan glares at me with a myriad of emotions shining in his eyes: anger, frustration, confusion, but the most prominent is hurt. I hurt him with my actions. I was strictly thinking about my own self-preservation when I made the decision not to tell him about our baby. I was blinded by the distance between us, but now that he's standing in front of me, I can clearly see how wrong I was.

With the door open, our parents are standing in the doorway. Everybody is quiet now with their attention on me. I stay focused on Ryan, though, because he's the person I owe an explanation to. The person who was affected by my choices.

"I know it was wrong, but I was scared," I admit, just as my stomach tightens with a contraction. I wrap my arms around myself, closing my eyes momentarily to get through it. When I open my eyes, they're filled with tears, but I refuse to let them fall. I did this, created this tension, and I need to take responsibility. "I told myself if I didn't tell you, then you weren't the dad, so when something happened to you, and you didn't make it back here, I wouldn't be losing the father of my baby because you never knew you were." Somebody gasps from behind me, but nobody says a word.

"Please don't fight," I plead, making eye contact with everyone. "It was my choice, not my parents'. Mine. I didn't do it to hurt any of you, but I get now how it did. But please don't blame them. I'm an adult and I chose not to tell anyone."

I look back at Ryan. "I know that's messed up," I say, taking a deep breath as another contraction hits. "But you know how messed up I am from losing my husband. Every time I thought about telling you, I imagined you getting killed over there, and I couldn't do it. I'm so sorry. I know it doesn't help, and I can't—" My breath is knocked out of me as another contraction overtakes my body, the pain almost unbearable. "Take it back," I finish.

"It hasn't been twenty minutes," Ryan says.

"What?"

"You said your contractions are about twenty minutes apart. It was only maybe five minutes between them in the house and then not even two just now."

"Two?" my mom says. "Are you sure?"

"Every time she has one she holds her stomach," Ryan says, pointing at me as another contraction hits, this one worse than the others. I squeeze my eyes shut, taking deep breaths in and out until it passes.

"Micaela, is that true?" Mom asks.

"I think so," I breathe. "They're coming closer now and"—I double over in pain, and Ryan catches me—"they hurt."

"We need to get you to the hospital," Ryan says, wrapping his arms around me and walking me to his truck.

"We'll grab your stuff and meet you there," Mom says.

The drive to the hospital is filled with uncomfortable silence, and I hate that it's because of what I've done. I spent several days with Ryan, and from the very first minute we spoke, it was always comfortable. So the fact that it's not now makes me feel sick inside, especially since we're about to bring a baby into this world. A baby we created.

Ryan parks and we go in through the main entrance, going straight to the labor and delivery ward. I've preregistered, so once I give them my name and show them my license, they bring me back to a room so they can assess me. After I'm changed into a hospital gown, the nurse sets me up with monitors across my belly and chest to monitor the baby's and my heartbeat, and then the doctor comes in and checks me out.

"Your water hasn't broken, but you're almost completely

dilated. Since you're already thirty-eight weeks, I would like to break your water and push you along rather than send you home only to come back again."

I glance over at Ryan, whose face is completely devoid of any emotion. "Whatever you think is best," I tell the doctor, wishing my mom would hurry up and get here.

"Would you like any pain medication?" he asks. "Once you hit full dilatation you won't be able to get any."

A huge contraction hits, and I nod emphatically. I read on those moms groups how a lot of women like to go at it all natural, but I am clearly *not* one of those women.

After the doctor breaks my water, the nurse cleans the area up, and then an anesthesiologist comes in and gives me an epidural. Ryan stays the entire time, sitting on the couch and staring at me but not saying a word. I can't tell if he's mad or concerned, or if he's trying to give me space.

Once I'm situated, the nurse lets me know if I have any family who would like to visit, they can come in now. Ryan offers to go get them, and a few minutes later returns with our moms.

"The men said to let them know once the baby comes," Kayla says with a playful eye roll. "I just wanted to come in and make sure you're okay." She bends over and kisses my forehead.

"I'm okay. The drugs are already working," I joke, thankful she's not too mad at me.

"I texted Liza," Mom says, referring to my younger sister. "She's at a friend's house but is getting a ride here, and Liam is hanging out with your dad in the waiting room. They both said to tell you they love you."

"The doctor said it shouldn't be too long. He broke my water and I'm almost completely dilated." I shrug, not really sure what the hell any of that means. I've read a million books on what to expect once I have the baby, but I probably should've read at least one on labor and delivery.

"Good evening," the nurse says cheerily. "How's everyone?"

Everyone mumbles an okay or good.

She checks my blood pressure and then walks over to the machine that's monitoring the baby's heartbeat. She smiles, tells me she'll be back in a little while to check on me, then disappears.

"You guys don't have to hang out here," I say, once she's gone.

"I'm the only one who has to be stuck in this room." I laugh softly, my eyes feeling heavy from the pain meds.

"I'm going to go let the guys know everything is okay," Kayla says. She stops at Ryan and rubs a hand up and down his shoulder before she exits.

"I think I'll join her," Mom says after a beat, pressing a kiss to my forehead. "I'll be back soon," she whispers, letting me know she's giving Ryan and me a moment.

When she leaves, and it's only Ryan and me in the room, neither of us says a word for several long minutes. The epidural is working and I can barely feel the contractions.

Ryan stands and walks over to the monitor. "We're going to have a baby," he murmurs, lifting the paper that's printing out the baby's heartbeat. Unsure if he's talking to me or to himself, I don't respond.

"How are you feeling?" he asks, walking back over to me.

"Okay. He's kicking. Do you want to feel?"

"He?" He raises a brow.

"I don't really know. I decided to wait and find out. But I think it's a boy." Every time I would see him on the monitor I would imagine him with Ryan's and my brown hair and Ryan's cobalt blue eyes.

I place Ryan's hand on my belly. The baby presses one of his limbs against my stomach and Ryan's eyes light up. "Holy shit," he whispers. "There's a baby in there."

I choke out a laugh, for the first time feeling a little lighter since he showed up. "There is."

"I almost missed all this," he says, his hand and eyes not leaving my stomach.

"I'm so sorry, Ry." His gaze moves to my face, and his eyes soften. "I never meant to hurt you."

"I've been thinking about you for the last nine months," he admits. "I thought about writing you a million times, but I didn't want to put you in that position." He pauses for a moment. "Did you know... when I called and asked you to visit?"

"No." I shake my head to emphasize my answer. "I mean, I might've had a clue, but I was deep in denial. Then I went to visit Georgia and Lexi, and Lexi made me take a test. By the time I got it confirmed by a doctor you were already gone." It's becoming hard to keep my eyes open, but I try, needing to make things right with Ryan.

"I'm so sorry," I say again, the words coming out in a slur. "If I could do it all over again…"

Ryan pulls a chair over and sits in it, putting his hand back on my belly. "Shh, it's okay, I know. Just rest. You have a long night ahead of you. We'll deal with everything else later."

I nod, closing my eyes so I can rest them. Today has been emotionally draining, and when I leave here I'm going to have a baby. I need to get all the sleep I can while I can.

At some point, I must've drifted off, because the next thing I know, I'm hearing voices that weren't here before I fell asleep. I open my eyes to find Ryan standing by the monitor, along with my mom, the doctor, and nurse.

"I agree," the doctor says, looking at Ryan. "The heartbeat has decreased significantly and in a short amount of time." He glances at the nurse. "Let's prep her for an emergency cesarean. The baby appears to be in distress."

"Yes, sir."

"What's going on?" I ask, suddenly nervous and confused.

"Ryan was watching the heartbeat and noticed it dropped rather quickly," Mom says, "so he called for the doctor."

"Something's wrong with my baby?" I cover my belly with my hands, even though there's nothing I can do.

"No," the nurse says, moving the IV to a portable unit, "but when the baby shows signs of distress, we want to get him out as soon as possible so he doesn't remain in distress, and since you aren't fully dilated yet, it's best to perform a C-section rather than put him through the stress of a natural delivery."

The nurse hands me a medical cap. "Put this on." She holds a set of scrubs out for Ryan. "Only one person can go in, but you can bring a camera to take pictures."

Ryan glances at my mom, torn. "Are you okay with…"

"You're the father," my mom says before he can finish his question. "Make sure you take tons of pictures and come get us once you can." She gives him a hug then walks over to me. "Everything is going to be fine." She kisses my temple. "I love you, sweet girl."

With her words, it hits me. I'm about to become a mom. The

doctor is going to cut me open and take my baby out of me. My baby, who is in distress.

"Mom," I cry out. "I can't do this alone."

"You're not," she says. "Ryan will be there, and as soon as you're approved for visitors, we'll come visit. I'm not going anywhere."

I glance at Ryan, who's frowning at me, and my heart sinks. "But I'm scared," I admit, tears stinging my eyes. "I need you." I know I'm working myself up, but I'm freaking out. What if something's wrong with the baby? I can't do this on my own.

"It's going to be okay," my mom says, tears welling in her eyes. She gives me another kiss, then looks at Ryan before she leaves. "Take care of our girl, please." Ryan's eyes widen, but he nods.

The nurse comes back in with another nurse. "Put those on," she says to Ryan, pointing at the scrubs. "Nurse Rose is going to walk you to the OR while I wheel Micaela down and get her situated. Once she's prepped, we'll let you come in."

A few minutes later, I'm in a cold room with a blue separator blocking my view of my belly. The doctor walks me through what he's doing, but I'm not absorbing anything he's saying, almost positive I'm having a panic attack.

"Hey," a gravelly voice says. I turn my face slightly and find Ryan's face only a hairbreadth away from mine. "Breathe, Micaela, you got this." He takes my hand in his and squeezes it softly. "I'm here with you."

"I'm really freaking scared," I say through a sob.

"What do you need from me?" he asks in a voice that reminds me of our time together at the beach house.

"Can you stand and watch? Make sure the baby is okay, and take pictures?"

"I can do that."

"All right, Dad," the doctor says. "Get your camera ready."

Ryan stands and pulls his phone out of his pocket. I can't see the doctor or anyone else, so my eyes are trained on Ryan, watching his expression.

"And it's a… boy," the doctor says.

A boy. I have a baby boy. Ryan and I have a baby boy.

Ryan's eyes fill with emotion, but he doesn't take any pictures. And then it hits me. The baby isn't crying.

"Ryan," I say nervously. "Why isn't the baby crying?" My heart is beating out of my chest, and it's hard to breathe. Something is wrong. On every TV show I've ever seen, the baby comes out crying.

I hear the doctor and nurses talking, but it's hard to make out what they're saying.

"Ryan..."

"Everything is okay," Ryan says tightly, his eyes never leaving whatever it is he's looking at.

"I can't hear him," I cry. "He should be crying."

"It's okay," Ryan says softly. "They're working on him. He's beautiful... perfect."

"But he's not—"

And then I hear it. The most beautiful sound I've ever heard in my life. My son crying. Tears drip down Ryan's face as he holds the phone up and snaps some pictures.

A minute later, a nurse walks over with the bundled up baby. "Here he is," she says. "Say hello to your baby boy."

She holds him next to me and I lift my face mask to give him a soft kiss on his cheek. "Is he okay?"

"He was having a little trouble adapting to the world. I'm going to take him to the NICU to get him checked out. Once you're out of recovery, we'll take you to see him." And with those parting words, she whisks my baby away.

"Ryan, go with them, please," I plead.

"What about you?" he asks, his tone filled with concern and uncertainty.

"I'm fine." I lock eyes with him. "Go make sure our son is okay, please."

"Okay."

I lie, staring at the ceiling while the doctor closes me back up. It feels like hours before I'm finally rolled back to my room. When I get there, Ryan is waiting. I glance around, but there's no baby.

"Where is he?" I ask, panicking.

"Whoa, calm down. They want him to stay in the NICU so they can monitor him to be on the safe side, but he's perfect, Micaela. I promise." Ryan takes my hand in his and brings my knuckles to his lips. "He's so fucking perfect. He's eight pounds exactly. Twenty-two inches. He has a full head of curly brown hair. His eyes are a dark blue like mine, but the nurse said they can change... and his lips..." He traces my lips with his finger. "They're heart-shaped like yours. He's the perfect combination of us."

Chills run down my spine when he touches me. I've missed Ryan so much. When I was alone, I would imagine what it would be like if things were different. If he wasn't in the military and in Afghanistan. We would've taken the pregnancy test together. He would've gathered me into his arms and told me he loved me and couldn't wait for the baby. We would've moved in together and spent months decorating the baby's nursery.

Ryan pulls his phone out and turns the screen so I can see the pictures he took of our sweet baby boy. My heart swells with a love so strong I can barely breathe. "You got to hold him?" I ask, when he gets to a picture of him holding our son.

"Yeah. Your mom took the picture. She's with him now."

"I want to see him."

"The nurse said you have to wait for the epidural to wear off and then I can wheel you to the NICU."

"I want to see him now." I pout, my emotions getting the better of me. "I'm fine."

"That's because you're numb from the epidural," the nurse says, strolling in. "And once it wears off, you will feel everything. You will be prescribed something so you're not in pain, but it won't numb you."

"I want to see my baby."

"And you will, but we can't let you get up yet."

"Can you bring him here? Aren't babies supposed to stay in the room with their moms?"

"Because he was struggling when he arrived, he will have to stay in the NICU. It's hospital policy."

"For how long?"

"Until you both are released. The good news is you'll get some rest, so take advantage of it, but you will have to go visit him. Are you planning to breastfeed?"

"Yes, for as long as I can, then I'm going to try to pump."

"Okay, as soon as we can, we'll get you over to your baby."

I close my eyes in frustration. I want to see him now. He needs to see me, to know who I am.

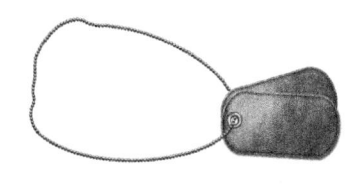

## CHAPTER NINETEEN

### RYAN

I watch as Micaela struggles to remain in bed and not try to bolt to find our son. She's so beautiful. So strong. She just had her baby ripped from her body and was glued back together. She should be exhausted, passed out, getting some rest, yet all she cares about is getting to our son. *Our son.* Fuck, I have a son. With Micaela. A beautiful, perfect son. This entire day has been crazy. I came home to visit my family, hoping to see Micaela. But I never in a million years would've thought I would show up at her house and find out she was pregnant with my son.

While we're waiting for her to be able to go to the NICU, our families stop in to visit. Her brother is carrying balloons, and her dad has a bouquet of flowers. My sisters each give her baby gifts, which keeps her occupied—opening the boxes of clothes and chatting about them—but I can see it in her eyes. She's being polite, but all she wants is to get to our son.

"I hate this," she says with the most adorable pout when everyone leaves so she can get some rest.

"I'm sure it won't be much longer."

She rolls her eyes, and I laugh. Fuck, I've missed her so much. I want to be mad at her, but my heart is too full. She gave me the most precious gift in the entire world.

"Do you have a name in mind?" I ask, trying to distract her.

"I thought of a couple, but I'm not set on one. Any names significant to you?" she asks. "Anyone you want to name him after?"

I give her question some thought. I was adopted, so I don't know where my name comes from or why I have it. I have no middle name. I don't know any of my biological family members. And then it hits me... This baby is the first biological relative I know. He has my blood running through his veins. I never not considered my family, *my family* just because we don't share blood. But knowing my son does has my heart pumping hard against my ribcage. I don't know who my biological father is. He was a piece of shit, and I don't care to know him. But I know who the man who raised and loved me is: Bentley Ryan Cruz. The man who took me in, gave me his last name, and loved me like his own.

"What are you thinking?" Micaela asks.

"Um... well... my dad's middle name is Ryan. He's named after his dad, which coincidently is also my name."

Micaela smiles softly. "I didn't know that. That's really cool. Like it was meant to be. Would you like to name him Ryan?"

"We don't have to," I backtrack. "What names were you thinking?"

"I like Ryan," she says. "It's a good, strong name. And we could give him my dad's middle name too. It's Alejandro."

"Ryan Alejandro..." I don't finish, unsure if she'll use my last name or hers.

"Cruz," she finishes. "Ryan Alejandro Cruz Junior. We can call him RJ for short."

"RJ." I find myself grinning like a fool. "I like it."

"Me too."

A few minutes later, the nurse comes in with a wheelchair and lets us know Micaela can go see RJ now. We help her from the bed and into the chair, and then the nurse wheels her to the NICU.

Micaela's mom is coming out as we're going in. "He's so perfect," Bella gushes. "You two definitely made a beautiful baby." She bends and hugs her daughter. "Congratulations, sweet girl."

"We picked a name," she tells her mom. "Ryan Alejandro Cruz Junior."

Her mom smiles. "Oh, what a perfect name!"

"We're going to call him RJ for short," I add.

"I love it. Can I let everyone know?"

"Of course," Micaela says, her eyes flitting to the NICU. She wants in there so badly, but she's trying to be polite.

After washing our hands and putting on gowns, we enter the area.

The neonatal nurse smiles warmly at us and walks over. "You ready to hold Baby Boy Anderson?"

Micaela's brows furrow in confusion right before a look of longing mars her beautiful features.

"They name them based on the mother's last name," I tell her, helping her out of the wheelchair and onto a leather sofa. She nods, but doesn't say a word, most likely thinking about Ian. Briefly, I wonder if she's wishing it were him here with her instead of me. Irrational jealously hits me like a punch to the gut, but I quickly force it aside. It's not fair to bring those feelings into this room. He was her husband, they planned a life together, and now he's gone. It's pointless to be jealous of a man who is no longer alive. I'm here with Micaela and we share a son.

The nurse takes RJ from the infant warmer—as the nurse called it earlier—they have to keep him in to monitor him. "Here you go, Mom." She sets him in Micaela's arms, and I pull my phone out to take pictures. Tears stream down Micaela's cheeks as she smiles down lovingly at RJ.

"Ryan," she breathes, glancing up at me, her brown eyes filled with liquid emotion. "He's so perfect." She kisses his forehead and his eyes flutter open. "I can't believe we created him," Micaela murmurs, and my heart swells. I never planned to have kids. My life was the military. When Laura suggested we start a family, I couldn't picture it. I didn't want it. But as I watch Micaela love on our son, I can see it all vividly: the walks through the park with RJ, pushing him on the swings, family movie nights cuddled on the couch, family pictures, family vacations. Everything my mom and dad gave my sisters and me. I want it all. And I want it with Micaela.

"Marry me," I blurt out.

Micaela slowly lifts her head, her eyes wide with shock. "Wh-what did you just say?"

"Marry me."

"Because of RJ?" she questions.

I drop down onto the couch next to her. "No, because what we had during our time at the beach house was unlike anything I've ever felt. My entire life I've always felt different, unsettled. I watched my parents live and love. They would laugh and smile, and there was this... calm about them. Like they were simply content just *being*. But no matter how much I tried, I couldn't find what they had. I couldn't figure out how to settle down."

"You were married before," she points out.

"And I was gone more than I was home. I kept searching for that calm, but it felt unattainable. Until you. At the beach house, I was calm, settled. It took everything in me to leave."

"Ever think it was the beach? That's why it's called a vacation house. It's meant to be relaxing."

I shake my head, getting frustrated. She doesn't understand, but I have to make her. "My heart and my head... they're always racing. I feel antsy in my own body, like I have to keep moving. But when I'm with you..." Fuck, this is going to sound so stupid. "I swear my heart slows down."

Micaela laughs. "Well, if that isn't the best pickup line I've ever heard." When I don't laugh, she stops. "You're being serious..."

"Yes, the last nine months in Afghanistan... I was losing my mind. All I wanted to do was get back here, back to you. I craved the calm you radiate. It's like..." I take a deep breath, trying to remain patient. "You center me."

Micaela nods slowly, trapping her bottom lip between her teeth. "Ryan..."

"Please, baby. Marry me."

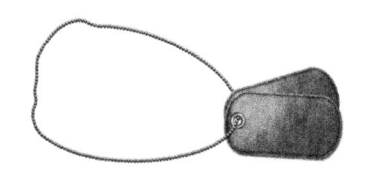

## CHAPTER TWENTY

### MICAELA

"*Please, baby. Marry me.*"

Ryan wants to marry me. At first I thought he was asking out of obligation because of RJ, but after his speech, I get it. Because I felt it too. Not the same way he explained it, but different. After Ian died, it felt like my heart was torn into a million pieces, but Ryan helped put it back together. He didn't push me to move forward, but instead walked beside me while I took each step. My heart wasn't completely put back together, but Ryan showed me that it could still be damaged and work. It would just beat differently, and that's okay.

The problem is, being with Ryan would mean putting a strain on my heart. And while it's working fine now, I'm not sure it could take the weight. It's fragile, barely holding on. I need to handle it with care. Ryan's in the military and will be leaving soon. It's the reason I didn't tell him about RJ. I might be fixed, but I'm not perfect, and I couldn't handle it if something happened to Ryan over there. And yeah, he'll be returning in a few months, but then what happens when he leaves again? It takes a certain kind of woman to be married to a man in the military, and that's not me. I thought I was... until I lost Ian.

"Ryan," I say slowly, hating that I'm about to hurt him. It

means the world to me that he was able to find that calm with me, but I can't be who he needs, not while trying to be who I need me to be.

Just as I'm about to explain this to him, RJ's eyes flutter open and his sweet little face contorts into a look of pain. My heart picks up speed in worry.

A soft mewl escapes his puckered lips, getting the nurse's attention.

"Is something wrong?" I ask nervously.

"He's hungry," she says. "The lactation specialist is on her way to answer any questions you have, but if you want, I can show you how to latch him on."

"Should I... umm... leave..." Ryan mumbles, his face turning a light shade of pink.

I bark out a laugh that has RJ jumping in shock. "Sorry, little guy," I coo, lowering my gown and exposing my breast to feed him. I read all about breastfeeding, even watched how-to videos.

"What's so funny?" Ryan asks.

"You." I bring RJ to my breast and his lips form the cutest little O as he moves his face from side to side trying to find his source of food. When he latches on, his crying immediately stops. "You're this big, bad, military man, but the mention of me breastfeeding has you freaking out."

"I wasn't freaking out," he argues.

"You were totally blushing."

Ryan leans in close so nobody else but me can hear him. "I know how it feels to have my lips wrapped around your breast," he says slowly, a taunting smirk pulling on his lips. "I was just trying to give the little guy some privacy... to eat."

"Oh my God! Ryan! You're such a perv!"

RJ jumps again from my loudness, popping off my breast and returning to crying. Shit, I really need to work on my voice level. "Shh... it's okay," I tell him softly, lifting my gown back up and lifting him over my shoulder to burp him. Once he burps, I move him to my other breast, latching him on.

"I can't believe you just said that." I glare at Ryan, whose eyes are dancing with laughter.

"You're a natural," he says, nodding toward our son, whose

eyes are fluttering closed, his lips barely hanging on. I remove him from my breast and lift him back up to burp again.

"I read a lot." I shrug. "I wanted to make sure I knew what I was doing. I had no idea how much is involved in having a baby. And they grow and change so fast. The book about their first year is bigger than the damn Bible." I laugh, but Ryan's face falls.

"What?"

"I won't be here," he says, his voice full of sorrow. "I have to go back in two weeks. I'm going to miss everything." His eyes shine. "Fuck." His head drops into his hands.

"Hey." I move RJ to my other arm and take Ryan's hand in mine. "Ryan, look at me."

He lifts his head, and my heart squeezes at how devastated he looks.

"I'll send you pictures and videos. I have this calendar my mom got me where I can write down what he does every day. I'll type it up for you. I promise." I can't imagine having to leave RJ for several months. I'm dreading putting him down to go back to my room.

"He's not going to know who I am."

"Of course he will. We can video you talking to him and I'll play it for him, and we can video chat, so you can see him."

"You'd do that?" he asks.

"Of course." I link our fingers together. "I know I was scared. I still am. But I was wrong. I promise, Ry, I'll make sure RJ knows who his daddy is, and once you come home, you can pick up where I left off."

"And what about us? Will we pick up where we left off?"

My thoughts go to our time at the beach house. The hugging and kissing and making love. The laughing and talking and connecting. I want that so much, but...

"I can't," I whisper. "I'm sorry, but I can't." I drop my eyes in shame. "My heart just couldn't take it if something happened to you. I'm sorry."

Ryan unlinks our hands and lifts my chin so I'm looking at him. "I'm going to let you have your way for now because I get it. What happened with your husband... But when I come home..."

I open my mouth to argue, but he shakes his head. "Uh-uh. I

*will* come home. And when I do, we're going to discuss you becoming mine."

I try to interrupt again, but he places two fingers to my lips. "The thing is, Micaela, I know what it feels like to be with you, to be *in* you. To be calmed by you. And I'm not going to stop until I can have you again, this time for good."

---

THE NEXT FEW days pass in a blur. Because RJ was admitted to the NICU, he has to stay there. After the first night, I no longer need a wheelchair, and every two hours Ryan and I walk from my room to see our son. Our parents visit, going back and forth between seeing RJ and us. They bring Ryan food, while I'm stuck eating the hospital crap. Ryan never leaves my side, except to take a shower in my room. On discharge day, my parents show up with RJ's car seat, and after filling out the necessary paperwork and showing the nurse the car seat is installed properly in Ryan's truck, we take our son home—well, to my parents' house, which is also my house, since I live with them, and Ryan doesn't have his own place. Because he's never home, he hasn't bothered to buy a home, instead staying in the guesthouse at his parents' place when he's in town.

Not wanting to miss a moment with his son before he has to leave, he asks my parents if it's okay to stay with me. Since RJ is little, he's sleeping in my room with me. I have a crib, bassinet, and changing table set up for him. My parents offered to turn a guest room into a nursery for him, but I'm not planning on staying here that long. I still have my dreams and goals I want to achieve, even if I've had to take a slight detour.

"You graduated," Ryan says, looking at the diploma, as I step out of my en-suite bathroom. The moment we got home, my family attacked RJ. My siblings argued over who would get to hold him, and I used that time to jump in the shower. There's nothing like showering in your own house, in your own shower. I glance over and see RJ is sleeping soundly in his bassinet, swaddled like the most adorable little burrito.

"Just my AS. I still have two years left. Finding out I was pregnant had me altering my plans, again. But I made sure to get my

AS before he was born, and I'm still planning to finish what I started."

Ryan glances over at me, raking his eyes down my pajama-clad body. I'm wearing comfy leggings that are easy on my incision and a loose nursing top my mom bought me. The front crisscrosses, tying at the side, which makes it easy to pull it to the side when I need to feed RJ. I cringe at what Ryan must see. I've put on a good thirty pounds from the pregnancy that my mom warned me weren't *all baby*. As soon as the doctor gives me the go-ahead I'll be at the gym with my mom working to get the weight off. But for now… well, this is me, and it's a far cry from the woman he spent time with at the beach.

"What?" I ask self-consciously after several long moments, when he doesn't look away.

"Being a mom suits you. You look beautiful."

"Oh yeah." I roll my eyes, climbing onto my bed to rest while RJ does. "Nothing is sexier than a woman in her breastfeeding pajamas."

"Damn right," Ryan growls, joining me on the bed. "But not just *any* woman. You. Nothing is fucking sexier than knowing under this top are your perfect breasts that not only supplied me with pleasure…" He winks, and I groan. He's such a damn perv. "But also supply our son with the nutrients he needs," he finishes, his face going from flirty to serious. At his words, my heart swoons, my cheeks heating up.

"I could watch you with RJ all day." His lips curl into a sad smile. "I only have nine days left. Can we just stay in here, the three of us, so I can soak up every second possible with you both?" I know he's joking, but the way his eyes bore into mine, I think there's a part of him that would be okay with just doing that.

Ryan scoots down and wraps me in his arms, and I lower my head onto his chest. We haven't discussed any more about his proposal, or what our future holds, and for that I'm thankful. Right now the only thing I can focus on is being a mom. He doesn't say a word as he threads his fingers through my hair. And suddenly all the excitement from the last few days catches up to me, exhaustion hitting me hard, and with the sound of Ryan's heartbeat calming me, I close my eyes and let sleep overtake me.

"MICAELA," a melodic yet gruff voice says. "Micaela, you have to wake up, baby."

Baby? Why is someone calling me baby? And why are they trying to wake me up?

"C'mon, baby, you just have to wake up long enough to feed RJ and then you can go back to sleep." Those words have me bolting up in my spot. I'm a mom, and I have to feed my baby.

"There she is," Ryan says, smiling softly. He's dressed comfortably in a pair of black basketball shorts and a gray T-shirt that reads ARMY across the front, his muscular biceps and forearms on display as he holds our son in his arms, like he's the most precious treasure that needs to be handled with the utmost care. RJ is staring up at his daddy, sucking on his pacifier, hard, like he's hoping if he sucks hard enough, milk will magically appear. Even though it's obvious he's hungry, he still looks content, and I don't blame him. Ryan has a way of making you feel protected and cherished without even trying.

Before I take RJ from him, I reach over and grab my phone, taking a picture of the two of them. Ryan is glancing down at RJ, love swimming in his gorgeous blue eyes. My heart swells at the sight, but quickly bursts when I remember he's going to be leaving soon, going back to Afghanistan and risking his life. There's a chance he won't return—or if he does, it could be in a body bag.

*Just like Ian did...*

My thoughts go to the last time I saw him, lying cold and lifeless in the coffin. He wasn't even in another country risking his life. He was merely training, a routine skydiving session gone wrong—way wrong.

"*Unfortunately it happens,*" they said, as if they were informing me about the weather instead of telling me my husband was dead.

"Micaela," Ryan says, snapping me from my thoughts. "Baby, you're crying." He reaches over and wipes a tear I didn't realize was falling.

I look at him and all I can see is Ian postmortem. Ryan might be alive right now, but the chances of him remaining that way are slim, and I have to protect myself, so when he does die, I can be strong for our son. It's no longer just my heart that's at risk, but RJ's as well.

"You okay?" Ryan asks.

"No," I choke out, taking RJ from him and cradling him to my chest. "I think it's best if you go home."

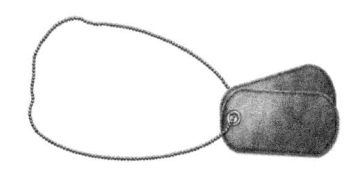

# CHAPTER TWENTY-ONE

## RYAN

It happened so fast. Like, with the quickness of one flicking a switch, she was transported from Vegas to Alaska. She went from warm and vibrant to ice-cold and hard. For a second, I was stunned by her words, confused as fuck. Everything had been going good. We were getting along great—more than great. We were taking care of RJ together. She was even cuddling in bed with me. And then *flick* her entire demeanor changed.

"There's no reason for you to sleep here. We're not together and I need my space. You can come and visit," she says, and it hits me—she's freaking out. I knew this was coming. Been waiting for it, actually. I spent almost two weeks with Micaela, watched her fight to take a simple step forward. I've seen her broken and lost, and I got to watch as she dragged herself step by step until she could walk again. To assume she's going to be perfect would be ludicrous. She had plans that didn't include me. It was why I walked away that day. Sure, I called and asked her to join me in Texas a couple months later. That was me being selfish. I missed her like crazy, missed the way I felt around her. But when she said no, I didn't push because I knew it wasn't personal. She was protecting her heart.

Which is exactly what she's doing right now. I don't know

what went through her head just now, but if I had to guess from the tears in her eyes, it was either thoughts of Ian, or of me leaving soon. Whatever it was, it was scary enough to erect that wall she's built to protect herself.

I should be angry that she's pushing me away, but the fact that she didn't include our son has my heart inflating. She's accepted I'm his dad and not going anywhere, and she isn't trying to keep me from him—only from her, because even though she can't protect RJ from getting hurt, she can still protect herself.

I lean over and give RJ a kiss on his forehead. I don't want to leave, but I'm not about to argue with Micaela. She's only given birth a few days ago. Her emotions are all over the place, and she's exhausted. "I love you, little guy," I whisper to my son before planting a kiss to Micaela's temple. "If you need anything, I'm only a phone call away. Text me later and let me know when I can spend time with RJ."

She swallows thickly and nods, refusing to look at me. I take one last look at her and RJ, then reluctantly leave. When I get downstairs, Bella is in the kitchen making herself a protein shake. She doesn't fight anymore, but she works out and trains other fighters.

"How's our girl doing?" she asks, taking a sip of her drink.

"She's having a moment," I tell her honestly. "She asked me to give her space."

Bella frowns. "You're not going to really do that, are you?" When I chuckle, she adds, "You're good for her. When she returned home, she was almost back to the old Micaela. She had a new plan and was a woman on a mission."

"She's stronger than she realizes."

"She is." She takes another sip of her drink. "She never mentioned your time together, but I could tell something was different. It was like she wasn't just healed but changed. Whatever happened between you two stayed with her when she returned."

I cough into my fist at her words, and her eyes widen, realizing what she just implied. "Not like that!" She laughs. "Well, actually..." She shrugs. "She did come home with a baby in tow." She mock glares, and I laugh.

"I'd like to say I'm sorry, but have you seen that baby upstairs?" I nod toward the staircase. "There's not a damn thing I regret about our time together, especially since it gave us him."

Bella laughs. "I get it. You going home?"

"I think I'm going to head to the Fight Club to get a workout in. Give her some time to get through whatever's going on in that beautiful head of hers. Can you keep an eye on her? She's still sore and exhausted."

She nods. "I can do that."

"Thanks."

After going home to see my mom and changing into my workout clothes, I head to the gym. Marco is standing at the front desk when I walk in. We haven't had a chance to really talk about me and Micaela since I returned. Between everyone arguing and then Micaela going into labor, we've been a little preoccupied.

"What the hell are you doing here?" he asks when I scan my card. I was expecting him to have words, but I didn't think I would be unwelcome here.

"The last time I checked I'm still a member. If that's changed just let me know."

"Whoa." His hands go up in mock surrender. "That's not what I meant. Just wondering why you're here instead of with Micaela and your son."

"She kicked me out," I grunt. "Said she needed some space."

Marco nods. "I was pissed when I found out it was you who got my little girl pregnant." I have nothing to say, so I wait for him to continue. "Then I blamed myself when I found out *where* you knocked her up." He eyes me for a second. "And then I learned you were the reason she was finally living again."

He walks around the desk and steps in front of me. "I'm hoping one day you'll make an honest woman out of her, but I know firsthand how stubborn the Cooper women can be."

"Cooper?"

"Fuck yeah, Bella and Micaela might have my last name, but their attitude is all fucking Cooper."

"Yeah, okay." I laugh. "And none of that attitude is from you." I pat his shoulder. "Micaela can be stubborn all she wants, but one day I *will* marry that woman, and it's good to know you'll be supportive." I look him in the eye. "I'm not proud of how it happened, but like I told Bella, I could never regret it. Micaela is the one for me. I can feel it deep in my marrow. Now, I just have to convince her I'm the one for her."

Marco nods. "She'll come around. And just for the record, I wanted to tell you about RJ. I would never keep something like that from another man. I know how that feels. I was just trying to give her time to handle it her way."

"I know. I get it. I was pissed, but it's hard to stay that way when I know why Micaela did what she did."

"She's scared as hell."

"Yeah," I agree.

"Any idea what you're going to do about that?"

"I have a couple ideas." I've actually been thinking a lot about our situations and how my life and hers can somehow come together. "I need to get through the next four months and once I get back, I'm going to figure shit out."

"Well, regardless of what happens with you two, as RJ's dad, you'll always be family." Marco pulls me into a hug and clasps me on the back, and I sigh in relief, knowing the man I've looked up to most of my life has my back.

After a good workout and a shower, I head over to my sisters' boutique downtown to spend some time with them. They insist on taking me to lunch, where they gush over all the pictures of RJ. Since I haven't spent much time with my nieces and nephews, I agree to have dinner with them. Mom and Dad join us, and we make it a family affair. It's nice to have all of us together. Unfortunately, with me gone a lot, it doesn't happen often enough.

While we're hanging out, I check my phone a million times, but Micaela never once texts. Eventually we say good night and I head back to my parents' place, to the guesthouse. I end up falling asleep on the couch while watching crap television and wishing I were with Micaela and my son.

I wake up in the morning and get ready to go to the gym, but before I leave, my phone goes off with a text from Micaela: **I'm taking RJ for a walk, if you want to join.**

I respond with: **Would love to. Can be there in ten minutes.**

She doesn't respond, instead giving the message a thumbs-up.

I laugh, knowing this is her way of letting me in while keeping me at arm's length.

I arrive at her house and find her standing outside with RJ bundled up in a large red badass-looking stroller that makes him look even tinier. It has three fat wheels with a handlebar that runs across the back. It's in the high sixties today, so Micaela is wearing a Fight Club hoodie, a pair of leggings that show off all her curves, and a pair of fluffy boots all women wear. She waves to me as I park and jump out of my truck.

"Nice stroller. You planning to go off roading with this thing?"

She laughs, the sound carefree, reminding me of our time in Venice once she let me in. "It's a jogging stroller. My parents bought it for me since I love going for runs outside." She pulls the canopy down, revealing a mesh cover. "This will protect him from the wind."

Before she closes it, I lean over and give RJ a kiss on his forehead, inhaling his fresh baby smell. It's something I hope he still has when I return in a few months.

We start our walk down the driveway and then make a left once we hit the road. At first, Micaela is quiet, looking everywhere but at me, and I don't say a word, not wanting to push her even farther away.

Then, after about a half a mile, she points to a house that's for sale. "This used to be my friend Jenny's house. She moved her senior year. I'm surprised the house is still for sale. It has the most beautiful floor-to-ceiling fireplace."

"The market is at a standstill. It was booming for a while and everyone was buying properties, but then people got greedy and started raising the prices. Now there are too many overpriced homes for sale and not enough buyers."

"Makes sense," she says. "Is that why you haven't bought anything?"

"Yeah," I say, leaving it at that. I'm not about to mention I'm rarely ever home, so it would be a waste of a house. Once I get back from this deployment, things are going to change. For years, I was restless, volunteering for deployments to try to find something to make me feel whole, connected, centered. But I never found it —not until Micaela, and now RJ.

"How are you feeling?" I ask, changing the subject.

"I'm okay. Still sore. The pain meds help. The doctor said it's good to walk. I'm just not supposed to lift anything heavy, so I had my mom carry the stroller out for me."

"For six weeks, right?" I ask, mentally calculating how long that is. I'll be gone soon and she'll still have four more weeks of needing help. Help I won't be here to give her. It's a good thing she's living with her parents. Between them, her grandparents, her siblings, and my family, someone will always be around to help her.

"Yeah," she says.

As we're walking past her grandparents' house, Liz comes barreling down the sidewalk with Cooper following after. "I knew that was you!" She pulls Micaela into a hug first and then me. "We just got in and were getting settled. We were about to head over to see the baby."

Cooper and Liz are best friends with my parents, so I practically grew up here. They now live half the year in Florida since they're retired, but they must've come back early when they heard Micaela had her baby.

"Congratulations," Cooper says, shaking my hand and then hugging his granddaughter.

"Thank you."

"Come inside," Liz insists. "It's too cold out here for the baby."

Micaela wheels the stroller to the front door and then Liz pulls him out, carrying him inside while giving him kisses and commenting how adorable he is.

We spend a little while with them, until RJ gets cranky, and then Micaela tells them she's going to feed him at home so she can lay him down afterward. After we say our goodbyes, we head back to Micaela's place. Shockingly, she invites me inside. We spend the rest of the day together, watching TV and taking turns holding RJ. When dinner rolls around, Bella invites me to stay, so I do, but only after asking Micaela if it's okay. After I've helped with the dishes, before Micaela can push me out the door, I leave on my own.

"Text or call if you need anything," I say to Micaela, handing her back RJ.

I can tell she's warring with herself, unsure if she should ask me to stay, but I'm not going to put her in that position. Whatever the reason she pushed me away, she's still not ready to discuss it yet. Besides, going for that walk with her made me think... and now I have some things I need to take care of before I leave.

"Good night," I murmur, my lips close to her ear.

She visibly shivers, telling me all I need to know. She still wants me... She just needs time.

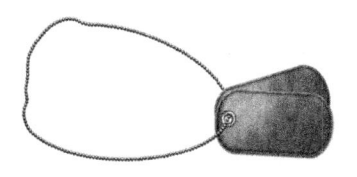

## CHAPTER TWENTY-TWO

### MICAELA

I WAKE UP, but delay opening my eyes, already dreading the day before it even begins. December twenty-fifth. Christmas. Also known as the day I lost my husband. It's also my son's first Christmas, so I take a deep breath and open my eyes, determined to make it a good day. But before I can do that, I need to do something first...

It's still dark out. Only five in the morning. When we were little, we would wake up before the sun would come up, excited to open presents, but now that everyone is older, we sleep in a little. After feeding RJ, we head out. The ride to the cemetery is short. Ian was buried locally since his entire family lives here. When I arrive, I take him out. My stroller is too big for the trunk of my car and I'm not supposed to carry the heavy car seat yet. RJ is half asleep, so I lay him out on a blanket next to me in front of Ian's grave.

"Two years." I stare at the headstone until the tears blur my vision. "I miss you so much." I clutch my hand to my heart and focus on calming my breathing. I have to drive home, so I can't get too worked up.

"The last time I was here I didn't even know I was pregnant. Now, I'm a mom." I lift RJ up and give him a kiss on his forehead. He snuggles into my chest and I welcome it, needing the comfort and warmth he brings to my heart. "His name is Ryan Alejandro Cruz Junior. He's named after Ryan and my dad."

I try so hard to control my sobs, but I can't stop them. I'm so torn. I miss my husband more than anything, but I also know that had he still been alive I wouldn't have RJ. It's such a complicated thing to think about. I guess when it comes down to it, I have to look at it like from the darkness of losing Ian—something that was out of my control—a light shone through, and that light was Ryan, and in turn, came RJ.

"I never planned to be a mom so young," I continue. "But he's quickly become my entire world. He's filled so many of the holes you created in my heart when you died."

I hold RJ tight, crying into his side. I used to dread crying because it symbolized me not moving forward, but now, it feels therapeutic. As if I'm cleansing my heart and making room in it for RJ.

"Ryan leaves next week." I take a deep breath. "I'm not sure if I should even talk to you about him, but I don't know who else to talk to, who would understand like you do. He's in the military. On a deployment in Afghanistan, but he came home for two weeks. He asked me to marry him." The tears continue to fall, so I set RJ down, not wanting to disturb his sleep. He's swaddled tightly, so he's nice and warm.

"I can't do it," I tell Ian. "Losing you was so damn hard. I can't even imagine what losing Ryan would do to me. I want to be strong for him like I was for you when you left for training, but I was naïve back then. I didn't fully comprehend the risks. Now that I've lost you, I get it, and I just can't bring myself to put my heart out there again. I have to be strong for RJ. He *needs* me to be strong."

"Oh, Micaela." A feminine voice comes from behind and I jolt up to find Ian's mom standing behind me.

"Mrs. Anderson."

"Oh, dear, please call me Jeanine. We're still family." She envelops me in a hug. "I've missed you so much."

"I've missed you too."

"And who's this little guy?" she asks, once we pull apart.

"I'm so sorry. I shouldn't have..."

"Stop." She pats my cheek. "I didn't mean to overhear, but I heard you talking to Ian when I was walking up. It's okay."

"This is RJ." I kneel next to my son, and Jeanine does the same. "He's only a week old."

Tears prick her eyes. "He's beautiful. And from what I heard, his father is serving overseas."

"Yes, he's in the military."

"Ian's dad was a SEAL for thirty years. His grandfather was one for thirty-five."

"Ian was following in their footsteps," I say, unsure where she's going with this.

"They're both still alive." She raises a single brow and I get it... I don't like it, but I get it.

"Life is crazy, sweetheart. We never know what today or tomorrow will hold. All we can do is live right now, in the moment, like it's all we have."

"I know, but it's hard. It's one thing to live life to the fullest, but it's another to know the man I'm considering giving what's left of my heart to is purposely going out and risking his life."

"I know right now your heart is aching. Even after two years, it still hurts. And I can't speak for Ian, but he loved you so much, and if I had to guess, I would like to think he would be so happy to know you've moved forward. You're so strong, Micaela. You stood by Ian's side and supported his dreams until his very last breath. But you still have so much love left to give."

She leans over and kisses my forehead. "Please don't be a stranger. I would love to spend time with you and that handsome baby."

"Okay." I pick up RJ and stand. "I'll give you two some privacy."

I press two fingers to my lips and then place them on the top of Ian's headstone. "Merry Christmas, baby."

---

"MERRY CHRISTMAS!" Mom says, pulling me into a hug, before taking RJ from me so she can give him some morning love. She does it every morning when I come down to eat breakfast before she heads out for the day.

"Merry Christmas, sweetie," Dad says, giving me a kiss on the cheek.

I glance over and see Liam and Liza are already sitting on the couch waiting to open their presents. Liam most likely doesn't believe in Santa anymore, but he hasn't confirmed it, so Mom insisted on playing along just in case. She said it's more fun when they come from Santa anyway.

"Sorry I made you guys wait. I went to the cemetery and ran into Ian's mom."

"We all just woke up," Dad says, handing me a cup of hot cocoa filled to the brim with marshmallows, while Mom hands RJ to Liza, who immediately goes about giving RJ tons of kisses.

"Did you have a good visit?" Dad asks.

"Yeah, I introduced him to RJ."

If what I said sounds crazy, nobody mentions it.

"That's good." Dad squeezes my shoulder and has a seat next to Liza on the couch.

"I love you." Mom kisses my cheek then sits next to Liam on the love seat.

I have a seat on the other side of Liza, so I'm close to RJ in case he wakes up hungry.

"Since Micaela is home, can we open presents?" Liam asks, bouncing in his seat.

Since RJ is too young, I didn't buy him anything. Between the baby shower Lexi and Georgia threw me and my parents spoiling their first grandchild, he has everything he could need, and more. Of course, as I glance at the gifts, I notice his name is on several things. It shouldn't surprise me, though. My parents, especially my mom, love spoiling us. Christmas is my mom's favorite holiday and she always goes all out.

"As soon as your grandparents get here," Mom says.

"Are Grandma and Grandpa Michaels coming over?" Liza asks.

"They'll be here for New Year's," Dad says. "They're still in Elko visiting your aunt Mackenzie." Dad's sister moved to Elko for a job promotion a few years ago, so Grandma and Grandpa bounce back and forth between our family and hers for the different holidays. Since we usually go to Breckenridge for Christmas, we're usually all together, but I couldn't go this year, so they went to her house thinking I wouldn't give birth until afterward, only RJ came early. I've been texting them pictures every day, and Grandma Hayley is dying to finally meet RJ.

"Is Uncle Nathan in town?" Liza asks, referring to Mom's brother.

"Nope," Mom says. "He's still traveling all over the globe." She rolls her eyes playfully. Uncle Nathan created an app and sold it to some company for a bunch of money. It set him up for life, and instead of using it to start a career, he's been traveling all over the world having the time of his life.

"But Aunt Lilly and Uncle Sean will be at your grandparents' for dinner," Mom adds.

"Yes!" Liam says. "I can't wait to show Shane my new games." Shane is Aunt Lilly and Uncle Sean's son. He and Liam are only six months apart and best friends. Both total gaming nerds.

"Who said you're getting any games?" Dad laughs.

"Because I asked Santa for them, and I was totally good this year." Liam shrugs like it's a given he'll be getting what he asked for.

"Define *good*," Dad says, leaning over and ruffling Liam's hair.

"Merry Christmas!" Grandpa says, walking through the door with Grandma following behind. They're carrying stacks of presents. Dad stands and grabs them from them, setting them on the table.

The adults talk and catch up for a few minutes, so I take a moment to text Ryan Merry Christmas. I include a picture of RJ in his adorable Christmas pajamas that I took earlier this morning when I put them on him. We discussed him coming over after he spends the morning with his family. His sisters both have kids and Bentley makes breakfast every year. I bought RJ this super cute Santa outfit and want to get some pictures of him under the tree later. It's crazy this is his first Christmas. Not that he'll even remember it, but I want to still have photographic proof of it for him to look at when he's older. Ryan texts back Merry Christmas and says he'll be over when they're done there.

The morning is spent with everyone opening their gifts— Liam, of course, got all the games he asked for. Liza got tons of clothes and shoes and makeup and her first cell phone since she's now in high school. Mom and Dad got me a gift card to the baby store and a gift certificate to the spa. Everyone got RJ cute clothes and toys. My brother, sister, and I all pitched in and paid for our parents to go on a cruise—since none of us are working, Grandma and Grandpa pitched in as well.

After opening presents and having breakfast, Ryan shows up carrying a single wrapped present under his arm.

"For you," he says, setting it on the table and taking RJ from me.

I wasn't sure if we would be exchanging gifts, but I wanted to give him something. Because we're at this weird impasse-slash-standstill right now, I wasn't sure what to get him. I mean, he asked me to marry him, so I know he wants us to be more than friends, but he's leaving in less than a week, so we're not together —but we have RJ. So I wanted to give him something that's meaningful, but isn't too personal. And I think I found the perfect gift.

"Yours is upstairs. I'll go grab it."

"Wait, open yours first," he insists. "It's for you and RJ."

"Okay." I unwrap the package and open the lid. Inside are a bunch of envelopes. I pick the first one up and open it. Inside is a packet of papers. I read through them, beginning to hyperventilate when I understand what they're for. Apparently Ryan has been busy this last week...

"Ryan... Tell me you didn't do what I think you did."

"Which one did you open?"

"The one that says you bought a goddamn house and need my signature for the deed!" I shriek, dropping the papers to the table like they're capable of burning me.

Ryan flinches like he's just been slapped. "Not exactly the reaction I thought you would have."

"What else did you do?" I open the next envelope and a key falls out. "A car?" I yell. "Have you lost your damn mind?"

I open the next envelope. This one is Ryan's will. The changes have been highlighted, indicating he's added RJ and me to it. If something happens to him, RJ gets his insurance policy and trust and I'm the guardian.

At this point, I'm shaking. My hands are literally trembling so badly it's hard to use them. But there's still one more envelope. I take a deep breath and open it. A bank account, needing my signature to have me added to it.

## CHAPTER TWENTY-TWO

I drop the papers and walk away, needing to calm down before I say something I might regret. I don't even know what to say, to be honest. I go upstairs, ignoring my mom calling my name, and slam my door shut. My eyes land on Ryan's present, which seems so stupid now. The guy just bought me a fucking car and a house and added me to a bank account that has more zeros than I would even know what to do with. My gift to him cost twenty dollars.

On some level, I should've expected this. Ryan comes from a very wealthy family—old money, as I heard my parents call it. While they don't act like it, they're loaded. Ryan and his siblings each received a huge trust fund from their grandparents, and I heard none of them have to work. His sisters, Chloe and Faith, used their trust to open a cute boutique downtown called A Clothes Affair, and Ryan joined the military because he wanted to. I guess I was just hoping Ryan wouldn't try to buy my love. I don't need or want a house or a car or money. I just want him. Alive and breathing and present.

There's a knock on the door, and I close my eyes, taking a deep breath. "Come in."

Ryan walks through the door minus RJ. "Your mom has him," he says, answering my silent question.

"Here's your present." I shove it into his chest.

He rips the wrapping paper until it reveals what's inside: a photo album. Silently, he opens the album and flips through page after page.

"It's not a house or a car," I mutter, feeling like an idiot. I took the pictures I had of Ryan and RJ so far and had them printed. I bought an old-school photo album and put them in there, decorating the pages.

When Ryan doesn't say anything, still flipping through the pages, I add, "I thought you could take it with you, so you have something to look at." I also included the few pictures I have of us from our week together in California, as well as a few of his family I was able to snag off social media.

He raises his head and his tear-filled eyes lock with mine. "You made this for me?"

"Yeah." I'm hoping the tears are because he likes it...

"It's the best fucking gift I've ever gotten," he says, setting it down and pulling me into a hug. He nuzzles his face into my hair, and I wrap my arms around his waist. "I never wanted this," he says, not letting me go. "The family... the kids... I could never imagine having any of it. But now." He sniffles and holds me tighter. "I want it all, Micaela. With you."

"Ryan," I breathe. I can't do this. Not a week before he's leaving.

"I know," he says knowingly. "But I just need you to know that it's you. You make me want it all. Make me want shit I never wanted before."

He releases me and backs up. "I know you freaked out over your present..."

"My present?" I squeal. "A present is that." I point to the photo album. "You set me up for life."

Ryan doesn't laugh. "Damn right I did. You and our son. The reason why you won't be with me is because you lost your husband. I have to leave in a week, but I'm not going until I know that if something happens to me, you and our son are both taken care of. The house is for you to create a life in. It's the one you pointed out. Only a half mile from your parents. It's yours to do with as you please, no strings attached. The car is safe and will fit the stroller. You complained your car was too small for it. I want you to be comfortable and safe while you're driving our son around. The money is so you can focus on taking care of RJ and not have to worry about how to pay for things. I know your parents will help, but RJ isn't their responsibility. He's ours. He's mine. He's going to need diapers and wipes and clothes... Babies have needs. I know my Christmas present was a little over the top, but I only have a week until I have to leave, and I needed to make sure that when I do, you and RJ will be okay."

Well, shit, when he puts it like that, he's not trying to buy my love. He's trying to make sure we're taken care of. But what he doesn't understand is that when Ian died, I didn't care that I had no money or a house or a new car...

"I appreciate all of that, but all I want is for you to come home safe. No amount of money can bring Ian back, and it can't bring you back either if something happens to you."

"No, but it will give me peace of mind to know you are both taken care of while I'm gone, or if, God forbid, something does happen to me. You may not need all of this now, but I need you to know it's available to you if you ever do need it."

I frame his face with my hands. "Thank you." I place a kiss to his cheek. "I'll sign whatever you want to give you that peace of mind, but please know all I *want* is for the father of my son to come home."

"I will," he says. "I prom—"

"Don't." I cut him off. "Don't make promises you know you damn well may not be able to keep."

He takes a deep breath, and I can tell he wants to argue, but instead he says, "All right, how about we go downstairs and I'll show you your new SUV? I drove it over here."

"Sounds good."

We spend the rest of the day celebrating Christmas with our family. We have dinner at my grandparents' house, where Ryan's family joins us.

The days following are spent making as many memories as possible. Every picture I take, I print and add to his photo album. Every morning I text Ryan with a different excuse to come over. We never discuss him leaving, or what will happen once he does. We just simply enjoy each other and our son.

Unfortunately, like anything good in life, it all eventually has to come to an end. And that's proven the day after New Year's, when I wake up and realize Ryan leaves in twenty-four hours.

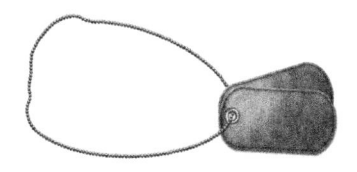

## CHAPTER TWENTY-THREE

### RYAN

You don't realize how quickly vacation can pass by until you're at the end of it, wishing it would go on forever. It's been two weeks since I found out I was going to be a dad. Since I *became* a dad. In those two weeks, RJ has gained a pound and a half. His eyes stay open for longer periods of time. And when he's hungry, he definitely makes it known. Those two weeks have been spent with Micaela and me hanging out every day. We eat, watch television, go for walks, all while spending time with our son. It would seem like doing that shit would be boring, but it's not. It's fucking perfect and there's no other way I could imagine spending my days. These past fourteen days have been the best of my life. It's like we've created the most perfect bubble. One I wish we could live in for the rest of our lives.

Unfortunately, that comfy little bubble I'm loving the hell out of living in is burst wide open with a single text from Micaela:

**Come over and wear your military uniform.**

And with those seven words, I'm forced back into reality. A reality where I realize I'm leaving tomorrow. I only had fourteen days, and all I want is more...

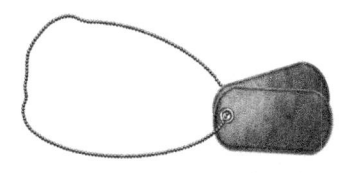

## CHAPTER TWENTY-FOUR

### MICAELA

Ryan walks through the door wearing his military uniform. I don't know what it's called officially, but it's a camouflage button-down jacket with matching pants. There are patches on both arms, but I don't know what any of it means, and combat-looking boots finish the ensemble.

I was worried when I texted him to come over wearing his military uniform, he would ask me why, but he didn't. And that's good because I wouldn't have been able to explain it through text. Even now, I dread what we have to do, but we only have less than twenty-four hours until he leaves, so it's now or never.

"Where's RJ?" he asks, looking around for our son. "And why am I wearing these? I don't leave until tomorrow."

"He's in my mom's room with her. She felt it would be best."

"Why?" He glances at me, his eyes filled with worry and confusion. "What's wrong?"

"Other than you leaving..." I force out a laugh. "Nothing. We need to make a couple videos."

"Videos?"

"Yeah, one for RJ to watch while you're away, and..." I swallow thickly, trying not to lose it. "One if you don't make it back."

Ryan's eyes widen in shock, his face contorting into an angry glare. "The fuck?" He steps closer to me. "I'm not making a video in case I die."

"Okay, so you'll just die and not have any final words for your son, who is only a baby and will never have any recollection of ever having met you, aside from the pictures I've taken. He'll have nothing from you. Not your voice, or your words, nothing."

He stares at me for several seconds, his breathing heavy, before he nods once in understanding. "Fuck," he mutters. "Okay."

We go outside on the back porch where it's bright and quiet. I set up the tripod with my phone and explain all he has to do is press play and then pause for each one. "Do that for each video, and I'll be able to show him the one while you're gone without mistakenly showing the second. I'll save them as separate files."

"Wait." He grabs my wrist as I walk away. "You're not staying?"

"I think it would be best if you do it alone. As if it's just a conversation between you and him."

Ryan nods and I go inside. A few minutes later, I peek outside to check on him and find him on the floor with his face in his hands. I rush out, unsure what happened, and find him sobbing.

"Ryan," I breathe, sinking down in front of him. "What happened?"

"I can't do it," he chokes out, refusing to look at me.

"I know it's going to be hard, but it will be worth it when I can show—"

"Not that," he mutters. "I can't leave." He glances up at me, his eyes red-rimmed. "I can't do this." His chest is rising and falling quickly. "I'm going to miss everything. His doctor appointments. When he smiles and laughs. He's not even going to fucking know who I am!" he booms.

My heart cracks wide-open, but I take several breaths to stay calm. Ryan needs me to be strong right now. He's been so strong for me—at the beach house, when I was giving birth to RJ—now it's my turn to be strong for him. "Do you know why I asked you to wear your military uniform?"

He shakes his head as tears of pain run down his cheeks.

"Because I want to make sure RJ knows that his daddy is a hero, and that's what this outfit symbolizes."

"I would rather just be his dad," he admits softly. "And your husband."

He pulls me into his lap and nuzzles his face into my neck. I don't know what to say to make him feel better, so I don't say a word, just letting him cry it out.

Eventually, he calms down and lifts his face to look at me. His cheeks are tear-stained and his eyes are swollen and puffy. He's no longer crying, but his chin is trembling.

"I hate this," I tell him. "But you have to go, and God forbid something does happen, RJ will have something from you."

Ryan nods in agreement. "All right." He scrubs his hands over his stubbled jaw. "I'll do it."

About twenty minutes later, Ryan comes inside and hands me my phone, asking to see RJ. His face is splotchy, telling me he cried some more, but he's more composed. I call my mom out and she hands RJ over to Ryan with a sympathetic smile. "For what it's worth," she says. "We're all so proud of you."

"Thanks," he says, snuggling his son to his chest and inhaling his scent. "But all I want is to get through these next four months and then get back home, so I can start my life."

His words bring tears to my eyes as I remember not even a year ago when we were at the beach house and he told me the military was his life.

We spend the rest of the day together. Ryan downloads texting and video chatting software to my phone that I can use to contact him when he's back overseas. Apparently he upgraded his phone to an international plan, and the base he's staying on has service. It's shitty, but it's enough we'll be able to talk. He also gives me his email so I can send him pictures of RJ. Of course he adds that I should also include pictures of myself.

Instead of him going home, he spends the night with his body wrapped around mine. He wakes up for every one of RJ's feedings and insists on being the one to change his diaper and burp him.

The morning comes too soon and he wakes me up when it's still dark out. "Baby, I have to go," he murmurs, kissing the corner of my mouth. "Wake up so I can say goodbye."

"Wait." I shoot up. "You're leaving... like now?"

"I have to be at the airport at five a.m."

"We're going with you." I throw off my blanket and stand.

"No, you're not," he says, shaking his head. "If you go, I'll never get on that fucking plane."

"Ryan, please," I beg. "We have to see you off."

"That's why I woke you up. But I don't want to wake RJ up. He's sleeping and will be cranky." He swallows thickly, glancing at our sleeping baby, who has no idea his daddy is about to leave and won't be coming home for several months.

"I have to go home and get my stuff," he says. "I'll text you before the plane takes off, but it may be several days before I can communicate."

When my eyes bug out, already freaking out, he explains, "I have to turn my phone off for security. I'll fly into Nova Scotia, then get on a plane to Germany, and from there, I'll take another plane to Kyrgyzstan."

"That's a lot of flying," I say dumbly. "You have to do all that just to come home for two weeks?"

"Yeah." He runs his knuckles down my cheek. "Four months is going to feel like forever."

"Probably," I agree with a half-smile, "but we'll get through it."

He leans over and kisses my forehead, the tip of my nose, and then the corner of my mouth. "I know how you feel about promises, so I won't make any. But I will tell you that I'll be counting down the days, hours, fucking seconds, until I'm back here with you guys."

He gives our son a soft kiss to his forehead and, closing his eyes, breathes in deeply as if he's trying to memorize his scent. When his eyes open, they meet mine. He gives me a sad smile that has my heart breaking in two, as he takes my face in his hands. "I love you, Micaela," he murmurs against my lips.

And then with one last soul-crushing kiss, he disappears.

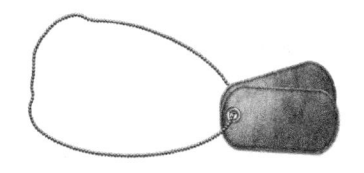

## CHAPTER TWENTY-FIVE

### FOUR MONTHS LATER

#### MICAELA

Ryan: Send me a pic of RJ

Me: <insert pic from earlier>

Ryan: He's in his pajamas from this morning. I want a current one.

Me: Can't... He's not with me right now.

Ryan: :(

Me: Don't give me that. It's been a long day. He was up all night, and I'm exhausted. I'm relaxing in the bath.

Ryan: The bath? As in... you're naked? I'll just take a picture of you then.

Me: Ha ha ha

Ryan: Who's laughing?

> Me: <insert picture of my feet>
>
> Ryan: Fucking sexy feet
>
> Ryan: <insert picture of his crotch> I'm hard.

I CRACK up laughing and text him back.

> Me: You must be really desperate to be turned on by feet.
>
> Ryan: Every part of you turns me on.
>
> Me: Should I send you a picture of my nose next? How about my knees? I've been told I have some sexy knees.
>
> Ryan: You already know I'll take whatever you'll give me.

I smile at his last text, knowing he's serious. The last four months have been rough for him. He's missing RJ—and me—like crazy, and he makes it a point to tell me that every day. Thankfully, with technology, we're able to text every day, as well as send pictures back and forth. We've even video chatted a few times, but the service isn't good and it breaks up. When he's out doing whatever he does—he's very vague on the details and I don't push—it can be several hours before he replies, but we haven't gone more than twelve hours without communicating.

At first, the texting was a little formal—kind of awkward. I was worried every day that he wouldn't respond and I would get a call similar to the one I got with Ian—and I *would* get that call, because he added me to his next-of-kin paperwork, so if anything does happen, I will be the first to know. Because of that, I tried to keep my distance. But when your only form of communication is texting, you have no choice but to eventually warm up to it. And since you're hidden behind a screen it's easy to say things you normally wouldn't say to someone's face. Late night chats have turned personal—although we steer clear of anything regarding the future, keeping it about our past and present.

And, along the way, those conversations have taken a flirty

turn. Knowing he's stuck in the desert with nobody but other soldiers, I tend to give in, giving him whatever he asks for. He never crosses the line, but we've definitely toed it plenty of times. Even though we haven't discussed being together, since he knows I can't handle that conversation until he's back on U.S. soil, he's mentioned on several occasions he has no desire to be with anyone else but me. I didn't realize how much I needed to hear it, until he said it. I've heard too many stories of soldiers being lonely while on a deployment and seeking comfort in someone over there.

**Ryan: You there?**

**Me: Yeah, tell me again how many days until you're home.**

**Ryan: Eight days, fourteen hours, twenty-five minutes, and thirty-six seconds.**

There's no way he could really know to the second how long it will be until he's home, but he always includes it all when he answers me.

**Me: I can't wait.**

**Ryan: Me too. You said you were up all night with RJ. Is he okay?**

**Me: Yeah, I think he's going through a growth spurt so he's waking up a little more often to eat.**

**Ryan: I miss him so damn much.**

**Me: We watched your video today. When you come home, he'll know who you are.**

After shaving my legs, I drain the tub and get out. After getting dressed, I head downstairs to find my sister and RJ. I'm so thankful to have my family. It's not that I couldn't handle taking care of RJ myself, but it's nice to have people I can count on.

Family who can watch him while I take a bath or go to the doctor. People to help me feel like I'm not doing this alone while Ryan is overseas.

The second I step into the living room, RJ spots me, his face lighting up. He's lying on the floor, smacking the keys to the toy piano he loves. As I walk closer, his arms and legs flail, excited to see me. There's nothing in the world better than seeing the way he lights up when I walk into the room.

"Did you have a good bath?" Liza asks, looking up from her homework.

"I did. Thank you." I pick up RJ and nuzzle my face into his neck. He giggles at my touch and my heart soars.

"A delivery came for you," Liza says, pointing to the box on the table. I don't need to ask who it's from since I already know. It's from Ryan—just like all the others.

I pick it up and RJ swats at it like it's his piano. Not wanting to open it in front of anyone, I excuse myself to my room, thanking Liza again for keeping an eye on RJ.

Once I'm in my room, I set RJ down next to me. He continues to bat at the package as I unwrap it. When I get it open, I find the most gorgeous hand-crafted bracelet. It's not identical to the necklace Ryan bought me when we were on Balboa Island, but it complements it perfectly. As I clasp the bracelet on my wrist, my thoughts go back to the last few times I received packages.

*"Micaela, you have a package," Mom yells up to me.*

*I run downstairs, thinking it's her way of surprising me, since today is my birthday. When I get to the living room, she's holding a small box that's wrapped with multicolored, shiny wrapping paper with balloons all over it.*

*I grin, taking it from her. "What is it?" I ask, shaking the box. It's kind of heavy.*

*"I don't know," she says. "A young man dropped it off."*

*"It's not from you?"*

*"Nope."*

*I tear the paper off the box and open it, finding an expensive-looking camera and a small bottle of Jack Daniel's. Taped to the inside of the box is a note.*

## CHAPTER TWENTY-FIVE

> *Happy Birthday to my favorite baby-mama,*
> 
> *The big 2-1, huh? I imagine you won't be going out since you'll more than likely be home with our little guy. But you can't turn 21 and not have a legal drink, so I included a bottle of Jack. It better be the only man you're celebrating with... I also included a camera. The guy at the store said it's the best. I know your phone takes sufficient pictures, but this one will take professional quality. While I'm gone, take tons of pictures, please. Of RJ, of you, of everything you guys do and experience. I want to feel like I was there with you. I look forward to seeing them all when I get home and adding them to my photo album.*
> 
> *I hope you have a wonderful birthday. Give RJ a kiss from me.*
> 
> *Xo Ryan*

Since Ryan had already been in Afghanistan for a week, I knew he had to have planned this before he left. It was so sweet and completely unexpected. I thanked him and did as he asked, using the camera to take pictures of RJ and myself. Every few weeks, I get them printed so they'll be ready to put into his photo album once he returns.

To say I was shocked when the next month rolled around and another box showed up at our door would be an understatement.

"Another one?" *Dad asks, checking out the box I'm carrying inside. It was dropped off by the same teenage boy who dropped off the last one—according to Mom.*

"I asked him if there was more, but he just smiled and walked away."

*I take the box upstairs and close my door. I don't think there'll be anything intimate in it, but it is Valentine's Day, so you never know.*

*I open the box and sift through the pink tissue paper. When I* pull out a vibrator, I nearly choke on my laughter. Next, is a framed photo of Ryan shirtless, his entire muscular upper body on display. He's smirking in the photo, exposing his dimples. The same dimples our son has, now that he's starting to smile.

I feel around and find a small bottle of KY warming gel and a small black box. I open the top and nestled inside is a beautiful ring. It's shaped like an infinity symbol and has the word mom in script along the edge with a turquoise stone—which is RJ's birthstone—in the center. I put it on, with tears pricking my eyes, and then go in search for a note, hoping there's one since the last package included one.

I find it at the bottom.

---

*Happy Valentine's Day!*

*I hate that I can't be here with you, but I'm counting down the days until I'll be back, and once I am... well, I told you I wouldn't make any promises, but I can tell you that you won't need that vibrator anymore. Until then, I've included the perfect self-care kit. Warming gel, a vibrator, and of course, a picture of me. Feel free to use as necessary. I hope you like the ring. I figured the best way to celebrate a day about love is by thanking you for the love you've given me—our son. I told you once I never imagined ever having a family, but now, all I can think about is getting back to mine. Yes, mine. Because for the rest of our lives, you, RJ, and me are a family. I love you, Micaela.*

*Happy Valentine's Day, baby.*

*Xo Ryan*

*PS. Feel free to text me if you need any more visuals ;)*

---

When March came around, I didn't expect a gift since there were no birthdays or holidays. So I was beyond shocked when I opened the door to find the same delivery kid standing there holding a box.

"Another one?" I ask, taking the box from him.

"Yep," he says with a smile.

"Wait here." I run to my purse and grab a twenty to tip him. "Thank you." I hand him the bill. "Hopefully this is the last time since Ryan will be home at the end of next month."

The kid doesn't confirm or deny, just smiles and thanks me.

As I close the door, eyeing the package, it hits me. Ryan will be home next month. We've almost made it. Then another thought occurs, this one morbid. What if Ryan has another box waiting to be delivered in case something happens to him? I shake the thought off and go upstairs to open my package, unsure of the reason for it.

Inside the box are two envelopes. One reads: open me first, so I do. It's a letter.

---

*Happy Anniversary!*

*I know... I know... technically we don't have an anniversary since we're not together, but this week is one year since you stumbled into the beach house, and my heart, for the first time, felt like it found its home. Growing up I knew I was adopted. My parents were always honest about it. But I never felt like I was adopted. My parents and sisters loved me like I was their own flesh and blood, but as I got older I felt different. I would see them with each other and I craved the connection and contentment they found in one another.*

*So, fresh out of high school, I married my best friend. She needed me and I was hoping to feel the connection my parents feel when they're together. Only, I didn't feel it at all. Not an ounce of what they felt. For a long time I thought, even though my parents told me blood doesn't mean anything, maybe they were wrong. Maybe what I felt was genetic. My biological parents clearly had trouble connecting with others. From what I was told, their relationship was toxic and they had no idea how to even begin to love their own child.*

*I was afraid I was like them, and the thought scared me so much I spent as much time as possible away from home. The more I was away, the less chance I had to fuck it all up. I used the military as my escape. I was searching for something that, at the time, I didn't know wasn't out there. Eventually Laura had enough and asked for a divorce. She deserved more than what I was able to give her, so I gave it to her, and then I took off on another deployment, and then another.*

*It wasn't until you walked through the door that night, I finally realized what I was searching for couldn't be found because what I was searching for all along was you. Your heart, your smile, your touch. It's everything I was searching for but didn't know how to find. The sucky part was knowing that even though I finally found you, I had to let you go. Walking away from you at the end of our time together was the hardest thing I've ever had to do. But I did it for you. Because I knew, even though you were everything I needed, I couldn't be who you needed.*

*Of course fate was on my side, and nine months later I found out you were carrying my baby. It confirmed what I already knew. You're mine. Go ahead and open the other envelope now. I can't make any promises, but... well, just open it.*

*Miss you and RJ.*
*Xo Ryan*

---

## CHAPTER TWENTY-FIVE

*I open the other envelope to find a one-week cruise for two for July inside. It stops at several islands and all the off-shore excursions have been booked. According to the itinerary we'll be spending four days snorkeling, scuba diving, and touring the different islands. It's a dream vacation for anyone who loves the ocean, which is why he bought it.*

*He can't make any promises, my ass. This is the definition of promise. That he'll be home in time to go on this cruise with me. I try not to get too excited, but deep down, I'm squealing, and for the first time since he left, I'm feeling like maybe this story will have a different ending than the one with Ian.*

I smile to myself at the memory of all the packages. With Ryan coming home in a little over a week, this has to be the last package. I find the note and read it.

---

***Micaela,***

*I saw this bracelet and thought of our time together on Balboa Island. I can't wait to be home so we can make new memories. I know I said no promises, but it's time to make them now. I'm heading home this week, and I'm coming for you, baby. So, be ready. Because I have months of missing you to make up for.*

***Xo Ryan***

---

I grab my phone to text Ryan and see there's a text from him. Caught up in my memories, I must not have heard it.

**Ryan: Packed and ready to get the hell out of here. Another compound is having a mechanical issue, so my squad and I are heading up there before we leave. It doesn't have service like I do here, since it's at a higher altitude, so if you don't hear from me, don't freak out. I'll text when I can. Give RJ a kiss from me. Love you and see you soon.**

Even though there's a chance he won't get it, I still send him a text back.

**Me: Thank you for the bracelet. I love it and can't wait to make memories with you. I love you and I'll see you soon. Be safe. xo**

It's the first time I've texted the words, and I almost consider deleting them, but the truth is I mean them, and once Ryan is home with RJ and me where he belongs, I'm going to say them in person.

And that's when it hits me, Ryan is coming home. We made it. And an idea strikes. I've put off moving into the house he bought for me, afraid of living in it alone, but now that he's coming home, I want to move in. He mentioned on a couple different occasions that he would love for the three of us to live together. He's given me all these gifts. What better gift for him than to be living in the home when he gets here. I can get his stuff from the guesthouse and have my dad and Bentley help me move everything in so it's ready when Ryan gets home next week.

"C'mon, little guy," I say to RJ, who is crumpling the wrapping paper in his fists. "Your daddy will be home soon. Let's go make sure he has the perfect home to return to."

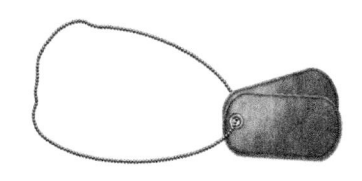

## CHAPTER TWENTY-SIX

### RYAN

"Fuck, I'm ready to go home," Julian, one of the guys in my squad, complains, handing me the electrical wiring. "My daughter's birthday is next week and I had my wife book us a trip to Disney." It's been four days since we got here. With the outpost located at an altitude of fifteen thousand feet, it's extremely remote. While we can communicate with command, our personal electronics and internet don't work at all up here. I can't imagine having had to spend the last four months without talking to Micaela and RJ. No pictures or videos, no texts. I would've gone mad.

"Maddy wants to visit every princess there is," Julian adds with a sigh.

I smile at him and continue to fix the frayed wire to the sensor, imagining what it will be like when RJ is old enough to go on trips, like to Disney. My parents used to take my sisters and me all the time. We would spend hours waiting in the long lines to go on every ride and they would always buy us ice cream to eat while we waited so we wouldn't complain. I can't wait to experience everything with RJ as his dad.

"Hey, Cruz," Sergio, another guy from my squad, calls over. "The motion detectors are acting up."

"Did you check the—"

Before I can finish my sentence, a howling scream with a violent explosion crashes near me. The violence of the shock rattles me, and I'm instantly on the ground, screaming, "Incoming!" But I can't hear my own voice.

I look up and see flashes of fire spitting from the barrel of the .50 cal in the guard tower. I feel the vibrations in my chest as more explosions flash all around me. Only one thought propels me as I sprint to my weapon and body armor: I'll be fucking damned if I made it this far, only to not make it home to Micaela and RJ.

But as the acrid smoke from the explosions billows in the air and the sounds of machine guns firing overhead fills my ears, a horrible feeling roils in my gut: Maybe it's a good thing I didn't promise Micaela I would be coming home...

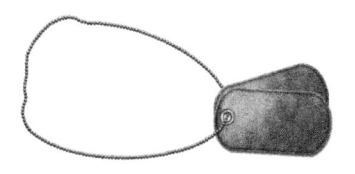

# CHAPTER TWENTY-SEVEN

## MICAELA

"That's it," Dad says, setting the nightstand on the floor. "You're the only person I know who could put a house together in less than a week."

Bentley laughs, placing the lamp on top. "She's a woman on a mission."

"I just want it to be perfect," I tell them. I also needed something to keep me distracted. I haven't heard from Ryan in seven days. He's not due to return until technically tomorrow, but this is the longest we've gone without talking since he left, and it's eating away at me. My mind can't stop questioning if he's okay, why he hasn't found a way to contact me. If he's due to return tomorrow, shouldn't he already be on his way? And if that's the case, he should've been able to message or call me. But he hasn't. Not a single word.

"And it is," my mom assures me, handing RJ over to me. "The home looks gorgeous. The pictures you hung up in the living room are beautiful."

"Thank you." I blew up nine pictures of Ryan, RJ, me, and our families and had them printed in black and white. I hung them up in black wood picture frames behind the couch. Not wanting to spend too much of Ryan's money, I only bought the essentials for now: living room and dining room furniture, as well as a crib for

RJ, so I could keep the one he's using now at my parents' place in case they ever need it. The rest of his stuff I brought here. Kayla and Bentley said I could bring Ryan's furniture from their guesthouse here for the master bedroom. My mom helped me pick up the little things we'll need like towels, a mop, and a vacuum. Since the house was in move-in condition, all it took was having the guys help move all the heavy stuff in.

"Are you planning to sleep here tonight?" Mom asks, her brows dipping together in what looks like concern.

"I was... Is there a reason I shouldn't?"

"No." She sighs. "I just can't believe my baby is moving out."

"I'm not even a half-mile away." I playfully roll my eyes. "I can stand outside, and if I scream loud enough, you'll be able to hear me."

Bentley chuckles, but Dad doesn't dare laugh. Mom glares. "Be nice." She embraces me. "I guess I should be grateful it's only a half-mile."

I swallow thickly at her words, as I remember my plan—before I found out I was pregnant. San Diego University. Scripps. I applied and got in. But then I found out I was pregnant with RJ, so I temporarily deferred. Eventually I'll have to decide—

"Bentley!" Kayla screams, rushing into the house.

"What's wrong?" he asks, grabbing her shaky hands in his own to comfort her. "Kayla..."

Her eyes dart over to RJ and me. He's busy playing with the necklace Ryan gave me. He loves to put it in his mouth. Her eyes lock with mine and my stomach drops. I know that look. It's the look my mom gave me the day Ian died.

No. This can't be happening. Not again.

"Kayla," Bentley prompts, not catching on.

"Is he dead?" I ask bluntly, needing her to rip the Band-Aid off.

Mom gasps, coming to my side.

"Is he?" I repeat. "Is Ryan dead?"

"Enough!" Bentley barks. "He's not dead."

Tears race down Kayla's face. "We don't know. A base in Afghanistan was attacked. Several were injured and a few were killed. That's all they're saying right now. I tried to text him, but—"

"That doesn't mean anything," Bentley argues. "He doesn't always respond."

"He went to a different base to do something," I inform her and Bentley. "He said it was too high up. No service. I haven't heard from him in a week. He was supposed to be home tomorrow."

"Oh, Micaela," Mom coos, approaching me carefully like I'm a rabid animal.

"I need to be alone," I tell them.

"Honey," Dad starts.

"Please." I swallow the lump in my throat, refusing to lose it.

"Do you want me to take RJ?" Mom offers.

"No." I clutch him tighter to me. "Can you let me know if you hear anything?" I ask Kayla.

"Yes." She nods, wiping her tears. "Maybe it wasn't even the base he's at. There are so many over there."

I shake my head, already knowing it was his base. Otherwise I would've heard from him. I always hear from him. There's only one reason why I wouldn't hear from Ryan—if he couldn't communicate.

I can feel it in my gut, in my heart. We were so damn close. "I need to be alone," I repeat, pushing everyone away. I can tell they don't want to leave me like this, but I can't do this with them. Not a-fucking-gain.

"We're only a phone call away," Mom reminds me, pressing a kiss to my forehead first and then another one to RJ's, who's still blissfully gumming the starfish on my necklace, ignorant to the fact that without him ever really knowing his father, he's more than likely lost him.

As soon as everyone reluctantly leaves, I sit on the couch with RJ. Grabbing my laptop, I pull up the video of Ryan. I should probably be checking the internet to find out the details of the attack, but it won't do any good. It doesn't matter what happened or why. If he's dead, nothing will bring him back. I know that all too well.

Instead, I click on the video RJ and I have watched over a hundred times in the last four months. Ryan's face comes onto the screen, his gruff voice getting RJ's attention. We watch the video every night before bed. RJ doesn't understand it, he's too young, but because we've done it every day, he squeals, excited to do something he knows.

His hands slap the screen as Ryan says hello to RJ. "Hey there, little guy. This is your dad, Ryan. You don't know it, but we have the same name."

Ryan's eyes water, but he takes a deep breath, refusing to let them fall. My mind goes back to that day, four months ago, when I told him he needed to make the videos. He broke down and lost it, not wanting to make them, but deep down he knew it had to be done, and this is why.

"I'm wearing this outfit because I'm in the military," Ryan continues, plastering on a smile for his son. "I'm a combat engineer." He laughs softly. "My job is to build and fix things." He shrugs awkwardly. "Umm... anyway, that's what I'm probably doing while you're watching this. Fixing things." He gnaws on his bottom lip, closes his eyes, then takes a deep breath and opens them. "I just want you to know how much I love you. I've only known you for a couple weeks, but fuc—I mean... Jesus, I suck—I mean stink at this." He chuckles humorlessly. "I just need you to know how much I love you and your mom. You don't know me yet, but I'll be home soon and I plan to spend the rest of my life getting to know you. My dad—your grandpa—and I are real close. He taught me how to ski and snowboard, took me fishing, and taught me how to fight. He taught me how to play sports. He was always the coach of every team I played on."

Ryan swallows thickly, sniffling back his emotions. "I can't wait to do all that with you. Watch you grow up... hear you say your first word... be there when you take your first step." He curses under his breath. "Just do me a favor and don't do anything until I get home." He laughs, shaking his head.

"I hope you're being good for your mom." He smiles a genuine smile, his dimples popping out. "Give her lots of hugs and kisses for me, okay?" He runs a hand along his shaved head. "I love you so much, RJ. And I love you, Micaela. I know you said no promises... but, I'll see you both soon." And with one last smile, his face disappears and the video ends.

I told him not to promise, but he still did. Not in a single letter or text, but in this video. He did. And now he's going to break his promise. I close my eyes, needing to calm myself. My nervousness and fear is turning into anger and I don't want RJ to see that. To feel that. He needs me to be strong. Nothing has been confirmed. There's still hope. He could be at a different base, perfectly fine and getting ready to head home. He's just running late. That's all it is… But deep down, I know that's not true. And lying to myself isn't going to do any good.

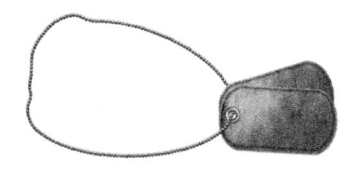

## CHAPTER TWENTY-EIGHT

### FOUR DAYS LATER

### MICAELA

"Sweetheart, please let me take RJ," Mom insists. Her eyes are filled with a mixture of pity and sympathy. It's been four days since Kayla dropped the bomb that a base was attacked in Afghanistan, and since then, nobody has heard anything. I want to believe that, since we haven't been notified of his death, he's still alive, but we also haven't heard from him. So that could easily mean whatever is going on over there is bad and they just haven't gotten around to notifying us yet.

"You need a break," she insists. "You've been holed up here for the last four days with RJ. Please, let me help."

"I'm his mom," I snap. "I don't need or want a break. RJ needs me." *I'm most likely the only parent he has left,* I think but don't say out loud.

Mom flinches, and I feel bad for the way I spoke to her, but I don't have it in me to apologize. She's right. I do need a break. I'm emotionally exhausted, and because I haven't slept more than a couple hours over the last few days, I'm running on fumes.

"And you're no good to him if you're not taking care of yourself." She wraps her arms around me and I inhale her soft-scented perfume, allowing myself a brief moment to escape. To pretend I'm fifteen again and my biggest problem is what to wear or who I should hang out with.

I'm so damn tired, but my mind is racing. It goes from believing Ryan is dead and trying to figure out where I go from here, to having hope he's alive, which has me trying to search for anything online indicating as such. Unfortunately, while the government will spoon feed little bits of information as they see fit, they won't give classified details until it's all been investigated. The only reason Kayla found out what she did was because she's close with Ryan's ex, who is still friends with other military wives, one whose husband is at the compound Ryan was at, until he left to go to another one. They can't give any details, so we don't know if he's at the one that was attacked, but the longer he goes without reaching out, the more likely he was.

"Micaela, you're an amazing mother," Mom murmurs into my hair. "But sometimes being a good mom means admitting you need a little help. And it's okay to have help." She backs up slightly, framing my face with her hands. "It doesn't make you any less of a mom." She kisses the tip of my nose. "There's a reason for the saying: it takes a village. Your dad and me, your brother and sister, Ryan's family...Even Lexi and Georgia...we're your village. Let us help."

I release a harsh breath, letting myself feel the weight of the situation. My head and heart hurt. My body is sore, and it's hard to keep my eyes open. "Okay," I choke out.

Mom smiles softly. "I'll take RJ home with me. Take a bath and relax. Read a book, watch crappy TV. Take a nap. Go for a walk. I know it won't be easy, but for a little while turn it off."

"Okay," I repeat.

"If you're up for it, come over for dinner. If not, RJ can stay the night." She picks RJ up, who immediately grins, excitedly cooing at his grandma.

"I love you, little guy," I say, kissing his cheek. "Thank you, Mom. Love you."

"I love you, too." She kisses my forehead one more time before she heads out the door with RJ.

Taking her advice, I run a hot bubble bath in the Jacuzzi tub. I spend the next hour shaving and relaxing. I use my iPad to read a couple chapters of the book I'm reading—although, I couldn't tell you what's actually happening. When the water turns cold, I

## CHAPTER TWENTY-EIGHT

jump in the shower and wash my hair, which hasn't been washed in days.

When I get out, with a towel wrapped around me, I pad into the bedroom to get dressed. I'm about to grab my underwear and pajamas from my drawer, when I spot Ryan's ARMY hoodie hanging in the closet. My stomach plummets, remembering all his stuff is in here. *Because he's supposed to be here...*

I snatch it off the hanger and pull it over my head, the scent of Ryan immediately enveloping me. Instead of putting on my underwear, I put on a pair of his boxers, rolling them up twice so they don't fall. Then, I climb into bed, knowing I probably won't fall asleep, but also knowing I need to try. Like my mom said, I need to take care of myself so I can take care of RJ.

When my eyes won't close, I grab my laptop from the nightstand and drag it over. My finger glides across the trackpad, waking it up, and Ryan's face surfaces. The last thing I watched was his video to RJ. I click out of it, and his other video taunts me. It's in the same file folder, named **Don't Watch.** Ryan named it that to remind me that it should only be watched if something happens to him—if he doesn't make it back.

My finger moves the cursor to the file, but I don't yet click. If I open this, it's like admitting he's gone, and I'm not ready to admit that yet. No, I won't open it until his body has been found, or at least until someone confirms his death.

I shut down the computer and snuggle into Ryan's blankets. Since we're using his bed, we're also using his sheets. Kayla suggested I wash them, unsure when the last time he washed them was, but I was too afraid they would lose his scent. If he doesn't come home, eventually his smell will disappear. Just like Ian's did. And all that will be left are the memories.

My heart squeezes behind my ribcage as I think about my memories with Ryan. While I had years with Ian, I only had less than four weeks with Ryan. Sure, we've spent the last four months texting and getting to know each other, but it's not enough. What will I tell RJ about him? I don't know enough to make sure he knows his daddy. I don't have memories to share. We never went to the movies, or experienced embarrassing moments. We didn't have any inside jokes. Hell, we haven't even gone on a single date. I guess his family will have to share their memories with him...

Sobs bubble up and over, racking my body, as I cry for a life I never got to have with Ryan. We created the most precious gift, yet we never got to experience parenthood together. There's so much more I want to know about him, and now it might be too late—I may never have a chance to get to know him.

Lifting the hoodie over my head, I snuggle deeper into the fabric, trying to make it feel like Ryan's body is wrapped around mine. As my heart thumps loudly and painfully in my chest, I weep into the blanket, until my lids can't handle the pain anymore, and my eyes close of their own accord, forcing me to fall into a fitful sleep.

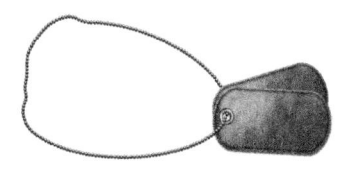

## CHAPTER TWENTY-NINE

### RYAN

"Fuck!" I fling the useless device across the vehicle. "Fucking piece of shit won't turn on."

"Well, it's been through hell," Sergio points out. "Literally."

I give him a pointed look, but can't argue. What we just went through over the past week is probably the definition of hell. If not, I imagine it's damn close. The ambush, which thankfully ended with the Afghani terrorists all dead—some by their own hands and some by ours—also ended with two of our men dead. I didn't know any of them well, since they weren't part of my squad, but it still hits each one of us hard as hell. We took a bad fucking loss that day. Once everything was under control, we spent days getting everything sorted. I knew my family would be freaking out, but I had no way of communicating with them. And even if I could've, I wouldn't have been allowed to. Because of the attack, we were under strict black out orders until we were back on U.S. soil.

"Can I borrow yours?"

"Yeah." He hands me his phone.

I go to type Micaela's number, but I realize I don't fucking know it by heart. Luckily, I know Marco's. He answers on the first ring. "Hello?"

"Hey, it's Ryan."

There's a long pause and then a deep sigh. "Thank fuck. You okay?"

"Yeah, just running a few days late," I joke, trying to make light of the situation. I can't go into details over the phone.

"Not funny," he snaps. "We've been worried sick. We thought..." He sighs. "Your mom said..."

"My mom?" *How the hell does she know anything?*

"Yeah, I guess someone told someone and that person told her. She showed up freaking out. Nothing was confirmed, but there was speculation."

Jesus, fuck. Micaela must be going out of her fucking mind. I'm not just running late...I'm missing.

"I'm okay," I choke out. "I need to get a hold of Micaela, but my phone is fucked. Do you have her number?"

"Yeah." He rattles off her number.

"Can you tell my parents I'm okay? I didn't realize something was said to my mom. I'm leaving the airport now. I have to stop at the base, but then I'll be on my way to you."

"She's at your house...Umm...the house you bought her."

"She's living there?" My heart swells at the thought. She never told me that.

"It's supposed to be a surprise. I'm sure she'll tell you once you get a hold of her, but just in case she's too distraught, that's where she is."

"Thanks."

We hang up and I dial Micaela's number. It rings several times before going to voicemail. Maybe she's not answering because she doesn't recognize the number.

"Hey, baby, it's Ryan. I didn't want to leave a voicemail, but I just want you to know I'm okay. I'm calling from a buddy of mine's phone. Mine isn't working. I'm on my way to you, but I won't have any way of talking until I get a new phone. I love you."

I hang up and hand Sergio back his phone. "Thanks. If she calls back, can you let her know I'll see her soon?"

Sergio nods.

As soon as we get back to the base, since all the paperwork was already done, I say bye to my men and head out. I'll deal with everything else tomorrow. Today, I need to get home to Micaela and RJ.

## CHAPTER TWENTY-NINE

Not having a phone is killing me, and the fact that Micaela didn't call Sergio's phone back has me feeling sick inside. She doesn't know I'm okay...

I pull up to the house I bought and see her SUV in the driveway. Leaving my shit in the vehicle, I slam the truck door and run up to the house, using my key to get in. The first thing I notice when I step inside is that it's furnished. It's still kind of bare, but there are all of the necessities. My eyes go to the photos on the wall behind the couch—of us and our families. They're all candid, but the way they're printed makes them look professional.

A phone ringing from somewhere in the house has me reluctantly tearing my eyes from the photos. I locate the phone on the end table and see Marco's name on the caller ID.

"Hello."

"Hey, you're with her?" he asks, sounding concerned.

"I'm with her phone. I just got here, but it doesn't look like anyone is here."

"RJ is with us," Marco says. "Micaela..." He clears his throat. "She wasn't doing real well, so Bella convinced her to let us take him so she could have a little break."

Damn it, I hate what she's been going through, and more so, that I'm the one to put her through it. This is exactly what she feared would happen.

"Maybe she went for a walk," he suggests.

"I'm going to check the rooms for her now and then I'll go from there."

We hang up and I go in search of Micaela. I find her in the master bedroom. My furniture from my parents' place fills the once empty space. She's lying on one side of the bed, cuddled into my blankets, and I immediately recognize my hoodie on her. Her face is scrunched up in what looks like pain, and I imagine she finally fell asleep thinking the worst.

I take a second to watch her sleep, then using her phone camera, snap a picture. She's so fucking beautiful with her curly hair splayed out across my pillow. Her heart-shaped lips are puckered, and her brows are furrowed like she fell asleep against her own will.

Needing to touch her, I undress out of my OCPs, then change

my boxers for a fresh pair. I should probably shower, but I can't wait that long to have her in my arms.

Edging across the bed, I align our bodies so her back is to my front. I nuzzle my face into her hair, inhaling deeply and drawing in her scent, rememorizing her smell: vanilla. It's a little different than before I left. She must've switched shampoos. I gently lift her head, pushing my arm under her and wrapping my other arm around her torso. I should probably wake her up, but she's sleeping so peacefully and her dad said she's been having a rough time. So instead, I snuggle into her back and close my eyes, finally feeling my heart calm for the first time in four months. My body and mind feel centered. Right here, with this woman, I finally feel at home.

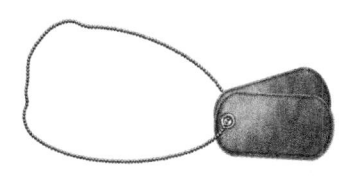

# CHAPTER THIRTY

## MICAELA

Taking a deep breath, I crack my eyes open, feeling refreshed. I'm not sure how long I slept for, but my eyes no longer feel like they weigh a hundred pounds and my body doesn't feel as sore. My head is no longer fuzzy. I feel rested. I listen for RJ but quickly remember my mom took him—because I was exhausted. Because Ryan is missing. Now that I've had a break, I should go get RJ and bring him home. I feel around for my cell phone, but instead my hand comes across a hard... body?

The second it sinks in, I roll over and scoot back, almost falling off the side of the bed. Strong hands catch me, though, before I do, and it's then I realize Ryan is in bed with me.

"Whoa, it's just me," he says, a soft smile on his face.

"If I'm dreaming this, I'm going to be seriously pissed," I blurt out, bringing my hand to his face to make sure he's real.

Ryan's mouth turns down into a frown. "You're not dreaming, baby." He runs his finger down the center of my face, starting with my forehead and trailing his fingertip along the center of my nose and down to my lips, tracing the outline of my mouth. "I'm here."

His words are like electricity to my body and mind, and it all clicks at once: he's here, alive, safe. With me. And without thought, I'm climbing on top of him and then peppering kisses all over his face. His forehead, his temples, his nose, both cheeks.

He chuckles as my hands roam across his bare shoulders and down his chiseled chest, making sure he's really okay. If possible he's even more muscular and toned than he was four months ago.

"I'm here," he repeats.

"I need to make sure you're okay," I explain through a relieved sob.

Our mouths connect in a passionate kiss that sends a bolt of electricity to my heart, reviving it after days of it barely beating. Fat tears roll down my cheeks and Ryan breaks the kiss to lick each one. "Shh, it's okay," he coos, gripping my hips and shifting us so he's sitting up against the headboard and I'm straddling his lap. "Don't cry, please."

I wrap my hands around him, clinging to his neck, while he kisses more of my falling tears that I can't control. "I didn't think —" Before I can finish my sentence, Ryan places his fingers to my lips.

"I know, baby. But I'm here. I'm so fucking sorry it took me longer to get to you, but I'm here, and I'm not going anywhere."

Before I can argue, *for now*, his lips crash against mine. Tasting, coaxing, consuming. My body sinks against his, but it's not enough. I need to feel closer.

I break our kiss, only long enough to remove his hoodie, then my mouth goes back to devouring his. With my body pressing against his, skin to skin, it's better but still not enough.

Sensing my irritation, Ryan pauses our kiss. "What's the matter?"

"I..." My brown eyes lock with his blue, and it hits me once again that he's actually here with me. I hoped and prayed and begged God for him to come home and he's here. "I *need* you," I breathe, meaning that in every sense of the word.

Without me having to explain, Ryan knows exactly what I need. He flips us over, so I'm on my back and he's on top of me. He brings his mouth down to mine and kisses me with abandon. I reach down and remove his boxers, then mine, so we're both completely naked. His lips leave mine, and he trails soft kisses down the side of my face, along my jaw. He kisses across my neck, and once he's to my breasts, he places an open-mouthed kiss to each of my nipples, sucking them gently.

"I missed you so much," he murmurs, massaging my breast

before he wraps his lips around the hardened peak again. My legs are wrapped around his thighs, and my center tightens in response.

"I never want to go another day without touching and feeling you," he says as he lowers a hand and inserts a finger into me. "Fuck." His face falls next to mine, his lips right up against my ear. "Your body missed me, didn't it?"

Unable to find my voice, I nod, lifting my pelvis as Ryan inserts another digit. He slowly pumps his fingers in and out, coaxing an orgasm from deep inside me. His thumb massages my clit gently, and I explode around him.

"Yes," he hisses, removing his fingers and replacing them with his hard length. With his arms caging me in, he thrusts into me, connecting our bodies in the most intimate way.

Our mouths meet once again, and his tongue strokes mine to the same rhythm he makes love to me. Heat floods through my veins, setting my body on fire. I didn't realize how cold I was, until now. Ryan's touch, his kisses, the way his body connects with mine, warms every part of me in the best way possible.

We're so close, I'm not sure where he ends and I begin. I can feel the thumping of his heart against my chest, the shakiness of his breath against my mouth, and when he finally lets go, whispering that he loves me, I can feel his entire body shudder as his warm seed fills me in the most delicious way.

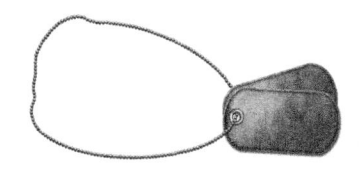

## CHAPTER THIRTY-ONE

### RYAN

"I want you again," Micaela says, her voice sounding upset by her admission.

After we finished reuniting, we made love again, this time with her on top. After that, I dragged her into the shower to rinse off, and from there, we climbed back into bed. She wrapped herself around my body, her soft legs tangling with mine. Her face found its place against my chest, and mine nuzzled into the curve of her neck. Neither of us said a word, instead choosing to just hold each other, reveling in the quiet moment of contentment.

It didn't take long before her warm body, rubbing against mine, caused my dick to get hard. I ignored it, not wanting the moment to be about sex, but simply about me holding her.

"And that's a bad thing?" I ask, lowering my eyes to look at her.

"I also want to go get RJ so you can see him."

"Ahh..." I say in understanding. I want nothing more than to go see our son, but I also want this time with Micaela. I *need* this time with her.

She moves from me and I frown, wanting her back. I assume she's getting up to get dressed so we can head over to her family's house, but instead, she scoots down, so she's eye level with my dick.

"I think I'll just have one more taste. And then we'll go." Wrapping her delicate fingers around my shaft, she guides my dick into her open mouth, only stopping when the head hits the back of her throat. The sight of her swallowing me almost has me coming down her throat. I groan in pleasure, and it spurs her on. She backs up slightly, exposing my wet shaft, then takes me all the way in again.

"Fuck," I grunt. I'm going to come like a goddamn pubescent teenage boy if she keeps doing that. She rolls us over so she's lying between my legs and her head begins to bob up and down, sucking my dick like she needs it to survive. I reach down and move her hair from her face so I can watch. Then I reach farther to pinch her pink nipples that are hanging like perfect teardrops, swaying back and forth as she fucks me with her mouth. She takes my ballsac in her palm, squeezing slightly, and I'm a goner.

Unable to form the words to warn her, I grasp her mane, trying to pull her off me, but she doesn't let up, taking every last drop of my orgasm.

Her mouth pops off my dick and she runs her tongue along the seam of her lips before she smiles sweetly. "Okay, I'm ready now."

"Yeah, but I'm not." Sitting up, I grip the curves of her hips and lay her down. "Now, it's my turn."

---

I'M quiet on the walk over to Micaela's family's place, and thankfully, she doesn't question it, just holding my hand and walking next to me. After I ate her pussy—twice—we showered again and then got dressed. I called my parents to let them know I'm okay, and they made me promise, once I'm settled in, to bring Micaela and RJ over. Micaela and I haven't talked about what happened during my last few days of deployment, why I was several days late. I know she knows we were ambushed, but she doesn't know anything else. It will be in the news soon, so I'm planning to tell her, but right now I just want to focus on her and RJ and being home with them. When I tell her what happened, I'm almost positive she's going to freak out. But right now she's pretending to be blissfully ignorant, like I was away on an

## CHAPTER THIRTY-ONE

extended trip and not almost killed by some crazy as fuck terrorists who had bombs strapped to their bodies to prove whatever point they were trying to make.

When we get to the door, I take a deep breath and she glances over at me. "You okay?"

"Yeah..."

"Then why are you squeezing the life out of my hand?" She raises our joined hands. "I lost all feeling of my fingers three houses back."

"Sorry." I loosen my grip but don't let go. "I know RJ isn't going to know who I am, but what if he's scared of me?"

"Why would he be scared of you?"

"Before I was adopted, I was sent to foster care. I don't remember a lot, but I do remember all the strange faces. I was passed around to different homes and not knowing who anyone was scared me. He knows you and your family. He knows my family...but he doesn't know me. So he might be scared."

"Were you scared when Bentley and Kayla took you home?"

I think about it for a second, remembering the day they saved me. At first, I was scared. Bentley was this huge, muscular, scary-looking man, but then he knelt down next to me and, with the softest voice, said, 'We'd like to take you home if that's okay.' He extended his hand, and in that moment, I had never felt so safe.

"No, I felt safe."

"That's because they loved you. Just like you love RJ. He might not know you, but he'll know you love him."

She takes my hand and walks us through the door. The second her mom spots us, she rushes over and envelops me in a motherly hug. "Oh, thank God. When Marco told me he heard from you, I was so relieved. You've spoken to your mom, right?" she asks, stepping back and assessing me to make sure I really am okay.

"Yeah, we'll probably visit her tomorrow so she can see me for herself."

"Oh, good." She gives me another hug. "RJ is in the backyard with Marco and Liam. They're grilling dinner. You guys will stay, yes?"

"Of course," I tell her, already following Micaela through the house to the backyard.

We step outside and the smell of grilled meat wafts in the air.

It's been a long ass time since I smelled food that good. Marco is standing in front of the grill, and Liam is sitting at the table, drawing or writing on a piece of paper.

Marco tilts his chin toward me with a grin. "There he is, and in one piece."

"Dad," Micaela chides, walking over to Liam. She gives the top of his head a kiss before she bends down. "There's my little guy," she coos, lifting RJ into the air. His smiling, pudgy face comes into view, and tears burn behind my lids. She blows raspberries on his belly and his eyes light up, the most beautiful fucking giggle ringing through the air. I've seen him in pictures and a couple times in video, but none of that did him justice. With my brown hair and bright blue eyes, he already looks like me. But when he laughs, his dimples, which are identical to mine, pop out, and if I had any baby pictures, I'm almost positive that's what they would look like.

Micaela lowers him, so he's vertical again. Unlike the last time I saw him, he's able to hold his head up, and his eyes meet mine curiously. His fingers go to his mouth, but Micaela removes them, popping a pacifier into his mouth.

"Want to hold him?" she asks, stepping closer to me. When she turns slightly, I can see the onesie he's wearing is camouflage and reads, *Some heroes wear capes, mine wears combat boots.*

A lump, the size of a hand grenade, blocks my airway. Micaela has every reason to despise that part of my life, and I know she's terrified of it, yet, while I was still in Afghanistan, she moved us into the home I bought for her. She dresses our son in outfits like the one he's wearing now. She's been kicked down, but she still remains so damn strong.

"Ryan," she prompts, shaking me from my thoughts.

"Yeah," I choke out, clearing my throat when the word comes out barely audible. "Yes, please." I extend my arms and she hands RJ over to me.

"RJ, this is your daddy," she says softly, as if he understands her.

His gaze locks with mine, and for a second I worry he's going to cry. But then his hands come up, rubbing on the short beard I have because I wasn't able to shave for over a week. He spits out his pacifier, and then his mouth opens like a hungry fish. Before I can figure out what he's doing, his drool-filled mouth lands on my nose.

Micaela giggles. "He's giving you kisses."

I stand there, frozen in my place, while my son gums the hell out of my nose—saliva dripping down into my mouth—and thank God that I'm able to be here with my family.

A minute later, RJ pulls away from my nose, replacing his mouth with his fingers. He squeezes my nostrils, his eyes going slightly cross-eyed as he stares intently at my face. I chuckle at how fucking curious he is.

"Hey there, little guy," I say, keeping my voice soft. "I've missed you."

RJ answers me by moving his hand from my nose to my mouth and pulling on my lower lip. When a laugh bubbles out of me, he grants me the most beautiful smile, and I'm almost positive, right here on the back porch of Micaela's parents' house, my heart leaps out of my chest and into my son's hands.

"See," Micaela says softly. "He totally loves you."

"Dinner's ready," Marco calls over. "Get inside, so we can feed you some good ol' American cuisine.

We all sit around the table, and Micaela offers to put RJ into his swing, but I'm not ready to let go of him yet, so I opt to eat one-handed. The conversation stays light, everyone getting me caught up on everything going on here, asking me questions like if the food we're eating is better than over there and if I've gotten to take a hot shower yet. I know they're doing it for Micaela's benefit, not wanting to bring up what happened, and I appreciate it.

Eventually RJ gets fussy and Micaela excuses herself to grab a bottle. When he was a couple months old, she wasn't producing enough milk, and he was cranky all the time. She made the decision to switch to formula. She cried on the phone to me that day, feeling like a failure, and I hated that I couldn't be here to comfort her.

When she returns, she hands me the bottle, knowing I'm still not ready to give him up. His heart-shaped lips form the cutest O as he dives for the bottle. I watch him as he devours his food, sucking every ounce down like he's starving. When he's done, I lift him up to burp him, but he won't stay still.

"You don't have to do that," Micaela says with a laugh.

Instead of eating, my attention stays on RJ, shocked and amazed at how much he's grown. Four months feels like a damn lifetime when it comes to babies growing. The last time I held him he was tiny, his skin soft and saggy. But now he's got muscles and baby fat filling him out. He's less like a baby and more like a tiny, living, breathing, little human.

When dinner's over, we hang out, bullshitting and catching up for a little while. When RJ gets cranky, Micaela informs me it's because it's nearing his bedtime. After saying our goodbyes, we head home. The walk with RJ is quiet, both of us lost in our own thoughts. I'm not sure what's going through her head, but for me, I'm excited to be home and ready to finally start living my life with my family. Because that's what we are—a family. I'm hoping Micaela and I being intimate wasn't a one-time thing, and when we get home, we'll be sharing a room together. I didn't expect to come home to find my stuff moved into her place. I had planned on wooing the hell out of her and convincing her to be with me. Not that I'm complaining, but I don't exactly know where we stand and I'm afraid to ask. Call me a coward if you want, but I don't want to mention it and fuck up my chance of being with my family.

"I need to give RJ a bath," Micaela says once we get through the door. "He's on a good schedule, for the most part. He goes to bed after a bath and a bottle, only waking up once in the middle of the night for a diaper change and to eat. He's even been sleeping in until six."

"Can I help?"

"Of course."

We work together to give RJ a bath, get him into his pajamas, and then give him one last bottle before putting him to bed. His eyelids are hooded over and he's already halfway to his dreams when Micaela sets him in his crib, splaying a blanket across his little body. She turns off the light and winds up a mobile that's hanging above his crib. It turns in a circular motion, playing soft music, and RJ's eyes close before it even makes it around one full time.

"I'm exhausted," Micaela says, removing her clothes and putting on her pajamas. "I don't even know how you're still standing erect and with your eyes open." She moves to the bathroom and brushes her teeth.

"Probably the adrenaline," I admit, following her lead and getting changed then brushing my teeth. My stuff is still in my truck, but Micaela bought everything new for me.

Once we're both ready for bed, she climbs onto one side, so I go to the other. This will be the first time we've slept together since our time at the beach house. We did spend a couple nights together when she had RJ before she asked for space, but we were up all night taking care of him, and the last night before I left I pretty much stayed up all night watching her and RJ sleep.

Micaela fits her body against mine and lays her head on my chest. "This feels good," she murmurs through a yawn.

"Being together?"

"Yeah, that... but also knowing you're home safe. I won't have to worry anymore. We can just... be together." With one last yawn, she cuddles closer to my body, and a few seconds later, her soft snores fill the quiet.

I should probably go to sleep, but it's hard coming back to civilian life after a year of being in the desert, sleeping on a hard as fuck bed, constantly having to be alert. It also doesn't help that while it's 9:00 p.m. here, it's 9:00 a.m. in Afghanistan. I will my body to shut down, but when I realize it's not happening, I instead focus my attention on Micaela and watching her sleep. Aside from the nights we spent together at the beach house, which were mostly spent under the stars or us falling into bed exhausted, I haven't spent much time in bed with a woman. I was married to Laura for years, but we slept in different rooms. She was going to school and studying late and somehow the office turned into her room. Then when she started working as a nurse and later a nurse practitioner, when I was actually home, we would work opposite hours, so she continued to sleep in the other room. Without realizing it, it became our norm.

Micaela shifts in her sleep, her head leaving my chest and her body flipping over like a fish out of water, taking the blankets with her. I glance down at my blanketless self and laugh. She did the same shit at the beach house. *Fucking adorable blanket hogger.*

Wrapping my arms around her from behind, I nuzzle my face into her neck and let the soft sound of her snoring lull me to sleep.

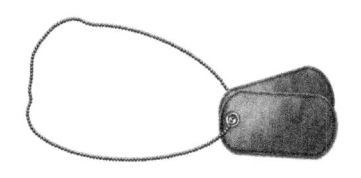

## CHAPTER THIRTY-TWO

### MICAELA

The sound of RJ whining through the monitor wakes me from my slumber. When I roll over, I bump into a hard wall that almost has me falling off the bed in shock and confusion. My eyes pop open, and I find Ryan sleeping next to me, snoring... not so softly. I smile, my heart happy that he's home safely in bed. We haven't discussed his time in Afghanistan and, if I'm honest, I don't want to. I'm perfectly content remaining ignorant as long as possible.

RJ's whines get louder, so I turn the monitor off and stumble out of bed so I can change and feed him.

Grabbing the bottle I pre-make every night so I don't have to do it when he wakes up, I pad into his room. Since he wakes up every night at almost the same time, this has become a routine I can practically do in my sleep—and most nights, like tonight, when I'm beyond exhausted, it feels like I do.

Like me, RJ is still half-asleep. I quickly change his diaper then feed him his bottle. He hasn't even finished drinking the entire thing before his eyes shut, his tiny chest steadily rising and falling. I lay him back in his crib, giving him his pacifier, and with a soft kiss to his forehead, quietly exit, more than ready to go back to bed.

After dropping the bottle into the dishwasher, I head back to the bedroom, turn on the baby monitor, and climb into bed next to

Ryan. He groans when the bed jostles him but doesn't wake up. I pull the cover up and over me, getting comfortable. My eyes are closing when a loud snort has my lids popping open. *What the hell was that?*

I glance over to where the noise is coming from. It's Ryan... snoring. Like he can't breathe. *What the hell... Is something wrong with him?* I watch him for a few minutes, but he seems okay. I close my eyes again, snuggling farther into my blanket, when I realize I need to go pee.

Damn it! Throwing the blankets off me, I pad to the bathroom. So I won't wake Ryan up, I leave the bathroom light off. There's enough light coming in from the hallway and outside. I'm not even a foot into the bathroom when something tangles in my foot and I fly forward. Before I hit the ground, my hands catch the side of the sink and I right myself. Grabbing the offending item, I lift it up and squint. It's Ryan's shirt. He left his clothes on the floor... two feet away from the hamper.

Rolling my eyes, I pick up his laundry and drop it into the wicker basket. I back up and, pulling my underwear down, sit to go pee. Only instead of landing on the toilet seat, my body keeps going down.

"Ahhh!" I shriek, as my ass hits the icy cold toilet water. I cringe, thinking about the amount of germs that are hugging my ass cheeks right now.

"Micaela!" Ryan yells, running into the bathroom. He switches the light on, taking in his surroundings like he's searching for an intruder.

"Help me," I complain, trying and failing to lift myself out of the damn toilet.

Ryan's gaze lands on me and his eyes widen in shock. "Oh, shit."

With my butt so far in, my legs are sticking straight out—with my underwear still wrapped around my ankles—and I probably look like a turtle on its back, struggling to flip over.

He grabs my hands and pulls me up into a standing position. "Are you okay?"

"Aside from my ass being drenched in nasty toilet water, I'm fine," I huff, pulling my pajama shirt off and throwing it into the hamper... which reminds me. "By the way, in case you didn't know, this is a hamper. Clothes go in it." I pull my underwear off and drop it into the hamper as a mock demonstration.

Ryan's brows furrow in confusion.

"You left your clothes on the floor," I explain, my tone annoyed. But Jesus, I'm freaking tired. "I tripped over them."

"And landed in the toilet?"

"No," I snap. "I landed in the toilet because you left the seat up." I flick the seat and it hits the porcelain with a loud bang.

"Shit, sorry." He winces.

"Aren't you supposed to be all neat and organized in the military? Like, people are depending on you to keep America safe..."

Ryan lets out a laugh, but quickly reins it back in. "I highly doubt me leaving my boxers on the floor will determine whether America remains safe."

"Well, it's going to determine whether you remain safe."

"Got it." He bites his bottom lip, hiding his smirk, and I sigh, suddenly feeling like the biggest bitch.

"I'm going to take a quick shower."

His eyes take in my body, as if just now realizing for the first time I'm naked. "Hmm, that sounds like a good idea." He waggles his brows.

"Not happening." I gently push him back. "I'm tired and RJ will be up way too soon. I'll be out in a minute."

Ryan pouts playfully. "Fine." He pecks my lips before exiting the bathroom.

After I take the quickest shower known to man, I throw on fresh pajamas and underwear. Ryan has already fallen back to sleep—and is snoring—so I climb into bed. After a few minutes of tossing and turning, I scoot closer to him to check out his snoring. I've never heard anything like this before. It literally sounds like he's struggling to breathe. Could something be wrong? I try to think if I've ever heard him do this before, but every time we've spent the night together I slept all night.

When he softly chokes, sounding like a congested pig, I pull up Google. It says sleeping on your side can help, so I push Ryan over. He goes willingly, and for a good minute, the room is quiet. Until it starts up again.

*My God, he's loud.*

I read some more recommendations, but they all involve surgery or suffocating the person...

I try to block it out, fluffing my pillow and closing my eyes, but it can't be ignored. So, I reach over and gently squeeze his nostrils for a few seconds. His eyes pop open and he sucks in a deep breath.

"Are you... trying to kill me?" he splutters.

"What?"

"For you falling in the toilet..."

"No." I shake my head emphatically. "You're just... snoring really loudly and I thought something was wrong."

He squints his eyes. "So you thought you would plug my nose so I couldn't breathe?"

"Well, when you say it like that it sounds bad..."

I roll over on my back and release a sigh. "I'm so tired," I whine, sounding like a baby. "I can't sleep with you snoring."

"You snore too," he volleys back.

I swing my head back toward him, shooting him a glare. "I do not."

"Yes, you do."

"Well, if I do, there's no way it sounds like whatever it is you're doing," I scoff. "Like you're literally sawing logs in our bed."

"Okay." He chuckles, pulling me into his arms. "How about you fall asleep first, so my log-sawing doesn't keep you up?"

I nod, laying my head on his chest. His arm comes around me, his fingers running soothing lines up and down my back. My lids become heavy and I'm almost asleep, my head feeling slightly fuzzy, when a loud choking sound has my eyes opening.

He can't be fucking serious. How the hell did he fall asleep that fast?

I move out of his hold and grab my iPad. It's obvious I'm not going to fall asleep right now, so maybe I can read a few chapters in my book. I always fall asleep while reading when I'm tired.

After reading the same paragraph several times and having no clue what I've read—because Ryan's snoring is so close on my radar, I can't *not* hear it—I grab my blanket and go to the living room. It's already three in the morning. If I don't fall back asleep soon, it's going to be a rough morning when RJ wakes up, bright-eyed and ready for the day.

Out here, I can't hear Ryan's snoring, but the couch obviously isn't meant to be slept on, because as I shift around trying to get comfortable, my back screams in pain. I finally give up and turn on my iPad. I read the remainder of my book and then start on another one before my body finally submits and I fall asleep.

---

"BABABABABA." The sound of RJ has me wrenching my eyes open. Not even on the monitor does he sound that close. Forgetting I fell asleep on the couch, I roll over and fall onto the hardwood floor with a thump.

"Ugh." I close my eyes and take a deep breath. My knees and back are both moaning in agony, and my head is pounding. I couldn't have gotten more than a couple hours of sleep.

"Are you okay?" Ryan asks, concern in his tone.

I glance up and find him standing in front of me, dressed for the gym and holding our son in his arms. RJ is no longer in his pajamas and is sucking down a bottle.

"Yeah," I grunt, slowly rising to my feet.

"Why did you sleep out here?"

"It was either that or suffocate you in your sleep," I say dryly, dragging my feet to the kitchen to make myself a cup of much-needed coffee.

"I'm sorry," he says, following me. "I had no idea I snored that loudly."

"Your wife never pointed it out?" Or tried to kill you...

"We slept in separate rooms," he says with a shy shrug.

RJ drops his bottle and reaches for me. I take him from Ryan and he picks the bottle up, throwing it into the sink.

"It goes in the dishwasher," I point out.

"Huh?"

"The bottle goes in the dishwasher, after you rinse it out. Otherwise it will stink up the bottle."

"Oh, sorry." He rinses it out and places it into the dishwasher, while I pour milk and sugar into my coffee.

"You're going to the gym?"

"Yeah..." he says slowly. "Is that okay? I work out every morning, but I don't have to—"

"No. It's fine."

"You sure?" he questions.

"Yeah. I have some stuff to do around the house." I stand on my tiptoes and give him a kiss. "I'll see you when you get back."

After he's out the door, I set RJ in his swing, put on a baby show for him to watch, and go about tidying up a little. I notice Ryan brought in his duffle bag and left it by the door. When I pick it up to move it to the room, I find it's seriously heavy. Emptying it out, I set his stuff—like the photo album I got him—on his nightstand, and then grab all the dirty clothes to put them in the hamper. When I go to lift the lid, I notice the boxers, sweats, and shirt he was wearing last night are on top of the hamper. Not inside... but on top. Really? Is it that difficult to lift the lid and place them inside?

Grabbing his clothes, I add them to the pile in my hands and put them all into the hamper. Since the hamper is now full, I figure I should probably just do a load of laundry. So, scooping all the clothes back out of the hamper, I bring them to the laundry room and throw them into the washer, along with some detergent. I read the dials on the washer to make sure it's set correctly. I've occasionally done my own laundry, but usually my mom—or the cleaning woman Dad hired to help out—handles it—I know, I know, I'm spoiled. But I'm not above learning.

When RJ squeals to get my attention, I close the lid, press start, and head back out to the living room to check on him before I throw the rest of the dirty dishes into the dishwasher and turn it on. While I'm in there, I take a frozen package of chicken out and set it in the sink. I'm not the best cook, but I'm trying to learn. And with Ryan home, I figure I can make us dinner tonight. He's all about eating healthy, so I figure it's best I learn.

When RJ fusses to be let free, I take him out of his swing and settle us on the floor on his fluffy blanket so he can stretch out. I'm exhausted from my lack of sleep, and my head is still pounding, but I push it aside, giving RJ raspberry kisses to his belly. He giggles and wiggles and my heart soars.

We're playing pat-a-cake—which means I'm playing while he smiles and squirms—when the washer buzzes that it's done.

"Be right back, little guy." I kiss the tip of his nose and run to the laundry room to rotate the laundry. As I'm pulling each item out and putting them into the dryer, I notice everything that was once white is now pink. All of Ryan's white shirts, white boxers, white socks... pink, pink, pink.

*What the hell? Why is everything pink?* I have jeans in here... different colored shirts... But nothing pink.

And that's when I see it—my brand-new red sweater my mom bought me. I only wore it once.

"Damn it!" I throw the last of the clothes into the dryer and slam the dryer shut, pressing start.

I go back to playing with RJ, until the dryer dings it's done. Hoping somehow the clothes miraculously will have gone back to white, I pull the dryer open, only to find dry, pink clothes.

I carry them to the couch, so I can figure out what's now garbage, when I hear something...

*Drip, drip, drip...*

Is it raining? I glance outside and see the sky is blue. I follow the sound to the kitchen, where I find bubbles leaking out the sides of the dishwasher.

"Shit!" I flick the handle and pull the dishwasher open. The entire thing is filled with soapy water. It's brand-new, so why the hell is it broken?

I grab the detergent from under the sink, confused, until I see that I used laundry detergent in the freaking dishwasher! I must've grabbed the wrong bottle.

Tears of frustration and failure prick my eyes, as the front door creaks open and Ryan's voice fills the house, letting me know he's home.

While I'm trying to get myself together, he finds me, holding a pair of his pink boxers, with a smirk on his face and one brow raised in amusement. "Was this your way of punishing me for leaving my clothes on the floor?"

I know he's only joking, but the dam of emotions breaks and I let out a sob, the tears that were threatening to spill falling over and sliding down my cheeks.

Ryan drops the boxers onto the counter and cuts across the kitchen to me. Only he doesn't see that the floor is soaking wet, and almost busts his ass on the puddle of water that's seeped out of the dishwasher.

"Oh, shit." He grabs the counter to stabilize himself.

"I used detergent in the dishwasher."

Ryan snorts, ready to crack up laughing, but when he sees the glare on my face, he schools his features. At that moment, RJ lets out a tired cry, ready for his nap.

"I need to lay him down," I say, stomping past him. I scoop RJ up and carry him into his room, change his diaper, and lay him in his crib. I put his pacifier into his mouth and his eyes roll back, ready to pass out.

I need to deal with the pink clothes and wet floor, but I'm too tired and cranky. So, instead, I go to my room, climb into bed—flicking the monitor on so I can hear RJ when he wakes up—and, covering my body and head with the blanket, close my eyes and go to sleep.

If it's one thing I've learned as a new mom, it's that when the baby sleeps, you sleep. Everything else will be waiting for me when I wake up.

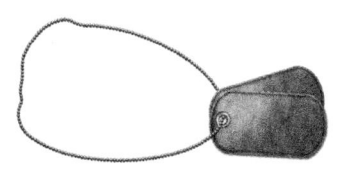

## CHAPTER THIRTY-THREE

### RYAN

I HAVE no fucking clue what just happened. It's obvious Micaela is upset, but I'm not exactly sure why. Sure, the clothes are pink and there's a puddle of soap on the floor, but it's not that big of a deal, right?

Giving her a minute to cool down, I find a mop in the pantry and mop up the liquid. I set the dishwasher to rinse and place a towel on the floor in case any more soap spills out. Then, I grab the pink clothes, keeping what I can and chucking what I no longer want. Pink boxers are fine, but I'm not about to sport pink socks. After folding the rest of the laundry, I grab the stack of clothes and set off to find Micaela, only to find her fast asleep in our bed. She must be tired since she couldn't sleep last night. I feel bad that my snoring kept her up and led her to sleeping on the couch. I'll have to make sure she falls asleep before me, since my snoring is so bad she can't fall asleep.

I leave the laundry on the dresser and jump in the shower, making sure to put my dirty clothes into the hamper this time. When I get out and am getting dressed, I hear RJ's voice come through the monitor. He's only been asleep for less than thirty minutes. I switch the monitor off and head into his room to grab him so Micaela can sleep a little longer.

While I'm changing his diaper, my phone buzzes in my

pocket. After I left the gym, I stopped by the store to get a replacement for my broken one.

"Hey, Dad."

"Hey, Son, how's it going?"

"Good...I think."

Dad laughs. "Everything okay?"

"Yeah, just..." I take a deep breath, unsure how to explain what happened. "I don't know..."

"You know I'm here any time you want to talk, right?"

"I know, and I appreciate it. So, what's up?"

"What's up is that your mom is chomping at the bit to see her baby boy. Any chance you're planning to come by today?"

I glance down at RJ, who's staring up at me with an adorable grin splayed across his face. His lack of nap doesn't seem to have affected his attitude—unlike Micaela, who clearly needs to finish *her* nap.

"Yeah, Micaela isn't feeling well, but I can bring RJ over."

"She okay?"

"Yeah, I think so..."

Dad chuckles. "How about we talk when you get here?"

"All right. I'm on my way."

After packing up the diaper bag Micaela uses full of diapers, wipes, bottles, and formula, I load RJ into his car seat, buckle it into my truck—make a note to buy one for my vehicle so we don't have to keep switching it from vehicle to vehicle—and head out.

"My baby!" Mom squeals when I walk into the house with RJ in tow a few minutes later. I assume she's talking about me, so I roll my eyes playfully, but then she snatches RJ from me and starts planting kisses all over his face. "I've missed you so much," she coos, leaving me standing in the foyer, while she walks into the living room and sits on the couch with her grandson.

"Wow, what am I? Chopped liver?" I joke, following her in.

"I missed you too," Mom says, blowing me a kiss. "But I haven't seen this handsome man in several days."

"You haven't seen me in four months," I scoff. "And I almost died." It was meant as a joke, but Mom stops what she's doing and glares, clearly not taking it as such.

"Don't go there," Dad warns, sitting next to Mom.

"It was a joke."

## CHAPTER THIRTY-THREE

"A bad one," Mom points out. "And, of course, I missed you too." She hands RJ over to Dad and walks over to give me a hug. "I'm so glad you're home safe." She hugs me tightly. "I'm too young to have all these gray hairs you're giving me."

She sits back down next to Dad and takes RJ from him, peppering more kisses on his cheeks. He giggles and squirms, loving the attention.

"Where's Micaela?" Mom asks.

"Sleeping."

Mom's brow rises at my one-word answer, silently telling me to elaborate, but before I can, the doorbell rings and in walks Marco and his dad, Caleb.

"What's up, G.I. Joe?" Caleb extends his arm and we bump fists. "How's it going?"

"Chilling."

"Where's my daughter?" Marco asks, glancing around.

"She...umm..."

"She, what?" he prompts.

Fuck, I guess I should just come out and try to explain this to someone.

"I don't know." I sigh in frustration. "Yesterday I got home and everything was perfect. But then last night...I left my clothes on the floor and she fell into the toilet...She turned our clothes pink, and I guess she used detergent instead of dishwasher soap and soaked the kitchen. Apparently I snore and she couldn't sleep... And then she cried and laid down for a nap."

I take a deep breath at the end of my long as fuck explanation, and everyone goes quiet. Mom is holding back a grin, and Dad is smirking, Marco's eyes are bugging the hell out, and Caleb is full-blown smiling like what I just said is hilarious.

"Welcome home, Son," Marco finally says, patting me on the shoulder.

I open my mouth to ask what the fuck he means by that, when my phone rings. It's Micaela.

"Hey, baby, you sleep good?"

"Oh, thank fucking God! Your phone works!" Micaela cries loudly through the phone.

"Yeah, I got a new—"

"RJ is missing! Please tell me you have my baby." I might not be able to see Micaela through the phone, but I can hear the tears in her words.

"Yeah, I'm at my parents'."

"You didn't tell her you were coming here?" Mom gasps.

"Ryan," Micaela breathes. "You can't fucking leave with my baby without telling me! I was about to call the police. I woke up and he was gone."

I'm about to ask where she thinks he could've gone without me, since he can't get out of his crib, let alone walk, but stop myself.

"I'm sorry," I say instead. "I didn't think..."

"No, you didn't," she snaps. "What time will you be home?"

"Uhm..." Fuck, I'm not sure what the right answer is here. "When do you want me home?"

Dad snorts and Mom slaps his chest.

"Will you be home for dinner?" she asks slowly.

"Yeah." I clear my throat. "I'll be home soon. Do you want me to pick something up?"

When she doesn't answer, I move the phone from my ear and see she's already hung up.

"You didn't tell her you were coming here?" Mom repeats.

"She was sleeping. I thought I'd take RJ so she could get some sleep."

"That was a very thoughtful gesture," she says. "Especially based off everything you said happened last night and today, but you can't leave with a mother's baby without letting her know. Our first thought is, what if someone stole him?"

"Yeah, I didn't think about that." I scrub the sides of my face. "Apparently I haven't thought about anything since I got home. I've fucked up more in eighteen hours..." I breathe out a sigh. "I don't know what I'm doing wrong."

"You're not doing anything wrong," Marco says, sitting next to me. "It's all new. Micaela has never lived on her own before. She doesn't know how to do the laundry properly or run the dishwasher. She's done it occasionally, but for the most part, her mom or our cleaning lady does it. The kids have always had chores, but they were also busy with school and extracurricular activities. She's going to have to learn."

"And it drives women nuts when you leave the toilet seat up,"

Caleb adds with a laugh. "Hayley almost killed me when she fell in once."

"No woman wants to pick up dirty clothes from all over the floor." Mom scrunches her nose in disgust.

"And you have to always let the woman fall asleep first," my dad says. "Especially if you snore. Your mom needs absolute silence to fall asleep. I can't even watch the television in the room."

"I didn't think about any of that," I admit, feeling like shit. "I might've lived with Laura for years, but I was rarely home, and when I was, we were like two ships passing in the night. More like roommates than spouses. We didn't even share a room."

"It just takes time and patience," Mom says.

"So, what do I do now?" I ask. "How do I fix this?"

"I buy Hayley spa days," Caleb says.

"I take your mom away," Dad adds.

"I buy Bella houses," Marco deadpans.

When everyone looks over at him, he shrugs. "How do you think we acquired the beach house in Venice, the cabin in Breckenridge, and the condo in Jupiter? I tend to fuck up a lot."

"I would start with flowers," Mom says. "And an apology."

---

AN HOUR LATER, I'm walking into the house with RJ in one hand and dinner and flowers in the other. I'm not even completely through the door when the scent of burnt food hits my senses. The smoke has clouded the living room and kitchen, so I swing the door back open to air it out. I set RJ down by the door so he's not affected and go in search of Micaela.

I only make it as far as the dining room when I see her sitting at the table. With her head in her hands, she's softly crying.

"Babe."

She looks up at me and frowns, not even bothering to wipe her eyes that are filled with liquid. Her hair is up in a messy bun, and her face is all splotchy.

"Is there a fire?"

"No," she says, her voice devoid of all emotion. "Just ruined dinner."

It's obvious we need to talk, but I first need to lay RJ down since he's passed out in his car seat. I shut the front door and open a couple windows. Then, I carefully take him out of his car seat and lay him in his crib. He starts to fuss, his lips puckering, but the second I give him his pacifier, he calms, falling back into a content sleep.

"He's asleep," I say, sitting next to her at the table.

She nods and mutters, "Thanks."

"I brought dinner." I lift the bag I left on the table.

She eyes the bag for several long seconds before she shifts her gaze to me. "I made dinner."

"I thought you said it burned."

"Yeah, but you didn't know that." She huffs. "I asked you if you would be home for dinner and you said yes."

"And I am." Fuck, this woman has me so damn confused I don't even know which way is up.

"My God, we suck at this," she says, fresh tears filling her lids and falling. She shakes her head and covers her face with her hands.

Needing to touch her, I pull her into my lap, so she's straddling me, and remove her hands from her face. "Stop it. Nobody sucks at anything."

"We've only been living together for less than twenty-four hours and we're failing badly."

I can't help the laugh that escapes. "We're not failing." I kiss the tip of her red nose. "There's no pass or fail. We just need time." I think about what my parents, Marco, and Caleb said earlier. "This is new to us, and there's going to be a learning curve. I've been in Afghanistan for the last year, and before that, I was gone more than I was home. And you've been living at home with your parents."

She opens her mouth to argue, but I cover her lips with my hand. "We've got this, Micaela. I promise. I'll put my clothes in the hamper and you won't turn them pink." Her eyes narrow, and I laugh. "You can buy me a nose plug so you don't kill me and a blanket so I don't freeze my ass off."

"I do not—"

"You don't what?" I ask, cutting her off. "Keep the AC at arctic temps? You damn sure do. And then you steal all the blankets and use them as your own personal igloo." I press my lips to hers before she can argue. "And it's fucking adorable."

She sighs, finally calming down.

"I'll make sure to put the seat down, so you don't go swimming in the toilet, and I'll cook so you don't burn the house down," I continue. "And we'll get a whiteboard for the door so I remember to let you know where I'm going."

She wraps her arms around me and smiles a watery smile. "I love you, Ryan Cruz."

"And I love you. You're right. It's only been twenty-four hours. We've never done this, but we *are* doing it, and it's going to be fucking amazing."

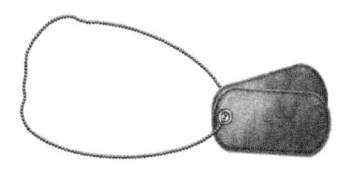

# CHAPTER THIRTY-FOUR

## MICAELA

"W E'VE NEVER DONE THIS, *but we are doing it, and it's going to be fucking amazing.*"

His faith in us is an aphrodisiac. Everything that could've gone wrong, has, yet he still has all the confidence in the world that we're going to be okay—because he believes in us. Just like I need to. We've come too far to give up now. While I was crying over burnt chicken and pink clothes, he was buying me flowers and dinner. He was thinking of solutions to make things better.

With his strong hands cupping my cheeks, his mouth gently presses against mine. His lips part and his tongue darts out, seeking my own. When his tongue finds mine, I release a soft sigh that seems to set him off. His hands glide down my neck, shoulders, arms, landing on my ass, as he deepens the kiss. His mouth devouring mine, taking my breath away.

He lifts me off his lap and sets me on the edge of the table, spreading my legs and standing between them. We're all teeth and tongue and lips as we work frantically to remove each other's clothes. Shirts and pants go flying. My bra gets thrown somewhere. He peels my underwear off, tossing it behind him, at the same time I push his boxers down his muscular calves. His dick springs up and I fist the thick member. Precum seeps out of the tip, and I use it to help stroke him up and down. He feels soft and smooth like velvet and all I can think about is taking him in my mouth.

As if he can hear my thoughts, he breaks our kiss and says, "As much as I want you to suck my dick, I need to be inside you." His lips find the slender column of my neck and he trails open-mouthed kisses along my heated flesh. His fingers part my folds, and when he finds out that I'm soaked, he moans against my skin. "Yeah, I need to be right the fuck inside you. *Now*."

Gripping my thighs, he parts my legs and, in one fluid motion, sinks inside me. And everything I was upset over melts away as I get lost in Ryan. In his touch. In his love. Nothing else matters but being with him, letting him love me. My legs wrap around his torso and his hands release me. One palm slaps the table to hold himself up and the other finds the apex of my thighs, going straight for my clit. The man has got to be the best damn multitasker I've ever met. I can barely focus on not yelling too loud so I don't wake up our son, while he manages to bring my entire body to life. He kisses down my throat, suckling on my collarbone, before he dips lower and takes my breast into his mouth.

He wraps his lips around my nipple and bites down at the same time his finger swipes across my clit, sending waves of pleasure coursing through my body. Being with Ryan is like having access to the most potent, addictive drug. It doesn't matter how much he gives me, how much I take, it's never enough.

I always want more.

His taste. His touch. His words. His love.

I want it all.

His time. His smiles. His patience. His heart.

And he gives it all to me. Everything I want. Everything I need. He hands it all over on a silver platter.

Tugging on his hair, I pull his face to mine, and my mouth crashes against his. His orgasm rips through him, and he shudders above me, groaning against my lips as he releases his hot seed inside me. For several long minutes, even though we've both come and are sticky and sweaty, we stay where we are—kissing, touching, loving each other—refusing to break the connection.

Until our son's shrieks ring through the house, letting us know he's awake.

## CHAPTER THIRTY-FOUR

"LET'S GO AWAY," I murmur against Ryan's lips. RJ is down for the night and we're snuggled on the couch with a movie in the background that neither of us is paying attention to.

"What?" he asks, confused.

"Neither of us has any obligations," I explain. "Let's take RJ to the beach house. Back to where all this started. We can introduce him to the sand and the ocean. Spend some time with Lexi and Georgia. Maybe have Tristan and Charlie babysit so we can all go out. Charlie's offered several times."

Ryan considers this for a moment before he says, "I don't want to run, baby." He kisses me softly, as if to lighten the blow. "I know you're scared, but we're in this together. Running to another state isn't the answer."

I want to argue that that's not why I want to go away, but deep down I know he's right. Living in a bubble with Ryan is amazing, but every time that damn bubble bursts and we're smacked with reality, something goes wrong. If we could run to the beach house, that bubble has a better chance of staying intact.

"Why don't you invite them here for the weekend?" he suggests. "We can have one of our parents watch RJ so we can go out. You're twenty-one now, so you can even legally drink." He waggles his brows playfully. "Then I can bring you home and have my way with you." His smirk tells me he's remembering our time at the beach house when we went out and I got drunk—only this time he wouldn't have to play nice.

"Fine, but I still want to take RJ to the beach."

"And we will." He presses his lips to mine. "Once you've gotten the hang of the laundry, we know the kitchen is safe from fires and flooding, and I know you won't kill me in my sleep."

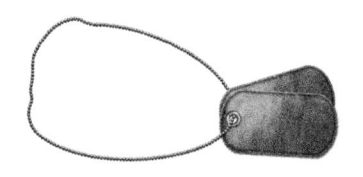

## CHAPTER THIRTY-FIVE

### MICAELA

"Аннн!" Lexi throws her arms around my neck and molds her body to mine, hugging me tightly. "I've missed you so much! This semester almost killed me." She steps back and pouts. "Please tell me you've secured a babysitter. I need to have some fun."

"And what, spending time with my son isn't fun?" Ryan says, joining us.

"He's the best kind of fun," Lexi argues, "but I also need some pre-mom Micaela fun. The kind where we're too drunk to remember the trouble we got ourselves into."

She walks into the house like she owns the place, rolling her luggage behind her.

Georgia stifles a laugh, giving me a one-armed hug. "She took three art classes," she says with a playful eye roll.

"And a math class," Lexi points out. "One very exhausting and traumatizing math class. Why anyone needs to take math when they're majoring in art makes no sense."

Ryan snorts, snaking his arms around me from behind and kissing my cheek.

"Hey, don't laugh," Lexi says, pointing a manicured finger at Ryan. "I'm an artist. I create. I don't do math. Math is... structured and I don't do structure." She points to Georgia. "She does structure."

"And *she* did most of your homework," Georgia says, referring to herself in the third person. "So, if anyone deserves a fun night out, it's me."

Lexi snorts a laugh. "Oh, really? A fun night, huh?" She steps into the living room and picks RJ up, giving him kisses. "What kind of fun are we talking here, dear sister? The drinking kind?"

"Maybe." Georgia shrugs.

"Oh, I can't wait to see this," Lexi says, cracking up laughing. RJ joins in, not having a clue why he's laughing but still laughing nonetheless.

"Your house is beautiful," Georgia says, looking around.

"Yeah, very... grownup," Lexi adds with a wink.

"Thanks. My parents are going to take RJ for the night," I tell them, showing them to their rooms. Since the house has four bedrooms, two of them have been turned into guest rooms for the time being. When we confirmed they would be staying with us, Ryan ordered two bedroom sets and had them delivered.

"Once we're ready to go, I'll just run him over and then we can take off. We'll order an Uber so nobody has to drive."

"Sounds like a plan." Lexi kisses RJ's cheek then hands him to Ryan, who takes him into the other room, while Lexi, Georgia, and I climb onto the queen-sized bed together. Georgia and I sit against the headboard, and Lexi sprawls out across the end of the bed. "Is anyone else going besides us?" she asks.

"I considered inviting a few friends from school." I shrug. "But I stopped talking to most of them when Ian died. And the few who kept in touch kind of disappeared after I had RJ. I guess having a baby isn't exactly most people's idea of fun."

"Then they're not friends," Lexi points out. "Real friends stay by your side, even when shit gets tough. You need to move to LA so we can be closer."

"I agree," Georgia adds. "You could go to school with us."

"And where would I live? I can't exactly live with you and your parents."

"We're moving out," Lexi says with a mischievous grin. "And we convinced Dad to pay for it."

"How the hell did you pull that off? You live like ten minutes from the school."

"We told him we're growing up." Lexi shrugs, like it was just that easy. I'm not buying it, though. Uncle Tristan is super protective of his daughters.

"And," Georgia adds, "we also told him that if we had gone away somewhere, he would've paid for dorms, but we lived at home instead, which saved him a ton of money, so we asked if we could use it toward an apartment, and since we're both doing well in school, he agreed."

If it weren't for Ryan paying the bills here, I'd be living with my parents forever. It's expensive to live in Vegas, and without a degree, whatever job I were to get would never pay enough. They had offered to pay for my dorm in San Diego after Ian died and I told them I would still like to go to school there, but that feels like so long ago.

"Have you found a place yet?"

"No, but we're looking. We're hoping to be moved in soon. I want to throw a party to celebrate summer. You could move in with us," Lexi offers, and I love her even more for that.

"One, I wouldn't want to cramp your style." She opens her mouth to argue, but I continue. "And two, if I were to go away to school it would be to San Diego. Right now, I'm just focusing on RJ and Ryan. I'll figure my schooling out later."

"So, does that mean you and Ryan are..." She waggles her brows, and Georgia giggles.

A huge grin breaks out across my face, remembering the last couple weeks since Ryan returned home. The first few days were rough, even after I kind of lost it and we talked then had the best makeup sex on the table, but every day gets easier. We spend our days with RJ and our nights together. Some days Ryan works out on his own, while I hang out with my mom. Other days, we work out together. Since RJ is five months old, he can hang out at the gym daycare, but usually one of our parents are around and insist on taking him.

Since Ryan is an exceptionally good cook, something I forgot about from our time together at the beach house, he's been showing me how to make different meals. And I'm proud to say nothing else, since that first day, has burned. He also makes sure I fall asleep before him, and thankfully, he doesn't snore every night. He thinks it was from the dust in Afghanistan. It had his sinuses clogged.

Don't get me wrong, things aren't perfect. He still leaves his clothes on the floor more than he remembers to put them in the hamper. I fell into the toilet once more before he made a conscious effort to remember to put it down. We learned I have a tendency to leave the cabinets open, and he's hit his head on them no less than five times. He also curses my amount of 'girly products' on a daily basis. I leave them all over the sink—my deodorant, hair products, makeup, lotion—and every time he uses the sink, he manages to knock everything to the floor. I'm working on putting it all away after I use it, I swear.

But even with all that's not perfect, we're together and happy and spending time as a family with our son. I couldn't ask for anything more.

"We're together," I tell them.

"Remember when we were younger, and he was in town for the holidays." Lexi giggles. "He was in the hot tub with his wife..."

"Oh my God!" I exclaim, remembering what she's talking about. We were probably twelve... maybe thirteen years old. We were all in Breckenridge for Christmas and had snuck out to go use the hot tub at Bentley and Kayla's place, since they were the only ones with one—only Ryan and Laura were already out there.

"That body." Lexi whistles. "He became the star of my older man fantasy. All wet and hard..."

"Who was wet and hard?" Ryan asks, scaring the shit out of all of us.

"You," Lexi says without apology.

Ryan's one brow arches in confusion.

"We saw you and Laura in the hot tub when we were younger. You were shirtless," I explain.

Lexi nods, and Georgia blushes.

Ryan laughs. "I don't remember that, but I know damn well nothing happened in that hot tub."

"Doesn't matter," Lexi says. "We were barely teenagers and you were a good eight years older. You simply in a hot tub with a woman was like watching porn for us."

"You ladies are insane." Ryan shakes his head. "RJ is at your mom's. He was getting tired, so I brought him over so he could fall asleep there."

"Thank you," I say, getting off the bed and walking over to

## CHAPTER THIRTY-FIVE

give him a kiss. "We're going to go get ready," I say to Lexi and Georgia without taking my eyes off Ryan.

"Uh-huh, sure you are." Lexi laughs. "More like thinking about Ryan in a hot tub got you all *hot* and bothered and now you're going to go bone him since you can."

"Don't say bone," Georgia chides. "She's not hooking up with him. She's making love to him."

Lexi and Georgia both laugh.

"Be ready to go by nine," I say, dragging Ryan out of the room.

"Is that true?" Ryan asks, once we're alone. "Did me in the hot tub get you all hot and bothered?"

He pulls me into his arms and dips his fingers into my pajamas shorts, under my panties. "Fuck, woman. You're drenched."

"It's not my fault," I whine. "You're hot and you know it." I pull his face down for a kiss. "And it makes me very happy to know Laura and you didn't do anything in the hot tub."

"Oh yeah," he murmurs against my lips. "And why is that?"

"Because I fantasized about us doing it in the hot tub many, many times when I was younger, and now that we're together, I'm going to have to insist on that fantasy coming true."

"We can definitely make that happen," he says, swiping his tongue across the seam of my lips. "But since there isn't one here, how about we shower together and consider it a warm-up?"

"That sounds absolutely perfect."

---

"FOR FUTURE REFERENCE," Lexi says, strolling into the living room. "Your bathroom presses up against the guest bathroom." She saucily winks, and my face flushes, as I recall what went on in the bathroom.

"Oh, don't get all shy now. It made for some great shower entertainment. Way better than porn. But you might want to keep it down if you have anyone besides me staying in there. Or you know... if you have more kids."

She laughs, and Georgia snorts. They're both dressed in gorgeous dresses, perfect for the clubs here. Lexi's is tiny and black, showing off her pert breasts and toned, pale legs. She's wearing tall, black heels to match. Her blond hair is pin straight and her makeup is barely there. Where Lexi's is sexy, Georgia's is more classy. It's a deep crimson red with long sleeves. It's not as tight or short as Lexi's and it completely covers her chest. She's wearing black heels to match. Her hair is down in loose waves and her makeup is also lightly done.

"You look beautiful," Lexi says, already moving on to another subject, as if telling us she got off to us having sex in the shower isn't a big deal. "A total MILF." She winks.

"Thanks." I'm back to my pre-pregnancy weight, but my body is thicker, more shapely than it was before I had RJ. My breasts, even though I'm no longer breastfeeding, are bigger, and my hips are a bit wider. When the girls confirmed they would be coming down this weekend, since their finals ended a couple days ago, my mom and I went shopping so I could buy a couple new outfits.

The dress I'm wearing is an olive green tie back dress. It's short like Lexi's and dips in the front, showing off my cleavage, but is long-sleeved like Georgia's dress. I'm wearing nude heels, my hair has been straightened, and I'm only wearing a bit of mascara. I tend to sweat when I dance, and I don't want my face coming off.

"I would agree," Ryan says, entering the room, looking sexy as hell. He's wearing a black button-down collared shirt with the sleeves rolled to his elbows, exposing his corded forearms. His jeans fit snuggly against his muscular thighs, and his shoes are brown suede. He's even trimmed his beard, so it's neat.

"But she's *my* MILF," he adds, pressing his lips against mine. "You look fucking sexy as hell, babe," he says, tugging on my bottom lip. My body sags against his and a soft moan escapes past my lips.

"Oh, no," Lexi says. "Let's go. If we don't leave now, you two will end up back in the shower. And based on how long you were moaning, your man has some stamina."

Ryan nuzzles his face into the curve of my neck and chuckles. "You need to find new friends."

"She's not my friend," I joke. "She's family."

"I'm both," Lexi cuts in, grabbing my hand and pulling me away from Ryan. "And there's nobody like me."

We take an Uber to the Strip and have him drop us off in front of a popular Italian restaurant for dinner. We each order a martini, and after begging Ryan to please loosen up, he orders a whiskey. We spend dinner talking and laughing, having a good time. I might live several hours away from Lexi and Georgia, but distance has never prevented us from remaining close. Two—maybe three—martinis later and we're ready to get our dancing on.

After Ryan pays the bill, insisting if any of us tried it would chip away at his masculinity, we head over to Club LA. It's a new club Lexi heard about and is dying to check out. When we arrive, there's a line fifty people deep. I'm about to suggest we go somewhere else, when Ryan takes my hand and walks us to the front of the line. He shakes hands with the bouncer, quickly introducing us. Apparently he's one of the guys who is stationed at the same base as Ryan.

"Damn, Ryan, your cool factor just got raised a couple notches," Lexi yells over the music thumping through the speakers. "You're the last person I expected to know anyone working at a club."

"He's in the military," Ryan explains. "The guys who aren't active duty have to work full-time jobs to make ends meet. The military doesn't pay a whole lot."

I consider asking him if he's active duty, but push the thought aside. Being ignorant might not be the smartest decision, but it's the less stressful option. Ryan only got home a couple weeks ago. We have plenty of time to deal with reality. For right now I just want to live in our little bubble. He's home safe and in bed with me every night, and that's all I care about right now.

We step up to the bar and Ryan raises his hand to get the bartender's attention. She gives a small nod, indicating she saw him, and then walks over.

"What can I get you?"

"I'll take a rum and Coke," Lexi says. When Ryan's friend let us in, he stamped all of our hands assuming we were as old as Ryan.

"I'll have a lemon drop," I tell her.

"Water," Ryan says.

"No way," I argue. "You promised you would let loose. He'll have a whiskey neat," I tell the bartender since that's what he was drinking at the restaurant.

Georgia orders the same as me and then Lexi adds four double shots to the order.

"We're going to be crawling out of here," I warn.

"If we party right." She winks saucily, handing her credit card over to the bartender before Ryan can. "You paid for dinner. I got the drinks."

"Not happening." He snags her card from the bartender and hands her his.

The bartender comes back a couple minutes later with our drinks. We each take a shot, leaving the glasses on the bar top, and then take our drinks with us to a booth that's near the dance floor.

After Lexi begs Georgia to dance with her, they take off onto the dance floor, while Ryan and I get comfortable in the booth. He pulls me into his lap and runs his hands up and down the length of my arms, trailing kisses along my shoulder and collarbone.

"You look so fucking gorgeous tonight," he murmurs into my ear. "I can't wait to get you home and get you naked." His hand roams down my side and lands on my thigh, which is visible from my dress riding up, but hidden behind the table.

We spend the next several minutes making out like horny teenagers, until Lexi and Georgia return with another round of double shots.

Ryan warns us that we'll be cleaning up our own throw-up when we're upchucking our dinner into the toilet later, but still takes his shot.

"I feel good," I tell Lexi, taking the last sip of my lemon drop. "I don't want any more to drink."

"Well, someone has to drink it." She pouts.

Ryan lifts the shot and downs the liquid then goes back to kissing me. His tongue swipes past my parted lips, darting into my mouth. I suck on his tongue, tasting the sweetness of the alcohol.

"Come and dance with us," Lexi shouts, not caring that we're practically dry humping in the booth. "Please," she insists.

"We're watching the drinks," Ryan murmurs against my lips.

"There are no more drinks," she huffs, which makes Ryan release my mouth and chuckle.

"We're keeping the booth warm," he argues, his gaze locked with mine, humor glinting in his eyes.

"C'mon," I say, reluctantly climbing off his lap. "They're only here for the weekend."

Ryan grumbles but stands, wrapping his arms around my

waist. We make our way onto the dance floor, the four of us finding our own little spot. The music is pumping, playing a mix of old-school and new tracks, and Lexi, Georgia, and I dance facing each other, creating a small circle, while Ryan stays behind me, his body grinding against mine. He barely even moves but still manages to look sexy as hell. *Guys have it so damn easy...*

We spend the next few hours drinking and dancing and having a good time. Every time Lexi gets more shots—how her tiny little behind is able to hold it all remains a mystery—Ryan downs my shot for me. When she returns with another tray of shots—this time Georgia bowing out—she calls us lightweights and swallows back Georgia's while Ryan drinks mine and his.

Ryan and I are all over each other on the dance floor. It's obvious by the way he's acting, the alcohol has done what I was hoping it would do—loosened him up. Our bodies, completely in sync with one another, are swaying to the music, and with his face only a hairbreadth away from mine, he tells me how much he loves me and everything he wants to do to me once we get home. Ryan drunk is exactly how I pictured: sweet and sexy and so damn adorable.

At some point, a couple of guys find their way over, trying to hit on Lexi and Georgia. Even though Ryan's paying full attention to me—grinding his body against mine, and peppering kisses along my jawline and neck—I can tell he's making it a point to keep an eye on them as well, which only makes me love him that much more. He's protective by nature, and when I'm with him, I feel safe. I also know any time he's with our son, he'll be safe.

I can't see what happens since my back is to Georgia, but I imagine it must have something to do with the guy who's been trying to chat her up getting handsy. Because one second Ryan is running his fingers through my hair and kissing the sensitive spot below my ear, and the next, he's in the guy's face. With his hand in mine, he's stepped between Georgia and the guy.

"Hey! The lady said no," Ryan says, towering over the guy and getting in his face. I peek around him and see the guy shooting daggers at Ryan, obviously pissed he just put a dent in his plans. He looks like he's about to start shit, but once he realizes Ryan's not only several inches taller, but probably has a good fifty pounds of muscle on him, he steps back, deciding it would be a fight he would undoubtedly lose.

Lexi has now moved over to Georgia and has her arms around her in a comforting way, glaring at the guy like she's about to step around Ryan and take him out herself—and by the look in her eyes, I'm almost positive she could.

"I think I'm ready to go," Georgia says nervously, once the guy walks away. Her hands are shaking, and she looks uncomfortable. Georgia has never been comfortable in situations that involve a huge group of people. She usually only goes along with it for Lexi, and even then, it's rare she'll actually join in.

Lexi nods, not even attempting to argue. While Lexi has a thick shell, blocking out anything bad in the world and rarely taking life serious, Georgia is softer, more sensitive, and that hard shell Lexi carries on her back shelters and protects them both.

When we arrive back at our house, Georgia and Lexi retreat to their rooms, and Ryan and I do the same. I peel off my dress and shuck off my heels, leaving me in only my undergarments. I'm about to head into the bathroom to rinse off, when Ryan's arms encircle my waist from behind.

"Fuck, there's only one thing hotter than you in that dress and heels." His hand glides down my stomach, landing on my cotton-covered mound. "You in nothing but a sexy bra and this tiny thong." He slips his fingers under the material and pushes through my folds. I part my legs to accommodate him, and he sinks his finger into me, finding my clit.

"I feel like I've been hard since you stepped out of the room in that dress." He dusts my hair to the side, pushes the bra strap down, then places a soft, lingering kiss to my bare shoulder. He cups my breast with his hand, massaging it before he zeros in on my nipple, pinching and tweaking it. Bolts of electricity shoot straight to my core, which is already on fire from him rubbing delicious circles on my tiny, sensitive nub. I'm already close to coming, and he must sense that, because he pulls his hand out.

I whimper at the loss of his touch, but before I can complain, he twirls me around and lifts me, setting me on our dresser. "I need to see you," he says, his sapphire eyes meeting mine. The love and lust shining in his eyes are enough to take my breath away.

He pulls my thong down my legs slowly, kissing my flesh as he goes. When I'm naked from the waist down, he parts my thighs and drops to his knees. With his tongue and fingers, he makes love to my pussy, worshipping me. Every lick, every kiss, every bite is done languorously, with my pleasure in mind. He doesn't stop until I'm screaming out my orgasm, blinding lights overtaking my vision as I come hard and long.

When I open my eyes, he's standing in front of me, his eyes glittering in the soft light coming in from outside. He runs his tongue across his lips, and I know he's tasting me. A soft smile spreads across his face, and my stomach tightens. I rarely compare Ryan and Ian. It's not right or fair. They're two different people, and Ian is gone. But in this moment, I can't help but notice the way Ryan is looking at me. With Ian, I knew he loved me. I could see it in his eyes, feel the warmth from it in my heart. He gave me the best kind of butterflies. But with Ryan, when his eyes meet mine, like they are right now, it's as if I'm his entire world. And his love... it doesn't stop at my heart or my belly—it flows through my veins, blazing through my entire body.

"Marry me," he says, his eyes locked with mine. My heart picks up speed at those two simple yet heavy words, until I remember...

"You're drunk," I point out, trying to make light of his request. The last time he *asked me* to marry him was right after RJ was born. We were both high on love for our son, and I knew I couldn't say yes. I couldn't agree to marry Ryan for the sake of doing the right thing for our son. But now things have changed. My feelings for him have grown, and I'm in love with him. But I can't say yes when I know he's been drinking and might not be thinking clearly.

His lips part, like he's about to argue, but I cover his mouth with my fingers. "You want to marry me? Ask me when I haven't just delivered a baby and you're about to leave for several months, or when you haven't been drinking and I'm going to worry if you really mean it or if you're just drunk and thinking with the wrong head." I laugh and Ryan rolls his eyes. I know he isn't proposing to get in my pants—I'm a sure thing. But is there something wrong with wanting him to propose when he's sober and something life-altering isn't taking place?

"I love you and I would love to marry you one day. But I need you to ask when you're in the right state of mind so I know you mean it."

Ryan nods, and I remove my hand. He takes a step back, his mouth forming a slight frown. He's assuming this has put a damper on the mood, but I'm not about to let that happen.

Wrapping my legs around the back of his thighs, I pull him toward me, until he's back between my legs, our chests flush against each other. "We have an entire night without our adorable little cock-blocker," I point out. "So, I'm going to need you to fuck me now."

Ryan's frown morphs into a lopsided grin—it's not big, but it's enough to make the sexy dimple on his left cheek pop out. I bring my face close to his and dart my tongue out, running it along that dimple. "Show me how bad you want to marry me." I press my lips to his cheek. "Show me what I have to look forward to *if* I agree to marry you."

Gripping my thighs, Ryan pulls me toward him at the same time he thrusts his hips forward, sinking deep inside me. "Oh, I'll show you what it'll be like to be with me," he taunts. His mouth connects with mine, and he kisses me hard. "I'm going to fuck you so hard, make you come so many times, you're not going to be able to walk without thinking about me." Tingles of excitement pulse through my body.

He pulls out halfway, then pushes back in, filling me completely. "But I need you to understand one thing..." He grips my hair and tugs on it slightly, so our eyes lock. "When I'm sober, I'm going to ask you to marry me, and the minute you say yes..." He thrusts into me again, and my body clenches around him. "And you will say yes," he growls. "I'm not waiting..." With the hand that's not holding my mane, he brings his fingers to my already sensitive clit and massages circles along it, working my body back up into a frenzy. "We're getting married, and I'm making you mine." His mouth crashes against mine, and he kisses me with abandon. "You're mine, Micaela, and I'm yours."

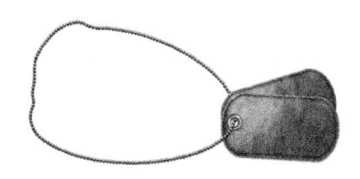

## CHAPTER THIRTY-SIX

### MICAELA

"Oh, my sweet girls!" Mom rushes into the living room and wraps her arms around Lexi and Georgia. "How are you?" She steps back to appraise them. "How's school? Your parents? Oh! How's your brother? I can't believe he's in high school."

"Mom, breathe," I joke.

"Sorry, I just can't believe it's been so long since we've seen them. Marco," she calls out to my dad, who must be in the other room with RJ. "We should take a trip to California soon."

"Yes, dear," Dad says dutifully, making me snort out a laugh. That's been his go-to answer for anything she wants for as far back as I can remember.

Mom playfully rolls her eyes. "Did you girls have a good night out?"

"Ugh." Lexi moans. "My head hurts. I swear I'm never drinking that much again." She plops onto the couch and drops her head back against the cushion.

"Shouldn't have been drinking at all," Dad says, walking into the room with RJ in his arms, who spots me and squeals in excitement. "Where's Ryan?" he asks, handing my sweet baby boy over to me.

"At the gym," I tell him, taking RJ from him. I kiss his cheek and inhale his sweet baby scent. *God, I missed him so much.*

"I'm heading there now." He kisses my forehead. "There's mail for you on the counter. Make sure you grab it. One looks like a bill."

He kisses my mom. "I'll see you later."

"So, what are you up to today?" Mom asks once Dad is gone.

"I'm not sure." I shrug. "Probably just hanging out."

"I was thinking we could go shopping," Mom suggests. "Then go to the spa and get manis and pedis."

"Oh, yes!" Georgia agrees. "I'm dying for a good foot massage. I've been too busy with school."

"Eh... I don't want to drag RJ along. He'll get bored and fussy."

"Actually, Ryan said he would be over to get him after his workout."

"You talked to him?" I ask my mom, confused.

"Just a quick conversation." Mom waves me off and stands. "Why don't I make something to eat to help with your hangover, and once Ryan gets here, we can take off?"

"Yes," Lexi moans. "That sounds wonderful."

We follow my mom into the kitchen, and I grab my pile of mail. I need to do a change of address so it comes to my house. I'm sifting through the stack, and most of it is junk. There is one bill, like my dad mentioned, from when I had RJ. My insurance only covered so much, so I've been making payments on the balance. At the bottom of the pile, I spot a letter from the University of San Diego and open it. It's from the admission's office. I requested to defer for one year when I found out I was pregnant with RJ, and they agreed. Now, they're wanting to know—

"Everything okay?" Mom asks, peeking over my shoulder.

"Yeah," I croak out, then clear my throat. "Yeah, everything's fine." I stuff the letter back into the envelope to read later, when I'm ready for my protective little bubble to burst.

An hour later, we're fed and Ryan, as my mom mentioned, comes by to pick up RJ for the day. We spend the morning shopping—where Mom buys each of us a couple cute outfits—and the afternoon getting manis and pedis.

"You should get your hair done," Mom says, while we're sitting at the hands and feet dryers.

"For what?" I pat the top of my head. My hair is up in a messy

CHAPTER THIRTY-SIX 223

bun, which is the norm for me since RJ is going through a hair-pulling phase.

"Just because." She shrugs. "My treat." She smiles a tad too wide, and I glance at her speculatively. She's up to something...

"There's nothing wrong with pampering yourself once in a while," she adds. "Just because you're a mom doesn't mean you can't feel pretty."

She has a point, and it has been a while since I got a good trim. "Fine."

Once our nails are dry, we walk next door to the salon. I'm assuming we're walk-ins, and the place is busy, so I'm not sure if I'll actually get in. But then Mom gives the lady at the front desk my name, and I realize she made an appointment.

Before I can ask her about it, I'm ushered to a chair, where I spend the next couple hours getting a trim, having my balayage redone—since I haven't gotten it done in over a year—and then having my hair straightened. When the stylist is done, Lexi, Georgia, and Mom gush how beautiful I look.

"While we're at it, why don't we do her makeup?" Mom suggests.

"I don't think—" I begin, but am cut off by the stylist.

"Yes! Perfect." She flits around, applying my makeup, and when she's done, I look like I have somewhere to go—kind of a waste if you ask me, but it does feel nice.

"Here, put this on," Lexi insists, thrusting a bag at me. It's from earlier when we were shopping.

"Are we going somewhere?" I ask, confused.

"We're not, but you are." Lexi winks. "Now go! We only have a few minutes. The heels are in the bag too." Before I can do as she says, she pulls me into a hug. "Have a good time tonight."

"Yes! Text us later," Georgia says.

"Well, *tomorrow*," Lexi adds with a laugh.

"You're leaving?" I ask, separating from Lexi.

"Yeah, we're going to head home," Lexi says. "We have an apartment to find." She winks and kisses my cheek. "Love you."

"Love you both," I say, pulling Georgia into a hug.

After we finish saying our goodbyes, I head into the bathroom to change. The halter dress in the bag isn't one I've seen before. They must've snuck it in while we were shopping. It's navy blue and short, showing off my legs. I slip on the black peep-toe heels and stuff the clothes I was wearing into the bag.

When I step out of the bathroom, I look around for my mom but don't see her anywhere.

"They're outside," the receptionist says with a smile.

"Thank you."

When I step outside, my gaze lands on the most gorgeous man standing in front of a stretch limo. Our eyes connect and he smiles wide, his two dimples popping out.

"You look fucking amazing," he says, stepping forward.

"Look at you," I say back, drinking him in. I thought he looked sexy last night in a button-down shirt, but that look has nothing on the suit he's sporting right now. Black jacket and dress pants that look like they were tailored just for him. He's wearing a metallic silver shirt underneath—no tie, with a few buttons undone. His shoes are shiny and black. He looks like he's going to a...

"We're not getting married, are we?" I blurt out.

Ryan throws his head back with a laugh. "No, babe. We're not getting married. But we are going on our first official date." He shoots me a flirty wink and takes my hand in his.

"Who has RJ?"

"He's with your parents at their house."

I slide into the limo and Ryan edges in after me. I notice a bottle of champagne sitting on ice and lift it. "Want some?" I waggle my brows.

He shakes his head. "No, but you should have some."

I hand him the bottle so he can open it for me. He pops the top and pours me a glass. I take a sip and the bubbles go to my nose. I've never had champagne before. I assumed it would be sweet, but it's kind of... bitter. I take a few more sips, then set my glass down.

Ryan leans in and runs his tongue along the seam of my lips, sending shivers down my spine and straight to the apex of my legs. "Mmm, you taste good," he murmurs against my lips.

"You sure you don't want any?"

"Nope, I'm enjoying tasting it on you."

A few minutes later, we arrive in front of a well-known restaurant that I know costs a fortune to eat at. I mentioned last night when we walked by that I've always wanted to eat there.

# CHAPTER THIRTY-SIX

"If this is where you're taking me to eat on our first date, you're setting the bar high," I joke as we get out. "I mean, how in the world will you top this place for our second date?"

Ryan chuckles. "I'm sure I'll figure it out."

With his hand splayed across my lower back, he guides us to the elevator and up to the top floor, where a maître d' is waiting. Ryan gives her his name and we're immediately shown to our table, which is outside on a terrace.

"Wow, this view is gorgeous," I say, looking down at the Strip.

"I'd have to agree," Ryan says.

I look over at him and he's staring at me. "You're such a cheeseball," I say playfully, rolling my eyes.

"Maybe, but it's the truth. You look beautiful tonight." He pulls out my chair for me and I sit, taking a sip of the water the waitress dropped off.

"Thank you for bringing me here," I tell him, setting the water down. "You didn't have to do all this."

"I wanted tonight to be memorable," he says. "You only get one first date."

The waitress returns and reads off the drink specials. Since I had enough to drink last night, I stick with water, and Ryan does the same.

We both peruse the menu, and when the waitress returns and we both order the same thing—steak and scallops—we laugh.

"Is it weird that I'm missing RJ like crazy, even though I just saw him a little while ago?" I ask, when the waitress walks away.

"Am I that bad of company?" Ryan jokes, pouting dramatically.

"No!" I reach across the table and slap his arm. "I'm enjoying your company. I always do. But I feel like I haven't seen him in a while. He spent the night at my mom's last night and then I spent the day out without him today." I shrug a shoulder, hoping I don't sound like some crazy helicopter mom. "It's just that... he's a part of me, and when I'm not around him, it's as if a piece of me is missing."

Ryan smiles softly, moving his chair closer to me and taking my hand in his. "It's because you have the biggest damn heart," he says, bringing my knuckles up to his lips. "And you're an amazing mom."

"He makes it easy," I joke. "The real test will be when he's a hormonal teenager, fighting us tooth and nail to be his own person. Sneaking out of the house to meet with his girlfriend or to go to parties..."

Ryan chuckles. "Is that what you were doing as a teenager?"

"Well, duh... weren't you?"

He shakes his head. "I was in JROTC and spent my weekends at drill or robotic competitions."

"You dated, though, right?" We haven't touched on our past. I know he was married, even met her a couple times, but I don't know much about him before our time at the beach house, except that he was overseas more than he was on U.S. soil.

"Laura and I hung out, but we were just friends. We met in science and sort of hit it off. I wasn't much of a talker, so I didn't really make friends easily, and she kind of attached herself to me. She didn't mind that I was quiet. She just liked not being so alone." His lips tilt into a shy smile.

"You talk to me."

"Yeah, but I wasn't outgoing. I wasn't looking to party or get drunk. I loved MMA, which is why your dad and I are close. I would hang out there after school, or with Laura. I got by in school, but I knew from the moment I joined JROTC, I wanted to join the military. When I was in that class, I felt a sense of belonging. I excelled at it. I joined Raiders and the drill team, and it kept me busy."

He entwines our fingers together, and my heart pumps quicker. I love when he touches me. "What about you? Book nerd or cheerleader?"

"Why does it have to be one or the other?"

"So, what, you were both?" He quirks a single brow.

"I was a straight-A student... and a cheerleader."

"Ahh." He nods, smirking. "So, you were smart *and* sexy in high school. I bet you were named homecoming queen, weren't you?" He chuckles, but when I divert my eyes, his laughter rises. "You were, weren't you?"

"Ian was a football player—the quarterback—and homecoming king." I roll my eyes, feeling kind of embarrassed. "Kind of cliché, I guess." Ryan spent his high school years preparing to join the military, to make our country better. I spent it shaking my pom-poms and sneaking out to hang out with my football star boyfriend.

"Hey," he says, tucking a piece of stray hair behind my ear. "It's not cliché." He leans forward and presses his lips to mine. "I hope our son has your brains *and* personality. I hope he has plenty of friends and is involved in school like you were."

My heart stutters in my chest at his praise. "I hope he's protective and strong like you."

"You're strong too," he says. "The way you moved forward after Ian died. That takes strength."

"Well, you're smart too," I volley, making him smile. "Not anyone can get a degree in mechanical engineering."

"No matter who he is, or what he does, we'll be there for him... supporting him... together. Because, you're right, he's a part of both of us."

I nod in agreement, a lump of guilt forming in my throat. "I really am sorry I didn't tell you right away that I was pregnant. You could've missed out on his birth, his first couple weeks of life, if not months, and it would've been my fault."

"I've already forgiven you," he says, curling his fingers in the back of my hair and bringing my face toward his. "It was a weird situation and you made the decision you felt was best at the time. In the end, it all worked out."

The waitress steps up to our table, setting our plates in front of us. After asking if we need anything else, she disappears. We eat our meal while making light conversation, including making plans to go to the beach house soon. When the food is gone, the waitress clears our plates and asks if we would like dessert. Before I can answer, Ryan orders us a chocolate cake to share.

"While we wait, I have something I would like to ask you," he says.

When I give him my full attention, I notice he looks kind of... nervous. I'm about to ask him what's wrong, when he slides off his chair and gets down on one knee.

"I might've been drunk last night when I asked you to marry me, but I wasn't when I bought this ring," he says, pulling a small, black box out of his jacket pocket. "I bought it shortly after you gave birth to RJ, but I've been waiting for the right time to ask.

Obviously, last night, after I'd been drinking wasn't the right time." One side of his mouth tips into a boyish grin.

I release a nervous laugh as he opens the box and a beautiful diamond engagement ring glints in the light. One large square diamond sits in the center with several smaller diamonds forming an infinity on either side. It reminds me of the ring he gave me when he was overseas.

He plucks the ring out and sets the box on the table. "The first time I married I was young and didn't understand what it fully meant to be married. I was helping out a friend. I don't regret it because at the time, it was what we both needed. I loved her, but it was different than the way I love you. Until you, I didn't know there were different kinds of love." His indigo eyes meet mine. "I know when you married Ian it was supposed to be forever..."

I clutch my hands to my chest, willing myself not to cry.

"And if I could bring him back, I would. Just so you would never spend a single day being heartbroken."

Tears well up in my eyes as I listen to his admission.

"But I can't," he continues. "And while I hate what happened to him, I'll always be thankful, that through something so heartbreaking and tragic, you came into my life. Those two weeks on the beach with you changed everything for me. My heart had never felt so damn full."

I can feel my broken heart heal. With every word he speaks, he's slowly healing me. Piece by piece, word by word, he's putting it back together.

"And then you did something I wasn't expecting," he says. "You gave me our son, and the love in my heart spilled over. I'm in love with you, Micaela, and all I want in this world is to spend my life with you. Will you marry me?"

I don't have to think about it. Everything he said, I was thinking—feeling. There's nothing I want more than to spend my life with Ryan. To be loved and cherished and adored by him.

"Yes," I choke out. "Yes, I will marry you."

The most breathtaking grin spreads across his face, as he pushes the ring onto the third finger on my left hand. Then he stands and takes me into his arms, lifting and twirling me in a circle, kissing me hard.

The waitress returns with our cake, but Ryan asks her to box it up, so we can eat it at home. I can see the glint in his eyes—he wants to celebrate our engagement in private, and I'm totally onboard with that.

We're barely through the door of the limo before Ryan and I are attacking each other. I pull my dress up to my hips at the same time he unbuttons, unzips, and yanks his pants halfway down his muscular thighs. His dick juts out, swollen and ready. Neither of us wastes any time, guiding me onto his hard length.

"Jesus fuck," he groans. "I can't believe I get to spend the rest of my life buried deep inside you." His mouth crashes against mine, devouring me as he fucks me from the bottom. His thumb massages my clit, giving it the perfect amount of pressure to set me off. We both come at nearly the same time, hard and fast, clinging to one another like we're each other's life lines.

When our breathing has calmed down, Ryan lifts me so I'm back on the bench. Taking a wet napkin, he wipes up my center so I'm not dripping with his cum. After he cleans himself up, he presses the intercom and tells the driver he can take us home. It's then I remember where we are...

"It's a privacy window," Ryan says, answering the question I haven't yet voiced. "He couldn't hear anything."

"Can we go get RJ?" I ask, looking up at him as I snuggle against his side.

"Damn, woman, so it's like that, huh? You have your way with me and then throw me to the side?" He smirks playfully, and my insides warm.

"Yeah, it's only eight thirty," he says, glancing at his watch. "We can go get him. Are Lexi and Georgia spending the night?"

"No, they went home. I said bye to them before you picked me up."

After the driver drops us off at our house, we go inside and change and then head over to my parents' place to pick up RJ. My mom had texted he's close to falling asleep but is still awake for the moment.

When we walk inside, my mom's gaze goes straight to my left hand. "Let me see!" she gushes, grabbing my fingers and bringing them up in front of her face. "Oh, Ryan." She sighs. "You did good." I figured she knew what was going to go down since she's the reason I was pampered today.

"Congratulations, Son," Dad says, stepping into the room with RJ in his arms.

"Have you guys thought about when you want to get married?" Mom asks, hearts shining in her eyes. She's not the biggest girly-girl, but she, like any woman, loves a good wedding, and since Ian and I got married on the whim, she's probably hoping this one will be more traditional.

"As soon as possible," Ryan says, sliding his arm around my shoulders and pulling me into his side.

"I was actually thinking a beach wedding. At the beach house where it all started. Maybe later this summer." I glance up at Ryan, who nods and smiles.

"Whatever you want is fine with me." He presses his lips to mine.

"That sounds perfect," Mom says. "Think about the date and then we'll get to planning."

I take RJ from my dad, and after saying our goodbyes, we head home. I give him a bottle, then Ryan gives him a bath, while I take a quick shower. When I come out, RJ is fast asleep in his crib. Gently, I kiss him good night, then head out to the living room to join Ryan.

"I was thinking of the first weekend in August," I tell him. "My brother and sister won't be back in school yet, so they'll be able to join us for a long weekend."

Ryan pulls out his phone and scrolls through his calendar. His hands still, and his mouth contorts into a frown.

"What's wrong?" I ask. "I know you said as soon as possible, but we're going to need a couple months to get—"

"No, it's not that," he says, cutting me off. "These last few weeks, since I came home..." He sets his phone down to give me his attention, and a horrible foreboding feeling comes over me. Maybe it's the way he's staring at me with such serious eyes, or the way his tone is lacking all emotion, but something tells me whatever he's about to say is something I'm not going to like.

"What?" I push. "The last few weeks, what?"

"We've been in this bubble... I knew you didn't want to talk about what happened in Afghanistan..." He twists his body, so he's completely facing me.

"Well, of course I didn't want to," I admit. "You almost died.

Who the hell wants to talk about that?" I cross my arms over my chest in an attempt to somehow protect myself.

"But now we have to," he says solemnly. "I used some of my leave I've accumulated to spend time with you and RJ when I got back, but next week I go back."

My heart stills. "Go back where?" I ask slowly.

"To work. I'm active military." He moves to grab my hand, but I back up before he can. "Micaela..."

His eyes lock with mine, silently begging me to understand. And I do... I knew this. I might've ignored it, swept it all under a rug, but deep down I knew Ryan returning home wasn't the end of his military duties. I don't know enough about the military or his situation to know how he was able to come home and be with us for as long as he has been, and at the time I didn't want to know. I still don't. Ignorance is bliss, and all that jazz.

But now, as I watch our perfect little bubble explode, exposing us to the reality of our situation, it hits me: I'm engaged to a man in the military. A man who spends more time gone than at home.

He's going to leave us.

Go back to Afghanistan...

*Or worse.*

And while he's doing that, I'll be doing what? Staying home and praying for him to return safely? My thoughts go back to the letter in my purse, the one I folded up and pushed to the bottom, in an effort to remain in our comfy bubble. Only that bubble burst anyway. Because you can't hide from reality. And the reality is, Ryan's life, his dreams, his world is the military. Which leads me to ask myself the question: why am I not chasing my own dreams?

"I can't do this." I stand, knocking into the coffee table.

He stands as well, his eyes widening in fear. "You can't do what?"

I walk around the table and he meets me on the other side. "Micaela, please. Listen to me. My job in the military isn't what you're thinking. I'm not risking my life. I work a regular nine to five job. I go in around seven for PT, which is pretty much working out. After I shower, I report to work. Then, at the end of the day, I come home. I even have off weekends."

"But you're still active, so at any time they can make you go overseas. You can be put in a situation like in Afghanistan where you're risking your life... where there's a chance you can die."

He closes his eyes and takes a deep breath, and I know I have my answer.

My heart, that felt like it was finally healing, is now being shattered all over again, and I'm not sure if it will be possible for it to ever be put back together again.

I glance down at my ring, and Ryan steps toward me, snatching my hand. "No, don't do this," he commands. He takes my chin between his fingers and tilts my face to look at him. "Please don't fucking do this."

"I have to," I choke out, peeling my hand out of his. I remove the ring from my finger and place it into his palm, closing his fingers around it. "When we were at the beach house, you told me to follow my dreams."

I go to my purse and grab the letter from the University. "My dreams are in San Diego. I pushed them aside while we were living in our bubble, but I can't do that anymore. I can't give up my dreams, so I can watch as you risk your life while you follow yours."

I hand him the letter, but I don't wait for him to read it. Instead, I go to my room to pack a bag, then go to RJ's room to pack him one. I know I'm being a coward and running, but I can't stay here, knowing we can't be together.

"Don't do this," he begs, joining me in RJ's room. "We can figure it out together." His voice is gruff, filled with emotion, and I'm afraid to look at him. If he's crying, I don't know what I'll do.

"Figure what out?" I shove RJ's clothes into the luggage. "I've always wanted to live on the beach, study the ocean and marine life. Your job is here, working for the military. Going overseas and risking your life."

"Where are you going?" he asks, grabbing my bicep to stop me.

"To my parents'."

Ryan entwines his fingers in my hair and tilts my face up to look at him. "This isn't over. I'm letting you go for now because I don't want to fight with you, especially not in front of our son. But we're going to figure this out. I'm not letting either of you go."

He crushes his mouth to mine. He doesn't use his tongue, but his lips linger on mine, like he's needing to drink me in, get his fill because there's a chance it might be the last time we ever kiss. The thought devastates me.

"This isn't over," he murmurs against my lips. "*We're* not over."

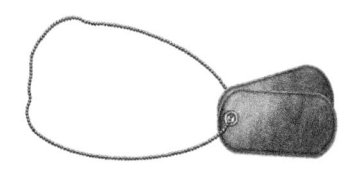

## CHAPTER THIRTY-SEVEN

### MICAELA

"We can go with you," Mom offers, as I pack a small bag for RJ and me. I've been staying with them for a few days, and I've spent most of the time crying. But not anymore. I meant what I said to Ryan. I have dreams, a future, and I need to follow it. He's the reason why I have them. He helped me heal last year, and when I returned home, I applied to San Diego and Scripps, determined to keep taking one step in front of the other. And I can't push my future and dreams aside, so I can stay here in Vegas while he keeps following his dreams. I need to be near the beach to do what I want. Vegas has no beach, no ocean.

*But it does have Ryan...*

No, not going there. I've already lost one husband. I'm not about to lose another.

"And I appreciate it," I tell her, zipping the bag up. "But this is something I need to do on my own. I'll be the one moving to San Diego."

She sighs in acceptance. "Okay, fine, but we're only a phone call and a plane ride away." I'm planning to drive there once I have everything figured out, since I'll need my vehicle, but since this is just a quick trip to meet with the admissions office and take a look at the apartments near campus, we're flying there.

"I know, and I love you for that." I kiss her cheek and smile wide, trying like hell to remain strong and not cry again.

She frowns, knowing me too well. "You know, Ryan—"

"Nope, can't go there," I say, lifting RJ from his crib. My parents setting up a nursery for when RJ comes over worked in my favor when I ran the other night. They already had everything here, so I only had to take my stuff. I'm assuming Ryan's back at work this week, like he mentioned. I've taken a few walks around the neighborhood and his truck wasn't there. He's texted a few times asking how I'm doing and asking to see pictures of RJ, but he hasn't brought us up. I guess he's accepted we can't be together, which is probably for the best—even if there's a small—okay, large—part of me that was hoping he would at least try. Which is unfair of me to want, when I know in order for both of us to follow our dreams we can't be together. Eventually, we're going to have to sit down and figure out how to co-parent, since we'll be living close to five hours away from each other, but right now, I can't do it. I just need to take one step at a time, and at the moment, that step is going to San Diego to figure out my school and living situation.

Several hours later, RJ and I are on the campus of the University of San Diego. Since my appointment with admissions and my advisor aren't until later, I'm meeting with a leasing agent to discuss off-campus housing. She's going to show me the two-bedroom apartment they have available. Since my scholarship covers living expenses, I'll be able to live right off-campus in their approved apartments. They also have daycare on campus. I'm not thrilled about RJ going to daycare at only eight months old, but from what I've been told, it's small and clean, and the caregivers are college students majoring in early education.

I find the leasing office, and roll RJ's stroller inside. "You must be Micaela," an older, gray-haired woman says, standing from behind her desk. "I'm Sonia. We spoke on the phone."

I step around the stroller and shake her hand. "It's nice to meet you."

"The apartment we have available is on the first floor, so you won't have any stairs to climb with your little guy," she says. "It's not far from the office, so we can walk there if you're up for it."

"Sounds good."

She's right, the apartment is only a block away from the office.

# CHAPTER THIRTY-SEVEN

When we enter the apartment, the first thing I smell is chemicals. It must've been cleaned since the pervious tenants moved out.

"Take a look around and let me know if you have any questions," she says, stepping to the side so I can check out the place.

The foyer is small, and the living room is just off it to the right. The walls are all stark white and empty, unlike the cream-colored walls at home. I can paint them, though, and add pictures. I try to imagine recreating the walls of candid photos I did at the house, but when I picture it, my heart drops into my stomach. Would I include pictures of Ryan? Just because we can't be together, doesn't mean he isn't RJ's dad... But would it be weird to have pictures of him on my wall? What if I meet someone?

The thought causes my heart to pick up speed, and before I know what's happening, I'm standing in the middle of the living room, damn near hyperventilating.

*Calm down, Micaela. You made this decision because it's for the best. It might hurt right now, but in the long run...*

I suck in a sharp breath, but it's hard to get air into my lungs. I push the stroller out of the living room, hoping it will help calm my nerves to leave the room. But when I enter the master bedroom, my freak out only worsens, as I try to imagine having to buy all new furniture... having to sleep in my bed without Ryan.

I poke my head into the bathroom. It's simple and clean. But all I can think about is when Ryan and I made love in the shower. The way he organizes my toiletries around the sink. How he wrote an actual note on the mirror to remind himself to throw his clothes in the hamper.

I glance in what would be RJ's room and visualize where his crib and changing table will go. The rocking chair in the corner—where Ryan has spent every night reading to him before bed.

*Oh my God, he won't be able to read to him.*

I choke back a sob and take a deep breath. It won't matter if he reads to him every night, because when he dies during a deployment, he won't be alive to read to him anyway.

*But what about all the days he's not away? All the moments he'll miss...*

I head to the kitchen, and a flashback of me burning dinner and then Ryan making love to me on the table hits me straight in my chest.

I can't do this...I can't live without him. Even if it means there's a chance I lose him...

I need him. I love him. He's my world, my future. What's the point of any of this without him there by my side?

I pull my cell phone out of my purse and dial his number. It rings several times before it goes to voicemail.

"Ryan, it's me," I say through a sob. "I-I need you. I'm so sorry for leaving, but I'm standing here in this apartment in San Diego and I miss you and I need you. RJ needs you. I can't do this without you. I'll change my major. I'll—"

"No, you won't," a deep voice says from behind me. I whip around and find Ryan standing where the dining room table is supposed to go. He's dressed casually in a blue T-shirt and jeans. His head is shaved, and he has light stubble along his jawline. All I want is to run into his arms, so he can hold me.

"I was just leaving you a message," I say dumbly, hitting end on the call and dropping the phone back into my purse.

"I know, I heard you," he says, stepping toward me. "I went by to see you this morning, to talk to you, and your mom said you left."

"And you flew here that fast?"

"Drove," he corrects. "I couldn't let you do this. I told you I wouldn't let us end and I meant it. I just needed a few days to figure everything out. I didn't want to say anything without knowing the facts."

"What facts?" I ask, confused.

"I'm leaving the military." He presses his palm to my cheek. "You said you can't give up your dreams while I follow mine, but what you don't understand is that my dreams, they all revolve around you and our son. Your dreams are *mine*. The military was my way to escape. It gave me purpose, stability. But when I'm with you, I feel all of that and more. I feel centered. Complete. My heart is so damn full."

"But you love the military."

"No." He frames my face with his other hand. "I love you and RJ. I love our life together. I'm out. I signed my release papers. My contract was up for renewal when I returned, but I didn't sign it."

He's out.

No more risking his life.

## CHAPTER THIRTY-SEVEN

No more leaving to go overseas.

"What will you do?"

He chuckles. "I have an engineering degree and a bank account with more money than most dream of. I'm sure I can figure it out. Until then, I was thinking I could follow in my dad's footsteps and be a stay-at-home dad for a little while, while you follow your dreams."

"I was coming back," I say. "My voicemail..."

"I know, I heard, and I love you even more for that. That you would be willing to give up your dreams to be with me is the most selfless thing anyone has done for me, besides my parents adopting me. But that's not what I want for you...for us. You deserve to finish school and create a future for yourself. And I want nothing more than to be here with you while you do it."

"What do you think?" Sonia asks, making her presence known. I completely forgot about her being in here.

"We're going to have to pass," Ryan says politely. "There's been a change of plans."

"There has?" I ask.

"Yeah, we have all summer to find a home where we can place roots."

"A home," I mimic. The sound of that word brings fresh tears to my eyes.

A home here in San Diego, with Ryan and RJ.

"I was thinking on the beach," he says. "I don't know about you, but the beach is kind of special to me." He winks, and heat warms my insides.

"The beach sounds perfect."

"Good." He takes my hand in his and slides my engagement ring back onto my finger. "No more taking this off. You're mine, and I'm yours. We're in this together...forever."

## EPILOGUE

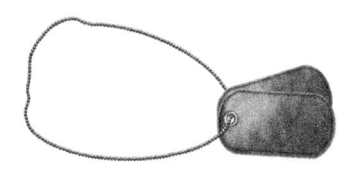

### RYAN

*Fourteen Months Later*

"Daddy, I help!" RJ insists, grabbing a handful of strawberries and dropping them onto the waffle I've just placed on the center of the plate.

"You're a big help," I tell him. "Can you do the blueberries too?"

"Yes!" He digs into the container and pulls out several blueberries, releasing them on top of the strawberries.

"I have some too?" he asks, already plucking a couple off the plate and into his mouth. "Mmm..." His bright blue eyes light up. "Foot cream next!"

I laugh, handing him the bottle of whipped cream. "Whipped cream," I correct.

He ignores me, pressing the top. The whipped cream shoots out, all over the waffle, plate, and counter, making him giggle in excitement.

"Perfect," I tell him, pouring the coffee and mixing in some milk and sugar.

"To Mommy!" he exclaims, jumping off the stool and onto the floor.

He grabs the flowers we picked up at the store, while I grab the tray and place the plate, mug, and silverware on it.

"Mommy!" he yells, when we enter the room. "Happy 'Versary!"

Micaela groans, and her eyelids flutter open and closed a few times, adjusting to the light. "What?" she asks, sitting up and wiping the sleep from her eyes.

"Happy 'Versary!" RJ repeats, thrusting the flowers at her.

"Happy Anniversary," I say, placing the tray on her lap. I give her a quick kiss, and she grins happily.

"Happy Anniversary," she says back.

"I made dat." RJ points to the waffle filled with fruit and whipped cream.

"You did?" Micaela asks, lifting him up and placing him next to her before I can stop her.

"Babe, be careful," I say, knowing she's not going to listen.

She rolls her eyes. "I'm pregnant, not disabled."

The day we found out she was pregnant, I started doing my research, reading every book I could get my hands on about pregnancy. Most of which scared the shit out of me. Since she's only a couple months pregnant, we haven't told anyone yet. I read you can miscarry early on, and it's best not to tell anyone until you're in the second trimester. I know. I know. I'm being overprotective. But in my defense, I wasn't around for the first pregnancy, so while this is nothing new to her, it's all new to me. And it's scary as fuck.

We weren't supposed to get pregnant. Micaela thought we should wait until she was done with her degree and she still has a year to go, but fate had other plans, and even though she was on birth control, several pregnancy tests and a blood test later, and we found out she was pregnant. And we couldn't be happier.

"This is delicious," she says through a moan, taking a bite of her waffle, then giving RJ a bite.

"Delicious," he agrees with a wide, whipped cream covered grin. Of course, his word comes out as *de-ish-is*, but it's adorable the way he tries to copy everything we say. He's a tiny little sponge, absorbing everything around him.

"I also got you a little something." I hand her the small wrapped gift.

She opens it, then looks up at me with tears in her eyes. "It's beautiful," she says, referring to the charm bracelet. She told me once she loved the one her grandmother was given by her grandfather years ago. So, I had Bella find out who made it and had one made for her. It has a heart from RJ that reads *Mom* in the middle, and a dolphin to symbolize her love of marine animals. The third and last charm is of a heart with a key.

*"You hold the key to my heart,"* I told her when we said our vows on the beach in Venice in front of our friends and family. And I meant it. Until Micaela, I thought my heart was broken—that nature overpowered nurture, and even though I was raised in a loving home, I wasn't capable of having what my parents had. But it turns out Laura was right. I just had to stop running and open my heart. I just didn't know at the time, that Micaela was holding the key. And with one click of the lock, my heart was opened. She owns my heart and soul and everything in between.

"We need to get ready to leave for Georgia's graduation," she says. "And we still need to finish packing for our trip to the beach."

She emphasizes the word beach, knowing it will get RJ's attention. The kid is obsessed with the ocean, just like his mom. "Yay! Beach!" he squeals.

"I finished," I tell her. "Luggage is in the back of the truck." I don't mention that I also booked us a hotel for tomorrow and Sunday night. Since Bella and Marco are in town for the next two weeks, and we'll be staying at their beach house with them in Venice, I spoke to them. They'll be keeping RJ with them for two nights, so Micaela and I can have a couple days to ourselves and they can spend some time with their grandson. It couldn't have worked out better.

"You're too good to me," she says, handing me her empty plate. "I'm going to take a shower to help me wake up. Can you get RJ ready?"

"Of course."

## Micaela

I step out of the shower and wrap my towel around myself. My bracelet dangles from my wrist, and the charms clink against each other. It's perfect. Ryan might've gotten the heart and key charm to symbolize his vows, but that heart means so much more to me than that. It symbolizes the way he took my heart and, with his love, put each fractured piece back together. Then, once it was whole again, he kept it and protected it. Cared for it. Nurtured it.

"I don't know how it's possible, but I swear just knowing you're carrying my baby makes you even sexier," Ryan says, startling me.

"I didn't see you there." I wrap my arms around his neck and kiss the corner of his jaw. "And I hope you feel that way when I'm sixty pounds heavier and look like a beached whale."

"Mmm... I can't wait."

"Thank you," I say, my throat clogging with unshed emotion.

"You're welcome." He kisses the tip of my nose. "I'm glad you like the bracelet."

"Not for the bracelet," I correct. "For showing me that there are different kinds of love. That no love is the same, and the amount of time you have with that love isn't guaranteed. All we can do is love with everything we have and make sure the ones we love know just how loved they are."

"That's a whole lot of love," he jokes, his mouth connecting with mine. We spend the next few minutes kissing, until we hear the doorbell ring.

"Are we expecting someone?" I ask.

"Nope, I better go get it." He kisses me one last time before disappearing.

I drop my towel and throw on my clothes, and am about to head out to the living room to see who's here, when Lexi enters my room. "Were we supposed to—" My words are cut off when she throws her arms around my neck and cries into my chest.

"Lexi, what's going on?"

"I shouldn't have run." She sobs. "But I-I." Her cries get louder, so I hold her tighter, letting her get it all out. She's one of the strongest people I know—despite the shit she's been through recently—so if she's crying, something bad has happened.

"Can I stay here?" she asks softly. "Just until..." She chokes on another sob. "I didn't know what to do. Where to go."

"You can always come here," I tell her, rubbing my hand up and down her back. "You know that, but what about your sister's graduation today and your—"

"No," she says, cutting me off. "I can't be there... I just... I can't." I want to ask her what's happened, but I know she'll tell me when she's ready.

When she's all cried out, she takes a step back. Her eyes are red and her face is puffy. "There's something I need to tell you. Something nobody knows. Not even Georgia."

"Okay."

"I'm pregnant."

**The End.**

# MY KIND OF *Beautiful*

*A Finding Love Novel*

# NIKKI ASH

*To my daughter, for showing me every day how beautiful life is.*

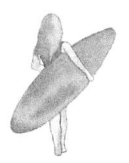

# CHAPTER ONE

## ALEC

"It's your turn to cook, bro, and I'm thinking burgers." Chase grins wide and throws two packages of ground beef into the shopping cart. "I'm also thinking baked potatoes." He pushes the cart over to the produce section and grabs several potatoes, tossing them into a produce bag and then the bag into the cart.

"Yeah, yeah. Why is it when it's your turn to cook, you buy pre-made meals, but when it's my turn, I actually have to cook?" I pick out a few tomatoes and onions and add them to the cart.

"Maybe because you can actually cook. Trust me, I'm doing everyone at the station a favor." He chuckles, throwing a head of lettuce into the mix. "Who'll put out all the fires in Los Angeles if all the guys are sick with food poisoning?"

I throw a couple cans of baked beans into the cart. "Maybe you should give those words of advice to Lexi. The woman is determined to learn how to cook, and I'm pretty sure it's going to end with her killing all of us."

"Food poisoning doesn't kill." Chase laughs.

"No, but fires do." I shake my head as I think about the last few times my best friend and roommate has attempted to cook and failed. "I'm telling you right now, if that damn fire alarm goes off one more time while I'm trying to sleep, I'm going to find a way to padlock the oven so she can't cook."

"When are you going to admit you have the hots for Lexi Scott?" Chase shoots me a knowing look, which I choose to ignore, instead grabbing a package of buns from the shelf and throwing them at him.

"Oohhh, that hurt." Chase groans dramatically. "Seriously, though, in the last year, since I was transferred to this station and have gotten to know you, not once have I seen you treat the women you're talking to the way you treat that woman."

"That's because I'm not *talking* to Lexi." And if I'm honest, I'm barely talking to other women. But when the guys and I go out, it tends to send up a red flag when they're all trying to hook up with various women, while I'm wallowing in my drink, trying to fight my feelings for a woman I'll never make mine. It'd probably be smart to actually hook up with one of those women—fuck my feelings for her straight out of my system. But the few times I tried ended with me walking out the door, leaving the woman hanging—sexually frustrated and pissed—so I decided to take a short hiatus from sex, get my shit together, and then try again. Only that hiatus has lasted way longer than I planned. I've been abstinent so long now, my dick has probably disowned me. If it could, it would detach itself from my body and find another guy to get it laid.

"She's my friend," I tell him for the millionth damn time, hoping this time he'll believe me. "Just like Georgia is my friend. And if you want to stay friends with women, you don't *talk* to them."

"I'm not buying it. I've seen you with both of your roommates. You don't give Georgia the same look you give Lexi."

"And what look might that be?" I regret the question the second the words come out of my mouth. I thought I've been good about hiding my feelings, but it's hard when we share a living space. When she flits around in her tiny little cutoff shorts and bikinis. When she lays her legs across me on the couch, begging me to give her foot massages. Or when she snuggles up next to me to watch a movie, and her tiny, perfect body rubs up against mine. I try so damn hard to ignore the way my heart clenches in my chest, or the way my dick stands at attention at her touch. If Lexi's noticed, she hasn't said anything. So, she's either blind to my feelings, ignoring them, or I'm doing a good job at hiding them—at least from her.

"The look that says you want to lock her up in your room and fuck her until the sun comes up," Chase says. "Then, when all the condoms run out and she can't take any more, you cook her breakfast in bed." He waggles his eyebrows.

"Chase, you're seeing shit that isn't there," I deadpan, lying through my teeth. "And speaking of breakfast in bed, when are you planning to sleep in your own bed?" I give him a pointed look.

Without answering me, Chase pushes the cart into the checkout line and starts loading the items onto the conveyer belt. I could push him to answer, but I don't. For one, Chase sleeping on my couch when he has his own home and a wife can't be a good sign, and if it means he's having marriage troubles, the last thing I want to do is make him feel like he can't crash at my place. And two, it might cause him to further push the subject of me hooking up with Lexi, and the last thing I need is to visualize my best friend in my bed: under me, on top of me, me fucking her from behind. Pulling her long blond hair while she calls out my name. *Damn it!* I look around to make sure nobody is watching me, then adjust my pants.

Chase pays the cashier while I bag the groceries and then we head back to station one-fifteen, which is located in Los Angeles near UCLA. We're one shift away from having three days off, and once we're off, I plan to spend at least one of those days in my bed asleep.

We get back to the station and the guys are all hanging out in the workout room. Chase and I work shift B with four other guys. This shift consists of two twenty-four-hour shifts every other day and then four days off. Chase has been a firefighter for ten years and was recently promoted to Battalion Chief—he's in charge of the guys on our shift. He took the place of a guy who was promoted to Fire Chief when ours retired. I've been working as a firefighter-slash-paramedic for the last five years at this same station and was promoted last year to Lieutenant. The other guys on our shift are Luke and Thomas, who are both firefighters-slash-paramedics like me, Carter, who is the Driver Engineer—he drives the fire truck and manages the equipment—and Scott, who just recently finished the academy and is still working on his EMT license.

"What's for dinner?" Carter yells from the treadmill.

"Burgers," I yell back, throwing the bags onto the counter while Chase lights the grill.

I've just finished putting everything away and am in the middle of prepping the burger patties when the tone goes off throughout the station. It doesn't matter how long you've been working as a firefighter, when the ridiculously loud ringing hits your ears, you cringe. Then you jump into action. Because all of our bunker gear is kept on the truck, all we have to do is jump on once Chase comes out with the information from the dispatcher to let us know where the fire is.

"Westwood Village condos," Chase calls out, looking straight at me. "Alec's address," he adds with a smirk. The guys all groan. *Dammit, Lexi.* Even though the fire probably isn't anything to be too concerned about, we still treat it how we would treat any fire that's called in.

We arrive at my complex in less than two minutes and head up to the second floor. The door is already open and you can smell the smoke leaking from inside. The smoke alarm is blaring throughout the house, and is Lex in the kitchen trying to put the fire out? Nope, her ass is standing on a chair with a broomstick in her hand, jabbing at the smoke alarm to shut it off. Chase and a couple of the other guys head into the kitchen to make sure the oven fire is under control while I go straight for Lexi.

Grabbing her by her waist, I pull her off the chair. She shrieks in shock, until she sees it's me, then her eyes go wide. I lower her to the ground before I reach up and press the button to silence the alarm. When the room goes quiet, Lexi sighs, and I can see it in her face that she's trying not to laugh.

"Lex," I groan, about to lay into her, but then her deep blue eyes meet mine and I shake my head. It's damn near impossible to be mad at her. "This is the third time this month. Maybe you could...I don't know...practice cooking at your parents' place." At least then it would fall on another station.

"I wasn't cooking." She shakes her head emphatically, and several strands of her blond hair fall from her loose ponytail. I give her a pointed look and she grins wildly, reminding me of a rose:

# CHAPTER ONE

beautiful to look at from afar, but filled with thorns, making her impossible to touch. And if you do attempt it—thinking you can somehow get around them, so you can experience her beauty up close—there's no doubt she'll prick you, leaving you bleeding and in pain.

"Happy Birthday to you! Happy Birthday..." The guys begin singing, and I turn around to see a charcoaled cake in Chase's hands, a huge smirk splayed across his face. The guys are all shaking with laughter as he sets down what I'm assuming was Lexi's attempt at baking me a cake for my birthday. They finish singing and start clapping, thinking they're fucking hilarious.

"See? I wasn't cooking. I was baking." Lexi shrugs innocently. "It's your favorite...white cake."

Her eyes go to the black cake that could pass for burnt brownies, then back to mine, her top teeth biting down on her bottom lip. "Sorry about Ms. Holden calling nine-one-one." She rolls her eyes. "She could've just come over and asked if everything was okay. She doesn't have to be so dramatic all the time."

I throw my arm across the back of Lexi's shoulders and pull her into a side hug. "Lex, you know I love you, right?"

"Yeah..." She tilts her head up to look at me, and I ignore the stirring in my gut at the sight of her. Of her plump, kissable lips, of the way her blue eyes remind me of the deep ocean—full of life, yet mysterious and uncertain.

"You've gotta stop trying to cook and bake. Paint, surf, go graffiti the hell out of some of those abandoned buildings." I give her forehead a kiss to lighten the blow. "But for the love of God, woman, don't touch our oven, please."

"Ugh... fine. I did find some crock pot recipes I've been wanting to try out. Maybe I'll ask my mom if I can borrow hers." The guys start to chuckle, but when Lexi glares at each of them, they all stop laughing at the same time.

"Lexi, I'm home." The door slams closed and in walks Georgia, Lexi's sister and my other roommate. "Please don't tell me that firetruck outside is for..." Her feet and mouth come to an abrupt halt when she sees all of us standing in the kitchen.

"Hey." She shyly waves at the guys. "I guess it is..."

"Lexi, here, was baking me a birthday cake." I point to the cake pan.

"I was gone for less than an hour." Georgia sighs. "How do you even burn a cake in that amount of time?"

"Well...I..." Lexi looks at her sister sheepishly.

"You what?" Georgia grabs the pan and throws the entire thing into the garbage can, not even bothering to try to clean it out and at least save the pan. "I wasn't even gone long enough for you to burn a cake. What did you do?"

"Well, Ricco may have called and said the waves are killer. There's a storm brewing, you know. But I had already put the cake in, and you were gone. I just thought if I doubled the temperature, I could cut the bake time in half. It makes sense, right?" Lexi's shoulders shrug and her head tilts to the side.

I cover my mouth from laughing, knowing it will only encourage her. But holy shit, she's so fucking adorable. She's just so lost in her own world. Chase's gaze meets mine, and he raises one knowing brow.

"Anyway," Lexi continues when nobody answers her. "I figured while I was waiting for the cake to finish, I could paint some, so I put my earbuds in and got to work. The next thing I know the fire alarm is going off and the condo is all smoky."

"It's okay, darlin'," Carter says. "You know..." He approaches Lexi, who eyes him speculatively. "I've been known to make a mean omelet"—he nods slowly—"the morning after." He shoots her a flirtatious wink, and the guys' gazes go to me, and it's in that moment I realize they *all* know my feelings for Lexi. I thought I've been doing a good job of hiding them over the years, but apparently not. Does that mean Lexi knows too? If she does, and hasn't said a word, wouldn't that mean she doesn't return my feelings?

Lexi scrunches her nose up in disgust, and I bark out a laugh. "And on that note, let's go." I give her a kiss on her cheek. "Be careful surfing."

"Always." She beams.

The guys all say goodbye to the women and then we head back to the station to finish our night.

## CHAPTER TWO

### LEXI

"How's it going?" I throw myself onto my sister's bed and peek over at her computer screen. She's working on designing a new website for Jumpin' Java—our favorite coffee shop in Larchmont Village, where our mom has a painting studio and our dad owns a UFC training facility. While we both take after our mom creatively, I'm more of a paintbrush-in-hand kind of artist, and Georgia is all about the digital. Technically, Georgia is my stepsister. Her mom married my dad when we were little and they each adopted us. But to anyone who doesn't know that, we're sisters—and she's my favorite person in the entire world.

"It's going." She smiles softly, pushing a wayward strand of brown hair behind her ear. "Finishing this up." She points to the screen.

"Want to come watch me surf tonight?" Georgia's made it known she doesn't particularly care for the people I hang out at the beach with, but I hate that she almost never goes anywhere, so I invite her everywhere. She's either at school, at our mom's studio helping with the children's parties, or at home working behind her computer.

"Max is coming to take some pictures," I add, knowing if I say our younger brother is going to be there, she might actually go.

Georgia gives me another smile—the one that tells me she

loves me and doesn't want to hurt my feelings, but she doesn't want to go. When I look up at her, her bright green eyes are dimmed, and my heart hurts for my sister. Somewhere in there I believe there's a woman who's begging to come out and be carefree, but that woman is being pushed down by another part of my sister who shies away from the public and all social situations. She's more comfortable sitting behind a computer than hanging out with living, breathing people—except for me. Georgia is the yin to my yang. She's more than my friend, more than my sister. She's the other half of my soul.

"I received a weird email today," she says.

"Oh yeah? From who?"

"She said she's my grandmother. She emailed my business page."

I sit up, confused. We only have one grandma and grandpa, and they're currently traveling through Europe. "Did it sound like Grandma?"

"No, she said she was my biological father's mom."

"Oh my God!" I push the laptop away from Georgia. "Did you tell Mom?"

"Not yet. She never talks about my bio dad. I never thought about the fact he could have siblings or parents out there."

"Did she mention why she's emailing you now?"

"All she wrote was that she would like to meet with me to discuss some matters. I replied not to contact me again. I didn't know what else to do… and please don't mention anything to Mom. You know she gets upset at any talk about her old life."

"Okay," I agree. "But if she emails again, you should ask her why she wants to meet with you. I doubt she just wants to get to know you. You're about to turn twenty-one. She's had years to contact you."

"Maybe."

"So, no to the beach tonight?"

"Not tonight. Have fun and ride all the waves."

"Fine. Want to watch some more of *The O.C.* when I get home?" Binge watching older shows is Georgia's and my thing.

"Sure."

Grabbing my surfboard and art supplies, I throw it all into the back of my Jeep and head over to Santa Monica Beach. When I get there, several people are already out in the water. There is only about three hours of light left, and most people prefer not to night surf because it can be dangerous and not worth it. But with the storm heading this way, the swells are coming in between ten and fifteen feet compared to the normal surf of three to five feet. Usually, in order to get bigger waves, we have to drive a couple hours south.

Before I head over to my friends, I stop at the taco stand and buy a bunch of tacos, then drop them off to my friend Aiden. He wasn't expecting me, so he's not there—probably going for a walk along the beach. I leave them for him in his tent, knowing he'll be surprised and happy when he returns and finds them there.

"What's up, Lexi!" Shane, a surfer and friend of mine, calls out as I make my way over to him and set my stuff down. Taking my clothes off, leaving me in just my bikini, I pull on my Roxy wetsuit and zip it up from the back. Then I cover my art stuff with my towel, so it doesn't get dripped on.

"Lexi! How's my sexy little artist doing today?" Jason, another friend of mine, stabs his board into the sand and pulls me in for a hug.

"Chilling... How long have you guys been out here?"

"Long enough to see all the Barneys about kill themselves. Already seen two guys break bones and had to call an ambulance." Shane shakes his head.

"Ugh! Why does everyone who owns a surfboard see big waves and think they can all of a sudden surf?" I ask through my laughter.

"I don't know, but these waves are seriously bitchin'. I swear some of them have hit a good twenty feet." Jason reaches into his bag and pulls out a joint, lighting it up and taking a drag. Then he passes it to me. Not wanting to be fucked up while on the waves, I decline.

"Later... Right now I want to hit the waves." I grab my board to head down the sand, but before I can walk away, Jason grabs my cheeks and pulls me in for a kiss. The smoke he was holding in transfers from his mouth to mine.

I push him away with a cough of laughter. "Jason," I whine, making him laugh. "Don't be a douche. Let's go!"

He takes one last hit then pinches the joint between his

fingers to put it out. After throwing it back into his bag, he grabs his board, and we run down the beach. Just as my feet hit the water, I hear my name being called. When I look back, I spot my brother, Max. I wave to him, and he waves back. Then he throws a blanket down on the sand and has a seat, camera in his hand. Max is sixteen and a sophomore in high school. His true love is photography, and you'll never see him anywhere without a camera.

Jason, Shane, and I paddle out, and once we're far enough, we meet up with several other guys and a few girls, who are all watching the waves. Some I don't recognize and others I've grown up surfing with. Everyone's talking and bullshitting, but I'm not here to gossip. I'm here to surf. I watch each wave, and when I spot the one I want, I drop to my belly and start paddling. The wave hits and my back arches as I'm lifted. Just as the wave begins to pick me up, I pop up and catch it, riding the wave all the way back to shore.

I spend the next few hours riding wave after wave, taking the occasional break to talk to my brother and to give Ricco a hug when he shows up. When the sun is almost all the way down and nearly everyone has headed home, I drop my board into the sand and peel my wetsuit off my body.

"You staying to paint?" Max asks.

"You know it." I drop onto the blanket and grab my bag of supplies and canvas.

"Want me to stay?" he asks, looking around. There are still a few straggling surfers, including Jason and Shane, who'll be here for hours night surfing.

"No, I'm good. I just want to paint the storm that's brewing."

"Text me when you get back to your Jeep, yeah?"

"Of course."

The storm breeze is a perfect mixture of humid with a hint of coolness to it. It has me grabbing the orange and blue paints. My hair whips around my face, so I throw it up into a messy bun and begin painting. The waves are gorgeous. Dark blue with white crests roll into the shoreline. The sun is now a faint yellowish-orange in the background peeking out from behind the now black ocean. I get lost in my painting, until I hear my name being called. When I look up, I find Ricco, Shane, and Jason standing to the right of me, drinking and getting high—a typical night for them.

"Damn, that painting looks like the real thing." Jason glances from my canvas out to the sea. "One day, when you're a famous artist, will you still find time to visit us lowly surfers?" he jokes.

"Shut up." I throw my paint brush at him and he catches it. He lunges toward me and wraps his arms around me. I've known Jason's had a crush on me for a while, but I ignore it. There's only one guy on my mind—*one I don't stand a chance at being with.*

My phone dings, giving me the perfect excuse to pull away from him. *And speak of the devil...*

**Alec: How are the waves?**

I type back a quick response: **Awesome! I wish they were like this all the time.**

I snap a picture of my painted canvas with the ocean in the background.

**Alec: Looks beautiful. We should hang it in the hallway.**

I smile to myself. There isn't a picture I've painted that Alec hasn't found a spot for in our home. At this point, it looks more like an art gallery than a home.

I notice it's already nine o'clock, so I start packing up my stuff.

"Heading out?" Shane asks.

"Yeah." I stand and shake off the blanket.

"Here, we'll help you to your car," Ricco offers, taking my still-wet painting from me.

"Thank you, but I'm perfectly capable of carrying my stuff." I laugh at how crazy my friends are acting.

"We know," Ricco says, "but did you hear about that girl who was attacked on the beach the other night?"

"No." A shiver runs down my spine. Sure, the beach is filled with homeless folks, and the city is riddled with crime, but it's not often you hear of someone being assaulted on the beach where I surf and spend a lot of my time.

"They haven't caught the guy yet," Shane says. "But the girl didn't make it..."

"Damn, well, thanks for looking out for me." I give the guys a grateful smile. I'm lucky to have so many people in my life who love me and care about my well-being.

We carry all our stuff up, and they help me load everything into my car, refusing to leave until I'm safely inside and driving away. When I get home, I text Max to let him know I'm home safe. Georgia's sitting at the kitchen table, working on something on her laptop.

"Hey you," I say, walking over to her.

"Hey! Good night?"

"The waves were perfect."

Georgia sniffs the air then glances up at me. "Were you smoking tonight?" she asks, disappointment laced in her tone. I hate when she acts like this. For one, smoking weed is common on the beaches of LA. Hell, doing harder drugs is even more common. But also, because I hate the thought of Georgia being disappointed in me, and let's be real, I'm pretty much a walking disappointment. Sure, I'm in college, but what exactly am I going to do with that degree? No fucking clue. While Alec has known he's wanted to be a firefighter since he was a kid, and Georgia has always wanted to follow in our mom's footsteps and do web design, I have no clue what I want to do with my future. I love painting, but the thought of having to do it to earn a living makes me cringe. I do it because I love to do it, not because I need to. And if I had to do it to earn money, I fear I would resent it.

"No, the guys were," I tell her, already making my way down the hall to jump in the shower. Once my body is clean and rid of the saltwater, I get out and get dressed in a pair of pajama shorts and a tank top.

When I come out, I find Georgia in her room. She has the next episode of *The O.C.* ready to play. I cuddle up in her bed next to her, and my head falls onto her shoulder. I'm not sure how many episodes we watch before we both pass out.

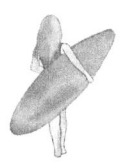

## CHAPTER THREE

### ALEC

"You're more than welcome to crash at my place," I tell Chase as we walk to our vehicles. It's finally eight in the morning, which means we're off for the next four days. "I was only fucking with you yesterday about squatting on my couch."

"I know, man, and I appreciate it, but... I need to go home." Chase shrugs. "I'll see you tomorrow night."

Because my birthday is today, I'm celebrating with my family tonight and my friends tomorrow night. Both parties were completely their doing and not mine. It's funny, when you're little, you can't wait to get older, but then once you're older, you want time to stop. Not that I'm old. I'm only turning twenty-five today. But I'm pretty sure I'm too old to still be having multiple parties. I laugh when I think about Lexi arguing with me, insisting she throw me a birthday party at Club Hectic. We both know the party is more for her than me, but I'll let her have it. Lexi loves finding any reason to party, and I love watching her party.

I'm pulling up to my house, when my phone rings. Seeing that it's my dad, I answer the call.

"Hey, old man."

"Don't talk shit, Son. You're getting up there in age, too."

"If I'm getting old then that must make you ancient," I joke.

"Not ancient, just wiser. I wanted to be the first to wish you a Happy Birthday."

"Thanks, Dad. I'll see you tonight, right?" My mom and stepdad, Mason, are having a dinner party at their house to celebrate my birthday. I'm one of the lucky kids whose parents are divorced and actually get along, so everyone, including my dad and my stepmom, are invited.

"Of course. You just getting off your shift?"

"Yep, I'm off for the next four days." My eyes are already starting to close of their own accord—we were up all night putting out a house fire and didn't get any sleep—but I will them to stay open so I can finish this conversation with my dad and then head upstairs to bed.

"I was wondering if you'd like to have brunch with me on Sunday."

"That sounds great." Every year for my birthday we always go to brunch just the two of us. Even if it didn't fall on his weekend with me, he would come and pick me up for the day.

"Eleven okay?"

"Yeah, and, Dad?"

"Yes?"

"How about this year you bring Lacie? I know it's always just been the two of us, but she's part of our family too now." They've been together for a few years and were married last year. I don't know her well, since I'm older and don't live with my dad, but she's sweet and good to him.

He's silent on the phone for a beat before he says, "Thank you, Alec. That means a lot to me, and I know it'll mean a lot to her."

"I'll see you guys tonight."

"I love you, Alec."

"Love you too, Dad."

I open the door and the place is quiet. The girls must be sleeping. Because they're on summer break, they don't have any classes, which means they'll sleep until noon. I spot them both sleeping in Georgia's room, and after getting changed out of my uniform and taking a quick shower to rinse off, I slip into bed with them. Lexi must feel me, because she rolls over and lays her head down on my chest.

I dip my head to give the top of her head a kiss. I can smell her coconut-scented shampoo mixed with saltwater. It doesn't matter how many times she showers, I think she'll always smell like the ocean, and I'll never be able to go to the beach without thinking of her. As my fingers run up and down her back, my thoughts go back to last year, right after Georgia and Lexi finished their sophomore year at UCLA and Lexi insisted it was time for them to live on their own. Of course, she had to bring it up during a barbecue when everyone was there...

"It's time for Georgia and me to move out," Lexi says nonchalantly.

Tristan, Lexi and Georgia's dad, chokes on his beer. "Excuse me?" His eyes are wide, and he looks like he's about to lock his daughter up in her room without a key.

"It's time, Dad. We talked about this a while ago. I'm going to be twenty-one in October and Georgia will be twenty. We're both adults and need to spread our wings. Right, Georgia?" She looks at her sister like she always does when she needs her on her side. Of course, Georgia agrees, just like she always does.

"And how are you paying for this apartment?" Tristan argues, which has everyone grinning because we all know he's going to be paying. Lexi and Georgia are his little girls, and he would sell his kidney to make sure they were happy.

Of course, Lexi wouldn't be Lexi if she didn't have all the answers. "Well, I was thinking we could get a roommate. There are plenty of apartments near campus, and we could split the bills. Georgia makes money working at Mom's art studio, and I have money in my savings from the surfing lessons I've given and the competitions I've won." She smiles sweetly, and Tristan groans.

"You're not using your savings," Charlie says.

Lexi beams, knowing if she's got her mom on board, Tristan is screwed.

"I don't know," Tristan says. "We live in LA. It's a scary world out there beyond this gated community. We would have to find you somewhere safe with a gate, and we would need to have an alarm system installed. I don't like the idea of my girls being alone in an apartment, nor do I want you moving in with some stranger."

"Dad, we're not babies anymore." Lexi pouts. "We're perfectly capable of living on our own."

"Weren't you just calling me to come over because you couldn't figure out how to open the oven?" I ask.

"How was I supposed to know when you press clean on the oven, it locks it to clean it!" Lexi yells.

"You thought the oven was on fire." I laugh. "You called me at the fire station freaking out."

"I thought when I clicked to clean it would shoot out cleaner! I didn't know it locks and heats up!" Lexi growls.

"And what about the time when you clogged the vacuum and couldn't get it to work?" I chuckle.

"I didn't know it fills up!"

"Where did you think it all goes? Back into the ecosystem?" I taunt. "Oh! And remember the time when you clogged the toilet and—"

Everyone laughs.

"Aleczander Sterling, if you don't shut up right this second, I'm going to tell everyone about the time I caught you—"

"Whoa! Okay, chill, woman." I hold my hands up in surrender. Because no one needs to know what she caught me doing when we were younger. And no, I'm not saying—you can use your imagination.

"I was just trying to point out maybe you aren't as ready to live on your own as you think." I shrug a shoulder.

"And you are?" Lexi argues.

"I'm a grown man, Lex. I'm a firefighter and a paramedic," I point out smugly.

"Oh, whatever, Mr. Paramedic. Remember when you choked on that pizza cheese?" Lexi giggles. "Your hands were flailing everywhere, and I had to reach over and do the finger sweep to save your life!" Her hands flail through the air as she mocks me. "You wouldn't eat pizza for like a year after that!"

Everyone cracks up laughing.

"That was before I became a paramedic. Now I'm a trained professional. Just the other day my neighbor had an emergency, and luckily I was there to help her."

"Are you referring to that ditsy, slutty neighbor of yours? What did she need help with? Locating her panties?" Lexi's hand goes to her hip, and I stifle my laugh, not daring to answer that question. If there's anything my dad, stepdad, and Tristan have taught me over the years, it's not to walk into traps like those.

"Ha!" Lexi yells. "Not answering because you know I'm right."

Damn, woman...

"Okay, okay," Tristan says with a laugh. "While this has been extremely entertaining, it's given me an idea. While I have to accept you and your sister want some freedom, I also want to make sure you're both safe."

"Okay..." Lexi says slowly.

"What if you move in with Alec?" Tristan looks at me. "You mentioned you're looking for two new roommates since yours got married and moved out. It would be perfect. And I would make sure their part of the bills is paid."

Is he fucking crazy? There's no way I'm living under the same roof as Lexi. It's hard enough being best friends with her while living in separate homes. Now he wants me to share a small area with her? My mom might've raised me to be a gentleman, but that still makes me a man, and I'm not sure how the hell I'll be able to hide my feelings for her if I have to share a roof with her. Every day, coming home to her, knowing she's naked in the shower, watching her lounge around in her tiny fucking pajamas...

I glance toward my stepdad, Mason, and he cringes, knowing the feelings I have for Lexi. He also knows I would never go there. Her friendship is too important to me. She's too wild and carefree. She's never been in a relationship that's lasted more than a couple months. She does what she wants, when she wants, and she doesn't like to answer to anyone. She's the most independent woman I've ever known. I love all of that about her, but it also scares the shit out of me, because I'm not sure, if I told her how I feel, I could be the man she needs. I'd like to think I could since I know her better than anyone—aside from her sister. But what if I couldn't be? It would end with us breaking up, and then I would lose her completely—because everyone knows, couples who break up rarely remain friends. And that's just not a chance I'm willing to take. Maybe in the future, when she's older and has calmed down a bit...

"Yes!" Lexi squeals, throwing her arms around me. "That would be so awesome!"

I hug her back, and my eyes meet Georgia's, who's grinning from ear to ear. When I cringe, she smirks. Georgia might be soft-spoken and shy around people she doesn't know, but that doesn't mean she isn't paying attention. And based on the look she's giving me, it's safe to bet she knows damn well how I feel about Lexi.

"Georgia, what do you think?" Lexi asks her sister.

Georgia smiles. "I think it's the perfect plan."

"It's settled then. We'll move into Alec's condo!" Lexi jumps up and down, her hands clapping in excitement, which causes my palms to sweat in nervousness. My gaze meets Mason's again, and he's grinning a knowing smile, certain there's no way I'm going to tell Lexi no.

My eyes close, remembering what it was like the first few months of living with Lexi. I took so many cold showers, she thought I had mysophobia—fear of germs—and was trying to get me to see a therapist. When she mentioned it one night while we were all out to dinner, Mason cracked up laughing, and the next day showed up at the station with several pornos and a bottle of lube as a joke.

---

I WAKE up to someone knocking on the door. When I look around, the bed is empty, and the condo is quiet. The girls must've left. I grab my cell phone to check the time and see there's a piece of paper on top of it.

### Happy Birthday! See you tonight! Xoxo Lexi and Georgia

I open the door and find Mason standing on the other side with a coffee in his hand and a smile on his face. "Happy Birthday, Son." He hands me the coffee then pulls me in for a hug.

My mom and Mason married when I was eight years old, and while my biological father is in my life, Mason has become just as much of a father figure over the years as my dad. Mason is now a retired UFC fighter who trains other fighters at Tristan's gym, but when I was younger, Mason was my idol. I worshipped the ground the man walked on, in and out of the ring, and while I might've tamed down my obsession with him the older I got, he's still someone I look up to. And not just because he was a UFC fighter, but because of the way he loves my mom, my sister, and me. I couldn't have asked for a better stepdad than Mason.

"Thanks, man, but you didn't need to come all the way over here to say it. Aren't we meeting up tonight?" We walk back into the condo, and that's when I notice Chase is sleeping on the couch. One of the girls must've let him in.

"We are, but I was thinking we could get a workout in."

"Sounds good." I check my phone and see it's already three in the afternoon. "Let me get dressed and grab a change of clothes. I'll just shower at the gym."

"Is there a reason Chase is sleeping on your couch?" Mason asks when I come back out.

"He's having marital issues. Hasn't really said much."

"Wanna wake him up to go?"

"Nah, let him sleep. I don't know what time he got here."

We get to the gym, and the place is packed. There are fighters practicing in the octagons, several using the weights. Even the treadmills are all taken.

"Alec!" Tristan yells from over near one of the octagons. "Get over here!" He gives me a hug. "Happy Birthday, kid."

"Thanks."

"You here to get a workout in?"

"You know it." The octagon we're standing next to is empty. "Hey, Mason, wanna spar?"

Mason grins like a fucking Cheshire cat. "I'd hate to beat your ass on your birthday."

A bunch of the guys who're standing around laugh.

"Well, I'm okay with beating your ass on my birthday," I volley.

"All right, Bruiser," Mason says, calling me the nickname he dubbed me with years ago, when I knocked him to the ground and busted his lip open. "But when you show up to dinner tonight all bruised up, make sure you let your mom know it was your idea."

"I'm a grown ass man," I scoff. "I don't need to explain shit to my mom."

All the guys crack up.

"Yeah, okay." He laughs. "Keep telling yourself that. Get some damn gear on."

## CHAPTER FOUR

### LEXI

"Mom, Dad!" I call out when Georgia and I walk through the door. "Max!" I yell. "Where is everyone?" I ask Georgia.

"Their cars are in the garage, so they must be here," she says.

We head out back and find our parents in the pool. Mom is wrapped around Dad, and they're making out like a couple of horny teenagers right in the middle of the pool. When I look closer, I notice Mom is topless!

"Oh my God! Please tell me you guys aren't seriously fucking in the pool!" I screech, covering my eyes with my hands.

Georgia lets out a snort-laugh. I can't see her, but I'm sure she's covering her eyes as well.

"Young lady, watch your mouth!" Mom scolds me through her laughter.

"If you don't want to walk in on your parents fornicating, maybe you should call first," Dad adds.

I hear the pool water shift, and then wet feet padding across the pool deck.

"We're decent." Mom giggles a minute later. I lower my hands from my face and find them both in towels. "And to what do we owe this pleasure?" She gives me a kiss on my forehead, then heads over to Georgia to give her one as well.

"We had to pick up Alec's birthday present before the

dinner tonight, so we thought, since we had time, we'd stop by here to see you guys," Georgia says. "Sorry." She smiles apologetically.

"Don't apologize. It's not our fault our parents can't keep their hands off each other." I give my dad a kiss on his cheek.

"Did you hit the waves last night?" Dad asks.

"I did! You should've seen them! Max took some pictures. Wanna see?"

"You know it." He puts his arm around my shoulders, and we all head inside. "Just let us change into dry clothes and then we'll meet you in the living room."

When Georgia and I walk into the living room, Max is now sitting on the couch with his laptop open. "Did you just get home?" I ask.

"Yeah, I was hanging out with Anna, but she needs to get ready for tonight." Anna is Alec's sister and my brother's best friend.

"Can you show Mom and Dad the pictures you took last night?" I plop on the couch next to him. When he clicks on a file, several photos come up, but they aren't of me. They're of Ricco—my brother's unrequited love interest. Max smiles sheepishly before scrolling down to the ones he took of me surfing. Then he turns the laptop around for everyone to see, as our parents walk in fully clothed—thank God.

"Wow! That sunset is gorgeous!" Mom gushes. "That's a beautiful image, Max."

"Umm... hello, look at me on the surfboard." I point to the perfect image of me barreling deep in the hollow of the wave.

Dad chuckles. "Oh, sorry, we didn't see you there, front and center."

Max and Georgia laugh.

"I signed up for the Vans Surf Classic at Huntington Beach. It's in July this year."

"That's awesome, Lex," Mom says. "Will you have time to practice, though, with school?"

"I was actually thinking I would take the summer off. I was only planning to take a couple classes anyway. I can start back up in the fall. It's not like I have to graduate by a certain date, so I could take a couple extra classes in the fall or spring or finish in the summer..." I hold my breath, waiting for my parents to freak out.

"Have you figured out what you want to do yet?" Dad asks.

"Aside from illegally tagging the walls all over LA," Max adds with a laugh.

Mom and Dad glare at him, and Georgia groans.

"I think it's time to head to the Street's house," I point out. There's no way I'm touching that subject with a ten-foot pole.

Since Alec's parents only live one street over from my parents, we walk over there. With the storm having passed through earlier this morning, there's a gentle breeze. We get to their house and Anna answers the door with a huge grin.

"Alec totally told you, didn't he?" I huff.

"You burned a cake!" She cracks up laughing, and both my parents' eyes dart over to me.

"You didn't." Mom tries to stifle her laugh, but fails.

"She did, and the chief said they're charging her this time." Alec shakes his head. "Three hundred and fifty-three dollars." He chuckles.

"You would've been better off just buying the cake," Max says.

I shoot daggers his way, but he isn't fazed.

"Hey, leave your sister alone." Alec pulls me into his side. "It's the thought that counts." He gives me one of his panty-dropping winks, and my insides turn to mush. Why couldn't my best friend be ugly? Like seriously? Did I do something in another lifetime where God decided I needed to be punished? Or maybe Alec just did something really good. It had to have been something amazing, though. For him to have been given those gorgeous milk chocolate eyes, that strong nose and chiseled jawline. Not to mention, his perfect, silky smooth hair that has my fingers always twitching to run through the strands. And let's not forget his hard, muscular body that has every woman drooling when they see him. Ugh! And that ass! My God, I hate the gym with a passion, but sometimes I go just to watch the guy run from behind. His tight, muscular ass bouncing as he runs on the treadmill.

*Sigh.*

In another lifetime, he must've saved tons of kittens who were stuck up in trees, or maybe he cured some crazy disease that, if not for him, we'd all be dead. Something. Because there's no way God just makes someone that damn beautiful for no reason. It just doesn't make sense. And not only is he beautiful, but he's seriously hung. I'm talking about huge! Like when he goes to the store, he's definitely buying king size, and I'm not talking about candy bars. And in case you're wondering, no, I've never gone there—not that I haven't fantasized about it. But you can't live with someone for close to a year without accidently—or on purpose—walking in on them naked at some point.

Oh, and did I mention he has tattoos? Yep! The man's bulging biceps are covered in them! And not shitty ones like most guys get. Nope, all sexy, meaningful ones. His body is literally the equivalent of a perfect canvas that I just want to paint—or lick—my way across.

Unfortunately, there will be no licking—I mean painting—for me. I just get to be the best friend. You know the one I'm talking about. The girl who gets to meet all of the other girls he dates, while cursing each one to hell while smiling way too brightly. Luckily, Alec isn't a manwhore, so it doesn't happen often. Actually, now that I'm thinking about it, it hasn't happened in a long time, but when it does, it takes everything in me not to kick them out and beg him to take me right there on the coffee table, and on the couch, on the kitchen counter, in the shower. Oh hell, if Alec were mine, I would make him take me on every inch of every surface in our condo.

And I know what you're thinking: why not just beg him now? What could you possibly lose? Well, I've obviously thought about that, and the answer to your second question is *everything*. I'm only twenty-one years old. Alec isn't much older. The odds would be stacked against us, and if it didn't work out, I would lose him. I don't care what people say. You can't fuck your best friend then go back to being friends once it doesn't work out. I would rather have Alec as my best friend long-term than as my boyfriend temporarily.

The truth is I kind of suck at relationships. Being Tristan and Charlie's daughter has made it easy for me because in their eyes I can never do any wrong. Their rose-colored glasses probably stem from the fact I was abandoned by my mother at birth—from the little bit my father told me, Gina was a drug addict who felt I was better off with my dad. She walked out the door of her hospital room without looking back, caring more about her drug addiction and drug addict boyfriend than me. Eventually, she overdosed and died.

My parents would never say it, but I'm almost certain I take after Gina in several ways, including my 'free spirit' as my parents like to put it, which is really just a nice way of saying I'm a hot fucking mess. Sure, my parents say they love how carefree I am, but I see the worry in my dad's face every time he asks me what I want to do with my life. Or there was the time when Max let it slip that I occasionally smoked cannabis while hanging out with my friends at the beach. My dad nearly lost it, afraid I would end up just like Gina—which is how I found out the truth about her.

My mom says the way I am is just the artist in me, but if that's the case then why is she so put together? Both my parents went to college, started their own businesses, and years later are still successfully running them. Georgia is a year younger than me, and she's already running a successful web design business. Me? The only reason I'm in college is because it was the only way I could keep slacking off—painting and surfing—and make my dad happy. If it wasn't for Georgia keeping me on track with my classes, I would've failed out my first semester in.

Aside from my parents, I've had three successful friendships in my life: Georgia, my pseudo cousin Micaela, and Alec.

Georgia is my sister and, just like our parents, she wears beautiful rose-colored glasses when it comes to me. She doesn't always agree with my choices, but she never judges me, and she always supports my decisions.

Micaela probably only remains my friend because she's long-distance and doesn't have to deal with me on a daily basis. She grew up in Las Vegas, but now lives in San Diego with her husband, Ryan, and their son, RJ.

And then there's Alec. I've been in love with him for God knows how long, and every relationship I've been in was doomed from the get-go because of it. Not that it took much for them to fail. All I had to do was be myself and they practically ran for the hills. The truth is, Alec deserves more than I could ever give him. A woman who knows what she wants in life. A woman for him to get married to and have tons of babies with. She'll be as put together as Alec is—as put together as my parents are—and they'll live happily ever after. And she won't be able to cut him out of my life because I can honestly say that Alec and I were never anything more than friends.

"Hey, you okay?" Alec asks, his arm still slung over my shoulders, snapping me out of my thoughts.

"Yep, just thinking about what an old man you are now." I stick my tongue out, and Alec laughs.

The doorbell rings, and Alec lifts his arm up, leaving me to go answer the door. I sit next to Georgia on the couch. She's talking to Alec's grandma, Denise, about the program she runs: *Keeping Kids off the Streets*. It's a non-profit organization that helps to keep single moms and their children off the streets and in safe homes. Georgia is in the middle of updating their website for them.

Alec walks back into the living room with his dad, Gavin, and stepmom, Lacie, by his side. Mason and Mila come out of the kitchen and give each of them a hug, then Mila announces that dinner is ready. Everyone finds a seat at the table and starts passing the delicious food around. Alec's favorite is stuffed shells, so that's what Mila's made, along with a huge salad and garlic knots.

"How's work going?" Gavin asks Alec, who smiles wide.

"Good, it's been pretty busy lately, but with the rain finally coming through, it's quieting down. Aside from the occasional oven fire, that is." Alec smirks at me, and I shove his shoulder playfully.

"Leave Lexi alone," Gavin chides playfully.

"Thank you." I smile at him.

"I can't help it." Alec laughs. "It's just too easy to rile her up." Alec's hand comes up to my hair, ruffling it, and I'm sure messing it up.

"Oh my God, you're so annoying!" I duck and swat his hand away.

"It's like he's still ten years old," Gavin says with a wink. "Saying he wants nothing to do with you, yet messing with you to get your attention."

Mason laughs. "Remember when Alec used to tell everyone how much he hated Lexi?"

"I didn't say I hated her," Alec says defensively. "I just said she was annoying." He shoots me a wink that makes him look like his father, only younger and more handsome.

"Whatever." I roll my eyes. "You were just as annoying, and you still are." I take a bite of my garlic knot and swallow. "That's why you're still single." I poke my tongue out, and Alec chuckles.

"You are too," he points out.

"Yeah, but I'm still young. You're practically an old man now."

Everyone laughs, and Alec groans.

"He's still young," Gavin says. "He has plenty of time to find the love of his life." His arm goes around his wife. "I didn't find mine until a couple years ago." He presses his lips against Lacie's cheek.

"I was thirty when I met Mila," Mason adds.

"Love knows no age," Mila says. "You don't find love… it finds you."

"I love that," Anna says, raising her glass of water. "To love finding you."

"But not too soon," Mason adds, giving his daughter a pointed look.

She rolls her eyes, and everyone laughs.

"Are you enjoying your summer?" Gavin asks Anna, changing the subject.

"Yes," Anna says with a smile. "I'm catching up on my sleep. It's been fabulous."

"And," Max adds. "When we go back, we won't have to ride the bus anymore since I'll be driving." He looks at my dad, who laughs. Max turned sixteen recently and got his license. He's been begging Dad to get a vehicle. Anna is the same age, but she isn't a fan of driving, so she has no desire to get her license.

"Real subtle, kid. Maybe, if you're lucky, I'll let you borrow one of my vehicles." Dad laughs.

"Yeah right, Tristan." Mom cackles. "We both know you'll be buying him a car simply because you won't want him to touch your precious Ford truck."

When I turned sixteen, Dad reluctantly bought me my jeep. And I say reluctantly because he wanted me to drive a Ford, but I wanted a jeep. He gave in and bought me my baby. It's the same jeep I drive today. Georgia, on the other hand, let Dad have his way, and she drives a Ford F-250. The thing is huge! Dad had to have a side-step installed, just so she could get into the damn thing, but she loves it, and she loves that it made Dad happy to buy her a Ford.

"FYI," Max says, "I'm totally okay with a Ford." He looks at me and laughs.

"Whatever, I'm okay with being the black sheep of the family. I love my jeep. It holds my surfboard perfectly."

"As long as it holds your books perfectly," Dad volleys.

"You girls only have about a year left, right?" Gavin asks.

"Yep, we both have one more year to go." Even though Georgia is a year younger than me, she's so smart, she took extra classes in high school and graduated early, with me.

"Actually," Georgia says. "I met with my advisor and since I've been taking extra classes every semester, she told me if I go full-time this summer, I can graduate early."

"How early?" I ask.

"At the end of the summer," she admits.

Everyone congratulates her, and she blushes, not keen on all the attention.

"I'm really proud of you, Georgia," I tell her. "It sucks we won't walk together, but at least once you're done, you'll have more time to help me with my classes." I wink playfully, and she rolls her eyes.

"Any plans for after college?" Gavin asks.

"I want to expand my graphic and web design business," Georgia says.

"Great goal," Gavin says before he turns his attention to me. "How about you?"

"I've actually been thinking about doing a little bit of traveling," I blurt out, having no clue where the hell that even came from. I feel everyone's eyes hit me, and I immediately want to take it back, but it's too late now.

"Really?" Lacie asks. "I did quite a bit of traveling in my twenties. Where are you planning to go?"

I think about this for a second. Where would I go if I could go anywhere? My mind goes to what I love most: surfing. "I would like to visit all the best places to surf: Sydney, Ireland, South Africa, Bali... I could check out the different cultures and art..."

"I heard Tahiti and Fiji are known for their surfing waters," Lacie says.

"Yeah," I agree. "The only places I've surfed are here and Mexico."

It doesn't get past me that my family and Alec haven't said a word. They're all just staring at me, most likely in shock since I've never once mentioned wanting to travel after I graduate. Well, that's because I never thought about it. But now that I'm thinking about it, it actually sounds like a really great idea.

"Traveling can be expensive," Lacie points out. "If you need any tips, let me know."

"Thank you," I say, not bothering to tell her that when I graduate my grandparents on my dad's side will be giving me my trust fund. They've set one up for each of their grandchildren to receive once they graduate from college or turn twenty-five. It's not enough to live off of, but it's enough to buy a house, or in my case, go traveling. They set it up to help us start our lives. My dad used his to open his own gym.

Nobody else says anything, but I can feel Alec's searing glare on me, as well as Georgia's hurtful stare.

Finally Mason, who must sense the tension, speaks up. "We've decided to finally purchase a cabin in Breckenridge," he says. "Mila and I are going to be heading up there for winter break with Anna."

"Sounds good," Alec says. "I'll put in for it. It's been a couple years since we've been."

After dinner, Alec's birthday cake is brought out and we all sing Happy Birthday. Then everyone gives him his gifts, while he whines that he's too old, but thanks everyone. I save mine and Georgia's for last.

"Here you go." I hand him the small box. "It's from Georgia and me."

He opens the box and inside is a Casio Men's G-Shock Solar Atomic watch. Georgia and I searched online for the perfect watch for a firefighter after Alec's got messed up while on a call a while back.

"The guy at the store says it's the perfect watch for a firefighter. It has a digital compass, a barometer, a thermometer, an altimeter, five different alarms, and is solar powered."

"Thank you." He leans over and kisses my cheek, then gets up and hugs Georgia.

Everyone stays for a while afterward, talking and hanging out, until it gets late and we all say good night. Georgia rode with me in my jeep, so we head back home together, Alec following.

"I'm going to head to the beach," I tell her once I pull up into my parking spot.

"It's late," she points out.

"I know. I'm just going to go paint."

"You're just trying to leave so you don't have to explain yourself... It's okay if you want to travel, Lex." She looks over at me, a sad smile splayed across her lips. "I just wish you had said something."

"Honestly, I wasn't sure until Alec's dad asked me about my plans."

"So, when are you planning to leave?"

"I don't know. I still have a year of school left. I was thinking next summer, if I graduate on time."

We're both quiet for a couple minutes, and I know I need to make this right between Georgia and me. Explain to her where I'm coming from, so she'll understand.

"Hey, sis," I start. "Sometimes I feel a little lost." My words come out as a whisper. I'm not good with being vulnerable, and Georgia is great about accepting me the way I am, which is why we're not only sisters but best friends.

"I do too," she agrees, her green eyes meeting my blue ones.

"It's like we have this amazing life. The perfect parents. The sweetest brother." Hot tears burn behind my lids. "We're so blessed."

"We are."

"But sometimes I feel like I don't fit in."

"And I do?" She laughs softly.

"At least you know what you want to do in your life. I have no clue what I want to spend my life doing after graduation."

"Oh yeah, my life is looking so glamorous. My goal in life has been to make sure I have a job where I can hide behind a computer screen," she says, her words throwing me for a loop. I always assumed Georgia just preferred to stay behind the scenes.

But now she's making it sound like she's unhappy *not* putting herself out there.

"I'm afraid," I admit.

"Of what?"

"Of ending up a loser like my real mom."

"That's not possible. You're like the most beautiful, coolest person I know." She grins, trying to lighten the mood. "I don't think it's possible for you to be a loser."

"My mom was pretty too. She was actually pretty freaking gorgeous. And she was the life of the party." One day, without my dad knowing, I found her on social media and stalked her pictures. Even though she's not alive, pictures never go away. Her pages are still up, but nothing has been added to them in years.

"That doesn't mean anything."

"I think I would feel better if I knew what I wanted to do with my life."

"I think it's okay to not know," Georgia says. "After listening to you, I'm definitely questioning everything."

"What do you mean?" I bring my hand down on top of hers.

"When you said you wanted to leave, it hit me that all these years I've been hiding from life, using you as a crutch."

"Why have you been hiding?" I feel bad that I've never asked that before. Georgia's always been the way she is, and the same way she accepts me without question, I accept her. But maybe I should've asked...

She quickly averts her gaze, something I've only seen her do when she would lie to Mom and Dad to cover for me. They eventually caught on and it became a joke in our family. "When I was younger and we would go places, I would get nervous. I would feel like I was going to have a panic attack."

"I remember." She would go quiet and hide behind our parents or me. Mom would tell people she was just shy.

"When I'd be at home, or it would be just us, it wouldn't happen. So, eventually I made it a point to not leave." Something in her voice, in the way she's refusing to look at me, tells me there's more to this than she's admitting. But I don't call her out on it. When she's ready, she'll tell me.

"Maybe if you put yourself out there, you can overcome it. I mean, I'm not a doctor or anything, but I can be with you. If you don't want to be stuck behind a screen, then you shouldn't be."

"You're right. I think it's time I get out of the house."

"Really?" I grin, so proud of her for wanting to take this step.

She nods. "If you can be brave enough to travel the world on your own, I can be brave enough to put myself out there. Instead of saying we're lost, how about we just say we're looking down each road for the perfect path to take?"

"Finding our perfect path... I love that."

"Me too. And I was thinking I could borrow something a little sexier for Alec's birthday..."

"Really?"

"Yeah... Maybe I'll... I don't know. Dance with someone besides you." She smiles shyly. Georgia has been to the club with me on quite a few occasions. She's never missed anyone's birthday celebrations, but she tends to dress more formal, so as not to get noticed. Even though she's so gorgeous she could probably wear a garbage bag and get noticed.

"I bet we can find you the perfect dress in my closet." I lean across the middle of my jeep and give my sister a hug. "I love you, Georgia, and I'm so proud of you."

"I love you, too."

## CHAPTER FIVE

### ALEC

I'm sitting in a booth in Club Hectic, surrounded by several of my friends, as well as some of the guys I work with who have tonight off. I'm pretty sure between Lexi and Chase, everyone I know has been invited to celebrate my birthday. I'm watching Lexi and Georgia shake their asses on the dance floor to an old-school remix. Right now "Hypnotized" by Plies is pumping through the speakers, and my eyes are stuck on Lexi's sexy-as-fuck body. When she and Georgia came out of their rooms dressed in tiny—way too fucking tiny—black dresses and fuck-me heels, I about lost my shit. For one, Georgia doesn't dress like that. In all the years I've known her, I've never seen her in anything that shows off every damn curve she has.

When I asked what the hell was going on, Georgia smiled and said, "We're finding our perfect path." I have no clue what she meant by that, and I didn't ask because I was too focused on Lexi, and how gorgeous she looked. She tends to be a ripped jean shorts and tank kind of girl, so when she dresses up, it makes it all the more special.

"Holy fuck, man." Chase comes over and sits next to me. He grabs a shot off the tray and downs it. "When the hell did she get so hot?" He nods toward Lexi and Georgia, who are now grinding up against each other to "Me & U" by Cassie, completely oblivious to the fact every fucking perv is staring at them. If this is how they plan to find their perfect path, I'm about to be getting into a lot of fights.

"Who's *she*?"

"Obviously Georgia. I wouldn't dare talk about your precious non-girlfriend. But she's definitely looking good as well."

"Aren't you a married man?" I might not have the same type of feelings for Georgia as I have for Lexi, but I'm just as close to her as I am with her sister. I've known her almost as long as I've known Lexi, and she's just as much of a sister to me as my own is. I'll be damned if any guy is going to fuck with her—friend or not.

"Not for long." Chase downs another shot and slams it down.

"Damn, man, I'm sorry."

"It's all good." He shrugs. "I found out she's been fucking around with another guy. I think it's time I do a little fucking myself."

"That's rough, bro." I take a shot then look Chase dead in the eyes, so he knows what I'm about to say is serious. "I don't blame you for wanting to get laid, but it won't be with Georgia."

"Are you seriously cockblocking me?" Chase asks incredulously.

"Call it whatever you want. There are hundreds of women in this club. Go fuck 'em all if you want, but Georgia is off-limits, *especially* since you're still married."

Chase opens his mouth to argue, but whatever he sees in my face must tell him I'm not playing, because he just nods. "All right, but can I at least dance with her?" He points to the women who are now surrounded by a bunch of men.

"Yeah, let's go." We take one more shot before we head over to Georgia and Lexi, not so subtly pushing through the guys. Chase makes eye contact with Georgia, his hands going to her hips. At first, she looks like she's about to hyperventilate just from his simple touch alone, but when he leans down and whispers something to her, she smiles and nods, then wraps her hands around his neck.

When I know Georgia is okay, I pull Lexi's back into my front. She spins around, her hand coming up about to slap me, but when she sees it's me, her hand lowers and a beautiful smile appears.

"I thought you were one of those guys." She nods toward the guys who're moving on to other women now that they see Georgia and Lexi aren't available.

"Good to know you would've handled yourself." I take her hand in mine and bring it up to my lips. Lexi's eyes go wide. I should really stop the flirting. I know my boldness is thanks to the tequila, and tomorrow morning when I'm no longer buzzed, I'll regret what I've done. Not because I don't want Lexi, but because I've worked hard to keep that thin line neatly drawn and in place.

"Damn right, I would've." Her arms snake around my neck, and she continues to dance seductively, using me as her own personal dance pole.

I'm not sure how long we dance, but when the club lights and music lower, I realize I've spent my entire night with Lexi in my arms, and it feels so damn good that, when she removes her hands from my body, I almost pull her closer, not wanting her to let go. And that thought has me sobering because Lexi isn't mine to hold on to. No matter how much I wish she were.

"I'm meeting my dad and Lacie for brunch later. Want to join me?" I ask Lexi when we're back home and heading to bed.

"Sure, just wake me up," she says before heading into her room. "Good night, Birthday Boy."

---

MY ALARM GOES OFF ALL TOO SOON, and after hitting snooze several times, I finally drag myself out of bed. *What the hell was I thinking agreeing to go to brunch the morning after going clubbing?* Knowing Lexi will need some time to get ready, I make my way to her room. Her door is partly open, so I don't bother to knock, instead quietly entering. She's sleeping on the left side of her bed like always. I constantly joke with her that she has a king-sized bed for no reason since she never sleeps on the entire thing. Georgia says she's waiting to share a bed with someone.

With her eyes closed and her face free of her makeup, she looks all natural and even more beautiful. Her body is snuggled into her blanket, and she's snoring lightly. I look at the time on my cell phone. Maybe I have enough time to lie with her for a little while...

Setting my alarm for a little later, I drop it onto the nightstand and climb onto the right side of the bed. Lexi startles slightly when she feels the bed dip, but when her eyes open and she sees it's me, a small smile makes its way upon her lips. She groans softly and edges closer so that her neck is snuggled in the area where my shoulder meets my chest. She throws her arm over my stomach and immediately falls back asleep. I should close my eyes and get another hour of sleep, but all I can think about is how perfectly her body fits with mine.

---

"ALEC, it's time to wake up." I open my eyes and look around. I must've fallen back asleep after all. "Your alarm was going off, but I hit stop." Lexi's chin rests on my arm as she smiles up at me. "Did you have trouble sleeping?"

"No, I came in here to wake you up, but you looked so adorable sleeping and snoring, I decided to join you." My comment earns me a swat to my arm.

"You don't tell a woman she snores." Lexi sits up and pouts. "Now get out, so I can get ready. What time do we need to leave by?"

"Ten thirty."

After I get ready, I head out to the living room to wait for Lexi. Chase is lying on my couch, scrolling through his phone.

"Have a good night?" he asks.

"Yeah, it was a good birthday. You?"

"Yeah, until Georgia—"

"Until Georgia what?" Lexi asks, stepping into the living room.

"Left me hanging for another guy," Chase finishes, shocking the hell out of not only me but Lexi.

"What?" Lexi gasps. "What are you talking about?"

"Last night... You two were too into each other to notice, but while I was dancing with Georgia, some asshole asked to cut in, and she let him."

"Well, you *are* married," Lexi points out.

"And he's not an asshole," Georgia says, joining the conversation. "His name is Robert and he's very sweet."

Lexi's mouth falls open. "You got his name?"

"And his number." Georgia smiles. "I figured it was a good first step to find my perfect path."

"What the hell is up with you and these paths?" I ask.

Georgia blushes and Lexi actually looks at me shyly.

"It's none of your business," Lexi says. "It's a sister thing." She walks over to Georgia and envelops her in a hug. "I'm so proud of you. I think that's a great first step."

I'm not sure what they mean by a path, but so far, it's involved Georgia dressing sexy and getting a guy's number. I have a feeling this path bullshit isn't something I'm going to like. Especially if it involves Lexi getting a guy's number.

Lexi and I arrive at the restaurant at eleven on the dot, and I spot my dad and Lacie already seated. I texted him before we left to let him know that Lexi would be joining us, so he could get us a table for four.

"Good morning, you two." Dad stands and gives me and Lexi a hug. Lacie does the same. The waiter comes over and we order our drinks.

"How was your night out?" Lacie asks after the waiter walks away.

"Good, but I don't think my body is able to handle those long nights out like it used to," I groan.

Lexi laughs. "You're twenty-five, not sixty, and we were home by three."

"You'll understand when you're my age," I joke.

We spend the next hour or so enjoying our meal. My dad talks about a new client he and Lacie have picked up at their real estate firm. He's one of the majority stakeholders in a large investment firm, so it's a huge deal for their firm. Lexi gushes about a storm she heard is coming in soon and can't wait to get out on the water. My dad, of course, warns her to be careful.

"You sound just like your son," she says, right before she shoots a playful glare my way.

"That's only because I love you and can't imagine what my life would be like if something happened to you," I tell her truthfully.

Her glare softens. "I know. That's why you're my best friend."

My dad gives me a knowing look, but I just laugh it off. My

family will forever be rooting for Lexi and me, but like I've said a million times, I'm not about to risk losing our friendship just to have a chance at something more with her. Lexi is wild and untamed. She isn't meant to be tied down. She's meant to soar and be free.

While we're finishing our meal, Lexi's phone dings with a text. When she checks it, she frowns.

"Everything okay?"

"Yeah, that guy Georgia met at the club last night..."

"Robert?"

"Yeah, he asked her to meet him for lunch."

"What's wrong with that?" I ask.

"Nothing, I guess. It's just that Georgia has never dated before, and now she's going from zero to sixty. She should take her time and get to know him first, before meeting with him."

"You've hooked up with guys with less conversation," I point out. I'm not trying to judge, but I'm surprised she's being so judgmental toward her sister.

Lexi's eyes meet mine. "Exactly, and I know how empty it feels. I don't want that for my sister."

It takes everything in me not to pull her into my arms and beg her to let me show her how meaningful it can be. I haven't personally experienced meaningful sex, but I know without a doubt if Lexi and I were to get together it wouldn't be without emotions.

Instead, I nod. "You're a good sister."

When the bill is paid, my dad and Lacie walk out with us to my truck.

"Thank you for brunch," I tell my dad, giving him a hug.

"Anytime. You know this new client I have? He's offered me tickets to some country music festival next weekend. Apparently, the company he owns has ties to the Empire Polo Club." The Empire Polo Club is a large concert venue in Indio. "Lacie and I thought about going, but to be honest we couldn't even tell you who half the bands are that are playing at the festival. I'm starting to realize I'm no longer the cool guy I used to be."

"It's okay, Dad, you're still cool in my book." We both laugh. "I'll see if Lexi wants to go. She loves country music, so I'm sure she'll be down." I glance over at her chatting with Lacie, giving my dad and me a minute to talk alone.

"He said he'll have four tickets for me at will-call. I'll let him know you'll be the one picking them up."

"Sounds good." I give my dad another hug. "Thanks."

## CHAPTER SIX

### LEXI

"This feels soooo good," Georgia groans, dropping her head against the back of the salon chair. "Aren't you glad you drove up for a girls' day?" She glances over at Micaela, who has her eyes closed, also thoroughly enjoying her pedicure.

Even though my toes end up getting ruined from the sand and saltwater, every two weeks, Georgia and I go to get pedicures. She loves them, and I love spending time with my sister, so it's a win-win. This morning, Micaela drove up to join us. After going to breakfast, we came to our favorite salon to get pampered.

"I am," Micaela gushes. "Summer classes start Monday, so it's nice to relax for a little while."

"How are Ryan and RJ doing?" I ask. Ryan is staying home with RJ while Micaela goes to school full time. He posts the most adorable pictures on social media, but I really should make my way down to visit soon. RJ is so cute and growing up too fast.

"They're good." Micaela smiles. "I can't wait to be done with school so things will slow down a little. Between school and interning at Scripps... and being a wife and a mother..."

"You're like superwoman," Georgia tells her.

"Hardly. I couldn't do it without Ryan, that's for sure."

"You're both amazing parents," Georgia says.

"I can't even imagine having a baby," I admit. But then I

picture a brown-haired, brown-eyed little boy who looks like Alec, and my belly flip-flops. I bet he would make a wonderful dad, what with his big heart and all his patience. He would teach him how to fight and I would teach him how to surf...

"What are you thinking about?" Micaela asks.

"What? Nothing." I shake myself from my ridiculous thoughts.

"Bullshit. You got this goofy look on your face," Micaela accuses.

"I was just thinking about my adorable godson and how glad I am you're the one with the baby, so I can spoil him rotten and then hand him back when it's time for him to be fed and changed." I poke my tongue out and Georgia and Micaela both laugh.

"This color?" the nail tech asks me, holding up a bottle of blue nail polish.

"Yes, please."

After we finish getting our toes done, and Georgia gets a manicure, we get our eyebrows threaded and then each get a facial. Once we're completely pampered, we head over to the Santa Monica Pier to have lunch. I stop at the taco stand and order some tacos, then tell Georgia and Micaela I'll be right back.

"Hey, Aiden," I say when I approach. He's sitting in the sand and drawing in his sketchpad, something he does often.

"Hi, Lexi," he says back, his brown eyes meeting my blue ones. "Did you bring me tacos?"

"I did." I hand him the bag.

"Thank you. I'm drawing a picture. You want to see?"

"Of course, but then I have to go. My sister and cousin are waiting for me."

"Okay." He turns his sketchpad toward me.

The drawing is of the ocean with several dolphins swimming around. It's in pencil and the details are flawless. Every line, every shadow done with perfection. "Did you see these?" I ask, pointing to the dolphins.

"Yes, they were swimming right there." He points out toward the water.

"It's a beautiful picture," I tell him, hating that nobody but me ever sees his art. He deserves to have his art hung up where everyone can see it.

"Thank you, Lexi," he says, opening the bag so he can eat his food.

"You're welcome. I'll see you soon."

I head back up to the pier and find Georgia and Micaela sitting at a table with our food and drinks.

"How's Aiden?" Georgia asks when I sit down. She's only met him once, when she came with me to the beach, but she knows I feed and visit him on the regular.

"Good... drawing."

"Who's Aiden?" Micaela asks.

"A friend of mine who's homeless and has lived in a tent under the pier for the last several months. I brought him something to eat." I met Aiden one day when walking by him. I offered him some food I had packed and, even though at first he was reluctant, he accepted my offering. Now, every day I'm here I either buy him tacos, which is his favorite meal, or bring him food from my house.

"That's so sweet of you," Micaela says.

I shrug. "I wish there was something more I could do."

We eat our lunch and then Micaela takes off back home. Georgia and I spend the rest of our afternoon getting ready for tonight's music festival.

---

"THIS LINEUP IS AMAZING!" I yell as Luke Bryan thanks everyone for coming out tonight, and the crowd screams and shouts their love for the man.

"It is!" Georgia sports a wide grin that tells me she's enjoying herself. I was shocked when she agreed to come to the music festival with Alec, Chase, and me. I know she's already made steps toward finding her perfect path, like going to the club and dancing with Chase and Robert, and then meeting Robert for lunch the next day—which she told me went really well and they're planning to go out again soon. But I kind of expected her to say the music festival was too much too soon. However, when I told her about it, she squealed in excitement, shocking the hell out of me and making me proud at the same time. It probably helps that she's a huge country music fan and it's just the four of us in the owner's box, so while it's loud all around us, we're not actually in the middle of the craziness.

I can't deny that her willingness to find her perfect path has me thinking about mine. Since we made that pact in my jeep, she's made a pointed effort to get out of her comfort zone, while I haven't done anything. I think my issue is that I don't even know what path I'm looking for, what getting out of my comfort zone entails. Georgia's issue has always been that she's shy and isn't comfortable around a lot of people, so finding her path seems so cut and dry: put herself out there in crowds. I'm not saying it's easy for her, but at least she knows what path she's looking for.

Me? Not so much... I know I'm lost, unsure of what I want for my future. I've thought a lot about how I said I want to travel, and I have to wonder if maybe it's my way of trying to escape. But at the same time, maybe traveling will mean finding my path. I guess, for right now, I'll just keep moving forward and hope to eventually see that perfect path.

Rodney Atkins makes his way out onto the stage, and a couple minutes later, we're singing our hearts out to "These are My People" while we wait for the guys to return with our drinks.

"You better drink every damn bit of this," Alec says when he hands me the most adorable drink I've ever seen. I don't even know what's inside of it, but the cup is shaped like a fish bowl and it lights up. I saw someone else walking with it and begged Alec to find it for me.

"Twenty-five dollars," he adds with a groan.

"Thank you!" I grab the drink from him and take a sip. It tastes like lemonade with a bit of a kick to it.

Chase hands Georgia the bottle of water she asked for, and then both guys have a seat, with their beers in their hands, in the chairs behind us. Georgia and I sing and dance to several songs, but when Kane Brown hits the stage with "What Ifs", a song that always makes me think of Alec, I set my drink down and pull Alec out of his chair to dance with me.

Turning around so that his front is flush against my back, I start shaking my ass. I sneak a glance back and see he's shaking his head, but his eyes are silently laughing. His hands grip my sides, and his face dips down. He's so close, I can feel his cool breath hit my overheated skin. I assume he's leaning in to tell me something, so I'm shocked when his lips brush up against the curve of neck, sending shivers straight down my spine. He places several kisses along my sensitive flesh, and I find myself tilting my head slightly to give him better access as I get lost in Kane Brown's words about being made for each other and Alec's touch.

Needing to see his face, I twirl around in my spot. His dark brown eyes, filled with lust and want, lock with mine. I recognize the look because it's exactly what I'm feeling. The sexual tension in the air is so thick it's almost suffocating. My heart picks up speed and my brain screams *abort!*

Afraid the moment is getting too deep, I take his hat off his head and place it on my own with a playful smirk. In return, his hands glide down my sides and land on my ass, and then he shocks the hell out of me when he lifts me up. My legs wrap around his waist and my arms snake around his neck. We sway to the music, our eyes never leaving one another. No words are spoken, and I haven't the slightest clue what any of this means. This is Alec. The guy I've had a crush on since I was old enough to understand boys don't really have cooties, and it's just something dads tell their daughters to keep them from chasing the boys. I've seen him date various women. I was there the day he decided to join the fire academy. I can remember the moment I realized my crush wasn't just a crush, but actual love. He's my roommate, my best friend. And as good as it feels to be in his arms, I can't let myself get lost in him. Whatever is happening between us will end in destruction, heartbreak. I'll lose him. And I *can't* lose him.

Needing to put some distance between us, I open my mouth to ask him to set me down, when he leans in and softly brushes his lips against mine. It's barely even a kiss, more like a sensual whisper that leaves me wanting more. His tongue darts out and slowly licks across the flesh of my lips before it finds its way into my mouth. My lips curve around his and our tongues swirl around each other. My arms tighten around his neck and his fingers massage circles into my ass cheeks. Everything and everyone around us fades away as we get lost in our kiss, in each other.

The kiss ends, and I faintly hear the current song fade out and a new one begin. It's slower, more sensual, and I can't handle being in Alec's arms like this, without knowing what that kiss means to him. I was just thinking we can't be together, I can't risk losing him, but with that one kiss, all I can think is how much I want him and need him. Fuck the risks. Fuck the consequences. What if *he's* my perfect path?

I stare into his smoldering gaze, as both of our chests heave like we've just run a marathon. I silently beg him to say something, anything, but he remains quiet, the look on his face a mixture of lust and confusion. Reluctantly, I release my legs from around him. Understanding what I'm silently asking, he gently sets me onto my feet. I turn back around to face the concert, but Alec doesn't sit back down. Instead, he wraps his arms around my waist from behind and nuzzles his face into my hair, his scruff tickling my neck. My body sways to Kane Brown as he sings about lying next to the woman he loves, comparing it to what heaven must be like.

I don't realize my butt is rubbing against Alec's crotch, until he pushes my hair to the side and whispers into my ear, "That's not wise, Lex." His fingers dig into my hips, stopping my body from moving, and that's when I feel it—his hard erection pressed up against my ass. Before I can react to it, he snatches his hat off my head and sits back down. I glance back at him and see the hat is covering his crotch. I throw my head back in a loud belly laugh, and he rolls his eyes.

When I look over at Georgia, I see her and Chase standing next to each other, laughing and swaying to the music. Her eyes meet mine and she shoots me a knowing wink, telling me she didn't miss what happened between Alec and me.

The rest of the concert goes by way too quickly. The four of us dance and sing and Georgia even drinks some of my drink. Before we know it, everyone is making their way back onto the stage to say good night, and then we're piling into my jeep. Alec only had one beer, so he drives us home.

We all go our separate ways once we're inside. Georgia says she's exhausted and is going straight to bed. Alec says he's jumping in the shower, and I do the same. When I get out, I throw on a pair of boxers I stole from Alec years ago and a comfortable tank top and pad into the kitchen to grab a bottle of water. I'm on my way back to my room when Alec steps into the hallway in nothing but a pair of loose sweats hanging low on his hips. His hair is still wet and beads of water are dripping down his taut muscles. His tattoos are shining bright from being wet. I watch, mesmerized, as the tiny droplets of water glide down his torso. *Damn, I'm thirsty. I wonder if he'd let me lick him...*

If Alec notices me staring like a damn perv, he doesn't point it out. Instead he says, "I had a good time tonight."

I give him a small smile. "Me too."

There's so much going through my head, but I'm afraid to voice my thoughts. If I say the wrong thing... if I'm overthinking what happened tonight, it could potentially ruin our friendship. Everyone witnessed what happened between Joey and Dawson on *Dawson's Creek*. You don't date your best friend unless you're okay with ruining your friendship. Their experience should be a warning for everyone.

"Listen," Alec says, stepping toward me. The way his brows are furrowed has my stomach twisting into a knot. This can't be good. Nothing that begins with *Listen* is ever good. "Tonight, what happened between us..."

"Yeah?" I hold my breath, waiting for the blow to come, but praying it doesn't.

"It shouldn't have happened," he says, knocking me right onto my ass.

"Okay." I nod robotically. There's more I want to say, but I don't. The moment is already awkward, which is exactly why he's right... Tonight shouldn't have happened. All we did was kiss and everything's changed. What would happen to us if we hooked up, or if we decided to give a relationship a chance?

"It's just that—" he starts to explain, even though he doesn't need to, because I get it. I do. No matter which way we go, we'll end up at a dead end, and then nothing would ever be the same again. I would lose my best friend. Georgia would have to pick sides. Family get-togethers would be weird.

Alec isn't my perfect path. And I need to accept that and stop trying to make this into something it's not. Something it can never be.

"Sorry," Chase mutters, cutting off Alec. "I'm just going to take a quick shower." He slips by us and into the bathroom, shutting the door behind him.

Alec's eyes never leave mine. His lips part, about to continue, but I can't deal with whatever he has to say, so like the coward I've apparently become, I speak first. "I'm going to head to bed. Good night." And without waiting for him to respond, I slip into my room, closing the door behind me.

## CHAPTER SEVEN

### ALEC

I WAKE up to my phone ringing, and when I look at the time, I see it's already ten in the morning. I rarely sleep in this late, but between the late night at the club and then last night at the music festival, I was exhausted. The phone stops ringing then starts again. When I look at my caller ID, I see it's Lacie. She's probably calling to see how the concert was.

"Hey, Lacie."

"Alec." When she doesn't say anything else, I'm immediately on alert.

"Lacie, is everything okay?"

"Oh God, Alec," she cries out. "No, everything is *not* okay. Your father has been in an accident."

I sit up, trying to focus on what she's saying, but my entire world feels like it's being shaken.

"He didn't make it," she adds, and I was wrong, my world hasn't been shaken—it's been blown to pieces.

"What happened?" I whisper, the lump in my throat too big to allow me to speak properly.

"It's all my fault. I told him I was hungry." She sobs through the phone. "We hadn't been by the store, so we didn't have anything to make for breakfast." She cries harder. "He offered to go pick us up breakfast at the diner. The paramedics believe he had a heart attack while he was driving, and by the time the ambulance got there it was too late."

"Fuck!" I feel the burning behind my lids and know I'm crying. "Where are you?"

"I'm at the hospital. I-I don't know what to do," she admits softly.

"I'll be right there." I jump out of bed and quickly throw some clothes on. I step out of my room and the house is quiet. My hand presses to Lexi's door to tell her what happened, but I quickly back away, instead heading down the hall to the living room. Chase is passed out on the couch, and I consider waking him up but don't. If I have to say the words out loud then they'll be true. My dad will really be dead. And right now, I'm still in denial.

The entire drive to the hospital, I come up with a million different scenarios where my father is still alive—from Lacie being misinformed, to my dad playing a sick joke on me. But deep down I know none of the scenarios are going to pan out. I can feel the heaviness in my chest. My dad is gone.

I arrive at the hospital and find Lacie sitting in a waiting room chair by herself. Her head is resting in her hands, her quiet sobs racking her body. Sitting next to her, I slide my arm around the top of her shoulders. She looks up, her eyes swollen and her cheeks blotchy.

"Oh, Alec," she cries. "I'm so sorry. I didn't know. If I had known that—"

I shake my head and pull her into my embrace. "Don't do that. It's not your fault. People leave the house every day. Don't blame yourself." I see this happen all the time. A husband leaves the coffee pot on by mistake, or a wife forgets to turn a burner off. The house burns down, and they blame themselves, blame each other. It doesn't matter, though, who did what. It happened, and no matter who you point your fingers at, it's not going to change the outcome.

"They said they're doing an autopsy to confirm how he died, and once they're done..." She can't finish her sentence, her cries now coming too hard for words to form. She holds me tighter, and I rub her arm in a soothing gesture in an attempt to comfort her.

When she finally stops crying, I notice her breathing has evened out. I dip my head slightly and see she's cried herself to sleep. The nurse sitting at the desk across from me gives me a sad smile.

"Sometimes our bodies and minds just need a small break," she says. I nod in understanding. I haven't shed a single tear since I arrived, and I'm almost positive I'm still in denial. My mind and body are numb, refusing to acknowledge my dad is gone.

Instead of calling anyone, I drop my head back against the wall and just sit here while Lacie sleeps. When she wakes up, we're going to have to deal with this. We'll have to speak to the medical examiner, have my dad's body moved to a funeral home, then, we'll have to plan a fucking funeral. We'll have to tell each and every one of our family members, friends, and his employees that he's dead. But for right now, while Lacie is asleep, I can pretend for a little longer that my dad isn't gone.

Lacie eventually wakes up, and when she does, for a brief moment, I can see it in her eyes that she's confused. She's wondering if this was all a horrible nightmare. She's looking around and wondering why she's in my arms and not my dad's. She's disoriented, curious as to why we're sitting in a hospital waiting room. I can see the moment when she remembers. Her throat bobs as she swallows thickly, her top teeth biting down on her bottom lip. Her eyes widen and fill with devastation, and her head tilts slightly to the left in a silent attempt of asking me if what she's remembering is indeed real.

"It really happened," I confirm, saying the words out loud for the first time. "He's gone."

She shakes her head back and forth and closes her eyes. The tears race down her cheeks, and she drops her head into her hands. "No, no, no, no..." She continues to repeat the same word over and over again, not wanting it to be true, and I know exactly how she feels.

## CHAPTER EIGHT

### LEXI

"Oh, man, those waves!" I yell over the music blaring from someone's speakers as I jab my board into the sand. I drop onto the blanket, grabbing a cold bottle of water from my cooler, and down the entire thing. It must be ninety-five degrees outside right now, and the saltwater may cool my body down, but it does nothing for my thirst. "Adulting seriously gets in the way of my surfing time."

"Hell yeah, it does," Jason agrees with a laugh, grabbing a water as well. He flops onto my blanket, soaking the entire thing. I've known Jason for about a year or so now, but I don't know a lot about him. From the little he's mentioned, he's a trust fund kid who spends the majority of his time fucking off and surfing. According to him, when he's not at the beach, it's because his dad is making him learn the company he owns, so he can one day take over. He doesn't seem too thrilled about the idea.

"I told my parents I'm taking the summer off to train for the Vans Surf Classic."

"The winners get a sponsorship for next year's world tour," Jason says. "If you win, you would have to quit school. You prepared to do that?"

Before last night, I would've said no. Surfing has always just been for fun. I wouldn't give up school, something that's important to my parents, to leave here—*leave Georgia and Alec*—and travel the world surfing. When I had mentioned traveling at dinner the other night, I wasn't really one hundred percent sure. I was just lost and wanting to escape. And then Alec kissed me, and if he had told me right then and there he wants to be with me, I would've given up anything in the world to be with him. But he didn't. Instead, he told me it shouldn't have happened. Which means if I stay around here, one day I'm going to have to watch Alec fall in love with another woman. Get married, have kids, create a life together. And I can't be around for that.

Alec was right. That kiss shouldn't have happened, because it changed everything for me. It was one thing to love him from afar, but to actually feel his body against mine, to know how his mouth tastes when entwined with mine, changes everything. Because now I've had a glimpse of how good it could be with Alec, and it hurts to know I can never have that—to know he doesn't want that.

He once told me he wants what his mom and Mason have, what my parents have. Maybe the reason why he doesn't want me is because I'm nothing like them. I'm too wild, too carefree—too unpredictable. I don't know what I want for my future. I live in the moment. I've always been the black sheep of my family—even if my parents swear they love me the way I am. I've always worried I'm too much like my biological mom, that my dad wants me to go to college so I don't end up like her. But what if finding our own perfect paths isn't possible? What if my path has already been decided, and I'm just fighting the inevitable?

"I saw your recent tag," Jason says, snapping me from my thoughts. "On the abandoned building near Luciano's." Luciano's is an authentic Italian bakery in the rougher part of LA. It's the only business in its neighborhood that hasn't been shut down yet. The city has been shutting down or buying out each business, so they can tear the buildings down to create condo developments.

"I've never admitted to anything." I give Jason a side-eye, and he rolls his eyes. Everybody who knows me knows I've been graffitiing all over the abandoned buildings in LA for years. Everywhere I graffiti, I leave my tag: a silhouette of a surfer chick holding a surfboard. In a city that's filled with so much darkness and chaos, I've always been drawn to adding my own color and brightness. People think LA is so glamorous, so beautiful, but those people have never lived here. It's not like what you see in the movies or on TV. There's a small percentage of wealth and the rest is poor. The beach is beautiful but filled with homeless people. The businesses are thriving but too expensive for the common folk to shop at. For every fancy restaurant, there's fifty people who can't afford to even eat. They fill the alleyways, the beaches, the sidewalks, and I fill the walls with hope and beauty.

"You don't have to admit to it." Jason laughs. "I would know your work anywhere. It's beautiful... just like you."

"Thanks," I say, my cheeks heating up from his compliment. Jason is a good-looking guy. He can be a huge flirt, and I know he sleeps around. I also know he's interested in me. He's made it known on several occasions without actually saying it. And if I weren't completely in love with my best friend, I would probably give in to his advances, but I am, and no matter how many times I've tried over the years to get under someone else to get over Alec, it never works. Eventually I stopped trying. Too many meaningless one-night stands led to me giving up. Now, it's been so long, my vagina would probably go into shock if it was touched by anything other than my fingers or vibrator.

"So, I was thinking..." he begins.

I bite down on my bottom lip, praying he doesn't ask me out. Things are already awkward with Alec. The last thing I want is for things to be awkward with another one of my friends.

Then I remember why things are awkward with Alec. *It shouldn't have happened.*

"...maybe we could go out sometime," he finishes.

I expected him to say something sexual, like he wants to hook up. I wasn't expecting him to actually ask me out. Maybe this is my path: moving forward, finding a nice, good-looking guy who wants to go out with me.

I'm about to tell him okay, when my phone rings.

Alec's name appears on the caller ID, and I take a deep breath, worried as to why he's calling. Maybe he feels the need to finish telling me why our kiss shouldn't have happened... *Or maybe he's changed his mind...* I tamper down that thought, refusing to get my hopes up.

"Hey," I say nervously, jumping to my feet. Jason is still on the blanket, watching me intently, so I lift a finger, silently asking him to give me a minute.

"Hey," Alec echoes softly.

The silence between us is awkward, and I know right away, he isn't calling because he's changed his mind. I'm suddenly very thankful the only thing that happened between us was a kiss. Joey and Dawson were still okay after their kiss. It wasn't until after they decided to take the leap from friends to a couple that everything changed between them. Which means Alec and I will get through this. We'll get past this awkwardness and go back to being best friends.

"Alec? Is everything okay?" I ask slowly, when he remains quiet on the other end of the line.

"It's my dad... He was in an accident." My hand goes to my mouth with a gasp. "Lacie and I just left the hospital, and we're heading to the funeral home. He's gone." He chokes out the last word, and my heart feels like it's just imploded inside my chest. Leaving everything where it is, I grab my keys and take off, running to my jeep. My only thought is that I need to get to Alec. The kiss, the unrequited feelings, the awkwardness, none of it matters anymore.

"Which one?" I ask, turning my ignition. "I'll be right there."

Alec gives me the name of the place, and I tell him I'll see him in a few minutes. On my way, I call my parents and then Georgia to let them know. When I arrive at the funeral home, I see Alec's silver truck parked in the front. Remembering I'm still in my wetsuit, I strip out of it and throw on a pair of cutoff jean shorts and a tank. I look like shit, but this will have to do. I'm not driving all the way home to change.

I get inside and immediately spot Alec speaking to an older gentleman. His stepmom is sitting in the corner with her face in her hands, her shoulders moving up and down while she cries quietly.

"Hey," I say softly, making my presence known but not wanting to interrupt the two guys conversing. Alec stops talking and turns to me. His eyes are bloodshot, and when they meet mine, a single tear falls. If I had to guess, I would say that, up until now, Alec's refused to acknowledge his grief. Not knowing what to say in this situation, I do the only thing that comes natural and wrap my arms around him and hug him tight. Alec's body sinks into mine, his face nuzzling into my neck. His hot tears hit my skin as he cries over the loss of his father. I don't bother speaking. There's nothing I can say that will make this better.

When Alec's body calms down, and he goes still, I lift my head up slightly to meet his eyes. "Tell me what you need."

"You here is all I need."

---

WHEN I WAS FIVE, my biological mom died. There was a funeral, but my dad said he felt it was best for me not to attend. We visited her grave once, but I don't remember it, and I haven't been back since then. When I was eight, my great-grandma passed away, but once again, wanting to shelter me, my dad and mom insisted Georgia and I stay home. So, at twenty-one years old, I've just attended my first funeral, and if this is part of growing up, I must admit, I'm not a fan of getting older. To say it was sad would be a gross understatement. Gavin's wish was to be cremated, so Alec and Lacie picked out a lovely wooden urn that was placed for everyone to see. Georgia created the most beautiful slideshow of images and videos Lacie and Mila gave her. I had some images blown up, and since I couldn't sleep, I painted a portrait of Alec and his dad, which Alec insisted be shown. His stepmom read a poem, and Alec spoke of fond memories he had with his dad.

When the funeral was over, everybody went back to Mila and Mason's home. I'm not sure what the point of it was. Maybe to reminisce? I don't really know. Food and drinks were brought in, but most people didn't eat. Everyone gave their condolences to Alec and Lacie, and eventually one by one people trickled out.

From beginning to end, Alec's had me by his side. Even the last four nights he's slept in my bed with me. He holds me close until he thinks I've fallen asleep, and then he cries softly into my chest for hours. Alec has taken some personal time off work and hasn't said when he plans to return. We haven't discussed what happened between us the night of the concert. It's as if, with the death of his father, everything between us went back to normal. It solidifies why we can't ever be together. We need each other too much, and we can't gamble what we have, in hope of something more.

Now, the funeral is over, the meals everyone made for Lacie

are in her fridge, and we're back home. For the first time in days, there's nothing to do. No funeral to plan, no pictures to create. It's done. Gavin is gone, and he isn't coming back. All that's left is for everyone to start living their new life, one without Gavin in it.

Alec has been quiet since we got home, and I imagine he's struggling with this next part. Now that everything is calm, there's nothing for him to do to keep busy. He excused himself to shower the second we walked through the door, and when he got out, he went straight to his room to get dressed, closing the door behind him. I thought about knocking to see if he's okay, but if he wanted or needed me, he wouldn't have shut the door, or he would've opened it back up after he got dressed.

Chase is sitting on the couch—which now seems to be his new, permanent bed—messing with his cell phone, and Georgia's next to him texting on her phone—probably with Robert.

Unable to take the silence another second, I stand, needing to get out of here. "I'm gonna head to the beach." I haven't been since Alec called me with the news of his father passing away. I left my board there, and Jason texted me to let me know he would hold onto it for me.

"You're going to leave Alec?" Georgia asks, her brows furrowed in confusion.

"He obviously needs some time to himself." I nod toward his closed door. "I'll be back in a few hours."

After changing into my bikini and grabbing my wetsuit and keys, I head to the beach. I send Jason a text, and he replies that he's already there and has my board.

With the daylight limited, when I get to the beach, after getting Aiden some food and bringing it to him, I don't waste any time putting on my wetsuit and getting my board from Jason. He tries to bring us up, but I shake my head, telling him I can't do this right now. Thankfully, he doesn't push. I spend the next couple hours in the water. Paddling out and riding in. The waves are good, but it wouldn't matter if they weren't. I needed this. To feel the saltwater against my skin. To be out in the Pacific Ocean with nothing but the water and my board.

When I finally decide to take a quick break and grab a drink, I notice Alec is sitting in the sand. His knees are bent with his arms around them. His sandals are next to him, and his toes are digging into the wet sand.

"Hey," I say, shocked that he's here. "What are you doing here?" When I get closer, he stands, shaking the sand off him. He's in a plain white T-shirt and khaki cargo shorts. His face is freshly shaved, and his brown hair is messy.

"You look amazing out there, Lex." He smiles, but it doesn't reach his eyes like it usually does. I wonder how long it will take for him to smile like he used to before his dad died. It's probably selfish, but I hope it doesn't take too long. It's only been four days and I already miss his real smile.

"Thank you." I push my board into the sand.

"Can we go for a walk?" He worries his bottom lip nervously.

"Sure." I reach behind me and pull the zipper on my wetsuit down, shrugging out of it and leaving me in only my bikini.

"Do you have clothes?" he asks, his eyes raking down the front of my body.

"Oh, yeah. In the car."

Alec's hand rises behind him, and he grabs the back of his shirt, pulling it up. My eyes dart to his muscular torso and up to his hard chest as his shirt rises higher and higher, until it's off his body. He hands it to me, and I take it, throwing it over my head. Immediately, the signature cologne Alec wears hits my nostrils, and I force myself not to bring the material to my nose to inhale it like a crazy person.

I drop my board onto the ground and throw my wetsuit on top of it, then call out Ricco's name. "Can you keep an eye on my board?"

He's sitting on a blanket with a bunch of our friends, smoking a blunt and listening to some oldie's rock. He nods once and smiles, taking another hit. My eyes land on Jason, who's also sitting there, only he isn't smiling. He's shooting daggers my way. At some point I'm going to have to speak to him, but right now Alec needs to come first.

Alec looks like he wants to say something, but he doesn't. Instead, he starts walking in the opposite direction toward the pier. Nervous as to why he came here to talk to me, I stay quiet and wait for him to speak first. When we reach the pier, he stops in his tracks and faces me. The sun is just about gone, and the only light shining on us are the pier lights.

"The last few days have been hard," he starts. I simply nod in response, letting him speak. I can't even imagine what he's going through or how he feels, and I'm not going to pretend like I do. "When we got home today, my first instinct was to push you away." Now him shutting his door makes sense. "I called Lacie to see how she's doing, and she's a mess. She's pushing everyone away: my mom, me, her sister..." He stops speaking, and I'm not sure if I'm supposed to say anything, so I don't. I have no clue what's going through Alec's head right now, but he obviously drove over to the beach because he has something he needs to say to me.

Taking a deep breath, his eyes meet mine. "I called Mason, worried about Lacie, and he said when his father died, his mom did the same thing. She pushed him away, not knowing how to deal with the grief. Then he said something that made me think." Alec takes my hand in his, and I look down at our fingers intertwined. His large, masculine hand swallows my smaller one whole.

"He said the dark, ugly moments, like death, have a way of pushing people together or tearing them apart." Alec's voice cracks, and in the faint light I can see his eyes are glossy with unshed tears. "I don't want my father's death to tear us apart, Lex."

I start to shake my head because there's nothing that could tear us apart. Before I can voice my thoughts, though, Alec presses two fingers against my lips, stopping my words from coming out. He runs them across my lips then smiles softly.

"Life is too short. Too uncertain. My dad didn't find his soul mate until he was in his forties, and his time with her was cut short because of a clogged artery he didn't know about. He left to go get breakfast and will never return home. Now, only a few years after meeting my dad and falling in love, Lacie is alone again."

Alec's grip on my hand tightens as he pulls me closer to him. "I don't want to one day die with regrets. I'm in love with you, Lex, and I'm done pretending that I'm not."

"Alec," I breathe. He's saying the words I've longed to hear for years, but I'm scared he's only saying them because he's grieving over the loss of his father. He just told me the other day the kiss shouldn't have happened.

"I mean it, Lexi. I want you. I want to be with you. I want to hug you, kiss you, make love to you. I want to spend every day of our lives loving you up close, instead of from afar like I've been doing for years."

His hands lock behind my back, and he pulls me closer to him, our bodies flush against one another. "Tell me you want that too. Tell me you need me the way I need you. I've seen the way you look at me, the way you touch me. The other night at the concert, the way your body fit perfectly against mine. The way your lips molded against mine. It's like you were made just for me."

I want so badly to say yes. To wrap my arms around him and tell him I want him the way I want to spend my days surfing. I need him like I need to paint, to create. I love him like I love the smell of the saltwater. He's my addiction. I crave him every day. But I can't tell him any of that. Because when the grief lessens and he realizes I'm not what he needs, I'll lose him. He thinks he needs me as his girlfriend, but what he really needs is me as his friend. And that's exactly what I'm going to be—his friend.

"I love you so much," I tell him, wrapping my arms around his neck. I breathe in his scent and my eyes momentarily close, getting lost in everything that is Alec. "But I can't be with you."

He tightens his hold around me before loosening his grip so he can back up slightly and make eye contact with me. "Lex, please."

"You don't mean this. You're hurting. You just lost your dad and your heart has a gaping hole in it. But I can't be the one to fill it. I love that I'm the person you turned to for comfort. It means the world to me. And I'm here for you. But we both know we can't have anything more than friendship."

His gaze sears into mine. "What I *know* is that losing my dad made me realize how short life is, and I don't want to spend it in denial. I'm in love with you. And yeah, maybe it looks bad admitting that right after my dad died, but it doesn't make it any less true."

God, I want to believe that, so damn badly. But I can't chance it. If he changes his mind... If he regrets it later... He's hurting and not thinking clearly, and I have to be the clearheaded one for both of us, so we don't make any decisions we'll regret later. Decisions we can't take back or come back from.

I cup his face with my hands. "I'm sorry, but you're my best friend and it can't be anything more."

Alec sighs, shaking his head. "There already is something more. I was part of that kiss we shared *before* my dad died."

"The kiss you told me shouldn't have happened?"

"Because I was scared," he barks. "Just like you are."

"Hey, Lexi," Jason calls out. "Everything okay?"

Alec tenses, tilting his head slightly to the side. "Everything's fine."

"I asked Lexi," Jason says.

"I'm okay," I yell back. "I'll be over there in a minute." I turn back to Alec. "I'm supposed to be practicing for the upcoming surfing comp, but if you want to go somewhere—"

"No," Alec says. "Go surf." He grips the curves of my hips and pulls me into him until our bodies are flush. His face is so close to mine, I can feel his warm breath on me when he whispers, "This isn't over, Lex." He kisses the corner of my mouth, and a shiver runs down my spine. "I know you feel the same way I do, and I'm going to prove it to you."

He walks me back to where my stuff is and then takes off. Once he's gone, Jason walks over. "Your boyfriend?"

"No, just a friend." But as the word friend leaves my lips, I know that's not entirely true. Alec is so much more than that, even if I don't want to admit it.

"Let me take you out," Jason says. When I hesitate, he closes the distance between us. "Please. Just one date."

I should tell him no, admit that I have feelings for someone else, but does it matter what feelings I have for Alec when I refuse to act on them? Maybe going out with Jason will help me force the idea of Alec and me from my head—and heart. At the same time, I want Jason to understand…

"I'll go out with you, but I'm not looking for anything serious right now."

"Got it," he says with a nod. "Just one date."

## CHAPTER NINE

### ALEC

It's been almost a week since I made it clear to Lexi, I'm not giving up on us. The problem is, since then, she's been avoiding me like the plague. Most days and nights, she's at the beach surfing. The few times I've tried to hang out there, she's made it a point to act like she's too busy to spend time with me. And when she's home, instead of watching television in the living room, she stays in her room. At night, when she goes to bed, she shuts her door. I'm trying to be patient. I know this is her way of fighting the inevitable, but I'm getting a little antsy.

Especially since I overheard her talking to Georgia earlier about going on a double fucking date with that dick Jason. I've seen him hanging around her, and if I thought for a second that Lexi really liked him or that he would be good for her, I would throw in the towel and let her be happy. But I know damn well he isn't her type. For one, he has no ambition. He literally just hangs around the beach, drinking and getting high. Lexi might hang out with them, but she wants more in life, even if she's a little lost right now. She paints the walls to spread her hope and beauty because she sees the good in everything. She's in school—even though she hates it—because she knows it will better her future. And she's not your stereotypical surfer, looking to get high and party, like the idiots she hangs out with. She surfs because it's her passion.

"We're going out," I tell Chase, who's in his usual spot on the couch, watching TV.

"Seriously?" He pops his head up and quirks a brow. I haven't been out in some time, not since my dad died.

"Yeah, but don't say a word." I gesture my head toward the hallway, silently indicating I don't want the girls to know. They're currently in Georgia's room getting ready. They don't know I overheard, and I don't want them to. I heard Lexi mention she doesn't want Jason to pick her up here—probably because she knows I'll lose my shit—so they're meeting the guys at the bar downtown. I considered busting in there and demanding she not go, but decided to take a different approach. Show her it's me she wants.

"Be ready to go after they leave."

Before the girls come out, I make myself scarce, not coming back out until I hear the front door close, indicating they left.

"Where're we going?" Chase asks, once we're in my truck.

"To The Black Sheep. Georgia and Lexi are going on a double date there."

Chase laughs. "Well, this just got interesting."

We walk into The Black Sheep and my eyes immediately go in search of Lexi. I haven't the slightest clue how this is all going to play out. I have a few options: I can stay hidden, watch and see how her date goes. I can make my presence known but keep a distance, or I can—

"Holy shit! Look who's here," Chase exclaims, taking the choice out of my hands. "Lexi, Georgia, what the hell are you guys doing here?"

Chase grabs a chair from another table—without even asking—and drags it between Georgia and Robert. With a smile plastered on his face, he plops his ass into the chair and sits back, crossing his arms over his chest.

I stifle a laugh and follow along, only I sit between Lexi and Georgia, since Lexi's date, Jason, is sitting too close to her for me to move in between them.

"What are you guys doing here?" Lexi stiffly asks.

"We heard this place has great burgers," Chase answers, dropping his arm onto the back of Georgia's chair. Robert notices and shoots him a possessive glare that Chase either doesn't pay attention to or doesn't notice. Georgia snorts a laugh, knowing Chase's full of shit, and her eyes dart between Lexi and me, at the same time Robert turns his glare on her. Call me an overprotective friend, but that move just added him to my shit list.

"Well, in case you didn't notice," Jason speaks up, leaning over so his eyes meet mine, "we're on a date."

"Oh, shit," Chase says like he wasn't aware. "Our bad. But you guys don't mind us joining, do you?" He glances at Georgia, who covers her mouth to stop herself from laughing.

"Alec, can I talk to you for a second?" Lexi asks, already standing and grabbing my arm before I can respond. She drags me down the hallway, until we're hidden in a darkish corner, away from prying eyes and ears. "What the hell are you doing?" she shrieks, jutting out her cute-as-fuck chin, like the little badass she is.

"As Chase said—"

"No." She covers my mouth with her hand. "Don't you dare lie to me. We don't do that, ever." Her plump lips form a flat line. She removes her hand and crosses her arms over her chest. She's wearing a formfitting tank top and it takes everything in me not to dart my eyes to her breasts I know are peeking out of the top.

"I warned you I wouldn't give up." I grip the curves of her hips and gently push her until her back is against the wall. "You don't like that guy, not like you like me. And you're wasting all of our time by going out with him. If I learned anything from my dad's death, it's that we should never waste our time because we don't know how much time we have."

"You can't do this, Alec," she begs, her eyes shining with raw emotion.

"Can't do what?" I place a palm above her head and lean in, so she's forced to look up at me. In this position I could easily take her mouth, but I won't do it, not until she agrees to be mine. "Can't show you that I'm in love with you?" I tuck a blond hair behind her ear, and she visibly shivers. "I know you want me, *you* know you want me, hell, everyone at that fucking table knows you want me. You want to fight this, fine, but I'm not going to make it easy for you, and I'm not going to give up until you're mine."

Lexi closes her eyes and takes a deep breath and for a second,

I think maybe she's going to give in. But when she opens her eyes, I instantly see the defiance in her irises. "I'm on a date, Alec. You and I are friends, and if you keep this up, you're going to ruin that friendship."

She turns to walk away, but before she can, I tug her toward me, so her back is against my front. I dip my face so my lips are right at the shell of her ear. "I get that it's going to take you a bit longer to get on board with the idea of us, and I'm okay with that because I know in the end we'll be together, but I need you to promise me something."

She sighs. "What?"

"Until you're one hundred percent sure he's the man you love, please don't sleep with him."

Her breath hitches, and then a few seconds later, she nods before she walks away.

I follow after her, but instead of sitting, I nod to Chase that it's time to go. I'd like to say I'm a good enough guy to wish them a good date, but I'm not. With a squeeze to Lexi's shoulder and a smile to Georgia, I do the hardest fucking thing and walk out of the bar.

---

"I WANT to be with her, and I know damn well she feels the same way." I'm sitting at a local diner having lunch with Mason and Chase. It's been damn near two weeks since I told Lexi how I feel and almost a week since her date with dick-face. Since I walked out of the restaurant, we've barely spoken, let alone seen each other. She swears it's because she's busy surfing, getting ready for her competition in July, but I know her and she's definitely avoiding me. "How the hell do I get her to admit her feelings for me?"

Mason laughs, and Chase shakes his head.

"Maybe it's for the best," Chase says. "I married young and look where I ended up... divorced."

"You signed the papers?" I ask. Chase was served divorce papers a couple weeks ago. After throwing them on the table, he took off and didn't come home for a few days. When he returned, he didn't say a word about them and I didn't want to pry. I figured when he was ready to talk, he would bring them up.

"Yeah. Since neither of us really has any assets, it'll go through quickly," he says, taking a sip of his coffee. He looks like shit, like he needs to take a long as fuck nap, but I don't point that out. No need to kick the guy while he's down.

"I'm sorry, man," Mason adds.

"It's all good," Chase says. "She was a cheating druggie. The more I tried to get her help, the more she pushed me away. I should've known how it would all end."

"Maybe you're right." I sigh, crossing my arms over my chest. "One of the reasons I didn't pursue Lexi before is because of how young we are. My parents married young..." I swallow thickly, trying to keep it together. Any time I bring up my dad, I lose it. It's been almost three weeks since his death, and it doesn't hurt any fucking less.

"You aren't your parents," Mason points out. "Sure, as people grow, they change, but plenty of people who get married young last. And you can't not be with someone because there's a chance it won't work." He glances at Chase. "Did you love your wife?"

Chase nods once.

"Did you have good times with her? Create memories?"

"Yeah."

"Then you don't regret it. Every moment, every situation happens for a reason," Mason says. "I had a shit life growing up, but I would go through it all again if it meant it would lead me to right here—with your mom, you, and your sister." He quirks a brow. "And I know your parents feel the same way. Had your mom not been with your dad, they wouldn't have had you. And I know damn well neither of them could ever regret their time together *because* it gave them you."

"Yeah, well, I'm just glad Victoria and I didn't have any kids," Chase says, referring to his soon-to-be ex-wife. "I didn't grow up in a perfect home where my parents got along and we all sat around having meals together like you guys do. My parents barely got along. And after..." He clears his throat, his face all of a sudden looking pained. "After my sister died, it only got worse, until my dad drank himself to death."

"You had a sister?" He's never mentioned having a sibling.

Chase nods. "It's not something I like to talk about. We grew up in a shitty neighborhood, surrounded by shitty people, and it led to her making shitty choices. Now she's gone. Where I come from, that elusive happily ever after people talk about is only found in those bullshit Disney movies." His sad eyes meet mine. "And since we were so poor, we couldn't even afford to watch them anyway." He shrugs.

"I didn't get it at first either," Mason says. "I actually came from a similar home. It took me finding Mila to understand what real love is all about."

"Oh, I know what it's all about," Chase says bitterly. "I loved Victoria with every ounce of my being. But look what loving her got me: ten years wasted, homeless, and sleeping on my best friend's couch. I think I've had enough of that love bullshit to last me a lifetime."

"You're too young to be this bitter," Mason says. "Take it as a learning experience and move forward."

"Oh, I am." Chase chuckles. "Every night since I signed those divorce papers I've moved forward." He waggles his brows, and Mason and I both groan.

"Well, I'm not trying to move forward," I say, wondering how the hell we went from me trying to convince Lexi to be with me, to Chase transforming into a manwhore. "I'm trying to figure out how to get Lexi to admit she wants to be with me."

Mason grins. "That's easy. Do what I did when I needed to convince your mom to stay married to me... Show her how good it can be with you."

"It's kind of hard to do when she's avoiding me." *And going out with another guy...* Thankfully, from what I've seen, she hasn't been out with Jason again, and the night she did go out with him, she got home only an hour after me, so I know she didn't go with him back to his place.

"You're just going to have to try harder." Mason smirks.

The waitress drops off our food and we eat in silence. I think about what Mason said. Maybe he's right. Maybe the key to getting Lexi to give in, isn't to beg her but instead to show her.

After we finish eating, we talk for a little while, then head to the gym to get a workout in. Afterward, I stop by Lacie's place to check on her. She's finally starting to come around. She's not back to work or even leaving the house yet, but she's at least showering. I bring her some food from one of her favorite restaurants and she thanks me. When she stands to take it, I notice something is different... her stomach has a bump.

"Lacie?" My gaze darts between her face and her stomach.

Her eyes well up with tears. "I'm thirteen weeks."

"Did my dad know?"

She nods. "It wasn't planned, and because I'm almost forty, we were worried about the possibility of a miscarriage, so we were waiting to tell everyone." Tears slide down her cheeks. "I can't believe I have to do this alone."

"Hey, you are *not* doing this alone. You have me and my parents. Your sister... I know it's not the same, but I promise you, you aren't doing this alone."

She chokes out a sob. "Thank you, Alec. That means a lot to me. Your brother is going to want to know all about his daddy, and you know him the best."

"Brother?"

"Yeah. I had a blood test done. It's a boy."

"Congratulations." I give her a hug. "My brother will know exactly who his dad was. I promise."

After Lacie updates me on her pregnancy, I head home. On the way, I call my mom to let her know about Lacie, and she promises to stop by to check on her. While Lacie and I were talking, she mentioned possibly moving in with her sister. She lives a couple hours north, and she felt bad for leaving and taking my brother with her. But I assured her that no amount of distance would stop me from being part of their life, and if moving in with her sister is what's best for her, then that's what she should do.

I get home and find Chase on the couch, texting on his phone. "Want to go out tonight?" he asks. Tonight is his last night off before he's back on shift.

"Nah, tonight starts Operation Get Lexi."

Georgia walks out of her room and laughs. "Operation Get Lexi?" She shakes her head. "Only my sister would require an actual operation to get her to see what she already knows." She grabs her purse off the end table. "I'm heading over to Robert's. Be back later."

"Things are moving a little fast with him," I mention, making Georgia roll her eyes.

"Not everyone waits twenty years to admit they like someone. Bye!" she yells, closing the door behind her before I can say another word.

## CHAPTER TEN

### LEXI

I open the front door and tiptoe inside. It's late—I stayed out surfing later than I planned. Okay, let's be honest, I did it on purpose. Ever since Alec told me he wants more, I've been avoiding him. And since the night he showed up to my date, I've been double-y avoiding him. I know it's immature, but I don't know what else to do. I almost gave in that day at the beach, and again, when he cornered me in the restaurant, and I know if he keeps pressing it, I'll eventually give in. My plan is to stay away long enough that he comes to his senses and realizes he's not actually in love with me, but in love with the idea of being in love. Then, once he admits it, I'll tell him it's all good and things will go back to normal between us.

*But then why did you tell Jason you needed to hold off on going out with him again?*

Pushing that thought away, I set my surfboard against the wall and notice Chase is lying on the couch, texting on his phone.

"Hey," he says, without looking up. "You can sneak in all you want, but Alec is on to you."

I glare at him. "Shouldn't you be out screwing your way through LA?" I immediately regret my snippy comment. Chase is a good guy. He's just hurt over his wife cheating. I can't really blame him for wanting to get lost in other women to get over his wife. I'm not sure how I would react if I were in his shoes.

"Leaving soon," Chase volleys, as I walk down the hallway toward my room.

"There she is," Alec says, appearing out of nowhere.

"Jesus, you scared me." My hand clutches my chest.

"Sorry, I heard you talking to Chase."

"Is he like officially living with us?" I whisper.

"I'm not really sure." He shrugs. "He's got a lot of shit going on. Are you okay with him crashing here? Because if you aren't..." I love that Alec would be willing to kick his friend out if it makes me uncomfortable, but I would never ask him to do that, and truthfully, I don't mind Chase here.

"No...He's fine staying here. I was just thinking that maybe you should offer to share your bed, so he doesn't have to keep sleeping on the couch." I smirk playfully.

"Men don't share beds like you women do. The couch is all he's getting." He steps closer, invading my personal space, and I suddenly find myself backed up against the wall in our hallway. "But I wouldn't mind sharing a bed with you." He waggles his eyebrows, and the butterflies that were dormant in my belly take off. This is exactly why I've been avoiding Alec.

"I don't think that would be a good idea," I breathe out.

"On the contrary." Alec rests his palms on either side of my head. "I think it would be a great idea." He runs his nose along my cheek and down my jawline. "What do you say, Lex?" He presses his lips to the rapidly beating pulse point on my neck. "Share a bed with me, and we can give Chase his own room."

"Shit, sorry, guys," Chase says, walking past us and snapping me out of the moment. "I'm jumping in the shower and then I'll be out of your hair."

"Actually," I say, ducking under Alec's arm. "Alec and I were just talking."

"We were?" Alec says, his voice perking up.

"Yeah. We were saying, instead of you sleeping on the couch, you can have one of the rooms."

Chase's brows go to his forehead. "You don't have to do that."

"We know, but we want to. I have to talk to Georgia, but I'm sure she'll agree. I'll move my stuff into her room and then you can have my room."

"You sure?" Chase asks.

"Yeah."

"Thanks." He smiles appreciatively. "Let me know how much the bills are, and we'll split them," he says before he disappears into the bathroom.

Once he's gone, Alec is back in my space. "Georgia has a new boyfriend. Don't you think she'll want her own space? You can share a room with me."

"Good one." I pat his chest. "Not happening."

He chuckles. "Oh, it will definitely happen. You *will* be sharing a bed with me soon enough." He lowers his head and brings his lips to my ear. "And when it does, it's going to be fucking amazing."

After I shower, since I'm not tired but don't want to leave my room, I lie in bed and pull up surfing videos on my laptop. With Alec on my mind, it's hard to focus on what I'm watching. A few videos in, there's a knock on my door. I consider pretending I'm asleep in case it's Alec, but worry it might be Georgia. She's been hanging out with Robert a lot lately. I need to make it a point to hang out with her soon so we can talk about him.

"Come in," I call out.

Of course it's Alec who steps through my doorway. Dressed in a pair of red basketball shorts hanging low on his hips, a white T-shirt stretched across his chest, and a knowing smirk on his lips, he saunters into my room like he owns the place.

"What do you want?" I groan.

"I thought we could watch TV." He shrugs, nodding for me to scoot over. When I ignore his silent request, his mouth quirks into a lopsided grin. "Have it your way."

Before I can protest whatever he's thinking of doing, he's scooping me into his arms. He plops onto my bed and settles me across his lap, his arms encasing my body tightly, so I can't try to crawl off him.

"Alec!" I shriek, wriggling to get free.

"I wouldn't do that if I were you," he warns.

Confused, I continue wriggling, until I feel something hard against my ass, and then it hits me—I'm grinding against his crotch. My neck and cheeks warm in embarrassment, and Alec barks out a laugh.

"Fuck, you're so adorable."

When I glare at his choice of words, he sobers. "Hey, there's nothing wrong with being adorable."

"Little kids are adorable." I pout. "Puppies are adorable..."

"*You* are adorable," he repeats. "Ninety-nine percent of the time, you're this badass, wild little thing who takes no prisoners. Nothing bothers you; nobody fazes you. But then, every once in a while, you let a select few see the *real* you. The you that's vulnerable and insecure and shy." Alec runs his fingers through my hair and, stopping at the back of my nape, tugs softly so my chin is jutted out and we're locking eyes. "The way your skin turns the most beautiful shade of pink, giving away your true feelings. It's so fucking adorable, and beautiful, and sexy."

I swallow thickly at his words, trying to push the golf ball-sized lump down my throat so I can breathe. He warned me he wasn't going to give up, but I wasn't prepared for all this. His words, his touch...

"You're not playing fair," I whisper, my heart beating erratically.

"I never said I would," he murmurs. His fist tightens on my hair and he pulls my face to his. "Your excuse for not giving us a chance is that I only want you because my dad died, but that's not the truth and we both know it. You're scared to let me in, and I get it, Lex. I was scared too. Hell, I still am. I told you the kiss shouldn't have happened because I was terrified of what it would mean to admit my feelings for you. But now, I'm more terrified of you never knowing how I feel. Of us never getting our chance." He brushes his lips against mine, and a shiver erupts down my spine.

"I'm in love with you, Lexi," he says against my mouth. "And all I want is to show you just how much..."

"Alec," I breathe, but the argument can't get past my lips.

"I love you," he repeats. "And I know you love me."

I should tell him it would be better to wait until he isn't so emotional to make a decision like this. Give him more time to grieve over his father. There's a chance he's going to wake up in the morning and want to take this all back, but he's right. I do love him. I've been in love with him for years, and what if he wakes up in the morning and still feels the same way? Sure, there's a chance we end up like Joey and Dawson, but what if we're not them? What if we're actually Joey and Pacey, and taking this chance means we'll get our happily ever after? It's a chance I have to take. Because if I don't, I know I'll always regret it.

"I do love you," I admit. "I've been in love with you for as long as I can remember. I don't even know when it happened. Maybe it was when we were younger and you would help me defend Georgia against the mean kids at school. Or it might've been when you would pick me up at five in the morning to take me surfing because you had your license and I didn't, and you would sit in the sand and watch me for hours without complaining. I don't know. I just never..." My voice wavers as I'm overcome with emotions I never thought I'd be able to express. "I never thought you would ever feel the same way, and now that I know you do, I'm scared shitless."

"Don't be scared," Alec murmurs, his lips now only mere centimeters away from mine.

"How can I not be? If we do this and it doesn't work out, I'll lose you." I twist my body so I'm straddling Alec, then push him so he's lying on his back, his head resting against my tall stack of fluffy pillows. "I can't lose you."

His hands come around and cup the backs of my thighs, grinding my center against him. "You're not going to lose me," he promises. "No matter what happens, we'll always be in each other's lives." His brown eyes plead for me to believe him, to believe *in* him, in *us*.

There are so many things that can go wrong. I'm not a relationship expert by any means, but I'm old enough to know the odds are against us. Every adult in my life didn't find their forever until they experienced heartbreak. If we give in to what we want, there's a huge chance we might end up breaking each other's hearts.

"Don't do that," Alec says, fisting the back of my ponytail. "Don't think of everything that can go wrong." He pulls my face down to his. "Don't set us up for failure before we've even begun. Let's just take it one day at a time."

"One day at a time," I repeat, taking a deep breath. I can do that. One. Day. At a time.

"One day," he murmurs against my lips. "One moment... One kiss..."

I wrap my arms around his head, and my fingers thread through his short hair. His lips part mine, and his tongue sinks inside. Warmth floods through my veins as his tongue strokes mine. He kisses me gently, with patience, proving through his actions that he really is taking it one moment at a time. And I have to say, this moment feels damn good.

Since I'm in only a tank and a pair of cheeky underwear, Alec massages the globes of my ass, gently grinding our bodies against one another, the friction hitting my clit in all the right ways.

Needing to feel more of him, I break our kiss and pull at the bottom of his shirt, silently telling him what I want. With eyes screaming of love and desire, he sits up and yanks his shirt over his head, revealing his perfect body. I rub my hands down his sculpted, tattoo-covered chest, then place open-mouthed kisses to each of his nipples, before I begin to work my way down each of his rippled abs. His skin is soft yet firm, only a sprinkle of dark hair running down the center. I've fantasized so many times about what Alec would feel like... taste like... but none of my fantasies did him any justice.

I pepper kisses down his happy trail, excited to be so close to the Promised Land. When I arrive at my destination, I lower his shorts and his dick springs free. It's thick with a single vein running from root to tip, and my mouth waters at the sight, wanting to taste him. I fist his hard shaft gently, then wrap my mouth around the swollen head. It's smooth and tastes clean, the scent of the soap he uses in the shower lingering on him.

I take him into my mouth, as far as I can go, dragging my teeth along his entire length. Alec hisses, gripping my nape, as I run my tongue along the same area, licking away the sting.

"Jesus fucking Christ," he growls, tugging my head off his dick. My mouth makes a popping sound and saliva drips down my chin.

Alec flips us over so I'm on my back and he's hovering above me. He licks his way up my chin then sucks my bottom lip into his mouth before releasing it.

"It's my turn," he murmurs, pulling my top down and exposing my breasts.

"But I didn't get to finish." I pout.

"Patience," he says, as he wraps his lips around my pebbled nipple and sucks on it. Electric waves shoot through my body, as if there's a direct path from my breast to my core. Wrapping my legs around Alec's waist, I clench my thighs together.

"I need—"

The door swings open, making us both jump. Alec's head swings to the side as my eyes pop open to see who's there, realizing when Alec came in to talk to me, he never closed the door.

"Hey, Lex, I—Oh my God!" Georgia squeals, at the same time I shriek, "Georgia!" as I try to cover my breasts—which is really pointless since my sister has seen me naked plenty of times over the years. But in this moment, I'm not exactly thinking clearly...

"Sorry!" she yells, slamming the door behind her.

Alec glances back at me, his face a bit flushed, and his eyes wide in shock and embarrassment. Makes sense since Georgia probably got a nice peek of his butt since, at some point, he removed his shorts and boxers.

"Well, that was one way for her to find out about us," he finally says.

"Yeah." I laugh, covering my chest back up since the moment has been ruined. "I should probably go talk to her."

"Okay." Alec drops his hands to either side of my head and presses his mouth to mine. "But when you're done, we're moving your stuff into my room."

It takes me a second to understand what he's talking about, but when I do, I shake my head. "No way, it's too soon. I'm moving into Georgia's room with her."

Alec eyes me for a brief moment, as if he's trying to think of his argument.

"Fine," he finally says with a shrug. "You want to share a closet with her, so you can tell yourself we're taking this slow, have at it, but you'll be in my bed every. Single. Night."

## CHAPTER ELEVEN

### ALEC

"There." I drop onto the bed in Chase's new room. "Everything has been moved out and into Georgia's room." I shoot Lexi a mock-glare, and she giggles. She can laugh all she wants, but there's no way she's spending a single night in bed with her sister instead of with me—at least not on the nights I'm home. If she wants to share a bed with her when I'm on shift, she's more than welcome to. But the nights I'm home, her warm body will be wrapped around mine—just like she was last night.

"Maybe we should get him a more manly comforter," Georgia suggests, glancing around the room. Since Georgia already has furniture, we left all of Lexi's in here for Chase. All we did was move his clothes, which were shoved into the corner of the living room, into his new room. The girls hung them up and folded them neatly into the drawers.

"It's a room and has a comfortable bed. Chase won't give a shit about the color of the comforter." I stand and pull Lexi into my arms, fucking stoked that I get to touch her and kiss her and hold her whenever I want now. "Want to grab something to eat?"

"Sure," she says, pecking me on my lips. I want to drag her to my room so I can continue exploring her body, but I hold back—there will be plenty of time for that.

"Georgia, want to ask Robert to join?" she asks her sister.

"He's still at work," Georgia says. "And I have homework to get done before class tomorrow. You guys go ahead."

"You sure?" Lexi asks.

"Yeah, but if you want to bring me home something, I won't stop you." Georgia smiles, then exits the room.

"Since it's late, we can just grab something at the pier," Lexi suggests.

"Sounds good."

It's a nice night, so we jump into Lexi's jeep. The beach is only a short drive from where we live, and a few minutes later, we're parking.

"I'm starved," Lexi groans, taking my hand in hers. I glance down at our joined hands, loving how easy it was, once we gave in, for us to move from best friends to more. It's only been a few hours, but her taking my hand tells me she isn't second-guessing shit.

We place two orders of fish and chips then find an empty table. Lexi sits next to me and I pull her into my arms, kissing her while we wait. Now that I've knocked down that wall, and I know I get to have her this way, I can't fucking get enough of her.

"Lexi?" a gruff voice says from behind us.

We both turn and find Jason standing there with his board in his hands. He's in his wetsuit, the top half unzipped and pulled down to his waist. He must've just come up from surfing.

"Hey," Lexi says slowly.

"What's this?" Jason asks, nodding toward us. It's obvious by the way we're sitting what *this* is, so I'm assuming he's asking out of shock not ignorance.

Lexi tries to pull her hand out of mine, and when I tighten my grip, she whips her head back around and glares. "I need to talk to Jason real quick," she says, her tone even. "Can you give me a minute?"

Not wanting to be a possessive dick, I nod, but when my eyes land on Jason, who's glaring my way, I can't help myself.

Holding on to her hand, I pull her face toward mine and kiss her hard. My tongue pushes past her parted lips and I devour her. The kiss is short, but my point is made.

When the kiss ends, Lexi sighs in contentment, and then, as if her foggy head has suddenly cleared, she pulls her hand back and her mouth forms a flat line. "Not cool, Alec."

"Maybe not." I shrug. "But he needs to know you're mine." I lean in and press my mouth to hers. "And I'm yours."

"When you say shit like that, it's hard to be mad at you."

Without waiting for me to respond, she stands and approaches Jason. Of course, at that moment, our order number is called. Figuring it's best to give her a minute, I get up and grab our food from the counter.

As I'm walking back over to the table with our food, my eyes find Lexi, who's still talking to Jason. Her back is ramrod straight and she's shaking her head. Jason's glaring at her, his eyes filled with anger. I don't want to interfere, but I'm not about to let him make her feel bad for choosing to be with me.

I set our tray of food on the table, then walk up to them, wrapping my arm around Lexi's waist. The second she glances over and sees it's me, I feel her instantly soften into my side.

"You mind?" Jason snaps. "We're talking."

"Not with that tone, you're not." I remove my arm from Lexi and step into Jason's space.

His glare moves from Lexi to me. "That isn't up to you."

"Lexi, you done?" I ask, without looking at her.

"Jason, I really am sorry," she says, her voice filled with remorse. "I didn't plan for this to happen…"

"You don't have to explain shit to him," I tell her, backing up from Jason and taking her hand. "Our food's getting cold." I pull her away from him, refusing to give him any more of my time. He's pissed he lost his shot with her, and I get it, but it's not my damn problem, and quite frankly, it's not hers either. And it sure as hell doesn't warrant him giving her shit.

"You okay?" I ask, when I notice she's eating her food in silence.

"Yeah." She shrugs a single shoulder. "I just feel bad."

"For what? You went out with him once and it didn't work out. That's called dating. It doesn't always end up in marriage."

"I know," she says with a sigh, "but he called me a tease, said I led him on. And maybe he's right…"

"Bullshit," I argue, refusing to listen to her put herself down.

That guy is damn lucky he's already left. If I see him again, we're going to have some words.

"I did only agree to go out with him with the hope of knocking you out of my thoughts." She glances out at the water, her eyes full of guilt.

"Hey." I press my palm to her cheek, forcing her to look at me. "He's a grown ass man. No, you probably shouldn't have agreed to go out with him if you weren't interested, but it doesn't matter. You followed through and went on your date. You weren't interested in going out again, so you didn't. Some guys have trouble with being let down, but that's not your fault. It's his, and he needs to get over it."

"Okay," she says, twisting her mouth into a small smile. "I'm done. Want to grab Georgia something to eat and then head home?"

"Yeah." When my lips pull into a grin, Lexi's own smile widens.

"You're totally thinking about getting laid." She smacks my shoulder playfully. "I should make you wait..."

"Until when? Marriage?" I volley, imagining Lexi walking down the aisle in a beautiful wedding dress.

"Yeah," she smarts.

"Fine."

Her eyes widen. "Fine?"

"Yeah, I have no intention of waiting long to marry you anyway. I've waited years to be with you, what's a couple more months?"

"A couple months?" she shrieks. "You're crazy!"

"About you." I pull her into my arms. "I don't want to waste any time, Lex. I love you and you love me. I want to marry you... and soon."

"Are you proposing?"

I shake my head. "When I propose, I'll have a ring and it will be romantic. You deserve that."

"Well, that's good to know," she says with a soft laugh. "Now I'll be waiting and wondering when."

She snakes her arms around my neck and threads her fingers through my short hair, then climbs into my lap, not giving a shit that there are people surrounding us. "But until then, I don't want to wait. Like you said, we've both waited a long time to be together. With anyone else, it would feel like we're rushing, but you're my path, Aleczander Sterling."

"I don't know what the hell a path is, but I like that I'm yours, Alexandria Scott."

She giggles, and the sound does shit to my insides. "Georgia and I made it up. It's not a real path... It just represents us trying to find our way because we both feel lost."

"We're young, Lex, and we're not always going to know which way to go, but I can promise you, no matter what, I'll be by your side while you're trying to figure it out."

"I like the sound of that," she says, softly pressing her mouth to mine. Her tongue slides through my parted lips, and I taste the lemonade she was drinking mixed with Lexi. We kiss for a few minutes, until she grinds her center against my dick, and I remember where we are.

Something prickles in the back of my neck, like a sense we're being watched. My eyes scan the area, not seeing anyone paying attention to us, but I still don't like it. "Let's take this back to the house," I murmur against her lips. "Where I can explore every inch of your body without an audience."

After getting Georgia's food, we jump into Lexi's jeep to head home. When we arrive, Georgia is sitting on the couch with Robert watching a movie.

"Hey," she says, jumping up to grab the bag from me. "Thank you. All that studying has me famished." She sits back down and opens the box. "Mmm... this smells so good." She takes a bite of the fried fish and moans. "And tastes just as good."

Robert scrunches his nose in disgust. "Yeah, if you're into clogged arteries."

"Not all of us can eat healthy twenty-four-seven," Georgia says, taking another bite.

"You're an adult, Georgia. A little discipline won't kill you," Robert replies with an eye roll. *Real fucking adult...*

Georgia laughs him off. "The movie just started." She points to the screen. "Want to join us?"

Lexi gives her sister a strained smile, and I can tell she's holding back from saying what's on her mind. We haven't discussed Georgia's boyfriend, but based on the glare she's shooting his way, I'm going to guess she isn't a huge fan.

"Actually, we have somewhere we have to go," I tell her.

Lexi's gaze swings over to me. "We do?"

"Yeah." When I had placed Georgia's food into the back seat I saw Lexi's backpack that I know is full of supplies—which gave me an idea. "We'll be home later."

Taking Lexi's hand in mine, I pull her out the door and back to her jeep.

"Where are we going?" she asks with a playful pout. "I thought you were going to explore me in your room."

I chuckle at how adorable and sexy she is. "When I explore you, I'm planning to be so thorough you'll be screaming my name. And that's not something I want to do with your sister and her *boyfriend* in the living room."

"Not a fan of his either?"

"Something about him just rubs me the wrong way."

"I agree. But Georgia is happy, and he's her first real boyfriend. I don't want to be a Debbie Downer."

"We'll keep an eye on him." I don't give a shit how excited Georgia is to finally have a boyfriend. If that fool doesn't treat her the way she deserves, I'll kick his ass to New York.

"So, where are we going?" she asks when I open her door for her.

"I saw your art supplies in the back. I was thinking we could take a little field trip."

"You want to watch me graffiti a wall?" she asks incredulously.

"I've seen your work all over the city, but I've never actually seen you do it."

"If we get caught, we'll be arrested," she warns. "I don't have anything to lose, but you have a job you love, and…"

"I'm not worried." I dip my head and press my lips to hers. "Show me a night in the life of Alexandria Scott."

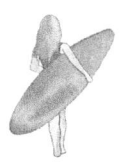

## CHAPTER TWELVE

### LEXI

As I drive down the back streets of LA, Alec and I are both silent. I've never allowed anyone to witness my work firsthand. Sure, my close friends and family know which pieces I've graffitied, but it's always been something I do on my own. When I'm feeling down, and the world is feeling a little uglier than usual, it's my way of adding beauty to it, making my small little mark in the big bad world.

I was prepared to go home and have sex with Alec, something that is considered to be the most intimate act between a man and a woman, yet somehow the thought of him watching me paint feels as if I'm baring myself to him—cracking my chest open and pouring my heart and soul into his hands.

I find an abandoned building the city has bought but hasn't torn down yet and park around the corner. Reaching back, I grab my backpack that contains my spray paints, then hop out of my jeep. Wordlessly, Alec follows after me, over to the giant brick wall. There are already several tags littering the wall, but I find a good blank spot I can make my mark on.

Unzipping my bag, I grab the different colors I want to use and begin to create my picture. Tonight's image is Alec-inspired. He stands behind me, watching, but doesn't say a word the entire time. I get lost in my creation. With every spray of paint, a piece of ugly is transformed into something beautiful. A bit of darkness is brightened.

When I'm done, I draw my moniker on the bottom of it—a multi-colored silhouette of a woman holding her surfboard—then step back to check out the finished product. It's my signature night sky with bright, twinkling stars above the ocean, but tonight, I added a boy and a girl facing each other. They're small in comparison to the large sky, because in the grand scheme of things, we all are—just two people in a world filled with billions. Next to them is the quote Alec's mom recited at his birthday dinner: *You don't find love... it finds you.*

"Holy shit, Lex," Alec says, finally speaking. He snakes his arms around me and rests his chin on my shoulder. "Do you have any idea how fucking talented you are?"

"It's just graffiti." I shrug a shoulder nonchalantly. "Talent is Picasso or Van Gogh... Monet or Magritte."

Alec's hands grip the curves of my hips, and he twirls me around, backing me up against the brick wall. "I don't know who half those people you named are, but I know that that painting"—he juts his chin toward the wall behind me—"is fucking amazing. How you were able to take something as simple as spray paint and turn it into something so awe-inspiring blows my mind. It's us, right?" His eyes bore into mine. "The boy and girl... love found them."

"Yeah," I choke out, swallowing the lump in my throat. "It's us." Tears prick my lids as I'm suddenly overcome with emotion. Usually I draw a painting and then leave it behind. I'm not forced to face what I draw or why I draw it. But standing here with Alec, I want—no, I *need* him to know what this painting means to me.

"I have this amazing, beautiful life that's filled with supportive, loving parents, a sister who is more like my soul mate, and friends and family like you and Micaela. But even with all the good, I still feel like something is off. Like something is missing. I don't know if it's genetic..." I swallow down the raw emotions I feel when I talk about the woman who gave birth to me and then abandoned me. "My biological mom, Gina, was a druggie who was unhappy until the day she died."

"You're not her, Lex."

"That's the problem. I don't know *who* I am, what I want to do with my life. It's why Georgia and I made that pact about finding our perfect path, so we could find our way." I raise my hands and frame Alec's face—the scruff tickling my palms. "Georgia took off out of the gate, making all these changes, and I was worried she would leave me behind, but then you came along and found me —*love* found me, found *us*, and now... I'm still lost. I have no idea what my future holds, but that dark, scary path just got a whole lot brighter because of you."

"I've always been here, Lex, and I always will be." Alec kisses the tip of my nose, and the simple act sends sparks through my body. "You *will* find your place in the world." He dips his face and brings his mouth to my ear. "Watching you in your element was the most beautiful thing I've ever witnessed, and I have no doubt that one day you will find exactly where you belong. But here's the thing..." He trails kisses down my neck and then suckles on my pulse point. "Life isn't about the destination, so while you're searching for where you want to end up, we're going to enjoy the beautiful journey we're going to take together to get there." His lips move up my neck and he peppers kisses along my jawline. "Every step..." He kisses the corner of my mouth. "Every detour..." He kisses my chin. "Every moment will be beautiful in its own way."

Our mouths fuse together and our tongues unite, stroking, teasing, caressing one another. Without breaking our kiss, Alec grabs the globes of my ass and lifts me. My legs wrap around his torso at the same time my fingers weave through his hair. Since I'm in a jean skirt, the denim scrunches up to my waist, leaving only the barrier of my thin panties between us. As we devour each other, I grind against his hard stomach, and it's almost as if we're skin to skin. My center rubs up against him, my clit receiving the perfect amount of friction to send me soaring, as my orgasm rips through me. He deepens our kiss, swallowing my moans of pleasure. My legs are shaking, my breathing erratic. My clit is overly sensitive. But I want more. I need more.

I reach down to undo Alec's pants, but he stops me. "Not here," he murmurs against my lips. "Not where anyone can watch. You're mine," he growls. "Only mine."

Alec kneads my ass cheeks, digging his fingers into my flesh, as he lifts me off the wall. With me in his arms, he dips down, grabs my backpack, and carries me to the jeep. He sets me in the passenger seat then rounds the front of the vehicle. The entire drive home, I can't keep my hands off him. I run my fingers through his hair, palming his denim-covered crotch. I pepper kisses along his neck and stubbled jaw. More than once, I beg him to pull over so I can climb on top of him and fuck him, but he refuses, telling me he's going to take his time worshipping me.

When we finally get home, we rush through the condo and head straight to Alec's room. Georgia's door is closed, and since I saw Robert's car in the guest parking, I know he's in there with her.

The second Alec's door is closed, he's on me. He lifts and drops me onto the center of his king-sized bed. I part my thighs and smirk knowingly when his eyes land on my exposed panties.

"They're drenched," he growls, lifting his shirt over his head and dropping it to the floor. "I can see the wet spot where you came. Take your skirt off," he demands, unbuttoning and unzipping his jeans. With his pants like that, I can see his happy trail leading to his black briefs, and my first thought is how badly I want to lick down it, until I get to the top of his hard shaft and—

"Now," Alec says, shaking me from my own little fantasy.

I undo the buttons on my skirt and shimmy it down my thighs. My eyes stay trained on Alec, who's pushing his jeans and briefs down his muscular thighs. His hard length springs from its confines and bobs once against his stomach before it points straight out at me.

I lick my lips and squeeze my thighs together at the sight in front of me. I can't believe Alec is actually mine. Mine to kiss, mine to touch, mine to love.

All. Fucking. Mine.

He steps out of his clothes and saunters over to the bed. He crawls over to me and pushes my thighs back apart. I watch, unsure what he's going to do first. Will he kiss me? Fuck me? Touch me? The possibilities are endless, and the best part is, whatever we don't do right now, we can do later. Tomorrow, the next day, next week. We have our entire lives ahead of us to do whatever we want with each other.

He dips his face between my legs, and even though I can't see him, I can feel him run his nose along my damp center. And then, he inhales. Actually breathes in my scent, and I damn near orgasm on the spot.

"Fuck, Lex," he murmurs. I've never had a guy this up close and personal before. I should probably feel a little self-conscious, but with Alec, I feel nothing but comfortable.

He finally hooks my panties and pushes them down my legs. He places kisses along the insides of my thighs until he gets back to my center, and then he devours me—licking, sucking, nipping at my clit. He works me over until the most intense orgasm hits me like a tidal wave, wave after wave washing through me.

When I can't take it anymore, I pull him up and crash my mouth against his. He tastes like *me*, and hot damn, if that isn't a turn-on.

"I need you inside me, now," I whisper against his lips.

Alec leans over me and lifts my shirt over my head. Then reaching behind me, he unsnaps my bra and peels it off me, leaving me completely naked and under him. As he backs up, he trails kisses along my collarbone and down my chest, giving each of my breasts a kiss. He quickly licks my nipples before he sits back up. With him positioned between my thighs, he lifts my legs and hooks them over the crook of his arms. His palms land on either side of my face, forcing my legs to almost hit my chest.

With his mouth seared to mine, he enters me in one fluid motion, so deep my back arches off the bed. With our bodies flush against one another, he fucks me with abandon while devouring my mouth. With every swipe of his tongue, thrust of his pelvis, explosions of chills race up my spine. Butterflies swarm in my belly, and all too soon I'm losing myself to another orgasm. Alec's pace picks up, and then he quickly pulls out. He drops my legs and grips his shaft, stroking it tightly. His chest is rising and falling in quick succession, and his skin is glistening with sweat. His brown eyes watch with lust and fascination as cream-colored beads of cum spurt out and onto my belly and chest.

When there's nothing left for him to release, he drops his now-soft dick and sighs. "If I could, I would keep you just like this. In my bed, covered in my cum." My thighs squeeze at his dirty talk. This is a side of Alec I've never seen, and holy hell, if it doesn't make me want him that much more. What's that saying? *A gentleman in the streets, and a freak in the sheets...*

His gaze lifts and meets mine. "I've waited so fucking long for this, Lex." His fingers swipe up the sticky cum and he trails it up my torso and onto my breast. He swirls it around my hard nipple. "Now that you're mine, I hope you realize I'm never fucking letting you go."

My insides knot at his words, and I pull at his shoulders to bring his mouth to mine. "That's good, Alec, because I never want you to let me go."

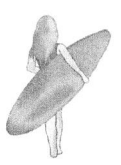

## CHAPTER THIRTEEN

### ALEC

I WAKE up to the sound of Lexi softly snoring. Her body is draped across mine, and her head is nestled against my chest, with my arm wrapped around her. Since she was covered in my cum—something I was completely okay with but at the same time understood why she wasn't keen on going to sleep in that condition—we jumped into the shower together. Since I have the master bedroom, I also have an en suite bathroom. We stayed in the shower, kissing and washing each other, until the water ran cold, and then, after she dressed in a shirt of mine—and nothing else—we climbed back into my bed, where we made out like teenagers until we eventually passed out.

Now it's morning, and I wish we could stay in bed all day—hell, if it were up to me, we would stay in bed all fucking year. When Lexi is in my arms, the ache I feel over losing my dad hurts a little less. I know she can't replace him—nobody can. But for years, he was rooting for Lexi and me to get together. It's actually bittersweet when you think about it. I finally got the girl, but I lost my dad. He's not here to congratulate me, to be by my side when we one day get married—which, if I have it my way, will be sooner rather than later. He won't be here to hold his first grandchild when we have kids.

"What's going through that head of yours?" Lexi asks, running her fingers up my bare chest.

I glance down at her, and her brows furrow. "Alec," she says, scooting closer, so she's lying on me, our faces close. "Why are you crying?"

I blink rapidly and can feel what she's referring to. Thinking about my dad brought tears to my eyes. Not wanting to ruin our time together, I shake my head, but Lexi immediately shakes hers back.

"Don't tell me nothing. You have tears in your eyes." She lifts her hand and swipes at a tear that escaped. "Talk to me."

"I was thinking about my dad," I admit. "Of everything he'll miss. Everything I won't be able to share with him because he's gone."

Lexi nods in understanding, then climbs on top of me, so we're face-to-face. Her thighs grip my torso, and I can feel her heat against my skin. "I won't even pretend to know what you're going through," she says. "I've never lost anyone, except my bio mom, but really, I never had her, so I know it's not the same. But, I knew your dad, and he loved you so much, and I'd like to think he's in heaven watching over you."

"I hope you're right," I tell her, and then to lighten the mood, I add, "but hopefully not *all* the time." I waggle my brows and flex my hips, making Lexi giggle.

"You're such a perv." She swats at my chest playfully.

"And I'm *your* perv."

She snorts a laugh. "What are we doing today?"

"Is staying in bed an option?" I half-joke.

"I need to go to the beach later to get some surfing in. And I was thinking we could ask our parents to go to dinner so we could tell them about us. I don't want them to find out from anyone else but us."

I love that she wants to tell our families. It means she's serious about us, which is good since I'm dead fucking serious about her.

"That sounds good. I want to go by Lacie's to check on her. Want to go with me? We can grab a late breakfast afterward." I told Lexi about Lacie being pregnant and her plan to move closer to her sister. I offered to help her pack up, but she insisted on hiring a service.

"Of course."

After calling our parents and texting Georgia, we head out. As we're walking past Lexi's jeep to my truck, she stops and gasps. "What the hell?" Keyed into the driver side of her jeep, reads, *slut,* the line from the t continuing across the entire side of her vehicle. "Who would do this?"

"If I had to guess... Jason." I pull my phone out to call the police so we can file a report. "He's pissed you didn't want to date him and now he's being fucking immature."

Lexi's head whips around to look at me. "That asshole... When I see him, I'm going to kick his ass."

"You're not going anywhere near him. If he has the balls to do this shit, who knows what else he's capable of."

She growls, and I chuckle at how feisty my woman is.

After filing a report with the police, and then calling Lexi's insurance company to file a claim, we finally take off as planned.

Our first stop is to visit Lacie, who, for the most part, is doing okay. She tells us she's not ready to sell the firm she and my dad own, but she's going to delegate from her sister's. I tell her whatever she wants to do is up to her. My dad left me a nice-sized nest egg with his life insurance policy he had, but everything else was left to Lacie, which I completely agreed with. She was his wife, his partner.

She also tells us how happy she is that Lexi and I are finally together. "Your dad would be so happy for you," she says, tears filling her eyes. "He would always say you two were meant to be together."

"I wish he were here," I tell her, missing him so fucking much and hating that I'll never see him again.

"Me too," she agrees, rubbing her belly.

After talking with her for a little while longer, we say our goodbyes and then go to breakfast at Jumpin' Java in Larchmont. It's Lexi's favorite coffee shop. We've both known the owner since we were little, so when we walk in holding hands, her face lights up. She runs around the counter and gives us both a hug. "I knew it! I knew one day you two would end up together. I'm so happy for you both."

After placing our order, Lexi suggests we take it to go, so we can walk around Larchmont since it's a nice day out. While we walk down the sidewalk, we hold hands and talk. Since my dad passed away, I've felt like I'm always one step away from losing my shit, but when I'm with Lexi, it feels like I can breathe. She chats away about the upcoming surfing competition and how excited she is, and I listen to her, enjoying her company.

"Dinner with our parents isn't until later," she says when we return to my truck. "If you want to drop me off at my jeep, I can take it to the beach to get some surfing in and meet you back at home later."

"I only have a little more time until I go back to work. I want to go." I also want to make sure Lexi doesn't confront Jason. I would hope he wouldn't do anything to her in person, but you never know what someone scorned is capable of, and I'm not about to risk Lexi going to the beach alone right now.

After stopping at the house so Lexi can grab her beach stuff, we head back out. When we get there, we find an area where there aren't too many people and spread out a blanket.

"I'll try not to be too long," she says, peeling her shirt off her.

"Take as long as you want." I pull her by the wetsuit that's hanging at her waist and tug her toward me. She falls gently onto her knees between my legs, and I pull her up so she's lying across the top of me.

Our mouths connect, and my tongue slips past her parted lips. I find her tongue, sucking on it until she moans into my mouth. She tastes like the mocha coffee she was drinking—sweet and fucking addictive. I slide my hands to her ass and squeeze her ass cheeks, pulling her closer, until she's on top of me and rubbing her warmth against my dick.

"Get a room!" someone yells, making Lexi groan and attempt to move off me. Not wanting her to go anywhere—and yeah, maybe I'm staking my claim—I grip her hips and pull her into my lap.

She squeals in shock, then laughs, but doesn't move. "Alec, I need to hit the waves."

"I need your mouth," I argue, fisting her ponytail and pulling her face to me for another kiss.

"So, this is why my sister called a family meeting," Lexi's brother, Max, says, dropping next to us with his camera in his hands.

"What are you doing here?" Lexi asks.

"Summer break," Max smarts.

Lexi glances around, and when her eyes land on a couple guys walking over, she laughs. "You're hanging out with Ricco?"

Max blushes. "I ran into him at the pier and he asked if I wanted to hang out." He shrugs.

"He's older than you, Max," she points out.

"Lex, be my sister, not my mom, please."

"I am being your sister," she says softly so the guys can't hear. "He's more experienced than you... Just be careful, okay?"

"Got it," Max says quickly.

"Well, looky here," Ricco says to Lexi. "I heard the rumors, but I wasn't sure if there was any truth to them." His eyes are filled with humor, so I know he isn't hating on us, but I also know the only person he could've heard the rumor from is Jason, since he's the one who saw us last night.

My eyes go to the owner of the *rumor*, Jason, who's standing back with his board in his hand, glaring at Lexi and me. Our eyes lock and I make it a point to wrap my arms around her waist, nuzzling my face into her neck and kissing her flesh.

"I want to say something to him," she whispers into my ear.

"Not worth it," I tell her. "Let the police handle it." The cops mentioned if we say anything to Jason, he can try to cover up his tracks, so the best thing is to not say a word and let them investigate.

"So, the rumors are true?" Ricco asks. "You two an item?"

"Yeah," Lexi says, giving my cheek a kiss and then standing. "We're a couple."

"About damn time," Max says, leaning over and patting me on the shoulder. "Welcome to the family, man."

"We're just dating," Lexi points out. "He's not family until we're married." She winks flirtatiously, then, grabbing her board, jogs down the beach.

"Semantics!" I call after her.

Max laughs. "Marriage, huh? Just make sure you ask Dad's permission first. You know how he is about his little girls."

Shit... I didn't think about that. I'm dating Tristan Scott's daughter. I'm going to be having dinner with him, and he's going to take one look at us and know I'm sleeping with her. Fuck!

Maybe we can get married today, before we meet them for dinner. Then I can say I've made an honest woman out of her...

"You okay?" Max asks with humor in his voice. "You're looking a little pale."

"Maybe I should go pick up a ring now," I suggest, freaking the hell out.

Max cracks up laughing. "I'm pretty sure Dad knows Lexi isn't a virgin."

I swing my head around and glare at him. No guy wants to be reminded his woman has been with anyone before him. Of course, this only makes Max laugh even louder.

"Okay, my bad." He puts his hands up. "But seriously, we've all been waiting for you two to come to your senses for years. He's not going to be shocked that you're together. Just treat her right and you won't have any problems... with any of us."

"Got it."

I look out at the ocean just in time to see Lexi riding a rather large wave, and Jason sidling up to her. I don't know shit about surfing, but I do know from listening and watching Lexi, encroaching on someone's wave is a huge fucking no.

He comes so close, their boards almost touch, and Lexi ends up wiping out.

"What the hell," Max says, removing the camera from his face.

"He has a thing for your sister," I explain, "and he's pissed he didn't get her." I don't mention he's also most likely the guy who keyed her car, since she hasn't told her parents yet. She's planning to tell them about it tonight at dinner.

I stand, wanting to make sure Lexi is okay. She pops up and grabs her board. Even from up here, I can see the pissed off expression on her face. She is one sexy fucking feisty woman. She paddles to shore, following Jason, and once they're both out of the water, she's stomping toward him, yelling.

I can tell by the way Jason is smirking he got exactly what he wanted: Lexi's attention. The guy seriously rubs me the wrong fucking way.

"I apologized for things not working out between us," she says. "We went on one freaking date! One! For you to call me names and key my jeep is bullshit!" So much for not confronting him...

"But fucking with me in the water is taking this shit too far. You don't. Fuck. With someone. In the water!"

"What do you mean he keyed your car?" Max asks.

"Someone keyed slut into the side of my jeep... hours after Jason called me a tease because I chose to date Alec instead of him."

"You did what?" Max says, stepping up to Jason, who still has a shit-eating smirk plastered on his face. "What the fuck is wrong with you?"

"You have no proof of that," Jason says with a shrug. "Maybe I'm not the only guy your sister was leading on. Who knows how many guys she's letting dick her."

Max punches Jason square in the face. "Don't you ever talk about my sister like that."

Jason stumbles back slightly, and once he gets his footing, steps toward Max.

"You need to get the fuck out of here," I tell Jason, stepping between Jason and Max. "You didn't get the girl, deal with it like a man, not a little bitch."

"Whatever you say," he says through a laugh, already walking away.

"I can't believe him." Lexi huffs.

"Forget him," I tell her. "He's gone now. Go surf and show me how you're going to win this competition." I pull her toward me and kiss her. At first, she's wound up tight, but eventually she softens into the kiss.

"Okay," she murmurs against my lips. "Sorry I let it slip about him keying my jeep."

"Don't worry about it. Just promise me you'll stay away from him." My request isn't coming from a jealous boyfriend, but from someone worried about what that asshole is capable of. I could tell by the smug look on his face he didn't give a shit about being called out or caught.

"I will," she says. "I promise."

For the next few hours, I watch Lexi surf. She's amazing out there. Completely in her element. Eventually Max and Ricco decide to head out, saying they're going to grab a coffee.

While I wait for her, I look up jewelry stores on my phone. I wasn't kidding when I said I'm planning to make her my wife sooner rather than later. I know without a doubt she's the one for me.

While I'm scrolling through rings, my phone goes off with a text.

> **Chase: I crashed on the couch after my shift. Woke up and realized all my shit was gone. Luckily Georgia was here to tell me you moved it all into Lexi's room. Thanks, man. And please tell Lexi thanks.**
> **Me: It's hardly a hardship having Lexi in my room.**
> **Chase: I figured as much. But still... thanks.**
> **Me: We're going to dinner at the Scotts' tonight. Wanna join?**
> **Chase: Thanks, but I'm going to crash. Shift tomorrow. You know, the job you haven't been to in weeks...**

His text reminds me that I go back to work soon. I needed the time off to deal with my father's death. I knew in the state of mind I was in, I wouldn't be of any use to anyone at the fire station, especially if there was an emergency. But now, I'm looking forward to going back to work. I enjoy my job.

> **Me: Yeah, yeah... I know you miss me, sweetie pie. Don't worry, I'll be back next week.**
> **Chase: Oh, thank God, pookie bear.**
> **Me: If you change your mind, just let me know.**
> **Chase: Thanks.**

"You ready to go?" Lexi asks, standing in front of me. She's already unzipped her wetsuit and is pulling it down her toned body, exposing her tiny yellow string bikini she's wearing underneath. Her hair is up in a messy bun, and droplets of water are dripping down her neck and disappearing into the swell of her breasts. Her belly button is sporting a tiny navel ring, and on the curve of her hip is her moniker—a multi-colored silhouette of a woman holding a surfboard.

"What?" She glances down at herself.

"Come here." I grab her hand and pull her down to me. My mouth closes over hers for a hard kiss. "I can't keep my eyes and mouth and hands off you." I drag my hands down to the globes of her perfect ass. "You smell like the ocean," I murmur, kissing her again. Lexi laughs—it's light and carefree and it does crazy shit to my insides.

"We're really doing this, aren't we?" she asks, her ocean-blue eyes sparkling with happiness. I love that I'm the reason for her happiness—that *we're* the reason for her happiness.

"If I have it my way, for the rest of our lives."

After we're packed up, we head up the beach toward her jeep. We're about halfway there when Lexi stops and says, "Do we have any waters left in the cooler?"

"Yeah," I say, confused. It's not that long of a walk to her vehicle. Does she really need to stop and take a drink break?

She grabs a couple waters out of the cooler, then grabs the bowl of fruit we didn't finish. She drops her board where it is and runs toward the pier, yelling that she'll be right back.

Unsure where the hell she's going, I leave the cooler and her beach bag next to her board and follow after her. When she arrives under the pier, there are several tents popped up in the shade. This is common in LA, especially in the parks and on the beaches. Homeless folks sleep in tents anywhere they can pitch one up.

Lexi stops at a particular blue one and says, "Aiden, it's Lexi."

A second later, a tall man steps out of his tent. He looks to be in his late teens, maybe early twenties, dressed in a pair of raggedy jeans and a holey shirt. His long hair is on the greasy side and his face is covered in facial hair. He's wearing a pair of bright green glasses that look like something a child would wear. With a bright smile on his face, he removes the glasses, that is until his eyes land on me, then he immediately puts them back on.

"Lexi, someone is here," he says. "I don't know him, Lexi."

Lexi glances back at me, before turning her attention back to Aiden. "It's okay. That's Alec. He's my boyfriend."

Aiden's fists clench at his sides. "Boyfriends are bad, Lexi. My mom's boyfriend was bad." He grabs Lexi and pulls her behind him. "You go away, Lexi's boyfriend. You are bad."

"No, Aiden. Alec isn't bad. I promise," Lexi says.

"Boyfriends are bad," he repeats. It's clear there's something going on with this guy, but Lexi isn't fazed, which tells me she knows this guy on a deeper level.

"Aiden," she says calmly. "Why was your mom's boyfriend bad?"

"He hurt us," he tells her matter-of-factly. "He yelled at us and he hit us."

"Oh, Aiden, I'm so sorry," she says. "You're right. Your mom's boyfriend was bad, but not all boyfriends are bad. Alec doesn't yell or hurt me, and he's a firefighter. He saves people. He's a good guy."

"Like Fireman Sam?" Aiden asks.

"I don't know who Fireman Sam is," Lexi says honestly, but I know who he is.

"He was a cartoon fireman on YouTube," I tell her.

"He's my favorite hero," Aiden tells her. "But he isn't wearing his fire suit."

"No, he only wears it when he goes to work. I brought you some stuff," Lexi tells him, holding up the bag she placed the food and drinks into.

Aiden looks into the bag and smiles softly at Lexi. Then he pulls her into a tight hug. "Thank you, Lexi," he says. "I like water and fruit. But I like tacos more."

"I know," she replies with a laugh. "But you have to eat food that's good for you too. Not just tacos."

"But I like tacos," he argues.

"I know you do," she says. "I have to get going, but I'll see you soon, okay?"

"Okay! Bye, Lexi, and bye, Lexi's fireman boyfriend."

When we get back to the jeep, Lexi says, "Aiden is autistic... Well, I think he is. I searched his mannerisms on Google and that's what popped up. I don't know much about him except that he loves drawing and he's homeless. He's been living in that tent for the last several months. I always give him food and drinks when I come to the beach."

"Have you thought about telling someone?"

"Who? The police? No way." She shakes her head. "They'll cite him, or worse, arrest him. You saw how he reacted to you. It took months before he warmed up to me. What do you think would happen if the police approached him? No. He's better off where he is. At least he's left alone."

On the ride home, we're both silent, and I can't stop thinking about Aiden. There has to be something we can do to help him. He's not just homeless... There's clearly something more to him, like Lexi said. I make a mental note to ask the guys at work if there's anything in LA that helps or supports homeless people who have special needs.

"Want to shower with me?" Lexi asks once we're home.

I watch as she makes a show of untying the strings that hold her bikini top together and dropping it to the ground, exposing her perfect tits. Next, she pulls the strings on her bottoms and they fall to the floor, leaving her completely naked. I take a moment to take her in: her milky skin that doesn't match how often she's at the beach. Since her dad is naturally tanned, I would bet she gets her creamy complexion from her biological mom, but she never talks about her.

Her blond hair is down in waves. I can remember the day she dyed it. She said she needed a change, and after Georgia talked her out of getting a tattoo—which was a damn good thing since she wasn't eighteen yet—she showed up with her hair dyed blond. I loved Lexi as a brunette, but something about the blond fit her personality better. It was wilder, like her.

My eyes cut to her toned abs and thighs. She doesn't work out at the gym, but she surfs daily, which keeps her in shape. She's tiny, maybe five-foot-four, compared to my six-foot-three self, but for such a little thing, she's all badass. And I love how low-maintenance she is. She prefers to be in a bathing suit and flip-flops. And when she's not at the beach, you can find her in cutoff jean shorts, a tank top, and Vans. What you see is what you get, and I love that about her.

"Alec," she says, taking me out of my thoughts. "Shower?"

Not needing to be asked again, I cut across the room, shedding my shirt along the way, and lift her into my arms. When we get inside the bathroom, I slam the door closed, unsure if my bedroom door is shut, and set her on the counter next to the sink. I part her legs and step between them. She wraps her arms around my neck and her fingers thread through the strands of my hair.

"Fuck, Lex. You're so damn perfect." I take her breast into my hand and wrap my lips around the rosy pink nipple. As I suck on the hardened peak, her back arches and she pushes her chest forward, silently demanding more.

I feel like the luckiest guy in the world that I get to be with Lexi. I hate that we wasted so much time trying to ignore what was right in front of us, but there's nothing we can do about the past. All I can do is try like hell to make up for the lost time, and right now my plan to do that is by making love to her.

Spreading her thighs farther apart, I push a finger inside her. She's already wet, so I don't waste any time pushing another inside. I fingerfuck her until I know she's more than ready, kissing her all over—her neck, her breasts, her lips—and then I pull her to the edge of the vanity.

With my dick as hard as a steel rod, I guide myself into her warmth. Our eyes lock briefly before hers roll back in pleasure. I will never get tired of being the one who brings her pleasure.

Her legs wrap around my waist, and I fuck her slow and deep, enjoying how hot and tight she is. My thumb finds her clit, and I massage circles, working her up until she's screaming out her release.

"Fuck me harder," she demands. "Faster."

Grabbing her thighs, I tug her closer and pick up my pace, doing exactly what she wants. Her cunt clenches around me and she comes again all over my dick. Remembering I'm not wearing a condom, I pull out at the last second and am about to stroke myself, when Lexi drops to the ground and grabs my dick, taking over. Her warm mouth covers the swollen head, and, knowing she's tasting not only me but her own juices, I lose my shit, coming straight down her throat.

"Jesus Christ," I breathe through heavy pants. She looks up at me through her lashes and grins around my dick. Then, the little minx licks the excess cum off my flesh before she stands and runs her tongue along her lips.

"Shower?" she asks, quirking a single brow.

"Shower," I agree.

## CHAPTER FOURTEEN

### LEXI

"You ready to go?" Georgia asks, stepping into our room. I had assumed Alec and I would be driving together to my parents' place for dinner, but instead he told me he needed to meet me there because he had a couple errands to run.

"Yeah." I lean over the dresser and apply a thin coat of lip gloss. "Is Robert coming?" I ask, locking eyes with her in the mirror.

"Maybe, he's still at work." Georgia plasters a smile on her face, which has me turning around, concerned.

"Everything good with you two?"

"Yeah..."

"Don't do that." I walk over to her. "We don't lie to each other, ever."

Georgia nods. "I know. I'm sorry. This is all just new to me. I think everything is good, but I don't have anything to compare it to."

"What has you questioning it?"

Georgia's cheeks turn a light pink. "He, umm... He wants to have sex, and I told him I'm a virgin, and..."

"And he's respecting that, right?" I straighten my spine. I'll be damned if that guy thinks he can bully my sister into doing anything she's not ready to do. "He's not pressuring you?"

"Yeah, no." She shakes her head. "But when I told him I wasn't ready, he kind of looked... disappointed."

"Oh well." My voice rises in annoyance. "You've only been together for a short minute. He can wait as long as you make him, or he can skip rocks."

"You and Alec have had sex," she points out. Then, quickly, she adds, "I'm not judging."

"I know you're not." I take her hand in mine. "You're right. Alec and I made the decision to be together and went from zero to eighty. If he has it his way we'll be married by the end of the week," I joke—kind of. The truth is, I actually believe if I agreed, he would marry me tomorrow. Between the years we wasted not giving into our feelings and him losing his dad, Alec has no desire to waste a second of precious time.

Georgia laughs. "I'm glad you guys are finally together. I just don't know if or when the right time to have sex is. I feel like I've waited this long... Do I just do it and get it over with? Or do I wait for a sign? And if so, what sign am I waiting for? Is there ever a perfect moment to lose your virginity, except for on your wedding night?"

This time it's my turn to laugh. "I love you so much." I pull her into a hug. "As you know I lost mine our senior year. I wish I had waited for Alec, but I never thought we would actually get a chance to be together. I obviously can't change anything, so there's no point in dwelling over it. I don't think there's ever a perfect time, but I can tell you that if I could do it over again, I would've at least made sure I loved the guy I was giving my virginity to. Not because the act is so sacred or whatever, but because once I was with Alec, a man I love, it made it so much better. Every kiss and touch is so much more meaningful. Sex with Alec isn't just sex. We make love. He worships me, makes sure I'm taken care of. So, I guess to answer your question, make sure you love Robert."

Georgia nods. "Thank you, Lex." She hugs me. "He's not going to be thrilled, but I'm going to wait."

"And if he doesn't respect that," I say, pulling back and looking into my sister's bright green eyes. "Then dump his ass." She laughs softly. "I mean it. A man who cares about you will wait until you're ready. You're fucking beautiful, Georgia. Robert might be your first real boyfriend, but that's only because you chose not to date until now. Trust me when I tell you, you can get any damn guy you want."

Georgia rolls her eyes. "Whatever, Lex, let's go."

When we walk outside, Georgia sees the damage to my vehicle. "I can't believe Jason did that," she says.

"I know, we have no proof, but I would bet it was him." I tell her what happened at the beach earlier, everything Jason said to me, and how Max punched him.

"Good," she says, her nose scrunching up. "What a loser."

We take Georgia's truck to our parents' place, and when we arrive, I see Alec's truck already in the driveway, along with Mason's BMW.

We walk into the house and the first person I see is Alec. He's wearing a Station 115 shirt that's taut across his chest and a matching hat. He's talking and laughing with my dad, but when he hears the front door close, he stops and turns. Our gazes collide and my stomach does a small flip-flop. We're actually doing this. Alec and I are together.

Without thinking about anyone else who might be watching us, I cut across the room, straight to Alec. It's only been a few hours since I've last seen him, kissed him, but I already miss him. Our mouths crash against each other, as he takes me into his arms.

"I think we were supposed to tell everyone first," he murmurs against my lips when we break our kiss.

It takes me a second, but once I process what he's just said, I glance around the room and find everyone is watching us. My mom and Alec's mom, Mila, both have huge grins on their faces. My dad's face is a mixture of a smile and a glower. My brother and Georgia are both laughing, and Mason is sporting a knowing smirk.

"Well, I guess you all know now." I shrug, feeling a slight blush upon my cheeks.

"We do," Mom says matter-of-factly. "And we're very happy for you both."

She wraps her arms around me, and I sigh into her warm embrace. I might come across like I do whatever I want, but I still care about what my family thinks. Their opinion matters to me because they matter to me.

"Dad, you too?" I ask, just to make sure.

"As much as I hate the idea of my little girls growing up, I know it's inevitable, and it makes me feel a little better to know you're with a man who loves you and will support and take care of you." Dad kisses my cheek. "I love you, Lex."

"Thank you. I love you too, Dad."

---

"THEY TOOK IT WELL," I tell Alec, running my hand up his naked chest. We're lying in bed and have just finished making love for the second time. After we got home from dinner with our parents, we beelined straight to his room and to bed, where we've spent the last couple hours.

"Of course they did." He places a kiss to my temple. "We were apparently the only people who weren't on board with us."

"Hey, I was on board with us." I poke him in the chest and then roll over onto my elbows. "I just didn't think you were, and then once I knew you were, I was afraid you would change your mind, or if we did this and it didn't work out, I would lose you... I'm still worried about that last one."

Alec pulls me on top of him. "I love you, Lex, and I can't say what the future holds because anything can happen." He swallows thickly, and I know he's thinking about his dad. "But as long as I'm alive and you're willing to let me love you, I'm going to spend every day loving you."

Since we're both still naked, I reach behind me and take his hard length into my hand, guiding it inside me. I sigh once I'm completely seated and our bodies are connected in the most intimate way. Leaning forward, I take Alec's face into my hands and whisper against his lips, "And I'm going to spend every day loving you back."

## CHAPTER FIFTEEN

### LEXI

"That was the perfect fucking air wave," Shane says, dropping onto the sand next to me. "If you hit the waves at the comp like you've been doing, I wouldn't be surprised if you take the entire thing. Your life will be changed. Tours, endorsements..."

"That would be awesome," I admit, grabbing a bottled water, twisting the top off, and taking a large gulp. I let Shane's words bump around in my head for a few minutes. For as far as I can remember my world has revolved around art and surfing, but up until now, they felt like hobbies. My parents always tell me how creative I am, and my friends comment on how good of a surfer I am, but none of that means anything if I can't create a future with them. But Shane is right, if I win this competition, I can make a career out of it.

My phone pings from somewhere, and I grab my bag to find it. It's Alec asking where I am. I left him sleeping in bed to get some surfing in. He goes back to work in a few days and can use the sleep. Even though he seems happier with us being together, I know he's still having trouble sleeping at night. He misses his dad and his heart is still broken. I imagine it will be for a long time.

Just as I'm about to text him back, droplets of water hit the phone, making me shove it back in my bag. "Hey!" I exclaim, glancing up. With the sun shining, it takes a second for my eyes to adjust, but once they do, I find Jason standing above me.

"You're soaking my stuff," I tell him, pushing his thighs so he stumbles back.

"Where's your boyfriend?" He runs his fingers through his shaggy blond hair, flinging water all over me like a wet dog.

"Go away, Jason," I say, ignoring his question and pulling my phone back out so I can return Alec's text. I let him know I'm at the beach and will be home soon.

"I was hoping we can talk," he says as I stand, ready to leave.

"There's nothing to talk about."

"Look, I was being a dick." He shrugs a shoulder and scrubs his hand along his scruff. "I shouldn't have gotten that worked up over you and that pretty boy. Everyone knows you don't do serious. Pretty Boy will come and go, and I don't want to lose you in my life." Oh my God! Did he just admit to keying my car, and is acting like it's not a big deal? What the hell is wrong with this guy?

My phone goes off with another text from Alec: **I have the day planned. Meet me at home when you're done.**

I grab my towel from my bag and then throw my phone into it. "His name is Alec, and he isn't going anywhere," I tell Jason, looking him dead in the eyes so he knows I'm serious. "I love him, and it's serious. As for you and me... our friendship is over. Friends don't do the shit you did to me."

"Are you fucking serious?" he spits, stepping closer to me.

"You heard her," Shane says, popping up and stepping in front of me. "What you did wasn't cool, man. Now you gotta deal with the fallout. Walk away."

Jason's nostrils flare, and his fists tighten at his sides, but he does as Shane says and walks away.

"I can't believe him," I say once Jason is gone. "Thank you."

"It's all good," Shane says. "I heard about what happened, and he's way fucking wrong."

"Yeah, just sucks I have to see him here all the time now." Maybe I need to consider finding another surfing spot... "I'm going to head out," I tell him, giving him a hug. "I'll see you later."

On the way to my jeep, I spot Aiden sitting in the sand next to his tent. Remembering I have some extra bottles of water, I head over to give them to him. It's hot out and I bet he can use the fresh, cold water.

"Hi, Aiden. How are you?"

"Hi, Lexi," he says with a smile, his bright green glasses on his face. "I'm okay. I found some crabs. Look." He points to a small bucket with two crabs in it.

"Wow, how cool. Are you going to keep them?"

"No." He shakes his head. "I'm drawing them. See?" In his sketchpad is a drawing of the bucket and two crabs. "I won't hurt them, Lexi. I will let them go."

"That's really good," I say, pointing to the sketchpad.

"Thank you. Wanna see more pictures?"

"Sure." I sit next to him and take the pad from him.

"Be careful. Are your hands clean?" he asks, his head turning toward me.

"They're clean," I promise.

"Okay, good." He sighs, then removes his glasses and clasps them onto the front of his shirt. I noticed a while ago he only removes them when it's just us. A few times that I've been with my friends, he would say hello, but he wouldn't remove his glasses. My guess is he uses them as protection, only removing them when he feels comfortable.

I flip through the pages of his book, in awe of how talented Aiden is. I've seen his drawings before, but every time I see new ones, I'm amazed by just how good he is. It's also obvious he sees everything around him. There are several new drawings of people surfing and swimming. A family having a picnic. There are a few of people kissing and one that looks like two people having sex. I wonder if Aiden knows what he's drawing. If he knows what sex is.

"Aiden, what's this?" I ask, pointing to the drawing of the couple on top of each other.

"That's a man and a woman loving each other," he states matter-of-factly.

"Do you see this a lot on the beach?"

"Yes. I thought the man was hurting the woman, but when I tried to save the woman, they yelled at me and said they love each other."

I stifle my laugh, imagining poor Aiden hearing some woman

getting fucked and screaming and him thinking she was being hurt. He's too innocent and sweet for his own good.

"These are really good," I tell him, handing him back his book. I wish there were something I could do to help him, but I have no clue where to even start, and I'm scared if I speak to the wrong people, I could do more harm than good.

"Thank you, Lexi," he responds, beaming with pride.

"I have some water for you." I grab the bottles of water from my bag and hand them to him. "Are you hungry?"

"I had breakfast," he says honestly. "Brian gave me extra bagels."

Brian is the owner of the breakfast restaurant on the pier. Instead of throwing out the food from the day before, he puts it out for the homeless to take.

"Okay, good. Then I'll see you soon." I always say soon instead of later or tomorrow. I made that mistake once and Aiden accused me of lying because I didn't return later that day or the next.

Fifteen minutes later, I'm stepping through the door as Georgia is walking down the hall with her backpack slung over her shoulder. It's crazy to think in a couple months she'll be graduating from college. I wish I had the motivation for school she does, but if all goes well, I'll win the Vans Surf Classic and be on my way to a career in surfing, which will hopefully open other doors of opportunity. I still plan to finish school, especially since it's so important to my parents, but at least I'll be able to say I've created a future for myself.

She doesn't see me walking up, since she's staring down at her cell phone with a frown marring her face. "Hey," I say to get her attention. Her head pops up and she gives me a strained smile. "What's wrong?"

"I don't know. Hilda sent another email requesting a meeting with me." Hilda is Georgia's biological father's mother—her biological grandmother. Her bio dad died when she was little and she's never had any contact with his family. Our mom is a lot like our dad, tightlipped about their past. I know they're that way to protect us, but we're not babies anymore and deserve to know the truth, even if it's hurt us.

"Have you told Mom?"

Georgia scoffs. "Yeah, right. She'll freak out, probably beg me to delete my email address."

"Maybe, or maybe she'll support you and be there for you. I think she would want to know, and if she finds out from someone other than you, she's going to be hurt. What if Hilda contacts her because you won't respond?"

"Since when did you get so wise?" Georgia jokes. "You're right, I'm going to set up a meeting with her."

"And you're going to tell Mom?"

"Not until I know what's going on. I don't want to upset her. Every time her past gets brought up I can see the pain in her face. I'm not putting her through that if I don't have to. If I feel like I need to tell her, then I will."

"Okay, if you need me, I'm here."

"I know. Thank you. I better get going to class before I'm late. I'll see you later."

I head back to Alec's room and find him in the bathroom brushing his teeth. He's dressed in a pair of jeans that hug his perfect ass and is shirtless, his back glistening with tiny droplets of water from his shower. He glances up at me and smiles, and my insides turn to mush.

"I'm going to take a quick shower," I tell him, stripping out of my clothes and sliding into the shower. When I get out, I towel dry my hair, brush my teeth, and put on deodorant. Unsure of where we're going, I wrap my towel around my body and go in search of Alec to find out how I should dress. When I don't find him in the room, I venture out to the living room, only to find him standing next to Chase and some woman.

*Shit, I didn't think about him being home. And who's that woman?*

At the sight of my towel-clad body, Alec's eyes burn with lust, while Chase glances at me with laughter in his own. The woman next to Chase glares.

"Sorry," I say, quickly backing up. "I wasn't sure where we're going, how I should dress."

"I can show you," Alec says, walking toward me like a lion stalking his prey.

"Oh no!" I exclaim. "You showing me will lead to us never leaving." I turn and race down the hall with Alec following after. I swing open my bedroom door and am about to shut it on Alec, when he slips inside at the last second, slamming it closed behind him.

Gripping my hips, he pushes me against the wall and pulls the knot holding my towel, so it falls to the ground, pooling around my feet. "Fuck, Lex," he growls, capturing my mouth with his own. Heat floods through my veins, warming my entire body. Our kiss deepens, as Alec lifts me up. My legs wrap around his waist and my back hits the wall with a thud. Before my brain can even compute what's happening, his pants are undone and he's entering me. With his mouth devouring mine, he fucks me against the wall.

Every time we're intimate, it's as if the world around us disappears. I hope it's always like this. This hot, this intense, this emotion and lust filled. I rag on my parents for them being all over each other all the time, but now I get it. When you feel the way my parents feel about each other, the way I feel about Alec, all you want to do is show them. It's as if words aren't enough. You can try to explain it, but the depth of your feelings is lost in translation and the only way to completely make it clear is through your actions. Every kiss, every touch, every time we make love, I hope it conveys every emotion I'm feeling.

My body trembles as a mind-blowing orgasm slams into me, taking Alec right along with me. We continue to kiss through our orgasms, until he goes soft inside me, until I can feel his cum leaking out of me and dripping down my leg, and then it hits me...

"You came in me."

Alec's eyes widen and he pulls out, dropping me to the ground. "Shit, sorry, Lex." He winces. "We probably should've had a talk about protection. I've been so consumed with you..."

"Same," I agree. "I'm on the pill, but I'm a slacker about it. I haven't had sex in a while, so..."

Alec grins, liking the fact my sex life has been lacking.

I roll my eyes. "I'll make it a point to be more consistent."

He shrugs a single shoulder. "Worst-case scenario you end up pregnant."

"And my dad kills you," I half-joke, bending and grabbing my towel to wipe myself.

"We'll be married soon," he volleys. "And life is short. If we start a family sooner rather than later, would it be the worst thing?" His lips curve down into a frown. "I meant it when I said I don't want to waste a single day I have with you."

My heart cracks at his words, knowing they're stemming from his dad passing away. "And I want that too," I tell him, dropping the towel and framing his face, "but we're also young and I don't want to rush into anything. I'm hoping to pick up a surfing contract, and..."

"And getting pregnant and surfing don't exactly go hand-in-hand," he finishes.

"No, they don't. But surfing contracts are usually short-term." Which makes me realize the hole in my plan. After the few years of traveling and surfing, what then? I'll be right back to where I started.

"Lex, you okay?" Alec lifts my chin so I'm looking at him. "We don't have to get—"

"It's not that," I say, cutting him off. "I just feel like every time I think I've got my future planned out, something I'm missing pops out and blocks my path."

Alec shakes his head. "That's the beautiful thing about life, Lex. You don't have to pick a path and follow it. You don't have to know your future. Anything can happen at any time, so all you have to do is live and love. Enjoy the beauty in the moment. That's what I'm doing." He kisses the corner of my mouth. "I'm enjoying the beauty in us and finally finding our way to each other. And if you want to talk paths, I think that's a pretty fucking awesome path."

"It's easy for you to say that when you have a career. You're this amazing firefighter who keeps getting promotion after promotion. And if you hadn't chosen to be a firefighter, you could've easily had a career in the UFC. I'm a half-ass college student who surfs and graffitis walls."

"No, Lexi, you're a talented artist and a badass surfer who is only twenty-one and still finding her place in the world, and there's nothing wrong with that. Life isn't a race and in the end we all end up in the same place," Alec says, his jaw clenching. "Dead."

"Alec," I breathe, hating that our hot love-making has turned to this.

"It's the truth. My dad busted his ass to build up his business. He threw his marriage away and didn't find love until years later. Now he's gone and all that's left of him is his pregnant widowed wife and his son who misses the hell out of him." Tears glisten in his eyes. "Don't worry about what you think you should be doing. Focus on what you want to be doing, okay? Live your life and live it for you."

"Okay," I agree. "But what happens if I do win and get a contract? It would mean traveling..."

Alec smiles softly. "Then you travel. You see the world. When I can, I'll join you, and when I can't, I'll be right here waiting for you." He presses his lips to mine, and I sigh into the kiss.

"Nothing is going to keep us apart," he promises once we separate. "Let's get going. I had a plan for today and you're putting us behind schedule."

"Me?" I laugh. "You're the one who attacked me!"

"Because you walked out in a towel."

"I didn't know what to wear."

Alec chuckles. "How about something that covers your body, so I can control myself long enough to get us to our destination."

"Fine, I'll get dressed." I saunter around him, purposely brushing against his body.

"I'll wait for you outside," he groans.

I bark out a laugh as he darts out of the room, leaving me alone to get dressed.

## CHAPTER SIXTEEN

### ALEC

"Where are we going?" Lexi asks once we're in my truck.

I glance over at her and take in how beautiful she looks. Today, in the place of her usual cutoffs and tank, she's sporting a T-shirt and skinny jeans that of course make her look sexy as hell. Her gray shirt, which has Billabong written in big letters across the front, hangs off her shoulder, revealing her bright pink bra strap, and her ripped jeans show more of her flesh than they actually cover, and what is covered is plastered to her like a second skin. Instead of her signature flip-flops, she's sporting a pair of white Vans. And to top her look off, because all of that isn't sexy enough—insert eye-roll—her blond hair is down in messy waves and she's wearing my Station 115 hat that she stole.

Lexi in my hat is enough to make me want to pull the truck over, drag her into my lap, and fuck her while she's wearing nothing but my hat.

"Earth to Alec," she says, knocking me from my fantasies.

"Sorry." I clear my throat. "I was picturing you riding me in nothing but that hat."

She snort-laughs then her lips curl into a gorgeous grin. "In nothing but your hat, huh? We can *definitely* make that fantasy come true," she says, leaning over like she's about to make it *literally* come true right now.

When she reaches for her seat belt, I cover her hand with mine. "Not now."

Her brows hit her forehead. "Wow, already turning me down for sex. Does this mean the honeymoon period of our relationship is over?" She quirks her head to the side and pouts.

"No," I tell her, laughing at how adorable she is. "But I want to take you out, and if you're going to ride me in nothing but my hat, I would rather it be in our bed where I can enjoy it completely."

"Our bed?"

Huh? *Oh...* "Yeah, *our* bed... You can keep pretending you're sharing a room with your sister, but you've yet to actually sleep in there. My bed is now ours."

Lexi surprisingly doesn't argue, instead sitting back and bringing her knees to her chest.

"So, where are you taking me?"

"On a date."

She whips her head around and smiles. "A date?"

"Are you a parrot today?" I joke.

"A parrot?"

I laugh. "You keep repeating everything I say in the form of a question."

She rolls her eyes. "Whatever. Tell me more about this date."

"It's a surprise." I put my truck in drive and pull out.

"If I guess correctly, will you tell me if I'm right?"

"Sure." There's no way she's guessing.

"Lunch and a movie."

I give her a quick side-eye before focusing back on the road. "Give me some credit. It's our first official date. I'm not that cliché."

"Well, I've never been on a date before," she says, shocking the hell out of me.

"You've never been out with a guy?"

"Nope. I've only had a few boyfriends. They were either too young to drive, or once we were old enough, we just hung out." She shrugs. "Most guys don't want to actually date... They just want to hook up."

I want to argue, but she isn't lying. I can't even remember the last time I took a woman out on a date. We live in a world where people text more than talk, and hook up more than hang out. And when they do hang out, they spend more time taking pictures and going on social media than actually getting to know the person they're with.

That isn't happening with Lexi. She's my forever, which means we have to establish a solid foundation. Something Mason said when I went over to Tristan's to talk to him about wanting to ask Lexi to marry me.

My thoughts go back to that awkward conversation...

*I knock on the Scotts' door and Tristan answers. "Alec, how are you? Come in."*

*He opens the door wider and I step inside. "I'm good. I was wondering if we could talk."*

*"Sure," he says.*

*I follow him back to his home office-gym-man cave Charlie had made for him. It consists of a desk in one corner and a treadmill and workout bench in another. On the wall between two windows hangs a ridiculously huge flat screen television, and facing the television are two comfy-looking leather couches—one of which is currently occupied by Mason, who is lounging on it with his feet on the wood coffee table and his phone in his hand.*

*When he hears us enter, he looks up and smiles.*

*"Son." He drops his feet to the ground and stands. "How are you?" he asks, enveloping me in a hug.*

*"Alec is here to talk to me," Tristan says, trying and failing to contain his laughter.*

*"Oh yeah?" Mason quirks a brow at Tristan.*

*They both sit next to each other, crossing their arms over their chests and bringing their ankles up to their knees at the same time.*

*Fuck, can these two have any more of a bromance?*

*"So, what's up?" Tristan asks. "First." He raises his hand. "How are you holding up?"*

*So, we're going to do small talk first... well, okay then. "I'm hanging in there," I tell them honestly. "I miss my dad like crazy. We used to talk in the morning when I would get off my shift, while I was driving home. Sometimes I go to dial his number and it hits me all over again that he's gone."*

*Mason nods and leans forward, dropping his elbows onto the tops of his thighs. "I can't replace your dad, nor would I ever try to, but if you ever need to dial a number to talk, I'm here."*

"I know," I tell him. "And it means everything to me."

"You have a lot of people who love you," Mason says. "You'll get through this."

And cue my perfect transition... "That's actually what I wanted to talk to Tristan about."

Mason and Tristan both laugh. Of course these assholes aren't going to make this easy for me.

"Go on," Tristan prompts.

Fuck it, I might as well just come out and say it... "I'm in love with your daughter."

"Which one?" Tristan asks. Fucker knows damn well which one.

"Lexi."

"Yes!" Mason fist pumps. "You owe me a hundred bucks."

Huh?

"Damn it!" Tristan says, grabbing his wallet from his back pocket and pulling a bill out, smacking it on the table. "I thought for sure you would wait until after Lexi graduated."

"I knew you wouldn't wait that long. At the rate Lexi's going, she could be in school forever," Mason says, swiping the bill up and stuffing it into his front pocket. "I do have to give you credit, though. You waited longer than your mom thought. She predicted you would give in once Lexi graduated from high school."

"What the hell... Did you all seriously bet on when Lexi and I would get together?"

"I didn't," a feminine voice says. I glance back and see Charlie standing in the doorway. When the hell did she get here?

"Oh, don't play innocent," Mason says. "The only reason you didn't bet was because you didn't think he would get the guts to admit his feelings."

"Really?" I ask, slightly offended, but also, not, because it did take me a long ass time to finally speak up and tell her how I feel.

She laughs and sits next to her husband. "Well, in my defense, I kind of figured Lexi would hightail it out of here after graduation."

Like she's planning to do if she wins her comp and gets a surfing contract...

I push the thought of Lexi leaving from my brain. I just want to be part of her life, even if it means she needs to travel and surf. I want to be there to watch her spread her wings and fly, not be the reason she feels like they've been clipped.

"So, I take it you finally reeled her in?" Mason asks.

"Do not refer to my daughter as a goddamn fish," Tristan says, pointing his finger at Mason in warning.

Mason raises his hands in surrender and laughs. "You know what this means, right?" he says to Tristan. When Tristan just glares, Mason continues, "We're about to be related." He waggles his eyebrows and Tristan's gaze swings over to me.

"Is that why you're here?" Tristan demands. "To drop the bomb you're dating my daughter and to ask my permission to marry her?"

"Eeek!" Charlie squeals. "I get to plan a wedding!" She stands and does some weird dance, which has Tristan wrapping his arm around her and pushing her back down.

"Alec," Tristan prompts, his brows furrowing in... anger? Fuck, this isn't going as planned.

"Yes," I croak out.

"Yes, what?" Tristan says.

"I'm in love with Lexi and I'm dating her and I want to marry her," I rush out.

Mason slaps his hand on his leg, and I glare at him. "You're seriously not helping."

"What did I do? This is great. I wish your mom were here to see you sweating bullets." He pulls out his phone. "Can you start over, so I can record it?"

I shoot him the finger, which only makes him laugh.

"Of course you have our blessing to marry Lexi," Charlie says, ignoring Mason. "And I think it's so sweet you came to ask her father for permission."

"Oh, yeah," Tristan adds sardonically. "Really fucking sweet."

"Oh, stop," Charlie says, slapping his chest. "Alec is a good man, with his life together."

"Thanks," I tell her, still waiting for Tristan to give his approval.

"When are you planning to ask her?" Tristan asks.

"Soon," I admit truthfully. "I don't want to wait. Life is too uncertain."

"Are you doing this because of your dad's death?" Tristan asks. "Because I get how something like that can rock your entire world, but if you're wanting to marry Lexi because you think life is short and you want to seize the day and all that shit, you need to consider there's a chance she'll live to be a hundred. Are you sure you can handle her for the next eighty years?"

"Umm..." I begin, unsure how the hell to answer him. I think there might be a joke mixed in there somewhere, but I can't say for sure. "I'm okay with handling Lexi for the next eighty years."

Mason snorts out a laugh, which has me replaying the words I just said in my head. "That came out wrong," I say, trying to backtrack. "Nobody can handle Lexi."

Mason laughs again, and this time Charlie joins in.

Fuck, this is all coming out wrong. "What I mean is, I love Lexi and I just want to spend the rest of my life with her, however long that is."

Tristan finally smiles. "You're right, nobody can handle Lexi, and the fact that you know that and still want to marry her speaks volumes. You have my blessing." He extends his hand and I meet him halfway shaking it. "Besides, you marrying her means she's no longer my problem." He shrugs. "It's the husband's job to take care of his wife... emotionally, financially..."

"Oh, whatever," Charlie scoffs. "Stop acting like you're so tough. Lexi and Georgia will always be your little girls, and you will forever give them everything and anything they want and need." She leans in and kisses Tristan's cheek. "It's one of the reasons why I love you. You're the best damn dad."

"I know you're only joking," I say, "but I do have a good job, and with my recent promotion I make a decent living. I'm prepared to take on the role of being Lex's husband in every way. I know we're young, but I love her and know she's the one. Whether it's her dream to travel the world surfing, or to paint, I plan to fully support her. I just want to spend my life with her."

"Good man," Tristan says.

"When are you planning to ask?" Charlie adds. "Can we throw you guys an engagement party?"

"I'm thinking this week, before I go back to work. I know it's soon but..."

"Hey," Mason says. "When it's right, it's right. I married your mom in a chapel in Las Vegas on a whim. Almost twenty years later and we're still going strong."

"You mean I'm still putting up with you?" my mom says, walking into the room.

"Semantics," Mason says with a laugh, standing and walking over to my mom to give her a kiss.

"What's with the powwow?" Mom asks, sitting on Mason's lap. I should be disgusted, but I'm used to it. They've always been all over each other since as far back as I can remember.

"Alec came over to ask Tristan's permission to marry Lexi," Mason says.

"What?" Mom shrieks. "You're marrying Lexi? I didn't even know you two were dating! About freaking time. I thought the two of you would've—"

"Gotten together when she graduated high school?" I finish dryly. "Yeah, I heard all about your bet."

Mom at least attempts to look a little sorry.

"I won," Mason says, pulling out his hundred-dollar bill. "How about I take you out to dinner tonight?" He lifts his brows up and down playfully, and my mom laughs.

"It's a date," she says. "Oh, can we go to The Melting Pot?"

Mason groans. "Woman, you know I hate that place."

"But I love it," Mom quips.

"See this?" Mason says to me. "This is marriage. Making sacrifices like eating at an overpriced cheese place that makes you cook your own damn food."

Mom smirks. "It's hardly a sacrifice when afterward, when we get home, you always get to—"

"Whoa now," I say. "Nobody wants to hear what happens once you get home."

Mason laughs. "The beauty of marriage. You give and then you receive." His brows bounce up and down and I swear I throw up a little in my mouth.

"Any real advice?" I ask. The truth is, no matter how disgustingly sweet they are together, I'm sitting in a room with two couples who have been married for almost twenty years. Something that doesn't happen often these days.

"That is real advice," Mason says. "You give and receive. I give by going to that restaurant your mom loves, and I get by..." He grins and winks.

"What Mason is trying to say is," Mom adds, "in order for a marriage to be successful, you have to be willing to give and take."

"And keep it fresh," Charlie adds. "Surprise her with flowers just because. Don't wait for a holiday." She beams at her husband. "I love when Tristan comes home with dinner or my favorite candy on a random night."

"Start your relationship with a firm foundation," Mason says. "What you do now will set the tone for your entire relationship. Make sure she knows she comes first. Take her out, order in, cook her dinner, find time to spend alone time together. It doesn't have to mean spending money, just being there is what creates that foundation."

Mom smiles softly at Mason, as I soak in every word he says. He might be one of the biggest smartasses I know, but he makes my mom happy, and I want nothing more than to make Lexi happy.

"Always communicate," Mom says when he's done speaking. "No matter how hard the truth is, always give it."

"Don't run," Charlie adds softly. "There will be ups and down along the way, but never run, unless it's to each other. Face whatever comes your way together."

Tristan kisses her cheek then says, "If you ever need anything, we're here. Always."

"Thank you," I tell them. "Lexi is planning to tell everyone we're dating at dinner tonight, so try to act surprised."

"Oh, that's why she texted me she wants to do dinner with all of us," Charlie says with a laugh. "I thought for sure she was going to announce she's dropping out of school and wanted an audience so her father wouldn't kill her."

"Have you bought a ring?" Mom asks.

"Yeah." I pull it out of my pocket and show them. The guys congratulate me, and the women ooh and aah over it.

"Once I figure out when I'm going to ask her, I'll let you know, so you can plan the celebration," I tell Charlie.

"Sounds perfect," she says. "We better head out before Lexi gets here and finds us all together." She and Tristan both hug me then leave.

Once it's just Mason, my mom, and me, they both stand and walk over to me.

"I wish your father were here," Mom says, getting choked up.

"I know," I tell her. "Me too."

"He would be so proud of you," she says into my shirt.

When we separate, Mason says, "I've told you this before. I can't and won't attempt to replace your dad, but I'm here if you need anything."

I choke out a laugh. "You've said that to me so many times over the years, but what you don't get is, you're just as much of a dad to me as mine was."

With tears in his eyes, Mason nods and pulls me into a hug. "Thank you, Son, that means the world to me."

"Alec, are you okay?" Lexi asks, pulling me out of my thoughts. "You have tears in your eyes."

"Yeah." I clear my throat. "I was just thinking about my dad." Not a complete lie… But I can't tell her the entire truth without admitting I met with her dad before the barbeque.

I pull into the parking garage and Lexi looks around. "I wasn't paying attention to where we were going. Where are we?"

"You'll see."

We get out of the vehicle and walk through the garage, ending up on Seaton Street. Immediately, Lexi's face lights up. "We're in the Arts District!"

"Yep, I figured you could show me around since it's your favorite place. We can go by a couple of the galleries, and then get lunch."

Lexi stares at me for a long second, then nods. "That sounds like the perfect first date."

She takes my hand and, since she knows this area like the back of her hand, proceeds to show me around. We walk up one street then down another, while Lexi and I discuss each graffitied piece.

"This is the Colette Miller Angel Wings Project," Lexi says when we step onto Colyton Street.

"What's that?" I ask, as we walk over to the life-size angel-looking wings that are painted on the wall.

"She created this project to remind people that we are the angels of this Earth. It's our job to be the good." She steps between the multicolored wings and turns around. "Take a picture of me."

I pull my phone out and snap the picture. "You are without a doubt the most beautiful angel," I tell her, putting my phone away and pulling her into my arms.

"This is what I want to do," she says, pointing to the wings.

"Draw on the walls? You already do that, Lex, and your pieces are amazing."

"No, not that. I want to make a difference with my art. I want it to be something people recognize, and not because it's graffitied on a wall or because it's good, but because it means something."

"Then make it mean something."

Her eyes lock with mine and she nods. "Yeah, maybe one day." She shrugs. "Let's go look at some more art."

She tries to pull away from me, but I hold on to her. "Hey, don't do that."

"Do what?"

"Brush off your passion. You love art and want to make a difference. You just have to think about how you can do that. What's important to you and how you can use art to accomplish whatever it is you want to accomplish."

"You make it sound so easy."

"I didn't say it would be, but that doesn't mean you can't do it. You're one of the most passionate people I know. You feel lost right now, and you keep talking about finding your path... Maybe combining your passion of art and your want to make a difference is where your path leads. You just have to figure out how to make them work together."

Lexi's lips curve into a beautiful smile. "You're right. I just need to take some time to think about it."

"And you have plenty of time."

After we check out more art on the buildings, we stop at a German restaurant neither of us has been to and eat lunch.

"I had a really good time today," Lexi says on our walk back to my truck. "You know this date set the bar high, right? Every date following will be compared to this one."

I laugh, remembering what Mason said about setting the tone of our relationship, and pull her into my side. "I'm okay with that. I have every intention of raising that bar higher and higher."

## CHAPTER SEVENTEEN

### LEXI

"Lex, your alarm," Alec groans into my ear, tightening his hold on me.

I pry my eyes open and grab my phone, pressing end so the noise will stop. It's 5:00 a.m. and I need to head to the beach to get some surfing in, but the only thing I want to do is stay in bed with Alec. He returns to work in a few days and all I want to do is soak up as much time with him as I can. I know him going back to work isn't life-changing. He actually has a pretty cool schedule that gives him four days off in a row. I'm just not looking forward to sleeping without him the two days he's gone for his twenty-four-hour shifts. I've gotten used to sharing a bed with him, and it will suck to be in it by myself.

With a deep breath, I pry myself from Alec and sit up. With one more inhale and exhale, I stand and head into the bathroom to get my bathing suit and wetsuit on. When I come out, Alec is up.

"What are you doing?" I ask, grabbing my beach bag. "Go back to bed. I'll pick up breakfast on my way home."

He shakes his head. "I want to go."

"You don't have to do that. Surfing is my thing, and I don't expect you to come and watch every day."

"I know, but I hate you going out in the dark alone, so if I can go, I want to." He grabs the fabric of my wetsuit and tugs me toward him. "I know you like to surf early, but when I'm at work and you're going alone, can you consider going when the sun is up since you don't have classes to get to?"

"Alec..."

"I know," he says. "You're a strong, independent woman, and I love that about you. But LA is a scary place and Jason giving you shit doesn't help any." To say Alec was pissed when I told him Jason approached me would be an understatement. He flat out said the next time Jason comes near me, he would make him regret it.

"Fine," I say, giving in.

"Thank you." He gives me a kiss that makes me want to go back to bed with him instead of going to the beach.

I spend the morning surfing while Alec hangs out and watches. I run into Shane and Ricco, and luckily Jason isn't around. Maybe he finally got the hint...

After I'm done, we stop for breakfast and I grab an extra meal for Aiden. When he sees me, he removes his glasses and gives me a hug. Alec stays back but waves and Aiden waves back.

When we get to my jeep, I immediately notice two of my tires are flat. "What the hell," Alec says, bending down to check out one of the tires. "This tire isn't just flat, it's been slashed."

"What?" I look around, as if the person who did this would've been stupid enough to hang around afterward. "I only have one spare."

"Yeah, and you need two new tires," Alec says, fuming. "We'll have to get your jeep towed to a garage nearby."

While we wait for the tow truck, Alec finds an officer who's patrolling the area and tells him what happened. The officer takes down my information so we can make a formal report. We also tell him about my jeep being keyed and how Jason all but admitted to doing it. He says they'll look into it, but doesn't sound very hopeful.

We're just finishing up with the police officer when the tow truck arrives. The guy quickly loads up my jeep and gives us a ride.

Luckily the garage has my size tire and I pay for two new ones. While we're there, Alec has them change my oil and rotate my tires. Once my car is ready, we head home.

"I have somewhere I want to take you," Alec says once we're home. "Shower and dress in something nice."

"Nice? Like a dress or just something without holes?"

Alec laughs. "A dress would be good."

---

"WHAT ARE WE DOING HERE?" I ask when we pull up in front of my mom's paint studio and my dad's gym—they're located directly next to each other—and Alec kills the engine.

Ignoring my question, Alec says, "Wait here," before he gets out and runs around the front of the hood and over to my side to open my door. He extends his hand to help me climb out—even though it has a sidestep he had installed so I could get in and out without breaking my neck—and kisses the top of my hand once I'm down.

I assume we're going to visit one of my parents, so I'm confused when we bypass both of their places.

"I've known since I was nineteen years old that I was in love with you," Alec says, stopping once we get around to the side of the building. He grants me a soft smile that has my insides twisting into knots. "You had snuck out of your mom's paint studio and run over here. I followed you and watched while you painted the entire wall." He nods toward the wall I graffitied years ago. Since my parents own the building, it's never been painted over.

I laugh, recalling that day. It was the first time I graffitied a public wall and signed it using my moniker. "It was because you followed me, I got caught." I roll my eyes, remembering how Uncle Mason went looking for Alec because he was supposed to be sparring with him but had disappeared.

"You painted the Starry Night by Vincent Van Gogh," Alec says, glancing up at the wall. "Do you remember why?" His eyes move back to meet mine.

The memory comes back to me like it was just yesterday. "A woman was visiting the paint studio and talked to my mom. When my mom asked how she was liking LA, she said she was disappointed because there were no stars in the sky. She said it's supposed to be a city where people go to make their dreams come true, yet there wasn't a single star to wish upon." I smile sadly, remembering Zoe tell my mom that her mom had passed away years ago from cancer.

"Her name was Zoe, and she was looking for local businesses to participate in the charity gala to support cancer awareness. The Delilah Cross Wish Upon a Star Charity. Charlie donated several paintings to the gala to be auctioned off." We were given tickets in exchange for her donation and attended the gala. It was the most beautiful event I'd ever been to. The entire theme was about wishing upon a star.

A wayward strand of hair falls in front of my eye, and Alec smiles softly, tucking it behind my ear. "When your dad came out and saw that you had recreated the Starry Night, he said you could've done that on a canvas for it to be auctioned off for the cause. That your graffiti on the wall couldn't be sold. It was of no value. You stood right here with your hands on your hips and said, 'My painting is worth more than a charity can raise. The city lacks all the beautiful stars, and now everyone who walks by will have a star to wish upon, so they can all make their dreams come true.'"

"I was like fifteen." I laugh, remembering how inspired I was by her story. I knew I needed to paint it on something bigger than a two-by-two canvas.

"Your age didn't matter," Alec says, shaking his head. "It wasn't even what you painted. It was your heart. It was how passionate you were about the meaning behind the painting. In that moment, I stopped seeing the messy, clumsy little girl with paint permanently in her hair and saw your beautiful soul. You're like this ray of sunshine in a dark, cloudy world. It's why Georgia gravitates toward you. You light up everyone's life around you without even meaning to."

Tears prick my eyes at his kind words because I definitely don't see myself the way he sees me.

"And now you're twenty-one and still drawing hope all over the walls of LA, and one day you're going to figure out how to change the world, and I can't wait to be there when you do."

Alec takes a step back and pulls something—a ring box—out of his pocket. "I knew back then what a big heart you had, and it's only grown over the years. I want that heart, Lex. I want it to be mine. I want your heart, baby."

He drops to one knee, and my hands cover my mouth, realizing what's happening.

"Alexandria Scott," he continues, opening the box and revealing the beautiful heart-shaped diamond engagement ring. "Will you marry me?"

I don't even have to think about it. I may not have any idea what my future holds, but I do know one thing. I want Alec by my side while I figure it out. "Yes!" I tell him. "Yes, I will marry you."

Alec rises to his feet and swoops me up into his arms, twirling us around in a circle. His lips connect with mine and he kisses me hard, showing me how happy he is with my answer.

When he sets me back onto my feet, he takes my hand in his and slides the ring onto my third finger. "I don't want to wait," he says, bringing my hand up to his mouth and kissing the finger that now holds my engagement ring. "I want to get married as soon as possible."

I'm not shocked by his admission, since he's made his intentions clear every step along the way. But what I am shocked about is the fact I'm completely okay with marrying him as soon as possible.

"How about in August or September?" I offer. "It will give us enough time to plan the wedding after the competition is over."

"Okay," he agrees. "We can discuss it with our parents and set a date."

Oh shit... our parents. "Alec, we just told everyone we're dating not too long ago. Don't you think they might freak when they learn we just went from dating to engaged in less than a couple weeks?"

"Nope," Alec says confidently. "Everyone already knows."

"What?" I sputter.

"You don't really think I would ask you to marry me without asking for your dad's permission first, do you?"

"You asked for his permission?" I choke out. "When? Where?"

"When I told you I had some errands to run the day we all got together for the barbeque, I went to pick up your ring and speak to your dad."

"And how did that go? I mean, you're still alive, so at least we know he didn't kill you..." I half-joke.

"It went well. I'll tell you about it later, but right now, we have people waiting to help us celebrate our engagement."

Alec takes my hand in his and walks us around to the front of the building. Before we get to his truck, he pulls his phone out. I glance at it and see he's texting someone.

"Everything okay?"

"Yeah." Instead of steering us toward his truck, he turns at the last second and steps in front of my mom's paint studio. Before I can ask what he's doing, he opens the door and pulls me through.

The second we enter, everyone yells, "Congratulations," and my parents are on me, hugging me.

Next, Georgia envelops me in a hug. "I'm so happy for you," she says, holding me tight.

"Thank you," I tell her, my heart so full. "You'll be my maid of honor, right?"

"Oh, so what am I, chopped liver?" a feminine voice says.

Georgia and I separate, and I find Micaela standing there with her hand on her hip and a playful smirk on her face. "Micaela!" I shriek, running into her arms. "I can't believe you're here."

"And miss your engagement party?" She scoffs. "Not on your life."

"Are Ryan and RJ here?" I ask, looking around for her husband and son.

"Yes," she says, a smile gracing her lips. "They're around here somewhere. Probably at the dessert table. RJ is obsessed with the cupcakes."

I give her another hug because I've missed her. The last time I saw her was at Alec's dad's funeral, and that wasn't exactly a social visit. "I'm so glad you're here."

"I was just kidding about the whole maid of honor thing," she says with a laugh. "But I better at least be invited to the wedding."

"Oh my God, stop! You will be in my damn wedding and you know it."

We both separate and laugh.

"Go on and make your rounds," she says. "We're in town for the weekend at the beach house."

"Oh, yay! We're totally hanging out. We should have a barbeque."

"Sounds good," she says.

## CHAPTER SEVENTEEN

My eyes lock with Alec's mom and she pulls me in for a hug. "I'm so happy love found you and Alec," she says. "Welcome to the family... officially."

"Congratulations," Mason adds. "About damn time that boy hooked you." He winks, and Mila smacks his chest.

"How many times do I have to tell you?" my dad says, coming up next to me. "My daughter is not a damn fish."

Mason throws his arm around his wife's shoulders and shrugs. "There's nothing wrong with being a fish. I hooked Mila and it was the best damn catch of my life." He bends slightly and kisses her cheek.

"You mean I caught you," she says playfully.

"Damn right, you did, and there was no throwing me back in."

"You guys are so damn cheesy," Anna says, rolling her eyes. "Please promise me you and my brother will never be as gross as they are." She gives me a hug.

"Too late," Chase says, walking over. "You should hear the noises coming from their room." He fake gags, and my dad chokes on the drink he's holding.

"Chase!" Georgia scolds. "Like you're one to talk. All those women you've been sneaking into our place." She makes a gagging sound.

"What women?" I ask, confused.

"The women you wouldn't have noticed because you've been too busy in your little bubble with Alec," Georgia says with a laugh. "But I know, because I can hear them through my wall. 'Oh, Chase, right there, no, not there... right there!'" She mocks in a fake nasally voice.

Everyone cracks up laughing at her interpretation of Chase's women. Well, everyone but Chase.

With a straight face, he leans in close to Georgia, so nobody but her can hear him—and the only reason I can hear him is because I'm standing so close to her—and whispers, "At least my women make noises. I don't hear shit coming from your room, which tells me one thing..." He moves closer, so I can't hear what he says, but based on the look on Georgia's face, whatever he's said upset her, because as soon as he's done speaking, she's running away from him toward the back of the studio, where the bathroom is.

"Nice going," I tell him before I run after her.

When I get to the bathroom, I open the door and find Georgia sitting on the toilet seat, sniffling back tears.

"I forgot to lock it," she mutters.

I sit on the decorative chair across from her. "What did he say?"

"The truth." She smiles sadly. "That nothing is going on with Robert and me in the bedroom... Well, that, and if something is going on, he must not be satisfying me."

"Which is it?"

"Nothing's going on."

"So, you told him you weren't ready?"

"Yeah." She nods. "He wasn't thrilled, but he said he would wait until I am."

"Good," I tell her. "And fuck Chase. What you're doing or not doing in the bedroom isn't any of his business."

"No, it's not," Chase says from the doorway. "But maybe Georgia shouldn't play with the big dogs if she's gonna pee like a puppy."

"What?" I laugh.

"It's an old saying," Chase says. "You know... if you can't take what's being thrown at you, you shouldn't be throwing it yourself."

"Look here, mister." I stand, about to rip him a new one, when Georgia stands as well and steps between us.

"He's right. I shouldn't have made fun of... your women's sounds."

I snort a laugh. "Are they using our bathroom? If so, you're going to need to pitch in more. We shouldn't have to clean up after your one-night stands."

Chase rolls his eyes. "You don't clean at all. You have a cleaning lady." True... That was a great housewarming gift our parents got us when we moved in.

"We should go on a double date," I tell Georgia. "Since our last one got ruined." I glare at Chase, remembering how Alec and Chase crashed it.

"Damn right, we ruined that shit," Alec says, joining the mini bathroom party. "Because you belong with me." Alec pulls me into his side and kisses my temple. "Everything okay in here?"

"Yeah," Georgia says. "Again, I'm sorry," she says to Chase, who at least has the decency to look ashamed at the way he upset Georgia.

"Sorry for what?" Alec asks, looking at each of us confused.

"Nothing," I tell him. "Let's go celebrate our engagement."

We exit the bathroom, and I notice Georgia and Chase stay back. I make it a point to glare at him, silently warning him that he better apologize to her.

We spend the rest of the evening celebrating with our friends and family. Once it's late and people start making their exit, we thank everyone for coming and, after thanking our family for throwing us this party, go home.

---

"I LOOKED up the Women's International Surfing tour dates," Alec says. "If you win the competition and snag a spot on the tour, the next tour date is in September."

"That's a big if," I point out. There will easily be a couple hundred women competing for a slot.

"You will."

We're lying in bed, with my body wrapped around his, his fingers drawing circles along my back. After we got home, we hung out with Georgia and Robert for a little while and then retreated to our room. After participating in our own little engagement celebration—which involved both of us naked with Alec inside of me—we showered and then fell into bed, exhausted.

"I think we should get married in August," he says, rolling onto his side so we're facing each other. "Whether you're going on tour or going back to school, August comes before either one and after the competition."

"Micaela got married in August. We would have to make sure it's on a different weekend."

"Done."

## CHAPTER EIGHTEEN

### ALEC

"Welcome back!" the guys holler as Chase and I walk into the station. They all surround me, giving me a hug. Some congratulate me on my engagement and others express how sorry they are for my loss. It's crazy how quickly time flies by. In the last several weeks, I've lost my father, found out I'll be a brother again, finally admitted my feelings to Lexi and got engaged, Chase officially moved in, and my stepmom moved away. Life is fucking crazy and if you blink too slowly it will all change before your eyes.

"Thanks, guys." I want to say it's good to be back, but the truth is, I've only been away from Lexi for twenty minutes and I'm already missing being in bed with her. "So, what did I miss?"

The guys get me caught up with everything that's been going on here, then Chase and I head to the workout room to get a workout in. The day flies by, with only one text from Lexi wishing me a good morning and letting me know she's going surfing. I hate the thought of her heading to the beach on her own, but I can't act like an overbearing fiancé. Surfing is Lexi's passion and I can't stop her from doing it while I'm at work.

The afternoon flies by with a couple calls involving an oven grease fire and a vehicle that caught on fire. In the evening, I text Lexi and she tells me she's home from surfing and hanging out with her sister and they're planning a double date for us tomorrow night. I tell her that sounds good and I'll see her in the morning.

When nighttime rolls around, she sends me an image of her sleeping in our bed, and in place of where I should be, she's drawn in a stick figure guy.

An accompanying text comes in right after: **Pretending you're here with me.**

Finally, eight o'clock comes and Chase and I head home. We both go straight to our bedrooms, and when I open the door to mine, the sight in front of me has my dick hardening.

Lexi, lying in our bed with her legs wrapped up in my blankets. Her back is completely bare, telling me she's not wearing a shirt, and her ass cheeks are on display, only a thin black scrap of material running down the center of her ass.

Not wasting any time, I strip out of my clothes and slide in behind her. She stirs but doesn't wake up, and her ass juts out, rubbing against my hard-on.

I encircle my arms around her, my hand massaging her breast while I trail kisses along her smooth shoulder blades and up to her neck. I brush her hair to the side and kiss the spot she loves just below her ear, which makes her moan softly and squirm.

"Lex, baby," I murmur into her ear. She stiffens against me, and I know she's now awake. I tweak her nipple between my thumb and finger, turning it into a hard peak, and she groans softly, the sound vibrating straight to my dick. Fuck, I've missed her so damn much and it was only twenty-four hours without her. I don't know what will happen if she wins that sponsorship with Vans, but if I have to use personal time to chase her ass around the globe that's what I might have to do because there's no way I'm going too long without having her in my arms.

Moving my hand down her stomach, I dip it inside her underwear and find her center. I work my fingers between her warm hole and sensitive clit. Stroking and massaging her. She wriggles her body, clenches her thighs together, and moans, spurring me on. I suckle on her neck, working her over until she's dripping wet.

"Alec," she breathes, on the same page as me.

Shoving her underwear down, I part her legs and guide my dick into her. The feeling of her pussy sucking me in is the equivalent of coming home after a long as fuck shift. Right here, with Lexi, in Lexi, is the only place I want to be.

While I thrust into her from behind, I work her clit over. She's so fucking close, I can feel her cunt squeezing my dick. And then she releases a loud moan as she comes completely undone. Her legs shake and her pussy spasms. She screams out my name so loud I'm positive anyone home can hear her. She clenches tightly around my shaft, and I bury my face into the crook of her neck, coming right along with her, draining every drop of my seed into her.

"Is this how you're going to wake me up every morning when you get home from work?" she asks, her breathing labored. "Because if it is, you going to work won't be half bad after all." She giggles, and if I hadn't just drained myself into her thirty seconds ago, the sound would have me hard and ready to go.

I pull out of her and flip her onto her back, climbing over her. "Oh yeah?" I drop my hands onto the bed on either side of her. "So, you're willing to go twenty-four hours without seeing me, if it means I fuck you?" I part her legs and she wraps them around my waist, pulling my hips toward her. My dick is already hardening, and I enter her again.

"Jesus, Lex," I groan, my hard length pushing into her cum-filled pussy. "I missed you so fucking much." I give her a chaste kiss then pull back slightly. "I could live right here, in you, for the rest of my life."

"I'm completely okay with that," she says, grabbing ahold of my neck and pulling my face to hers. "How about you show me *exactly* how much you missed me?" Her mouth crashes against mine, and her tongue delves between my parted lips. She holds me close to her, kissing me, while I make love to her again, showing her exactly how much I missed her.

---

"WHAT DO you mean Robert doesn't want to go on a double date?" Lexi slowly asks her sister. "Like he can't because he has to work?"

"No." Georgia shakes her head, the expression on her face filled with embarrassment. "He didn't like the way Alec and

Chase crashed our double date before." She rolls her eyes then glances my way. "I'm sorry. He's been stressed about some case at work and I don't want to add to that."

I can tell Lexi is fuming, but she's holding back, not wanting to get into an argument with her sister. I figure it's best to say something before Lexi does. "It's okay, Georgia. Give it some time. Maybe we can all get together at your parents' place for a barbeque and he can get to know me in a neutral setting." He was supposed to come to the barbecue the night Lexi and I told our family we were together, and then again, the day I proposed, but he bailed both times, saying he had to work. I'm definitely seeing a pattern here, and if it continues, Robert and I will need to have a chat.

Georgia exhales a deep breath. "That would be good. I'm going to study for my exams. First half of summer classes are almost over."

"But what about going out?" Lexi's bottom lip juts out in disappointment.

"I really need to study," Georgia says.

"Seriously, Georgia?" Lexi asks, her tone now annoyed.

"I have to study," Georgia argues.

"If Robert had said yes to going out you wouldn't be using that excuse."

"Maybe not, but that doesn't mean it's not true. I really do need to study. Just go out with Alec and have a good time. I promise we'll go out soon."

Before Lexi can argue further, Georgia retreats to her room.

"She's going back into her shell," she says once Georgia is in her room with the door closed. "Robert was supposed to help her break out of it. Now, because of his stuck-up ass, she's sinking back in."

"Just give it some time," I tell her, trying to remain neutral. One thing I've learned over the years is not to get in the middle of Lexi and Georgia's shit. They'll argue and make up quick enough to give you whiplash.

Lexi glares. "She's my sister. I'm not giving it time. If her boyfriend doesn't want to be around her best friend and sister, then we have a problem."

She stomps to Georgia's room. I stay where I am, unsure of

what I'm supposed to do. Thank God I'm a man. Men don't have these issues.

"Alec," she hisses. "C'mon." Okay then... Guess I'm part of this.

She swings the door open and Georgia looks up from her books that are spread across her bed. I stay back, trying to camouflage myself against the wall, still not wanting to get in the middle of this.

"I'm your sister," Lexi says. "And he"—she points to me—"is your best friend." So much for camouflaging myself. "If Robert doesn't want to double date with us, then fuck him!"

Georgia's eyes go wide in shock. As much of a spitfire as Lexi is, she always handles her sister with kid gloves. No matter how many times I've seen them disagree, Lexi has never yelled at her sister.

"I'm serious, Georgia," Lexi says. "So far, I've seen him talk shit about what you choose to eat, not show up to any of our family functions, give you shit about you not wanting to sleep with him, and—"

Whoa, now that has my attention. "What the hell does she mean giving you shit about not wanting to sleep with him?" I ask, cutting Lexi off. "Don't tell me that asshole is giving you a hard time because you're not jumping into bed with him as quick as he wants."

Georgia's cheeks turn a light shade of pink and she opens her mouth to say something, but before she can get a word out, Lexi speaks first. "Yes, that's exactly what's happening, and now, he's refusing to hang out with the two most important people in her life."

Georgia opens her mouth again, but Lexi continues. "This is not happening, Georgia, I mean—"

"Stop!" Georgia yells, and Lexi's mouth closes quickly in shock. "If you would let me speak, then you would know I agree, which is why I just ended things with him."

"You did?" Lexi asks, sitting on the bed next to her sister.

"Yes, through a text." Georgia shrugs. "Then I blocked him because you know I hate confrontation."

Lexi laughs and hugs her sister. "I'm so proud of you. The right guy for you is out there, I just know it."

"Yeah, maybe." Georgia's voice cracks, telling me even though she's trying to appear nonchalant she's upset. "For now, I think I'll just focus on school."

Lexi's lips twist into a grimace. "Don't let one dumbass ruin all men for you."

"I won't," Georgia argues, but we can all hear the lie in her words. She put herself out there for the first time and the guy was a dick. For most women, that wouldn't be a big deal, but Georgia isn't most women, and it will take time for her to put herself back out there.

"Okay," Lexi says. "I know you're studying, but how about taking a little break and coming out to dinner with us? We can skip the movie."

Georgia is already shaking her head before Lexi can even finish her sentence. "I really do need to study. I promise another time."

"Okay," Lexi repeats, clearly at a loss as to what to do.

We exit Georgia's room and Lexi says, "I don't want to leave her."

"Of course not," I agree. "We can order in and get her favorite and then drag her out here to watch a movie with us."

Lexi wraps her arms around my neck. "Thank you, Alec. That asswipe Robert needs to take some lessons on how to be a boyfriend from you."

"But I'm not a boyfriend," I say, holding up her hand. "I'm a fiancé."

"And the best one ever."

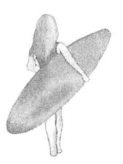

## CHAPTER NINETEEN

### LEXI

"Yay!" Mom shrieks. "So, we have a date? You're sure?"

"Yes," I tell her, taking a sip of my coffee. "That's the date. It's before fall semester starts, after Micaela and Ryan's anniversary, and the surfing comp will be over. Alec already put in for that weekend and the following week. He's insisting we go on a honeymoon, but he won't tell me where. He says it's a surprise."

"We have less than two months," Mila says, scrolling through the calendar on her phone. "It's not a whole lot of time, but we can do this. We're going to need a venue—"

"We're thinking Micaela's parents' beach house in Venice," I tell them. "I love the beach and they have a private one. It's free and simple..."

"Sweetie," Mom says, putting her hand on mine. "You only get married once." She flinches at her own words, but quickly recovers, smiling extra hard. "You want to make sure your wedding is what you want. Your dad and I are paying for it, so please don't go with what's free and simple."

As if I didn't think I could love my parents any more... "I know that, and I appreciate it, but you know me, and I like simple. If you have this dire need to spend money, make a donation to a cause for the arts. All I need is Alec and me standing in front of someone who can legally marry us. I love him and just want to become his wife."

Mom and Mila both sigh.

"Okay, fine," Mom agrees. "But how about a hotel on the beach instead, so we can have a reception there? The beach house won't fit everyone."

Knowing this is important to her, I agree. "All right, just promise me you'll keep it simple," I say, standing.

"Where are you going?" she asks.

"Surfing."

"Don't you usually go at the crack of dawn?"

"Yeah, but since Jason keyed my car and my tires were slashed, Alec made me promise to only go when it's daylight out. When he's off, he gets up early with me and watches me surf."

When we told our parents about Jason, my dad and Mason were damn close to going after him, but since nobody seems to know his last name—which is kind of weird—and he's been MIA from the beach, they wouldn't even know how to find him. So, my dad called the station to ask about my jeep and was told there are no cameras in our complex or in the parking lot at the beach, and with no eyewitnesses, there isn't much they can do.

"You raised a wonderful young man," Mom says to Mila, who smiles at the compliment.

"It's so crazy to think that in less than two months we'll officially be family," Mila gushes.

"I know! Go ahead, Lexi," Mom says. "Have fun surfing. We'll put together a list of things we need to do, and we'll get together soon to go over it all."

"Thanks, Mom." I give her a kiss on her cheek. "Thanks, Mila." I kiss her cheek as well.

When I get to the beach, I text Alec I'm here, so he knows that if he texts or calls why I might not answer him right away. He's on shift, and I've noticed when he's at the station and there are no fires, he gets bored and will text me. As much as I hate being away from him, I enjoy our nightly conversations. Sometimes they even get heated and end with us having phone sex.

After I get a good practice in, I head home. As I'm walking toward the door, my phone goes off. I check it and see it's Alec:

**Happy Anniversary.**

**Anniversary?** I text back. We've only been together for a few weeks.

**Alec: It's been one month since you agreed to be my girlfriend.**

I laugh at how cheesy he is.

**Me: Is this your way of ensuring you'll get laid when you get home? Because I can assure you, I'm a sure thing.**

I pull up my calendar and set a reminder to notify me every month so I can be as cheesy as he is. When I type in the event, I notice there are only a few weeks until the surfing comp. It's kind of crazy how quickly a month has passed and how much has changed during that time. In August, Alec and I will be getting married, and then shortly after, I'll either be heading off to tour the world surfing or signing up for my fall classes. My stomach sinks at the thought. I know Alec said we would make it work, but when I signed up to do this competition, I never imagined leaving to follow my dream would mean leaving him. It's definitely something I need to think about.

**Alec: Getting to be inside you is always a positive, but all I need is you in my arms when I get home.**

I smile at how sweet he is, and then an idea hits...

---

"ALEXANDRIA SCOTT!" Georgia yells, covering her ears. "What are you doing?"

"I was baking brownies for Alec's and my anniversary," I yell back, trying to stab the smoke alarm with the end of the broom.

"Your what?"

"It's our one-month anniversary," I explain, bashing the alarm.

"Go tell Ms. Holden not to call nine-one-one!" I grab a chair and stand on it, reaching up to press the button. I keep hitting it, but it doesn't stop alerting everyone in the vicinity that I once again fucked up something I was trying to bake.

"Oh my God!" Georgia yells. "Did you turn the oven off?"

"Oh, shit! I forgot." I was too busy trying to shut the damn alarm off. I jab my finger into the alarm and it finally silences it.

Jumping down, I run over to the oven Georgia just turned off and open it to take the brownies out, so they'll stop cooking even more.

"No, wait!" Georgia says, but it's too late. The smoke fills the air, and the alarm starts blaring again.

"Go tell Ms. Holden not to call nine-one-one," I tell her again, dropping the burnt to a crisp brownies on top of the stove.

"Too late," a deep voice says. "If you wanted to see me, all you had to do was ask."

I remove the oven mitts and run into Alec's arms. Since he was gone before I woke up this morning, I haven't seen him since last night.

The blaring comes to a halt, and I find Chase and a couple of the other guys Alec works with standing there, dressed in matching uniforms, wearing matching smirks. I back up slightly and run my eyes down Alec, who's wearing the same thing they all are. There's just something about a man in a uniform...

"Lex," Alec groans, shaking his head. "What happened?"

"I was making you brownies for our anniversary. I was going to bring them to the station."

Alec's face lights up before he quickly schools his features.

"I'm telling you there's something wrong with that oven." I point to the offending object that keeps burning my shit. "It said to bake for fifty-five minutes. I set the timer and it hasn't even gone off yet. I don't understand how it could even be burnt."

"One," Georgia says. "Fifty-five minutes is for an eight-by-eight pan. This is eight-by-thirteen, so it should've only been twenty-five minutes." Oops... "And two, the timer isn't on." She presses the blinking numbers and the timer starts. "You never hit start."

"You know they're going to charge you," Alec says with laughter in his voice.

I swivel around and step close to him. "Maybe tomorrow when you get home I can work on paying off some of it…"

Chase snorts. "Alec isn't the one who charges you. It's the city."

"Shut up," I quip, making Alec grin.

I take another step toward Alec, until we're so close our bodies are flush against each other. "While you're here," I whisper, "you think we can go to our room and—"

"No," Chase says, cutting me off. "And FYI: you suck at whispering almost as badly as you suck at baking. Stop trying to do both."

The guys chuckle, and I glare. "Careful," I warn him. "You might come home and find out you're homeless."

Georgia snorts out a laugh, and Alec encloses his arms around me. "I have to get going," he says. "Thank you for the brownies." He kisses me, and the guys all groan.

"Do you realize you just thanked your fiancée for brownies she burned?" Chase asks. "You are so fucking pussy-whipped."

"Hey," Alec says, pulling away from our kiss. "Don't be talking about my woman's pussy."

Chase raises his hands in surrender, then heads out the door with the other guys.

Once they're gone, Alec says, "I'll see you in the morning. No more baking. I appreciate the thought, but next time, maybe buy them…"

"Yeah, yeah." I roll my eyes. "Ricco texted me he's heading to the beach. I might meet him there to get some more waves in."

"All right, baby," he says, kissing my cheek. "Have fun and be safe."

## CHAPTER TWENTY

### ALEC

- **Hey baby**
- **Lex?**
- **You still at the beach? Text me when you get this.**
- **Lex, I'm getting worried. I haven't heard from you in a while.**

I STARE AT MY PHONE, confused and worried. I'm probably overreacting, but any time I text Lexi, she texts me back. If she's surfing, it may take a little while, but not hours.

I pull up Georgia's name and hit call.

"Don't worry, she hasn't attempted to bake anything else," she says with a laugh.

"She's at home?" I ask, getting straight to the point.

"No, she went surfing. I haven't seen her all afternoon."

"It's dark out."

"It won't be the first or last time she's surfed after the sun went down."

"She agreed she wouldn't," I say, feeling like an overprotective crazy asshole. "With her jeep being vandalized and Jason starting shit..." My heart pumps harder. Maybe it's nothing, maybe I am overacting, but something feels wrong...

"I'm sure she's fine," Georgia responds, her tone no longer light and carefree. "She's probably hanging out with her friends. You know she spends more time at the beach than home. She probably has her phone on silent and lost track of the time."

"Can you call your brother and get Ricco's number? She said she was meeting him at the beach."

"Yeah, don't worry, though. I'm sure she just got caught up in the waves."

We hang up and I try calling Lexi several more times, each time getting no answer.

I'm grabbing my keys to drive over to the beach to look for her when Georgia calls back. "He was there with her and then left with Max. Last time he saw her was hours ago."

"Fuck. I'm heading to the beach to look for her. Call your parents and anyone she might be with."

"Okay, will do."

"Where're you going?" Chase asks, walking up next to me.

"I'm going to the beach to see if Lexi is there. She's not answering or returning my calls. I'm worried something's happened to her."

Chase opens his mouth, I'm sure to make a smartass comment, but when his eyes meet mine, he nods in understanding. "I'll come with you."

The drive to the beach is filled with silence. Georgia calls me and lets me know nobody has seen or heard from Lexi, and she hasn't posted anything on any social media platform.

"It shows she's at the beach," Tristan says when I answer his call. "I have a tracker for all my kids. It shows she's been at the beach for the last eight hours." I'm assuming Georgia or Max told their dad I'm looking for her.

"Thank you."

"Keep me updated."

"Will do."

We hang up as I'm pulling into the parking lot for the beach. I immediately spot her jeep and drive over to it. I glance inside, but it's empty.

"She must still be surfing."

"Yeah, but it's not like her to go this long without texting or calling me."

We head down the sidewalk and onto the beach. I go straight for the area where she usually surfs, but she isn't there. It's late now and the beach is dark and empty.

"Maybe she's eating on the pier," Chase suggests.

"Maybe... Can you go check? I'm going to walk down the beach, see if she's somewhere else." My eyes land on the dark area under the pier. It's a long shot even getting Aiden to talk, but maybe he's seen her and can at least tell me that much.

I run toward his tent, slowing down the closer I get so I don't spook the guy. As I step up to his tent, I notice Lexi's board and beach bag are lying next to it. My heart goes erratic. I've seen her stop here and talk to him, but I've never seen her actually go in his tent. And the thing is small, would barely hold the two of them.

"Aiden," I call out.

There's some shuffling and then the material is being unzipped. Aiden pops his head out and puts his glasses on. "Lexi's boyfriend," he says. "Lexi is hurt. She's bleeding and won't wake up."

That's all I need to hear to sprint into action. Quickly unzipping the tent the rest of the way down, I gently push Aiden out of the way so I can get to Lexi, but stop when I see my fiancée laid out in front of me. Because of the lantern that's lighting up the area, I am able to see every feature of her, and the sight in front of me almost brings me to my knees.

She's lying on her back and her eyes are closed. Her hair is soaking wet and all tangled. And on her head is a giant gash with blood pouring down the side of her face.

"Lexi is hurt. She's bleeding and won't wake up," Aiden repeats.

"What—"

"Alec!" Chase screams before I can finish my sentence. "What the fuck is going on?" he yells, his eyes bouncing between Aiden and me.

Aiden falls backward. "I don't know him. This is my home. You can't be here." He shakes his head and backs into a corner of his tent. "Lexi's boyfriend, I don't know him," he repeats.

"What happened to Lexi?" Chase asks.

"I don't know," I tell him honestly. "It looks like she hit her head. We need to get her to the hospital." My shock from seeing her like this is wearing off and my EMT training is kicking in. "Call the ambulance. I don't want to move her in case she's injured anywhere else." Chase pulls out his phone and steps away to make the call.

"Aiden, can you tell me what happened?" I ask, dropping down next to Lexi and checking for a pulse. It's there, and she's breathing. Since she's not awake and has a huge gash on her head, this can be brain related.

"The man hurt her," Aiden says. "He wasn't loving her."

"Who?" If it was Jason, so help me God, I'll fucking kill him.

"The mean sur—"

"They're on their way," Chase says, cutting off Aiden. "I don't know what the fuck you did to Lexi, but I'm calling the police."

"I didn't do that," Aiden says, shaking his head. "I didn't do that."

"Then who did?" Chase yells.

"I didn't do that," Aiden repeats. "I didn't do that."

"Chase, stop," I bark. "He's autistic."

As I check out the gash on Lexi's forehead, Aiden rocks in the corner repeating the same thing over and over again. Any chance I had of him telling me what happened has been thrown out the door, but right now all that matters is getting Lexi to the hospital. The fact she hasn't woken up yet isn't a good sign. I lift her lids and her pupils are dilated, concurrent with a head injury.

I run my hands down her body, checking to see if she's injured anywhere else. Her knees are torn up, both of them covered with fragments of rock and blood, but aside from that she looks okay. She's wearing her bathing suit, so she must've been surfing.

"EMTs are here," Chase calls inside. He had run up to meet them so he could show them where we are.

"Aiden, I need you to step out so they can get in here to help Lexi. Can you do that?"

"Lexi is hurt," he says. "They'll help her?"

"Yes, they'll help her."

"I didn't do it," he repeats.

"I believe you." And I do, but I still don't know what happened. Right now, though, I just have to focus on getting Lexi help.

Aiden steps outside and I explain to the EMTs what I know,

which isn't much. After they carefully move her onto a gurney, they bring her up the beach and roll her into the ambulance. Aiden asks if she's going to be okay and I tell him I'll let him know before jogging to my truck so I can follow them to the hospital.

"Let me drive," Chase says. "You need to call her family."

"Thanks."

I call Tristan first, since he's her dad, and tell him I found Lexi passed out and we don't know anything else. He says he and Charlie are on their way to the hospital now and he'll call Georgia, Max, and my parents, so I don't have to.

"Who the fuck was that guy?" Chase asks when I end the call.

"Aiden. He's a friend of Lexi's. He's homeless and lives in that tent."

"We need to call the police. He could be the one who did that to her."

"No," I argue. "He said someone hurt her. My guess is he saved her. No police until she tells us what happened."

"If he didn't do anything wrong, he has nothing to worry about."

"No," I repeat. "She's protective of him and if he's arrested and didn't do anything wrong, she'll be upset."

We get to the hospital and head straight for the Emergency Room since that's where they'll bring her through. Since I'm also an EMT, I have a card that lets me through. Chase offers to stay back and wait for our families.

They wheel her into a room, and my heart sinks when her eyes are still closed. Her not waking up can't be good. I stay out of the way while the EMTs explain their findings to the doctor, who immediately orders tests and asks that I wait in the waiting room.

The next few hours are long. We all sit together, waiting for information. It's late and everyone is exhausted. Our nerves are frayed. Nobody bothers to say a word or make fake conversation. The nurse comes out once to let us know the doctor is still running tests, and once he has answers, he'll let us know.

"Family of Alexandria Scott," the doctor says.

We all jump to our feet.

"Yes," Tristan says. "I'm her father."

"Alexandria was brought in with a head injury. After running tests, we've found that she has a traumatic brain injury. There doesn't appear to be any permanent damage to the brain itself, but from speaking with Miss Scott—"

"She's awake?" I blurt out.

"Yes, she woke up a little while ago. We asked her a few questions, and it's clear she's disoriented. She knows who she is and where she is, but she can't recall the last several hours leading up to the incident, which is very common amongst brain injury patients. She suffered a severe concussion, but luckily the swelling has gone down. We'll need to monitor her for the next forty-eight hours and run another MRI to make sure everything's okay."

"Can we see her?" I ask, trying like hell to be patient, but freaking the fuck out. She has a concussion, swelling in her head... She can't remember the last few hours. This could've been worse, way worse, but it's still bad. And whoever the fuck did this to her is going to pay.

"Yes," the doctor says. "Let's start with one at a time, and once she's moved to her private room, she can have more visitors."

## CHAPTER TWENTY-ONE

### LEXI

My head is pounding—a mixture of the hit I took to the head and the obsessive need to know how I hit my head. The constant *thump, thump, thump* feels like my skull is being drop-kicked over and over again like in the MMA fights the guys my dad trains participate in. I'm down, tapping the hell out, only the ref isn't stopping the fight. The harder I try to remember what happened, the worse the thumping gets.

With my eyes closed, I try to rest and calm down. The doctor said he was going to let my family know how I'm doing and allow them to come back. Hopefully someone will have some answers for me. Did I hit my head while surfing? And if so, who saved me? All the doctor could tell me was that I took a hit to my head, which caused me to get a bad concussion. It's the reason I feel nauseous and lightheaded. Apparently there was even swelling to my brain, which thankfully went down. And now they're just monitoring me to make sure I'm in the clear.

The door opens and in walks Alec. His face is pale and he has purplish-black bags under his eyes. He looks like he's aged several years. The second he lays his eyes on me, they well up with tears. He rushes over and gently cups my face in his hands. Taking a deep breath, he kisses my forehead.

"Seeing your beautiful blue eyes open is the best fucking thing," he murmurs, his lips lingering on my skin.

"Why wouldn't you see them?" I ask, confused.

Releasing my face, he pulls back and snags a chair, quickly dragging it over so he can sit close to me. He takes the hand closest to him and threads our fingers together, bringing it up to his lips to kiss. He closes his eyes again and inhales, like he's taking in my scent.

"Alec, what happened?"

He opens his eyes. "What do you remember?"

"Nothing...Well, nothing that would lead to me being here. The last thing I remember is going to the beach." I try to conjure up a single memory past that, but all that happens is the thumping worsens, making me flinch in pain.

"What's wrong?" he asks, his eyes widening in fear.

"My head hurts, and when I try to remember what happened, it gets worse, like I'm straining my brain or something."

"Don't do that."

"How did this happen?"

Alec sighs. "I don't know. When you didn't return my calls or texts, I went looking for you. It was dark out, and I was worried..."

"The last thing I remember was surfing and it was day time. Ricco and my brother were there."

"Anyone else?"

"Shane had stopped by but left with some friends."

"What about Jason?"

"No, not that I remember."

"Aiden found you. Based on the little he said, you were attacked by someone. By the bump on your head and your knees being torn up, I think you hit a rock. Aiden brought you to his tent but didn't know what to do. You were knocked out."

I hear everything he's saying, but none of it makes any sense. I don't remember any of this. Surely, if all this had happened, I would remember something, anything.

"When I got to the beach, I went to Aiden's tent and found you. Chase called an ambulance and you were brought here."

"None of that sounds familiar," I tell him honestly. "Where's Aiden? I want to talk to him."

"He's at the beach. Chase yelled at him, not knowing his condition, and he kind of freaked out."

"He must be so worried." I glance around as if I can somehow get up and leave. Alec must sense what's going through my head because he shakes his.

"You're not going anywhere. You took a damn blow to the head, Lex. I could've lost you. Your fucking brain was hit."

"I know, but I'm okay, and I need you to go to Aiden and let him know that I'm okay. He's got to be freaking out. Please."

Alec exhales a deep breath. "Okay. I'll go in the morning."

"No, now. And bring him some food and water," I plead. "I once saw some surfers upset Aiden and he retreated into his shell. Refused to leave for days. I had to bring him food and water and coax him to come out."

"All right," he reluctantly agrees. "But before I go, I think we should report this to the police."

"Report what? That I hit my head and scraped my knees, but we don't know how it happened?"

"Okay." He stands and kisses the top of my head. "I'm going to go talk to Aiden and hopefully he'll be able to tell me who did this to you, and then we're filing a report."

"Alec, don't upset him," I argue as he steps back. "If you get there and he's upset, do not make it worse."

"Lex," he barks, then closes his eyes for a brief moment to calm himself down. He opens his eyes and his gaze sears into mine. "You could've died tonight. Chase thinks Aiden—"

"Nope, do not fucking go there," I yell, making my head explode. "Aiden would never do this to me. Chase doesn't know him like I do. If someone did this, it wasn't him. You can ask him, but if he gets worked up, leave him alone. I'm alive and safe in the hospital and that's all that matters."

He stares at me for a long minute like he wants to argue, but he must think better of it because he lets out a loud sigh. "Fine, I'll be back."

He exits the room, and a few minutes later the nurse comes in and says they're moving me to a private room since I'll be here for the next couple days. Once I'm situated, my family comes to visit.

Georgia cries that she was worried and feels bad she didn't worry sooner. Of course, I tell her that's ridiculous. My parents coddle me, asking if I'm okay and if I need anything. Max stands in the corner, feeling guilty because apparently he left me at the beach alone, which I tell him is an absurd reason to feel guilty since I've been going to the beach by myself since I was sixteen and have stayed after dark too many damn times to count. Mason and Mila visit with Anna but leave shortly after so I can get some rest. Micaela calls Georgia, who tells me she's thinking about me and loves me.

Once everyone has seen I'm okay and alive, I tell them all they can go home. It's late—or rather early—and they all look like zombies.

A couple hours later, while my family is still hanging out and refusing to leave, Alec walks through the door. He says hello to my family and then says, "I spoke to Aiden."

"Aiden?" Georgia asks. "You think he did this?" I can hear it in her voice, she doesn't believe he's capable of doing something like this. I don't know who did this or why they would want to hurt me, but my gut tells me it wasn't Aiden.

"Who's Aiden?" Dad asks.

"He's the homeless boy, right?" Mom says, remembering the times I've talked about him.

"You think a homeless guy did this?" Dad rises to his feet.

"No, calm down," I tell him. "Aiden is homeless and I believe also autistic. Alec went to talk to him because he's the one who found me."

Everyone looks at Alec. "I didn't mention it because I knew Lexi wouldn't want him brought in until we knew all the details," he explains. "And Lexi would've been pissed if they'd brought him in for questioning and upset him." My heart warms at his words.

"Thank you." I take his hand and squeeze it. "What did he say?"

"He was worried about you and on a one-track mission to make sure you were okay. I told him you're okay and once he calmed down, he said the same thing he told me when I found you. That a man hurt you."

"He doesn't know who?" Dad asks.

"If he does, he couldn't say. He was worked up and that's all I could get out of him."

"We need to file a police report," Dad says. "We need a record of what happened."

"We don't know what happened," I spit out, frustrated that I can't remember. "For all we know a guy hurting me means I was walking past someone and tripped over them and hit my head."

Alec glares. "My guess is Jason did this. Can you remember getting into a fight with him?"

"He wasn't there," Max says. "Hasn't been around since he tried to get Lexi to talk to him and Shane told him to go away...But that doesn't mean he wasn't around where we couldn't see him."

"Exactly," Alec agrees.

"We can't jump to conclusions," I insist. "This could've been an accident." But even as I speak the words, my gut is telling me this was anything but an accident. Jason was pissed at me the last time I saw him. I could see it written all over his features.

"I think we should let the police know," Dad adds. "We can be honest with what we know."

"Which will have them harassing Aiden. No." I shake my head. "At this point it would be his word versus whoever's and they would destroy him."

"Fine." Dad sighs. "But no more going to the beach alone."

"Then he's won," I argue. "I'm not going to let some asshole steal the most important thing to me." The throbbing in my head intensifies and I close my eyes.

Alec must notice because he says, "How about we let Lexi rest. She's been through a lot and needs to sleep."

"I agree," Mom says.

Lips brush my forehead. "We'll be back tomorrow to see you. I love you, sweetheart." When I open my eyes, Mom's are filled with tears.

"Mom, don't cry. I'm okay."

"I know," she says. "But any time something bad happens to your children it's scary. We don't know what happened, but we do know that we could've lost you."

"We love you," Dad says. "I know you're strong, but whoever did this could've hurt you and I'm going to find out who it was."

"I love you too, Dad."

One by one everyone files out. Everyone except Alec, who's adamant about staying since he has the next few days off anyway.

He gets as comfortable in his chair as he can and insists I get some sleep.

I close my eyes, when a weird flash of something—a memory?—hits me.

"*Ow! That hurts. Please don't do this.*"

My eyes pop open and I glance around, chills running up my arms. Alec's eyes are already closed, and I can hear soft snores, telling me he's asleep.

Where did that come from? Was I attacked? Did I fight back? The voice is muffled in my head, so I can't make out who it is. I try to close my eyes to remember more, but nothing else comes, and soon, I'm lost in a fitful sleep.

## CHAPTER TWENTY-TWO

### LEXI

"YOU'RE A FUCKING TEASE! *And teases like you deserve what they get.*"

"Ow! That's hurts. Please don't do this."

"Lexi, Lexi, wake up, baby."

I snap my eyes open and the light from outside attacks me, forcing my eyes to close. It's been almost a week since I was released from the hospital and my headaches have only lessened slightly. The only time I can escape them seems to be when I'm asleep, but the problem is every time I fall asleep I'm hit with nightmares that wake me up. It's a never-ending cycle that has me exhausted and irritated.

"Hey," Alec says softly, concern etched into his features. Every time I'm trapped in a nightmare, he wakes me up. I know he wants to ask what's going on, but he hasn't, which is good since I wouldn't know how to explain it.

With every nightmare that plagues my sleep, I question if they're just that—a nightmare—a story my conscience is conjuring up out of fear of not knowing what happened that night—or if, subconsciously, I'm remembering pieces of the attack. I'm not sure if I'd rather it be the former or the latter. On one hand, if it's not real then I still don't know what happened, but on the other hand, if it *is* real, then I'd almost rather not know what happened.

Because if my nightmares are any indications as to what went down that night... well, I don't even want to consider that.

"Lex, I need you to talk to me," Alec pleads, picking me up and settling me into his lap. His arms encircle my body, making me feel safe. I close my eyes and rest my head against his chest. Whether it's his incessant texting—both me and Georgia, who is on babysitting Lexi duty while he's at work—to make sure I'm okay, or waiting on me hand and foot when he's home, he's been here in some shape or form since the second I was brought to the hospital.

Up until now, he's made sure not to do or say anything that might upset me, but based on his tone, I think he's getting frustrated. And I don't blame him. Every time I go to sleep, I wake a few hours later screaming and crying, dripping in sweat.

At first, he thought it was because I was in pain, but then I apparently spoke in my sleep, begging someone to stop, and he knew then something else is going on.

"I don't know what you want me to say," I murmur into his chest, inhaling the clean scent of his bodywash. He must've showered when he got home from work, because even though he's wearing a T-shirt, I can smell his body wash through it. "I'm having nightmares, but I don't know what's real and what's made up."

Alec tightens his hold on me. "Can you tell me about them?"

*No, because if I do, I'm afraid that will make them real.*

When I'm silent for too long, he says, "What about seeing someone? Like a therapist...someone you can talk to who isn't close to the situation." His suggestion tells me he's thinking the same thing I am. The only reason I would need or want to speak to someone on the outside is if I didn't feel comfortable talking to him, and there's really only one reason I wouldn't feel comfortable talking to him...

"Lex, please." He kisses my forehead. "I'm worried about you. You're barely talking when you're awake, you haven't gotten out of bed except to use the bathroom, you're screaming in your sleep... There's this wall that you're building between us and it's scaring the fuck out of me."

I close my eyes and swallow thickly, silently willing the tears burning behind my eyelids not to fall. He's not wrong, but I don't know what to do, what to say. I need answers, but I don't know how to get them. Unless...

"I want to go talk to Aiden."

Alec nods. "When?"

"Now..." While I'm having a moment of fearlessness.

"All right."

After throwing on a pair of cutoff jean shorts and a tank, and throwing my hair up into a bun, we head to the beach in Alec's truck. The closer we get, the more my heart rate accelerates, and that makes me sad as hell because the beach has always been the place I go to relax. It's almost an extension of myself and now I'm scared to be here.

After I insist on grabbing Aiden something to eat and drink from the pier, we walk toward where Aiden's tent is located. As I glance around for anyone who might be watching us, I realize just how scared I actually am, and that pisses me off.

Alec holds my hand, and I know he can feel me squeezing with every step we take.

When we get near Aiden's tent, I let go. "I need to talk to him alone."

"Lex..."

"He trusts me and is comfortable around me, and if we're alone he might give me details he didn't give you."

Alec scrubs his hands over his face in frustration. "Okay, I'll be right here." He grabs me by my hips and pulls me close, his mouth fusing with mine. Before I can kiss him back, several flashbacks hit me, one after another.

*A mouth attacking mine.*

*Hands gripping my hips.*

*A pelvis grinding into my front.*

The onslaught of horrific images has me pushing Alec away.

"Lex?" The hurt in his voice has me opening my eyes and remembering that I'm here safe with Alec.

"I need to talk to Aiden," is all I say before I turn my back on Alec and head over to the tent.

When I get there, he's sitting in the sand, sketching in his sketchbook with his neon green glasses on. He must hear or sense me because he glances up and then drops his book.

"Lexi!" He pops up onto his feet and meets me halfway,

engulfing me in a hug. It's in this moment, I know with certainty Aiden would never hurt me and if anyone tries to accuse him of such, I'll fucking destroy them.

"I was worried about you," he says. "That man wasn't loving you."

Our conversation from not too long ago pops into my head.

*"That's a man and a woman loving each other,"* he states matter-of-factly.

*"Do you see this a lot on the beach?"*

*"Yes. I thought the man was hurting the woman, but when I tried to save the woman, they yelled at me and said they love each other."*

Bile rises up in my throat. "What man?" I ask him slowly.

"The mean surfer man."

I swallow thickly at his words. "Can we sit and talk? I brought you tacos."

Aiden releases me and nods, taking the bag from me. "Thank you. Tacos are my favorite."

We sit in the sand where he was sitting a moment ago.

"Thank you for saving me," I tell him after a few seconds of silence.

He removes his glasses and looks into my eyes, something he doesn't do often. "The man yelled at me. He said I hurt you. I wouldn't hurt my friend, Lexi."

"I know you wouldn't. They were just really scared and didn't know what happened."

"The man hurt you." He takes his book and opens it, then thrusts it at me. "See? The man wasn't loving you."

I take the book from him and stare at the page for several long seconds. It's of a man and a woman. She's wearing a bathing suit top with her bottoms around her ankles and is bent over a cluster of rocks. He's pulling her hair, his front flush against her back. It looks like they're lost in a moment of passion, and the thought makes my stomach roil. Before I can stop myself, I'm running toward the edge of the water and throwing up.

"Lex, what's wrong?" Alec comes running over. "What happened?"

"I'm okay," I insist, hating that I'm lying to Alec.

Aiden stands. "I didn't hurt her. I didn't hurt her," he repeats, pushing his glasses back on to protect himself.

"I know, buddy," Alec says slowly.

"I'm not buddy. I'm Aiden, and I didn't hurt my friend Lexi."

"He knows," I tell him. "It's okay." Not wanting to upset him any further, or risk him showing Alec the picture he drew, I change the subject. "Eat your tacos before they get cold."

"Tacos are my favorite," Aiden says, sitting back down with his bag of food.

"Here." I pull a few bills from my back pocket and hand them to him. "For tacos."

Aiden eyes the money. "I didn't work. I only get money when I work."

He shoves my hand away, refusing the money, and I sigh.

The first time I tried to give Aiden money to eat, he told me this, so instead of giving him money, I always make it a point to give him food. But since I'm not sure when I'll be back to the beach, I won't be able to buy him food, and I need to make sure he's taken care of.

"Okay," I tell him, not wanting to argue. I'll have to think of another way to get the food to him. "I'll see you soon, okay?"

"Okay, Lexi," he says, devouring his tacos. "See you soon."

When we get home, I head straight for the shower. It's too late, it's been days since I was attacked, but seeing that picture makes me feel dirty and gross. I can't remember it, but the picture is clear as to what happened, and based on his mean surfer comment, there's only one guy I can think of who would be mad at me enough to do this to me.

I let the hot water rain over me as I use my loofah to scrub every inch of my body, until my skin is red and sensitive and the water has turned cold.

When I finally get out, Alec is waiting for me, a frown marring his face. I need to tell him what I think happened. This isn't something I can keep from him, but first I need to find out if it was Jason who attacked me. Because the second I tell Alec, I know without a doubt he's going to go after him.

"You were trying to give him money because you're not planning to return to the beach," he says, calling me out.

"Yeah," I croak.

"Why? What did he tell you?"

"He said what we already know," I half lie. "I was attacked."

"And..." Alec prompts.

"And I'm scared," I admit, giving him some of the honesty he deserves.

"So, you're going to let whoever attacked you win?" He steps toward me and tucks a wayward hair behind my ear. The soft contact of his flesh touching mine sends sparks through my body. "You said in the hospital you weren't going to let whoever did this to you win. You have your surfing comp in a couple weeks..."

"I'm not doing it."

"Bullshit," he hisses. "You've been busting your ass for this. Georgia, Max, me...we'll go with you while you practice, but you're not giving up. This is what you want more than anything, and you're not letting some asshole take that from you."

He's right, and I love him even more for saying it. He could easily tell me to forget it. I suffered a concussion and he's been worried sick about me, but he's putting my wants over his fears, and I need to do the same thing.

"Thank you," I tell him, pressing my mouth to his. Our lips curl around each other, and Alec's hands find my face, deepening the kiss. I can tell he's treating me like glass, worried I'll break, and I hate that I'm scared that he might not be wrong.

I focus on staying in the now, refusing to let any of those horrible flashes ruin the moment. But the second his hand glides to the back of my head and his fingers thread through the strands of my hair, tugging gently on my bun, the picture Aiden drew flashes behind my lids.

*Me being thrust onto the rock.*

*My knees screaming in pain*

*A man behind me, fisting my hair.*

*My scalp is burning.*

*My neck is straining.*

*He's squeezing my breast.*

*Pain is radiating through my body.*

*And then....Everything goes black.*

"Lexi!" Alec screams, snapping me back to the present.

My eyes dart around and I realize I'm huddled in a corner, in a fetal position.

"Baby, you've got to talk to me," Alec begs. "Why are you

crying? Did I hurt you?"

He's so confused and worried and I owe him an explanation. I hate what this is doing to him, to us.

But the moment the words leave my mouth will make them real, and I don't think I can handle that. It's hard enough thinking them, I can't actually speak them.

"You didn't hurt me. I—" I take a deep breath. "I'm having flashes from the night I was attacked."

Alec drops to the floor and sits Indian style, giving me space and his full attention.

"I think it was Jason who attacked me."

Alec's eyes widen slightly.

"Aiden said it was a mean surfer," I add. "So it would make sense." I swallow thickly. "In my flashbacks, the guy calls me a tease." Just like Jason did the night he saw me with Alec.

I can tell he's trying really hard to remain calm for my sake, but his hands are fisted and turning white, and his jaw is ticking like it's about to crack, giving away he's anything but calm.

I consider telling him what else I think, but before I can, he stands and says, "I'm going to kill him."

"Alec, you can't." I stand as well. "You would go to jail, lose your job. I can't lose you." I wrap my arms around his waist.

"You have to report him. The cops need to know."

"It will be my word versus his, and all I have are some flashes, which may or may not be real. They've yet to get him for keying my jeep or slashing my tires."

Alec sighs. "What about Aiden?"

"I don't want to put him through that." I place my hands on his chest, hoping it'll calm him. "I know this is a lot to ask, but whatever he did, he did to me, and as of right now I don't even know what that is. I've seen all the shows. A woman goes into the station and accuses a man of something she isn't sure he did. Nobody takes her seriously."

"This isn't a show, Lexi. This is your life."

"I know, and if I was sure of what happened, I would go. But I'm not, and I don't want to throw shit out there that won't stick."

He nods. "Okay, I don't like it, but I'll do whatever you want. But I'm telling you right now, if I see him somewhere with no one around, all bets are off."

## CHAPTER TWENTY-THREE

### ALEC

It's four in morning and I need to wake Lexi up soon so she can get ready to head to Huntington Beach for the surf competition. It's a day she's been working toward for months. But as I watch her whimper in her sleep, something that's become the norm since she was attacked on the beach, I don't have the heart to wake her yet. On one hand, her whimpering means she's probably having a nightmare, and if I wake her it would stop, but on the other hand, since she rarely sleeps anymore, I hate to wake her up when she's actually sleeping.

Her lips form a soft pout and I run my thumb across them, trying to straighten them out. I hate to see her like this: lost in herself. I can't confirm what's been going through her head, and I know she isn't giving me all the pieces, but I've put enough of the puzzle together to take a guess as to why she's struggling. Why she jumps when I kiss and hold her. Why we haven't had sex since that night. I want to be there for her, but I'm trying to give her space. I'm afraid if I push too hard, Lexi will break.

Her hand reaches out, and when it finds me, she snuggles into my chest. I love that even in her sleep she's drawn to me. I've spent the last few weeks asking around for Jason. He's apparently gone MIA and nobody knows anything about him. Not his last name, where he lives. It's almost as if the guy doesn't even exist. I'm hoping for Lexi's sake he isn't at the comp today, but a small part of me would love to finally be able to get my hands on him.

"You look like you're in deep concentration," Lexi says, her voice gravelly.

"Just watching my beautiful fiancée sleep."

"I don't know if I can do this," she says softly, making my entire body go rigid.

"Do what?"

"Surf today."

I release a sigh of relief. I finally have Lexi in my life, there's no way I'm letting her go now. I don't know what the hell I would do if she said she meant she couldn't be with me.

"I'm not going to tell you that you have to." I pull her on top of me, then pull us up the bed, so I'm sitting against the headboard and she's straddling my middle. "But if your reason for not wanting to surf today is because of that asshole, I'll say what I said before, don't let him win."

"I'm scared," she admits, so unlike the Lexi I've known most of my life. I hate this for her and would do anything to make sure she's never scared again.

"Of what?"

She averts her gaze—something both she and Georgia do when they're lying—telling me that whatever she says won't be the entire truth. "Of choking out there...I haven't practiced in the last couple weeks."

"The Lexi I know wouldn't let fear stand in her way." I kiss the tip of her nose. "Everyone will be there, watching you, supporting you. My family, your parents, brother and sister, Micaela and Ryan will even be there. If at any time you don't feel up to it, then we leave."

"Okay." She leans forward and kisses me. "I'll go get ready."

We get to Huntington Beach, and I remain by Lexi's side the entire time she's setting up and getting checked in. The beach is packed with hundreds of people since this is a pretty big competition.

We find our families, who have a spot on the beach with a blanket and beach chairs. Lexi hugs them all and thanks them for coming, then heads off to practice. There's a short window of time allotted to surfers practicing before the competition begins. I watch as she grabs her board and drops it into the water, then paddles out.

"How's she doing?" Tristan asks.

"She's having flashes she thinks might be memories, some nightmares," I tell him. "She won't really talk about it, though. I told her she should see a therapist."

"I'll find a couple who take her insurance," he says. "She'll get through this. We just need—"

"What's wrong with Lexi?" Max asks, cutting his dad off.

My eyes quickly find her. She's standing along the edge of the water, her fists at her sides. Her board is in the water floating away, and she isn't moving, isn't attempting to grab it. I follow her line of sight, and that's when I see him: Motherfucking Jason.

"Grab Lexi!" I yell to her dad, as I jump to my feet and run toward Jason. I'll be damned if he's going anywhere without me finding out who the fuck this guy is.

I try to keep eyes on him, as I run up the beach, but there are too many people, the beach is too packed, and I lose him. I scour the area, the parking lot, combing the beach, but I can't find him.

When I get back to the area where everyone is, Lexi has a large towel wrapped around her and her sister is hugging her tightly, her mom and dad both hovering over them with pained expressions on their faces.

"What did he do?" I ask her, taking her from Georgia.

"He didn't do anything," she says, her voice cracking with emotion. "It was just...the way he looked at me." She visibly shivers. "I don't want to be here. Please take me home."

My eyes meet with her dad's, and his jaw ticks, but he nods once, silently asking me to do as she wants. I fucking hate this asshole for getting to Lexi, for fucking with her, and I'm not going to stop until I find him and uncover what he did to her. Lexi needs answers, and if I have to beat them out of him, I will.

After saying our goodbyes to everyone, we head home, where Lexi excuses herself, saying she's tired. Unsure if I should lie with her or give her some space, I pace the hallway, until finally I've had enough and I go in.

She's curled up in our blankets, her eyes closed. I know she's not sleeping because she isn't softly snoring, but she must want me to think she is. So I edge onto the bed next to her and wrap my arms around her carefully, holding her close but not too hard. She sighs in contentment and a few minutes later the snoring comes.

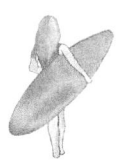

## CHAPTER TWENTY-FOUR

### LEXI

"Oh, Lexi," Mom breathes. "You look absolutely gorgeous."

"I agree," Mila says. "Stunning."

Georgia nods. "Most beautiful bride ever."

"It's perfect." Micaela sniffles. "Sorry, I'm just kind of emotional right now." She wipes a tear, and everyone laughs. She recently found out that she and Ryan are expecting their second baby and she's been crying over everything.

I glance at the three-part mirror that shows off every angle of me and try like hell to smile. They're all right. The dress is beautiful. It's classy, not too girly. Ivory instead of white like I wanted. It's a floor-length, sleeveless, A-line design, which will keep me cool during our summer wedding.

It's the perfect wedding dress, and I should be happy that after only trying on a couple I found the perfect one. But it's hard to be here, in the moment, and be happy, when I can't get Jason out of my head. The way he evilly smirked at me when our eyes met at Huntington Beach, I could feel it in my bones. He was the man who attacked me on the beach that night, and by the smarmy look on his face, he didn't give a shit that I knew. He knew he got away with it, and the thought equally has me fuming and makes me sick to my stomach.

"Lexi," my mom prompts. "What do you think?" Her sympathetic eyes meet mine in the mirror and I hate that I'm ruining this. Today should be a happy day. I should be laughing and smiling and so excited. We've had this day booked for weeks, and when she offered to cancel, I insisted we go. There are only so many weeks left until our wedding and so much still to do.

"It's perfect," I tell her. "And it doesn't even have to be altered."

She comes up behind me and smiles warmly. "You're going to make a beautiful bride."

"Thank you, Mom." I turn around and wrap my arms around her, needing to feel her warm motherly touch. "I love you so much."

"Oh, sweetheart, I love you too."

Since we're keeping the wedding small, we're not doing bridesmaids or groomsmen. Alec has asked Chase to be his best man and Georgia is my maid of honor. They'll be the only people up at the altar with us and will sign as our witnesses. So, after I confirm with the saleswoman I would like this dress, she helps me out of it and bags it up, and then we're on our way.

"Lunch?" Mila suggests.

"Sure," we all agree.

We stop at a deli we all enjoy and order soups and sandwiches to eat out on the patio. While we eat, Mom and Mila go over the details for the wedding, and Georgia and I look at the latest pictures Micaela took of her son RJ. He's so adorable and seems to be a little terror. He definitely gets that from Micaela and not his daddy.

I'm taking a bite of my sandwich when my phone dings with an incoming text.

**Alec: Have a bag packed when I get home. We're going away for a few days.**

My heart and stomach both flutter at the thought of some time away with Alec. The last couple weeks, even though we've slept in the same bed whenever Alec isn't working, has felt like we're floating in the water, and each of us is being pulled in separate directions. Alec has been trying so hard to get to me, but I've been so lost in myself, I haven't even attempted to meet him halfway.

Maybe this is what we need. Some time away from here to find our way back to each other.

**Me: I'll be ready!**

"Everything okay?" Georgia asks carefully, turning her attention to me. She's been practically walking on eggshells when she talks to me lately, scared the wrong thing will send me over the edge. Me going away will also give her a little break.

"Yeah, Alec and I are going to go away for a few days."

Georgia's brows dip together. "For how long? My graduation is next Friday."

"You think I would miss your graduation?" I scoff. "Only a few days."

Georgia releases a sigh of relief, then frowns. "Oh, great. You're leaving me alone with Chase." She scrunches her nose up in disgust.

"What's wrong with Chase?" I know they've gotten into it a few times in the past, but I didn't realize things between them were bad enough she doesn't want to be alone with him.

"Nothing," she says quickly, shaking her head.

"Don't do that." I lock eyes with her. "I know I've been...a little lost lately. But don't walk on eggshells around me, please. I already feel like things between Alec and me are rocky. I can't handle you and me not being us."

Georgia sighs. "I'm sorry. I just don't want to upset you."

"I'm not going to break," I promise her. If I haven't broken yet, I think I'm in the clear...

"Okay, well, you're right about being a little lost," she says. "Because if you were paying attention then you would've noticed Chase and his overactive dick." She rolls her eyes, and I crack up.

"His overactive dick?" She's mentioned he's hooked up with a few women since his divorce was finalized, but it's to be expected. He's young and was married for years, and his ex-wife hurt him.

"Yeah. Every day he's off, he has a different woman in his room, sometimes two." She gags. "I think Alec asked him to tone it down a bit since the day at the beach, because he's actually been quiet. But the second he finds out you and Alec are leaving he's probably going to throw an orgy." She fake shivers. "He's definitely proven a dick can't fall off from overuse."

Micaela and I both laugh, and Georgia glares. "You wouldn't be laughing if you had to hear him and the bimbos he's with every night."

"Hear who?" Mom asks.

"Chase," I tell her.

"The women are ridiculous," Georgia complains. "Oh, Chase, your dick is so big." She huffs. "If I have to hear one more woman stroke his ego, I'm going to kill myself."

"Sounds like that's not the only thing they're stroking." Mom snorts.

"Oh my God, Mom!" Georgia shrieks. "No, just no."

"Good one," Mila says to my mom, giving her a high five as Micaela and I crack up laughing.

After lunch, we head to the bakery and pick out the cake, then go shopping for my shoes and Georgia's and Micaela's dresses. When we're all completely shopped out, we say goodbye to Micaela, who only came up for the day, and then head home.

Since I'm not sure where Alec and I are going, I pack a couple casual outfits, a bathing suit, and something nice to wear out. Then I find Georgia so we can hang out.

"Up for some O.C.?" I ask from her doorway.

She glances up at me from her laptop, more than likely studying for her last final, and smiles brightly. "Always." She shuts the lid and sets it on her nightstand, then pats the mattress next to her.

I hop onto the bed and cuddle up next to her, as she clicks the remote, turning on the television. She finds the show she left off on and it starts: Marissa and Ryan are arguing and Seth is begging Summer to give him attention.

We watch in silence for a few minutes, before Georgia lays her head on mine. "I've missed you," she whispers. My throat fills with emotion, and I close my eyes, so tears don't escape.

"I've missed you too."

We watch one episode after another, until neither of us can keep our eyes open and the program asks us if we want to continue to watch. I should probably go back to my bed, but I'm comfortable in here, with my sister, so instead, when she clicks off the show, I snuggle up next to her and wrap my arms around her.

"Night, Georgia."

"Night, Lex."

---

STRONG ARMS WRAP around me from behind, jolting me awake.

*"Ow! That's hurts. Please don't do this."*

*He pulls on my bathing suit bottoms and then his fingers—*

"Lex," Alec prompts, shaking me slightly and knocking me back to the present.

I take a deep breath and roll over, away from Georgia who's still asleep, and into my fiancé's safe arms. I bury my face into his chest, inhaling his scent, reminding myself over and over again, he's who I'm here with. I'm in my sister's bed, in Alec's arms. I'm safe.

Alec doesn't say anything, just holds me tightly, until I lift my face up and make eye contact with him. "I'm ready to get out of here."

The pained look on his face tells me he wants to ask me what just happened, but he doesn't. Instead, he nods once. "Okay, let's go."

When I climb off the bed and stand upright, a sudden bout of dizziness hits me, making me wobble slightly. Alec notices and clasps onto my forearms. "Hey, you okay?"

"Yeah, I just felt a little lightheaded. I must've gotten up too fast."

He stares at me for several heartbeats and then says, "All right, let's get you something to eat. You haven't been eating much lately."

He's not wrong. I think I've lost an entire clothing size the last few weeks. Between the nightmares and the thoughts while I'm awake, I haven't had much of an appetite.

Alec grabs my overnight bag and his and throws them into the back of my jeep and then we're off. He hasn't mentioned where we're going, and I haven't asked. I like that he's surprising me. Something sweet and fun is just what I need right now.

The drive is done in awkward silence and I pray this isn't how the next couple days will be. Neither of us knowing what to do or say. Alec not wanting to say the wrong thing, and me having no damn clue what to even say.

We arrive in Santa Barbara and pull up to a beautiful hotel that's right on the beach. We get out and Alec tells the valet his name.

"Your luggage will be in your room, Mrs. Sterling," the gentleman says to me. Being called Alec's last name has me smiling, like a real smile, for the first time in a long time.

"Did you hear that?" I say to him as I hook my arm in his. "Mrs. Sterling. Has a nice ring to it."

"It sounds fucking perfect." He leans over and kisses my temple.

We get situated in our room and once the bags arrive, we change into our swimsuits. As I step out of the bathroom, I notice Alec is standing on the balcony staring out over the water.

I take a moment to admire him from behind. My best friend, my fiancé, and my soon-to-be husband. He's wearing a pair of board shorts and is shirtless, his arms resting against the top of the railing. From here, I can see his roped neck and back muscles, and his corded muscular forearms that don various tattoos he's gotten over the years. Alec is without a doubt the strongest man I know—and not just on the outside. He lost his father not too long ago, and instead of drowning in his grief, he turned it around, taking control of his life and living not only for himself but for his dad as well.

It makes me realize how much I want to be like Alec, be strong like he is. I can't change what happened to me... hell, I don't even know what happened to me. But I can change how I react to what happened. Every day I dwell on what happened is another day Jason wins. And I'm done letting him win.

I step up behind Alec and circle my arms around his torso, resting the side of my face against his back. He stiffens slightly, and I close my eyes, hating that he's shocked his fiancée is actually trying to touch him. He doesn't know what to do, what to say. And it's my fault because I've pushed him away.

"Alec," I say, sliding around and under his arm, so we're face-to-face. My back is against the railing and I'm standing between his arms. He glances down at me, assessing me, wondering what's wrong.

"I've missed you," I tell him, running my hands up his six-pack abs and over his taut chest. I encircle my arms around his neck and bring his face down to mine. My lips softly caress his. Tasting him for what feels like the first time. He doesn't move, letting me lead. But when my tongue pushes against his lips, he grants me access. I've missed how he tastes, how he feels.

The kiss deepens, and I pull him closer to me. "I need you," I murmur against his lips. His eyes pop open, searching my face to make sure I mean what I say. "Please, I need us."

My words must be what he needed to hear, because the next thing I know, I'm being lifted and brought back into our suite. He carries me over to the big bed and gently lays me down, climbing over me. Our mouths reconnect, this time with more passion. It's been weeks since we've been intimate, and it shows in our moves. The way Alec possessively nips at my bottom lip, then trails kisses down my neck. The way I thread my fingers through his hair, pulling him toward me, needing him closer.

He kisses his way across my collarbone and stops at my breasts. Pulling the triangle material to the side, he sucks on one nipple and then the other. Electric currents zap through my body, going straight to my core. I need Alec, to feel close to him. To replace any possible flashback with memories of him.

I watch as he kisses along the center of my belly, stopping to tug gently on my belly button ring. He continues his descent, placing a small kiss to my hip where my tattoo is. Then he works his way down to the apex of my legs. He spreads my legs open, then pulls on the strings on my hips to remove my bikini bottoms, leaving me completely bare to him.

He places an open-mouthed kiss to the hood of my pussy, before he opens me and licks up my center. I want to close my eyes and get lost in the sensations of what he's doing to me, but I keep my eyes open, memorizing every lick, every suck. Replacing every flashback, every nightmare with Alec. His kisses, his touches...

He pushes a finger, and then two, inside me, and our eyes lock. "You're mine," he growls, as if he knows exactly what I'm doing, what I'm thinking.

"Yours," I breathe in agreement.

He goes back to fucking me with his tongue and fingers and I make sure to stay right here in the moment with him. When my orgasm rips through me like a tidal wave, I scream out his name.

"Fuck me," I beg, needing him inside of me. Not wanting this moment to end.

He pushes his shorts down and hovers above me, his strong arms caging me in. "Lex, when I'm with you, I don't fuck you," he murmurs against my mouth. "I make love to you. Understand me?"

Tears prick my eyes. "Yes," I choke out. "Make love to me, please."

"My pleasure," he says as he pushes into me, filling me completely. His mouth crashes against mine. My hips rock against his. I tug on the ends of his hair as he makes love to me. And for the first time in weeks, my body relaxes. My heart slows. My brain feels free. This is exactly what I needed. Alec.

I allow myself to close my eyes, to enjoy the moment, to get lost in the feeling, but before I can stop it from happening, flashes from that night surface.

*The beach.*

*The sand.*

*The rocks.*

*Hands, not Alec's, hurting me.*

"Lexi," Alec says, "stay with me, baby."

I wrench my lids open and my eyes meet his. I focus on Alec, on his warm, chocolate brown eyes that look at me with love and adoration. On his perfect lips that say the sweetest words to me. On the way he feels inside of me, as if I was made just for him.

With Alec's eyes locked with mine, we both find our release, and I know without a shadow of a doubt, this man is everything I need. He's my path. My forever. And it's time I get the help I need, so I can be everything he needs.

# CHAPTER TWENTY-FIVE

## ALEC

"I'M GOING TO SEE A THERAPIST," Lexi says to me when she steps out of the shower from rinsing off. I'm pulling my board shorts up, and I stop, meeting her eyes in the mirror.

"Yeah?"

"Yeah. There's a chance I'm never going to know what happened that night, but I need to speak to someone about it. Get my thoughts out and find a way to move past it."

I finish putting on my shorts and turn around to face her. "I think that sounds like a good idea."

"Thank you for being patient with me these last few weeks."

"You never have to thank me for that," I tell her, drawing her naked body into my arms. "I love you, and we're in this together."

She smiles, a soft, genuine smile. One I haven't seen in a while. "I love you too, and I can't wait to become your wife."

"And I can't wait to become your husband." I bring her hand up to my mouth and kiss her engagement ring. "Have you thought about where you want to go from here?" Lexi had been hoping to get picked up by Vans, but because she left the competition without even competing, that's no longer an option. She hasn't mentioned it, but I'm worried she's been dwelling on it.

Lexi chews on her bottom lip. "Honestly, I don't know." She

shrugs as her eyes turn glossy. "Would it be okay if maybe we just focused on us while we're here?"

I open my mouth to argue, but she adds, "I know I have to deal with it, and I will. But right now I just want to be with you."

"Okay," I agree, hating that she's pushing shit aside, but hopefully when we get home and she meets with a therapist, she'll start dealing with everything. "What do you say we head out to the beach? Catch some sun, some waves. We can have dinner downtown..."

"Sounds perfect."

And the next three days are spent just like that. On the beach, in the water, in Lexi. Little by little, day by day, we find our way back to each other. We make love all over the hotel room: in the bed, in the shower, on the balcony. We check out the art galleries and do some shopping downtown. By the time check-out comes around, I consider quitting my job and extending our stay.

But since I kind of need my job, and we can't actually stay here indefinitely, after we have one last lunch downtown, we head home.

When we walk through the door, there's yelling and screaming, and Lexi rushes in, worried. I drop our luggage by the door, and we both go in search of where the voices are coming from.

"We have to share a bathroom," Georgia yells. "Is it too much to ask that you make sure your conquests don't touch my stuff?"

"I said I was sorry," Chase says. "I'll replace your shaver."

"I could've used it!" Georgia shrieks, sounding like she's ready to cry. "What if she had an STD?"

"I'm sorry," Chase repeats.

"Hey, what's going on?" Lexi asks, stepping up next to her sister and glaring at Chase.

"He had some girl over last night and she used my stuff," Georgia says. "My shampoo and conditioner and my shaver!"

"Ewww..." Lexi thumps Chase on the top of his arm. "Keep your hoochies out of my sister's stuff."

"I'll just...bring my stuff into my room," Georgia says, stepping out of Chase's room. "It's fine," she mumbles.

"No, it's not," Lexi says, shooting me a glare that says *this is your friend, you better handle this*.

Before I can say a word, though, Chase speaks up. "Look, I'm going to look for my own place, but until I find something, I won't bring any more women here."

"You don't have to find your own place," I tell him. "But yeah, maybe you could hang out at their place instead..." We talked about this before, but it was because I didn't want to upset Lexi. I'm assuming since Lexi and I were gone, he thought it would be okay.

"Done," he says. "I'm going to head out." He walks over to Georgia's room. "It won't happen again. I promise."

"Okay," she says softly. "Thanks."

He steps back out, and with a shake of his head, he grabs his keys and disappears out the door.

The rest of the afternoon is spent watching reruns of the girls' favorite shows and eating pizza that we have delivered. We all fall asleep in the same bed, just like old times, and in the morning, when I get up to go to work, leaving them both asleep, I feel like shit is finally getting back to the way it was before that asshole Jason fucked everything up.

When I get to the station, Chase is already there, talking with the other guys. "You never came home last night?" I ask.

"I did, after you guys were asleep, and I left before you. Figured I would give them some time to calm down. I also replaced Georgia's stuff. Left it in the bathroom for her."

"Thanks, man," I tell him. "They'll get over it. You don't have to find a new place to live." After he left, and Georgia calmed down, she felt bad for making Chase feel like he needed to move out.

"Eh, I'm newly single, and you're about to be married...I never planned to stay with you forever." He shrugs. "Are you and Lexi planning to get your own place after you get married?"

"We haven't really discussed it." I can't imagine her living anywhere without her sister. Those two have been inseparable for as far back as I can remember.

My phone dings with a text from Charlie, Lexi and Georgia's mom, letting everyone know they'll be hosting a dinner Friday night after Georgia's graduation and to please RSVP, so she knows how many people to order for.

"You going to the dinner?" I ask Chase, who laughs.

"Ah, no. That girl can't stand the sight of me. I think me

breathing personally offends her. I'm not about to ruin her graduation by being there."

"I don't think *you* offend her," I say with a laugh. "Just you fucking all those women so loudly that Georgia feels like she's forced to listen to a porno." I clasp him on his back. "I'm going to get a workout in, you coming?"

"Always."

# CHAPTER TWENTY-SIX

## LEXI

"Lexi, you ready to go to the meeting?" Georgia asks through the door.

"Yeah, just give me a minute." I climb onto my feet and flush the toilet, then wash my mouth out and brush my teeth for the third time this morning. The last several days I haven't been feeling so hot. It started when Alec and I were away, but I ignored it. It wasn't too bad, and I figured I probably just ate something that didn't agree with me, or I was stressed and exhausted from everything that's happened the last few weeks.

But then, the morning Alec left to work after returning from our trip, I went over to my parents' house to visit with them and get my insurance information so I could make an appointment with a therapist. As I walked through their door, the smell of bacon cooking hit my nostrils and I ran to the bathroom to throw up. I knew right then something was wrong. Very wrong.

I step out of the bathroom and Georgia is standing there, assessing me with her knowing, sisterly eyes. I release a harsh breath and she envelops me in a hug. She doesn't ask and I don't say anything. We don't need to.

Twenty minutes later, we walk into Klein's, an upscale bistro downtown. Our gazes both search for the woman we're meeting. "I think that's her," Georgia says, nodding toward a gray-haired older woman sitting in the corner. She's dressed in an expensive looking pant suit and her hair is pulled up into a tight chignon.

"You can do this," I tell her, squeezing her arm. "And I'll be with you the entire time."

"Are you Hilda Reynolds?" she asks when we approach.

The woman glances up and smiles stiffly. She has brown eyes, as opposed to Georgia's green and nothing about her reminds me of Georgia. They might be related, but they don't look it. "I am." She stands and extends her hand, which Georgia takes. Kind of weird that a woman meets her granddaughter for the first time in years and she shakes her hand instead of hugging her. Our grandma from our dad's side can't hug us enough when she comes home from traveling.

"Thank you for finally meeting with me." Her words are polite, but her tone is strained, like she's forcing herself to be civil. It's a good thing I'm here with Georgia, because if this woman says anything to hurt my sister, I'll have no problem throat punching her.

"And who is this?" She juts her chin toward me.

"I'm Lexi," I tell her. "Georgia's sister."

"You look to be the same age," Hilda says. "Impossible."

"Not biologically," Georgia says softly, clearly intimidated by this bitch.

"But we might as well be," I add.

The waitress comes over and we order drinks. Once she walks away, Hilda cuts straight to the chase. "I've asked you here today because you're about to graduate. Your father, Justin Reynolds, left in his will that until you're twenty-two or graduate college, I was to oversee the company he left behind."

When Georgia squints in confusion, Hilda says, "Of course your mother didn't tell you." The way she spits out the word mother has my hackles rising. She doesn't know shit about our mother.

"If she didn't, it was with good reason," I tell her. "Please get to the point of this meeting." I've had about enough of this uptight stuck-up woman.

"My point is"—she keeps her eyes on Georgia—"he left you a multimillion-dollar empire, and now that you've graduated, I would like for you to sign it over to me." She pulls out a folder from her purse and opens it up like she didn't just drop a huge bombshell.

Georgia gasps, and I glare. "Why would he do that?" she asks as the waitress sets our drinks down. One whiff of my caramel macchiato and I almost upchuck right here at the table. Discreetly, I push it away, so I don't have to smell it. Georgia eyes me curiously but doesn't question it.

The waitress takes our orders and I go with a parfait, hoping it will be easy on my stomach. Hilda orders one as well, and Georgia orders pancakes.

"Contrary to what your mother has probably told you," Hilda says, once the waiter has stepped away, "your father was a good man who loved you."

Georgia flinches. "She didn't tell me anything...and I barely even remember him." She quickly averts her gaze, and I immediately wonder what's going through her head.

Hilda huffs. "That's because your mother killed him when you were little." This time we both gasp. "Of course she didn't tell you any of this. I'm surprised she even let you meet with me."

When Georgia stays quiet, Hilda laughs evilly. "She doesn't know, does she?"

"Whatever she knows or doesn't know isn't your concern," I say. "So, her bio dad left her a company...and you want it...She's not going to just sign it over to you."

"I don't think—" Georgia begins, but I cut her off.

"You said it's worth millions. I'm not completely sure how it all works, but if she owns a company and you want it, I think you would have to *buy* it."

Hilda shoots daggers at me. "My husband and I have been running it for years."

"My grandfather?" Georgia asks. "I thought he was dead."

"He is. Thomas Faulding is my husband and the COO of Reynolds Oil. He's been running the company since your father was killed."

There she goes with that shit again... "You need to stop saying that," I warn. "Our mother wouldn't kill anyone. Now, if you want the company, you'll have to buy it from Georgia."

"Listen here, little girl," Hilda says, finally losing the little bit of restraint she had. "This is my damn company. Justin wrote that will before he knew Charlotte was a lying, cheating whore."

"We're done here." I stand, taking Georgia by the arm. "Georgia's attorney will be in contact." I pull her out of the bistro, all the way to my jeep, not stopping until we're inside.

"We have to tell Mom about her. That woman is fucking crazy."

"I can't." Georgia shakes her head. "It would break her heart that I went behind her back."

"She'll understand." Our mother is the most understanding person I know.

"Okay. Will you go with me?"

"Of course."

---

"YOU DID WHAT?" Mom gasps, glancing from us to our dad. "Why would you meet with her?" Mom's bottom lips wobbles and tears prick her eyes. Dad envelops her in a side hug to comfort her.

"I thought I could go there, find out what she wanted, and you would never know," Georgia says. "I'm sorry."

"Oh no," Mom tells her, "you didn't do anything wrong. I just wish you had told me so I could've gone with you."

"Did you know my..." Georgia's words falter, unsure what to call the man who is her biological dad. "Umm... my... I don't know what to call him," Georgia finally says.

Dad moves from Mom to Georgia. "You can call him whatever you're comfortable with," he says. "Your dad, your father, Justin...I won't take offense."

"You're my dad," Georgia says. "This is just so confusing. She said he loved me..."

Mom sniffles. "I can't do this."

"You never can," Georgia snaps, shocking the hell out of me. "She said you killed him."

Mom gasps, and Dad curses.

"Why would she say that?" Georgia asks. "I need you to tell me, because all I've heard about him is from my grandmother, who said he loved me and that you killed him. And she said other stuff too..." She trails off. She might be upset and want answers, but she would never intentionally hurt Mom's feelings.

Just as I'm wrapping my arms around Georgia, so she knows I have her back, my stomach roils, and I'm jumping up. "Need to go pee!" I yell, as I sprint to the bathroom. I spend the next few minutes dry heaving, since I haven't eaten since last night. When I'm done, I attempt to wash my mouth out and then go back to join my family.

"Charlie," Dad says. "I think it's time we talk to the girls." I sit next to Georgia, taking her hand in mine in support.

Mom shakes her head, closing her eyes, but then nods. "Hilda was right," she says softly. "I did kill Justin."

"It was in self-defense," Dad adds. "Your mom left him and he came after her. He had a gun and they fought. Had she not shot him, he would've killed her."

Tears stream down Mom's face, as Georgia and I both fly off the couch and hug her tightly. "I should've told you," Mom says. "It was just a horrible time and I never wanted you to be tainted by it."

"She said I own his company," Georgia says. "Reynolds Oil, and she wants me to sign it over to her."

Mom's lips turn down into a frown.

"I think she should have to buy it," I add. "I've seen enough shows to know if it's worth millions, Georgia should be getting money. That woman tried to meet with Georgia to get her to sign it over so she wouldn't have to pay her. I told her we would have Georgia's lawyer contact her. There's no way Georgia is giving that dreadful woman anything for free."

Dad chuckles. "You sure you don't want to major in law?" His comment is meant as a joke, but it reminds me of how uncertain my future is. I have a year left of school in a major that will lead to nowhere, and a surfing career that, if I'm right about why I'm throwing up, won't be happening any time soon.

"So, what do I do?" Georgia asks, thankfully bringing the attention back to her.

"We'll hire an attorney, as Lexi said," Dad tells her. "Request to see the will Justin had drawn up and go from there."

"And don't worry," I tell her. "We'll all be here with you every step of the way. That evil woman might think she could get one over on you, but she doesn't know who she's messing with."

"Thank you," Georgia says, giving me a hug, then standing to give Dad and then Mom one.

When we get home, it's almost four o'clock. I place a call to my doctor, and the scheduling nurse tells me they can get me in this week.

"Do you know roughly how far along you are?" she asks.

"Umm... I'm not sure." I try to remember when my last period was, but I suck at keeping track. *Just like I suck at taking my pills...*

"No problem, the doctor can figure it out when you're here."

"Thanks."

I end the call and consider texting Alec, but figure I should wait to tell him tomorrow when he's home from work, in person.

What the nurse asked about my period has me curious, so I pull up my calendar and try to remember when I got my last period. I think about since Alec and I got together...We haven't used protection, and I haven't gotten my period once. I swipe back to the previous months, unable to recall when I got it last. My period has always been all over the place, and since I suck at taking my birth control pills, that doesn't help any.

I should probably be more anxious about possibly being pregnant, but the thought of having Alec's baby kind of excites me. We're getting married next week... He has a good job... He mentioned before that if I did get pregnant, it wouldn't be the worst thing in the world, since he's all about seizing the day.

I lie back in my bed and close my eyes, imagining our life. Him coming home from work and us spending the day with our baby. Going to the parks and the beach, teaching him how to swim and one day surf. Teaching him art. I bet Alec will love to teach him MMA, just like Mason taught him.

As the imaginary reel of images scrolls through my head, my heart picks up speed at the idea of becoming a mom. I would make sure I'm a good mom like Charlie. I would be there for our baby, love him with my entire being. Maybe this is what my future looks like... being a mom. Maybe this is what I was meant to do, the path I'm meant to take. Charlie runs her paint studio, but aside from that, growing up, she was always around, hands-on. I'm not saying I don't want to figure out what else I want to do with my life, but maybe being a mom and wife is what I'm meant to do. And over time, I can figure everything else out.

Suddenly excited, I pull out my phone to text Alec that we need to talk when he gets home, but before I can get the words out, a text from him comes in.

**Alec: Luke and Finn are both out with flu. Chase asked me to fill in with him. I won't be home until Friday morning.**

Damn, not only will he not be home for me to tell him our news, but he won't be able to go to the doctor with me. As I'm texting him back, telling him to stay safe and that I'll see him Friday morning for Georgia's graduation, the need to throw up hits me again. I probably shouldn't have eaten so much at my parents' place. But I was starving and my dad's burgers smelled and tasted so good.

I run to the bathroom and throw up my entire lunch, and then it hits me. What if I'm not pregnant? What if I'm sick? I feel like if I were, I would have other symptoms, but just to be sure, I should get confirmation from the doctor, and then once I know for sure, I can tell Alec, and hopefully he'll be as excited as I am, and we can celebrate.

**Me: Sucks. Miss you and I'll see you Friday.
Alec: I'll be off through Sunday. We should do something fun.
Me: Sounds good!**

## CHAPTER TWENTY-SEVEN

### ALEC

Ninety-six-hour shifts suck. Sure, it means overtime, which is great, but it also means four days without seeing Lexi, four days of sleeping at the station without her.

"Thanks again for staying," Chase says as we walk up to the condo. "The last thing we needed was one of them giving everyone else the flu."

"No worries," I tell him. "You know I got your back."

"I'm going to sleep for the next twenty-four hours," Chase half-jokes before he slips into his room.

Since there were three pretty big fires yesterday—a dryer that was left on and caught fire and a building with faulty wiring—and another one last night—a candle that caught a curtain on fire while a family with little kids were sleeping—we're both exhausted as fuck. But today is the day of Georgia's graduation, so the last thing I'll be doing is sleeping. It's later this afternoon, but she said we have to head to the university auditorium early to get good seats. I'm hoping Lexi will at least be in bed, so we can cuddle for a few minutes before we both need to get ready.

When I enter our room, the bed is empty. She's probably sleeping in Georgia's bed. But when I walk in there, Georgia is up and typing away furiously on her laptop.

"Have you seen Lexi?" I ask.

"No." She stops typing and turns toward me. "Actually..." Her brows furrow in thought. "I haven't seen her since yesterday." She glances at her phone. "Shoot! It's already eight fifteen. I need to get ready for my graduation."

"What do you mean you haven't seen her since yesterday?"

Flashbacks of the last time Lexi disappeared flash before my eyes, and I'm running to the bathroom to make sure she isn't there. "Lexi!" I call out. No answer. "Lex!" Still nothing.

I grab my phone and pull up our conversation. Our last text was yesterday afternoon. I got so busy with putting out fires, I lost track of time.

"When's the last time you saw her?" I ask Georgia.

"Umm...Yesterday afternoon," she says.

"Not last night?"

"No." She shakes her head. "This company I work for...their site crashed and I've been working all night getting it back up. I lost track of time."

I call Lexi's phone, but it goes to voicemail. "I'm going to check the beach."

Georgia's eyes meet mine. "Alec, there's no way..."

"I have to make sure."

I run out the door and hop into my truck, noting that Lexi's jeep isn't in the parking lot. Fuck, where the hell is she? There's no way she would go to the beach, right? As far as I know, she hasn't been back there since she went to talk to Aiden. And to go without saying a word to anyone...No, no way. This doesn't make sense.

I dial her dad's number, hoping this is just some kind of shitty miscommunication. "Alec," he says.

"Have you seen Lexi?"

"No."

My heart squeezes in my chest. It's fucking hard to breathe. "Nobody has heard from her since yesterday afternoon."

"Fuck," he curses. "If that asshole..."

"I'm almost to the beach now. If he has anything to do with this, I'll kill him. Can you check her phone for the tracking?"

"Yeah, give me a second." A few seconds later, he says, "Her phone is off."

"Damn it." I slam my fist against the steering wheel.

## CHAPTER TWENTY-SEVEN

"Keep me posted."

We hang up and I pull into the parking lot. I don't spot Lexi's jeep anywhere, but I still head down to where Aiden is to see if he's seen her.

"Hi, Lexi's boyfriend," he says when I walk up. I want to correct him and tell him I'm Lexi's fiancé, but right now it really doesn't fucking matter. He's sitting in the sand, drawing in his sketchbook. He grabs his neon green glasses and puts them on.

"Hey, Aiden," I tell him, trying like hell to remain calm. If I upset him, he'll shrink up and I won't get any answers. "Have you seen Lexi?"

"Yes. She brought me dinner." He goes back to coloring in his sketchbook.

"Last night?" I ask to confirm.

"Yes, she brought me my favorite tacos," he says, not looking up.

*Fuck, Lexi, what the hell were you doing here alone?*

"Hey, Aiden, remember that bad man who hurt Lexi?"

Aiden's head pops up. "I didn't hurt her. It was that mean surfer."

*Mean surfer...Jesus, if that doesn't prove it was Jason...*

"I know. Did you see him here last night...with Lexi?"

"No. He isn't Lexi's friend. He's mean and he didn't love Lexi. He hurt her. She's not his friend."

"I know," I agree, trying to piece together what he's saying. "Did Lexi say where she was going last night?"

"She was sad. She was crying."

Fuck. Fuck. Fuck. This just keeps getting better.

"Did she say where she was going?" I repeat. "She never came home."

"No, she brought me tacos and cried. I gave her a picture to make her happy."

"When she left, was she alone?"

"Yes."

"And did she say where she was going?" I try again.

"No, but she said she'll see me soon. And my Lexi doesn't lie, so I'll see her soon. I'll tell her when I see her you want to see her."

I sigh in frustration. "Okay, thank you."

"Bye, Lexi's boyfriend."

I walk up to the pier and find the taco place where Lexi always buys Aiden his tacos. "Excuse me," I say to the gentleman who's wiping down the counter. "My fiancée, Lexi Scott, comes here a lot to buy tacos..."

"Yeah, I know her," he says before I can finish.

"Was she here last night buying tacos?"

"Yeah, she was. Real nice girl. She paid in advance for me to have tacos, every day, delivered to that homeless guy down under the pier."

Of course she did. Fuck, Lexi, where the hell are you? And why were you here?

"She showed up last night and gave me enough money for the next couple months, then bought some tacos and said she would bring it to the guy herself."

"Did you see her leave?"

"Nah, after she got the tacos and left, I didn't see her again."

"All right, thanks."

I'm heading to my truck, when I see that asshole walking down the sidewalk with a board under his arm. He's talking to some woman, who is laughing at whatever he's saying.

Without thinking, I stalk over to him. He doesn't see me coming, until it's too late, and my fist is connecting with the side of his face. He stumbles back, his board hitting the ground. The girl screams. I punch him again and again, landing each blow, not giving him a chance to get a single punch in.

He's on the ground, his face covered in blood, and I'm about to yank him back up to hit him again, when someone comes up from behind and pulls me off him. His body falls to the ground.

I try to shove whoever it is off me, so I can finish this, but the guy is too strong. "Alec," Mason barks. "What the fuck are you doing?"

"Get off me," I yell, trying to go after Jason again. He's now crawling backward, spitting blood onto the concrete. The woman he was talking to is at his side. "He's the asshole who attacked Lexi."

Mason pauses for a second, and then Tristan steps up. "This is him?" Tristan asks, walking up to Jason.

"Yeah, and Lexi was seen here last night and now I can't find her."

"You see my daughter?" Tristan asks.

Jason laughs. Fucking laughs.

"Let me go!" I shout at Mason, who's still holding me back.

"No, you handle this shit right. The last thing you need is him charging you with assault." Too late for that shit.

"I asked you a question," Tristan says. "I suggest you answer me."

"I don't have to answer shit," Jason spits, rising shakily to his feet.

"Then I'll call the cops and you can answer to them." We already know the cops won't do shit. There's no proof Jason attacked Lexi that night and she couldn't confirm it. Except... Aiden. Holy shit, he witnessed it, and when I asked him about last night, he seemed like he knew who Jason was. Maybe he can identify him.

My phone goes off and I pull it out. It's Ryan. **Thought you should know Lexi is here. She asked us not to tell anyone, but if Micaela ran, I would want to know she's safe.**

What the fuck? She ran. Why?

"Tristan, I found her," I tell him.

He turns around. "She okay?"

"Yeah."

He glances back at Jason. "I know damn well it was you who attacked my daughter. And now that I know what you look like, you better watch your fucking back." He picks up Jason's board, and while holding it, he uses the weight of his foot and snaps it in half. Then he walks toward Mason and me. "Let's go."

We follow him over to my truck. "Ryan texted me that she's at their house."

"In San Diego?" Tristan asks, sounding as confused as I am. "Her sister's graduation is in a few hours. What the hell is she doing there?"

"I don't know. He said she ran and asked them not to tell anyone, but he knew I would be freaking the fuck out." Speaking of which...

**Me: Thank you. Is she driving back down with you guys?"**
**Ryan: I don't think so. She's crying and Micaela is talking to her. She said she's not going. I just wanted you to know she's okay.**
**Me: Thanks.**

"He said she's not planning to go to the graduation."

"What the hell happened?" Tristan asks. "She would never miss her sister's graduation."

"Did you two get into a fight?" Mason asks.

"No, I haven't even been home in four days. Had to pull a ninety-six-hour shift. Got home and she was already gone. She came by here last night and saw Aiden. Bought him tacos. He said she was crying and he drew her a picture to make her happy. Then she left."

"All right, well, she's safe," Tristan says. "I need to get to Georgia's graduation. Then, afterward, we can figure this out."

"What?" I give him a look I'm sure matches my frustration. "I'm going to San Diego."

"She doesn't want you to know where she is," Mason says.

"And going to her will throw Ryan under the bus," Tristan adds. "She's safe there. Nowhere near Jason. Whatever is going on can wait until after the graduation."

"And like you said," I argue. "Lexi would never miss her sister's graduation. Something is fucking wrong." I glance at the time on my phone. "It's a two-hour drive. If I leave now, I can get her back in time."

Tristan blows out a harsh breath. "I want to tell you not to, but..."

"But you know damn well if that was Charlie, you would do the same thing." I look at Mason. "And you would too."

Mason nods. "Yeah, I would."

I open my truck door and get in. "I'll keep you updated."

The drive to San Diego is filled with me questioning every conversation from the last few days, trying to figure out what happened from the time we got back from our trip to now. None of it makes any sense. I'm missing a piece, and until I find out

## CHAPTER TWENTY-SEVEN

what it is, I won't know what's going on. When I'm halfway there, Ryan texts me to let me know they left to the graduation and Lexi stayed behind.

When I arrive at Micaela and Ryan's house, I see Lexi's jeep in their driveway. Since I don't have a key, I knock on the door. When nobody answers, I walk around the house like a creepy stalker, peeking into every window. Finally, I find the one I'm looking for. Lexi is lying on the bed, curled up into a ball and crying. Fuck.

I bang on the window and she jumps. "Lex," I yell. "Let me in."

Her eyes go as wide as saucers. She walks to the window and raises the blinds, giving me a full frontal view of her. Her eyes are bloodshot and puffy from her crying. Black rings underneath from lack of sleep. She's paler than usual, almost ghostly looking. Her blond hair is up in a messy bun and she's wearing my Station 115 hoodie with a pair of tiny cotton shorts barely peeking out from under it.

"You scared me, baby," I tell her.

Instead of telling me she'll open the door, she unlocks the window and lifts it slightly. "I'm sorry I didn't tell you I left."

"It's okay. We need to get to Georgia's graduation, though. So, why don't we talk on the way back?" I'll deal with getting her car later.

She flinches then shakes her head. "I'm not going with you."

"Lex, whatever is going on, we can deal with it...together. But you can't miss Georgia's graduation. You will never forgive yourself. This is a big day for your sister."

She sniffles and fresh tears surface. "You're right."

I sigh in relief. "I'll meet you in the front." I walk around the house and a minute later, Lexi steps out. "We can come back and get your jeep."

"No, we can't," she says, stepping up to me. "Because..." She releases a sob that hits me in the chest. It's as if someone is gripping my heart with a vice grip. "We're not together anymore." She slides her ring off her finger and tries to hand it to me.

"What the fuck are you doing?" I step back as if the ring has the potential to burn me. "What's going on?"

"I'm calling off the wedding...our engagement," she says, tears streaming down her face. She grabs my hand and forces the ring into my hand, closing my fingers around it.

"Why?" None of this makes any damn sense.

"Because I'm pregnant," she sobs. My eyes go to her belly. She's pregnant...We're having a baby. Then why the fuck would she leave me? I'm about to ask, when her next words stun me into silence. "And I don't know if the baby is yours."

## CHAPTER TWENTY-EIGHT

### LEXI

The look of pain and confusion on Alec's face damn near makes me throw up. I didn't plan to tell him like this, not right now, which is why I ran, so I could take some time to figure out how to tell him. I should've known Ryan would tell him I was here. I'm not mad, though. I shouldn't have left without telling anyone where I was going, especially Alec. He must've been so worried. I was going to text him that I was okay, but my phone died last night, and I didn't bring a charger with me. By the time I thought about it, after Micaela and Ryan left, I couldn't find one. They must've taken the chargers with them.

"Lex," Alec croaks. "You're going to have to explain this to me, because I know damn well you would never cheat on me."

He's right, I wouldn't. Because he's my entire world. Which is why I had to break up with him, because he deserves more... better... than what I can give him.

My head feels fuzzy, probably from all the crying and throwing up and lack of eating. "Let's sit down and I'll explain."

We have a seat on the porch swing, and it makes my heart hurt. Micaela and Ryan have the cutest little family home. They have a large backyard with a jungle gym for RJ, a wraparound porch with a swing that fits the three of them, and there's even a white picket fence. My hand goes to my belly, as I think about how badly I wanted this: the house, the family, the white picket fence. Only a few short days ago I was fantasizing about being a mom. Now, I...

"Lex, please," Alec pleads.

"Sorry." I take a deep breath. "As I said, I'm pregnant...and it might not be your baby." My thoughts go back to yesterday...

*"Alexandria Scott," the nurse calls out with a smile on her face.*

*"That's me," I tell her, standing.*

*We go through the standard visit stuff: weight, blood pressure, temperature check.*

*"It says you're here to get your pregnancy confirmed," she says once she's done jotting it all down on her iPad.*

*"Yes."*

*"Go ahead and change into this gown and pee in a cup in the bathroom. Write your name on it and slip it through the metal door." She hands me a white gown. "I'll be back in a few minutes."*

*Once she's gone, I do as she says, then have a seat on the table. As she said, a few minutes later, she returns, bringing with her my doctor.*

*"Lexi," Dr. O'Neil says, shaking my hand. My mom, Georgia, and I have been seeing her for years. "How are you?"*

*"I'm okay."*

*"The urine test confirmed you're pregnant."* I expect to suddenly feel nervous or worried. I mean, this is it. It's been confirmed. I'm pregnant. But I don't. I feel happy. Images of me telling Alec and him being as excited as me flit through my head.

*"It said in your chart you weren't sure when your last period was,"* she adds. *"So, we're going to do an ultrasound so we can give you an estimated date."*

*"Okay."*

*She rolls a condom onto the probe and explains she's doing an internal ultrasound because if I'm not too far along, she won't be able to pick up a heartbeat with the external one.*

*She turns the screen on and almost immediately a loud whooshing sound fills the room. "That's your baby's heartbeat," she explains.* My eyes stay trained on the small fluttering heart as I tear up. A heartbeat. My baby has a heartbeat. There's a living being in my body and in several months I'll be able to hold him or her in my arms. I immediately regret not telling Alec. I didn't want to get his hopes up if I was wrong and wasn't pregnant, but now he's missing out on this amazing, magical moment.

"Based on the size of the fetus, I'm estimating your due date to be March twenty-first," she says. "It might change give or take a couple days." She clicks on her iPad, then turns to me. "That puts you at roughly seven weeks."

Jeez, has it been that long since I got a period? I'm almost two months along. I do the math in my head. That would've been around... And like a bucket of ice water has been poured over me, I sit up quickly, trying to take in oxygen. My heart is going erratic and I can't catch my breath. It feels as though all the blood has drained from my body. My trembling hands clutch my chest as I try to slow my heartrate.

"Lexi, are you okay?" Dr. O'Neil asks, concerned.

"Can you tell...based on your calculations...when the baby was conceived?"

The doctor's brows dip in confusion, but she doesn't question my question. Instead she clicks on her iPad, then says, "We can't pinpoint the exact date, since days of ovulation for everyone differs, but based on your due date, it would be around July first."

July first.

The day I was attacked.

That date remains engrained in my brain. And I'm pretty sure it always will.

One hand roughly grips my mane, tugging my head back.

My knees slam against the rocks.

"Stop!" I plead.

The other hand slides under my bikini bottoms.

"Please don't do this," I beg.

"You're a fucking tease! And teases like you deserve what they get."

"Ow! That's hurts. Please don't do this."

"Lexi...Lexi, baby. Come back to me." Alec. His soft voice.

I open my eyes, and I'm back on the porch swing with Alec.

"I think he raped me," I whisper, my eyes refusing to meet his. It's the first time I've said the words aloud, and they feel like sandpaper as they leave my lips. "All the flashbacks in my head..." I choke out a sob. "They lead to him raping me. And the doctor... she said my estimated date of conception was July first."

When Alec doesn't say anything, I glance up at him. His jaw is hard and his eyes are closed. I can't imagine what's going through his head. This baby...it's supposed to be our baby. But there's a chance it's not. And it's not fair to put him through this.

"That's why I can't marry you," I explain. "I can't ask you to commit to spending your life with me when there's a chance I'm carrying another man's baby."

Alec opens his eyes and looks at me, and the pain radiating in them is enough to cripple my heart. "I should feel disgusted that I'm possibly carrying a baby by a man who raped me, but I can't find it in me to be. Because even though it's possibly half his, this baby is also half mine, and when I saw him on the monitor—"

"Him?"

"I don't know. It just felt wrong calling him or her an it. He had a heartbeat..."

Alec nods. "Why didn't you tell me about your appointment?"

"I wasn't completely sure if I was pregnant. When you mentioned the guys at work had the flu, I wondered if maybe I had it too. I wanted to confirm it and then tell you so we could celebrate. But then the doctor gave me the dates and I realized celebrating wouldn't be happening."

Alec turns his body toward me and takes my hands in his. His gaze locks with mine, and I feel sick to my stomach. He warned me to be careful. Not to stay on the beach too late. I didn't listen...

"I need you to listen to me very carefully," he says. "I love you with every part of my being. I knew years ago you were the one for me, but I was a coward, too scared to lose you to tell you how I felt. But then my dad died, and it gave me the courage to not waste a single moment. I realized from his death how precious life is. How short it is. You can do everything right and it can still end before you're ready for it to."

His words cause my throat to fill with emotion.

"You're mine, Lexi Scott," he continues. "You've been mine our entire lives in some way or another, and if you think this news is going to change that you don't understand how strong my love for you is."

"But—"

"No," he says. "No buts. This baby you're carrying is ours. End of story. We're going to go home and get ready and then go to

Georgia's graduation. And then when it's over we'll go to your parents' house for the graduation party. Tonight, I'll hold you in my arms and we'll talk about our future..."

A fresh round of tears form and spill over. My body racking with sobs.

"Next week we'll get married in front of our friends and family, and when we're ready we'll announce that we're expecting a baby. And in seven months we'll welcome that baby into the world. We'll love him and protect him and he will be ours." His eyes and tone carry such conviction, goose bumps cover my arms.

"But what if he isn't—"

"He is," Alec says, speaking the two words slowly.

"I can't let you—"

"You can't let me do what? Love a baby that's part you? An innocent baby who will have your blood flowing through his veins. When I was eight years old, I met Mason, and from the moment he moved into my mom's house, he loved me as if I were his own. And you know why? Because I was my mom's son, and he loved her. He treated me like his flesh and blood, the same as my sister even though she really is his. The same way your dad treats Georgia, and your mom treats you."

Tears course down my cheeks. I'm crying so hard I can't speak. I'm hiccupping between sobs, and it's hard to breathe. "I know, but you deserve better than this."

"What I deserve is you," he says. "What I want is you...the good, the bad, and the ugly. I want it all with you. Life isn't always beautiful, Lex." He reaches out and tucks a hair behind my ear.

"Sometimes it's downright ugly. And it's during those times we want to give up, hide so we don't have to deal with it. Like when my dad died...I wanted nothing more than to wallow in my grief. But it's because of those ugly times, we're able to appreciate the beautiful. What might've happened to you, the possibility that that asshole might've raped you is really fucking ugly, but, baby, you have a healthy baby growing in you, and if that's not fucking beautiful then I don't know what is."

Alec edges closer and wraps his arms around me. I close my eyes and inhale his fresh scent, immediately calming down, my body relaxing. I don't know what I was thinking running from

Alec. He's the other half of me. My path. My past. My present. My future. My forever.

Alec takes my hand in his and slides my ring back on. "Don't ever take this off again. This is where it belongs and where it needs to stay."

He kisses the top of my forehead and I sigh into his chest, feeling like I can breathe for the first time since finding out the date of conception. But then I remember what the doctor told me...

"Dr. O'Neil, my OB/GYN, said that in California, even if I can prove Jason raped me, if he's the father he can fight for rights to the baby." I couldn't believe what she said, so I looked it up when I left her office and she was right. In California, on several occasions, the men who were tried and found guilty, later went on to receive some sort of visitation.

"It's not going to happen," Alec says. He lifts my chin, so I'm looking at him. "That baby is ours and nobody will ever know anything different."

## CHAPTER TWENTY-NINE

### ALEC

Lexi is pregnant and she ran because she was scared I wouldn't be able to love her and the baby she's carrying if it turns out he's not mine. I hate that she didn't have enough faith in our love, in me, to know that I could never stop loving her, and I would die for that baby in her belly. But at the same time, I get it. She was scared. She still is. What she went through, is still going through, is traumatic as fuck. She still doesn't know what happened that night she was attacked, and she more than likely will never know. And now she's carrying a baby that was possibly conceived out of hate instead of love. But I meant what I said: nobody will ever know that. As far as everyone will ever know, that baby is ours, created out of love. And that asshole, Jason, will never know that Lexi is pregnant or that the baby might carry his DNA. I'll make damn sure of it.

I pull into our complex and Lexi parks next to me. I tried to convince her to leave her vehicle there, but she wanted to get it over with and bring it home now, so I followed her home. We need to run inside and quickly change and then head to Georgia's graduation. We'll just barely make it there, but at least we'll be there, and Georgia will have her sister there when she walks across the stage.

As I step out of my truck, I take a look around at the complex with new eyes. This place isn't exactly family friendly. It's adjacent to a busy road. The majority of the tenants are college students and young couples. There's a park, but it's about a half-mile down the street. When my parents bought me the place as a gift for graduating from the fire academy it was perfect, but now...

"What are you looking at?" Lexi steps closer to me and glances around, trying to see what I'm seeing.

"We need to buy a house. This place isn't meant for a family." I take her hand in mine and bring it up to my lips to kiss the top of her knuckles. Her skin is warm and soft and smells like her vanilla body wash. I miss the scent of the ocean on her. It's been a while since she's been surfing, and I guess with the baby coming, she'll have to wait a while longer.

"I want to buy a house on the beach," I tell her. "So you can go surfing on a private beach. I don't want you going back to that beach." I don't want her anywhere near where Jason might be.

"What about Aiden?" she asks.

Of course that's her concern. Lexi has such a big heart, and she's going to make an amazing mom.

"We're going to figure out how to help him," I promise her. "Get him off that beach and somewhere safe."

"Thank you," she says, standing on her tiptoes to kiss me.

We make it to Georgia's graduation on time and cheer for her as she walks across the stage. While we're there, Lexi tells me she's not sure if she wants to go back to school. She's not sure what she wants to do, but she knows she's excited to be a mom. I tell her she has plenty of time to figure it out. I make more than enough to support us, and with the life insurance money my dad left me, I can buy us a house to start our family.

---

THE NEXT WEEK FLIES BY. When I'm home, we hang out with everyone who's in town for the graduation and wedding. And at night, when we're alone, we lie in bed, wrapped up in each other, talking about our future, about the baby, about us. Lexi read that twelve weeks is when you're supposed to announce you're expecting, so we plan to tell everyone then. She hasn't even told her sister, which I'm surprised about. I think she's still grasping at the reality that she really is pregnant and in seven months she'll be giving birth to a baby.

When I'm at work, we text and video chat. I can see it in her eyes, she's scared. Of me changing my mind, of me regretting my words, my promise. She's waiting for me to tell her I can't do this. But it's never going to happen. I love Lexi and I'm going to marry her. The odds of this baby actually not being mine are slim. *If* he raped her, it was once, compared to the dozens of times we had unprotected sex during that time. Sure, it only takes once, and if he did rape her, the baby she's carrying could carry his DNA, but that baby, regardless of his blood type, is mine. He will carry my last name and will be loved by both of us. From the moment she told me, there was never a doubt in my mind.

But even though Lexi is one of the strongest women I know, I also know she's insecure when it comes to this topic. Her own mother, her flesh and blood, walked out of the hospital without her and never looked back. So, through my actions, I'll show her that I'm serious. That I'll love and protect her and this baby. That she and I are forever.

Starting with marrying her, which is what I'm about to do. With the wedding march playing in the background, I watch, mesmerized, as Lexi walks down the wooden walkway that is doubling as a makeshift aisle. On either side are white and pink flowers. She's dressed in a beautiful off-white dress that shows off all of her curves. In her hands is a bouquet of matching pink and white flowers. She's wearing a see-though veil that covers her face, and her hair is down in waves. When she steps down to where Chase, Georgia, and I are standing with the marriage officiant, she lifts her dress slightly, showing off her sparkly shoes. Of course my girl would wear Vans instead of heels.

She hands Georgia her flowers, and then, with tear-filled eyes, her dad leans over and kisses her cheek, murmuring something to her that makes her smile.

"I love you, Dad," she says.

"Love you too, Lex."

He extends his hand, and we shake. "I don't need to tell you to love her and take care of her. I know you will," he croaks.

I nod once. "Damn right I will."

He pulls me into a hug and then takes a seat next to Charlie and Max.

I take Lexi by the arm and walk her up to the altar then lift her veil. She smiles softly and her indigo eyes sparkle with happiness and love.

"You look breathtakingly beautiful," I tell her, not wanting to take my eyes off her.

"You look very handsome," she says. "But nothing beats your firefighter uniform."

She speaks loud enough that everyone hears, and they all chuckle, making her blush.

The officiant begins speaking, but I don't hear any of what he's saying. I'm too entranced by the woman in front of me. My soon-to-be wife, mother of my child, best friend. I never thought I would see the day when she would officially become mine.

"Do you, Aleczander Sterling, take Alexandria Scott to be your lawful wedded wife, to have and to hold, for richer or poorer, for better or worse, until death do you part?"

I laugh at the similarity of our names. Once upon a time, when Lexi was born, my mom was there and helped name her. It's like it was fate.

"I do." I slide the wedding band that matches her engagement ring onto her finger.

"Alexandria Scott, do you take Aleczander Sterling to be your lawful wedded husband, to have and to hold, for richer or poorer, for better or worse, until death do you part?"

"I do," she says with a watery smile, as she slides my fire-proof wedding band onto my finger. We decided to go with traditional vows, since everything we wanted to say was said between us when we were alone.

"I now pronounce you husband and wife," the gentleman says. "You may kiss the bride."

I step up to Lexi and, cradling the side of her face with my palm, press my lips to hers. The kiss is soft and sweet, unrushed. But then she wraps her arms around my neck and deepens the kiss, sliding her tongue past my parted lips. And the next thing I know, I'm lifting her into my arms as everyone around us claps and cheers.

Lexi pulls back, with the most gorgeous smile on her face. "Whoops," she says, not at all sorry.

I set her down and, with our fingers intertwined, we face our family and friends, ready to start our lives together as husband and wife.

We walk back down the aisle, and after taking pictures, we make our way onto the back deck of the resort. The reception is being held outside. There are tables set up all around, a bar in one corner, and on the other side is a buffet of food. In the center of the large area is the dance floor.

The deejay announces us, and everyone claps, welcoming us. Before we have time to speak to anyone, the deejay asks us to the dance floor for our first dance.

"I can't wait to hear the song you picked," Lexi says. She handled most of the details for the wedding, but she left the first dance song up to me, and I took the job seriously, making Chase and the other guys listen to dozens of songs before picking the one that was perfect.

"I wanted 'Love You Like I Used To,'" I tell her. "But Chase said it would be too fast to dance to."

Lexi smiles. "I love that song."

"You and Me" by Lifehouse starts and I take Lexi into my arms. Her lips curl into the most beautiful smile and I kiss her softly. "It's just you and me, baby."

"Yeah, it is," she agrees.

As we sway to the music, neither of us can take our eyes off each other. Words don't need to be spoken, as the song is saying everything that needs to be said in the moment. When it ends, I kiss her one more time before we make our way off the dance floor, since the next song will be the father-daughter dance.

As we're walking over to her dad, Aiden approaches us. Lexi insisted he be at the wedding. Chase was nice enough to bring him and Georgia promised she would keep an eye on him for us.

"Congratulations, Lexi," he says with his bright green glasses on. "Congratulations, Lexi's husband."

I laugh. "Thank you, Aiden."

"Thank you," Lexi says, giving him a hug. "And thank you for coming."

"I drew you a picture," Aiden says, handing Lexi the paper.

It's a picture of the two of us saying our wedding vows. He must've been drawing it while we were up at the altar.

"Oh, Aiden," she says, choking up. "It's beautiful." Tears slide down her cheeks and she tries to swipe them away.

"Lexi," Aiden says. "Lexi's husband loves you."

"He does," she agrees. "He loves me, and I love him too."

## CHAPTER THIRTY

### LEXI

The deejay announces that it's time for the father-daughter dance, so I thank Aiden for the beautiful picture and give the paper to Alec to hold for me.

My dad comes over and takes my hand, guiding us onto the dance floor. He's the strongest man I know, but today I've seen him shed tears no less than three times.

The music starts to play, and it's a song I've never heard before. For several seconds I listen to the lyrics, as my dad and I dance. It's about a father who loved his daughter first, before her husband. He prayed she would find a good man, but it's still hard to give her away. As the lyrics continue, the tears I was trying to hold back fall.

"Oh, Lex," Dad says, holding me closer. "I love you so damn much."

"This song is beautiful," I tell him, resting my head against his chest.

"It's called 'I Loved Her First' by Heartland." We dance for another minute, before he says, "I can't believe my little girl is all grown up."

I glance up at him and sniffle back the tears. Realistically nothing is changing. I'm still living in LA with Alec, only a few minutes from my parents, but it feels like everything is changing.

"I can still remember when you were little," he says. "Coloring everywhere, so damn carefree... I know I've been pushing you to find your place in this world, but, Lex, I need you to know how proud I am of you. Whether you go back to college, or surf again... or continue to paint the sides of those damn walls." He chokes out a laugh and I join in. "I know whatever you decide to do you're going to be amazing, because you already are."

"Thank you, Dad." He has no idea how much I needed to hear that right now.

The song ends and Mason comes over to dance with me. "First my goddaughter, and now my daughter-in-law," he says. "That boy better treat you right, or I'll throw his ass over the pier."

"You helped raise him," I tell him. "So you know how good of a man he is."

"Yeah, I do," he says, "and I'm so happy that you both found your way to each other."

"Thank you."

We dance as the song plays, and once it's over, Alec takes me back into his arms as the deejay announces that everyone is welcome to join us on the dance floor.

After we finish our dance, we eat and spend time with our friends and family. We cut and feed each other cake and Chase and Georgia give emotional and funny speeches. The day couldn't be any more perfect.

When it gets late, Alec reminds me we have a plane to catch. We thank everyone for joining us, and then after hugging and kissing our family, we take off on our honeymoon.

---

"HEY, MRS. STERLING, YOU READY?" Alec asks.

I glance over at him, a huge smile splayed across my face. I'll never get tired of him calling me that, and I know he says it because he loves hearing it just as much.

"Hell yes, I am, Mr. Sterling." I wink, and Alec laughs, pulling my face to his for a kiss.

We follow the crowd through the airport, then, after grabbing our bags, head outside to snag a cab. The honeymoon he planned is a week in London, visiting the art galleries and exploring the city, and I couldn't be more excited. I hated leaving Aiden, but Georgia promised she would check on him, and Greg has been paid for the tacos for the next few months.

The ride to our hotel doesn't take too long, and since Alec planned everything so well, check-in goes smoothly. When we step up to the door leading to our room, Alec scoops me up into his arms and walks us through the door. "Not our threshold," he says, "but it will do."

He sets me down and pulls me into his arms. "I need you," he murmurs against my lips.

"And you can have me."

"We're supposed to go sightseeing," he says.

"I'd rather see you."

Since our flight left right after the wedding, this will be our first time making love as husband and wife. Slowly, Alec removes my hoodie that has *Just Married* scrawled across the back and then my tank top.

He cups my breasts, which are sensitive thanks to being pregnant, and kisses the top of each one gently before he reaches around and unclasps my bra, exposing my hardened nipples.

"I can't believe you're mine," he says, wrapping his lips around a nipple and sucking. "These are mine." He takes my other breast into his hand and sucks on it the same way, sending zaps of pleasure through my body.

Stopping momentarily, he reaches behind him and removes his shirt, and I take a second to admire my husband. His tight abs and taut chest. I'll never tire of looking at him.

We both reach for each other's pants at the same time and laugh. After we're completely naked, he lifts me into his arms, carrying me to the bed. He lays me out in the center and climbs over me. He trails kisses down the center of my breasts and stops when he gets to my belly.

"I can't believe there's a baby growing in there," he says, awe in his tone. He kisses the spot just below my belly button. "I can't wait until your belly is big and I can feel the baby kicking."

Butterflies flood my belly and my thighs clench in want. I love when he talks about the baby and how excited he is. Since I told him, he's already started looking for houses and saving baby furniture websites. At night, he looks up information about pregnancy and babies and tells me all about it. He reminds me every day how blessed we are and that everything will turn out okay.

"Make love to me," I tell him, grabbing his shoulders and pulling him back up to me. "Make me yours."

"It would be my pleasure."

---

THE NEXT WEEK is filled with seeing the sights. We visit so many art galleries, and I take millions of pictures. When we aren't out sightseeing, we're holed up in our room, making love. I wish our honeymoon could last forever, but all too soon, it comes to an end and we're forced to return home…back to reality.

## CHAPTER THIRTY-ONE

### THREE WEEKS LATER

### LEXI

"How'd it go?" I ask Georgia as she walks through the door, her heels click-clacking against the wood floor. She looks so grown up and professional in her blazer, pencil skirt, and heels that she wore to court. Dad walks in behind her, also dressed smartly in a gray suit.

"Hilda settled." Georgia smiles softly. "I am no longer the owner of Reynolds Oil."

"What does that mean?" Mom asks.

We all wanted to be with Georgia, to support her, but her attorney felt it was best for only her and our dad to go. He managed to fast track it, and he didn't want Hilda to feel like she was being ganged up on and, in turn, create more problems. So, we've been waiting all morning at my parents' house to find out how it went.

"It means your sister is a millionaire," Dad says with a laugh.

"What?" I screech. "She bought it for a million dollars?"

"Way more than that," Georgia says. "But based on what the attorney said, she still got it for a lot less than I could've sold it for. And it turns out, Justin left me a trust fund as well."

"She should be thankful Georgia is so generous," Dad says, kissing Georgia on her temple.

"Wow, congratulations!" I hug her. "I'm glad this is all past you now." I know she's been stressed out over it, wanting to get it all settled. "So, what are you going to do now that you're a mega wealthy millionaire?"

Georgia snorts. "I don't even know. It's all so weird... and I hate that it's all from a man who tried to keep me from our mom and then tried to kill her."

"Hey," Mom says. "That money is rightfully yours. Put it away, invest it... you have time to figure it out, but don't feel guilty for having it."

Georgia nods. "Okay."

"Congratulations," Alec says as Mila and Mason walk through the door with his sister, Anna. Since I'm officially twelve weeks today, we're planning to tell everyone that we're expecting. Alec went with me to my last appointment and the baby's heartbeat was strong. We got new pictures of the little bean and we're so excited to finally be able to share our news with everyone.

"Hey, sweetie," Mila says to Alec, kissing his cheek. "Lexi." She kisses my cheek as well, then has a seat on the couch next to her husband. Dad tells Mason and Mila how court went while we wait for Max and Chase to get here.

Once they both arrive, and everyone is seated, Mason says, "So, let's have it. Mila has been dying to know your news. You can't text your mother that you have something to tell us and leave her hanging. She's been driving me crazy."

"I agree," Mom says. "I've been going nuts."

"Oh, c'mon," Chase says. "Like you guys don't know." He scoffs.

"Know what?" Mila asks.

"I'll let them tell you," he says with a smirk.

"Since you think you know, tell us," I taunt. There's no way he—

"Fine, Alec knocked up Lexi."

Everyone gasps, and Alec grabs the magazine off the coffee table and smacks Chase with it.

"You're pregnant?" my dad asks, his eyes going wide and straight to my still flat belly. I've started to put on a little weight and my clothes are fitting differently, but I don't have a present baby bump yet.

"Yes," I tell everyone. "I'm twelve weeks pregnant."

"I knew it," Georgia says. "I can't believe you tried to keep it from me, though." She side-eyes me half-jokingly.

"We wanted to wait until the twelve-week mark," I explain.

"Yeah, yeah." She stands and gives me a hug. "Congratulations."

"Wow," Mom says. "I'm going to be a grandma!"

Everyone jumps up and hugs us... Well, everyone except my dad and Mason. They're now standing against the wall, next to each other, with their arms crossed over their chests.

"Are you mad?" I ask my dad nervously.

"No," he says, tears pricking his eyes. "I'm just trying to figure out how the hell you went from my little girl, the one who colored all over the walls and hated boys, to being a wife and now a mother."

Mason huffs. "If I didn't love Alec as much as I do, I'd threaten to kick his ass for knocking up my goddaughter."

Both guys step forward and envelop me in a hug, each congratulating me. "We're really excited," I tell them.

"Hey, Lex," Max says. "Lex, you gotta see this."

I pull away from my dad and Mason and go to Max, who has his phone out. He hands it to me, and when I read what it says, I stumble back in shock.

"What's wrong?" Alec asks, taking the phone from me. "Holy shit," he murmurs, when he reads what it says.

"What is it?" my dad asks.

"Jason was found dead under the pier and Aiden has been arrested," I tell him. "We have to go to the station."

"Lex, you're pregnant," Alec says. "You can't be getting stressed out. Please, baby, calm down. We'll figure this out."

"Aiden saved me," I snap, grabbing my purse and heading to the door. "Had he not found me, I could've died. He needs us. Now."

"He needs an attorney," Dad says. "I'll call mine. Let's go."

We get to the station at the same time the attorney that my dad called does. We explain to him about Aiden and how he's homeless and it's likely he's autistic and has no one.

"I want to make sure he's protected," I tell him.

The attorney speaks to the authorities, who then agree to let us go back and see Aiden.

"He's not under arrest," the officer says as we walk down the hallway. "The woman who was attacked has confirmed that Aiden saved her, but we need him to walk us through what happened, so we have it on record. Then we can let him go."

I sigh in relief, thankful Aiden's not in trouble. "I'll go talk to him."

"Lexi," Aiden says when I walk through the door. "I want to go home. I need to go home. The nice man who brings me my tacos will be there soon." He's wearing his green glasses, but when I enter, he removes them.

"I'll make sure you get your tacos. Can you tell me what happened?"

"If I'm not there, he won't know where I am," he insists, only concerned with his tacos.

"I promise you, I'll make sure he knows, but I need you to tell me what happened, so you can go home."

Aiden sighs in frustration. "The mean surfer man didn't love her. He wasn't loving the girl," he says, shaking his head. "I told him he had to love the girl, like how your husband loves you, but he didn't listen. He yelled at me and hit me, like how my mom's boyfriend used to hit me. I told him it's not nice to hit, but he kept hitting me. He hurt me, Lexi." Aiden frowns and points to the black eye forming on his left eye, and my heart breaks. If Jason were still alive, I swear I would find a way to kill him myself.

"Then the police officer yelled at me and told me I had to leave my house and come here. I told him I didn't hurt her," Aiden continues. "I told him I had to be home for my tacos. Can I go home now and have my tacos?"

A part of me was hoping somehow Aiden would imply, through his words, whether Jason actually raped me, but to Aiden it's all the same. He doesn't actually understand the sexual act, only whether you're nice or mean. He might be an adult, but he sees things as a child does.

"Yeah," I tell him. "You can go home and get your tacos."

Aiden smiles. "Thank you, Lexi." He throws his arms around me in a bear hug. "I love tacos."

"I know you do."

He stands and puts his glasses back on, having no clue that he not only saved me but saved another woman. I'll never know how far Jason went, but what I do know is that had Aiden not been there, it could've been worse. Jason would've left me for dead, and had Aiden not been there last night, that woman could've been left for dead as well. Instead, she's safe at the hospital and Jason will never lay his hands on another woman without her permission again.

Aiden gets in the car with my dad, Alec, and me. He talks the entire way to the beach about wanting to go home and get his tacos, not caring that his home is a fucking tent under the pier. Not understanding that he's a hero.

When we get to the beach, he walks with me to the taco stand.

"Hey, Aiden," Greg, the taco stand owner, says. "I brought you your tacos, but you weren't there." He hands him a brown bag of food.

"The police made me leave," Aiden says. "I won't leave again unless they make me leave again. Will you bring me my tacos tomorrow?"

"Yeah," he says. "I'll bring you your tacos tomorrow."

Greg smiles sadly at me, obviously knowing what happened since it's been all over the news.

I walk with Aiden to his tent, and he sits in the same spot he always sits and starts to eat his tacos. I hate that I have to leave him here, but I still have no idea how to help him.

"I'll see you soon, okay?" I tell him, not wanting to leave, but knowing my dad and Alec are waiting for me.

"Okay, bye, Lexi."

## CHAPTER THIRTY-TWO

### ONE WEEK LATER

### LEXI

"Wʜᴀᴛ ᴀʀᴇ ʏᴏᴜ ᴅᴏɪɴɢ?" Alec yells over the smoke alarm as I pull the burnt to a crisp bread out of the toaster and toss it into the garbage can.

"I was trying to make toast!" I yell back, swiping my tears off my face.

Alec reaches up and presses the button, turning the alarm off. "Lex, we've talked about this. You're going to burn the place down if you keep trying to cook shit."

He turns around and when he sees I'm crying, he pulls me into his arms. "Baby, what's wrong? It's just burnt toast."

"It's not *just* burnt toast," I cry out. "How am I supposed to feed my own baby if I can't even toast bread?"

Alec laughs. "We have a long time before you need to cook for the baby. Plus, don't babies take bottles until they're like four?"

"Four?" I glare at him. "I'm pretty sure that's not accurate. RJ doesn't take a bottle anymore and he's only one. But I don't know," I hiccup through a sob, "because I have no idea about babies, and apparently neither do you. How the hell are we going to raise a baby if neither of us knows anything?"

Alec almost laughs again, but quickly stifles it. "We have our family and friends. We'll read up on it all. Every new parent has to start somewhere, but, Lex... no more cooking, please. If I have to, I'll hire someone to cook for us."

"Fine," I huff.

"I love you," he says, giving me a kiss. "I'll see tomorrow morning."

"Love you too."

---

### One Week After the Burnt Toast

"WHAT ARE you doing lying in bed?" Georgia accuses.

"What else am I supposed to be doing?" I flip through the shows, trying to find one I haven't watched yet. "I can't surf because I'm pregnant. I'm not allowed to cook or bake anything. Alec forbade me from going out and graffitiing the walls..." I roll my eyes as I recall the fight that ensued. I know he was right, and had I gotten caught, being pregnant and in jail would've been a bad thing, but I'm fucking bored.

Aside from visiting Aiden every day, I have nothing else to do. "I'm a college drop-out...I can't figure out how to help Aiden..." I've tried calling several organizations but none of them were helpful because Aiden is an adult. The only thing I can do is report him, which would get him arrested. I looked into assisted living for him, but it's more than I can afford. I would use up my entire trust fund in three years, and then what? "Pretty much, I'm a loser."

Georgia grabs the remote and turns the TV off. "It's your birthday. I'm taking you to lunch."

"Fine." I can always eat. At fourteen weeks pregnant, the morning sickness is gone and my appetite is plentiful. Since Alec is working and couldn't get off, we're planning to celebrate my birthday this weekend.

We arrive in the Arts District and walk to my favorite deli. I haven't been here since Alec took me on our first date. The walls are filled with art, and it makes my heart both full and sad.

"I miss this," I tell her, when we walk past one of my drawings.

"Well, maybe instead of creating illegally, create *legally*."

I roll my eyes. "Have you ever searched my hashtag?" I pull

my phone out and type it in, then show her. "Four million tags. Four million people took pictures of my art."

"And imagine how many would buy it if you created it on actual canvases instead of on the side of buildings."

"It's not about the money. It's about the purpose of the art. Using it to make a difference. I just...I want to make a difference."

I continue walking down the sidewalk when I notice Georgia is no longer next to me. "What are you doing?" I ask, looking back and seeing her standing in front of the abandoned building.

"You said you want your art to make a difference," she says.

"Yeah..."

"And you want to help Aiden..."

"Uh-huh."

"I have an idea."

"Well, don't be all suspenseful. Tell me."

"An art gallery, here. It can be a non-profit organization to help autistic children and adults. We could create an entire program that allows them to create, and the pieces we sell can help fund the program."

I stare at the large, empty building and can picture everything she's saying. Aiden could come here and have a safe place to draw. I could paint and teach and help others like Aiden. There's only one problem...

"How would I afford this?"

"I said 'we'," Georgia says. "In case you forgot, I have money, and I met with my financial advisor the other day, who told me I should consider making donations to help with the tax write-offs at the end of the year."

"This would be more than a donation. This would cost a lot and it would be time-consuming."

"I have the money," she says, "and you have the time. You would be in charge. Our grandparents run the rec center in Las Vegas. They would know what to do. How to set it all up."

She's right. Years ago, before we were born, our grandparents started a recreational center for kids to get them off the streets because Micaela's dad, Marco, was one of those kids on the street. They've been successfully running it for years and would gladly help us.

"And if Aiden agrees, we can pay him to work here, to help us..."

"Which would pay for him to live in assisted living." I throw my arms around Georgia. "You're a freaking genius, and the best sister ever! Thank you! Thank you! This is the best birthday ever. I can't wait to get started and tell Aiden..." I hug her tighter. "I love you, Georgia, thank you."

"You don't have to thank me, Lex. I'm your sister. I just want you to be happy."

I pull away from her and glance back at the building. "This is it, Georgia. I can feel it... This is my path."

# EPILOGUE
## LEXI

*Seven Months Later*

"Is that everything?" I ask, taking a look around the place one last time.

"I think so," Alec says, coming up behind me and wrapping his arms around me. "And if it's not, it's not like we can't get whatever we forgot... Your sister and Chase are still living here."

I groan. "I can't believe she'd rather live here than with us in our new house." Two months ago we closed on our first home. It was days before I was due to give birth, and we thought we would have time to fix up the small things we needed to fix up and then move in. Only our daughter surprised us by coming early. We stayed in the condo for two months, which was actually great since Georgia was around to help. Since I had a C-section, I couldn't lift anything for six weeks. Now, Abigail is two months old, sleeping almost through the night, and we're moving out.

"She wants us to have our own space," Alec says for the millionth time.

"Yeah, I know." I pout. "But she's staying here with Chase? She can't even stand him..."

"I own the condo," I remind her. "Instead of them having to find another place to live, I told them they can continue to live here. It saves me the hassle of having to find new tenants or sell the place."

"Umm…in case you forgot, my sister is rich. She can afford to live anywhere she wants."

Alec laughs. "Maybe she doesn't want to live alone." He shrugs. "Chase stopped bringing women around a while ago, and they haven't fought in a long time."

"I guess." I huff. "I'm just going to miss her."

"We'll only be ten minutes away," he points out, kissing me. I sigh into him and thread my fingers through his hair.

"Lexi," Aiden says, ending the moment. "Lexi's baby, Abigail, is crying."

"I'll go get her," I tell Alec. "You make sure we have everything."

I walk into the living room and find Aiden rocking Abigail's car seat. She's barely whining, but to Aiden that's crying. Any time she makes any noise that isn't happy, he wants us to make her happy. The moment she was born and he came to visit, he became attached to her.

"Here you go, sweet girl." I put her pacifier into her mouth that fell out and her eyes roll backward, as she instantly falls back asleep.

"Can we go paint now?" Aiden asks, referring to Through Their Eyes, the non-profit art gallery that's set to open soon. Right now, we're painting the inside. Georgia and I have contacted dozens of artists and celebrities and have gotten many donations. When it's done, it will be an art gallery people can visit and buy from, as well as an educational center. We're planning to run year-long programs, where kids can come to learn how to create, and all the proceeds will go to help support autistic children and adults.

"Go ahead," Alec says, walking over and kissing my temple. "I'll handle the rest."

"You sure?"

"Yeah."

Twenty minutes later, we arrive at the gallery and Aiden goes right to work, painting his masterpiece. He spends the afternoon painting while I work on the business side of things. When it's time to go, I take him out front where the private bus from his assisted living center picks him up.

"I'll see you tomorrow?" he asks, like he does every day, Monday through Thursday.

"Yes, I'll see you tomorrow."

"And baby Abigail, too," he says.

I laugh under my breath, realizing I said I instead of we. "Yes, we will both be here."

"At nine o'clock, right?" It's taken a little bit of time for Aiden to adjust to living in a new place and having a new routine. At first, it was rough. We even had to bring his blue tent with him and set it up in his room. But he's slowly adjusting, and the most important thing is he's happy and safe. The assisted living center provides a private bus that drops him off and picks him up every day during the week. I would love to take him myself, but they said he needs consistency, so it's best to let him ride the bus every day.

"Nine o'clock," I assure him.

"Okay," he says. "Bye, baby Abigail." He gives her a kiss on her cheek. "Bye, Lexi."

He steps onto the bus, and once he's seated, waves to us.

"All right, sweet girl, you ready to go home?"

She doesn't respond, fast asleep, but I take it as a yes.

A little while later, we arrive at our new home. It's a beautiful four-bedroom, three-bath, two-story house near the beach. As much as we wanted to be on the beach, those houses were ridiculously priced. But we found the perfect house, that's in a cute gated neighborhood and is only walking distance to the beach. It's not too far from Alec's fire station or from our parents. It's perfect.

When I walk inside, I'm amazed by what I see. Alec must've been busy because everything is put away and organized. The boxes that were everywhere are gone.

I set Abigail down, who's still sleeping in her car seat, and walk over to the fireplace, where he set up several photos in frames. One is from our wedding day. We're both smiling at each other with such love, I can still feel it as if it were yesterday. The next photo is of the day I gave birth to Abigail. She's all wrinkly and frowning, but Alec and I are grinning like fools. I'm looking at Alec, and he's looking at our daughter. *Our daughter*. We made the decision not to get them tested. Alec said he doesn't want to know because as far as he's concerned, she's his and always will be. He's listed as the dad on her birth certificate and the three of us share the same last name. They also share the same blood type, which isn't the same as mine. That means, either Jason had the same one as them, or she's Alec's biological daughter.

"Hey, you're home," Alec says, walking down the stairs. "I put away most of the stuff, but there are a couple boxes left for you to go through. I put them in our closet."

"Thank you." I wrap my arms around his neck. "I can't believe this place is ours."

"Well, you better believe it," he says. "This is our home..." He kisses the tip of my nose. "Our daughter." He kisses my chin. "Our life." His mouth connects with mine. "And it's damn beautiful."

---

## Alec

*The Next Day*

**Georgia: Thought you should know Lexi is out graffitiing the walls.**

I CLICK on the picture accompanying the text and see Lexi stuffing spray cans into a backpack, unaware that her sister is taking a picture of her. I left them in the box for her to either keep or get rid of. I guess she's putting them to use.

**Me: Did she mention where she was going?**

**Georgia: No, but she did say she needed to go finish something she started...**

**Me: How long ago did she leave?**

**Georgia: About thirty minutes ago. I figured I'd give her a head start.**

**Me: And I take it you have Abigail?**

A moment later, a picture comes through of my beautiful daughter sleeping soundly in her crib—her belly down and her bottom popped up in the air.

**Me: Give my daughter a kiss for me.**

**Georgia: Will do. Try to keep my sister out of jail...**

**Me: Will do.**

I exit out of our conversation and pull the tracker app up, clicking on Lexi's name to see where exactly she is. When I zoom in on her location, I can't help but laugh to myself.

"Hey, Chase, you mind covering me for a little bit?"

"Sure." He shrugs. "Everything okay?"

"Yeah, I just need to run a quick errand."

A few minutes later, I pull up to the abandoned building I haven't been to since the night I was here with Lexi. Her jeep is parked along the side, and when I walk around the corner, I find her, with her back to me, spray painting the wall.

She doesn't know I'm here, so I stay quiet and watch her as she creates, lost in her own world. When she finishes and backs up to check out her work, I clear my throat, startling her.

She spins around, her eyes wide at having been caught. But when she sees it's only me, her shoulders sag in relief. "You scared me!"

"Shouldn't be doing bad stuff..."

She rolls her eyes. "My sister rat on me?"

I laugh, not answering her question, and walk over to her. "It feels like forever ago since we were here and I was watching you paint." I tug on the bottom of her tank top and pull her toward me, connecting our mouths for a brief moment. It's only been twelve hours since I last tasted her, but I'm already missing the hell out of her.

"A lot has happened since we were here," she murmurs against my lips.

"Very true," I agree. "We've gotten married, had a baby, bought a home...We've created a life together since that night."

Her lips curl into a mesmerizing smile, and I capture her

mouth again. Her lips are soft and she tastes like her favorite raspberry drink from Jumpin' Java.

"I needed to paint one last time," she says when we break apart.

"One last time?" I quirk a brow in disbelief.

"I'm a mom now," she says with a shrug. "I can't be graffitiing the walls of LA...But I needed to complete the painting."

I glance at the work of art in front of us, really looking at it for the first time tonight. Earlier, my eyes were only on Lexi...The painting is the same one from before: of a couple facing each other with the backdrop of the night sky and twinkling lights. Next to them is the quote my mom said: *You don't find love...it finds you.*

But when I look closer, I see the addition she's made. In the middle of the couple is a tiny baby—our baby.

"Love found us," she says softly, wrapping her arms around my waist. "That dark, scary path...it led us here. To our baby girl. I feel like I've finally found my place in this world—with you and our daughter. As a mom and a wife. Our picture..." She looks up at me, her blue eyes twinkling from the hue of the streetlamp. "It's complete."

**THE END.**

# MY KIND OF Perfect

*A Finding Love Novel*

## NIKKI ASH

*To Bret, for loving me imperfectly perfect.*

## PLAYLIST

Apple Music

*Feels Great - Cheat Codes*
*House Party - Sam Hunt*
*Ain't My Fault – Zara Larsson*
*Blue Tacoma – Russell Dickerson*
*Sorry – Justin Bieber*
*Eenie Meenie – Justin Bieber & Sean Kingston*
*Feelings Show – Colbie Caillat*
*This Feeling – The Chainsmokers*
*I'm Yours – Alessia Cara*
*Behind These Hazel Eyes – Kelly Clarkson*
*Just the Way You Are – Bruno Mars*
*The Difference – Tyler Rich*
*I Don't Care – Ed Sheeran & Justin Bieber*
*Gold – Britt Nicole*
*Take Back Home Girl - Chris Lane*
*Give Your Heart a Break – Demi Lovato*
*Wanted – Hunter Hayes*
*There's No Way – Lauv*
*What Do You Mean? – Justin Bieber*

*Can't Take Her Anywhere* – Dylan Scott
*Tie Me Down* – Gryffin & Elley Duhé

# CHAPTER ONE

## CHASE

"Hey... Yeah, I'm on my way," my wife whispers into the phone, thinking I'm asleep.

I had to pull an extra shift at work because two of the guys called out, and then we were up all night putting out a fire that resulted in a mom and her baby both losing their lives. I love my job as a firefighter, but some days it's harder than others. We want to save them all, and it sucks when we can't.

"I'll see you soon," she says softly, using a tone very unlike her. I crack an eye open and see her standing in front of our dresser, putting her big hoop earrings into her ears. She's dressed in a short, tight, leopard dress and tall as fuck heels that show off her mile long legs. Her long, dyed, black hair has been straightened, and her face, which is being reflected in the mirror, is covered in makeup.

She's going out without me... again.

I take a moment to assess her features. My wife is hot. Always has been. And dressed the way she is right now, she looks every bit like the model she once was—before fame got to her head and destroyed her career. But if you remove the makeup, you'll see the wrinkles around her mouth from years of smoking. And if you look closely at the creases in her arms, you'll see the scars from the needles. She's been clean for a while now, but those scars are permanent. Just like the damage she's causing to our marriage by the choices she's making.

Before she can escape, I roll over and sit up. She doesn't notice me right away, so I clear my throat. She jumps, startled, and swivels around. "Chase... you're awake." Her striking blue eyes meet mine.

"I am. Where are we going?" I throw the freshly washed blanket off me—noting how she's been doing the sheets several times a week, when she used to barely wash them once a month—and stand. I don't really have any intention of going anywhere. I have to be back at work at 8:00 a.m., but my fake threat forces a reaction out of Victoria—shock tinged with a little bit of guilt—that tells me everything I need to know—something I've been suspecting for a while now.

My wife, the woman I've been married to for almost ten years, have been friends with for even longer, have been through ups and downs with, was by her side every time she fell off the wagon and needed help getting back on, is having an affair.

When she came home the first time smelling like another man's scent, I questioned her. She told me I was crazy, that I was starting shit for no reason. The next time, she said the club she and her friends were at was crowded and a guy probably rubbed up against her. It was a dumb as fuck excuse, but I swallowed it down, not wanting to believe my wife would cheat on me.

But now, it's time I open my eyes and stop being a dumbass.

"I'm going out with Fiona and Jezibel," she says, referring to her washed-up model friends.

"Cool. I'll join you."

Her eyes widen, but she quickly schools her features. "It's a girls' night," she retorts.

"I don't think they'll mind me crashing... Plus, I miss you." I walk over to her and cage her in my arms.

"Don't you have to work tomorrow morning?" She moves my arm and steps away like she's repulsed by me. I can still remember the days when we would spend hours at a time with me inside her. Even the last year, since she's been pushing me away, we haven't gone more than a couple days without having sex. But the last couple months it's gotten worse. I can count on one hand the amount of times I've been intimate with my wife. She starts fights all the time, which end with me sleeping on my friend Alec's couch. And when I'm home, she's either out with her friends or doesn't feel well and wants to be left alone. Something is definitely up, and I'm going to find out what—or *who*—it is.

"I do," I tell her, answering her question. "I actually have to work a double." A lie.

She chews the inside of her mouth. "Then you better get some sleep."

"Yeah, you're right," I say, a plan forming in my head. "Guess I'll see you in a few days." I step close to her and kiss her cheek. "I love you."

"Me too," she chokes out. "I, uh, I gotta go."

I watch as she grabs her purse and rushes out the door, and then I fall back into bed, knowing if I don't get some sleep, I'm going to be useless tomorrow, and as much as I want to follow my wife and catch her in the act, I have a crew of men who need me to lead. I worked hard to get to where I am, and I can't lose everything I've accomplished—especially since there's a good chance I'm going to lose my wife anyway.

---

"YOU'RE MORE than welcome to crash at my place," Alec says as we walk to our vehicles. It's finally eight in the morning, which means our twenty-four-hour shift is over and we're off for the next four days—unless another guy calls out and I have to come in. This has been one long as hell week. "I was only fucking with you yesterday about squatting on my couch," he adds.

I laugh at his remark. Yesterday I was fucking with him about not owning up to his feelings for Lexi, his best friend whom he's in love with but won't admit to. And in return, he called me out on sleeping on his couch several times the last few weeks.

"I know, man, and I appreciate it, but... I need to go home." I don't bother mentioning that my wife has no idea I'll be home in a few minutes, and if I'm right about my suspicions, there's a good chance I'll catch her with another man, in our home, dirtying those clean fucking sheets. "I'll see you tomorrow night." Alec's birthday is today, and we're all going out tomorrow night to celebrate.

I jump into my charcoal gray BMW 3 series—a gift to myself last year when I got my promotion as Battalion Chief—and head the few blocks home. I pull through the gate of our community and smile to myself at how far I've come. Victoria and I grew up in a small, poor neighborhood in South LA. We would talk of one day getting out of the ghetto. She would become a huge model and I would fight fires. We both achieved our dreams, but unlike Victoria, who couldn't deal with the dark parts of your dreams coming true, I remained grounded. She wanted to purchase a mansion in Hollywood Hills with the money she was making, but I refused, instead telling her we could do that in a few years.

It's a good thing I won that argument, because not too long after, she was caught with blow up her nostrils during a fashion show. Her career tanked, and I found out she spent all her money on partying and getting high.

When I got my promotion, I moved us away from Hollywood and into a two-bedroom apartment near UCLA. It's more laid back—less temptations for her. I paid for her to go to rehab and when she got out, I had everything set up and ready. At first when she got out, she was on board, focusing on herself and us, but all too quickly, she was back to her old self. Going out and partying. She swears she hasn't done any drugs, but I wouldn't doubt she's lying.

I go to pull into my designated parking spot, but there's already a newer-looking Porsche parked in it. I glance over and see Victoria's Mercedes in hers. I bought it for her when I got my promotion, hoping it would make her happy. Spoiler alert, it didn't.

I park in a guest parking spot and then head up to our second floor apartment. After unlocking the door, I open it slowly and quietly, and then close it the same way. I walk through our foyer and living room and stop in the doorway of our bedroom. The door is wide-open and she's in bed, sleeping on her side. Her hair is splayed out across the pillow, and her lips are forming a little pout. And behind her is a man I've never seen before with his arm thrown over the side of her, his hand resting on her bare, fake breast—something else she wasted her money on, thinking she needed them to be successful.

I knew there was a damn good chance this was what I would

find when I walked through the door, but I wasn't prepared for the hurt and betrayal I would feel seeing my wife in another man's arms.

I met Victoria when we were ten, fell in love with her when we were seventeen, and we were married when we were twenty. Now, at twenty-nine years old, we're about to be divorced. Because there's no coming back from this. I could forgive her for just about anything, but fucking another man... I can't do it. No matter how much I love her.

I clear my throat and Victoria's eyes pop open. It takes her a second for it to click: her husband is home and she's in bed with another man. But once it does, she jumps out of bed, in nothing but a tiny G-string.

The guy groans, stretching out his arms. He has no clue what's happening.

"Chase," she squeaks, her eyes darting between me and her fuck buddy. She runs over to the bathroom door and grabs her robe, throwing it on.

"Huh?" the guy says, opening his eyes and meeting mine. "Oh, shit. Look, man... I don't want any problems." He climbs out of bed, wearing only a pair of boxers. Human nature has me checking him out. He's about the same height as me, has tattoos donning his arms, whereas I'm tattoo free. He's skinny, tiny abs, but nothing like the muscle I have from working out daily. I'm not sure what's drawn Victoria to him, until he sniffs and wipes his hand back and forth under his nose. And then it hits me: he's a druggie, like my wife.

"Look, Chase, I wanted to tell you, but I didn't want to hurt you," she says, stepping over next to the guy.

"You told me you two were over," he says to her.

At this point, most guys would've pummeled the man who was sleeping in his bed, but that's not who I am. I'm married to Victoria, not this guy. Should he have been fucking a married woman? Hell no. But I got a glimpse at her left hand and saw she removed her ring. She's been lying to both of us.

"We are now," I tell him calmly, refusing to go ballistic and throw shit. I gave this woman my all. I loved her and supported her. I was faithful to her. And in return, she cheated on me God knows how many times.

My gaze meets Victoria's. "Let me know when I can come back and pack my shit. I don't want you to be here. And I'll file for divorce... you know, since you don't have any money to file yourself."

I turn my back on my cheating wife and walk out the door. She doesn't bother to chase after me, and I don't expect her to. She made her decision a long time ago.

A few minutes later, I'm pulling into Alec's complex. It's nicer than mine, located in a wealthy neighborhood. He comes from a well-off family—stepdad is a retired UFC fighter—and was given the place as a gift after he graduated from the fire academy.

I knock on the door, and Georgia answers. She's Alec's roommate, along with her sister, Lexi. She's holding her laptop in one hand and the door with the other. Her brown hair is up in a messy bun, and her eyes, green like the grass after a good rain, shine in sympathy.

"Hey," I mutter, "Alec mentioned..."

"Yeah, of course," she says, thankfully not making me finish my sentence. If I had to, I might fucking lose it. I'm barely holding it together as it is.

I grab the door from her and walk through it, closing it behind me.

"The pillow and blanket are where you left them," she tells me. "Lexi is at the beach, surfing, and Alec is asleep."

"Thanks." I fall onto the couch and drop my face into my hands, trying to figure out how the hell my life has come to this.

My phone dings and I pull it out.

**Victoria: You can come by and get your stuff tomorrow. And I'll file for the divorce. I want it done ASAP.**

She'll file for divorce?

**Me: With what money?**

There's no way her cheating ass is getting a dime from me.

**Victoria: Raymond said he'd pay.**

Raymond... Guess that's the guy's name. Must've been his Porsche parked in my spot. What a fucking dumbass. He finds out the woman he's fucking is a liar and offers to pay for her divorce? Must be the powder he's been snorting.

**Me: Cool, he paying for your apartment and Mercedes too?**

We both know her broke ass can't afford to pay for either one. Speaking of which... I pull up my bank app and quickly transfer my money from our joint checking to my sole savings account. I'll need to visit the bank as soon as possible to close that checking account and open a new one.

I wait a few minutes for her to answer, and when she doesn't, I put my phone on silent and throw it onto the coffee table. Fuck her and her cheating ass.

Grabbing the pillow and blanket next to the couch, I lie down and close my eyes, trying not to let myself get worked up. But fuck, it's hard. I gave her everything, all of me. My money, my time, my love. And what did I get in return? A cheating wife. At least we didn't have any kids. The divorce will go through quickly and then I can move on, start my life over again. I can tell you one thing, there's no way in hell I'm ever giving a woman that much of myself again.

Lesson. Fucking. Learned.

## CHAPTER TWO

### FIFTEEN MONTHS LATER

### CHASE

"Hey, what are you up to tonight?" I pop my head into Georgia's room and ask, even though I already know what she's up to... the same thing she's *always* up to.

She looks up from her laptop, and her emerald eyes meet mine. "Working." She lifts her laptop slightly.

"Any chance you want to go to Club Illusion with me?"

In the last two years, since I've known Georgia, I've only seen her actually go out a handful of times—usually when Lexi would drag her out for a celebration. But since Lexi and Alec moved out —after getting married and having a baby—Lexi has been too busy to go out, which means Georgia hasn't been out either.

"No, thank you," she says softly, shaking her head to emphasize her answer. She glances back down at her laptop, resuming her work. The woman practically lives in her room, on that thing. The only time she ever leaves it is to either visit her family or check on the art gallery she helps Lexi run. Hell, she even has her groceries delivered.

"All right. Not sure if I'll be home tonight, but text or call if you need anything, okay?" I tell her the same thing every night before I go out, or before I leave for work. In the several months we've been living together, she's never once texted or called me.

"Will do." She smiles sweetly up at me. "Have a good night."

As I'm about to dip out, I notice her smile quickly fades into a frown. I do a double take, and her eyes are already back on her laptop, but something about the way her lips quirk down rubs me the wrong way. I should probably ignore it. My friends are waiting, and while Georgia and I get along, we aren't exactly friends. The only reason we ended up living together was out of circumstance—Alec was too lazy to sell the place, Georgia wanted to give her sister some space, and I didn't want to deal with finding a new place to live.

"Hey," I say, getting her attention.

She glances back up at me, her eyes slightly glassy.

"You okay?"

"Mmhmm." Her gaze goes back to her laptop.

"You sure?" I assess her features, not buying her noise of an answer.

"Yeah," she chokes out, her voice contradicting her response.

"No, you're not," I say, stepping into her room.

I glance around, realizing in all the time we've been living together, I've never actually stepped foot in her room. After Lexi and Alec moved out, she took over the master bedroom. The walls are filled with a mixture of art her sister has created over the years and family pictures. Her furniture is all feminine, white-wash wood, and her area is clean and organized, barely lived in.

"Umm...yes, I am," she volleys without looking up.

"Look at me," I demand. When she ignores me, I step closer and pull her laptop away from her.

"Hey! What are you doing?" She scampers off the bed and comes after me.

I hold it over my head, and she tries to jump to grab it, but she's a good half-foot shorter than my six-foot self, and with my reach being longer, she doesn't stand a chance.

"Chase," she whines. "I have work to do.

"First tell me why you're upset."

"I'm not upset." She huffs.

I can't help but chuckle at the way her lips form the most adorable pout.

"Are you laughing at me?" she accuses, her eyes turning into thin slits. It's not often Georgia gets mad, but when she does, it's sexy as hell.

The first few months of us living together were rough. Our rooms were butted up next to each other and when I would have women over, they would be a bit...vocal. Georgia would get hella pissed and let me know. And then there was this one time when a woman used her shaver... Yeah, she damn near killed me.

It wasn't until I agreed to stop bringing women around that things calmed down. Then, after Alec and Lexi moved out, she moved to the master bedroom, which gave her her own bathroom. She told me I could bring women over again, but for the most part, I prefer going to their place. That way I can leave the morning after.

"Chase! My laptop!" she complains, jumping up to grab it.

"Not until you tell me what's wrong."

She drops her hands and sighs. "I just... I miss my sister," she admits with a shrug. "I guess... I'm kind of lonely." Tears fill her eyes, but she quickly blinks them away. "Now can I have my laptop back, please?" she whispers.

I knew she and Lexi were close, but I didn't consider that Lexi moving out would be this hard for her. I've been so busy focusing on my own shit, like moving forward after my divorce, that I haven't paid attention.

"Come out with me tonight," I suggest.

"So I can play third wheel to whichever woman you're planning to dick tonight?" Her face scrunches up in disgust. "I'm good."

I bark out a laugh, shocked and kind of turned on that she said dick. How very unlike Georgia. "I'm not going to *dick* anyone. I'm just going to have a drink with the guys." I had every intention of getting my dick wet tonight, but I can hold off one night to get Georgia out of the house.

"C'mon," I press. "You might even have fun." I mock gasp and she rolls her eyes.

"Fine." She sighs, trying to sound like going out is such a hardship. "I guess I could use the change of scenery."

"And an alcoholic beverage," I add. "Get dressed, so we can go."

I head out to the living room and drop onto the couch to wait for her. Women take hours to get ready, so I text the guys I'm meeting that I'm running late and warn them Georgia will be tagging along, so they know to be on their best behavior. Since Georgia sometimes stops by the fire station with Lexi to visit Alec, they know her. But since she's kind of a recluse, nobody besides her family *really* knows her.

I'm texting Carter back, when I hear the click-clack of heels on the wood floor. I look up, mid-text, and am shocked as shit by the sight in front of me. For one, I swear she's gotten ready in under twenty minutes. Something I've never seen a woman do before. But also, I've seen her occasionally dress up, and it's always on the conservative side. However, right now, what she's wearing is anything but.

Her black tank top is a turtleneck, hiding her cleavage, yet it's form-fitting, showing off the outline of her perky tits and slim waist. You can't technically see anything, but you can damn sure imagine what's underneath. She's wearing tiny—and I mean *tiny*—white shorts that show off her creamy, toned legs. Holy shit! My eyes land on her feet, and she's donning black open-toed heels with little ribbons on the tops and red soles on the bottoms. My mind immediately goes to her legs wrapped around my waist with those heels digging into my back as I fuck—

Jesus! I. Cannot. Go. There.

"Do I look stupid?" she asks, forcing my eyes to go to her face. Her hair is down in waves, and the glasses she wears when she's reading or working on the computer are absent. Her lashes are coated in a thin layer of mascara and her lips are shiny. But aside from that, she's all natural, and fucking beautiful. I knew she was pretty. Once upon a time, I even considered trying to hook up with her, but Alec pulled the best friend card, and I never bothered to look again. I mean, she's always in sweats and oversized shirts when she's lounging around the house. And when she leaves, jeans and a T-shirt. I had no fucking clue what was hiding under there.

"I'm going to go change," she says with a sigh, knocking me out of my thoughts.

"No!" I yell too loudly, causing her brows to rise in confusion. "I mean, no," I choke out, clearing my throat. "You look good."

Every night I go out, I come across women in expensive outfits and caked-on makeup trying way too hard—which is the norm in

LA—yet here she is, wearing shorts, a simple top, and a pair of heels, and she blows any woman I've ever come across away.

And the worst part... she has no damn clue.

"Are you sure?" she asks cautiously. "Lexi left these here... Well, except the shoes. These are mine. Lexi bought them for me..." She rambles on, and all I can do is stare at her pouty pink lips. "I don't really have any going out clothes, and I didn't want to embarrass you, or myself."

*Huh?* This shakes me out of my trance.

"One," I say, standing, hating that she thinks she would embarrass me based on her wardrobe. "You could wear a burlap sack and look sexy as hell."

She snorts. "You're such a liar."

"No, I'm not," I tell her truthfully. "And whatever you want to wear is up to you. Nothing you put on would embarrass me."

She flinches, quickly trying to hide it with a smile.

"What were you just thinking?" I ask, needing to know what's going through her head. She's the most soft-spoken person I know. Aside from getting upset about the women I used to bring home, she never complains about anything.

"Robert hated the way I dressed."

"Fuck Robert."

Robert was her short-term boyfriend. He thought he was fucking special because he worked for Daddy's law firm, and he treated Georgia like shit. A few times I considered letting him in on a little secret: Georgia was way too fucking good for him. But I didn't want to start shit that wasn't my business. Luckily, she's smart and dumped his ass.

"You ready to go?"

She takes a deep breath, then exhales harshly. "Yeah."

We take an Uber to the club because I'm planning to drink, and when we arrive, since I'm friends with the guy at the door, we get right in without having to wait in line.

"What do you want to drink?" I ask her when we reach the bar.

Her brows furrow in thought. "A lemon drop, I guess." She shrugs and squints, and I can tell she's uncomfortable. But this will be good for her. She's a young, single woman. She should be out having a good time, not cooped up in her room.

I shout our order to the bartender, and a minute later, he returns with my beer and her lemon drop. "Let's go find the guys," I tell her, handing her her drink.

As we make our way through the throng of people, several of them stop me to talk. Since my divorce last year, I've been making up for all the years I was home, trying to be a good husband. At first I was worried I'd run into Victoria at the clubs, but I've yet to see her since the day I picked up my shit. Given I agreed to what she wanted in the divorce, I had my attorney stand in my place to have it all finalized, and from what he told me, she had hers do the same.

I spot Carter and Luke, and grab Georgia's hand to guide her over to them, so she doesn't get lost in the crowd. Her hand is small inside mine, and I think about how long it's been since I've held a woman's hand. Victoria was never really the touchy-feely type, unless she wanted something, and the women I hook up with are just that—a hookup.

When I glance back at Georgia, she smiles weakly, looking completely out of her element, and I vow to show her a good time tonight, to make her see there's more to life outside of her four safe walls.

"What's up!" Carter yells over the music. He extends his hand and reluctantly I drop Georgia's.

"Georgia, you remember Carter?" Carter works with me on the same shift at the fire station.

"Yes," she says shyly, making him grin wide. In LA, we're used to women who are coy or have an agenda. Almost all of them are here to be the next big model or actress, and they'll soak up attention anywhere they can get it. A woman who is genuinely sweet and innocent like Georgia is rare.

"Nice to see you again," Carter says with that look in his eye he gets when he's interested in a woman. "Would you like to dance?"

At his bluntness, Georgia's eyes comically bug out. "Oh…umm…"

"We just got here," I cut in. "We're going to have a seat for a few minutes."

Georgia smiles up at me, liking that idea, and the way she looks at me like I'm some sort of white knight has me chugging my beer. Georgia is off-limits. For one, she's Alec's best friend, and he would kill me for going there. But also, I have no desire to settle down. I was tied down for twelve years, and look how that worked out for me. I just don't think I have it in me to give myself over to another woman. And Georgia is the kind of woman who deserves it all.

We slide into the booth, just as Luke and Scott walk over, each with a beer in their hands and a woman tucked under their arms. Both of them work the same shift as Alec, Carter, and me. Since we all have the same days off, we've gotten close. There's one other guy, Thomas, who works with us as well, but he's married with kids.

"Georgia... Luke and Scott," I tell her, ignoring the women. They won't be with them tomorrow, so there's no point in introducing them.

"Nice to see you again," she tells both of them, taking a sip of her drink.

"You too," they both shout over the music. Luke's eyes meet mine, and his brows go up in a silent question. I shake my head, and he nods with a laugh.

The guys all excuse themselves to go dance, leaving Georgia and me at the table alone. "Is your drink good?" I ask, making conversation.

"Yeah. If you want to go dance or whatever, you can."

"Nah, I'd rather chill with you." I shoot her a playful wink and her entire face turns pink. Fuck, she's adorable. "So, tell me about you."

"You know me." She laughs, bumping my shoulder with hers. The sound shouldn't affect me the way it does, hitting me straight in the chest. It's genuine and sweet. No motives behind it.

"Yeah, I know you, but I don't *know* you. Aside from the fact that you do web design for a living, I don't really know anything else."

She thinks about this for a second. "That's really all I do," she admits, so softly that if I wasn't sitting so close to her, I wouldn't have heard her. "I design websites for different businesses, maintain them... I do some graphic design..."

"What do you do for fun?"

Her eyes meet mine, and her pink lips form a frown that has

me wanting to put a smile back on her face. "I guess nothing," she says, lifting her cup and downing the rest of her drink. She cringes as she swallows, then sets the glass down. "I had this plan," she admits. "Well, Lexi and I had this plan... We were going to find our perfect paths."

I want to laugh at that. I learned a long time ago there's no such thing as perfect, but from what I've seen, Georgia, Lexi, and Alec were raised in a sheltered, cushy life, so it makes sense she would believe perfect exists.

Not wanting to jade her with my truth, I keep my thoughts to myself. "And how's that going?"

"Lexi found hers. She and Alec fell in love and got married and had Abigail..." She smiles brightly, genuinely happy for her sister. "And she found her calling with Through Their Eyes."

Through Their Eyes is an art gallery that's set to open soon. It'll help raise money for autistic children and adults, focusing on those who are low income or homeless.

"You're the reason Through Their Eyes even exists," I point out. Georgia inherited an oil company from her biological father who died when she was little. She sold it for millions of dollars, making her a millionaire at twenty-one years old. You would never know it, though, when you're around her. Especially since she still works like she needs the money—something I respect the hell out of her for.

"I provided the money, sure," she says. "But the rest is all Lexi. From the second I shared my idea with her, she made it her own, which is what I wanted. That gallery is going to do amazing things for a lot of people."

"But..." I prompt, sensing one coming.

"It's hers, not mine. She found her path, but I haven't found mine. And since she moved out, I haven't really been looking."

"What interests you? Besides web design."

She ponders my question for a few seconds. "I like reading... and watching cooking shows," she says with a laugh. "And eating."

"So, you should try cooking." I cringe when I say the words, thinking about all the times her sister tried to cook and the fire department was called because of the smoke alarm going off. Hopefully being a horrible cook doesn't run in their family.

As if she can hear my thoughts, she laughs. "I've cooked a few times with my mom and I've never burned anything." She winks, actually fucking winks, and my dick flexes in my pants. My guess is there's more to Georgia, but she hasn't allowed her true self to come out.

"Then you should definitely cook. I can be your taste tester." I can't even remember the last time I had a home-cooked meal, aside from the food the guys grill at the station. I can't cook for shit, and Victoria would never even attempt it.

"What else?"

"I don't know. I guess it's something I need to think about."

"Well, while you're thinking, what do you say we dance?" I stand and extend my hand.

"I don't know..." She eyes my hand speculatively.

"C'mon," I push. "We've danced together before and I was a complete gentleman."

"All right," she says, giving in and placing her hand in mine.

As I escort her to the middle of the dance floor, I push away any thoughts of how perfect her hand fits in mine, wondering what the hell I'm doing.

## CHAPTER THREE

### GEORGIA

WHAT THE HECK am I doing? One minute, I was updating a website, considering if I should order Chinese or Thai, and the next, I'm at a club, talking to Chase about my path. And now, I'm in his freaking arms, dancing with him to some old Jason Derulo song.

I'm so out of my element here. I can feel the panic attack creeping up, and I mentally beg it to stand down. My body and mind are confused, wondering what the hell I was thinking coming here—without Lexi, no less. She's the only person who really knows me, knows every one of my weird quirks, and doesn't judge me for them.

I'm not good at this—being in public, *peopling*. That's Lexi, she's the life of the party. And I'm good at standing behind her.

"Hey," Chase says to get my attention. "You okay?" He has his arms wrapped around my waist, and we're swaying to the music. He's so confident in everything he does. So good at fitting in.

When I don't answer quickly enough, he pulls me off the dance floor and over to a small, darker corner away from everyone. "Georgia, what's wrong?" he asks. "Your heart..." He presses his palm to my chest. "It's beating so hard."

That's because I'm in the middle of a panic attack. Because I'm a freaking loser and can't handle being in crowded places.

I try to open my mouth to explain, but I can't speak. I'm too worked up. From the outside, I look like a normal woman standing close to a man, but on the inside, my heart is thumping in my throat. It's hard to catch my breath. Tears are burning behind my lids. I close my eyes, trying to calm myself down, but it only makes it worse when memories from when I was younger surface, like they always do. Of my biological father yelling at me and throwing me in my room because I was crying for my mom. Of me being forced to stay there for days, by myself, all alone. Begging my grandmother to let me out while he was at work. I didn't know where my mom was at the time, but I knew she wasn't there with me.

I was little, too little. I shouldn't even remember what happened, but I do. I used to think they were nightmares, but the older I got, the more I realized they were memories. Memories I've never told anyone about—not even Lexi.

"Shit, Georgia, you're shaking," Chase says, rubbing his palms up and down my arms.

"I need..." I croak out. "I need to leave."

I take off running through the crowded club in search of the entrance. I don't stop until I push the door open and fall outside, gulping down pockets of air, finally able to breathe a little easier.

Jesus, I'm so messed up. I need to grow the hell up. I'm almost twenty-two, for God's sake. My biological father is dead, and I've been safe and loved for years. Tristan, the man who adopted me—and is my dad in every way that counts—and my mom love me more than anything. I've lived a life most dream of. I should be normal—like Lexi.

But I'm not.

"Georgia!" Chase yells, catching up to me. "What the hell happened back there?"

Not wanting to embarrass myself any further, I shrug. "I'm not feeling well."

"Bullshit," he hisses. "I felt your heart. You were shaking and—"

"Can you just drop it?" I snap. "I never should've come here."

Chase steps closer to me. "You were having a panic attack. Being in that club, with all those people..." His hazel eyes lock with mine as the pieces fall into place. "That's why you don't go out and stay in your room all the time..."

"Yeah, I'm weird. I'm going to catch a cab home. You should stay and have a good time." I turn to leave, but Chase grabs my forearm, stopping me.

"You're not weird. You have social anxiety. Have you talked to anyone about it?"

*No because that would mean telling my family...*

I shake my head. "I'm okay now. Really, you should go back in. I'm sorry for ruining your night. At least next time you'll know better than to invite me," I half-joke.

Chase doesn't laugh. "You didn't ruin anything." He flags down a cab and opens the door for me. I slide in, and then he gets in as well.

"You don't have to—"

"I'm not sending you home alone," he scoffs. "It's fine."

The ride home is quiet. When we get up to our place, which is on the second floor, we go our separate ways. I take a quick shower, then get dressed in a tank top and sweats.

I'm standing in the kitchen, getting a drink of water and checking my phone, when Chase walks in. He's dressed in black basketball shorts sans shirt. My eyes trail down his body. He works out almost every day, and his muscular body is proof of that. His skin is tattoo free, with only a light spattering of hair across his hard chest. His six-pack abs look almost airbrushed on. And the V that disappears beneath the waistband of his shorts... Jesus. My hand tingles, wanting to run my fingers down them to make sure they're real.

Chase clears his throat, and my eyes pop up to meet his, which are dancing with laughter because he just caught me blatantly checking him out. His chocolate brown hair is wet and messy from his shower, and a few droplets of water drip down his temple.

My phone pings with a text, and I glance down at it. I must frown at it because Chase says, "Something wrong?"

"No, I'm—"

"Can you please not lie to me?"

I look up and his jaw is ticking.

"I was lied to by my ex-wife for years. If you don't want to tell me something, just say that, but don't lie."

I swallow thickly at his request. I'm so used to saying I'm okay, it's become my go-to answer. I didn't intentionally lie to him.

"Lexi and I were supposed to meet tomorrow for lunch and to get our nails done. It's our thing..." Or at least it was until she had her daughter. Now I feel like I barely see her anymore. "She has to meet with the event coordinator for the gallery opening. It's not a big deal," I say flippantly, hoping my tone matches my words.

I send Lexi a text back, telling her it's okay and we'll get together soon. When I glance back up, Chase is staring at me. "What?"

"I never realized how often you lie. Do you ever tell the truth?"

"I'm going to bed," I mutter, not wanting to argue with him. I don't do well with confrontation and I'm finally not feeling like I'm going to hyperventilate, so I'd like it to stay that way. Before he can argue, I hurry into my room, shutting the door behind me.

---

"HEY, SLEEPYHEAD," a deep voice says. "Time to get up."

I groan and roll over, coming face to face with Chase, who's sitting on the edge of my bed. "What time is it?" I ask, my voice gravelly with sleep.

"Nine o'clock."

"Ugh! I'm sleeping. Wasn't my door closed?"

"Yeah, but I knocked and you didn't answer."

"Because I was sleeping," I whine. I was up until almost four o'clock working on a large website I'm creating for a fortune five hundred company.

"And now you're up. Let's go. We have things to do today."

I sit up, confused. "I don't have anything to do today." I glance at him and he's dressed in a Station 115 shirt, which is the number of the fire station he works at, and a pair of jeans.

"Yes, we do," he argues. "Now, up." He pats my thigh. "The day is a wasting."

He stands and grins. "I'll meet you in the living room when you're done getting ready." Then he disappears.

Twenty minutes later, I'm dressed in a pair of jeans and a shirt, ready to go. "Want to tell me where we're going now?"

"Who's your book boyfriend?" he asks, his eyes on my chest.

I glance down and then laugh. My shirt reads: My book boyfriend is better than yours. "It's a joke. I got it at a book signing I went to last year in San Francisco. A book boyfriend is a fake boyfriend from a book."

I turn around so he can see the list of names on the back of my shirt. "It's all my favorite heroes from the books I've read."

"Carson Matthews, Ridge Beckett, Kostas Demetriou, Reece Hatfield." Chase tilts his head to the side slightly in confusion.

"I told you I'm weird. The only serious relationships I've ever had were with fake guys."

"Stop saying that. You're not weird. I was just wondering how good those guys can be if they can't even really please you." He shrugs.

If I were drinking, the liquid would be all over him. "Well, I've only been with one guy," I admit, "and he was selfish in bed, so I think I'll take my fake men over real ones." The second the words are out, I immediately regret them.

"Wait... you slept with that douchebag Robert?" he asks incredulously.

"Not that it's your business..." But since I did bring it up first... "No, but we did stuff." He attempted to finger me, but nothing happened, and when I asked him about it, he got defensive and said sex would be better.

Chase's mouth gapes open. "You do *not* get to judge all men based on that asshole."

"Whatever, I'm dressed. Now where are we going?"

"It's a surprise." He grins mischievously.

Since I don't know where we're going, we take his car. It's a newer BMW, the interior all leather, and the gadgets all high-tech.

"This is a nice car," I say, realizing it's the first time I've been in his vehicle.

"Thanks."

"Too bad it's probably overpriced and will break down on you soon."

His head whips around to look at me. "What?"

"Yeah, don't you know what BMW stands for?" I ask, remembering all the jokes my dad threw at my godfather, Mason, over the years about his love of BMWs. My dad is a Ford man through and through, and Mason only buys BMWs. At first, I wanted a cute little car, but my dad wanted me to have a Ford truck so I would be safe. It took some getting used to, but it's kind of cool knowing I could run over any vehicle on the road—yes, my truck is that damn big.

"Really?" he scoffs. "You're going there? You drive a Ford," he accuses.

"First on Race Day."

Chase snorts. "Just don't be calling me when your truck is stuck on the side of the road, dead, to come pick your ass up in my BMW."

I laugh and turn the volume up on his radio, liking the song that's playing. When we drive into Larchmont, a small neighborhood I know well, since my parents both have businesses here, I glance around curiously.

"Coffee first," Chase says, pulling through the drive-thru of Jumpin' Java, my favorite coffee place. I smile on the inside that he knows this. I was with Robert for months and he didn't pay attention to anything. I hate mushrooms, yet every time he would order our food—because he insisted on ordering—he would forget to mention to the waitress to leave them off for me. And when I would complain, he would tell me that adults eat vegetables and to stop acting like a little girl.

A few minutes later Chase pulls into a parking lot and turns off his engine. I'm not sure why we're here, but I don't ask, instead, grabbing my coffee and following him.

When he steps up to a nail salon, I grin. "You're taking me to get my nails done?"

"*We're* getting our nails done." He winks playfully. "Just call me Lexi 2.0."

"Oh my God." I laugh. "Really? You're getting your nails done?"

"Whatever you two were supposed to do, I'm doing it too."

My heart swells. "Thank you, but you don't have to do that." And then without thought, I wrap my arms around him for a hug. I'm not expecting him to return the hug, so I'm taken aback when his hands slide around my waist and rest on the small of my back. I should back up... end the hug. But instead, I stay where I am, with my face pressed against Chase's chest. When I breathe in, I catch a whiff of his scent. It's clean and masculine and oddly enough smells like comfort.

I glance up, and our faces are close... too close. He looks down, his eyes landing on my lips, and I think for a second he's going to kiss me, which causes me to panic, unsure if I want him to. On one hand, I bet he'd be a good kisser... He definitely has the experience. On the other hand, he has all that experience because he's been with a lot of women, and I can't become one of those women... That's not who I am.

Before I can decide if I want him to kiss me, he retreats, clearing his throat.

"I want to," he says.

He wants to, what?

Kiss me?

Did I voice my question out loud?

Then he adds, "Plus, I've been needing to get a good pedicure." Oh! He's referring to wanting to get his nails done with me. I sigh in relief.

"Well, if you insist... This should be fun."

We walk inside and Chase surprises me when he tells the guy he has an appointment for us. We're told to pick out our colors. I go with my usual: pink, and Chase chooses blue.

"You can get clear, you know," I point out.

"Eh, what's the fun in that?"

We sit in our assigned chairs and the lady shows him how to turn his chair massager on. "Damn, this feels good," he moans loudly, his eyes rolling back.

Several of the employees and customers look over, making me laugh under my breath at how crazy he is. He glances over at me with a dreamy look in his eyes and shrugs, not giving a shit what anybody thinks.

I try to imagine Robert here with me and I can't do it. He would've scoffed at even the idea of a man getting a pedicure. Yet, Chase is one of the manliest guys I know—I mean, he runs into burning buildings for a living—and he's completely okay with sitting in a salon getting his toes painted.

Chase has made me laugh more this morning than I ever laughed with Robert. I was so stuck on the fact that I wasn't right for Robert... that I wasn't enough. When the truth is, Robert wasn't right for me.

"What's going through your head?" Chase asks.

"I want to find someone," I admit.

When his brows dip in confusion, I explain. "I want to find a guy who's right for me. Robert wasn't."

Chase nods in understanding. "You'll find him, Georgia, you just have to get out of the house to look."

He's right, and for most women that would be easy, but for me, it's a bit more difficult. It's probably why I settled so quickly for Robert. He was the first guy to give me attention. I was searching for that perfect path and there he was standing there. I thought at the time it meant something... And I guess in a way it did: a lesson learned.

"Damn, they massage your feet too?" Chase moans. "I'm going to have to get a pedicure every month."

I giggle and snap a picture of him. Since his head is back and his eyes are closed, he doesn't notice. I send a group text to Lexi and Alec.

> **Me: Look who's replaced Lexi! <insert winky face with tongue sticking out>**
>
> **Alec: LOL How the hell did you get him to do that?**
>
> **Me: His idea...**
>
> **Lexi: Nobody can replace me! <insert side-eye>**
>
> **Me: Well, he did. <insert shrugging brown-haired woman>**
>
> **Lexi: Tomorrow, let's do breakfast!**
>
> **Me: Sure! Sounds good.**

"Did you tell Alec I'm getting my toes done?" Chase asks. I look up and laugh. "Maybe..."

"You're lucky I can't get up right now, but once I can, you're dead, woman."

I laugh harder. "Okay, whatever you say. Lexi and I are meeting for breakfast tomorrow."

"That's good. See? You have nothing to be worried about with your relationship with your sister."

After getting our toes done, Chase gets a manicure, this time forgoing any polish, while I get my fills done on my acrylics. I get my eyebrows threaded, and he gets his trimmed. When the technician waxes the middle of his brows and he squawks like a duck, I crack up.

"Thank you for doing this," I tell him, once we're back in the car on the way home.

"You don't have to thank me. I had a good time, and I feel like a whole new man." He wiggles his clean fingers, making me giggle.

"So, there's this bonfire tonight," he says. I open my mouth to tell him no, but before I can, he adds, "And before you say no..." He side-eyes me. "It's at Carter's house. He's on a couple acres, has a big backyard that's backed up to the water. There won't be a lot of people there. Just a few. It'll be fun. We'll cook some hot dogs, roast some marshmallows, and I'll be with you the entire time."

It actually sounds fun, and before I can come up with an excuse not to go, I find myself saying, "I'll go... But if you want to leave me to do your own thing, I'll understand."

"My own thing?"

"You know... if you meet a woman and want to hang out with her..." The words taste bitter as they leave my mouth, but I push the thought aside. Chase is just being nice to me because I told him I miss Lexi and am lonely.

"If I wanted to hang out with some other woman I wouldn't have invited you," he says, leaving no room for argument in his tone.

## CHAPTER FOUR

### CHASE

We arrive at Carter's place, and there are a few cars parked in his driveway and along his front yard. Georgia is dressed in a pair of skintight jeans, a black hoodie that reads Fight Club, and black Vans. I love how low-key she is. Most women would be dolled up, but not her... She's dressed casual and it makes her even sexier. Her eyes are scanning the area, and I can tell she's nervous about being here. I promised her there wouldn't be too many people, but she's still scared. I told Carter a little about her condition and he ensured me there would only be a handful of people hanging out.

"He has a nice home," she notes absentmindedly.

"His parents left it to him." Carter lost both of his parents in a hotel fire when he was younger, which is the reason he decided to become a firefighter.

Taking Georgia's hand in mine—something I've grown to enjoy doing the last couple days—I walk us around the side of the house. The closer we get, the louder the music gets.

When we reach the backyard, Georgia comes to a halt so she can take everything in. There's a patio with tables and chairs, a decent size swimming pool, and a hot tub. Farther out, there are several lounge chairs facing the Pacific Ocean, and when you walk along the wooden path, it leads to his private beach where he has a bonfire going with chairs forming a circle around it.

If I had to guess, there are probably about fifty people here, a little more than I thought, but because he has so much room, it's not stifling like a club, so I think Georgia will be okay.

"There are a lot of people here," she says, mimicking my thoughts.

"They're spread out, though. Let's go find Carter to say hi, and then get drinks."

She nods, her hand tightening in mine.

"Hey, man." Carter extends his hand to fist bump me. "Nice to see you again, Georgia. Mi casa is your casa. Drinks are on the patio in the fridge and on the counters... food's cooking. You can also grab something to grill over the bonfire."

"Thank you," Georgia says politely.

"Of course," Carter says back with a smile.

We stop at the drink area and since I'm driving I grab a Gatorade. Georgia shocks me when she goes with a Mike's Hard Lemonade.

"I'm hoping a little alcohol will help with my nerves," she admits.

"Hot dog?" I point at the food.

"Yeah, can we grill it on the fire?" she asks, her face lighting up.

I chuckle. "Of course."

I pile a couple dogs on one plate and the ingredients to make s'mores on another so I won't have to come back up. Georgia makes us a plate of sides, and then we head down to the beach.

It's a nice night out, with only just enough breeze to make it cool and comfortable. We find two open seats and get situated. Thomas is sitting next to us with his wife in his lap. They must've gotten a babysitter because I don't see either of their kids running around.

"What's up?" I say, jutting my chin toward him.

"Date night." He grins.

After making introductions between Georgia, Thomas, and his wife, Hilary, we stick our dogs on a couple of skewers and hold them over the fire.

"You okay?" I ask Georgia quietly.

"Yeah." She glances over at me and smiles. "This is nice."

We watch our dogs cook, turning them until they're wrinkly

and dark brown, then we remove them and drop them into our buns.

"Mmm," she moans, taking a bite of her hot dog. "How is it that it tastes better cooked like this?"

I laugh and take my own bite, ignoring the way her moaning hits me straight in the dick. It's damn good. Crispy and cooked through.

"Looks like your first cooking mission was a success," I joke.

Georgia laughs. "I saved a couple of recipes online that I want to try."

"Once you know they're good, remember I'm your taste tester."

She cracks up. "You're supposed to try them to tell me if they're good."

I just shrug, taking another bite.

"Want some potato salad?" she asks, holding a forkful up.

"Sure." I'm about to set my hot dog down, when Georgia leans over and feeds me the bite, before taking her own. I watch as she enjoys the food, moaning and smiling with every bite. Georgia was right, she loves food.

"I'm going to make a s'more," she says, pushing a marshmallow onto the skewer and then hanging it over the fire. I watch her while she watches the marshmallow. I don't know what the hell is going on with me, but I can't take my eyes off her. The way she scrunches her nose up in concentration. How every once in a while, she drags her tongue across the seam of her plump lips, wetting them. I've been with several women in the last year, in more intimate positions, but none of them entranced me the way Georgia does without even trying.

"Shit," she hisses. "I burned it."

Reluctantly, I tear my gaze from her to see what she's talking about and find a charcoal black marshmallow engulfed in flames at the end of her skewer. "Here, let me help you," I say, taking the skewer from her and flicking the burned marshmallow off, then adding a new one.

"I wanted to do it." She huffs, her mouth forming a cute as fuck pout.

"C'mere." I nod toward my chair. She stands, unsure where I want her, and I grab her around the waist, pulling her into my lap.

"Now, the key to making the perfect marshmallow is to cook it evenly," I explain.

Placing the skewer in her hand, I wrap mine around hers. She leans back slightly to get comfortable, and with her face near mine, I can smell her sweet scent. I don't know what it is, but it's soft and feminine. Without thinking about what I'm doing, I run my nose along her neck.

Georgia stiffens, and I immediately stop. "Sorry," I murmur. "You smell good."

"It's Moonlit Path."

"Moonlit Path has a scent?" Weird.

She giggles. "Yes, it's what you're smelling."

"Well, okay then." I extend her skewer. "To make it perfect, you have to constantly turn the marshmallow in a three hundred and sixty degree circle. If you stop too long, the fire will attack it."

"And then burn it," she adds, like the fire has personally offended her by burning her marshmallow.

Slowly, we turn the skewer around and around until the entire marshmallow is a perfect golden brown. "All right, grab the graham cracker and chocolate," I tell her, pulling the skewer back.

She bends over to grab the plate and pushes against my dick. I let out a grunt and she pops up. "Sorry, did I hurt you?"

*No, you just woke up my cock and now it wants some attention...* "I'm okay," I croak out.

"Here you go." She holds up the plate, and I lay the marshmallow on the chocolate.

"Close it." She places the graham cracker on top, holding it down, so I can pull the skewer out. "All right, try it." I nod toward the snack. She lifts it up and takes a big bite, then sets it back down. Because of the hot marshmallow, melted chocolate drips out and coats her lips. It takes every ounce of restraint I have not to swipe my tongue across her chocolate-covered lips and taste her.

"Oh my God," she moans. "So good!" Her tongue darts out and licks up the chocolate, cleaning the mess from her mouth, and the entire time I wish I were doing it for her.

"Here, try it." She lifts it back up and shoves it toward my mouth. I open wide and take a bite. When she drops it onto the plate, her gaze zeroes in on my lips, and based on the way her eyes are now hooded, I would bet she's thinking the same thing I was just thinking a second ago—she wants to taste me.

Not giving a shit about anything besides tasting her, I lean in to do just that, but before our mouths touch, my name is called out, breaking the moment. Georgia scrambles off my lap and I stand.

"Hey, I thought it was you," Fiona says, walking over. She's dressed in a skimpy bikini and is holding a martini glass in her hand. She must've been walking down the beach from one of the bars. She looks the same as she did a year ago. Same fake face, hair, and tits spilling out of her top. Her skin is so tan, it's almost leathery looking.

"It's me," I say, plastering on a fake smile.

"How are you?" she asks, her enhanced lips forming a fake pout. Fuck, everything about her is so damn fake.

"I'm good. At a buddy of mine's bonfire."

"That's fun. I was so sad for you when Victoria divorced you. I always thought you were a good guy, but you know Victoria... So materialistic."

She rolls her eyes, and I stifle a humorless laugh at the irony of her words. She gained most of her money from marrying a guy three times her age and then getting everything of his when he died.

"I was worried about you, but I'm glad you're doing good... Oh," she says, looking around me at Georgia. "Who's this?"

I glance back and Georgia is nervously shuffling her feet, unsure whether to step forward or run away. "A friend," I tell her, giving her nothing more.

"*Girlfriend?*" Fiona asks, false sweetness dripping from her words.

"No," I tell her truthfully.

"That's too bad. With Victoria getting married and having a baby, I was hoping you would've moved on as well."

Her words hit me straight in the gut. Not because I'm jealous, but because it conjures up old memories of me begging Victoria to have a baby with me. I wanted nothing more than to start a family. When we first got married, she wanted that too. But then she let the modeling world get inside her head and changed her mind, telling me she didn't want a child to ruin her perfect body or life.

It's crazy how much someone can change. Who we were in our teens and early twenties is nothing like who we were when we parted ways.

"Such a cute little thing," she continues.

"So, she's good, then... Clean?" I shouldn't care, but it's hard not to. In some capacity, Victoria was a part of my life for damn near twenty years.

"Is anybody really clean in LA?" Fiona cackles. In other words, she's still a druggie. My heart goes out for that baby. I'm just glad it's not me who has to deal with that shit. Her cheating on me turned out to be a blessing in disguise. It saved me from years of heartache.

Which is exactly why I'm single.

I glance at Georgia, who looks uncomfortable as fuck, and sigh, thankful I didn't kiss her. It would've crossed us over a line I'm not prepared to step over. Sure, she's nothing like Victoria, but she's young and people change. No matter how sweet she is, I just can't risk my heart again. Not now... maybe not ever.

"We better get going," I tell Fiona.

"Okay, good seeing you." She waves, then traipses over to her friends, who were standing back, drinking and talking, while waiting for her.

"I'm not feeling well," I mutter to Georgia as we walk back.

She doesn't say anything and I feel like an ass for my change in mood. But it's for the best. Nothing can happen between us. We're friends, and that's the way it needs to stay.

## CHAPTER FIVE

### GEORGIA

It was like watching someone flip a switch. One minute I was in Chase's lap, inches away from being kissed by him, and the next, he's barely acknowledging me as he talks to some fake wanna-be Barbie about how his ex-wife is married with a baby. I watched as his entire demeanor changed. It was as if he completely shut down. Gone was the playful, fun, flirty Chase, and in his place was the closed-off, broken-hearted shell of a man.

I knew he wasn't available. He's made it clear so many times when he talks to Alec. He was with his wife for years, gave her all of himself, and when she cheated on him, it destroyed him. In the last year, he's never been with the same woman more than a few times. I would know since I would see them coming in and out of his room—until he agreed to take it to their place instead. Maybe that's changed in the last few months, but I would think if he were serious with someone, he would've brought her around or, at the very least, mentioned her.

The fact is, Chase has never pretended to be someone he's not. He's mentioned on more than one occasion he doesn't want to get married again. Alec told him he'd think differently once he met someone worth putting his heart on the line for, but Chase disagreed.

The ride home was quiet, Chase obviously in his own head. I

tried to talk to him, but he cut me off, telling me he didn't want to talk. And once we were through the door, without so much as a good night, he retreated to his room.

I was a little upset when he refused to introduce me to his... whatever she was... friend of his ex-wife? But what hurt even worse was the way he raised up a wall between us afterward. I thought we were friends, but the way he treated me on the way home was like I was nothing to him. I opened up to him, and he couldn't do the same for me.

Needing to take my mind off Chase, I lose myself in my work, and before I know it, it's already six in the morning and my phone is going off.

**Lexi: Abigail was up all night. I'm exhausted. Raincheck?**

My heart hurts, and the loneliness I feel has me wanting to throw my blanket over my head and disappear. So, after I text Lexi back that it's okay and we'll get together another time, that's exactly what I do.

## CHAPTER SIX

### CHASE

Fuck, I'm such an asshole. I was stuck in my own head last night and I completely shut Georgia out. I went straight to bed and passed out, just needing to shake off everything Fiona said. I'm so used to keeping women at a distance, I didn't even consider Georgia's feelings, just pushed her away and slammed the door on her face—literally and figuratively.

Now I'm pacing the floor, waiting for her to get home. She had breakfast plans with Lexi, and when I woke up, she was already gone. I texted her, asking if we could talk so I could apologize, but she hasn't responded.

Figuring she's busy with her sister and might be a while, I get dressed to go for a run. I can use the fresh air and time to think. But when I get downstairs, I notice Georgia's monster of a truck is in her parking spot. I pull out my phone and text Lexi.

**Me: Is Georgia with you?**

Maybe Lexi picked her up.

**Lexi: No, I had to cancel breakfast. Abigail was up all night…**

Fuck, does that mean she's still in her room? It's almost noon.

**Lexi: Everything okay?**

I should probably mind my own business, but my guilt over the way I treated Georgia, mixed with the way I know Georgia is hurting because of her sister, steers my next text.

**Me: Maybe you should ask your sister that… if you ever make the effort to spend time with her.**

I shove my phone into my pocket and run back upstairs to see if Georgia's in her room. When I knock on her door, she doesn't answer. I twist the knob and since it's not locked, I open the door. What if she hit her head or something? I need to make sure she's okay.

When I enter the room, she's sleeping in her bed. Her face is splotchy from crying, and even in her sleep she looks sad. My phone buzzes in my pocket, but I ignore it, going over and sitting on the bed next to her.

When the mattress dips, she stirs awake. Her bloodshot eyes meet mine, and if I felt bad before, it's nothing compared to the way I feel now.

"Lexi said she bailed…"

Georgia blinks several times, then flinches. "I left my contacts in," she says, sitting up and swinging her legs around. She disappears into the bathroom and a few minutes later comes out with her glasses on.

"I thought you were out with your sister."

"Nope," is all she says, grabbing her laptop and sitting back on her bed.

"I got worried when I found out you weren't with her and you weren't answering your phone. I didn't know you were asleep."

"Well, now you know I'm okay, so you can go."

I sigh, momentarily closing my eyes. I fucked up and now she's pushing me away. I deserve it…

"I'm sorry about last night."

She looks up from her laptop. "What are you sorry for?"

"For pushing you away. I was upset and shouldn't have taken

it out on you. We're friends and..." When I say the word friends, she flinches. I don't blame her. Before Fiona showed up, we were flirting and I was about to kiss her. But I can't go there. All we can be is friends. "I like hanging out with you," I finish.

"I don't need your pity, and I don't need you to hang out with me or babysit me or whatever it is you're doing."

"That's not why I'm hanging out with you," I argue. "I have fun with you. I just... I think we got swept up in the moment and I need you to know I'm not capable of anything more."

"Says every player." She rolls her eyes.

"Says every person who's been fucked over," I volley. "You've been in one short relationship, so you don't get it, but I was with Victoria for over ten years. She was my best friend for years before that. I loved her, and she screwed me. We went from agreeing to spend the rest of our lives together, to her lying and cheating on me."

I release a harsh sigh and shake my head. "So, yeah, I sleep around now. Because being single gets lonely, but meaningless sex beats getting my heart smashed again."

Georgia frowns. "I'm sorry. I shouldn't have said that, shouldn't have judged you. I spent years in school getting bullied and picked on because everyone assumed I was being stuck-up and thought I was too good to hang out. Guys thought I was playing hard to get... I hated the way they judged and labeled me without knowing the truth, and I shouldn't have done it to you."

"People are shitty. Me included." I shrug, and she grants me a small smile.

"You're not shitty. You're human."

Fuck, she's so damn forgiving. Whoever she ends up with is one lucky bastard.

"What do you say we go to lunch?" I suggest. "Neither of us has eaten."

"I meant what I said. You don't have to hang out with me."

"And I meant what I said. I want to. I like hanging out with you. I'm not hanging out with you because I pity you. I'm hanging out with you because I want to."

"You're sure?"

"Yes, now, c'mon. Get up, get ready, and let's go get something to eat. It's beautiful outside."

"Okay," she says. "I'll be ready in twenty minutes."

"I'll go change."

When I get to my room, I check my messages.

**Lexi: What's that supposed to mean?**

**Lexi: Hello?**

**Lexi: My sister and I are just fine.**

**Lexi: <insert ten middle finger emojis>**

Not wanting to cause shit, I text her back: **You're right, I shouldn't have texted that. Sorry.**

When she doesn't respond right away, I click out of the message, get dressed, and then shove my phone into my front pocket. When I step out of my room, Georgia is already dressed and ready to go.

"I was thinking we could go to the farmer's market," I tell her once we're in my car. "You mentioned finding some recipes to cook, so you could check for any fresh ingredients you need, and while we're there we can get lunch."

She smiles warmly at me. "That sounds great."

While I drive, she plugs her phone into my car and plays deejay. When her phone goes off with a text, it dings throughout the car and pops up on my screen as Lexi.

"She's sorry for bailing and wants to do a barbecue at her place tomorrow night," she says, rolling her eyes. I hate that what was once hurt is now turning to anger for her.

"You know, she does have a new baby... I don't think she's purposely bailing on you."

"I know," she says. "I'm not mad at her. I just miss her, and I guess in a way, I feel left behind. We had that perfect path pact, and I didn't think about what would happen if she found hers and I didn't find mine."

"You'll find yours," I tell her, reaching over and squeezing her thigh.

"Want to go to a barbecue tomorrow night?"

"Sure. Alec's been busy too, and I've only really seen him at work."

"Cool." She texts her sister back then turns up the music.

When we get to the farmer's market, we explore each of the booths. Georgia pulls up the recipes she found and buys several of the ingredients she'll need.

"I think I got everything," she says, popping a strawberry into her mouth. "I'm hungry. Where should we eat?"

I laugh that she's actually hungry. I swear for every item she bought, we ate two. Most women I'm around are so worried about their weight, they eat like rabbits. It's nice to be around a woman with an appetite.

"There's a Greek restaurant at the end." I point in the direction of where it's located.

"Mmm... I love gyros." She waggles her brows. "Let's do it."

We order our food, then find a table outside.

"Tell me something about you," I say, taking a bite of my chicken gyro.

"I love reading."

I snort. "No shit. Something else. Something I don't already know."

Georgia thinks for a moment. "I'm obsessed with *The Fast and the Furious* movies. I watch them at night when I can't sleep. I think I've seen each of them at least a dozen times."

"Those are the ones with that guy who died, right? Paul something or other..."

Her eyes bug out. "Paul Walker. And yes, those are them. Haven't you seen them?"

"Nope. Victoria wasn't really a movie person. She preferred all those reality shows..."

"Okay... but you haven't been with her in over a year. How have you not seen any of those movies?"

"I guess I'm not a sit-down-and-watch-a-movie-by-myself kind of guy."

"We're rectifying this tonight," she says, her tone dead serious. "I declare tonight a *Fast and the Furious* movie marathon night."

When we get to the condo, she puts away all of her farmer's market findings, while I get us set up in the living room at the coffee table. I was nervous that after the way I acted last night, things would be awkward between us, but I should've known they wouldn't be. Georgia isn't the type to hold a grudge.

"Today was nice," she says, sitting next to me. "Thank you."

"You don't have to thank me. Friends don't thank each other for hanging out with them. I had a good time too."

We watch the first movie, and then the second, and while we're on movie number three—technically it's number four because she insisted we skip number three—something about them needing to be watched out of order for it all to make sense—Georgia's stomach grumbles. "I think we missed dinner."

I glance at the time on my phone. "I think you're right."

We head into the kitchen to see what we have to make. I'm scouring through the cabinets, ready to settle on PB and J, when she says, "How about we make a flatbread? We can use some of the veggies I bought at the farmer's market."

"Sounds good to me." I close the cabinet.

She grabs a bunch of stuff from the pantry and fridge and gets to work making the dough. Apparently she found a recipe online and bought the stuff to make it but hasn't gotten around to it yet.

Once the dough is rolled out—that part was all me—and put on the wooden block, she starts slicing—and snacking on—the fresh mozzarella.

"What toppings do you like?" she asks, popping a slice into her mouth.

I laugh at the fact that she's eaten more of the cheese than she's put on the flatbread. "Anything." I steal some of the cheese from her and place it on top of the dough. "I'm not picky."

She chops up a tomato then takes a bite of one of the slices. "Oh my God, try this." She grabs another slice and brings it up to my lips. I open my mouth and she feeds me the tomato slice. When she doesn't retract her hand quickly enough, I playfully nip at the tips of her fingers, making her shriek with laughter.

"Not cool," she says with a laugh, placing the tomato slices on top. When she's done, she adds some basil then puts it into the oven and sets the timer. "Twenty minutes." She hops onto the counter. "What should we do while we wait?" She glances around like a bored kid, making me chuckle.

When she reaches for another piece of mozzarella, an idea comes to me.

"We could play the food game."

"What's that?" she asks, looking intrigued. The woman loves her food.

"You never played it as a kid?" I thought everyone did... When she shakes her head, I explain, "One person closes their eyes and the other feeds them a piece of food. The person being fed the food has to guess what it is. If they guess it correctly, it's their turn to feed the other person the food."

"What happens if they guess wrong?"

"They have to go again."

Her eyes light up. "This sounds like fun. I'll go first!"

"No way. I mentioned it. I go first."

She pouts playfully. "Fine. I'll close my eyes. I know food anyway, so I'll guess right."

She closes her eyes and I dash to the fridge to see what we have. I consider going with the hot sauce just to fuck with her, but instead go with something a *bit* more enjoyable.

"All right, open up." She opens her mouth and I slide the spoon between her lips.

Her face immediately scrunches up. "It's lemon juice." Her lips pucker and she coughs slightly. When she opens her eyes, she glares. "That was horrible."

"Hey, it could've been worse." I laugh. "I almost went with the hot sauce."

Her eyes widen. "I would've killed you." She jumps down. "Close your eyes. My turn."

I do as she says and a minute later, she's telling me to open up. I smell it before it enters my mouth. Cocoa powder. The spoonful is filled so high, I choke on the powder, my eyes opening in time to see plumes of it hitting her in the face. She coughs and splutters while cracking up laughing.

"Did you feed me the entire container?" I ask, spitting that shit out into the sink before grabbing a bottle of water and taking a large sip.

"Hey, cocoa powder is nicer than lemon juice!" She continues to laugh, and fuck if her laugh isn't the best thing I've heard in a long time. Her face is lit up and happy, and she looks so damn carefree. It's not often I see this side of her, but I fucking love it.

After going a few more rounds, where I make her eat mustard

and honey, and she forces me to eat soy sauce and butter, the timer goes off for our flatbread.

Once she's drizzled some balsamic vinegar over it, we slice and plate our food, then settle back onto the couch to continue our movie marathon. The flatbread is delicious and between the two of us, we devour the entire thing.

A few hours later, in the middle of the fourth—or is it the fifth?—movie, I hear the faint sound of snoring. I glance over at Georgia, who's snuggled up against my side, her face resting against my shoulder, and find her sleeping. Somewhere along the way, we ended up cuddled under a blanket together. I consider moving her to her room, to her own bed, but selfishly don't. I don't question myself—not wanting to have to consider the answer—as I shift us so we're both lying across the couch, with her head now tucked into the crook of my neck, and fall asleep to the sound of Georgia snoring.

## CHAPTER SEVEN

### GEORGIA

"What are you doing?" Chase asks, stepping into my bathroom. We've just gotten back from having breakfast and going for a walk on the pier and are hanging out until we have to head over to Lexi and Alec's place for the barbecue. "And why do you look like an alien who invaded Earth?"

I glance at him through the mirror and laugh. "I'm giving myself a facial. Want one?" It's meant as a joke, but I shouldn't be surprised when Chase shrugs and steps into the bathroom.

"Sure, will it make my face all smooth?"

"As a baby's butt," I joke.

"I've never felt a baby's butt," he says, taking the tube of face mud. "What do I do?"

"First, wash your face with warm water."

He does as I say, then turns to me. "Now what?"

"Now, this..." I squirt a glob out and smear it across his forehead, down the center of his nose, and along the tops of his cheeks. He has scruff along his cheeks and jaw, so I don't bother putting any there.

"Put it all over," he says, going cross-eyed as he tries to look down. "Maybe it'll make my beard soft too."

"Okay." I snort.

When I've covered his face completely, he looks in the mirror and smiles. "Take a picture with me."

"What?" I squeak. "No!"

"Yes," he says, pulling his arm around my neck and bringing me in front of him. He grabs his phone from the pocket of his sweats and snaps a picture. "This is totally Instagram worthy."

He types into his phone. "What's your name on there? I can't find you."

"I only have one for my business. I never really do anything worth posting…" And I don't exactly have many friends to follow or who would follow me.

"We need to change that. You're hanging out with me now. Everything we do is worth posting."

I shake my head and laugh. He's such a cocky ass. *And sweet, and sexy, and the perfect human bed*, I think to myself, remembering this morning when I woke up, lying on the couch in the comfort of his arms, both of us wrapped up in a blanket like we were burritos. He opened his eyes and smiled and my heart damn near stopped in my chest. I've never fallen asleep with a man before, but it's something I definitely want to do again. Too bad it won't be with Chase since he's off-limits… The thought feels like lead settling in my belly. Do other guys cuddle the way Chase does? Are their arms as strong and comforting? I guess there's only one way to find out—actually get out and meet someone.

"It's as hard as cement," Chase says, poking at his face while he stretches his mouth open and closed, making the mud crack.

"That means it's ready to be washed off," I tell him through a laugh. Hanging out with Chase is never boring. I hope whoever I meet is fun like him. I can't remember laughing as much as I have since I've been hanging out with him the last few days.

"We should go swimming."

"I'm not sure the association will be happy with us rinsing our faces off in their pool."

Chase cracks up. "After we rinse off. We have a few hours before we have to go to your sister's for the barbecue." He grabs a couple of washcloths and dips them under the water, then hands one to me.

"Wow," he says, admiring his face once the mud mask is all off.

"You're right. My face is smooth. Now, get a suit on, so we can go swimming."

I give him a two-finger salute and walk out of the bathroom. "Yes, sir!"

"That's what I like to hear," he says, following up his words with a hard slap to my ass.

"Ow!" I mock glare. "Keep your hands to yourself, or I'll slap you back."

"Don't tease me," he jokes with a wink.

After I'm in my bathing suit and cover-up, I meet Chase in the living room. He's sporting a pair of black board shorts and is shirtless, with a towel slung over his shoulder. I try to ignore how solid his body is, but it's so damn hard—pun not intended. Alec and Robert are the only two guys I've really paid attention to recently. And while Alec is like all muscular, and Robert was all... not, Chase is perfect. It's obvious he takes care of himself.

"Ready?" he asks, a smirk splayed across his lips.

Ugh, he totally caught me checking him out. I really need to stop doing that.

"Yep."

We walk down to the pool, and since this complex is mostly people in their twenties and thirties, there are a few people lying out, and a couple in the pool, but other than that, it's quiet.

We grab two available lounge chairs, and Chase throws his towel onto his, kicking his Nike slides off.

I take a deep breath and pull my cover-up over my head. I usually only wear my bikini when it's just Lexi and me at our parents' pool and we're lying out and tanning—well, I'm tanning, Lexi just burns. When we go to the beach or pool with other people, I tend to wear my one-piece or tankini. I don't know why. Maybe it's because I've never been comfortable with anyone paying attention to me, but now... it's time I made some changes. The other night at the club when I was dressed up, I felt good... sexy. And not because guys were checking me out, but because I felt pretty and feminine. I go jogging several times a week and have a nice body, so why cover it up all the time?

When my bikini-clad body is exposed, I glance down to make sure all the important parts are covered, and when I look back up, Chase is staring at me—and not like a friend.

"Is that new?" he asks, his voice gravelly. I know we're just friends, but I like that I have the ability to make his voice change. I've spent years hiding, and Robert barely paid attention to me. And with that thought, I vow to stop thinking about Robert. He's in the past and doesn't deserve a place in my present or future thoughts.

"No, I just don't usually wear it. Wanna swim laps?"

Chase clears his throat. "Yeah, sounds good."

Enjoying the fact that he's shocked at my bikini, I saunter past him, swaying my hips. I know I'm playing with fire, but the way Chase looks at me—even if he doesn't want to—makes me feel confident and sexy.

"So, it's like that, huh?" he calls after me.

I don't turn around, so when strong arms cage me in from behind, I shriek. "Chase!" I yell. "What are—" But before I can finish my sentence, he's hauling me over his shoulder, fireman style—pun intended—and running toward the pool. He leaps—yes, with my one-hundred-and-thirty-five-pound ass in his arms, he leaps—and drops us into the cool water.

When I pop up, pushing my wet hair out of my face, I lock eyes with him. "You're a dead man," I warn him.

"You'll have to catch me first," he taunts, taking off toward the deep end with me following after.

We spend the next couple hours swimming and messing around in the water. We swim laps and race, and then spend some time in the hot tub, until Chase reminds me if we're going to get to my sister's on time, we need to get out soon.

After I'm done showering and getting dressed, I check my emails, finding several from clients requesting work. Usually I don't have more than a couple, but as I scroll, finding one client who wants to know if I'm okay since I didn't respond within a few hours, I'm shocked by how behind I am. I never get this behind.

I keep scrolling and see I haven't checked my emails in a few days. I've been so busy with Chase I haven't had time to get work done.

I should probably feel guilty about that, but honestly, I don't. It felt good to get out and have a life. And the entire time—aside from that moment at the club—I didn't feel stressed. I make a mental note to do this more often. Maybe not with Chase, since eventually he'll want to go back to hooking up with women, but with myself. Lexi might be busy, but that doesn't mean I have to be holed up. It's time I find a life for myself.

---

"OH MY GOODNESS! Let me see my niece!" I say, snatching Abigail from Alec's arms. She's five months old and so freaking plump and adorable. I inhale her sweet scent and my heart skyrockets out of my chest.

"I missed you so much," I tell her, even though it's only been a little over a week since I've seen her. The one time I stopped by the gallery to see Lexi, Abigail was home with Alec since he was off work.

I sit us on the floor, so we can play with her toys. She smiles brightly and coos as she drops to her knees and makes like she's going to crawl away.

"Is she crawling?" I ask in amazement over how quickly she's growing up. One day she was this tiny little helpless baby and now she's giggling and cooing and moving all around.

"Not yet," Lexi says, sitting next to me. "We think she will be soon. She rocks on her knees, but doesn't actually go anywhere yet."

"She's so precious," I tell her, running my fingers through Abigail's soft baby hair.

"She is," Lexi agrees. "Can I talk to you for a second?"

I glance over at her serious face. "Yeah, sure."

"Outside?"

"Okay."

She tells Alec we'll be back, and then we head out to her backyard. The second the door opens, the smell of saltwater hits my senses. It's been a while since I've been to the beach. I should ask Chase if he wants to go soon. The thought immediately has me mentally berating myself. He probably has other friends he wants to hang out with. I can't monopolize all his time.

"What's up?" I ask, having a seat on one of her lounge chairs.

"Chase texted me yesterday."

"Okay."

"He implied maybe something was wrong... between us, I

think. Afterward, he kind of took it back, but I think he only did that so he wouldn't get in the middle. Is everything okay between us?"

A part of me thinks it's really sweet that Chase texted Lexi, but another part of me really wishes he had left it alone. I didn't confide in him for him to tell Lexi.

"We're fine. I don't know what Chase said, but I was just having a bad moment, and—"

"Georgia, please don't lie to me, or play it off."

"Look, I was upset that you bailed a couple times. I hadn't seen you in a while and I missed you. It's stupid and I vented to Chase, but it's not your problem. I was honestly just having a bad moment."

Lexi's mouth twists into a frown. "I'm sorry," she says, taking my hands in hers. "I'm still adjusting to everything and—"

"You don't have to explain yourself. I'm happy for you. You found the love of your life, found your calling with the art gallery, and you have a beautiful baby…"

"Finish your sentence."

Tears fill my eyes, and I try and fail to blink them away. "And it's everything I want," I breathe.

"Oh, Georgia." Lexi pulls me into her arms and hugs me tightly. "You will have all of that. You already have the career of your dreams, and you're the reason why I even have the gallery. You just have to get out there so you can find someone to share your life with. It will happen."

Her words mimic my earlier thoughts. In order for it to happen, I have to get out and make it happen. I'm not going to meet anyone sitting in my room. The other night at the club was a little hard, but I think the more I go, the easier it'll get. I've just spent so many years staying away from huge gatherings, I've gotten used to being alone, or being with only my family.

"And as for us," she says, pulling back. "I'm sorry for not making more of an effort."

"You have a lot going on. Chase shouldn't have said anything. I should be understanding of your new life."

"No," she argues. "You're my sister, my best friend. Don't make excuses for me. I've been a shitty sister and that's going to change."

"It's okay. I promise."

We go back inside and a little while later our parents show up. Shortly after, our brother, Max, arrives with Ricco, introducing him as his boyfriend. It's been a long time coming. Everyone congratulates them and then Alec and my dad get started on the grill—the rest of the guys joining them outside.

"How's everything coming along for the opening?" Mom asks Lexi, referring to the art gallery that's scheduled to open soon.

"It's going good," Lexi says. "I met with the event coordinator and she's taking care of everything, thank goodness. I can handle the art, but everything else is out of my area of expertise. I hired a manager too, so that will help."

"If you need anything, please let me know," Mom tells her. "I'm so proud of you. You really have found your place in this world."

Lexi smiles. "Thank you. I think as soon as Abigail starts sleeping through the night, it will be a little easier."

"She's still waking up?" Mom asks.

"Only a couple times, and now it's more out of routine than to eat. The women in that moms' group I'm in said to let her cry it out, but I just can't do it."

"You have to do what's best for you and your daughter," Mom says. "I remember when Georgia was little and..." She trails off, realizing she was about to mention the time before she met Lexi's dad. She doesn't like to talk about those times. She was married to my biological father and from the little I know, he wasn't a good man. After she was with Tristan, he went after her. They fought and she ended up shooting him in self-defense.

"Anyway." She clears her throat. "People will give you their opinions, but at the end of the day, Alec and you are her parents and decide what's best."

"I agree," Alec says, walking in and sitting next to Lexi. "If we want to let Abigail lie with us at five in the morning, while she kicks the shit out of my ribs, then we can do that."

Everyone laughs, and Lexi groans. "I might've started a bad habit. I was just so tired and our bed is so comfortable."

"And Abigail agrees," Alec says with a wink.

"And how are you doing?" Mom asks, turning her attention to me.

"Good."

She raises a single brow, silently saying, *"You're going to have to give me more than that."*

"I'm okay, I promise," I insist. "Just working..."

"You've been doing more than that," Chase says, walking in with a tray of burgers. "We went to get manis and pedis the other day, and then lunch. We went dancing at Club Illusion the other night, went to a bonfire Friday night, went to the farmer's market yesterday... Made homemade flatbread and watched way too many of those Paul Walker movies. We even went swimming and did facials this morning. You should feel my skin... Smooth as a baby's ass." He rubs his hand down his face, and I giggle, remembering the facials we did this morning. He doesn't even know what a baby's bottom feels like...

At the same time, Lexi and Mom both whip their heads around to look at me. "You did all that?" Lexi asks. "I knew about the nails, but I didn't know you were out painting the damn town red."

"I'm the new Lexi," Chase says. "Only manlier and sexier, and way more fun." He winks at me, and I can't help but laugh.

"I'd hardly call it painting the town... I was missing you and Chase got me out of the house." I pray my face isn't showing any of the feelings I'm catching toward him. I have to keep reminding myself we're just friends, but it's hard when I already started developing feelings for him before he pulled the brakes.

Lexi gives me a speculative look, not taking her eyes off me for several long seconds. "We definitely need to have a sister day soon."

I force a smile, remembering when every day was a sister day. Now we have to plan one because everything is changing, and I need to accept that.

It's time to find my perfect path.

## CHAPTER EIGHT

### CHASE

"So, you want to tell me what's going on with you and Georgia?" Alec asks, jumping off the treadmill and walking over to where I'm lifting weights. He grabs a paper towel from the nearby dispenser and wipes down his face. When we're not putting out fires, we're usually either working out, eating, doing chores, or sleeping.

I set the weights down and walk over to the legs station. The gym here isn't big, but it has everything we need to get a good workout in while we're on shift.

"What do you mean?" I ask, playing dumb. I know damn well he's about to hit me with the third degree. Alec's been friends with Georgia since they were little, and he's just as protective of her as he is of his wife.

"You know what I mean." He presses his hand against the leg weight so I can't open it. "You took her out to a club, to hang out at Carter's bonfire. Lexi's worried."

"Lexi needs to focus on herself." I don't mean for the words to come out as harsh as they do, but it is what it is. The entire reason I was hanging out with Georgia to begin with was because of Lexi.

"Seriously? What's your problem with my wife?"

"I don't have a problem with your wife," I tell him, standing back up since I'm apparently not going to finish my workout. "My problem is the fact that Georgia was in tears because she misses her sister so much."

Alec's face falls. "We offered for her to move in with us."

"And you really believe Georgia would do that?" I've only known her for a short time and even I know that's not how she rolls. "I get it, you and Lexi finally got together. You're happy and in love and you have a baby, but maybe you need to remember who you guys were before. Lexi and Georgia were stuck at the hip. Now... well, shit's changed."

"And so, what? You swooped in and gave her your shoulder to cry on?" Alec accuses.

"We hung out... as *friends*. She's actually a lot of fun to be around when she's not holed up in her room."

"And that's all it is?" he questions. "Friends?"

"That's it." I raise a brow, daring him to argue.

"Yo, Chase, get your ass out here," Luke yells. "You have a visitor."

Grabbing my towel off the bench, I wrap it around my neck and walk out to see who's here for me, with Alec following after. When I get to the main area, Georgia, dressed in another pair of tiny shorts—this time cut-off—and a hoodie with the logo of her dad's MMA gym on the front, is standing in the middle of the room holding a metal pan of some sort in her hands. Her hair is up in a messy bun and she's sporting her sexy librarian glasses.

She's tan from us being in the sun yesterday, and her face is makeup free aside from her lips being glossy. Jesus, she looks fucking stunning... and I'm so screwed.

"Hey, what are you doing here?" I ask, stepping over to her.

"I brought this for you guys." She shrugs a shoulder and her mouth quirks up into a shy smile.

I take the pan, which upon closer inspection is the kind you use to cook and store food in, and set it on our table. It seats six people, so all the guys on shift can eat together. When I lift the foil, steam wafts out, along with the smell of meat and cheese.

"Holy shit," Carter says, coming over. "Is that lasagna?" He inhales and rubs his stomach. "That shit smells good."

"Yep," Georgia says. "I even made the sauce homemade with the tomatoes and veggies we bought at the farmer's market."

"That better be for everyone," Alec says, sidling up next to

Georgia and throwing his arm over the back of her shoulders. My fingers tingle, wanting to push his arm off her and wrap my own around her. It's stupid. He's married to her sister, and we're only friends... But, even knowing all that, it doesn't change my reaction.

"Your sister can't cook, so it's been takeout or delivery every day," Alec adds.

"It's for everyone," she says softly, earning a kiss to her cheek from Alec. I damn near growl, wanting his hands and mouth off her.

"I hope it's good." She grabs a bag from the ground I didn't notice before and pulls out parmesan cheese and rolls. "These are homemade too," she boasts.

"Damn, Georgia, go big or go home, huh?" I joke, grabbing the plates and silverware and bringing them over.

"Eh... I think I'd much rather be at home," she says, scrunching up her nose. "It's safe there."

The guys all chuckle because she's fucking adorable, and my stomach knots. I have to remind myself she's not mine and we're better off as friends. Realistically, I know one day I'm going to have to let someone in, but I'm just not ready yet. And not with someone as sweet and innocent as Georgia. I come from a fucked up world and she was raised sheltered, always taken care of. We're too different and we'd never work. Then again, Victoria and I were from the same world and we didn't work either...

"Stay and eat with us," Scott says, pulling out a chair for Georgia. Alec has thankfully dropped his arm and is cutting the lasagna into pieces. Thomas grabs another chair and brings it to the table, so all seven of us can sit together.

"Are you sure?" Georgia asks. "I don't want to intrude."

"You're probably the most welcome person here," Luke jokes, taking a bite of his food. He chews and swallows and groans. "Damn, woman. Marry me right now."

Georgia snorts a laugh, and Alec glares, ever the protective pseudo brother.

"Is it good?" she asks.

"It's fucking delicious," Thomas says through a mouthful. "I'm going to need you to send me this recipe so I can have Hilary make it.

"No way." Luke shakes his head. "It's a secret recipe and my wife can only make it for me." He winks at Georgia and her face turns a light shade of pink.

"Why don't you take it down a notch," I growl at him, annoyed as fuck. Georgia and Alec both look at me. Alec's brow is raised and Georgia is frowning.

"I'm just saying, if you scare her off, she won't bring us any more food," I say, trying to play it off. All the guys are looking at me, so I dive into my food, ignoring all their stares.

When the food hits my tongue, the heavenly taste of meat and tomato and cheese hits my senses. Luke and Thomas were right. This lasagna is damn good.

"What do you think?" Georgia asks me.

"It's delicious. Even better than the flatbread we made the other night." I smile at her, and she beams. In the background, Alec's glaring and Luke is smirking.

*Just friends*, I remind myself. That's all we can be.

When we're done eating, since it's Luke's day to do the dishes, I show Georgia around the station. Where we work out, sleep, shower. Our gaming room...

"So," she says slowly as I walk her over to her truck. "Seeing Lexi and Alec and Abigail yesterday got me thinking about my future..."

My breath hitches wondering where she's going with this...

"I have my career, but I don't have anyone to share my life with," she continues, and I swear I stop breathing altogether. Is she about to ask me out? And why doesn't the thought have me wanting to run? I'm not ready. I should be thinking of a reason to bolt. Coming up with an excuse as to why I have to say no.

"I can't find anyone if I'm at home, so I want to get out... put myself out there. I want to one day get married and have babies, find a man I can cook for." She smiles softly, and I wait with bated breath for her to finish. Yes is at the tip of my tongue. It shouldn't be, but it is.

"I was wondering if..." She bites down on her bottom lip nervously. "Would you be my wingman?"

I'm about to blurt out yes, when it hits me... "Your wingman?" I ask, confused.

"Yeah. You like going to the clubs and picking up women, you know all the happening places in LA... And I don't really have any friends to go out with. I promise not to mess with your game." She laughs, and the melodic sound hits me like an arrow straight in the chest.

Jesus, I'm such a dumbass. She wants me to help her find a guy, not be her guy. It's probably for the best anyway. What the hell was I thinking?

"Yeah," I choke out, plastering a smile on my face. "I can be your wingman."

"Yay!" She jumps up and down and then throws her arms around my neck. "Thank you! I'm going to go shopping with my mom tomorrow. So tomorrow night, since you're off, want to go out?"

"Sounds good."

"Have a good night at work," she says, jumping into her truck.

"See ya." I wave as she drives away.

"So, just friends, huh?" Alec says, stepping up next to me as I watch her drive her monster truck away.

"Yep." I turn on my heel and walk back inside.

"You sure about that? Because when Luke mentioned—"

"Just friends," I bite out, cutting him off. "She even asked me to be her wingman."

"Her what?" Alec laughs.

"Her wingman. She wants to go out and find her Mr. Perfect, so she can marry said Mr. Perfect and move into a perfect house and have tons of perfect little babies running around." Yes, I'm aware of how bitter I sound.

Alec eyes me for a long moment then sighs. "I can't believe I'm even going to say this, but if you like her why don't you just tell her? It's obvious you do, and based on the way she blushed when you complimented her cooking, I would say the feeling is mutual."

Because it's not that easy... Because she's rich and comes from a great family and wants this perfect fucking life that I'm not capable of giving her. What do I even have to offer a woman like her? Not a damn thing.

"We're just friends," I tell him in a tone that says to drop it. "I'm going to take a shower."

Just as I'm walking toward the bathroom, the tone sounds through the station. I grab the receiver and take down the information from dispatch.

The six of us jump into the engine and take off to the location. And for the next couple hours, while we put out the fire, I push the thoughts of Georgia out of my mind and the fact that in twenty-four hours I'm supposed to help her find her perfect fucking guy.

## CHAPTER NINE

### GEORGIA

I CAN DO THIS. *I can do this. I can do this.* Those are the four words I keep repeating to myself as Chase and I walk through the Z Lounge. According to Chase, it's a little more down to earth. Instead of a deejay, they have live music. But as we walk through the main area toward the bar, I'm not sure Chase's definition of down to earth is the same as mine because the music is thumping so loud it's vibrating the floor, and the bodies—lots of bodies—are grinding against one another to the beat.

Maybe this isn't the way for me to meet someone. Surely, a club—or in this case, a lounge—can't be the only way to meet the person you hope to spend your life with. There has to be other ways. Like online... I cringe at the thought. I created a profile on one of those dating websites once after Mason, Alec's stepdad—who is also my dad's best friend and, as I mentioned before, my godfather—said he got together with Alec's mom through chatting on a dating site. I don't know if the times have changed, but the number of creepy men was astounding and almost convinced me to switch teams. So, no, a dating site probably isn't the way to go. But I don't think this is either.

When we get to the bar, Chase orders himself a beer and me a lemon drop, then we go in search of a booth. They're all taken, but we find a table with two chairs open, so we have a seat. Making sure my new little black dress doesn't ride up and expose my goods, I scoot onto the seat carefully.

"So, what's the game plan?" Chase asks, taking a drink of his beer. His hazel eyes meet mine, and my belly clenches. He's so ruggedly handsome. He hasn't shaved in a while, so his scruff is now practically a full beard. Idly, I wonder what it would feel like between my legs. I read it once in a book and at the time didn't get it, but now, looking at Chase, I kind of do.

"I don't know!" I shout nervously over the music as I try to remove the image of Chase's face from between my legs. "You're an expert at this," I joke. "How do you get all the women you do?"

I expect Chase to laugh, but instead he frowns and takes another sip of his beer. Is it possible I offended him? I don't know why. He's always owned up to sleeping around. And I'm not judging him. Not now that I know why he does it. He was hurt. And one day he'll meet a woman who will help him heal. But until then, he doesn't want to be alone. And I get that. Because I'm so damn tired of being alone.

"Hey, are you mad at me? I was only joking."

"No," he says, putting his beer down. "But I don't go after women." He shrugs. "They come to me."

I swallow thickly. The women go after him... Of course they do. Because most women aren't afraid to go after what they want. I down the rest of my drink in one swallow and slam my glass down.

"Then that's what I'll do," I tell him, standing.

"What?" He looks at me like I'm crazy, and I probably am. But so was Lexi once upon a time, and unlike me, she found her perfect path. Now it's my turn.

"I'm going to go to the guys." I glance around and spot a cluster of men at the bar. "And I'll start by buying them a drink." Just like guys do when they want a woman.

"Whoa, wait," Chase says. "Maybe you should think about this first."

"Why? So I can second-guess myself and then freak out and bail? No way."

"No." He wraps his fingers around my forearms to stop me. "Because the women who approach me are looking to fuck. They're desperate."

"So, what do I do then?" Why does meeting someone have to be so damn difficult?

"Let the guy come to you."

"Okay..."

We return to the table, and Chase goes back to his beer while I look around. There are a lot of different people here. Couples dancing, women dancing with women. Men, who look similar to Chase, nursing a beer. I look at one man in particular. He's sitting in a booth next to a woman. They're not talking, both just people watching like Chase and I are... and it hits me.

"How is anyone going to know I'm available?"

"Huh?" he asks, a V forming in the center of his brows.

"How is anyone going to know I'm available?" I repeat.

"I heard you. What do you mean?"

"Well, we've been sitting here for a little while and no women have approached you... It's probably because we're sitting together. They're assuming we're together. Maybe we should separate? Or I should come back when Lexi can join me." I clearly didn't think this whole thing through. If Lexi were here, guys would know I'm single.

"How about you stop focusing on meeting a guy and we dance?" Chase suggests, standing and taking my hand.

"But—" My argument is thwarted the second Chase pulls me into his arms and forces my hands to wrap around his neck. His hands slide down my sides and land on the small of my back. He bends and leans in so his face is close to mine. I can feel his warm breath against my ear, and it sends chills racing down my spine.

"You look beautiful tonight," he murmurs, pulling me in closer to him. My heart accelerates at his compliment. I should be focusing on finding a guy to get to know, but suddenly all I want to do is dance with Chase.

And that's exactly what we spend the next several songs doing. We're both sweaty—from the packed crowd, the hot lights, and the dancing—but I don't even consider leaving the dance floor —or Chase's arms—until he suggests we take a break and get a drink.

I follow him off the floor and over to the packed bar. "Do you want a lemon drop or water?" he asks.

"Water." I'm thirsty from all that dancing and alcohol isn't going to quench my thirst.

"Okay, be right back," he says, before cutting into the crowd.

I'm standing by myself for a few minutes, people watching, when a male voice speaks close to my ear. "Are you single?"

I twirl around and come face to face with a blond-haired, blue-eyed man. He's dressed in a white button-down collar shirt with his sleeves rolled up to his elbows and dark wash jeans. He's cute, and when his lip tugs up into a half smirk, he's even cuter.

I open my mouth to tell him I'm here with someone when I remember why I'm here... and that even though I was just dancing with Chase, I'm not here with him. "I am."

"Patrick," he says, extending his hand like a gentleman.

"Georgia," I say back, shaking his hand.

"Can I buy you a drink, Georgia?" he asks, his hand still holding mine.

"She already has a drink," a deep voice says before I can answer.

Patrick glances between Chase and me, and I can't see Chase because he's slightly behind me, but whatever he sees causes him to jump to conclusions, because the next thing I know, he's nodding and bowing out before I can explain.

"Hey!" I swivel around and slap Chase on the chest.

"What?" He hands me a bottled water.

"You totally just...cockblocked me!" Mind you, I don't have a cock, and I had no intention of having sex with that guy, but I don't know how else to describe what he just did.

"That guy looks like a douche," Chase says, shrugging and cracking open his water. He brings the bottle up to his lips and tips his head back, swallowing the entire bottle in one long guzzle.

"How would you know?" I ask, trying to sound annoyed but kind of distracted by the way his Adam's apple bobs up and down while he drinks.

"I could just tell."

"Well, my theory is correct. As soon as you were gone, he came over. Going out just the two of us obviously isn't the best idea."

Chase doesn't agree or disagree. "Want to dance some more?"

Well, tonight's apparently a bust anyway, and Chase is a good dancer... "Sure."

---

I WALK through the art gallery, amazed and in awe of the transformation. What was once a vacant, run-down building in the Arts district, is now filled with beautiful art from various artists, including Lexi. Lexi's plan is for the gallery to cater to all types of art, but every month a different theme and artist will be featured. A large portion of the proceeds will go toward raising money to help autistic children and adults, especially those who are low income or homeless.

I stop at a piece I haven't seen before and smile. On what looks like an eight by ten canvas, is a graffitied drawing of a woman standing with her back to the world, staring out at the ocean. She's holding her surfboard in one hand and her daughter's hand in the other. Seeing Lexi's art on display fills my heart with warmth. One day, someone will buy this painting and hang it up in their home or office. My sister's talent will finally be shared with the world—and not just in the form of graffiti on building walls.

"Lexi's sister," Aiden says, calling me over. "I painted this."

"Wow. It's beautiful."

Aiden is the reason this gallery came about. He's twenty-four years old and autistic. His stepdad used to hurt his mom and him and when he turned eighteen they kicked him out. He was homeless, living on the streets. Every day my sister would make sure he was taken care of the best she could, but she felt helpless. They became close and she wanted to save him. Now, he's living in an assisted living facility and works at the gallery.

"Thank you, Lexi's sister," he says, turning back to his painting. Lexi has various artists coming in to paint the gallery. Instead of it feeling stuffy like many do, she wants it to feel like you're immersed in the art.

"I called you last night," Lexi says, walking out with Abigail on her hip. The second she sees me, a bright smile lights her face, making my heart skip a beat.

"I was out with Chase." I take Abigail from Lexi and give her kisses. "I missed you, sweet girl." We move into her office and sit on her couch.

"You and Chase are close, huh?" Lexi asks, raising a brow.

"He was supposed to be my wingman." I roll my eyes. "Of course every guy just assumed we were together."

"And how about the women?"

"They were hot, but I don't swing that way." I wink playfully, making Lexi laugh.

"I meant for Chase."

"He didn't get hit on. We had a drink and danced. One guy actually did approach me, but Chase scared him off, saying he looked like a douche."

"Did he...?" Lexi's mouth twists contemplatively.

"Yeah, so now I'm not sure how I'm going to meet someone. I don't really have girlfriends, and you're busy being a mom to this cute little angel." I lift Abigail up and blow raspberries on her belly.

"I could have Mom watch her. It's been a while since I've been out."

"I wouldn't ask you to do that." I wave her off. "I'll eventually meet the right guy, when the time is right."

"You're not asking. It'll be fun. All these years I was waiting for you to finally go out and have a good time, and now that you're doing it, I'm at home." She pulls out her phone.

"Hey, Mom," she says. "Georgia is here and we were talking about going out one night this week..." She laughs. "Yes, that's why I was calling... Okay, love you, bye."

She hangs up. "I think I just made her life," she jokes. "She's so excited to take Abigail." Lexi tends to keep her daughter close. I don't blame her, though. The way she found out she was pregnant and the months following were hard on her. I think she just feels so blessed to have her, she doesn't want to let her leave her sight.

"She's going to take her for the night since Alec is working." She grins. "This'll be fun. The Scott women are going to paint the town red!"

I crack up. "In case you forgot you're no longer a Scott."

"Pfft, semantics. I'll always be a Scott. I'm excited for tonight."

"Me too. I feel like I'm finally making strides to overcome my social anxiety. I didn't freak out at all last night when Chase and I were out."

"Maybe Chase has the right touch." She winks dramatically.

"Or maybe I'm just finally getting past my issues." I shrug, refusing to acknowledge that she may be right. I thought the same thing last night in bed before I pushed it to the side and fell asleep.

I hand her back Abigail. "Want to come over and we can get ready together?"

"Yes." Lexi beams. "This is so exciting. It's like my little Georgia is all grown up. I get to pick out your outfit and do your makeup."

"Sounds good." I stand and so does she. "I'll see you tonight. I'm making the guys dinner... this new fettuccine recipe I found and want to try out. I'll save some for us."

"Yeah, I heard about your fabulous lasagna." Lexi side-eyes me. "Alec said we should hire you to cook." She rolls her eyes. "He won't let me use the oven when he's not home. He said the guys at the station we're zoned to won't be as nice when the neighbors call."

"That's funny," I say with a laugh. "Hey, maybe I should open a restaurant," I joke.

"You made one meal," Lexi deadpans. "I would make a few more dishes before you put on your official chef hat."

I spend the rest of the morning making the dish, and once it's done, I have to admit, I'm a damn good cook. After putting some aside for Lexi and me for dinner, I put the remainder of the pasta into one container and the homemade biscuits I made into another one, and then head over to the station.

"Oh, shit," Carter says as I walk up to the entrance. "Is that food you're carrying?" He grabs the containers from me.

"It is, but before you get too excited, you better taste it to make sure it's good."

"Thought I was your taste tester," Chase says, walking out from nowhere. His hair is wet like he just showered, and he's in the middle of pulling his shirt over his head, so his hard body is still on display. The shirt comes down and I internally pout.

Or at least I think I do...

Chase smirks, as if he knows exactly what I'm thinking, and my cheeks heat up.

"You are the taste tester," I tell him, "but you have to be a good boy and share." I playfully pat him on his stomach and note just how hard his abs are.

The other guys hear us and join in, grabbing plates and silverware. I open the containers and distribute some onto each of their plates. Chase is the first to take a bite, and I swear his eyes roll to the back of his head.

"It's official, Georgia," he says. "You're an honorary member of station 115."

I laugh. "And what does an honorary member get?"

"The right to cook for us forever," he says with a smile, while shoving more food into his mouth.

"Wow, I'm so lucky," I say, sarcasm dripping in my words. "But you better enjoy it while you can, because tonight Lexi and I are going out. She's going to be my wing-woman, and when I meet the man of my dreams, I'll be too busy cooking for him to cook for you guys."

Carter, Thomas, and Luke laugh, but Alec and Chase don't.

"What do you mean you're going out tonight?" Chase asks, dropping his fork onto his plate.

"Mom's going to watch Abigail. We're going to hit the clubs. I'm hoping she'll be a better wing-woman than you."

Alec groans. "I think you guys should wait until tomorrow night. We can all go, make it a group thing."

"I agree," Chase adds.

"I'm down," Luke says.

"Me too," Carter agrees.

"Then it's settled," Alec says before I can even argue. "I'll let Lexi know. Tomorrow night we'll all go out." What the hell just happened? I went from planning a girls' night out with my sister to it being turned into a group hang?

"Want some pasta?" Chase offers, like they didn't just railroad my plans.

"No." I pout. "I have some at home. But you enjoy. I need to go."

"You just got here," Chase notes. "Stay a while."

"I have work to do. Bye!" I give him a false smile, and after saying bye to the other guys, take off, annoyed as hell at the turn of events.

## CHAPTER TEN

### CHASE

"Did you see how pissed she was when she left?" Luke says with a shake of his head.

"Yeah, but oh well," I tell him. "Those women are crazy if they think we're going to let them go out without us."

"Yeah," Alec agrees with a sigh. I'd bet he's thinking about the shit that went down last year with Lexi. She was alone on the beach and was attacked. It was a fucked up situation and since then, he hasn't let her out of his sight other than to go to work. And I don't blame him. Underneath the thin layer of wealth and glamour, LA is a scary fucking place. I know that firsthand.

The rest of the shift flies by. We thankfully don't have any major fires—only one incident where a woman smelled gas, and after checking it out, we caught a leak—and at eight o'clock we change shifts. The guys all agree to meet at Boulevard, a new club that recently opened that Luke's brother is the bouncer at.

When I walk in the door, Georgia is standing in the kitchen in a racerback tank and yoga pants. She's dancing to whatever music is blasting in her headphones and shaking her peach of an ass while she blends something together.

I probably shouldn't do it, but I can't help myself as I quickly approach her and wrap my arms around her to scare her.

She shrieks, and her hand flings around to push me away.

When she does this, the top to the blender flies off and pink explodes everywhere.

"Oh my God!" she squeals, quickly grabbing the top and shoving it back on the blender before shutting it off. "Chase!" She turns back around and slaps my chest. We're both covered in...

"What is this?" I swipe my finger across her cheek and pop it into my mouth. "Mm, strawberry shake?"

"I found a healthy recipe. I was making one before I go for a run. It's a protein shake."

"Well, it tastes delicious."

She glares. "I wouldn't know."

I swipe some more, this time off her neck, and push my finger past her lips. "Good, right?"

Her tongue darts out and swirls around the tip of my finger, and my eyes go straight to her mouth, imagining a different appendage of mine is in between her lips.

Her eyes go wide, as if just realizing what I did, and pulls her face back, her lips gliding off my finger and leaving it glistening wet.

She clears her throat. "Yeah, it's good. I need to clean this up."

"I'll help," I croak, sounding like a horny fucking teenager. When she swivels around, I quickly adjust myself and think of old, smelly men, so my semi goes down.

We get the area cleaned up, and since there's still plenty of smoothie left, she pours us each some into a cup. The shake is delicious, but if I'm honest, the entire time I'm drinking it, I'm wishing I were licking it off her body.

Afterward, she invites me to join her on her jog. We spend the morning running to the pier, walking along the beach, and then run back.

"We should do this every day I'm off," I tell her when we get home.

"For sure. I'm going to shower. Alec and Lexi are coming over for dinner before we go out, and I'm making a new dish. I need to do some work stuff, but after, want to watch a movie?"

"Sounds perfect."

The more time I spend with her, the more time I *want* to spend with her. It's crazy that we spent months living together and I never bothered to get to know her.

*It's because you were too busy fucking anything with a vagina to get over your ex-wife...*

And now that I'm thinking about it, since the day Georgia and I started hanging out, I haven't even thought about hooking up with any women, nor have I dwelled on my divorce. For the first time it feels like I'm actually moving forward. I'm no longer bitter toward the way things ended, or the years I felt were wasted. With Georgia, I'm enjoying myself again. And not in the fake way I do when I stick my dick into some woman I don't know, but in a real way. Georgia and I laugh together, talk about shit. It's nice having someone to connect with.

I'm cleaning up my room, when my phone rings. "Hello," I answer without looking to see who's on the other end.

"Chase, I need you."

I close my eyes, listening to her slurred words. It's my mom, and she's drunk. Which makes no sense because the only time she ever gets drunk is... Shit! I pull the calendar up on my phone and the realization of what today is has sharp pains shooting through my chest. How could I forget?

"I'll be right there," I tell her before hanging up, grabbing my keys, and flying out the door. My mom and I aren't as close as I wish we were, but she's still my mom, and I love her and would do anything for her.

About fifteen minutes later, I arrive at my childhood home. It's located in a rougher part of LA, where the movies and television shows don't show because people would realize that the majority of LA isn't really all that glamorous.

Parking my vehicle in her driveway, I run up to the front door, and without knocking, go inside. I find my mom lying in her room with a bottle of vodka in her hands. The room is dark and smells like sex and alcohol. I gag a couple times, then open the windows, letting the light and air in.

Ignoring the fact that her sheets are probably full of sex as well, I edge onto the bed and pull her into my arms. There are only two days a year my mom gets drunk: the day my sister was born, and the day she died.

"Chase," she slurs. "You came."

"Of course I came," I tell her, cursing myself for forgetting the date. I always make it a point to visit my mom the night before and spend the night so she doesn't get like this. If I'm not here to stop her, she'll drink until she's sick and has to be hospitalized—it's happened more than once.

"I miss her so much," she cries. Her shoulders begin to shake, and when I push her hair out of her face, tears are racing down her cheeks. I don't bother to wipe them away, knowing they won't stop coming until she falls asleep.

Instead, I hold her close, telling her how much I love her, because that's all she really needs. To be comforted. The day we lost my sister, we also lost my father. My mom didn't take her death well, and my father couldn't handle taking care of my mom. He turned to the bottle and eventually his drunk ass left, leaving me to pick up the pieces. A few years later, he died from kidney failure.

"She would've been thirty-one today," Mom says. "My baby never got to live her life." I do the math in my head, and she's right. Audrina overdosed when I was seventeen and she was eighteen. It's one of the reasons why I decided on my career of choice. I first got my EMT license and then joined the fire academy. I wanted to save people, since I couldn't save my sister.

While my mom cries into my chest, I hold her, running my fingers through her hair and trying to calm her down. As long as I'm here, she won't drink, and since she's still awake, it seems I got here before she drank too much.

I don't know how long I hold her for, but when my phone vibrates for the millionth time in my pocket, I remember that I was so worried about my mom, I forgot to tell Georgia I was leaving.

Carefully, so I don't wake my mom, I pull my phone out. The time on the phone says it's four o'clock. I've been holding my mom for several hours. My heart breaks all over again for my mom. Some people rise up after a tragic event, others drown in it. If I weren't here to hold my mom up, she would drown.

The other three hundred and sixty-three days, she handles life. She works as a waitress at a local diner—the same one she's been working at since I was little—and pays her bills. She owns the home she lives in and refuses to move elsewhere. I've begged and pleaded, but she won't leave the home where Audrina grew up. Her room is the same way it was when she died, and she won't let anyone touch a thing. I've tried to get her to see someone, to get help, but she won't. I've spoken to a few people about it, and everyone says the same thing—unless she wants to get help, I can't make her. She's not an alcoholic, she doesn't do drugs, so there's nothing I can do.

**Georgia: Hey, you left… Everything okay?**

**Georgia: I'm worried.**

**Alec: Yo, where you at?**

**Alec: Everyone's worried. I called the station and nobody's heard from you.**

Gently, I set my mom down on the bed. She stirs but stays asleep. I type out a group text to Alec and Georgia.

**Me: Sorry I left in a rush. I won't be able to make it tonight.**

Alec knows I had a sister who died but doesn't know the specifics, and Georgia doesn't know anything about my family, so trying to explain it all in a text isn't exactly the best way to tell them. I hate that I won't be able to be with Georgia tonight, but my mom needs me. I'm all she has.

After a brief conversation through text with Georgia and Alec, who tell me if I need anything to let them know, I tell them to have a good time and then start cleaning up the house for my mom. The place is a disaster. My mom usually keeps the house clean. Everything in it is aged, but she's always made sure to take care of what she owns. Based on the dirty dishes and empty alcohol bottles all over, I would guess she started drinking last night, probably had whatever guy she's sleeping with over, and took her pain over losing my sister out on the place.

Just as I'm finishing up, Mom comes out of her room, her eyes glossy with new tears. "I'm so sorry," she says, enveloping me in a hug. "Every birthday, every anniversary of her death, I tell myself I won't do this…"

"It's okay, Mom," I tell her, hugging her back. "You're doing the best you can."

She glances around and sighs. "Thank you for cleaning up."

"How're you feeling?"

"I'm... okay. If you don't have any plans, would you like to go to the cemetery with me?"

"Of course. Why don't you go shower and get dressed, and then I'll drive us over."

"Thank you, Chase," she says, wiping a tear that's escaped, before heading back to her room.

The drive to the cemetery is quiet, and so is the walk over to where she was buried. But once we're there, Mom starts reminiscing about the past. We spend the next few hours talking about how smart and sweet Audrina was. The truth is, she had a bright future ahead of her. Until she met Danny. He was a bad boy, and she thought he was cool. She swore they loved each other and she would do anything for him, including drugs. Mom and Dad tried to get her away from him, but it only made her want him that much more. Everyone said it was just a phase and she would get through it... Unfortunately, she died before she could.

Tests revealed the drugs she took were laced with something that caused her heart to stop. She overdosed in the living room of Danny's house, and because he was too wasted, he didn't notice. And when he finally did, it was too late.

Once we're both cried out, we decide to grab something to eat. It's late, after midnight, so I take us to a diner, where we order breakfast for dinner, which was Audrina's favorite.

"How are you doing?" Mom asks.

I pop a piece of pancake into my mouth. "I'm good. Just working...chilling. The usual."

"Any new women?" she asks with a hint of a smile.

Mom used to be close to Victoria, considered her to be a daughter, and when she started doing drugs, she was right there, trying to get her help. She never wanted Victoria to end up like Audrina. But when she found out what Victoria did... let's just say blood is thicker than water.

Now, every time we talk, she asks me if I'm seeing anyone. She's mentioned on several occasions she would love to have a grandchild. Since I'm now her only living child, I'm the only one who can give her one.

"Nope," I tell her, refusing to think about Georgia and the fact that she's probably out right now, dancing with some guy who'll ask her for her number... Because she's gorgeous and any guy would be stupid not to.

Mom eyes me, and I can tell she's about to grill me, but my phone goes off. I glance at the text from Alec, reading it several times, refusing to believe what it says. The gods wouldn't do this... not today of all days.

"Chase," Mom prompts. "Everything okay?"

"No." I shoot out of my seat and pull a couple of twenties out of my pocket to pay for our food. I don't know how much it is, but it doesn't matter.

I'm out the door and in my car in seconds, heading to Los Angeles General Hospital. My mind is racing, and my only focus is getting there, so when my mom asks, "What's going on?" it hits me that she's in the car with me. I should've dropped her off at home, but I wasn't thinking.

"A friend of mine is in the hospital. Once we get there, I'll pay for a car to take you home. I wasn't thinking."

"Oh no," she says. "That's okay. What's wrong? Who is it?"

Shit, I don't want to tell her what's wrong. She doesn't even know Georgia, but I know she'll take it hard.

"It's Georgia..."

"Your roommate?" she questions. "I never hear you talk about her." I glance over at her and swallow down my emotions, thankful my mom is here with me right now.

"We've become close... friends," I choke out, hating that fucking word. "She was brought to the hospital because—"

Before I can finish my sentence, my phone dings with an incoming text from Alec letting me know her room number.

"Is she okay?" Mom asks.

"I don't know. Let me call you a cab..."

"No." She shakes her head. "This fancy phone you gave me for Mother's Day can do that. You go, and once you know what's going on, please let me know."

She pulls me into a hug. "I love you, Chase."

I look into her eyes. "You sure you'll be okay?" It's still Audrina's birthday, and the last thing I want to do is leave my mom alone.

"Don't you dare worry about me," she says. "I promise I'm okay now. Thank you for today. Now go."

We walk to the front of the hospital together, and then after hugging one more time, I take off inside. Since I'm in the system, they let me go through without asking questions. Every step toward her room has my heart thumping outside of my chest, and by the time I get there, I'm so worked up, it's hard to breathe.

With a quick knock, I walk in and find Tristan, Charlie, Lexi, and Alec all standing around a very still, very pale Georgia. If it weren't for the heart monitor beeping, I would think she's dead. Visions of my sister surface. Her ice cold body, blue lips, pale face. Her un-beating heart.

"What the fuck happened?" I growl, barely able to contain the anger that's radiating through my veins.

Everyone's eyes swing over to me, but Tristan is the one to speak. "She was drugged."

"Yeah, I got that from Alec's text. But what. The. Fuck. Happened?"

"She was talking to this guy..." Lexi starts, but her words are garbled from her crying and she can't finish her sentence. Alec wraps his arms around her and moves her to the couch.

"She was dancing with this guy, and she started to feel sick," Alec says. "He offered to take her home, but we told him no. She was complaining of feeling hot and lightheaded, and then she dropped to the ground and started having a seizure. The guy took off in the chaos of us calling for an ambulance. They ran tests and found GHB in her system."

Fucking GHB? "She was roofied?" My hands fist at my sides, ready to punch something. "Where is this asshole?" I will kill him, consequences be damned. There's no way another fucking murderer is getting away.

"The cops checked the cameras and are asking around, but we only know his first name—Kenny," Alec says.

"You should've been watching her!" I bark.

"I was!" Alec yells back. "You don't think I feel like shit? Of course I do!"

"Hey," Tristan says. "Shit happens. I'm pissed too, and if I ever see that fucker, he's dead, but Alec and your friends were all there. He called nine-one-one, and she's alive because of it."

I walk over to her and take her hand in mine, needing to calm myself down. I know realistically it wasn't Alec's fault, but he's the only person I can blame until I find the guy who did this to her.

Someone pushes a chair toward me, and I take it, sitting next to her. I entwine our fingers together and drop my face to her knuckles, trying to inhale her scent. She smells faintly of the perfume she wears, but mostly all I can smell is the hospital, and flashbacks from when I came to this same hospital to see Audrina surface. I try like hell to push them back. Georgia is alive. She's going to be okay—unlike my sister, who will never take another breath again.

"Damn it, Georgia," I say under my breath. "I never should've let you go out without me." Tears prick my eyes, and I swallow down my emotions. I wasn't there to save my sister all those years ago, and I wasn't there tonight to keep this from happening to Georgia.

"It still could've happened," Alec points out. "Nobody but that asshole who drugged her is to blame."

"Maybe not, but I started this. I told her to get out of the house so she could meet someone. Now look at her. She's been drugged and almost died." If I had been there, I never would've let any of those dickheads near her.

"People take shit every day and are fine," Tristan says. "Georgia just so happened to have a bad reaction."

"None of this is your fault," Charlie says, resting her hand on my shoulder. I glance up and she smiles sadly. "For years Georgia was stuck in that shell of hers. We accepted it because it's just who she was, but you got her out of the house. She's been so happy every time we talk. We even went shopping together for a dress, something we've never done. She's been cooking and baking, and she speaks so highly of you..."

I hear what they're saying, but I should've been there with her, protecting her. She's too fucking naïve, they all are. Raised with silver spoons, they don't know the bad and ugly out there. But I do, because it's what killed my sister and then pushed my father away. It's what destroyed my wife. What keeps my mom living in that shitty fucking neighborhood.

The heart monitor picks up and then Georgia's eyes flutter open. She starts coughing and wincing, and Charlie runs out to get someone.

"Chase," she croaks, looking a mixture of in pain and confused. "I... don't... feel good."

I grab a garbage can by her bed and raise it up in time for her to dry heave.

"Why isn't she throwing up?" I ask.

"She had her stomach pumped," the nurse says, walking briskly into the room. "Hello, there, Georgia, I'm Nurse Kelly. We're giving you nausea medication, but you might still feel sick. That's normal. I'll up the dose for you. Your abdominal muscles will also be sore for a few days. That's normal as well. We're giving you fluids because you're dehydrated." She goes about checking her, and Georgia, who is too weak to even talk, simply closes her eyes and nods.

We spend the next few hours watching her sleep. Alec's parents, Mila and Mason, stop by, and Alec leaves to go grab Abigail since Max, Lexi and Georgia's brother, was keeping an eye on her. But her parents, sister, and I stay.

She eventually wakes up but is groggy, and the doctor says that's normal. When she's discharged with a prescription for nausea medication and instructions to rest and drink plenty of fluids, Charlie suggests Georgia goes home with them. But of course Georgia doesn't want to be fussed over...

"I'm off until Monday," I tell them. "I can stay with her at the condo. I'll make sure she's okay." There's no way I'm letting her out of my sight.

Georgia gives me a small, grateful smile. "Thank you."

The nurse gets her into a wheelchair—per hospital rules—and I wheel her out.

"I'll go grab the car," I tell Georgia. "Be right back."

I run to where I left my car and pull it around to the entrance.

"I'll be by to check on you," Lexi says while I help Georgia into the passenger seat. She gives her a hug. "I was so scared."

"I know," Georgia tells her. "I'm sorry."

"You have nothing to be sorry about," Lexi says. "I just... all I could imagine..."

"I know," Georgia says again, knowing what she's saying without actually saying it. She could've been attacked the way Lexi was. Shit could've had a way worse ending.

"Take care of my baby," Charlie says, hugging me. "I'll be by with soup later."

"Sounds good," I tell her.

The ride home is quiet, with Georgia leaning against the window with her eyes closed. I know she's not asleep, but I don't know if she's resting or just doesn't want to talk.

Without thought, I scoop up her hand and thread her fingers through mine, needing to feel the warmth of her flesh. She's alive. Her heart is still beating. She's going to be okay.

She rolls her head toward me and briefly opens her green eyes, and like an electrical current straight to my heart, it hits me: I'm in love with Georgia Scott.

## CHAPTER ELEVEN

### GEORGIA

"All right, we've got blankets, pillows, your favorite red flavored Gatorade, some crackers for you to munch on in case you're hungry..." Chase glances around, and even though I feel like shit, I can't help but smile. I never imagined Chase to be such a good nurturer, but he is.

"Anything else?" he asks, the middle of his brows dipping in concern.

"I'm good," I assure him. "And if you have something—"

"Don't even dare finish that sentence," he says, his gaze searing into me. "The only place I want to be is right here with you. We're going to spend the next forty-eight hours binge watching whatever the hell you want while you rest and heal." His tone leaves no room for argument, so I don't.

"I'm going to shower real quick," he says. "While I do that, figure out what you want to watch."

"Okay." I cuddle into the blankets and grab my laptop so I can check my work emails.

"Nope." He snags my laptop from me. "No work. You need to rest."

Before I can argue, he's gone, with the laptop.

Using the remote, I click through the different options of what to watch, but as I'm going from show to show, my mind begins to wander back to last night.

Dancing with Lexi.

Drinking.

Meeting Kenny.

Dancing with Kenny.

Drinking with Kenny.

I was so caught up in trying to find Mr. Perfect, I wasn't paying attention. And it nearly got me raped... or worse, killed.

How could I be so stupid not to see what his intentions were? All he wanted to do was drug me. The thought is both scary and depressing. I watch women meet men all the time. They flirt and laugh and it leads to more. Why can't that happen for me? Why does the one guy I actually like not like me back? And the guy I try to get to know, to push the other guy from my thoughts, have to be a crazy psycho?

I sigh and cuddle farther into my blanket. Maybe I just need to take a little break from trying to find the perfect guy... So far this love stuff isn't all it's cracked up to be. Maybe my perfect path isn't finding the perfect man, maybe it's just finding myself. I can focus on cooking and my work...

But even as the thoughts flow through my head, it saddens me. The way my heart feels full when I hold Abigail. The way it thumps against my chest when Chase looks at me and talks to me. I want more. It's too bad I can't figure out how to get it. And clearly going to the club isn't the way to go about it. Not if I want to remain alive...

"What's going through that beautiful head of yours?" Chase asks, stepping into my room. His hair is dripping wet from his shower, and since he's still in the middle of putting on his shirt, his chest and abs are on display. Why must he always do that? Is it too much to ask that he finishes getting dressed *before* he comes near me? It's like his goal in life is to tease me...

My gaze drags lower. He's wearing a pair of basketball shorts that are hanging off his hips and show off how fit he is. He finishes putting his shirt on, hiding the goods, and I mentally pout, already missing the view.

"Georgia." He chuckles, having obviously caught me staring. Oh well, if he's going to walk around half-naked, then he can't be shocked when I stare. "Before I walked in you looked like you were deep in thought."

"Just thinking about that stupid perfect path."

"You know there's no perfect path, right?" He walks over and sits on the bed next to me. "Life isn't perfect and no path you take will be either as long as you're out of that shell and in the real world." There's a hard edge to his voice I've never heard before.

"You have no idea what real life is like," he continues. "Women get drugged every day, raped, killed. Only the rich and privileged think there are perfect paths because they don't experience the shit us poor people do." *Us poor people do...*

"You make six figures a year as a firefighter, drive a BMW, and live in a nice condo," I point out. "You hardly have room to judge." I don't know a lot about his childhood, but even if he was poor, he's not anymore.

"I lost my sister when she was eighteen," he says, shocking the hell out of me. "She overdosed after she became addicted to drugs because her asshole dealer boyfriend got her hooked. I found her in his house dead. I was seventeen. That's where I was yesterday... at my mom's. It was my sister's birthday, and like every year, my mom was drowning herself in a bottle."

Oh my God, no wonder he's freaking out. I was drugged on the birthday of his sister who died from drugs. Without hesitation, I sit up and pull Chase into a tight hug. "I'm so sorry. I can't even imagine what you're going through." I wrap my arms around him tighter and he sinks against me.

"I was so fucking scared for you," he grumbles into my neck. "When Alec texted... fuck." He pulls back and his glassy eyes meet mine. "I was the one who suggested you get out..."

"This isn't your fault."

"I should've been there," he argues. "Alec was focusing on Lexi and—"

"No, you shouldn't have been because you were where you were supposed to be, with your mom because she needed you."

"Next time you go to the club, I'll be going with you."

I scoff. "Trust me, that won't be happening. Me and clubs are done."

Before he can reply, there's a knock on the door. "I'll get it."

A minute later, my mom walks through my door with a sad

smile on her face. "I wasn't sure if you would be awake, but I told Chase I would be by with soup…"

"You don't have to come up with an excuse to check on me," I tell her. "You're my mom."

"I know," she says with a watery laugh. "How are you feeling?"

"I'm okay. Sore and tired, but I'm alive."

"You are," she says, tears pricking her eyes. She sits on the edge of my bed and pulls me into her arms. "I was so scared, Georgia. You're my baby girl and if something happened to you…"

Chase walks in with a tray at that moment and my mom pulls back. "I'm sorry. I guess it just really hit me. We could've lost you."

"You didn't lose me, and nothing like that will ever happen again."

Chase sets the tray on my lap. There's a bowl of chicken noodle soup I recognize from my favorite deli, a glass of orange juice, and some crackers.

"Thank you," I tell both of them. "It smells delicious."

"I'll give you guys a few minutes," Chase says. "Holler if you need anything."

When he's gone, Mom waggles her brows at me. "He's sweet."

I groan. "And just a friend."

"Your choice?"

"No, his. He was hurt and isn't looking for anything more."

"He seemed awfully worried about you for someone who's *just* a friend. He yelled at Alec and wouldn't leave your side."

"He blames himself. It was his idea for me to get out."

"Yeah, I heard that, but I don't know." She shrugs. "I just got a vibe."

"A vibe, huh?" I laugh as I take a spoonful of my soup. "Well, your vibe is way off. We're just friends. He was my wingman, but now that I have no intention of ever going back to a club, I have no idea how I'm going to find a man."

My mom eyes me for a moment. I expected her to appreciate the fact that I'm planning to stay away from clubs, so I'm shocked when she frowns. "What happened was scary, but you can't let one bad experience keep you from doing what you want to do."

I set my spoon down. "I was drugged, Mom. I went out to a

club a few times, hoping to find a guy, and I was drugged. I think I'll stay right here, in my house, where it's safe. Maybe I can try online dating or something," I half joke.

Mom doesn't laugh. "Do you remember last year when you were dating Robert?"

"Ughhh... How could I forget?" I groan.

"He wasn't a very nice man," she agrees.

"Hence why I broke up with him." I take a spoonful of soup.

"But afterward, instead of getting back out there, you went months without dating," she points out.

"Who would want to date after that?"

"And now, you've had something bad happen to you, and you're saying you're not going to go back to a club..."

"So?" I set my spoon down and take a sip of my orange juice.

"When I was married to your father," she says, her voice a tad shaky. "Not Tristan... But your biological father, Justin... He was abusive."

Her words have me abandoning my food and drink. My mom doesn't talk about her past life, ever.

"And not only verbally," she continues. "He would hit me too. He would come home and attack me." She visibly shudders. "As you got older, it got worse. I was terrified that one day he would hurt you, so I came up with a plan to run away with you, to get away from him." A single tear slides down her cheek and she swipes it away. "I slowly put away money so we could disappear. But before we could, he caught me. We fought and I hit my head. When I woke up, I couldn't remember what happened, and he claimed you were dead."

"What?" I choke out in shock.

"I was devastated and ran. I had no clue you were really alive and he was hiding you to punish me."

I don't even know what to say. What horrible person would do that to a mother? And I share DNA with him? But now it makes sense... My memories of my bio dad locking me away in my room. The way he treated me.

"I never told you," I admit, "because you hated to talk about Justin, but I have these memories of him yelling at me and throwing me in my room because I was crying for you. I didn't know why you weren't there, but now it makes sense."

Mom's eyes widen and several tears leak from her lids. "You never told me."

"At first I thought they were nightmares, but as I got older, I realized they were memories... I didn't want to upset you."

"Oh, Georgia. I wish you had told me. I'm so sorry. I should've told you about my past... *our* past. It's just that..." She sighs. "It's so hard to talk about it."

"It's okay, Mom. So, what happened after you left Justin?"

"After I ran, thinking you were dead, I ended up here in Los Angeles," she says with a watery smile. "I met Tristan and Lexi, and I fell in love with her at first sight." She sniffles back her tears. "But it took me a little while to let Tristan in. I was scared that what happened to me before would happen again."

"Well, who can blame you?"

Mom shakes her head. "I was so focused on the bad that already happened, I almost missed out on the good." Mom moves the tray off my lap and sets it on the nightstand. Then she takes my hands in hers. "What happened with Robert sucks. He was a shitty guy and will probably end up alone, but what I'm concerned about is the fact that after him, you didn't date for months. And now you're saying you're never going to a club again. You can't allow the bad to keep you from the possibility of the good."

She's right. It's exactly what I do. I stay in my room, in my little bubble, where I'm safe. It might've stemmed from when I was little and my bio dad kept me in my room for damn near a year, but I'm a grownup now and it's time to stop letting my fears dictate what I want in life. I want to be free...free to love, free to live. Just be free to do what I want.

"You're right. I've worked myself up over the years, creating a mountain out of a molehill, and it's time I take control of my life. I know what I want, and right now, the only person standing in my way is me."

---

"HOW ARE YOU FEELING?" Chase plops down on the bed next to me. He props his muscular forearm up against the side of his head and looks at me with his mesmerizing hazel eyes.

"Better," I tell him truthfully. "My mom and I had a really good talk, and I've come to a decision…" I twist my lips, unsure if I should tell Chase. He was really worried about me going to the club, and with his sister…

"Well, go on," he says through a laugh. "What's this decision?"

I take a deep breath, then in a rush, say, "I'm not going to give up finding the right guy… even if it means going to a club."

Chase blinks once. Then again. And then his mouth is on mine. He threads his fingers through the back of my hair and tugs me over to him. At first I'm in shock, wondering what the hell is happening right now. But then his tongue darts out, licking across the seam of my lips, and just like that, my mind goes blank, my body doing all the thinking for me.

I scoot closer, my body sighing into his, and he deepens the kiss. His lips mold with mine, our tongues tangling in one another. His hand leaves my hair and skates down the side of my body, until it lands on my hip. And then he's gripping my hip and rolling me onto my back. His legs push my thighs apart and he settles on top of me.

Our kiss is messy, desperate. Filled with all of our pent-up sexual tension. I run my fingers through his hair, and wrap my thighs around his waist, pulling him closer to me. When the hard bulge in his pants grinds against my center, I let out a needy groan, which spurs him on. He nips at my bottom lip, then sucks it into his mouth, before he breaks the kiss and moves to my neck. I tilt my head slightly, giving him better access, and he licks a trail along my sensitive flesh, taking his time and covering every inch.

I've only been kissed by a couple guys in my life, and none of them made me feel like this—as if my body is being wound up tightly in the best way. If he continues, I have no doubt I'll eventually snap. My lady parts are clenching in want. My nipples are hard, and as Chase works his way down my body, his fingers brush up against them, making me moan. How can such a simple touch elicit so much pleasure?

Needing to feel him, I pull his shirt over his head and toss it to the side. I run my nails along his hot flesh and laugh when a shiver visibly overtakes him.

"Fuck, Georgia," he murmurs, kissing his way along my collarbone. I'm wearing a tank top sans bra and he pulls the front down, exposing my breasts. As if asking for permission, he stops and glances up, his eyes shining with lust and desire.

The second I nod my permission, his lips wrap around my nipple. He sucks it into his mouth and bites down gently on the tip, causing my entire body to bow.

"Holy Jesus," I groan. "Do that again."

He chuckles at my demand, the rumbling vibrations shooting straight through me. My thighs tighten around him, and it makes him laugh harder.

I feel out of control. Every touch, every lick has me needing more.

As Chase is dragging my tank up and over my head, a door slams and then a few seconds later a feminine voice yells, "Hey, sis, I'm—Oh shit!"

*Lexi.*

"What hap—What the fuck?"

*Alec.*

"Oh God," I groan, at the same time Chase curses under his breath. "Give us a minute," I squeak, as Lexi's laughter rings out through the condo, no doubt remembering the time I walked in on her and Alec.

I scramble to right my tank top, mortified. What did we just do? Chase made it clear he doesn't want to settle down, and that's precisely what I'm looking for. I can't be another notch on his belt. It'll not only destroy me, but it'll ruin the friendship we've been building. A friendship I don't want to lose.

I try to push Chase off me, but he doesn't budge. "Move," I hiss in confusion. "And... put your shirt back on."

"Hey." He grabs my chin with his thumb and forefinger. "Breathe."

"What?" My chest is rising and falling in quick succession.

"I can see your brain is in overdrive. Don't second-guess what just happened."

"What *did* just happen?"

"You and me," he says, his lip quirking into a sexy grin.

I open my mouth to ask what he means by that, but before I can get the words out, Lexi yells, "We're still here and waiting!"

## CHAPTER TWELVE

### CHASE

Fuck. I've imagined how her pillow soft lips would feel against mine a million times. How her smooth skin would feel under my touch. I knew if I kissed her, if I touched her, I wouldn't be able to stop. And I was right. Her taste, her smell, her scent of pleasure, when I hadn't even pleasured her yet, are fucking addicting. And I'm fucked because I'll be damned if anyone but me will ever touch and taste her again. Fuck that, Georgia is mine. Fuck the risks, fuck my heart, just... fuck.

"We need to talk," Alec growls the second Georgia and I step into the living room. I raise a brow and he adds, "Alone."

"Stop," Georgia says softly, obviously embarrassed at having been caught. "Please."

Alec glares at me. He warned me to stay away, and he was right to do so... before I spent time with her. Hell, I don't blame him. This last year I've turned into an uncaring manwhore. But I wouldn't do that to Georgia. She's different.

"So, what..." Lexi says. "You two are together now?"

"No," Georgia rushes out, shaking her head quickly.

"Then what? You're just hooking up?" Lexi's glaring eyes meet mine, but I keep my mouth shut, letting Georgia and her sister have this conversation.

"What? No," Georgia argues. "It was just... a mistake."

And now I'm jumping in. "Like hell it was a mistake." Georgia's shocked gaze swings over to me. "Kissing you was *not* a mistake."

"I just meant we got carried away," Georgia backtracks. "Chase has been so nice to me and it was just... a moment."

"No, we didn't, and no, it wasn't," I argue again. I'm not going to let her play this off. Hell, I'm already thinking about the next time I can kiss her again. Unless...

"Wait, do you regret the kiss?" I never even considered she would regret kissing me.

"I—" she begins, her eyes darting toward Alec and Lexi, hoping one of them will save her.

"We just came by to check on Georgia," Lexi cuts in and stands, surprising me when she kisses Georgia's cheek then grabs Alec's hand and drags him to the front door. "We can see she's in good hands, so we'll go." She shoots me a wink. "See you guys later."

Alec grumbles his goodbye, but I don't miss the daggers he's shooting my way. He's protective as hell of Georgia, and as my best friend, he knows the way I've treated women this past year. We're definitely going to have a conversation soon.

Once they're gone, Georgia attempts to slip back into her room, but I catch her by her arm and stop her before she can run. "I meant what I said. I don't regret kissing you. It wasn't a mistake. I thoroughly enjoyed it, and if it's up to me, I'd like for it to happen again."

Georgia allows herself a small smile before she schools her features. "I enjoyed it too, but..." I raise a brow, waiting for her to make her argument so I can shoot it down.

"Well, c'mon, Chase," she finally says. "I'm a virgin... and you're..." She waves her hand at me. "You're not."

I crack up laughing. "No, I'm not. But so what?"

"So, as hot as you are, and as good of a kisser as you are, I can't be just another woman you stick your dick in."

Fuck, I love it when she says shit like that. It isn't often Georgia talks like that, but when she does, it's a goddamn turn-on.

I step closer to her and rest my hands on her hips. "What if I want you to be the only woman I stick my dick in?"

Her cheeks heat up, and I grin. Her innocence is so refreshing. "I would say you should reconsider because I'm not having sex until I fall in love." She raises a challenging brow at me, thinking her little confession is going to deter me, but what she doesn't realize is since we started hanging out, I haven't had sex at all, and surprisingly, I don't miss it. I would rather hang out with her and have a meaningful conversation than have meaningless sex.

"Before I got divorced, Victoria was the only woman I'd had sex with." Georgia's brows shoot up to her forehead. "This last year I was searching for an escape. I was hurt. I loved her and she cheated on me. She took something as sacred as our marriage and shit on it like it meant nothing to her."

I take her hands in mine, lacing our fingers together. I love how delicate and soft her hands are in contrast to my rough ones. "I can't take back how I've spent the last year, and honestly, I'm not sure I would want to. I handled shit the best I could, but that was all before you. And I know actions speak louder than words, so whatever I say right now isn't going to hold as much meaning as me showing you. But that's exactly what I would like to do... Show you that I have no desire to spend my time with any other woman but you."

Georgia releases a harsh breath. I expect for her to argue, to throw my past in my face, tell me there's no way I can be faithful, so I'm shocked when she simply says, "Okay, I'd like that... for you to show me."

I laugh softly. I should've known that once again Georgia is different. She's innocent and trusting and doesn't play games—just a few of the reasons why I'm attracted to her.

I pull her into my arms and hug her, giving her a kiss on the top of her head and inhaling her vanilla scent. "Thank you. You won't regret it."

She pulls back and smiles. "Does that mean no more clubs to look for the perfect guy?" Her green eyes twinkle with laughter.

"That definitely means no more clubs." Remembering she was in the hospital only a few short hours ago, I scoop her up into my arms bridal style and stalk into her room. I set her down on the middle of the bed and climb over her. We're in the same spot we were in before her sister barged in.

"No more clubs," I repeat, dipping my face down and pressing my lips to the curve of her neck. I nibble lightly and she giggles, so I do it again, loving the sound.

---

"WHAT THE HELL WAS THAT SHIT?" Alec barks the second I walk into the station. Everyone stops what they're doing and the place goes silent. After Alec and Lexi left, and Georgia agreed to give us a shot, we spent the rest of the weekend watching reruns of shows, eating takeout, and in between, making out like teenagers. We created our own little bubble, and it completely slipped my mind I would still have to deal with Alec.

"Georgia and I are dating," I say nonchalantly.

He gets in my face. "I warned you to stay away from her. You can have any woman you want. We might be best friends, but Georgia is family."

"And if we get married that'd make us family," I joke, but then the thought of Georgia and I getting married hits me, and instead of freaking out, I find myself smiling. Sure, it's way too soon for that, but that doesn't mean I can't still imagine it. Georgia, dressed in white, walking down the aisle...

"Holy shit," Alec hisses, "you're thinking about it."

"What?"

"You're actually thinking about what it would be like to marry Georgia."

"I really like her," I admit. Actually, I'm in love with her, but I can't say that yet. It's too soon. People will think I'm fucking nuts. "We've been hanging out a lot and we just click."

"If you hurt her, I'm going to have to beat your ass," Alec warns.

"Same," a voice says from behind me.

I turn around and find Mason and Tristan walking up.

"Just left breakfast with my girls," Tristan says, sizing me up as he walks over to us. I knew Georgia left early this morning to meet her mom and sister for breakfast. She was gone before I woke up and left me a note that she'd be by later with a new recipe for me to try. But I didn't realize her dad would also be there, or that we would be the topic of conversation. But I guess I should've expected that. I'm just not used to parents interfering. I mean, my mom cares, but she's not one to make a fuss. And Victoria's parents were barely around. Nobody ever cared or questioned anything we did.

"Breakfast's already over?"

"Nah," Tristan says, shaking his head. "They're still at the house, eating and gossiping. I overheard Lexi asking her sister about what she walked in on as I was walking out the door... Figured I must've misunderstood, because the last I heard, you promised to bring her home and take care of her." Tristan tilts his head to the side slightly. "Wasn't aware taking care of her meant almost sleeping with her."

I stifle a groan. "Nothing happened."

"Yeah, because Lexi and I showed up," Alec points out.

"Good job, Son," Mason says, patting him on the shoulder.

"Look, I get it," I tell them. "You guys are all protective of Georgia, but I'm not the bad guy here. I didn't plan for this to happen, but when she said she planned to go back to that club to find the perfect guy—"

"The fuck?" Mason hisses at the same time Tristan barks out, "Like hell."

"Exactly!" I throw my hands up in the air. "Anyway, she said that shit and it just happened. I kissed her, but nothing more than that happened." Not much anyway...

"So, you kissed her to stop her from going out?" Tristan eyes me accusingly.

"What? No. Don't twist my words." I hit Tristan with a pointed look. Georgia's father or not, I won't be accused of shit that isn't true. "I like her, and when she said that shit, it made me admit it."

"So what exactly are you two?" Mason asks.

"Dad!" Georgia yells. "I knew it!" She stomps up the station's driveway, and I can't help but smile. She's dressed in light blue skinny jeans that show off her sexy curves and a thin pink tank top. White Vans on her feet. Her hair is straightened, and she's wearing a little bit of makeup. Not a lot, but enough to make her emerald eyes pop and her lips look all silky and kissable. And I would totally kiss her, if it weren't for the scary way she's glaring at her dad as she stalks toward us.

"Georgia, honey, what are you doing here?" Tristan asks, his voice now soft. I've been around Georgia and Lexi long enough to know they have their dad wrapped around their fingers.

"The second the door closed, I knew where you were going!" She steps in front of me and turns around to face her dad. I can't see her facial expression since I'm now standing behind her, but I can see the way her arms cross over her chest and hear her humph in aggravation.

"Georgia, why don't you just let the men talk?" Mason says.

"Excuse me?" Georgia shrieks, making me snort out a laugh. Is he crazy? "This is *my* business, not any of yours."

"Well, it's kind of mine, too," I point out playfully, placing a reassuring hand on her hip and ignoring the way all three guys glare down at the gesture.

"Mine and *Chase's*," she corrects, glancing back at me with a soft smile. My stomach knots and it takes everything in me not to crush my mouth to hers right this second.

"You were drugged a few days ago," Tristan says, his eyes darting between Georgia and me. "You can't blame me for wanting to protect you."

"I get that," Georgia says. "And I appreciate your concern, but maybe next time talk to me."

Tristan nods and Georgia hugs him and then Mason. Lastly, she hugs Alec. "Thank you for looking out for me."

"I don't care if we work together, or that he's my friend," he says to her, making sure I can hear. "If he hurts you—"

"Then I get hurt," she says. "I won't allow it to affect your friendship. I know Chase's past, but I believe him when he says I'm his future." Fuck, and there she goes again, squeezing the hell out of my heart.

Alec looks like he wants to argue but instead nods. "All right." He hugs her again. "I need to get going on my chores." He hugs his stepdad and shakes Tristan's hand before disappearing inside.

"I've got my eye on you," Mason says, moving his pointer and middle finger back and forth between him and me. "Treat my goddaughter right."

"Uncle Mason," Georgia groans.

Mason pops his palms up in surrender.

"Let's do dinner soon," Tristan says, extending his hand out for me to take. "I've gotten to know a little about you as my daughter's roommate, but I'd like to get to know you now as her..."

"Friend," Georgia says before I can answer. "We're friends, Dad." *Like hell we're just friends*, I think but don't say out loud. She probably doesn't want her dad to give her a hard time, but we'll definitely be clearing that shit up when we're alone and I'm not at work. Georgia and I are more than friends. We might be in the early stages of this relationship, but she's mine.

"Let me know when you want to get together and I'm there," I tell him, shaking his hand.

Once he's gone, Georgia sighs. "I'm so sorry."

"You don't have anything to be sorry about." I tug on the front of her tank so she's forced to come closer. "You have a lot of people who care about you."

"I do," she says. "I better get going..."

"Yeah." I cup the side of her face and she looks up at me. "But first, I need to do this..." I dip down and capture her bottom lip with my own, then her top. She moans into my mouth, parting her lips slightly, and I push my tongue inside, quickly tasting her, before pulling back.

When I open my eyes, hers are still closed. I press one more soft kiss to her perfect mouth and then her eyes flutter open. "I really like kissing you," she admits.

"I really like kissing you too." I tuck a wayward strand of her hair behind her ear. I need to get inside, but fuck it's hard to let go of her.

"I better go," she says.

"Yeah," I reluctantly agree. "I'll see you later with dinner, right?" I couldn't give a fuck about the food. I just want an excuse to see her.

"Definitely."

After I watch her get into her massive truck and take off, I head into the station. The guys are all standing around bullshitting, but when they see me, like the assholes they are, they start hooting and hollering.

"So, it's true?" Luke asks. "Is Mr. Manwhore officially a one-woman man?"

I can see Alec standing in the corner, staring at me and

waiting for my reply. I look over at him and our eyes meet. "Yeah, as far as I'm concerned, I'm off the market."

The guys all cheer and laugh—everyone except Alec—but I don't take it personal. Just like I told Georgia, actions speak louder than words. Once Alec sees through my actions how serious I am about Georgia, he'll come around.

## CHAPTER THIRTEEN

### GEORGIA

**Chase: I have to stay late for a meeting. When I get home I was thinking we could do something.**

**Me: Sounds good.**

"WHO ARE YOU TEXTING WITH?" Lexi asks, a sly smirk on her lips. "Your boyfriend?" She scoops a bit of oatmeal up and feeds it to Abigail, who opens her mouth like a cute little birdy.

I was surprised to find Lexi, with Abigail on her hip and breakfast in her hand, standing on my doorstep first thing this morning. But since I'm always down for spending time with my sister and niece, it was a pleasant surprise.

"He's not my boyfriend," I correct her, popping a piece of blueberry muffin into my mouth. "We're just... talking... hanging out," I say, hoping I come across nonchalant. The truth is, I don't know what we are, and I don't want to get hurt thinking we're more while Chase is assuming we're less.

"Really? Does he know that?" She swipes up on her phone and types something quickly, then turns it around.

I stare at her screen to see what she's showing me, but I'm not sure what I'm looking at. "Is that his profile pic?" I look at a smiling Chase, dressed in his work uniform. His arms are crossed over his chest and his muscular forearms are bulging slightly. He's so damn sexy without even trying.

"Georgia, focus," Lexi says. "Yes, it's his profile picture and yours." I realize then, my picture is next to his. "He updated his status this morning, putting that he's in a relationship with you." Her eyes go wide. "Nothing says more serious than making it Facebook official."

I crack up laughing. "Does anyone even go on Facebook anymore?"

Lexi groans. "I don't know. Who cares. The point is he did, and when he did, he publicly announced that he's in a relationship with you. Didn't you get the notification?"

"I don't even have the app on my phone. I only go on it to see the photos Grandma and Grandpa post while they're traveling."

Lexi rolls her eyes and feeds Abigail another bite of her food. "Well, everyone saw this. Mom... Dad... All your guys' friends and family."

My heart pitter-patters at the thought. When I was dating Robert, I could barely get him to take me to a work function. Yet, Chase just announced to the entire Facebook population that he's in a relationship with me.

"I see that look on your face." She points an oatmeal-covered spoon at me. "You've totally fallen for him."

I nod, not even wanting to deny it. "I have, Lex. I mean, it's too soon, but..."

"Time doesn't determine anything. Look how quickly Alec and I got married once we finally gave in to our feelings."

They were married within three months, but... "You guys were in love with each other for years and just wouldn't admit it. Up until recently, I couldn't stand Chase, and I don't think he even noticed me."

Lexi snorts. "Oh, trust me, he noticed you. Alec is super pissed about all this. Apparently Chase wanted to ask you out a long time ago and Alec told him you were off-limits."

"What?" I shriek, shocked as hell.

"Yep. He didn't want to take a chance of you getting hurt by Chase. They got into it yesterday." She wipes Abigail's mouth with a wet-wipe, then hands her her sippy cup, helping her take a sip of water from it.

"I don't want Alec and him to be on bad terms. I'm a big girl and can make my own decisions."

"That's what I told him," Lexi agrees. "Plus, if Chase hurts you, I'll kick his ass."

She lifts Abigail from her mini high chair I keep here for when they come over and hands her to me. Abigail grins and giggles as I place kisses all over her cheeks. The sound wraps around my heart like the most beautiful rose covered vines.

I'm still giving her kisses when the door opens and Chase walks inside. His eyes meet mine, and those same vines tighten, forcing my heart to clench in my chest.

"Hey," he says, a small smile splaying across his face.

"Hey," I say back.

"Oh Lord." Lexi groans. "I'm getting out of here before I end up pregnant by just being in the same room as you two."

Chase snorts a laugh, but otherwise ignores her, coming over and giving Abigail a kiss to her cheek and then giving me a kiss to mine. "I'm going to jump in the shower," he says. My eyes stay trained on his body—on his ass—as he saunters down the hall and disappears into the bathroom.

"Oh em gee," Lexi says once he's gone. "You're totally going to F.U.C.K. him."

I bark out a laugh. "You know she doesn't know the word yet, right? And you could just say sex and it wouldn't be a bad word."

"Don't you change the subject." She wags her finger at me. "What happened to waiting until you're in love?"

I swallow thickly. "We're not going to have sex. We're just getting to know each other." But even as I say the words, I know if Chase wanted to, I totally would. I want him that badly.

"I gotta go," she says. "Have fun being in denial and call me afterward so we can talk deets. Bye!" She grabs her diaper bag and her daughter and flits out of the condo, slamming the door behind her.

I clean up the dining room table and kitchen, then head to my room so I can get changed and be ready to go when Chase gets out of the shower.

As I'm walking down the hall, Chase steps out of the steamy bathroom in nothing but a towel hanging low on his hips. He halts in place to let me pass by, but I'm flustered at seeing him half naked and dripping wet, and I stumble over my own two feet. He reaches out to catch me, and I would be thankful that he's the reason I'm not going to land face first on the wood floor, except when I go to grab a hold of him, my hands slide down his slick chest and abs and tug on his towel. The material drops to the ground, leaving him naked as the day he was born.

"Shit," he says, grasping my shoulders. "That was close."

Before I can stop myself, my eyes descend to where the towel was... to where it no longer is, and catch a glimpse of his dick.

He clears his throat and bends to scoop up his towel. My gaze goes back up to his face and he's sporting a knowing smirk.

Embarrassed, I scurry to my room and close the door, leaning against it once I do. Holy shit, I just saw my first dick... and it was Chase's. I didn't stare at it long enough to catch too many details, but the area above it was neatly trimmed and it was dangling between his legs. I drop to the ground and my head bangs slightly against the door. I close my eyes, trying to calm my erratic heart and start counting.

I've lost track of what number I'm on for the millionth time when there's a knock on my door. "Georgia, you ever going to come out?"

"I thought I would just die of embarrassment in here."

Chase laughs. "You have nothing to be embarrassed about. I'm the one who should be embarrassed. You saw my dick when it wasn't at its best."

"What?" I say through a confused laugh.

"Can I come in?"

I get to my feet and stand, slowly pulling the door open.

"There she is," he says, thankfully now fully dressed. I mean, I also enjoyed him without any clothes on, but... "You're blushing again," he points out. "Are you imagining me still naked?" He hits me with a cocky smirk.

"Oh God. Kill me now."

"Eh, then I wouldn't be able to do this." He entwines his fingers through my hair and crashes his mouth down on mine. I gasp and his tongue delves past my parted lips. It takes me a second to catch up, but once I do, I kiss him back. My belly flip-flops and butterflies soar in my chest. Nobody has ever made me feel the way Chase does with a single kiss.

He pulls back slightly, ending the kiss, and his hands palm the sides of my face. "That's much better," he says, his tongue swiping across his bottom lip like he's trying to savor my taste. "I've been dying to do that since I got home. Working twenty-four-hour shifts sucks." He presses his lips to mine for another brief kiss, and I sigh into him, not wanting it to end.

"You kissed me last night when I brought you dinner," I point out, playfully rolling my eyes, but deep down secretly loving that he's implying he missed me while he was gone.

"And then I had to go sixteen hours without doing it." His hazel eyes lock with mine. "A couple friends of mine are barbecuing at the beach. I think Alec and Lexi might swing by later. Wanna go?"

"Sure, just let me change into my swimsuit and then I'll be ready to go."

After stopping by the store to pick up some drinks and snacks, we head over to Venice Beach. It's a beautiful day, but hot, so I'm thankful I snagged Lexi's umbrella she left at the condo when she moved out. I strip out of my cover-up and shorts, leaving me in only my pink and black striped bikini, while Chase digs a hole and sets up the umbrella. Once he's done, I lay a blanket under it. He introduces me to a couple of his friends I haven't met yet, but most of them I already know from the fire station, and then we settle on the blanket in the shade. He removes his shirt and I notice, unlike his friends, he doesn't have a single tattoo on him.

"What?" he asks, when he catches me checking him out.

"You don't have any tattoos."

"Neither do you." He takes my hand in his and absently plays around with my fingers.

"I want one."

"Yeah? What would you get?" His fingers trail over my palm and up the inside of my wrist. I've noticed that when we're together he likes to touch me. His hands are always on me in some way. And when I'm talking, he always pays full attention to me. I like that.

"I don't know. Something meaningful since it'll be on my body forever."

"That's why I haven't gotten one. Growing up everyone in my neighborhood was covered in them. Usually shitty ones done in dirty basements." He cringes. "I told myself I wouldn't get one until I had a damn good reason to. Guess I just never had one."

"That makes sense."

His phone dings with a notification, which reminds me... "Lexi showed me something earlier... on Facebook."

He doesn't even look at his phone, instead focusing on me. "Oh yeah? What did she show you?" The way one side of his mouth is quirked up tells me he knows exactly what she showed me.

"Your relationship status."

Chase's grin widens. "That I'm in a relationship with you."

"Is that what we are? In a relationship?"

"Damn right, we are." He pulls my face close to his, and his mouth connects with my own. "You're mine," he growls against my lips. "And I'm yours." He closes his mouth over mine in a searing kiss that matches the tone of his words.

I'm his.

And he's mine.

I like the sound of that.

"Get a room!" someone shouts, forcing us to break apart.

"Go on a date with me tonight," he says, tucking a stray hair behind my ear. He's still holding me, refusing to let go, and my mind is all over the place.

"Why?" I blurt out.

His brows furl. "I thought we just covered this... we're in a relationship. That means you're my girlfriend and I'm your boyfriend." His face breaks out into a sexy boyish grin and I laugh, realizing he has me so all over the place I didn't finish my question out loud.

"Not why are you asking me out... Why did you change your mind about wanting a girlfriend?"

"You did," he says, kissing the corner of my mouth. "I couldn't see myself putting my heart back out there again, risking someone hurting me, until you."

I swallow thickly at the seriousness of his words. "Thank you,"

I tell him, not caring that we're having this conversation on the blanket at the beach, surrounded by his friends. "I'll be careful with it."

"I know you will. Now, how about that date?"

"A date sounds perfect."

## CHAPTER FOURTEEN

### CHASE

"Screw the date. Let's stay home." I'm only half serious. The half that's staring at Georgia, dressed in a sexy beige off the shoulder dress that stops mid-thigh and shows off every one of her perfect curves.

Georgia's eyes go wide, not picking up on my joke. "Why? What happened?"

I cut across the room and pull her into my arms. "You look too damn good. That's what happened." I kiss the corner of her mouth, not wanting to mess up the shiny lip gloss shit she's wearing. Later, I tell myself. Later, I'll mess that shit up.

"You're so cheesy."

"I'm dead serious." I glide my hands down her hips. Touching Georgia has become my favorite pastime, an addiction of sorts. She's soft and smooth and everything about her is so damn perfect.

"Let's go, silly!" she says with a giggle. She steps around me and I have the pleasure of watching her ass sway from side to side, her heels clicking across the wood floor, as she walks over to the front door.

"You coming?"

I quirk a brow, letting her comment settle in for a moment. Of course, she doesn't catch on because she's too damn innocent.

"Yeah," I say with a laugh. "I'm coming."

Twenty minutes later we arrive at Salvatore's, a small Italian restaurant on the beach that's reservations only. The hostess shows us to our table, which is outside, then leaves us with our menus. There are four chairs, and knowing I'm going to want to touch Georgia, I sit in the one diagonal from her instead of across.

"I've never been here," she muses, glancing out at the water. It's early fall, so there's a slight chill to the air. Not enough to be considered cold, but enough to make it nice out.

"A friend of mine owns the place." It's how I was able to get a last-minute reservation. "We grew up in south LA together."

Georgia smiles. "Does your mom still live there?"

"Yeah, she won't move away from there. It's the last place my sister lived."

Her smile fades. "I'm so sorry about your sister. I can't even begin to fathom what it would feel like to lose my sister."

Not wanting the night to take a sour turn, I shake my head. "Let's talk about something else."

"Don't do that," she says, taking my hand in hers. "I don't just want the good, the fun... I want all of you. The ugly, the scary, the shitty. I want it all."

Fuck, this woman. I raise her hand and kiss the tops of her knuckles. "Thank you."

We spend our date going from topic to topic. We talk about our pasts, our families, what we want for our futures. We laugh and joke and it's obvious the chemistry between us is there. The entire time we eat and drink and converse, we touch each other. I learn I'm not the only handsy one in this relationship, and I love that she can't keep her hands off of me.

It's honestly one of the best dates I've ever been on, and I know it's because it's with Georgia and what we're doing here is real. I spent the last year faking it, thinking it was the way to go about getting over the shit that happened with my ex-wife. But all I was doing was hiding behind a bunch of fake as fuck hookups. I don't regret it because they led me to this moment, but looking back I could've handled it better.

After we share a slice of cheesecake for dessert, I suggest we go for a walk on the beach.

"Actually," Georgia says, swiping her tongue across the seam of her lips. "I'd rather finish this date at home." Her green orbs burn into mine, and she doesn't have to tell me twice.

"Check, please!" I yell jokingly, making her laugh.

The second we're through the door of the condo, Georgia's arms go around my neck and I lift her off her feet, carrying her to her room. I drop her onto the bed and then take a moment to look at her. The way her hair is splayed out across her pillow as she looks up at me with her trusting emerald eyes and her perfect, pink, kissable lips. "You're so beautiful."

Her mouth curls into a shy smile. "Come kiss me."

"I will, but first I want to explore." Once my mouth touches hers, it'll be damn hard to stop.

After kicking my shoes off, I remove her heels, then kiss the instep of each of her feet. I trail kisses up her smooth, tanned legs, nip playfully at her hips through the material of her dress, and then settle over her.

I kiss my way along her neck, until I get to her pillow soft lips. Our mouths finally connect and my body sighs against hers. I could stay like this, kissing her, touching her for hours, maybe even days.

"Touch me, please," she murmurs against my lips. Her words are so soft, so shaky, I almost don't hear them.

"Where?" I ask, knowing our levels of experience are way the hell different and not wanting to take this anywhere she isn't ready for.

I open my eyes to wait for her to answer and hers pop open as well. For a moment, we just stare at each other. She licks her slightly swollen lips, which was caused from our kissing, and then says, "Anywhere... Everywhere."

Her legs tighten around me and I stifle a chuckle. She's turned on and is craving a release. "It would be my pleasure." I sit up and rake my gaze down her body. "Turn over."

Her eyes widen slightly, but then she does as I asked, flipping onto her belly and exposing the zipper that starts at the top of her dress and continues to just above her ass.

I pull the zipper slowly down, exposing her flesh. "It's like unwrapping a birthday present," I muse. Georgia shakes her head but doesn't say a word.

When the zipper hits the bottom, I pull the dress apart. Her skin is smooth and flawless, a couple freckles peppering her shoulders. I lay a kiss to each of her shoulder blades before I unclasp her bra. Her skin smells sweet. The same scent she always wears. It's a smell I'm finding myself craving all the time.

"Lift up," I tell her, leaning over her and kissing the shell of her ear.

She does so, and I pull her dress and bra down her body, leaving her in only a nude thong. Unable to help myself, I take a playful bite out of her ass cheek, making her yelp.

"Sorry, it just looks so damn delicious."

Before she can come up with a comeback, I massage the globes of her ass, causing her to release a moan. "Be right back," I tell her.

I hop off the bed and find her lotion in the bathroom. When I return, she's still in the same position. I squirt some into my hands and then begin to massage her shoulders. They're tight, telling me she's nervous. She's never exposed herself to a man like she's doing right now, and I don't take that shit lightly. I have no doubt when she asked me to touch her, she was expecting me to get her off, but I want more with Georgia and I need her to understand that. I want to make her feel good, and not just sexually.

As I massage her back and shoulders, the tension in her body slowly, little by little, bleeds away. When I work my way down to her ass, she tightens up momentarily, but then quickly relaxes.

Spreading her legs slightly, so I can kneel on the bed, I massage the globes of her perfect ass. She's toned and tight all over from jogging daily. She loves to eat, but she also loves to work out.

I dip my head and give the area I bit earlier, a kiss. She squirms slightly and when I look up, I catch her glancing back at me with lust-filled eyes.

Shocking the shit out of me, she spreads her legs wider, making it clear what she wants. But I'm not going to let her get away with keeping her mouth closed. She does that too often. But not with us. I want her thoughts, her words. "What is it you want?"

"I already told you. For you to touch me... everywhere."

I smirk. "Where exactly?"

She glares. When I quirk a brow, refusing to let it go, she releases a harsh breath then whispers, "My... pussy... please."

I chuckle softly. "So polite."

Gripping her thighs, I spread them farther, then run my fingers along the crack of her ass and then between her folds. I dip a single finger inside and find she's soaked.

"Turn over."

She does, exposing her perky tits, toned stomach, and neatly trimmed pussy. There are so many places I want to touch, kiss, lick, fucking worship, but before I can do any of that, I want to get her off. She's back to being wound tight, and I prefer it when she's relaxed.

And I know just the way to make that happen. Since she's a virgin and has never been properly taken care of, I focus on her clit. Using her juices, I massage soft circles across her swollen, needy flesh. Her eyes go wide, and her hips buck. The act making me realize something...

"Have you ever given yourself an orgasm?" Her cheeks tinge pink, giving me my answer. "Oh, baby. Be prepared to have your mind blown."

I drop down between her legs and lick up her center, inhaling her sweet musk. While I slowly lick her clit, I reach up and tweak her nipple.

"Chase," she breathes. "I'm... I think I'm going to—" Her words are cut off by a loud, guttural moan. Her knees tighten around my face, and her entire ass lifts off the bed. Her legs tremble as she rides out her orgasm. I don't stop stroking her clit until she drags her fingers through my hair and tugs on the ends, silently pleading for me to stop.

"Holy shit," she says, her smile lazy and sated. "That was so good." She giggles, and I laugh at how adorable she is. A few weeks ago, she was stuck in her little cocoon of safety... But now...

"What?" she asks, nibbling the corner of her mouth nervously.

"You remind me of a butterfly." I crawl over her and pull her blanket up to cover her naked body. Then I lie on my side, next to her. She turns over onto her side, so we're facing each other.

"A butterfly?"

"Yeah, like you've completed the final stage of metamorphosis and have shed your cocoon." I tuck a stray tendril of hair behind her ear and lean in to kiss her mouth. "You've been transformed from a caterpillar into a butterfly."

The corners of her lips tug into a huge smile. "Like I'm free."

A single tear skates down her cheek and I catch it with the pad of my thumb. "It's because of you," she says. "You help me spread my wings and fly."

"No, my beautiful butterfly. That was all you."

Georgia throws the blanket off her and climbs on top of me, forcing me onto my back. "It's my turn," she says with a mischievous grin.

"Your turn for—" Before I can finish my question, she's sliding down my body, taking my shorts and briefs with her. Once she's slid them off my legs, she throws them onto the floor then settles herself between my legs.

"I've never done this before, but I'm a quick learner," she says. "I know the women—"

"Whoa." I put my hand up to stop her. "Who's in this room with us?" Her brows furrow in confusion. "Us," I answer for her. "No other men or women. Just us. I don't give a fuck what any other woman did, nor do I want to compare what we do to anyone from my past."

Her eyes go wide. "I just don't want you to be disappointed."

I look her dead in the eyes, needing her to know how serious what I say next is. "Nothing you do could ever disappoint me." I have a feeling some shit went down with that dumbass Robert while they were dating, but I'm not going to go there. Just like I don't want any other women in this room with us, I don't want that fucking loser in here either.

"Okay." She sits up on her knees. "But like how you gave me that orgasm... It's because you're experienced. You know what a woman wants and how to get her off. I'm not going to ignore that fact."

When I open my mouth to argue, she raises her hand. "I'm not jealous, Chase. And I'm not going to hold your past over your head. But I shared a wall with you for months, so I know the women you've been with know how to please you."

Fuck, now I'm seriously wishing I never would've brought a single woman over to this place. It's one of the reasons why when I carried Georgia inside, I brought her to her room and not mine. Nobody's been in this room, in this bed, but her.

"I've never done this before," she says. "And I want it to be good for you, like it was for me."

"Whatever you do will be good because it's you."

She snorts. "How romantic. I've read enough romance novels to know the gist of how it's done, but there's so much to it. I want you to tell me if I do something you like or don't like. Okay?"

I nod once, agreeing, because I can tell she needs me to.

She smiles softly, then turns her attention to my flaccid dick. She takes my shaft in her hand and kisses the crown. And that's all it takes for my dick to get excited. It immediately perks up, and she smiles down at it before glancing back up at me.

"In my books, some guys like to be deep throated and some prefer to be licked and teased... What's your preference?"

Holy. Fucking. Shit. She did not just go there... "Georgia, if you do either of those things, both my dick and I will be happy. Just put your mouth on me and do whatever you want, babe," I choke out.

She looks like she wants to argue, but thankfully nods, then does as I suggested... puts her warm, wet, perfect mouth on my dick. She tongues the head, then licks my shaft. And then she parts her lips and takes me all the way into her mouth, and I damn near shoot my load down her throat.

I watch with rapt attention as she owns the hell out of the blow job, giving it everything she's got. When I'm ready to blow, I warn her and she pops off, finishing me off with her hand.

Ropes of cum shoot out, some of it landing on my thighs, and the rest on her tits. She glances down at the cum on her chest and swipes a bit up.

She isn't going to do what I think she is... She pops her finger into her mouth and sucks, her brows dipping in contemplation.

"I was wondering what it tastes like," she explains. "Some girls spit and some swallow... It doesn't taste horrible, but I'm not sure I would want to swallow that."

She scrunches her face up, and I crack up laughing. "I don't give a fuck if you spit or swallow."

I can honestly say I've never had a sexual experience like this before. And I fucking love it. Because it's real. It's honest. This isn't just a one-night stand. This is us learning about each other. Being in a relationship with one another. I never thought I would want any of that again. Until Georgia.

# CHAPTER FIFTEEN

## GEORGIA

I wake up to the feel of a hand gliding down my side. Remembering I fell asleep in Chase's arms last night, I don't bother opening my eyes. He reaches around and slides his hand under the material of my panties and cups my mound. I move my top leg over and hook it around his leg, eager for him to make me feel good again. He gave me multiple orgasms last night and I'm addicted.

Chase chuckles and kisses my neck, parting my folds and inserting a finger inside me, then another one. I moan, feeling full, and wondering if it's possible to take my virginity like this.

He moves me to my back, and while fingering me, takes a nipple into his mouth. I don't remember falling asleep topless, but I'm definitely considering never wearing a shirt again in bed if that means giving him easy access.

"This orgasm is going to feel different," he murmurs, lifting his face to kiss me. I consider warning him that Robert once tried to finger me, but it went nowhere. But then, his fingers move inside of me, eliciting pleasure I've never experienced, and any thoughts of Robert are gone. As Chase expertly strokes my insides, working me into a frenzy, I remember what he said last night: nobody belongs in this room but us. He was right. It's just me and him in this room, in this relationship.

He curls his fingers inside me, his thumb massaging my clit, and within seconds my orgasm is ripping through me. His mouth crashes against mine, swallowing my moans of pleasure. We kiss for several minutes, until his alarm goes off, reminding us both that he needs to get ready for his shift.

When he breaks the kiss and climbs off the bed, I pout. "Wait, what about you?" I nod toward the obvious hard-on he's sporting. "Come back here so I can... do you."

"Do me?" He laughs. "You sure you graduated from college?"

When I glare, he laughs harder. "I have to get ready for work." He leans over me and kisses me again. "But now I have something to look forward to when I come home."

He walks toward the bathroom and stops. "I can't wait to come home, so you can *do me*."

I chuck a pillow at him and miss, causing him to bark out another laugh.

After he leaves for work, I go for a jog around the neighborhood, make myself breakfast, and then get started on my work for the day. My mom sends a group text to Lexi and me, asking to do lunch one day this week, and we both respond that any day works. Which reminds me that I haven't eaten since breakfast.

I'm heading toward the kitchen, when there's a knock on the door. I open it to find a beautiful woman—in a fake, plastic, Barbie sort of way—standing in the doorway.

"Can I help you?"

When she eyes me up and down like I'm the gum on the bottom of her stiletto, I know she's here for Chase. This isn't the first woman to stop by, but I have to say, it's been a while. It used to happen a lot when he would bring a different woman home every night. It slowed down after he agreed to take things to their place, and it's only happened a couple times since Alec and Lexi moved out and I moved into the master bedroom—telling Chase he could go back to his extracurricular activities here, since we were no longer sharing walls and a bathroom.

"I'm looking for Chase. I left something here the other night."

The other night... That's a lie. Chase hasn't brought anyone home in a long time. But I'm not going to point that out. "He's not here, so whatever you left, you'll have to come back for another time."

I'm about to swing the door shut, when she places her hand on it. "I'll only be a second."

I sigh. "What is it you left?" Maybe I can find it for her and then send her on her slutty stiletto way.

She smirks. "My dildo."

It takes everything in me to keep a straight face. "Your dildo?" I heard her the first time, but I'm hoping she made a mistake.

"I'm sure you know how kinky Chase is..." She winks. "If I could just grab it, that'd be great. It's expensive and my favorite."

A lump forms in my throat. Too many times I heard the noises through the too-thin walls, so I know how sexually active Chase is, but it's hard to hear about it from the mouth of one of the women he's been with, knowing I'm not active at all.

"You'll have to ask Chase for it."

"I would, but I lost his number."

*Or he didn't give it to you...*

Grabbing my phone from my back pocket, I call him.

"Hey, butterfly," he says when he answers.

My heart pitter-patters in my chest at his nickname for me, and for a moment I forget why I'm calling. Until the woman clears her throat at the same time Chase says, "Georgia? Everything okay?"

"Yeah. There's a woman here for you, named..."

"Charleigh," she says.

"Charleigh left her dildo in your room and would like it back because it's expensive and her favorite."

"Fuck," he curses. "Georgia..."

"Do you want me to go into your room to get it, or give her your number?"

"Do not give her my number," he says quickly. "I never gave it to her."

*I didn't think so...*

"Fuck, umm... fuck!" he hisses. "Can I talk to her?"

"Okay," I tell him, handing her the phone, while mentally patting myself on the back for remaining calm, cool, and collected.

She says hello in the most obnoxious, nasally way, and I have to force myself not to roll my eyes.

"But, Chase, it was a hundred dollars," she whines. "How about if we meet up and—" He must cut her off because she stops talking and glares at me. "Okay, fine," she says with a huff before handing me back the phone. "He said I can go in his room and get it."

"Go for it." I open the door and let her in.

I hear Chase's voice, so I put the phone back up to my ear, realizing he didn't hang up. "Hello?"

"I'm so sorry. I told her she can grab what she left. Fuck, I'm—"

"It's okay," I say, not wanting to argue in front of Ms. Dildo. Not that there's anything to fight over. Chase has a past. I knew that.

A moment later she comes sauntering out of his room, holding a bright blue huge-ass dildo. She doesn't say a word, just glares, and then she's out the door.

"Georgia," Chase says. "You there?"

"Yeah, she just left..."

"I hate that I'm at work. Can we talk when I get home?"

"Chase, stop," I tell him, trying to shake the image of him shoving that huge dildo inside her. "It's okay. There's nothing to talk about." And then, because I'm awkward as fuck and can't stop talking, I add, "But maybe if you're holding anyone else's sex toys hostage, you could give them back. Maybe put out an ad for them to come get them..." It's meant as a joke, but it totally falls flat, making me sound jealous and petty. "I'm just kidding. I have some work to do. I'll see you later."

He says okay, sounding sad as hell, and then we hang up.

Since cooking has become something I really enjoy doing, I look up my bookmarked recipes I haven't made yet and get to work making a creamy chicken pasta.

While I'm cooking, I can't stop replaying what happened in my head. When I think about what exactly is bothering me, I come to the conclusion that it's not because he's been with other women, but because he hasn't been with me. And since my plan was to wait until I'm in love, he'll be waiting some time. I don't believe he would cheat on me, especially not after having been cheated on himself, but that doesn't mean he's not going to be left feeling unsatisfied.

When I finish making the food, there's way too much, and it's then I realize I doubled the recipe, making enough for the guys at the station, like I often do. I consider whether to bring them the food. I don't want to distract Chase at his workplace. I also don't want things to be awkward, but maybe showing up there with food will be like a little peace offering. *"It's okay you shoved monster-size dildos into your one-night stands..."* Oh geez, I seriously need to lay off the jokes, even if they're only in my head.

When I arrive, I see Alec first. He smiles and walks over to me, taking the pan of food from me. "We were about to do a run to the store to pick up food for dinner," he says, kissing my cheek. "Chase didn't say you were coming by."

"Shoot! I forgot to tell him." My mind was just so scattered. "I should've asked him first if I could come by."

Alec eyes me. "You don't have to call or ask before coming here, Georgia." Maybe not before, but doesn't that change once you're in a relationship with one of the guys who work here?

"Damn right she doesn't," Chase says, pulling me into a searing kiss that makes my legs feel like Jell-O. "Fuck, I missed you," he murmurs against my lips as he lifts and carries me toward the station.

I faintly hear Alec grumbling something about getting a room, but I'm too distracted by Chase's mouth on mine.

I assume he's just carrying me to the kitchen, so I'm confused when he keeps walking through the station and out another door.

When we finally stop, he pushes me against a wall. I don't know where we are, but my only focus is on Chase. The way he kisses me like he can't get enough of me. The way he makes me feel special and wanted and beautiful.

"Does this mean you forgive me?" he asks.

"There's nothing to forgive." And that's the truth. I refuse to be that insecure woman who gets mad every time her man's past gets brought up. He's thirty years old. Of course he has a past.

Gently, he releases my legs so I drop to the ground. His fingers slide up my bare thigh toward the apex of my legs, but before he makes it up the inside of my shorts, I cover his hand with my own.

"You gave me three orgasms last night and then one this morning. It's your turn..."

Chase's face contorts into a look of confusion. "This isn't a tit for tat..."

"I know, but I want to make sure you're taken care of." It's the least I can do since he's going without sex because of me.

He steps back and tilts his head slightly to the side. We're both quiet for a beat before he speaks. "This is about that woman..."

"It's not about her, but yes, her coming by and me seeing that giant dildo reminded me how different our sexual experiences are."

"I don't give a fuck about that."

"You say that now, but you haven't gone a long time without sex yet."

"A night of being with you the way we were last night means more to me than a thousand nights of meaningless sex." He cages me into his arms and kisses me softly. "I'm falling for you, and I don't give a fuck how long it takes before we have sex. Days, weeks, months, years. I. Don't. Care. I just want to be with you. Understood?"

Warmth spreads through my chest. "Yes."

"Good. Now let's go eat before the guys take all the food. I'm starved."

After we eat, Chase walks me out to my truck, where we make out like teenagers for several minutes before he reluctantly lets me go, only because the tone goes off and he rushes to get the information so they know where they have to go.

Instead of going home, I head to Lexi's, calling her on the way to make sure she's up for company. Since Alec is at work, she'll be alone with Abigail and it'll be the perfect time to have a sisterly talk. But first, I'll go by the coffee shop and get us a couple coffees.

---

"LIKE, HOW BIG?" Lexi asks.

"Big."

"Show me with your hands."

I spread my hands apart and her eyes go wide.

"Holy shit, I don't care how much I love Alec, you won't find me sticking a fake dick the size of an eggplant inside my cooch."

"It's not about the size of the dildo..." I tell her with a laugh.

"Okay, then what is it about?"

"I don't think I want to wait anymore."

She raises a brow. "You are not changing your mind about waiting until you're in love because Chase screwed some dumb skank with a giant squash."

I'm in the middle of taking a sip of my drink, so it all comes out, all over me and the table. Abigail giggles, thinking I'm a riot.

"Things have changed," I tell her, wiping down the table. "I'm going to be twenty-two next month and Chase is thirty. We're both grown adults."

"You're right," she says. "Just make sure you're doing it for the right reasons. Because you like him and want to be with him, and not because you think you have to keep up with the parade of women he had coming in and out of his room."

## CHAPTER SIXTEEN

### CHASE

I walk through the door of the condo, both mentally and physically drained. My eyes are barely able to stay open, but I force them to long enough to find Georgia, who is still asleep and cuddled into her blankets. I peel my clothes off me and then drag myself into her bed, wrapping myself around her body like a human burrito.

She squirms slightly, adjusting to my intrusion, and then turns over so she's snuggled into my chest.

"You smell weird," she says, her voice gravelly from sleep. "Like soap and... something else."

"We were putting out a fire all morning." I hold her tighter, thankful she's alive and safe. I love my job, but days like today suck. "It was out of our zone, but station 116 called for backup."

"Everyone okay?" she asks, her arms encircling my torso.

"The fire started in an apartment on the seventh floor. Everyone got out, except for two. A four-year-old and the babysitter. Parents were out and came home to find their child dead."

Georgia gasps. "I'm so sorry, Chase." She pulls me down to her and kisses the corner of my mouth.

"The babysitter made it... Admitted to smoking and leaving it lit."

"Oh no." She holds me tighter. "That's horrible."

"I'm so damn tired," I tell her, hearing the slur in my words. "I know I said we'd talk when I got home but—"

"Shh," Georgia murmurs. "There's nothing to talk about, Chase. We're good. Just go to sleep."

My eyes meet hers and my heart clenches in my chest, recognizing how different being with Georgia is. I just had a shitty night, the entire time questioning why this world is so fucked up and God is so cruel, but the moment I'm in her arms it's as though everything, even just for a brief moment, is perfect. I know it's only an illusion, and everything on the outside is still there, but maybe that's how it should be when you're with the person you love—as if the entire world, every shitty part of it, fades away while you're together.

---

I WAKE up to find Georgia sitting next to me, typing away on her laptop. When she feels me shift, she stops typing and glances down at me.

"Hey," she says softly.

"Hey." I drag myself up and lean against her headboard. "What time is it?"

"Five."

Shit, I slept the day away. Then I remember why and my stomach sinks. Losing someone in a fire always sucks, but a child... Fuck.

Georgia closes her laptop and sets it on the nightstand, then takes my hand in hers. "I wish there was something I could do or say..."

"You're doing it." I lean over and kiss her. "Why don't we get out of here? Go grab something to eat."

"You sure?"

"Yeah." It will do me some good to get out and be distracted. Especially since I'll be back at work at eight o'clock tomorrow and will need to be in my right mind.

"All right," she agrees.

After we're both showered and dressed, we head out. We're in my vehicle, trying to decide where to go, when my phone rings over Bluetooth, alerting me that my mom is calling.

"Hey, Mom," I say, answering.

"Hey, baby. What are you up to?"

"Nothing. About to grab something to eat. You?"

"I wanted to see if you'd like to go to dinner… You know since it's your birthday."

Georgia gasps. "Today is your birthday?"

*Shit, is it?* "What's today?"

"Chase, don't tell me you forgot your own birthday," Mom chides. "Is that why you ignored all my calls this morning?"

"I was sleeping. Was up all night putting out a fire."

"It's your birthday?" Georgia repeats, glaring at me.

"Who's with you?" Mom asks.

Georgia's eyes go wide, as if now realizing my mom can hear her.

"My girlfriend," I tell my mom, grinning at Georgia.

"What?" she shrieks. "You have a girlfriend? And she didn't know it's your birthday?"

Georgia's back to glaring at me. "He didn't tell me," she says. "Would you like to join us, Ms. Matthews?"

"Oh, please call me Sharon, and I would love to meet you. Have anywhere in mind?"

"Well, since it's Chase's birthday we should go somewhere nice."

I hold my breath, knowing it's going to be somewhere expensive. Georgia is from a different world than my mom and me.

"Oh! How about Zavarelli's in Venice since you love Italian. Have you guys ever been?"

When Mom doesn't say anything, I do. "I don't think either of us has been, but I do love Italian."

"Perfect!" Georgia beams, completely oblivious to the tension in the car and over the phone.

Mom clears her throat. "Okay, I'll, umm, see you guys soon." I know she was planning to pay since she always does for my birthday, but I have no doubt this restaurant will be out of her budget.

When we arrive, my suspicions are confirmed. The place is expensive. While we wait for my mom to arrive, Georgia puts our name down for a table and I glance at the menu. Shit, over fifty dollars a plate. There's no way my mom is going to be okay eating here.

"Hey, Georgia, if there's a wait we can go somewhere else."

She frowns. "It's only a few minutes, but if you don't want to eat here..."

"It's not that," I tell her, pulling her into my arms. "But my mom always insists on paying for my birthday dinner. Growing up we didn't have shit for money, but every year for my sister's and my birthday, my parents would take us out to dinner." It was literally the only time we ever went out to dinner.

Georgia's brows furrow in confusion. "You only went out to dinner twice a year?" She's not judging. She's curious. Because she wasn't raised like I was, where eating out was a luxury people in my neighborhood couldn't afford.

"Yeah, it became a tradition. And she's going to want to pay tonight, but..."

Georgia nods in understanding, her face falling. Damn it, I didn't mean to upset her. "I'm sorry. I didn't even think."

"No, don't be sorry. You didn't know and you were trying to be nice."

My phone dings with a message from Mom: **I'm sorry, I can't make it after all. Rain check?**

I try to hide the text from Georgia, but she sees it before I can. "How far do you live from here?" she asks.

"About thirty minutes. Why?"

"Tell your mom we'll be there in forty-five minutes." She takes my hand and speed walks to my car. I do as she says and then pocket my phone.

After a quick trip to the grocery store, I pull up to my childhood home, hoping my mom had enough time to pick up. She'll be embarrassed if we walk in on the place in less than perfect condition.

Georgia and I grab the bags of groceries she bought—without letting me see—and walk up to the front door. Before I can knock, Mom swings the door open. "I just got your text. What are you doing here?"

"The restaurant didn't have any availability," Georgia lies. "So, I thought we could make dinner here." She holds up the bags. "I'm learning how to cook and have been dying to make Margherita pizza. We could all make it and hang out... I also brought a cake."

Mom's gaze flits between Georgia and me and then her eyes light up. "That sounds perfect." Georgia walks inside, heading straight to the kitchen, while my mom and I hang back for a second.

She pulls me into a hug. "Happy Birthday. I'm so glad you're here."

"C'mon, you two," Georgia yells. "If I have to make it all myself, I'll be eating it all myself."

Mom laughs. "I've only known her for a minute, but I can already tell she's different..." *Than Victoria*, she means but doesn't voice.

"She definitely is," I agree.

When I step farther into the house, noticing how clean it is, she says, "Since the day you came over... that night..." Of the anniversary of my sister's death. "I've been making some changes."

"Really?"

"I saw how scared you were for that girl at the hospital and I didn't want you to feel that way toward me."

I take a look around again with new eyes and see just how clean the place is. "That's good, Mom," I tell her.

"I've also broken up with my boyfriend," she admits proudly. "He wasn't any good. I'm taking some time for myself."

"Good," I tell her again, kissing her temple. "I'm proud of you."

The night is spent with delicious food and great conversation. My mom and Georgia hit it off, despite how different they are, and I know it's because of Georgia. Because even though she's worth millions, she doesn't act like it. She's real and sweet and doesn't have a judgmental bone in her body, and fuck if tonight didn't make me fall even more in love with her.

"You know," she says, when we get home. "I saw in a movie once that the man gets birthday sex." She waggles her brows playfully.

I halt in my place. "Butterfly..." Is she saying what I think she's saying?

She saddles up next to me. "I like you and you like me..." Actually, I'm in love with her, but we won't go there right now. "And we're both adults. I don't see why we have to wait."

"Because you said you didn't want to have sex until you're in love," I remind her.

"So, my plans changed." She shrugs shyly.

I'm all about letting a woman make her own decisions, but the fact that she's saying this right after that chick showed up to get her fake dick tells me she might not be thinking clearly.

"There's no rush," I tell her, taking her into my arms and placing her on the bed. "We have our entire lives to be together." Before she can argue, I connect my mouth with hers, silencing her.

## CHAPTER SEVENTEEN

### GEORGIA

"He won't have sex with me."

Mom snorts and Lexi laughs.

"I'm being serious. Because I told him I want to wait until I'm in love, he won't have sex with me." It's been almost three weeks since Chase's birthday dinner and he meant what he said about it not being a rush. That night, while he refused to let me give him birthday sex, he did get a birthday blowjob... But that was it. He won't take things any further. We make out, give each other orgasms, but he always stops before we have sex.

I even tried to get him drunk the night of Lexi's and my birthday outing, but he wasn't having it. He did give me some amazing orgasms that night, before we fell asleep in each other's arms.

"I think that's romantic," Mom says.

Lexi and I both roll our eyes at the same time.

"Well, it's going to happen," I tell them. "And tonight."

"Tonight?" Lexi confirms.

"Yep. For one, I'm in love with him, and two, I'm ready."

"You're in love with him?" Mom asks, covering her heart with her hand.

"I am, and I want to take this next step with him. Even if we don't work out down the road, I won't regret being with him."

"Then it seems like you're ready," Mom says. "Are you on birth control?"

"Yep. And we've both been tested, so we know we're clean. I want it to be special... Chase has to work late, so I'm planning to cook him dinner when he gets home. I want to buy some lingerie."

Lexi laughs. "Alec never appreciates the lingerie. He just wants to rip it off."

"Same thing with Tristan," Mom adds.

"Mom!" We both groan at the same time.

"What?" she says. "It's girl talk. I can't help that your father is who I'm having sex with." She shrugs. "So, you want to buy lingerie? There's only one place to go: Agent Provocateur."

---

**Chase: On my way home. Want me to pick up dinner?**

**Me: Nope, dinner is made. ;)**

I SHAKE OUT MY HANDS, trying to get rid of my nerves. I'm not nervous about having sex with Chase. I'm ready. I've talked to my mom and sister about what to expect and researched as well. I know it seems like overkill, but I want to be prepared. What I'm nervous about is Chase turning me down. I'm putting myself out there and I'll be devastated if he tells me he doesn't want to have sex with me yet.

I considered serving dinner first then giving him me for dessert, but then I wondered if we would be too full and it would make us both feel gross—well, specifically me since I bought a skimpy piece of lingerie and want to look sexy in it. After eating a meal, I'll probably look pregnant with a food baby.

So, instead, I'm serving dessert first: me on a platter, er, well, in the bed. Since I'm already dressed in the lingerie, with my hair done—I went with natural waves—and just a bit of makeup on, I climb onto the bed and position myself in the center, ignoring how stupid, instead of sexy, I feel. The lights are dimmed and I lit a couple of candles on each side of the bed for ambiance.

The door opens and closes and then I hear Chase's footsteps

getting louder, the closer he gets. "Butterfly," he calls out as he opens the door. He stops in his place, taking me in, and I wait with bated breath for his reaction.

When he doesn't say anything for several long seconds, I curse myself. Maybe the candles were too much...

But then his hazel eyes lock with mine and I see the lust filled in them. He kicks his shoes off and then walks over to the bed, sitting on the edge. "Was expecting dinner, not dessert," he says, always on the same page as me. "This is a pleasant surprise."

He pulls his shirt off, exposing his six-pack abs he works hard for, and then crawls onto the bed so he's kneeling in front of me. He spreads my legs slightly so he can fit between them and drags his hands up my bare thighs. "You look gorgeous," he says, dropping his hands to either side of my head and kissing me. "I'm the luckiest fucking guy in the world to have you to come home to."

He kisses me again, this time slipping his tongue between my parted lips. Before things get hot and heavy, I have something I need to tell him, so I pull back slightly.

"I'm ready," I tell him, needing him to know this isn't just me getting sexy. "I know it's only a short time since we've been together, but you've quickly come to mean so much to me." I cradle his face with my hands, needing the connection. "I've fallen in love with you, Chase, and I know without a doubt I'm ready to have sex with you."

The most beautiful smile spreads across his lips. "It's about damn time you caught up to me," he says, shocking the hell out of me. "I've known I was in love with you since the night I saw you in the hospital."

I gasp. The night of the hospital? That was several weeks ago... "You've loved me since then?"

"Yeah, but I didn't want to scare you off." He shrugs. "I love you, butterfly, so damn much."

"I love you too."

Our mouths unite, and our tongues meet, swirling against each other. Chase uses one hand to hold himself up, and the other explores my body. When we break apart, coming up for air, he peppers soft, open-mouthed kisses along my jaw and neck. His face dips and his lips cover my nipple, sucking on it through the silky material.

"Did you buy this for me?" he asks, running his palm downward and landing on my hip.

"Yes," I breathe.

He smiles softly. "Then I won't rip it off your body."

He sits up and gently peels the straps off my shoulders, pulling them down my arms and exposing my breasts. He takes one into his mouth, swirling his tongue around the hardened nipple. I squirm, like I always do, wanting more.

I reach down and unbutton his jeans, and then Chase pulls them down the rest of the way, removing his socks and briefs, leaving him naked.

My gaze goes to his hardened length, excited to finally have it inside me. I wouldn't admit it to Lexi, since she lost her virginity when she was younger, but I'm glad I waited until now. Until I'm old enough to understand my body and Chase's. Until it was with someone I love.

Chase tugs my negligée off the rest of my body, leaving me in only the tiny G-string that barely covers anything.

He situates himself between my parted legs and then kisses the top of my mound through the thin material. I sit up on my elbows, so I can watch as Chase drags the material off my legs and drops it off the side of the bed.

The second the flat of his tongue laves up my center, my eyes roll upward and I drop onto my back. He plunges two fingers inside of me, filling me completely, and the pleasure intensifies. Every time he does this, I feel so full, I can't imagine how good it'll feel once his dick is inside me. I squirm at the thought, just as my orgasm hits me like a tidal wave, waves of pleasure washing through me.

I've barely come down from my high, when Chase is on me. His mouth crushes mine, as his body connects with my own. He parts my thighs with his and then he enters me. I try to stay relaxed, but it's hard when it hurts so badly.

"Breathe, butterfly," he murmurs against my mouth.

I do as he says, and then he pushes past the barrier of my virginity.

"You okay?"

"Yeah," I tell him, dragging my fingers through his hair. "Keep going."

With his arms caging me in, and our bodies flush against one another, Chase slowly and gently and deeply makes love to me. He tells me how good I feel, how much he loves me, and when he finds his release, draining every drop into me, I've never felt so cherished in my life.

## CHAPTER EIGHTEEN

### GEORGIA

*Beep. Beep. Beep. Beep.*

I pry my eyes open as Chase's alarm goes off, reaching over and hitting end so the noise will stop. Once it's quiet again, I glance over and find Chase passed out on the other side of the bed. He's lying on his back, naked, with one of his arms over his head, and the blanket covering the bottom half of him. My thighs clench in memory of both times we made love last night. The second time with him making sure I came as well.

My heart swells at how selfless and caring he is. I don't know why his ex-wife cheated on him, but I can't imagine wanting anyone but him for the rest of my life. Her loss is definitely my gain.

"Either stop staring, or get over here and ride me," he says, his voice raspy from sleep.

When I laugh at his grumpy playfulness, he smirks, wrenching open one eyelid. "I wasn't kidding." He throws the blanket off him and exposes his hard as steel dick.

I crawl over to him, ignoring the soreness between my legs, and climb onto his body. My hands go to his shoulders and his find my hips. We work together to guide his shaft into me, both of us moaning once he's completely seated in me.

"I could live like this," he says, reaching up and brushing my hair out of my face. "Inside you... It's my new favorite spot in the world."

He grips the back of my mane and pulls my face down to his. His tongue traces my bottom lip, then my top, before it slips past my parted lips—teasing, caressing. His skilled mouth devours mine, as he starts to move inside of me. I had assumed since I was on top I would be in control, but Chase's actions, as he fucks me from the bottom, deeply, steadily, say otherwise.

The way we move has my climax building quickly, and too soon, my entire body is trembling in pleasure as the most mind-blowing orgasm grips me.

"Fuck," he groans. "Your pussy is so damn tight." His eyes squeeze closed, and his dick swells inside of me. A second later, warm seed is filling me. As if coming drained him of all strength, he releases his hold on me and sighs deeply.

"Yep," he says softly. "I could definitely live right here inside of you. The outside world be damned."

After we've showered together, where he gives me one more orgasm, telling me it's to tide me over for the next twenty-four hours while he's on shift, he heads to work.

After meeting Lexi for breakfast, where I gush about how amazing being with Chase is, and we share stories about our guys, I go home and spend the next several hours working. When I'm all caught up, I lie on the couch, wishing Chase were here, and binge watch an old show.

As my eyes are closing, a text comes in from Chase: **I have to cover for a guy tomorrow morning, so I won't be home until later, but I want to take you out. Be ready for 5:00.**

Butterflies swarm my belly.

**Me: Will do.**

At five o'clock on the dot the next day, there's a knock on the door. I groan, seriously hoping it's not another one of Chase's sex toy skanks.

Reluctantly, I get up and open the door, mentally preparing myself. Only it's Chase on the other side, dressed in a pair of black dress pants and a royal blue button-down shirt with the sleeves rolled up to his elbows.

Before I can ask him why he's knocking on his own door, he pulls a bouquet of multicolored flowers out from behind his back, and my heart flutters. "For me?" I ask dumbly. I've never been given flowers before.

Chase chuckles. "For you."

"Thank you. They're beautiful." I take them from him and bring them into the kitchen. They're already in a pretty vase, so I just add water then set them on the center of the table.

"You look beautiful," he says, his eyes traveling down the length of my body. I'm dressed in a floral print dress that stops several inches above my knee and ties in the front, exposing a bit of cleavage. I've paired it with my black Saint Laurent peep toe heels.

"Thank you. Do you keep clothes at work?"

Chase's expression turns nervous. "I, um, well, I used to leave from work sometimes and go out..." Ah, during his playboy days.

He clears his throat. "You ready to go? We have reservations at six and you know how traffic is around here."

Flowers... reservations... "Are you trying to romance me?"

Chase throws his head back with a laugh. "Yeah." He closes the distance between us. "That's what boyfriends do, butterfly. We romance our girlfriends."

*Not all boyfriends do that,* I think but don't voice out loud.

"Okay, but just so you know, I'm already a sure thing, so if it's to get in my pants, it's unnecessary."

Chase chokes on his laughter. "Good to know." He kisses the corner of my mouth. "But it's not to get in your pants. It's to remain in your heart." My heart stammers in my chest. I didn't know love could feel like this, and I'm so thankful I didn't give up on finding it. If I had, I wouldn't be here with Chase.

We arrive at Cove 54 a few minutes before our reservation and are brought to our table right away. After the waitress reads off the drink specials, since it's a bit of a special occasion, I order an Apple Pie martini. Chase orders a Coke.

When the waitress walks away, Chase raises a brow. "An Apple Pie martini?"

"What? It sounds good, and we are on a date... I figured I would adult."

He laughs. "Okay, *adult*. How was your day?"

"Good. Yesterday, I met my mom and Lex for breakfast. It was nice. I got a lot of work done. Went for a jog..."

The waitress sets our drinks down and I take a sip. It's delicious. Fruity and sweet. We order our meals, and once she's excused herself I ask Chase how work was.

"It's been unseasonably dry, so the amount of fires have been higher than usual. Hopefully it rains soon."

We spend our meal flitting from one subject to the next. I love how well we click and how our conversations are comfortable and flow easily. I don't have to think about what to say, it all just comes naturally.

When dinner is over, Chase declines dessert, telling me he knows a place that has the best homemade ice cream sandwiches. When he was little and he and his sister would get good grades, his mom would take them here. It was a bit of a drive, but worth it.

It's within walking distance from the restaurant, so with his hand in mine, we walk there. There's a bit of a line, but it moves quickly.

"One chocolate chip cookie dough ice cream sandwich," he tells the woman.

"We're sharing?"

"Trust me, they're huge."

After he pays, she hands him the dessert. He's right. It's more than big enough for two people. The cookie is gigantic and is bent in half like a taco, with the ice cream in the middle.

"It's not a sandwich. It's a taco!"

"Yeah, a delicious taco."

We walk away from the ice cream place until we arrive at a more secluded spot. There's a small pond with benches surrounding the area. Instead of sitting on the bench, Chase and I sit on the grass near the water.

"How are we supposed to eat this monster-sized ice cream taco?"

"Like this." He lifts the taco and brings it to my lips, so I can take a bite. It's sweet and cold and delicious.

"Mmm... So good." I go to take another bite, but he pulls it back over his head, reminding me of when he stole my laptop and did the same thing.

"Uh-uh, you have to share," he says with a smirk.

Unlike last time, he's on the ground with me, and within reach. Before he realizes what I'm doing, I climb into his lap, straddling his thighs. Out of shock, he falls back slightly, just barely holding on to the ice cream.

I reach for the ice cream and pluck it out of his hand. "You share," I tell him, taking a big bite.

He laughs, then his arms go around my waist. He lifts his upper body up, colliding with my own, and his mouth crashes against mine. His tongue delves between my lips, swirling against mine. "Mmm... you taste delicious," he murmurs against my mouth.

My center grinds against his pelvis, and I feel the hard bulge in his pants. I glance around and it's dark, not a person in sight. It would be so easy... too easy...

I drop the ice cream into the grass and Chase groans, as if he knows what I'm about to do. "Baby, someone might see," he starts, but I shut him up with my mouth.

I quickly undo his zipper and pull his dick out of its confines. Since I'm in a dress, I simply pull my panties to the side and then guide myself onto Chase. To anyone walking by, it would look like I'm just sitting in his lap.

"Fuck, butterfly," he grunts, when I lift up slightly and then slam down. Without any foreplay, I'm tight around him, to the point it's almost painful.

His mouth latches onto my neck, sucking and licking my sensitive flesh. His fingers pinch my nipple, tweaking and pulling on the erect nub through the thin material of my dress and bra. His other hand finds its way under my dress and lands on my clit, massaging gentle circles across it. Soon, I'm soaking wet, sliding up and down his shaft. And then I'm coming. Hard. His mouth connects with mine, muffling my sounds of pleasure, as he chases and finds his own orgasm.

When we've both come down from our highs, out of breath and spent, he chuckles softly, his eyes meeting mine. "You never cease to amaze me," he says softly, kissing me hard on the mouth. "It's the most beautiful thing, to watch you spread your wings and fly."

## CHAPTER NINETEEN

### GEORGIA

**Me: You guys up for some lunch?**

I'VE BEEN WORKING all morning on designing a new website for a huge internet-based company and when I finally came up for air, I realized I hadn't eaten all day and I'm starving... and missing Chase. He's been busy at the station the last several days because one of the guys on another shift moved and they need to hire someone to replace him. Since they're short a man, he and a few other guys have been covering the guy's shift, which means, aside from the couple nights he slips into my bed and makes love to me before disappearing before I wake up, we've barely seen each other.

**Chase: Made by you? Always. We're just getting back from a house call, so we're all starved.**

I find a recipe I have all the ingredients for, and once I'm done making it, I package it up in a container and drive over to the station. I park my truck and grab the dish, and am walking up the drive, when I hear something. I stop and listen. Crying.

I glance around but don't see anyone. Setting the food down on a bench in the garage, I walk slowly toward where the crying is coming from, until I find a stroller with a baby in it near the front door. I rush over to it and look around for the owner of the baby. Who in the hell would leave a crying baby here?

Unable to handle the sound of the baby crying, I pick her up to try to soothe her. Luckily, it's fall in October and in the seventies. Even with the temperature on the cooler side, she's still warm. Her face is red and splotchy from crying and when she looks up at me with her beautiful, tear-filled hazel eyes, my heart is physically removed from my chest.

"Shh, it's okay, pretty girl." I hold her close, hoping to slow her crying down, and thankfully it works.

"Mamamamma," she stammers through her cries.

I wipe the tears from under her eyes. "I don't know where she is," I tell her. "But we'll figure it out."

"Georgia," Alec says, walking around the corner. "What are you— Is that a baby? What are you doing with a baby?"

"I found her here," I tell him, holding her close to my chest. Most likely exhausted from all the crying, she lays her head on my shoulder and snuggles into me.

"Let's bring her inside and see if there's a note or something in her stroller," Alec suggests.

He grabs the stroller and I follow him in, rubbing the baby's back. Her cries have finally stopped and she's quiet, twirling a piece of my hair with her finger.

We walk inside and the guys all swing their heads my way, each sporting a different look of confusion.

"That's not Abigail, is it?" Luke asks.

"No," I tell him. This baby is bigger, probably several months older than my niece. "I found her at the front door."

"What the fuck?" Thomas says. "Nobody rang the doorbell."

Chase walks in, taking in the sight in front of him, and says, "What's going on?"

"I heard a baby crying, so I went to check it out and found her in a stroller by the front door."

"What the hell?" Chase says.

"Maybe she thought she could leave the baby because of the SafePlace sign," I point out.

"It's for the youth, not for parents abandoning their children," Chase says in disgust.

"Well, she obviously cared enough to leave her somewhere safe," I tell him, sitting in a chair. "It's better than harming her or leaving her somewhere she could be hurt."

"I found a note," Alec says. His eyes meet Chase's and something about the expression on his face has my belly doing a flip-flop. "It's addressed to you."

"Me?" Chase walks over and takes the envelope from Alec. He takes one look at it and curses under his breath.

He rips it open and unfolds the note inside. While he reads it, everyone is quiet, but when the little girl in my arms lifts her head to look at me, and her hazel eyes meet mine, I already know what the note says.

"She's mine," Chase murmurs. "According to my fucking bitch of an ex-wife she's mine." His eyes meet mine before they land on the baby. "Her name is Hazel."

I find myself holding her tighter now that I know she's Chase's daughter. I don't want to judge Victoria, but that doesn't stop me from wondering how she could do this to him.

"Her birth certificate lists a Raymond Forrester as the dad," Alec says, "and based on this, she was born January first, making her ten months old."

"That's the guy she was cheating on me with," Chase says. "She was pregnant while we were still married and didn't say a damn word."

"What does the letter say?" I ask.

"She wanted her to be Raymond's but when she was born and had my hazel eyes she knew she wasn't. She didn't want to lose him, so she lied. Hazel had a herniated belly button and when they brought her in to have the surgery they asked for the parent with her matching blood type to donate blood in case there's an emergency since she has a rare blood type. Neither parent matched and he threatened to leave her, saying he won't raise another man's baby." Chase tosses the letter to me. "She chose him over her daughter."

I shake my head and place the letter on the table. I don't need to read it. All I want to do right now is hold this precious little girl.

"So, what do we do?" I ask.

Chase's hard expression softens. "Fuck, I love you."

"What?" I ask, confused.

"You said 'we'."

"Of course I did..." Because we're a *we* and I'll be by his side every step of the way.

"Mamamama," Hazel murmurs, taking my face in her hands. "Mama."

My eyes meet Chase's and he shakes his head. "I can't believe she did this."

"Do you want to hold her?" I ask, standing.

His eyes go wide. "I..."

"You hold Abigail all the time," Alec jumps in. "You got this."

I notice everyone else has left the room, obviously wanting to give Chase some privacy and space. "Hazel," I say, stepping over to Chase. "This is your daddy."

Slowly, I hand her off to Chase, but as we're making the exchange, she grasps ahold of my shirt. "Mamamamama," she screams, her eyes filling with tears.

"You found her, so she feels safe with you," Alec says.

I glance at Chase, who looks completely heartbroken. "Hey, she'll get to know you," I tell him. "She's just scared."

"And she knows how good you are," he says, cupping the side of my face. "I don't blame her for wanting to remain close to you. I feel the same way." He kisses the corner of my mouth.

"I think we should call DCFS," Alec suggests. "Make sure you do it the right way so she can't take her away from you since you're not legally the father yet."

"I agree." Chase pulls out his phone. "But first, I'm hiring an attorney."

He calls several attorneys, including the ones my dad and Alec's mom recommends, but at the end of each call, instead of hiring them, he keeps thanking them and hanging up.

"What's going on?" I ask him, concerned. After rocking Hazel, she fell asleep, so I laid her down on the couch, creating a barrier so she's safe. Since Carter was in the room watching TV, he said he'd keep an eye on her.

When Chase doesn't answer right away, I take his hand in mine. "Don't shut me out. What's wrong with all these attorneys?"

He sighs. "I can't afford them. LA is expensive as hell. I have some money in savings, but it won't be enough if we run into any problems, and then I'll have to switch attorneys. I have a couple credit cards, but I need to buy her stuff..." He sounds so damn defeated, and my heart aches for him.

"Who do you want to hire?"

He eyes the list he's made. "The guy Mila recommended sounded good. He's a little older, but handled her divorce."

"Then hire him," I tell him.

"Georgia, I can't let you—"

"Yes, you can, and you will. We're in this together. I have more money than I'll ever spend in my lifetime. Money I received from a man who hurt my mom and neglected me." Tears fill my eyes, but I force them back. "There's *nothing* I would rather spend that money on than to help a father get custody of his little girl."

Three hours later, Chase has hired attorney Ben Schneider. Ben has filed for emergency custody based on Victoria's note and has an appointment scheduled for Chase to take a court-appointed paternity test tomorrow, as well as a court date scheduled for next week.

Hazel has woken up, and after looking through her bag and finding some baby food but no bottles, and speaking to Abigail's pediatrician who assures me at this point it's okay to feed her regular soft food, I heat up some sweet potatoes I brought that was part of the lunch for the guys and feed them to her. I also shred some of the chicken and feed her that as well. She eats while sitting in my lap, the entire time banging on the table and giggling at Chase and Alec, who make faces at her.

"Chief said I can use the personal days and vacation time I've accumulated to take some time off and get Hazel situated," Chase says a little while later.

"Good. We can go by the store and order her stuff and have it delivered. While we're there, we can get anything else she needs like clothes and diapers and wipes..." I start making a mental list of everything she'll need.

"What about a car seat?" he asks.

"It's attached to her stroller."

After installing her car seat into my truck, since she doesn't want to leave my side, Chase and I head home to drop off his car and then go to the baby store.

I place Hazel into the shopping cart and she looks around curiously while I wheel it through the store. Noticing that Chase is completely out of his element, I take over, grabbing everything we might need. On occasion I ask him for his opinion and he gives it to me, but for the most part, he lets me do my thing. I'm not a mom, obviously, but I was there with Lexi while she was buying everything for Abigail, and my cousin Micaela also has two babies—RJ, who's two and a half, and Dustin, who's six months old.

While we're walking through the clothing section, Hazel reaches out and grabs a onesie, making us both laugh.

"Do you want this, pretty girl?" I ask, finding her size and handing it to her.

Her face lights up as she brings it to her mouth, munching on the fabric. "I think she likes it," Chase says with a soft smile aimed at his daughter.

After ordering a complete nursery and paying extra for next day delivery, we check out with the cashier and then head home. We're both exhausted, so we go through a Starbucks drive-thru to get caffeinated, and once we're home, I play with Hazel while Chase brings everything in and then sets up the portable crib-slash-play pen, so she has somewhere to sleep tonight.

"Where should we put it?" he asks.

"Either my room or yours..."

"About that," he says, gripping the curves of my hips. "I know we have an extra room, but I was thinking, what if we kept the spare room as is and cleaned out my room for her nursery?"

I tilt my head to the side, pretending like I have no idea where he's going with this, and he laughs.

"Fine, I'll spell it out for you." He tugs me closer, glancing over at Hazel, who's on a blanket on the floor, happily banging on her new toys.

"Will you officially move in with me?" His brows dip. "Or I guess, can I officially move in with you?"

I laugh at his silliness. "Yes, I would love for you to move in with me." I wink saucily, making him chuckle.

"So, we put her crib thing in my room?" he asks.

"I think since this is a new place and we're pretty much strangers to her, we should put it in our room."

"I agree," he says with a grin.

Once it's set up, we feed her and then give her a bath. By eight o'clock, she's half-yawning, half-whining, telling us it's time for her to go to bed.

"You want to try to put her to bed?" I ask Chase, handing him Hazel. In the last few hours she's really warmed up to him.

He's hesitant at first but nods in agreement, taking her from me. I hold my breath, praying she won't cry, and release it when she lays her head down on his shoulder.

I watch as he rocks her to sleep, and when he's not looking, I pull out my phone and take a picture. It's the first one of him and his daughter. Tomorrow, I'll print and frame it.

Since neither of us is ready to go to bed yet, after Chase lays her down in her temporary bed, while I click on the baby monitor, we tiptoe out to the living room, both of us dropping onto the couch in exhaustion.

"I couldn't have done this today without you," Chase says, pulling me into his lap. I straddle his thighs and run my fingers through his hair. "I was so damn shocked and scared... I didn't know which way was up."

"Yes, you could've. And you would've. Because you're an amazing man and her father, and I can already tell you love her."

"I do," he admits. "I'm so damn mad at Victoria, but I'm also so grateful that she gave me that precious little girl." He shakes his head. "It's so fucked up."

"You can't change what happened, but you can control how you handle it, and you're handling it." I kiss the corner of his mouth. "And I must admit, watching you rock her to sleep was the sexiest thing I've ever seen."

## CHAPTER TWENTY

### GEORGIA

"What are we doing with this dresser?" Chase asks.

I glance at it. It's Lexi's old bedroom set. It's in perfect condition, but we don't need it, and I doubt she'll want it. "Let's put it out front and call one of those donation places to pick it up."

Hazel cries from her crib, letting us know she's awake. "I'll grab her," Chase says.

I step over to the dresser and pull the top drawer out. It's filled with Chase's shirts. I pull them out and place them on the bed, then open the next drawer. Each one is filled with clothes. I'll need to make room in my dresser for all of this stuff.

"Hey, butterfly, do you remember how much—" Chase's words are cut off when I open the bottom drawer, finding what looks like an entire sex toy shop in there, and gasp in shock.

"Shit," he says. "I was supposed to clean that out, and then Hazel..." He thrusts the baby at me then slams the drawer shut. "This was before you... way before you."

I'm speechless. There must've been fifty different types of toys in there.

Chase hauls ass out of the room and then back in with a bag. But before he opens the drawer, he glances at me. "Hazel's hungry."

He's trying to dismiss me so I won't see all the toys. Too late for that. I nod and take her out to the kitchen, setting her in her high chair, and then go about preparing some mashed up veggies and meat, all while trying to rid my brain of the sight of all those toys. I have questions... so many damn questions.

A few minutes later, he passes by us with the bag in his hand, opening and closing the front door. He must be throwing it out in the dumpster. When he comes back in, we work in silence to rid his room of the furniture, and just as we're finishing, the furniture company with Hazel's stuff arrives. The day flies by, and by the time everything is set up and Hazel is in her own room asleep, we're both drained. Normally parents have months to prepare for a baby, not hours.

I'm showering the day off, when Chase steps into the shower to join me. His arms encircle me from behind, and he presses a soft kiss to my shoulder, making me sigh under his touch.

"I'm sorry," he murmurs into my ear.

"You have nothing to be sorry for."

"I said I didn't want anyone else in our relationship, in the bedroom, but by not getting rid of that shit, I brought them in."

"Can I ask you a question?" It's something I've been thinking about all day.

"You can always ask me anything." He spins me around so we're facing each other and backs me against the wall.

"Did you use those same toys on different women?"

He shakes his head. "Most of what you saw was still new. Only a couple toys had been used and I was planning to throw them away, but I forgot. I wasn't about to drop a dildo into our garbage can."

"So you keep a stash of toys for when women come over?"

"*Came* over," he corrects. "Past tense, because the only woman I've been with in several months is you. But yeah." He averts his eyes, looking slightly uncomfortable. "I kept them for when women came over."

I nod even though he can't see it since he's not looking at me. "I better get out in case Hazel wakes up." She's actually a very good sleeper, and independent. She rarely cries or fusses. I'm afraid to think it's because she was neglected.

He sighs but moves his hand so I can get out. After drying off and getting dressed, I go to bed, feigning sleep when Chase comes in a few minutes later. I feel the bed dip, but he doesn't try to hold me like he usually does. I want to roll over and say something, but I'm upset and don't know how to deal with it. He probably thinks I'm mad about the toys, but I'm not. I can't change what he did before us nor would I want to. I love Chase the way he is. What I'm upset about it is the fact that we've been sleeping together for a while now and he hasn't once tried or mentioned using a single toy.

---

**Me: Can we meet without kids?**

**Lexi: Sure! Alec is off today so he can stay with Abigail. Where?**

I TYPE out the address of the location and tell her to meet me in an hour.

"I'm meeting with my sister," I tell Chase, who's lying on the floor, playing with Hazel.

"Everything okay?" he asks. We haven't talked since I found the toys yesterday, and we need to. But first there's something I need to do.

"Yeah, I won't be gone long."

I bend at the knees and give Hazel a kiss. She glances up at me and grins her adorable toothy grin. "I can pick up lunch on my way back."

"Sounds good."

I'm about to stand, when Chase grips the back of my neck and tugs me into him for a kiss that feels like so much more than just a kiss. It's a plea, an apology, a declaration.

"I love you," he murmurs against my lips.

"I love you too."

---

"A SEX SHOP?" Lexi laughs. "You kinky little bitch!"

I roll my eyes. "I found an entire drawer of sex toys in Chase's room when we were moving his stuff from his room to mine."

Lexi's eyes go wide. "Damn, so Chase is the kinky one."

"Nobody's kinky," I groan. "I read an article on sex toys and a lot of them help heighten the pleasure."

"Hmm... Maybe I'll pick out a few things to surprise Alec with." Lexi waggles her brows.

We enter the store and the woman at the desk, who is dressed in sexy lingerie and wearing blood red lipstick, smiles. "My name is Jenn. Let me know if you need any help."

I pull out my phone and open the list I've made. "I need to buy this stuff," I tell her, turning the phone around so she can see it.

"Right this way." She stops in front of a wall of dildos. "Do you know which size you'd like?"

I think about the article I read. It said to get one around the same size as your significant other's. "Around eight inches."

Lexi snorts, then laughs. "Oh my God. Is that the size of Chase's dick?"

"Can you act like a mature adult about this, please?" I brought her here because I was scared to death to come alone, but now I'm rethinking that.

"Sorry. I'll take one too. But make mine eight *and a half* inches." She winks, and the woman laughs.

"Mine was a guess. I didn't actually measure him."

After we both pick out our choice of dildos, we move on to the next item.

"Oh, shit," Lexi says. "Butt plugs? You're totally going to let him in the back door, aren't you? Now, that's love."

Jenn shakes with laughter. "This one is a customer favorite." She hands me the silver teardrop-shaped toy. It's kind of heavy and has a pretty blue jewel at the front of it. "You'll need lube too." She plucks a bottle off the shelf. "Never allow anyone in the back door without proper preparation."

I read that in the article as well.

"I want one with a yellow jewel," Lexi says, grabbing it off the wall, along with a bottle of lube. "And I'm going to need to read this article you read."

We go from area to area, getting all the items on my list, and a

## CHAPTER TWENTY

few others Jenn suggests, and once we're done we both check out—Lexi having bought everything I did.

"This was fun," she says once we're outside in the parking lot. Then her face goes serious. "You're doing all this because you want to, though, right? Not because you feel like you have to, to keep Chase."

"Chase hasn't once asked me to use toys."

"So you're doing this because you think he wants to?"

I've thought a lot about this since that sexy toy slut came by to pick up her dildo. "I'm doing it because I want to. Because he obviously has the toys for a reason, and I've heard the way those women would scream in pleasure. Every time he touches me, he brings me pleasure. I think he hasn't brought up the toys because he sees me as this delicate little flower, and I don't want to be that person. I'm *not* that person." At least not anymore...

"He thinks I'm mad because he used those toys with women before me, but I'm hurt he doesn't want to use them with me. Up until now, we've been open and honest with each other. I don't know why he's shutting me out regarding this matter, but I'm going to force him to talk to me. Then hopefully, get him to use them with me."

Lexi nods thoughtfully. "You're a different person with him. And not in a bad way. I never would've thought he would be the guy for you, but after seeing you two together, I can see that you're both crazy in love with each other. You're good for each other."

After a few more minutes of talking, we hug goodbye, with the promise to meet later this week to get Abigail and Hazel together—and to discuss which toys are the best—Lexi's suggestion, not mine.

I stop by the deli to pick up lunch, then head home. Chase is sitting on the couch, watching a baseball game on TV. When I walk in, he pauses it. "Hazel just went down for her afternoon nap."

I set the food on the table, then head back to our room to hide the bag of toys in my drawer for later. We eat lunch, steering clear of any sex toy talk, focusing on Hazel and what the lawyer said, and once she's awake, since it's nice out, we take her for a walk to the park.

"No, pretty girl. Don't eat the sand," I tell her, removing her hand from her mouth.

Her cute little face scrunches up at the word no, making Chase and me laugh.

"How about the swings?" Chase suggests, lifting her up and flying her through the air like she's a plane to take her mind off the sand. He's so good with her, and I love to watch them both. The way she's accepted him so completely... it's as if she knows he's her dad. I don't have any other babies to compare her to, since I've never lived with one, but I thought the transition would be rougher. Instead, she shocked us by warming up to both of us.

Chase sets her in the swing and buckles her in. Her mouth immediately goes to the plastic piece in the front, and I half-gag, while Chase places a blanket in the front.

"She's like a puppy," he says with a laugh. "Chewing on everything."

"She's probably teething." We've been busy reading about babies every chance we get, since neither of us had any notice we'd be getting one, and we both want to know what to expect.

"I talked to your mom earlier," Chase says nonchalantly.

"Oh really?" They've spoken a few times since Hazel's come into our life. My mom is supportive, hell, both my parents are, and have offered to help in any way they can.

"Your parents are going to take Hazel tonight." His eyes meet mine. "So we can talk."

I swallow thickly, not liking this. What could he want to talk about that requires Hazel to be elsewhere? Is he planning to break up with me?

"She's only just become familiar with us. Don't you think it's too soon for her to spend the night somewhere else?"

"We'll pick her up tonight. We're dropping her off around four." He said we, so maybe he's not breaking up with me.

"Okay."

We hang out a little longer at the park, until Hazel whines she's hungry. While I take a shower and get ready, Chase feeds her. Then while he gets ready, I put together a diaper bag for my mom. Hazel's been around my parents, so when she sees them, she doesn't cry.

"Have a good time," Mom says with a smile. "We'll be here."

"Thank you for watching her," Chase tells her, kissing her cheek.

"Anytime."

"Where are we going?" I ask, once we're back in Chase's car.

"Home."

Home... Well, okay, then.

## CHAPTER TWENTY-ONE

### CHASE

I HAVE TO FIX THIS. Georgia and me. I couldn't fix my marriage, and now I know it was a blessing in disguise, but I can fix us. I'm determined to make this right. I have to. Georgia is different than Victoria. Our relationship is different. The love I feel for her is different. And I'm not going to lose her over sex toys.

Grabbing a bottle of wine I know Georgia likes, I pour us each a glass, then sit on the couch across from her. I'm not really a wine drinker, and she only drinks it on occasion, but it's the only alcohol we have here, and I'm thinking alcohol might be needed for the conversation we're about to have.

"Thanks," she says, accepting the glass from me and taking a sip.

"I'd like to talk to you about what you found in my drawer," I begin. "I want to explain."

Georgia nods, sipping more of her drink.

I take a deep breath, praying that opening up and being honest with Georgia doesn't mean losing her. "As I told you before, Victoria was the first woman I was with sexually. We were young and we both learned a lot about ourselves and each other through exploration. When she started using drugs, and I had her go to rehab, I resorted to porn and my hand." I shrug sheepishly, hoping Georgia understands it was my way of satisfying myself while my wife was gone and that I'm not some weird porn freak.

"Watching the porn, I came across videos with sex toys..." I clear my throat. "I was curious and bought a few so Victoria and I could try them out once she got out. The drugs had kind of messed with our sex lives, the intimacy between us put on the back-burner because she was too busy getting high. Only when she got out and I mentioned them, she freaked out on me, telling me I was sick and accusing me of cheating on her."

Georgia's eyes go wide, but I focus on finishing my story before I chicken out. "I never brought it up again. Sex between us went from hot and heavy to almost nonexistent and the intimacy between us was gone. We still had sex occasionally, but it was more due to marital obligation on her part. And then she started cheating on me. I didn't know it at the time, but looking back, it makes sense. She would only have sex with me once in a while to keep me from bitching."

I blow out a harsh breath and down the wine, setting the glass on the table. "When we got divorced, I started having one-night stands. One night a woman I was with busted out some sex toys. At first, by using them, I felt like I was sticking it to Victoria. Like a fuck you." I laugh humorlessly. "But I quickly learned toys can heighten the sexual experience. I picked some up at the store and would try them out with women who didn't mind."

I lock eyes with her so she knows how serious what I say next is. "I don't require toys in bed. I just want you, however I can have you. I was just having fun. I was a twenty-nine-year-old man who had only been with one woman. But the truth is, Georgia"—I set her drink on the table and take her hands in mine—"had I known what was on the other side of your door, I wouldn't have been with a single one of those women. I'm not trying to romance you," I say with a playful smirk to lighten the mood. "I'm just being honest. So please don't read too much into those toys, and please don't walk away thinking I'm some weird, kinky porn freak."

Georgia barks out a laugh. "I don't think you're weird or a freak, and even if you were, I'm okay with both." She stands and pulls my hand. "Come with me."

I follow her into our room and she pulls a bag out of her

drawer, handing it to me. It's black, and there's only one store I know of that uses black bags.

I open it up and peek inside it, finding all types of sex toys. "Georgia..." I shake my head. Of course, instead of running, she would try to please me. But that's not what I want.

"Before you give me some speech about how you don't need toys, yes, I bought these after seeing them in your drawer, but I didn't just buy them for you. I bought them for us. I love our sex life, and if these toys can make it even better then I'm up for trying them out."

Fuck, how the hell did I get so damn lucky to find this woman?

"And you swear you're not doing this because you think I need it?" I set the bag down and glide my hands down her side to her hips.

"I'm doing it because I want to. I promise."

I tug her close to me, until our bodies are flush against each other. "And if we do anything you don't like or you're not comfortable with, you'll tell me?"

"Yes," she breathes.

I move us to the bed, lifting her into my lap, and grab the bag of toys, dumping it out. There's so much shit here. I would've loved to see her buying all this, picking out what she wanted. I can tell by the stuff she bought, she put thought into it.

"I read an article about sex toys," she says, her cheeks tingeing an adorable shade of pink.

"Don't be embarrassed." I kiss her lips, loving how soft and warm they are. "You reading up on it, going to the store to buy this stuff, is not only fucking sexy but it means the world to me. You didn't make accusations, you didn't judge, and it made me fall in love with you that much more."

She smiles softly. "Lexi went with me and bought everything I bought. I'm sure Alec will be thanking you later."

I chuckle, elated that we're able to talk like this.

"So, while you were reading, did any of this stuff stand out to you? Anything you want to try first? We have a few hours before we have to pick up Hazel."

Georgia bites her bottom lip, looking over the items she purchased. "I don't know. I'm curious about all of them. It seemed like a lot of the women in the comments on the article like the butt plug and anal beads..." Her fingers run along the small bottle of lube. "They seemed to like anal in general. But a few said it hurts." She lifts a dildo. "I'm not sure how I would feel about using this instead of you. I like the feel of you inside me."

She glances up at me and shrugs shyly. "I'm okay with trying anything. You know more about this stuff than I do. I trust you to make sure whatever we do is good for the both of us."

Fuck. This. Woman. The way she opens herself up and puts her trust in me is so damn refreshing.

"Take your clothes off and lie on your stomach," I tell her, grabbing the blue jeweled butt plug and the anal vibrator and taking them with me. In the bathroom, I open both packages and wash the items with hot, soapy water, then dry them both off.

When I come back, she's lying just how I told her to, with her slim back and pert ass on display. Her head is resting sideways against her pillow, and her arms are above her head. I set the items on the bed, out of the way and then strip out of my clothes, leaving me in only my boxers.

I climb onto the bed and straddle the backs of her thighs. Squirting some oil in my palms, I begin at her shoulders, massaging her tissue. She moans and sighs, her body instantly relaxing. I work my way down her back, massaging any knots I can find. Once I get to her ass, I rub some more oil into my palms and then massage the globes, teasing at the crack. She tenses up slightly, assuming I'm going to take her ass, but I keep moving down, massaging her thighs and calves, and then giving her cute feet attention.

Once I've massaged every inch of her, and she's loose and comfortable, I work my way back up her body, stopping at her ass. I give it extra care, opening her cheeks and oiling it up, before I insert a single finger into her tight hole.

She tenses up, but quickly relaxes, spreading her thighs a little to allow me better access. I push my finger in and out of her, adding another one and then deepening my thrusts little by little, until she's writhing against the bed, moaning softly.

"This might burn a little at first," I warn her, as I push the butt plug in. It's on the smaller size, so her hole opens up easily and sucks it right in. When I know it's in there good, I roll her over onto her back.

"How does it feel?"

"I don't know," she breathes. "I can't really feel it so much. I felt it more when you were using your fingers."

"You'll feel it soon." I pull my boxers off then spread her legs, dropping on top of her with my palms landing on either side of her head.

I cover her mouth with mine. The kiss starts off slow and gentle, but soon we're ravenous, our tongues moving frantically against each other. I reach between our bodies and dip my fingers between her thighs, finding her soaking wet. Needing to feel her warmth, I guide myself into her until I'm balls deep in her tight pussy.

She breaks our kiss, her head going back with a moan. "I feel it," she says. "I feel..."

"Full," I finish for her. Between my dick in her pussy and the butt plug in her ass, she feels full. I know this because I can feel the hardness of the butt plug through her inside walls.

"Fuck me, Chase, please," she begs, tugging on my hair and pulling my face down to hers. I waste no time, drawing out slowly and then thrusting my hips forward, sinking inside of her again. And again. Her mouth moves to my neck, sucking on my flesh, while I bury myself to the hilt in her warmth over and over again until we're both groaning out our releases.

She sighs in contentment when I pull out, but I'm not done with her yet. "Don't move," I tell her, making her eyes go wide. I grab my boxers and wipe my dick off so I don't get cum all over the sheets, and then I slide down the bed.

"Chase, what are you doing?" She tries to close her thighs, but I push them open, watching as my seed drips out of her pussy. One day that seed will plant inside her and make a baby. The thought of her round with my baby growing inside her has my dick swelling.

I reach onto the floor and scoop up her shirt, tucking it under her ass, and then I lift her legs slightly, exposing the butt plug. I spread her cheeks and pull it out slowly. She moans, and I know what I'm about to do she'll love.

Grabbing the anal vibrator, I slick it up with a bit of oil then push it between her ass cheeks. Georgia groans as her hole sucks the object into her. I give her a moment to get comfortable and then I press the button on the end, making it vibrate. Her eyes go wide and she squirms.

"Feel good?"

She nods.

"It's about to get better." I drop to the side of her, taking one of her breasts into my mouth. I suck on her erect nipple, making her moan. At the same time, my fingers find her clit. I massage the swollen nub in gentle circles, working her up into a frenzy. The closer her orgasm, the tighter she squeezes her thighs, the louder her breathing gets. And the more turned on I am. I've been with more than my fair share of women, but not a single one of them compare to Georgia and the way she makes me feel.

I continue to stroke her clit, while the vibrator works her ass over. Until it all becomes too much and she falls off the edge, her entire body loosening as she comes. She screams my name in ecstasy, trembling all over. Her pussy gushes, covering my fingers with her juices, and I pull the vibrator out of her ass, making her moan loudly.

"Holy shit," she says, once she's come down from her high. "That was incredible." Her half-lidded eyes meet mine. "Which toy is next?"

I laugh, pulling her to me for a hard kiss. "No toys," I murmur against her lips, dragging her onto my lap. "Just me and you, butterfly."

## CHAPTER TWENTY-TWO

### ONE MONTH LATER

### CHASE

"Congratulations, Daddy!" Georgia says, throwing her arms around me. "How does it feel?"

Surreal, amazing, like my heart has been removed from the cavity of my chest and placed into my daughter's hands. "Really good," I tell her. "Thank you for..." Fuck, there's so much to thank Georgia for. I don't even know where to start.

"You don't ever have to thank me," she says, tears in her eyes. "I'm just so happy Hazel is finally legally yours."

Legally mine. Because Victoria signed over her rights. After the paternity test confirmed I'm Hazel's father, I petitioned the court for full custody. I wasn't sure if Victoria would fight me, maybe come to her senses that she's giving up her daughter. But she never did. A week after she was served, she signed the papers. I didn't actually see her do it. She sent the notarized papers in the mail like the coward she is, along with a note apologizing for being a shitty person and saying she's going to rehab.

Georgia, like the too good person she is, suggested maybe I should go visit her and see if she's okay. It's a big decision to give up your child. I told her Victoria's not my problem and as far as I'm concerned she's dead to me.

"Let's go get our little girl," I tell her, throwing my arm around her shoulders and walking out the door. Hazel might not legally be Georgia's, but she's the best damn thing in Hazel's life.

When we arrive at the condo, all of our friends and family are there. There's a huge banner across the back wall that reads, "Congratulations," as well as an assortment of food and drinks spread out along the counters and table. Pink and yellow streamers and balloons are decorating the entire area.

"Congratulations," Alec says, giving me a hug. "Is paternity leave over yet? You ready to come back to work?" he asks, making everyone laugh. I took time off to get to know Hazel and to also deal with her custody, but I'm definitely ready to get back to work. Georgia has offered to keep her while I'm at work since she works from home, so it'll work out well.

"Yeah, I'll be back at work Monday."

"Dada!" Hazel yells to get my attention. I glance over at my mom, who's holding her, and smile.

When Hazel wiggles for her to set her down, Mom does so. Hazel steadies herself on her feet and then with a huge smile, takes one step and then another, until she's over to me.

"Finally!" Georgia laughs. "I got it on video!" Every time she's taken a few steps, neither of us has had our phones on us. She's been determined to catch it on video.

"You're such a good walker," Georgia says to Hazel, tickling her belly. "Pretty soon you'll be running circles around your daddy."

"Dada!" Hazel says, pointing at me. Fuck, I'm a dad. To the most precious little girl in the world.

Georgia beams. "Yep! That's your daddy."

"*Dow! Dow!*" Hazel says, wiggling her tiny butt to get down.

"I can't believe she's going to be one soon," I say to Georgia as we watch Hazel walk like a cute little drunk person over to Lexi, who scoops her up into her arms for a hug.

"It'll be a Harry Potter party," she says with a laugh. We showed her a dozen different baby shows, but she had no desire to watch any of them. It wasn't until we were watching a Harry Potter marathon on TV one night that she stopped and watched like her eyes were transfixed to the television. We thought it was a one-time thing, but every time we put it on, she'll sit and watch the movies for hours.

"Did someone say Harry Potter?" Mason asks.

"It's Hazel's favorite," Georgia tells him with an eye roll.

"I knew that little girl was special," he says. "Harry Potter is the shit." He clasps my shoulder. "Congratulations, Chase."

"Thank you."

After everyone leaves—Charlie refusing to leave until the condo is cleaned up—and it's only Georgia, Hazel, and me, we settle onto the couch to watch a Harry Potter movie for the millionth time. Hazel snuggles up between Georgia and me and, within minutes, is snoring softly.

"I'm exhausted," Georgia says with a tired, happy smile on her face. "Today was a good day."

"It was." I lean over and kiss her. "Why don't you go take a bath and I'll put her to bed."

Her eyes sparkle. "Only if you join me." She winks, and my dick swells in my pants at the thought of fucking her inside the spa tub.

"Deal."

I lay Hazel down in bed, kissing her good night and turning the monitor on, then go in search for Georgia, finding her exactly where she said she would be—in the tub with bubbles filled halfway up her torso.

The lights are dimmed a bit and she's leaning against the edge with her head dipped back, her eyes closed. I take a second to take her in. The last few months she's come to mean so much to me. Every bump in the road, every obstacle, she's been there at my side. The positive in my negative. The light in my dark. The beautiful in my ugly. The fucking perfect in my way too imperfect world.

"Are you going to join me or just stare at me all night?" She lifts her head and her gorgeous green eyes meet mine.

I strip out of my clothes and, when she moves forward so I can situate myself behind her, her perky tits splash in the water slightly. The water is hot and she fits perfectly between my thighs. She backs up, her soft body using my front to get comfortable, and her head lulls to the side, resting on my shoulder.

"If I could, I would freeze this moment," she says softly.

"In the bathtub?" I joke. Absentmindedly, I run my fingers

along the underside of her breasts. She's soft to the touch, and I know if I were to taste her she would be sweet. Fucking perfect.

She laughs and it sounds lazy and content. "Maybe not exactly right here. I just mean in general." She takes my hand in hers and guides it to the top of her breast, indicating she wants me to massage her breast.

"I never imagined my life like this... With you and Hazel. I'm just so happy," she says with a sigh. "And it's because of you. Because you pulled me out of my room, refusing to let me hide."

I pinch her nipple between my finger and thumb and she moans softly. "I don't know what our future holds," she continues, "but right here, right now, it feels like I've finally found my perfect path."

I don't exactly believe in her perfect path shit, but I get what she's saying. Because with her in my arms, and my daughter under the same roof as us, things do feel pretty damn perfect.

I dip my head slightly and press a kiss to her bare shoulder and then her neck. I drag my hand across her stomach and find the apex of her thighs. "Spread your legs for me, butterfly," I murmur.

She does as I ask, and I push two fingers into her center, pumping in and out of her. Even in the water, I can still feel how wet she is. I use her juices to create friction on her clit. Sucking on the sensitive spot on her neck, I quickly bring her to a climax. Her entire body trembles in pleasure, her moans filling the quiet room. I love that I'm the only one who's done this to her. Has made her happy, made her feel like she's found that perfect path.

As she turns around and straddles my thighs, guiding her warm, wet pussy around my rock-hard dick, I capture her mouth with my own. My fingers dig into her hips, helping her ride me. As our mouths tangle, our tongues dueling with each other, my mind goes to what she said a few minutes ago about wanting to freeze time.

If I could, I would freeze this moment—me inside her, her wrapped around me. After my divorce, I couldn't imagine ever settling down again. Giving my heart and soul to another woman. But with Georgia, I can see it all. The lazy Sundays, the family dinners, the laughs and smiles and the love. So much fucking love. And with those thoughts, I know it's not about freezing time, but about having what we have all the time. Every day for the rest of our lives.

And I know just the way to make that happen...

---

"*OOH, OOH, OOH,*" Hazel says, trying to mimic the noise the monkeys make. It's Sunday and our last day together before I go back to work tomorrow morning, so Georgia suggested we take a family trip to the zoo. Which gave me an idea...

"That's right," Georgia says, kneeling next to Hazel. "Can you say monkey?"

"*Key-key,*" Hazel says, butchering the hell out of the word before she pushes off the fence and toddles down the sidewalk toward the next exhibit.

Georgia runs after her, scooping her up and peppering kisses all over her face.

"I love seeing Georgia so happy," Charlie whispers to me. "Thank you."

After Georgia mentioned the zoo, and an idea formed, I invited her family to join us, as well as my mom. I also invited Mason and Mila and Alec's sister since they're considered family. I wanted to invite Kaden and Ashley, Georgia's grandparents, but they're already in Breckenridge for the holidays, along with Tristan's younger sisters, Emma and Morgan, and their families. We'll be joining them next week for Christmas. Micaela, her cousin and best friend, is also here with her husband Ryan, and their two kids.

"You don't have to thank me," I tell Charlie, watching Hazel throw her head back in a laugh as Georgia lifts her up and moves her kisses to her belly, tickling her. "I'm the lucky one."

We go from exhibit to exhibit, then stop for lunch, before continuing on. The entire time, I'm half here, half in my own mind. I have a plan, but the closer I get to it, the more nervous I get. What if it's too soon? What if she thinks I'm crazy? What if we end up like my last marriage?

But the second we step foot into the butterfly exhibit and Georgia beams at me, with my daughter in her arms, as hundreds, if not thousands of butterflies flutter around us, I know I have nothing to be nervous or scared about. Because this is Georgia, and everything about her and us is different.

I glance at Lexi and our eyes meet. I nod slightly, so she understands, and her face breaks into a knowing grin.

"This is so beautiful," Georgia says, spinning Hazel in a circle as the butterflies fly all around us. "Hazel, do you see the butterflies?"

"*Bu-fy!*" Hazel squeals, trying and failing to capture one.

"Yes, butterfly," Georgia says, kissing her on the cheek.

I watch my two girls interact, until Georgia glances over at me and smiles oddly. "You okay?"

Her question snaps me out of my trance, reminding me what I'm about to do. "I'm perfect," I tell her, stepping closer. I give Hazel a kiss on her cheek, then turn my attention back to Georgia. "These last couple months with you and my daughter have been the best of my life."

Her lips curl into a smile that has the ability to light up the darkest of rooms.

"Remember when you said you wanted to freeze this moment in time because you're so happy? I felt that deep, because every moment I spend with you and Hazel are moments I want to freeze."

I pull the ring out of my pocket that I've been carrying around, waiting for the perfect moment. It's not in a box because it would be too bulky and obvious.

Georgia's eyes home in on it and widen. "Chase," she breathes.

"It's impossible to freeze time, but I don't think it's actually about freezing time but wanting those special moments to last."

She nods but doesn't say anything. Hazel, oblivious to what's happening, looks around at the butterflies, giggling and pointing.

"We can't freeze the moments, but we can spend the rest of our lives creating them, so many of them it'll feel like they're frozen in time." I drop to one knee and Georgia gasps, tears filling her eyes. "Marry me and spend the rest of our lives creating memories that are worth freezing. But not just with me as my wife," I add, "but as Hazel's mom."

Her becoming Hazel's stepmom isn't enough. She loves her as

much as I do, and I want us to be a family. I want her to adopt Hazel and raise her as her own.

I extend my hand so she can see the ring. It's a simple platinum band with a circle diamond in the center with butterflies made out of tiny diamonds hugging both sides. When I saw it, I knew it was the ring for Georgia.

"Yes," she says, tears trickling down her cheeks. "Yes, I will marry you."

I slip the ring onto her finger and then stand. Cradling her face in my palms, I tip her head up slightly and kiss her soft and sweet.

Hazel screeches, wanting our attention, and Georgia and I both chuckle into each other's mouth. "I love you," I murmur against her lips.

"And I love you."

---

"I DON'T WANT TO WAIT," I tell her later that night, after Hazel is in bed and we've finished making love.

We're both sweating and still catching our breaths, so it throws her off. "Wait for what?"

"To get married." I roll over onto my side and grip the curve of her hip. "For you to adopt Hazel. For us to add to our little family." We haven't talked about having our own children, but that hasn't stopped me from thinking about it.

Georgia's eyes widen. "So let's not." She kisses the corner of my mouth. "Let's elope. Go to Vegas and get married."

"Your parents and sister would kill us."

She shrugs. "So, we'll invite them."

"You don't want a big wedding?"

She shakes her head. "I just want to marry you."

"Then let's do it. Let's elope."

## CHAPTER TWENTY-THREE

### ONE MONTH LATER

### GEORGIA

"I can't believe you're doing this," Lexi says for the millionth time. "Who are you and what have you done with my sister?"

I laugh softly, trying not to jostle my arm.

"It's just like her tattoo," Chase says. "She's been transformed from a caterpillar into a butterfly." He winks my way and grins. I glance down at the work in progress on the inside of my wrist. A single butterfly. When the tattoo artist asked if I wanted it to be colored in, I told him no. The shades of gray represent the me before Chase and the butterfly is who I've metamorphosed into because of him.

My thoughts go back to earlier when we said our vows in a little chapel on the Vegas Strip in front of our family.

*"I, Chase Matthews, promise to love and cherish you, to protect you for the rest of our lives. I promise to stand by your side, to always support you, to be the person who cheers you on when you spread your wings, and like the beautiful butterfly you are, fly..."*

After we said our I dos, Chase surprised me with the papers for me to legally adopt Hazel. I knew I'd be signing them, but I didn't know he had them rushed to be ready in time for me to sign the day of our wedding. Afterward, we went to a nice restaurant with everyone and celebrated. The babies were all getting tired, and we were about to call it a night, when my mom and dad offered to watch my cousin Micaela's little ones and Abigail, and Chase's mom offered to keep Hazel for the night, so we could continue the celebration.

We were walking past a tattoo shop and I told Chase I wanted to get a tattoo to commemorate the occasion. I told him he didn't need to get one as well. I knew his stance on tattoos—that he didn't want to permanently mark his body until he found the right one. But he shocked me when he said he would like nothing more than to get one with me.

Chase, not giving a shit how girly some might think it is, insisted on getting a butterfly as well, only his is a bit darker, and with Hazel's and my name etched in the wings, and it's on his left pectoral muscle over his heart.

"All right," the tattoo artist says, wiping my wrist. "Check it out."

I glance down at the gray shaded beautiful butterfly and smile. "It's perfect."

I show it to Chase, who nods in agreement. "Perfect."

"Where to next?" Micaela asks once we're paid up and standing outside. "I'm for once not pregnant. I vote we get drunk." Her husband laughs.

"You guys can go," Chase says, wrapping his arms around me. "I'm taking my wife back to our hotel room and not coming out until tomorrow morning." I tilt my face up to look at him and he waggles his brows suggestively.

"I'm down for hitting a club," Lexi says. She pulls me into a tight hug. "Enjoy your wedding night. Congratulations. I love you and I'm so proud of you." She chokes up on the last word and hugs me tighter.

"I love you more, Lex."

We break apart—both of us wiping the tears from our eyes—and everyone else hugs and congratulates Chase and me, before we go our separate ways.

When we arrive back at the room, I tell Chase I'd like to freshen up, and of course he insists we shower together. The entire time we're washing up, we can't keep our hands and mouths off each other. I think we both want to have sex in the shower, but at the same time, we also want to make love for the first time as husband and wife in the bed. When we get out, I brush my teeth and am about to take my birth control pill when Chase plucks it out of my hand.

"What if you stopped taking this?"

"My pill?" I'm confused. If I don't take it, I'll... "You want to have another baby?"

"Only if you do." He smiles shyly. "You and Lexi are close in age and get along well. And my sister and I were too, until..." He swallows thickly. "Until the drugs, we were best friends."

I encircle my arms around his waist. "I wish I could've met her."

"I wish you could've too." He kisses the top of my head. "What do you think?"

I back up and he holds up the packet of pills. Doing the math in my head, I figure out that if we were to get pregnant now, Hazel and the baby would be just under two years apart. That's if I get pregnant right away. I've been on the pill for years, so it could take months...

"Okay," I tell him. "No more pill. Whatever happens, happens."

"Hell yes." Chase's lips curve into a sexy smirk. "Let's get started now."

He lifts me over his shoulder, fireman style, and stalks over to the huge bed, dropping me onto the center of the mattress.

"Wait! I didn't get to put on my sexy bridal lingerie." I picked it out especially for tonight. It even matches my wedding dress.

"You can show me after," Chase growls. "Right now, I need to be inside my wife." His mouth crashes against mine and all thoughts of my lingerie disappear as I get lost in my husband.

## CHAPTER TWENTY-FOUR

### FOUR MONTHS LATER

### CHASE

"I'm pregnant." Georgia lifts the stick with the bold word **PREGNANT** written out. "Oh my God! I'm pregnant." Her eyes light up and a huge grin splays across her face.

"You're pregnant." I pull her into my arms, both shocked and elated. Neither of us thought she'd get pregnant so quickly, so when she missed her period a couple weeks ago, she was in denial. Until the morning sickness started and we agreed it was time to take a test.

"Mama! Dada!" Hazel yells from her crib, letting us know she's awake from her nap.

Georgia wraps the stick up in toilet paper and drops it into the garbage, then washes her hands. When we walk into Hazel's room, she's bouncing up and down with the most adorable smile. "Up, please," she says, the word please coming out like *peeze*. I lift her out of her crib and place her on her changing table so I can change her diaper.

"I can't believe by the end of this year, we're going to have another little one," Georgia says, kissing Hazel's forehead. "I think we should look for our own place."

My head jerks up. "To buy?"

"Well, yeah." She shrugs. "Maybe in the same neighborhood as my parents or near Lexi..."

My brain starts calculating how much a house in one of those areas will cost. I spent the majority of my savings on Georgia's ring, and I still need to pay her back for the attorney.

"Hey," she says, picking up Hazel and setting her down. "If you want to stay here, we can. It was just a thought."

I watch as Hazel runs over to the corner of her room and drops into her oversized stuffed chair. It has her name stitched across the back and is pink, like most of the other stuff in her room. She grabs a book and opens it, mumbling to herself like she can actually read it.

"Chase, talk to me." I look back at Georgia, who's frowning. I consider lying to her, telling her I want to stay here, but the truth is, I would love to get a bigger place, buy a home we can call ours. The problem is, I can't afford anything like that—even with me up for a promotion at work, I still wouldn't be able to afford a down payment on a house where she's talking about.

But she can. Because my wife is wealthy as fuck. And despite her financial advisor suggesting I sign a prenuptial agreement, she refused, saying she won't go into a marriage with the idea that it will one day end. We haven't discussed money, both of us too busy focusing on Hazel and being newlyweds, but it's something we should've talked about.

"I only have a little bit of money in savings," I admit, making her frown. "And I know you're rich and can afford a million houses, but I want us to be equals in this marriage. I don't want to buy a house I can't afford."

Her face contorts into confusion. "So, because *you* can't afford it, *we* can't buy a house? How does that make us equals?" She crosses her arms over her chest. "The last time I checked, we're in this marriage together, and what's mine is yours and vice-versa."

I swallow thickly, having no response.

"You're right," I admit after a beat. "My words were based on male chauvinistic pride. I'm sorry."

Georgia nods. "I don't care about the cost of the house. I just want a place to call our own. With a backyard where our kids can run around and play. Maybe a porch swing where we can sit and grow old together. We have the money to live where we want and I want our children to grow up in a nice, safe neighborhood."

She's saying everything I've always dreamed about and I can't allow my pride to keep us from having what we both want. "I want all of that too." I tug on the bottom of her shirt, forcing her closer to me. "Let's do it. Let's buy a house."

"Thank you!" She squeals. "I can't wait!"

We spend the rest of the day playing with Hazel, and once she goes to bed, we check out listings for homes in the neighborhoods where her family lives. We find a few and email the agents, asking to set up a time to see them.

As we're turning off everything, preparing to go to bed, I get a text from an unknown number that has me stopping in my place.

**Unknown: Hey Chase, it's Victoria. This is my new number. Can we please talk?**

Can we talk? Has this bitch lost her mind?

**Me: There's nothing to talk about. Don't contact me again. You're getting blocked.**

I put her name into my phone, so I have her number then block her.

"Everything okay?" Georgia lays her head on my chest and drops her arm over my torso like she does every night.

"Yeah," I tell her robotically. Then I change my mind and go with the truth. "Actually, no." She sits up, concerned. "Victoria texted, wanting to talk. I blocked her."

Georgia's mouth turns down. "Chase... maybe you should hear her out. Before everything you guys were friends."

Fuck, can she be any more innocent and naïve?

"We're not those people anymore and her choosing to abandon our daughter proved that. I want nothing to do with her."

I can tell by the look on her face she doesn't agree, but she still nods and lies back down. "If you change your mind, I'll support your decision," she says, making me fall even more in love with her.

---

"CHASE... CHASE, WAKE UP." I wrench my eyes open and glance around. It's dark in the room, so it's late... or early. "Chase."

My vision clears and I see Georgia sitting up in bed with tears in her eyes. I immediately shoot up on alert. "What's wrong? Is Hazel okay?"

"Hazel's okay," she says softly, "but when I woke up to use the bathroom, I was bleeding." Bleeding... Fuck. "I think I'm losing the baby."

"It could be anything," I assure her, knowing nothing about how pregnancy works but trying to remain positive. "Let's get you to the hospital." I turn on my phone and call Charlie to come over and watch Hazel.

Georgia's quiet the entire drive and stays that way once we're checked in with the emergency room. Since she's only a few weeks along, it's not considered top priority, so we have to wait our turn. The entire time, I pray to God she's okay, that bleeding is normal. But when she flinches and I ask her what's wrong, and she says she has bad cramping, I know no amount of praying is going to save our baby.

Four hours later, we're told Georgia is in the middle of losing our baby. She was only six weeks along and it's apparently common for miscarriages to occur before the twelve-week mark. The doctor discharges her, warning her the next few days she'll bleed a lot, her body naturally releasing the fetus, and suggests she follow up with her doctor.

On our way home, I text Charlie to let her know, and she texts back she'll take Hazel to her house so Georgia can rest.

When we walk inside, Georgia goes straight to Hazel's room. "Where is she?"

"I had your mom take her to her house so you can have some time."

Georgia frowns. "I appreciate that, but I'd like for her to come home."

I step over to her. "Don't you think maybe you need a little bit of time to mourn? You just lost a baby. I know we only found out yesterday, but it still fucking hurts."

"I know, but losing the baby makes me appreciate what we have that much more." Tears fill her eyes. "I just really wanted to hug our daughter." She wraps her arms around her torso and I pull her into my arms, once again falling deeper in love with my wife.

"We'll go get her later. We don't want her to see either of us upset."

"You're right. You should probably get to work. You're already late."

"I called out. I'm not going anywhere. Get into bed and I'll run out and grab us some breakfast." There's no way I'm leaving her side right now. I have no experience with this sort of thing, but it feels like she's still numb, and I'm worried when the numbness wears off, she'll release every emotion she's keeping locked away right now.

"Can you also get me pads, please? I forgot I don't have any."

"Of course."

She climbs into bed and I kiss her forehead. "I'll be back soon."

On my way to the store, I get a call from Alec. "Hey, man."

"How's Georgia doing?" Lexi's mom must've told them.

"She's hanging in there. I'm going to get us breakfast right now."

There's a moment of silence before Alec speaks. "So, um, this is a bad time, but... Victoria is here and she's refusing to leave until she can speak to you."

Fuck. She can't be serious showing up at my goddamn workplace.

"I'll swing by there."

"Sorry," he says. "I tried to get her to leave, but she's being stubborn, and the only other option I'd have would be to call the cops, but I wasn't sure you would want that."

"I'll handle it. Thanks."

When I pull up, I see the Mercedes I bought her parked in the drive. I'm hoping I can get her to leave quickly so I can get back to Georgia. When I step inside, I find her waiting at the table. Her long black hair is up in a tight ponytail and she's wearing a face full of makeup. When she sees me, she stands, exposing her body. She's wearing a tiny yellow tank top, distressed jeans, and a pair of heels. She looks good. Clean. Sober. Good for her. But if she thinks she's going to waltz in here and make demands, she's about to be disappointed.

"This is my workplace," I tell her. "You don't come here. Ever. Well, unless it's to drop off my daughter." She flinches at my words, but I don't have it in me to feel bad.

"You didn't leave me a choice," she says softly, very unlike her. "I don't know where you live and you blocked me."

Not wanting a scene to be made in the station, I nod for her to walk outside with me.

"When someone blocks you that means they don't want to speak to you," I point out once we're standing in the back. Since the fire station is a home that was remodeled, it has a backyard. We put a swing set out here so the kids can play on it when we hold family barbecues.

Victoria steps closer to me, and I immediately see the look in her eyes. Seduction. Not over my dead body. "I'm married." I lift my left hand to show her my ring. Her eyes bulge out of their sockets. "And my wife legally adopted Hazel."

She splutters, shaking her head, at a complete loss for words.

"You didn't really think you'd come here months after abandoning my daughter and I would get back together with you and we'd be some sort of happy family?"

She clears her throat. "I messed up. Please, Chase. I just want to see my little girl."

I don't even have it in me to laugh at her audacity. Georgia is home, waiting for me to bring her food and pads because she just lost our baby while this bitch is begging to see the baby she left on a doorstop.

"I gotta go."

"Wait, please." She places her perfectly manicured hand on my arm. "Can I at least see a picture of her?"

"No, you don't deserve to see anything or hear anything regarding her. You don't even deserve to breathe the same air as her."

"Chase. C'mon, please," she whines, her tone grating my last nerve. "I was in a bad place. I'm better. I was scared to live without Raymond, but he's gone now, and you're... married," she chokes out. "All I have left is Hazel."

"Wrong," I bark out. "You signed the papers giving her up, which means you have no rights to her."

A single tear slides down her cheek. "I made a mistake."

## CHAPTER TWENTY-FOUR

"You've made a lot of mistakes," I agree. "But as far as Hazel goes, the best decision you ever made was giving her up." My phone vibrates in my pocket and I pull it out. It's Georgia asking if I can please get her pain medication. Because she's suffering from a miscarriage and is in pain, while piece of shit women like my ex-wife can get pregnant and carry a baby without a care in the world. Sometimes the world really is fucked up.

"I have to go." I put my hand on her shoulder to quickly guide her out. "Don't come back here. You made your decisions and now you have to live with them."

I don't bother to say bye to any of the guys, just focusing on getting Victoria into her car. "Chase, I'm begging you," she pleads as I open her car door.

"Get in the car, Victoria," I bark out. Thankfully, she listens. "Focus on staying clean, go to meetings, spend time with your parents, get a job, a hobby. But do not come around here again."

I slam the door closed and stalk away, refusing to even give her a second glance. She isn't worth my time or energy and my wife needs me.

# CHAPTER TWENTY-FIVE

## GEORGIA

"Park! Park!" Hazel yells as the park comes into view. It's been a little over a week since I miscarried and the only things keeping me together are Chase and Hazel. I saw the doctor and she assured me there's nothing wrong with me. She even said Chase and I are more than welcome to start trying again after my next cycle, but I think we're going to wait a little bit, so we can both move past the pain.

"Yes, that's the park," I tell her, pushing her stroller down the sidewalk. Chase is at work today, so we're meeting Lexi and Abigail to play and have a picnic.

We pull up and I unbuckle Hazel. The second I put her down, she takes off running toward the jungle gym. I glance around, looking for Lexi, but she isn't here yet, which doesn't surprise me. With her gallery opening a few months ago, she's been crazy busy working out all the kinks.

I follow Hazel around, keeping my distance, since she's going through this stage where she wants to be independent, but close enough that if something happens I'm right here.

There are a few other people at the park today, and Hazel makes a friend with a little girl who's playing in the sand with her sand toys. She runs to the stroller to grab her own sand toys and plops down next to the girl to play.

I smile over at the mom, wondering if maybe I should befriend her, but before I can go over and introduce myself, a woman steps in front of me.

She has jet-black hair and bright blue eyes. Her makeup is on the heavy side and she's dressed like she's going out to a club instead of to a park.

At first, I think she's just walking by, so I move to the right so I can see Hazel again, but she steps with me. "Can I help you?" I ask, moving slightly again so my daughter stays in my line of sight.

"I'm hoping so," she says. "My name is Victoria and that little girl is my daughter." She glances back at Hazel, and my hackles rise. Maybe it's the fact that I just lost a baby, or that she has the nerve to call her her daughter, but her attitude doesn't sit right with me.

"Actually, she's my daughter," I point out. "Just like Chase is my husband." Chase had told me she came by the fire station, begging him to take her back, for them to be a family again.

She clears her throat. "I'm sorry," she says softly. "That came out wrong. Can we please start again?"

"Or we don't have to start at all. Did you follow me here?" I look around to make sure there are still other people around.

"I did, but only because Chase won't talk to me. He blocked me and—"

"Can you blame him?" I ask, cutting her off. "You hid your pregnancy from him, tried to raise her as someone else's daughter, and only when he found out and you were going to lose him, did you tell Chase, by dropping her off at the fire station, where I found her bawling her eyes out all alone."

Victoria's face falls. "I was on drugs. I can't change what I did, but that's not who I am. I've been clean for almost six months now."

"And now that you're clean and your man won't take you back, you want Chase and Hazel?" I might hate confrontation and avoid it at all costs, but until now I never had any reason to fight. Chase and Hazel, they're my reasons to fight.

"No, I thought if I could get him back, he would let me see my —Hazel." Her eyes drop slightly. "I messed up... bad. But I miss her so much. And I know you adopted her... I'm just asking to see her, spend some time with her." Her tear-filled eyes meet mine. "I love her so much."

Just as I'm about to tell her this is between her and Chase, Hazel comes running over. "Mama!" she yells through tears. "Sand. Ouchy." She rubs her eyes, and I lift her into my arms. I carry her over to the table and grab a washcloth from the diaper bag, pouring some water onto it.

"Ouchy," she repeats.

"Don't touch it," I tell her, padding her eyes gently with the washcloth.

"Ouchy."

"I know, pretty girl." I sit her on top of the picnic table and wipe her eyes one more time. She looks up at me and blinks slowly, a small watery smile creeping up on her face.

"Better?"

"Yes. I hungry!" The word comes out like *ungry*.

"Aunt Lexi will be here soon with Abigail and then we'll eat lunch."

"Okay." Her beautiful smile widens and then her eyes go past me... to Victoria. I wait with bated breath for her to remember her. It's only been six months since she dropped her off, and she spent the first ten months of her life with her. Her top lip curls up into a shy smile and her hands lift for me to pick her up. I expect Victoria to say something, to tell Hazel who she is, but she doesn't.

"She's so beautiful," she chokes out. "Is she okay?" She's referring to the herniated belly button that was still healing when we found her.

"She's perfect."

Victoria nods. "I know right now isn't a good time to talk, not in front of her, but could we please talk? Mother to mother?"

Her words are like a knife straight through my heart. She's Hazel's biological mother. She gave birth to her. Her blood runs through her veins. I'm only her mother legally. And the baby that was growing in me... I lost.

But she doesn't know that, so when she says that, she's referring to the both of us being Hazel's mother. And in a weird way I respect her for saying that. Do I think she deserves the title of Mom? No. But she could've easily disregarded me as Hazel's mother as well.

"Hazel goes down for a nap at two o'clock. If you want to give me your phone number, I can call you."

She sighs in relief. "Thank you."

After giving me her number, she reluctantly leaves just as Lexi is walking up with Aiden and Abigail. "Who was that?" she asks, obviously having seen me talking to her.

"Chase's ex-wife."

Her brows shoot up to her forehead. "Hazel's..."

"Biological mom, yeah."

"What the hell did she want?"

"To see Hazel."

Lexi curses under her breath.

"Hey, Aiden, how are you?" I ask, changing the subject.

"Hi, Lexi's sister," he says back. "I'm hungry. Lexi brought me tacos." He holds up his bag.

"Tacos sound good."

"They are good," he says back. "Lexi, where do I sit?"

"On the blanket," she says, setting Abigail down so she can lay the blanket on the grass. I grab the cooler, and we sit on the blanket with the girls, getting their food ready, while Aiden eats his tacos and tells me about the gallery and all the painting he's doing.

"I have a new friend," he says. "Her name is Melanie and she paints."

Lexi grins and whispers, "She's his special friend."

"That's nice," I tell him, ignoring Lexi. "Does she paint at the gallery?"

"Yes, and she likes tacos."

"Her mom is the artist we're featuring this month. Melanie is the same age as Aiden and works with her mom. She's autistic like Aiden. They hit it off and have been inseparable."

"That's so sweet."

"It is. She asked him to come over and he actually agreed. I'm going to go with him, though, just to make sure he's comfortable."

"I'm done," Aiden announces. "Can Baby Abigail and I go play now?"

Abigail jumps up and grabs Aiden's hand. "I go play." She recently turned one and is now walking.

"Me too!" Hazel adds.

"Go ahead," Lexi says, picking up all the garbage and stuffing it into a bag. I shake out the blanket and fold it up, while she finishes cleaning up, and then we join them over by the slides. Aiden is standing at the bottom, while the girls take turns sliding down. He catches them every time, and then tickles them, making them squeal.

"Again!" Abigail yells, sliding down so Aiden can catch her.

"Be careful," he says when he sets her down and she toddles over to the steps. "Walk, Baby Abigail."

Lexi and I laugh at that. "I think he'll always call her Baby Abigail."

"Probably," she agrees. "Speaking of babies... How are you?"

"I'm okay. The bleeding stopped. The doctor said we can try again after I get my period."

"Are you going to?"

"I don't know," I admit. "I think Hazel is enough for right now."

"Because you're scared?" she asks, calling me out.

"Maybe."

"What are you scared of?"

"For one, losing another baby." I glance at her. "But also, my first thought when I found out I miscarried was, what if I can't have a baby of my own? What if there's something wrong with my body and I can't give Chase a baby that's part me and part him? And that made me feel guilty because in my eyes, Hazel is my own."

"You're human," Lexi says, "and your fears are normal, but you know firsthand that it's possible for a parents' love to be unconditional, even if they aren't biologically related to you."

Lexi's right. Lexi and I aren't biologically related, but you'd never know it. Tristan is my adopted father, but to me he's my dad. And my mom isn't Lexi's bio mom, but she loves her as if she's her real mom. I hope one day when Hazel learns that I'm not her biological mom, she'll still love me the same.

"Do you ever wish your bio mom had come to see you?"

Lexi takes a deep breath. "She was a druggy and she never once stopped long enough to try to see me, so no, I don't." Her gaze swings over to me. "Don't tell me you're considering letting Victoria see Hazel."

"She's clean, has been for several months."

"So what? She gave her up."

"Because she was on drugs. You said it yourself. Your mom never once stopped doing drugs long enough to see you, but what if she did? What if she had gotten sober and wanted to see you?"

Lexi shakes her head. "I don't know. Drugs ended up killing her. Maybe it was for the best I never knew her."

We play with the kids, until they're both wiped out, and then Lexi heads out and Hazel and I walk home. She falls asleep in her stroller, and I leave her in it for her nap, knowing if I move her, she'll wake up and won't go back to sleep.

I stare at Victoria's number for several long minutes before I give in and call her. "Hello," she says, picking up on the second ring.

"Hi, it's Georgia."

"Oh, hey, I was hoping you would call."

"I need to know what it is exactly you want," I tell her, getting straight to the point.

"To see Hazel. To be in her life in some way. I'm just asking for a chance to prove that I can be clean and in her life."

My thoughts go back to Lexi... She didn't get that chance because her mom never stopped doing drugs long enough to want her.

"I'll speak to Chase and let you know."

---

"YOU TOLD HER, WHAT?" Chase yells, making me jump. "What the hell were you thinking?" He's never yelled at me. Not once—but we've also never fought. But he's yelling now, and I don't like that. Memories from when I was little surface. My dad yelling at me, getting in my face, and then slamming the door closed. Me banging on the door and begging for my mom.

I shrink back, unable to have a conversation with him if he's going to yell. He must realize what he's done because he takes a deep breath. "I'm sorry, I shouldn't have yelled at you."

"No, you shouldn't have." I hit him with a hard glare, making it clear I'm dead serious. "Please don't do that again."

He nods and drops down onto the couch. "Georgia, you can't save the damn world, especially my ex-wife."

"I'm not trying to save the world." I sit next to him. "But the fact of the matter is, she gave birth to her, and when she was on drugs, instead of doing wrong by her, she gave her up, and now she's clean and wants another chance. And if I were in her position—"

"You would never be in her position. You can't even compare yourself to her."

"You never know what the future holds. Anything can happen, and I'd hope if I messed up and then tried to make things right, I'd be given a second chance."

Chase snorts humorlessly. "You're so fucking naïve. This world isn't perfect. It's not filled with rainbows and unicorns." He grabs Hazel's stuffed unicorn and tosses it to the side. "You just don't get it, and I'm glad you don't. It means you've lived a life without any hardship, and I would give anything to be able to say I've lived a life like that. But what you need to understand is that the big, bad, cruel fucking world is going to eat you alive if you don't recognize that outside your four walls everything is *not* perfect."

"I'm pretty sure there's a dig in there somewhere." I stand, refusing to continue this conversation.

"It's not a dig, it's reality."

"Okay, well, I'm just going to take my reality elsewhere because I don't want to fight with you."

Chase's brows fly up to his forehead. "You're leaving?"

"I'm going for a walk."

He sighs. "Fuck, butterfly." He shakes his head. "Don't go, please."

"I don't want to fight. Maybe it makes me naïve or sheltered, but I want to believe the good in people. Lexi's mom never changed. Drugs are what killed her. But Victoria is trying to change and I want to give her the benefit of the doubt."

"And I think that's great you want to see the good in the world, in her, but I'm trying to protect my daughter."

His words are a slap to my face. His daughter… like she's not mine. Because she isn't my blood. My baby, my flesh and blood, died before he or she was ever born.

"Your daughter... Right." I nod once.

Chase's face falls, understanding what he's just done, but it's too late.

Without saying another word, I grab my keys from the counter and leave. Chase runs after me. "Baby, please don't go."

"I have to," I tell him. "Because if I don't, things will be said... *more* things will be said. And words are powerful and can't be taken back once they're spoken."

Once I'm in my car, I drive to the closest parking lot and park. I cover my face in my hands and then I cry. I know a part of me is overemotional because of the miscarriage. My hormones are all over the place. But another part of me is hurt by what he said. The accusations he flung at me.

When my phone rings and it shows it's my dad, I pull myself together and answer.

"Where are you?"

"Like you don't know." I laugh. We have a tracking app on all our phones. "Chase called you?"

"He's worried. You've been through a lot recently and you took off."

"Then he should've thought about that when he was yelling at me and telling me how naïve I am."

Dad sighs. "Why don't you come home and we'll talk?"

"Okay."

A few minutes later, I pull up in my parents' driveway. Dad is sitting outside on the porch swing, drinking a beer. I sit down next to him, and he stretches his arm out behind my shoulders, pulling me closer to him. My head drops onto his shoulder and more tears fall. He doesn't say a word, just lets me cry it out until the tears finally stop falling.

"Chase said you want to give Victoria a chance to be in Hazel's life?"

I sit up and nod. "He doesn't agree. It's like he believes if someone messes up they should be given a life sentence."

Dad frowns. "Or he's given her a lot of chances and knows how giving her another chance will end."

"You're talking about Lexi's mom, Gina..."

"She wasn't her mom," he says flatly. "She gave birth to her, but she chose drugs over her. Walked away and never looked back."

"But Victoria did look back. She went to rehab and got better. If Gina had gotten better and wanted another chance, would you have given her one?"

Dad releases a harsh breath and meets my eyes. "At first, yes. I had hoped she would come around, especially when Lexi was little and I was exhausted and confused and lost as hell. I didn't think I was enough. But as the years went on and her drug addiction continued, I wished for her to die."

I gasp in shock. "What?" How could my sweet, caring father wish for anyone to die?

"If she died, it would mean she couldn't be a part of Lexi's life instead of just choosing not to be. It broke my heart that the mother of my daughter didn't want her, and I never wanted to have to tell her that."

My heart sinks. He didn't want her to die because he's cruel. He wanted to protect Lexi from having her heart broken. Because that's what a good parent does... protects their child. Which is what Chase is trying to do. So why am I pushing so hard for Victoria to see Hazel?

"I'm afraid," I admit, just as I spot Chase driving up the drive. He gets out of his vehicle and then takes Hazel out. Without stopping, he walks inside, and then a minute later, walks back out.

"I couldn't stay away," he says, leaning against the railing. "We're in this together."

I nod.

"Georgia was just about to tell me why she's afraid," Dad says, standing. "I'll leave you two to talk while I go play with my granddaughter." It warms my heart that my parents so easily accepted Hazel as part of our family. He bends over and kisses my forehead. "I love you, sweetheart."

"Afraid of what?" Chase asks once my dad has gone inside.

"I'm afraid that one day when Hazel is older, if we keep her away from her mom, she's going to ask about her and we'll have to tell her she tried to see her and we wouldn't let her, and I don't know if I can live with that. I know there's a chance she might fall off the wagon again, and if that happens then we know we tried and she made her choice. But people make mistakes and sometimes they just need another chance. I want to be able to tell Hazel that we gave Victoria the opportunity to be in her life. I want to teach her to have compassion for others and their situations, to give second chances. If that makes me naïve then so be it." I shrug. "But as you pointed out, she's your daughter and it's your choice."

Chase shakes his head. "When I said she was my daughter, it wasn't a dig at you. I just said it without thinking. When I made the decision for you to adopt her, I took that seriously. She's ours in every way that matters, and I promise you I will never imply again that she's not."

"Thank you. So where do we go from here?"

"We do it your way," he says. "We give her one more chance, but I need you to promise me if she fucks up, we're done. I don't want this to become a thing. I want to live my life with you and our daughter and whatever children we have in the future, and I don't want Victoria's shit to interfere."

"Okay," I agree. "She gets one more chance."

## CHAPTER TWENTY-SIX

### CHASE

"One chance."

"I understand." Victoria nods.

"Only supervised visits."

"Okay."

"And you will *never* get custody back."

She flinches. "I know."

"I'm only agreeing to this because my wife thinks you deserve another chance."

She looks over at Georgia. "Thank you."

Georgia nods. "Please don't make me regret it."

"I won't." She smiles softly, reminding me of a younger version of Victoria. Before the drugs took over her life. Maybe this will work out. Maybe Hazel can have all of us in her life. But the first time Victoria fucks up, she's gone. And I don't give a shit how sweet my wife is, I won't be giving in.

"We need a schedule. You can't be coming over here any time you want," I point out. "To start with, once a week. Then we can add a day or two once we see it's working out. Are you working?"

Victoria nods. "I'm working for my dad, answering the phones." She flushes, her telltale sign she's embarrassed about something. "They didn't know I gave Hazel to you," she admits.

"They had cut me out of their life when they found out I was using again."

Her parents are hardworking middle class folks. Her dad owns his own business and makes ends meet. They aren't well off by any means, but they bust their asses making an honest living.

"How did you pay for rehab?"

She flushes a deeper crimson. "Raymond and I signed a prenup. I received a settlement in the divorce."

I nod. "And where are you living?" Not that she'll be taking our daughter anywhere...

"I'm renting an apartment off Cypress."

"That's near the college." I know the area because it's in my station's zone. I'm surprised she can afford to live there on her own. She must've gotten a decent settlement in her divorce to Raymond.

"Yeah, it's in Cypress Gardens. I've applied to go to school too. I'm starting in the summer."

"That's good," Georgia says. "It sounds like you're getting your life back on track."

"I'm trying. My parents even seem to be coming around. Maybe one day they could see Hazel..."

"How about we focus on you seeing her first," I note. "Then we can consider other relatives."

As Victoria's about to respond, Hazel yells, "Mama, up!" Both women glance at the monitor.

"Georgia is Hazel's mother," I say, not giving a shit how rude I sound. "You're Victoria." Georgia's eyes go wide, and Victoria's lips curve down. "You wanted to be in her life, that's fine. But you gave up your right to being her mother. You're a friend of... Georgia's. Nothing more until we say so."

"I understand," Victoria says. "I just want to be in her life."

"Mama!" Hazel yells. "I want up!"

Georgia laughs and stands. "I'll go grab her."

When she's gone, I look at Victoria, who glances at me. "You might have Georgia fooled, but not me. Never me."

She opens her mouth then closes it like an ugly fish out of water. "Chase..."

"I hope you prove me wrong, but I'm not holding my breath."

Georgia walks out with Hazel in her arms. She looks around

and when her eyes land on Victoria, she nuzzles her face into Georgia's neck shyly.

"I'd rather not be around when you visit," I say to Victoria, standing. "So, figure out which day is good with Georgia." I kiss Georgia's forehead then Hazel's. "I need to get to work. I'll see you in the morning."

"Bye, Dada!" Hazel waves, warming my heart. I grab my keys from the counter and glance at my girls one more time before walking out the door. They're my entire life. My whole world. And if Victoria fucks with either of them... No, I take that back. *When* she fucks with either of them, I'm going to make sure she regrets ever stepping foot back into our lives.

I arrive at the station and find Alec waiting for me outside. "How'd it go?"

"She got what she wanted."

His eyes turn to slits.

"Victoria, not Georgia... Although, I guess she did too."

I walk inside and go straight to my office to check over the paperwork from the weekend. There were a couple house calls and one at the college, an electrical issue. I get started documenting everything, and am doing so when the tone sounds off. I jump to my feet to answer the call, taking down the information so we can head out. It's a single family home that caught fire while the family was out. Turns out they left the dryer running and it caught fire—something that's unfortunately common. The fire has us occupied for hours, between putting it out and doing damage control—the home is lost, but thankfully the family is safe and well.

Hours later, when we finally get back, we all shower and eat quickly, drained and ready for some shuteye. As I'm lying on my bed, Georgia texts me a picture of Hazel and her lying on the couch together, both of them in their pajamas and smiling.

**Georgia: Good night! We love you!**

**Me: Love you more.**

I trace the lines of their happy faces and fall asleep thanking God for both of them.

I WALK into the condo and it's quiet, which makes sense since it's only six in the morning. A couple of guys from shift A arrived early, so I figured I would surprise the girls with breakfast. I close the door and set the bag of food down, then head back, first stopping at Hazel's room. It's dark and she's softly snoring. She wakes up around eight every morning, which gives me a couple hours of alone time with my wife.

She's sleeping when I walk in, so I strip out of my clothes and climb into bed behind her. I nuzzle the back of her hair, inhaling her sweet scent. Fuck, I can't get enough of her. She's stopped bleeding, but we haven't had sex since she miscarried. She told me she's not sure if she wants to try again so soon, and I'm leaving it up to her, so I bought a box of condoms for when she's ready.

"Mmm... Chase?" she moans sleepily.

"Who else would it be?" I tighten my hold on her hip. "There better not be another man in this bed." It's meant as a joke, but because of my past, it falls flat.

Georgia turns over, framing my face with her delicate hands. "It will only ever be you in this bed," she says, not missing a beat.

I kiss her softly, reveling in how soft her lips are, and my hand skims down her waist, landing on her pert ass. "I missed you."

"What time is it?"

"Six"

Her eyes light up. "We have a couple hours..." She presses a kiss to the corner of my mouth. "Make love to me, Chase."

She sure as hell doesn't have to tell me twice. I waste no time removing our clothes and getting lost in her. We make love, not once, but twice. I could live inside my wife, and if it wasn't for our daughter waking up at eight o'clock on the dot and demanding breakfast, I probably would.

## CHAPTER TWENTY-SEVEN

### GEORGIA

"I have freshman orientation this morning. Could we meet up at the park afterward?" Victoria asks. We had agreed on Tuesday mornings at nine o'clock, and the last two weeks, she's shown up on time. She mentioned, depending on her school schedule, she might need to switch the days or times, so I'm not surprised when she mentions it.

"Sure, what time?"

"I should be done by one."

"It'll be hot. Why don't we meet at A Cup of Fun?" It's an indoor playground for kids between the ages of six months and six years old. Hazel loves it and when we're there and it's time to go home, she'll even throw a fit that she doesn't want to leave.

"Okay, sounds good."

We hang up and I text Lexi, asking if she wants to meet us there. She's been dying to meet Victoria, so this would be the perfect time. Plus, it'll be on neutral territory, in case my sister gets protective of me and her niece. She of course says she'll be there.

After Hazel's nap, we head out. The place has a café, so we'll get lunch there. After we arrive, get checked in, and put our socks on, Hazel takes off to the in-ground trampoline.

A few minutes later, Lexi and Abigail show up, and the girls squeal in delight, holding hands and jumping together. They're so cute together. I hope they have the close relationship Lexi and I have.

Lexi and I are taking pictures of the girls jumping when Victoria saunters through the doors.

"That's her," I mention quietly to Lexi, who glances around. I can tell when she figures out who she is because her lips quirk into a grimace.

"Did she not get the memo that this is a kids' playground?"

I look at Victoria again, noting her outfit. Unlike the last couple times we've met up and she was dressed in jeans and a simple top, today she's sporting a skintight minidress and heels.

"She just came from freshman orientation."

"Looks like she came from a strip club."

I cough to cover my laughter. "Be nice."

"Uh-huh."

"Hey!" Victoria says, super excited. "How are you?"

"Good. How was orientation?"

"I actually didn't end up going." Her face lights up. "I applied for my dream job, at LA Models, and they called me in for an interview."

"Wow, how did it go?" Chase doesn't talk a lot about her, but he did mention she used to model. I'm not sure why she quit, but that's good she's finding her passion.

"I got the job!" she shrieks.

"Congratulations!"

"Thank you." She finds Hazel, who has moved on to the pretend kitchen. "Can I go play with her?"

"Of course." When she walks away, Lexi eyes me. "What?"

"A model? I give her a month before she's back to snorting blow."

"What?" I gasp, whipping my head around. "Lexi!"

She shrugs. "Everyone knows most of the models in LA do drugs."

"Don't stereotype. It's rude."

"Whatever."

We spend the next couple hours at A Cup of Fun. The entire time I watch Victoria closely, Lexi's comment stuck in my head, but aside from her outfit being different, she's the same woman she's been the last couple weeks. She plays with Hazel with kindness and patience. We make small talk and, when the girls are wiped out and ready for their afternoon naps, head out, agreeing to discuss when to meet up next. With her new job, she has to see what her schedule will be like.

While Hazel naps, I do something I haven't done in a while—cook for the guys. After she wakes up, we drive over to the station to surprise Chase. The guys are all outside, sans shirts, washing down the trucks. They're all built and toned, and with the music blaring, they look like they're in the middle of a music video.

My eyes home in on Chase, who's glistening with sweat and water, and my lady parts tingle in anticipation. Since my period showed up a few days ago, we haven't had sex, but it's over now, and I'm most definitely going to be jumping him the first minute we're alone.

"Dada!" Hazel yells, getting his attention. His face lights up, and he drops the rag he was holding into the bucket and bends at his knees, scooping her up into his arms. It's the most beautiful sight, and I quickly snap a picture of them before grabbing the food in the containers and walking over.

"This is a surprise," he says, leaning over and kissing me.

"We brought food." I lift the containers and the guys all cheer.

"You're amazing," he murmurs into my ear, kissing the sensitive spot just underneath. Chills shoot through my body, making me visibly tremble. Chase notices and chuckles.

"I think we need a date night soon," he says, waggling his brows.

"Maybe Lexi and Alec can keep Hazel for a sleepover."

His eyes darken with lust. "Hell yes."

I giggle, shaking my head. "Watch your language."

We eat dinner with the guys, all of them fawning over Hazel the entire time, and then head to the backyard so she can play on the swing set for a little while.

"How was your day?" Chase asks.

"Good. Met Lexi and Victoria at A Cup of Fun." Knowing he hates to talk about Victoria, I don't get into the specifics.

He nods. "She doing okay?"

I'm assuming he's referring to Victoria. "Yeah."

He nods again, then walks over to Hazel to catch her coming down the slide. While he plays with her, I shoot Lexi a text, asking if she can keep Hazel tomorrow night, promising to keep Abigail one night. She texts back she'd love to and to bring Hazel over any time in the afternoon.

While I watch Chase and Hazel run around the yard, laughing and playing, I think about what it would be like to have another little one running around. Lexi and I were close growing up. We're close with Max too, but because he's several years younger, it's a little different. While Hazel has Abigail and they're close in age, I would love for her to have her own brother or sister that she's close in age with. I'm scared of losing another baby, but the one thing Chase has taught me is not to live in fear.

"What's going through your head?" Chase asks, startling me. I didn't realize he and Hazel were standing in front of me.

"I want to try again."

His eyes go wide, then his gaze drops down to my belly. "Really?"

"Do you?" He said it was up to me, but he lost a baby too.

"I would love to, as long as you're good with it."

"I am." I kiss him. "And I think we should start tomorrow night."

---

**Victoria: Can I see Hazel?**

I STARE AT MY PHONE. We agreed once a week, and she just saw her yesterday. I glance at the time. Chase is due home soon.

**Me: I can't today. Sorry.**

**Victoria: Tomorrow?**

**Me: We agreed once a week... You saw her yesterday.**

**Victoria: I'm sorry. I have to work next Tuesday. I was hoping to see her before then.**

I sigh, hating the position she's putting me in. Just as I'm about to respond, Chase texts me.

**Chase: Running late. I'll be home around five with dinner.**

**Me: Okay, I'll drop Hazel off with Lexi and meet you at home.**

**Chase: Sounds perfect.**

I switch back to my chat with Victoria. The bubbles show she's typing and a second later a text comes through.

**Victoria: Please. I really miss her.**

Because I hate confrontation, I give in.

**Me: Okay, you can come over this morning.**

**Victoria: Thank you!**

There's a knock on the door while I'm in the middle of feeding Hazel, so I get up and answer it. When I swing open the door, Victoria saunters in wearing another skimpy minidress and heels. Her hair is done, but it looks messy, like it's from last night. And her makeup is a bit smudged.

She's holding a small wrapped gift in her hand. "Morning!" she chirps a bit too loudly.

"Morning." I want to ask her if she slept in that outfit but bite my tongue.

She walks past me and straight to Hazel. "Good morning, sweet girl," she coos. "Did you miss Mommy?"

I'm stunned by her words but quickly recover. "Victoria..."

"Oops! Sorry." She bats her eyelashes at me. "It was out of habit." When her eyes meet mine, I notice they're glassy. My hackles rise. Something is wrong.

She sets the box down and lifts Hazel out of her highchair. "I got you a gift." She kisses her cheek then sets her down on the floor, handing her the box.

Hazel excitedly tears at the wrapping paper. She doesn't really know what a gift is, but she loves ripping paper apart. Losing patience, Victoria helps her rip the paper, until the box underneath is exposed.

She opens the box and inside is a... pacifier?

"This is from Tiffany's," she notes. "A platinum pacifier for my baby girl."

What the hell... "She doesn't use a pacifier," I point out, confused.

Victoria's gaze swings over to me, and for a second it looks like she was about to glare at me, but she quickly reins it in. "She did when she was with me."

I don't like her tone... at all. "That may be so, but she didn't have one when we got her, so we never gave her one."

She scoffs. "What are you saying? That you're a better parent than me?"

I flinch at how crazy she's acting. "Are you okay?"

She stands. "Of course I'm okay. And the last time I checked, you aren't my mother or my babysitter."

"No, but I am Hazel's mother, and I'm going to need you to leave."

Her face falls. "You said I could come over."

"And now I'm saying you need to leave."

I pull my phone out, ready to call the police, but thankfully, she does as I ask and walks to the door.

"I don't know what your problem is this morning, if you're jealous over my gift to Hazel, but I suggest you pull the stick out of your ass. I imagine it's painful."

And with those parting words, she walks out the door, leaving me gaping in shock. Who the hell is that woman?

Not wanting to upset Chase while he's at work, I lock the door and go about my day. I'll speak to him tonight when he gets home. Of course it'll probably ruin our night, but there's nothing I can do about that.

Hazel and I spend the day playing inside. I don't know what's going on with Victoria and the way she was acting has me all sorts of nervous. When two o'clock rolls around, Lexi sends me a text that she's going over to our parents' and will pick up Hazel on her way.

So, a couple hours later, when there's a knock on the door, I assume it's her. Only when I open it, I find Victoria, dressed in the same clothes as earlier, with her makeup running down her face.

"I'm so sorry," she cries, pushing through the door before I can stop her.

"You can't be here." I'm already grabbing my phone, ready to call nine-one-one. Something is wrong with her. It has to be drugs...or maybe she's drunk.

Hazel is finishing up her afternoon nap, so I'm thankful she won't see Victoria like this. Not that she'll remember it years from now. But I don't want her upset.

"I shouldn't have acted that way this morning," she sobs. "I'm just missing my daughter so much, and I got into a huge fight with my parents. My dad got mad when I told him I took the modeling job instead of going to school. And they didn't know about Hazel being Chase's..." Tears slide down her cheeks. "I know we agreed to supervised visitation, but if I could just bring her to their house to visit maybe they'll forgive me..."

Seeing the state of panic she's in, I don't want to upset her further. My goal at this point is to get her out of here so I can lock the door and call the police.

"I would have to ask Chase," I explain calmly. "And he's at work right now."

"Can you call him, please?" she begs. "Please."

"I can ask him tonight, but I can't call him while he's at work."

"That's such bullshit!" she yells. "I was married to him for years! I know damn well you can call him anytime." She gets in my face, and I reach for my phone, now scared.

"Okay. I'll call him."

"Thank you."

I glance down at my phone, debating whether to call Chase or the police, when the side of my face explodes in pain. My body flies backward, hitting the hard ground, and the back of my head smacks against the wall, causing me to become momentarily disoriented.

Before I can get up, a sharp object connects with my ribs—Victoria's heel. She kicks me over and over again. In the ribs. In the face. I'm trying to get up, to move away from her, but she doesn't let up. And when she finally does, and I open my eyes, she's hovering above me, her face inches from mine.

"I'm Hazel's mom, not you, bitch!" She grips my hair and lifts my head then slams it against the hard wood. Pain, like I've never felt in my life, radiates through my body. My head goes fuzzy, my brain feeling like I'm being stabbed with a million knives.

When I finally pry my eyes open, the house is quiet. Too quiet. Hazel! Oh my God, she took my baby. I grab my phone, dialing nine-one-one, as I roll over and climb into a standing position. My entire body groans in pain, but I focus on getting to my daughter's room, praying Victoria didn't do what I think she did.

The operator answers as I step into her room. Her bed is empty. She's gone.

"I need to report a kidnapping," I choke out.

I go through the details with the operator, but it's all a blur. My head is pounding, my side is in agony. I feel like I've been run over by a bus several times.

She tells me an officer will be over right away to get my statement and ask me more questions and that an Amber alert will be sent out immediately.

We're hanging up just as Lexi is walking through the door.

"What the hell happened?" she asks, setting Abigail down in Hazel's crib.

"Victoria," I sob. "She stole Hazel."

Lexi's eyes go wide. "Did you call the police?"

"Yeah. They've put out an Amber alert and an officer is on his way here." I clutch my phone in my hand. "I need to call Chase," I cry out, my body racking with sobs.

"You need to sit. I'll call him." She pulls out her phone and dials him. A few seconds later, she says, "Chase, it's Lexi. I need you to call me ASAP."

She hangs up. "I think you're going to need stitches."

"Forget about me!" I cry out. "I need to find Hazel. She said her parents wanted to see her... But I don't know where they live or what their names are. But Chase will know."

"Let me try Alec. He stayed late with Chase." She dials him on her phone and then says, "Alec, it's Lexi. Call me."

"What time is it?"

## CHAPTER TWENTY-SEVEN

"Five o'clock."

"Oh my God," I gasp. "I was out for hours. Victoria can be anywhere with Hazel. I thought..." The room around me spins, and I have to close my eyes briefly to make it stop. "I must've been knocked out."

There's a knock on the door and I rush over to answer it, ignoring the dizziness and pain. Standing at the door are two police officers.

"Please, I need your help," I tell them. "My baby was kidnapped."

# CHAPTER TWENTY-EIGHT

## CHASE

Today has been a day from hell. First, half of the guys on shift A caught the flu and are all out. Then, while helping an elderly woman put out a fire in her fireplace because she had no idea it was a real fireplace, I dropped my phone and shattered it. I should've called Georgia from one of the guys' phones to tell her, but we got a call about a car on campus that caught fire, which took hours to deal with.

Now, as I'm about to finally leave to pick up food for dinner, hours late, the tone sounds through the station. Stein, the assistant chief, who works shift C should be here by now, but he's stuck in traffic, so it looks like I'll be commanding this one. Dispatch relays the details and the station becomes a whirlwind of activity.

On the way, Alec calls my name. When I glance at him, he looks like he's seen a ghost.

"What's wrong?"

"Lexi called...Fuck! I had my phone on silent, and we were so fucking busy."

"What's. Fucking. Wrong?"

"Victoria stole Hazel. They're both missing."

And just like that, my entire world implodes. "Where's Georgia?"

"At the hospital. Victoria beat the shit out of her and she's getting stitches."

Fuck. Fuck. Fuck!

"They have an alert out for Victoria and Hazel. Lexi doesn't know anything else."

When we arrive on the scene, a clusterfuck of activity is swarming the front of the building. I want to leave to go look for my daughter, find out what the fuck is going on, but a portion of the building is fully engulfed in flames. I can't just walk away.

My eyes find the name of the complex and it sounds so damn familiar... Cypress Gardens... Where the fuck have I heard that name before?

And then it hits me. Victoria said she lived here... Fuck! This can't be happening.

As the guys and I jump out of the engine, we scan the scene, assessing the situation. Since I'm the Battalion chief, it's my job to command. But as I watch half the building go up in flames, there's no way in hell I'm standing out here on the sidelines.

"Hey, Rich!" I yell, as I charge to the back of the rig, grabbing gear and throwing it on.

"Chief," he calls back, looking shocked to see me gearing up. "What's going on?" There's protocol, a way shit gets handled, and by me going in, I'm breaking it. But I don't give a fuck. If that bitch has my daughter in that building, I'm going to find her or die trying.

"I need you to command!" I toss the radio at him.

"What the fuck are you doing?" Alec yells.

"I'm going in! Victoria lives in this building."

Alec curses under his breath. "All right, let's go. You're with me."

Reaching back, I turn on the air on my tank and pull my mask on. Thankfully, it's only a three-story building, and the fire appears to be contained to the east side. I send up a silent prayer that Victoria and Hazel aren't here, and if they are, they aren't on this side.

"Chase, you there?" Rich says over the radio.

"Yeah."

"The fire started in apartment 257. It's leased to a Victoria Burke."

"Fuck," Alec curses at the same time I do.

It's her damn apartment.

Taking my Halligan in my hand, I jam it into the doorframe of apartment 257 and pry the door open. When we break through into the apartment, the fire is out of control, thick clouds of smoke curling up toward the ceiling. Thomas and Carter work the pipe to knock down the flames, while Alec and I search the place.

With a thermal image camera in hand, I hold it up, scanning the darkness for any movement. The second I step foot into the master bedroom, my body goes numb. Victoria. She's lying on the bed, her arm draped off the side with a needle sticking out of her vein.

Rushing over to her, I try to shake her awake. Nothing. She's out, whether it's from smoke inhalation or from the drugs, I don't know.

I glance around for Hazel but don't see her anywhere.

Lifting Victoria into my arms, I radio down to command that I'm bringing her out. In the hall, I hand her over to Carter. "Take her!"

The second I go back in, the smoke is thicker, and the roaring of nearby flames can be heard over the piercing alarms. Dropping to my hands and knees, I search for my daughter, desperately throwing shit everywhere. She's not in the master bedroom or bathroom, so I move on to the rest of the apartment. I hear Alec yelling clear throughout the place, but I refuse to take his word for it. I need to see for myself she isn't here. The flames are licking the walls, the ceiling boiling and close to caving, and I know my time is limited. There's no way anyone, let alone a baby, would survive in this heat, in this smoke.

The call comes over the radio. "Command to all units. Evacuate the building. I repeat, all units, evacuate."

"Chase!" Alec calls out, struggling to get a line on the flames. "They ordered evacuation."

"Hazel is in here somewhere. I need to find her."

"The place is clear!" he yells back. "If she were here, we would've picked it up on the camera. We gotta go."

"I need to find her!" I go through a door I haven't gone through yet and find what was the nursery, fire rooted in every corner. Ignoring the command to evacuate desperately coming through the radio, I enter the room, crawling on my hands and knees with the camera in my hand.

Sweat pools inside my mask, the hiss of the tank and my heartbeat the only sounds. Fuck! This can't be happening. She has to be here somewhere. I check the guest bathroom again, then move on to the kitchen. Alec has cleared it, but I need to see it with my own eyes. And that's when I see it... One of Hazel's shoes. Georgia bought them for her last week because her feet had outgrown the old ones. I grab it to make sure I'm not seeing shit, but I'm not. It's half melted, but I know it's her shoe.

On my hands and knees, I search the other rooms for a third time. I'm crawling down the hallway when Alec yells, "We have to get out now! We've searched every part of this place and she's not here."

"She has to be!" I choke out. "She has to be."

His sad eyes meet mine. "Chase..." He can't finish his sentence, but I know what he's thinking. If she's here, there's no way she's still alive.

Command radios in that the fire's made its way to the boiler room, and Alec glances at me.

"Get out of here!" I bark, but he doesn't move. "I mean it! Go!"

With forty pounds of gear on me, sweat clings to my body. It's hard to breathe, hard to move. My hands and knees are burning with the boiling water beneath me.

I don't care about any of that, though. My daughter has to be somewhere in this fucking place. I refuse to believe she's dead. Alec is wrong. I'm going to find her and save her. As he reluctantly exits the apartment, I head toward the nursery again. Maybe she's hiding somewhere. She loves to play hide and seek. What if she's somewhere scared, waiting for me to find her.

A loud explosion shakes the building, stopping me in my tracks. I have to get out now if I want to make it out alive. For a brief moment, as I glance around, I consider staying. Is my life even worth living without my daughter?

"Chase!" Alec yells, shocking the hell out of me. "Let's go! I'm not leaving without you." He grabs me by my tank and yanks me out the door and down the stairs. When we make it far enough away, my feet give out. I drop to the ground and watch as the entire building explodes like fireworks on the Fourth of July.

A second and third engine pull up, working the fire together, but I can't move from my place. I can't stop watching my life go up in flames. And I don't budge until Rich says, "The EMTs called."

Ripping my mask off, I whip my head around, praying someone found my daughter. "Hazel?"

He shakes his head. "Victoria died on the way to the hospital. They don't know the cause of death yet."

I nod and stand. I know what it is. Overdose. She died doing the only thing she loves, the thing she put above everyone in her life, and she took my daughter with her.

"Maybe she wasn't in there," Alec says.

I hold up the shoe I was clutching in my glove and remove my tank. "She was there," I choke out. "This was her shoe."

Alec's face falls. "Fuck, man."

"I gotta go."

"Go," he says. "We'll handle this…"

I don't hear anything else he says. My head is fucking numb. I strip out of my gear, leaving it on the rig, and then start walking. I have no phone, no car, so I have no other choice.

I end up at the hospital. The nurse at the front desk glances at me with wide eyes. I'm sure I look a mess, but I don't give a shit.

I give her Georgia's name and she directs me to her room. When I walk in, she's in tears, crying into her phone. "Please, I just need an update. I—"

When her eyes land on me, her words come to an abrupt halt, before she speaks. "The police located Victoria's parents. She showed up with Hazel, but they got into an argument and she left. They haven't seen her or Hazel since. The police are searching for her, and I was asking them for an update—"

"I have an update," I say flatly, cutting her off.

"You found her?" Her tear-stained face brightens.

I hand her the half melted shoe and her face drops. "Chase…"

"She's dead."

Her head snaps up. "What? Who? How?"

"Hazel… and Victoria. They were in a fire. It hasn't been confirmed yet, but Victoria overdosed, and I couldn't find Hazel's body. I was too late. She's gone."

Georgia gasps. "No." She shakes her head, and it's then I notice she has bruises and cuts all over her face. Stitches above her brow. I should ask her if she's okay, but I don't have it in me to care.

"Yes," I bark out, my grief quickly morphing into anger. "She's dead! Because you, with your rose-fucking-colored glasses refuse to see the world for what it is! Fucked up!"

She flinches. "Chase, I'm..." She breaks into sobs. "I didn't mean—"

"Of course you didn't mean for this to happen. Because you never could've imagined it turning bad because you have no clue about how ugly this fucking world is!" I swipe the tray by her bed, the contents flying all over the place.

"Enough!" a deep voice barks from behind me. Tristan, Georgia's dad, walks inside. "I get you're hurting, but so is she."

"Good!" I bark. "She should be hurting because she caused this." I point my finger at Georgia. "I will never forgive you for this."

Fresh tears fill her eyes, and they're the last thing I see before I walk out of the room and out of Georgia's life. I should've known this would all end badly. She's too good, too sweet, too fucking innocent and naïve. She just doesn't understand how the real world works. How drug addicts like Victoria work. She wants to see the good in everyone and everything, but that's her reality, not mine. In my world, good doesn't exist.

When I get home, I stumble through the door. Robotically, I shower, and once I'm dressed, having no idea where to go from here, I end up in Hazel's room, sitting in her rocking chair and holding her stuffed animal.

I bring it to my nose, inhaling her scent, and then I fucking lose it. In a blink of an eye, I've lost my entire world.

# CHAPTER TWENTY-NINE

## GEORGIA

I can't stop crying. The tears won't stop falling. My body hurts so damn badly. But my heart...my heart has been destroyed. It's all my fault. I wanted to believe the good in her, and in the end, my naivety got Hazel killed. I should've listened to Chase. But I was so hell-bent on wanting to do the right thing, be a good person. I wanted Victoria to have the chance Lexi's mom never got. I didn't want Hazel to one day have to be told that we refused to let her mom see her.

And because of all that, she's dead. She died in a fire by herself. She was probably scared, calling out for us, and I failed her.

"Georgia, I know you're hurting, but you have to calm down," Mom says. "The doctor is going to admit you."

"I'm trying," I cry out, hiccuping through my sobs. "It just... hurts. I never meant for this to happen and now she's gone." I clutch my hands to my chest, wishing for God to take me instead of her.

"I know, sweetheart," Mom coos. "I know." She runs her fingers through my hair, but it does nothing to soothe me. Chase was right. This is all my fault. And nothing I do will make it right. We lost the most precious little girl today because of me.

A couple hours later, the doctor discharges me and I go to the police station to make my statement to get it over with. I can barely hold it together when I recount what happened. They inform me what Chase has already told me, that Victoria died from a drug overdose. As of now, Hazel's body hasn't been found, and until forensics can get in there and investigate, it will remain an open case.

Not wanting to go home and upset Chase further, I instead go to my parents' place. Exhausted and heartbroken, I lie in my childhood bed and, with the help of the prescription the doctor gave me, I fall into a fitful slumber, wishing when I wake up this all will be a horrible nightmare.

## CHAPTER THIRTY

### CHASE

*K*NOCK, *knock, knock.*

I wake up to the sound of someone banging on the door. I glance around, finding myself sitting in the rocking chair in Hazel's room and everything from yesterday hits me all over again.

Victoria beating up Georgia and stealing Hazel.

Victoria overdosing.

The apartment catching fire.

Hazel dying in the fire.

I consider closing my eyes, not wanting to deal with my new reality, one where I have to somehow move forward without my daughter in my life, but whoever is knocking on the door won't stop. I rise to my feet and drag myself to the front door.

When I open it, standing in front of me are two police officers. I know both of them from working as a firefighter. Have been on calls with them several times. "We were given your number from Alec at the station. We tried to call you."

"My phone is broken."

He nods. "We have someone that belongs to you." He steps to the side, exposing the other officer, who's holding my world in his arms.

My heart clenches in my chest, and for a second I wonder if

I'm going to have a heart attack. It's actually difficult to take in oxygen.

Please don't let this be a dream. It would be the cruelest of cruel dreams.

"Dada!" Hazel squeals, and I release a harsh breath. Her voice, the best sound in the world. A sound I didn't think I would ever hear again.

She wriggles in the officer's arms, reaching out for me to grab her. She's dressed in an overall dress with a pink and white striped shirt underneath. On her feet are pink striped socks and one shoe.

One fucking shoe.

Grabbing her from the officer, I pull her tight into my arms, burying my face in her neck. She shrieks in delight and the sound damn near brings me to my knees.

"She's alive," I breathe through a choked sob. "You're alive."

"She was turned in this morning. A gentleman by the name of Raymond Forrester said he showed up at Victoria Burke's home yesterday to speak with her. He walked in on her doing drugs and barely awake, so he took the child. When he returned this morning and found the building was burned down, he brought her to the station."

I close my eyes, tightening my hold on my daughter. "Please thank him for me," I choke out. Had he not taken her, she might not still be alive.

"Will do."

I close the door behind me and sink onto the ground, refusing to let go of my daughter. She's alive. She's living and breathing and giggling because she has no idea how close she came to having her life taken from her. She's happy and oblivious, the way a baby should be.

"Mama?" she coos, trying to get out of my hold. "Mama!" she yells.

Fuck, Georgia. She doesn't know Hazel is alive.

Thoughts of yesterday come back to me.

She was in the hospital, in bad shape, and I yelled at her, blamed her. She was at her lowest, we both were, and instead of holding her and comforting her, I kicked her while she was down. Fuck. I was so upset, but that doesn't excuse the way I behaved. I never should've said the shit I said.

# CHAPTER THIRTY

I stand, scooping my daughter into my arms, and grab my keys. I have no phone, so I can't call her. I'll have to drive over to her parents' place and see if she's there. Unless... Did she come home last night?

No, she would've heard the knock. Just to be sure, I check out the room and then the guest room. She's not in either one. Feeling Hazel's wet diaper, I quickly change it, then put her in clean clothes.

A few minutes later, we arrive at her parents' house. Her truck was still at the apartment, so someone must've driven her to the hospital. I knock on the door and Charlie answers. The second she sees Hazel in my arms, she breaks down into tears, pulling us both into her arms for a hug.

"Oh, thank God." She holds us for several seconds before letting us go. "Is she okay?" She runs her hands down Hazel's arms and legs, checking for herself. Of course, Hazel giggles, thinking she's tickling her.

"She's okay. Victoria's ex-husband found her and took her before the place caught fire. She was never near the fire."

"Hey, Mom, I think—" Georgia's words ring out and then stop. Our eyes meet, and I note how bad she looks. Her eyes are all puffy, and not just from crying, from being beat on by Victoria. Her lip is swollen and her cheek is bruised. Victoria didn't just steal Hazel, she assaulted Georgia.

A loud gasp echoes in the quiet house and tears slide down her cheeks. She moves to come closer but then stops. "She's alive," she whispers.

I nod. "She's alive."

A sob racks through her body, as she shakes her head. "Thank God."

"Mama!" Hazel yells, reaching out for Georgia, completely unaware of what's going on. When Georgia makes no move to come over and grab her, I step forward. Only she steps back.

"Georgia... Do you want to hold her?"

She shakes her head. "No."

Charlie sighs. "Georgia, honey..."

"I'm so glad she's alive," Georgia says, her voice shaky with emotion. "I—" She chokes on her sob. "I prayed for this all to be a nightmare..."

"I did too," I admit. "I'm so sorry about what I said. How I—"

"Stop," she says flatly, cutting me off. "You have nothing to apologize for. You trusted me with your daughter and I nearly got her killed."

The way she speaks, her tone devoid of all emotion, sends a chill up my spine. And then it hits me, she said my daughter. As if she isn't Georgia's as well. "I shouldn't have said—"

She cuts me off again. "Yes, you should've because you were right. I *am* naïve and gullible. You trusted me with your daughter and I let you both down."

She can't be saying what I think she's saying.

"I think it's best if you go," she whispers. "I'm going to stay here until I find a place of my own."

No. No. No, no, no. "Please don't do this," I blurt out, stepping toward her. She immediately steps back. "I was upset...I thought she had died and I lashed out. I didn't mean what I said... Hell, I don't even remember what I said." Unfortunately, that's the truth. I was so far gone, I couldn't even recall all that I said to her.

"It doesn't matter what you said. I'm not fit to raise a baby. My only job was to protect her and I failed. You both are better off without me." She glances at Hazel, longing in her eyes. I know she wants to hold her and kiss her and feel her warm flesh and beating heartbeat, but she's resisting because she blames herself. Because I blamed her. When we got married, I vowed to stand by her side, and when shit got rough, I turned on her.

And now she doesn't think she deserves to be Hazel's mom.

I have to fix this. Right now. I did this. And it's up to me to make it right.

Without giving her time to retreat, I cut across the room with Hazel still in my arms, backing Georgia into a corner. Hazel reaches for Georgia and she flinches.

"Chase, stop, please. You need to leave."

"No, you need to hold your daughter." I thrust Hazel at Georgia, not giving her a chance to refuse.

Not wanting her to fall, Georgia grabs Hazel, who clasps on to Georgia, excited to be in her arms.

"You can be mad at me all you want, I deserve it. But this little girl is your daughter. I was wrong for the way I reacted. Your innocence, how you see the world, is what I love about you. It means you haven't experienced the shitty parts of life, and I hope Hazel grows up with the same outlook on life as her mother."

She glances up at me with glassy eyes.

"I hope she grows up to be just like you. You're her mother in every way that counts and regardless of what happens between us, you will always be her mother. You trusted Victoria because it's who you are. You're trusting and good. Life hasn't hardened you yet, and I hope it never does."

"My good almost got Hazel killed," she murmurs, choking on a sob. Fresh tears spill down her cheeks, breaking my heart.

"I should've paid more attention. I knew the way Victoria was and I pawned the entire ordeal off on you. I knew she would fuck up, and to prove a point, I made you handle it all on your own. I should've been your partner. I'm your husband. If what happened to Hazel is anyone's fault, it's mine, because I knew what Victoria was capable of and I did nothing to stop the train wreck."

Georgia shakes her head. "If I hadn't gotten involved, none of this would've happened."

I step closer to her and run my knuckles down her cheek, wiping her tears away. "You don't know that. She still could've come after Hazel. When someone is on drugs, you can't predict what they're capable of." I wipe a falling tear from under her eye. "I know it's going to take time for you to forgive me for what I said, but I'm asking you to please come home with Hazel and me. I love you and I'm so damn sorry. I'm a jaded asshole, and I need you in my life to help me see the world with softer eyes."

She closes her eyes, and I fear she's going to push me away, but instead she moves forward and into my arms. Hazel giggles, being caught in the middle. I wrap my arms around my entire world. "I'm so sorry, baby," I murmur into her ear. "I'm so fucking sorry."

"No more apologizing," she says, resting her head against my chest. "I forgive you."

Of course she does. Because Georgia is good and pure. She's the perfect in this crazy, fucked up, imperfect world. I don't deserve her, but there's no way in hell I'm ever letting her go.

## CHAPTER THIRTY-ONE

### GEORGIA

SHE'S ALIVE. My sweet little girl is alive. When Chase showed up with her, I thought it was some sort of sick dream, but it wasn't. We came so damn close to losing her, but we didn't. At first, I was scared to hold her. After the situation I put her in, I didn't feel like I deserved to. But then he thrust her into my arms and I knew regardless of how I felt, I would never let her go again.

When Chase apologized for the things he said, I had two choices: either hold a grudge or forgive him. Some would choose the former, but I could see the sincerity and apology in his face, in his words, and so I chose the latter. Life is too short and I refuse to live it with a chip on my shoulder. Chase and Hazel are my world and I don't want to be without either of them.

After eating breakfast at my parents' place—where Lexi, Alec, and Abigail joined the second I called and told Lexi that Hazel was alive—we head home. It's odd walking through the door. It's been less than twenty-four hours, but it feels like so much has changed in those hours. While Chase lays Hazel down for her nap, I glance in the living room, where Victoria attacked me, and a shiver runs up my spine.

"You okay?" Chase asks, when he comes out of Hazel's room and finds me still standing here.

"Yeah, I just can't believe what happened. That Victoria is

dead and we almost lost Hazel... I could tell something was wrong with her. She was acting weird, like one minute she was on top of the world, telling me about how she's modeling and giving Hazel an expensive gift, and the next she was in tears. I was trying to call for help when she attacked me. I know you'll probably think I'm stupid saying this, but I wish I could've gotten help in time."

Chase smiles sadly. "I don't think it's stupid. I wouldn't expect anything less from you, butterfly. When I found her, she was passed out with a needle in her arm. She had a problem with drugs and nobody could help her but herself. And if she was modeling again, it all makes sense. For Victoria, modeling and drugs go hand in hand."

"Her parents said she got into a huge fight with them. They could tell she showed up high and they kicked her out. They apologized profusely for not forcing her to give up Hazel."

Chase sighs. "When I was searching for Hazel, I found a nursery in her apartment. I think she came here with the intent to take her. Drugs make people think they're invincible and do shit they normally wouldn't do."

He pulls me into his arms. "I know you said no more apologizing, but I need you to know how sorry I am. I fucked up big time and I'm going to spend every damn day making it up to you."

I shake my head. "That's not what I want. Everyone at one time or another says the wrong thing or handles a situation badly. Nobody's perfect." I stand on my tiptoes and kiss the corner of his mouth. "I love you, and all I want is to spend our lives together."

"Jesus, Georgia," Chase growls, lifting me into his arms. "You never cease to amaze me."

I screech, quickly covering my mouth so I don't wake up Hazel. "What are you doing?"

"I'm taking you to our room so I can make love to you." He drops me onto the center of the bed, then starts removing his clothes. When his boxers come down, his dick springs free, making both my mouth water and my thighs clench. It's been too long since he's been inside me.

He climbs up the bed and removes my shorts and underwear, then crawls up my body, pressing his mouth to mine in a searing kiss. "I need to be inside you," he murmurs against my mouth. "I need to feel your tight warmth wrapped around my dick."

His shaft pushes against the inside of my thigh and I assume he's going to thrust inside me, but instead he reaches over and grabs a toy out of the drawer. It's the anal vibrator.

"Lift up." He taps the side of my hip and I do as he says. He slides a pillow under my butt, then places my legs on either side of his shoulders. I'm completely open and exposed like this, but I'm too turned on to care.

His tongue lands on my hole, and I jump in shock. He chuckles, but doesn't stop licking the tight ring. He licks upward, from my ass to clit several times, each time slower, more controlled, and just when I think I'm going to come, he stops.

"Not yet, butterfly." He grabs the lube and squirts a little onto the vibrator, then slowly pushes it into me. Once it's inside, he turns it on, and I damn near come.

"Chase," I groan. "I need you in me. Now."

After making sure the vibrator is fully in, he crawls back up my body, settling between my legs, and enters me in one fluid motion. I'm so wet, he slides right in, both of us moaning at how good it feels. He stills for a second, so I can adjust to him, and then he begins moving in and out of me. His arms cage me in, and our bodies connect in the most intimate way. His mouth devours mine as if I'm his lifeline. As if he needs me to breathe, to survive. And I feel the same way. What we went through, it was eye-opening, a reminder of how uncertain life is. I spent so much of my life tucked away in my shell, but now all I want to do is live.

Between the vibrator and him, the ascent to my climax is swift, hitting me hard, and taking Chase with me over the edge. He pulls back, his beautiful hazel eyes locking with mine. They're filled with love and happiness. Butterflies attack my chest.

My path might not be perfect.

Our life might not be perfect.

But our love is.

# EPILOGUE

## GEORGIA

*Five Years Later*

"Fuck, you're so tight," Chase groans, gripping my hair and pulling it, as he thrusts into my ass from behind.

"Harder," I moan, nuzzling my face into my pillow while massaging my clit. The house is filled with people, but I'm horny and couldn't help myself. "Please, Chase," I beg, "harder."

Just because I'm six months pregnant doesn't mean I'm fragile. I like to be fucked and hard. And he knows that.

Thankfully, he listens, and within seconds, my orgasm rips through me. He pulls out, coming all over my ass, and I sigh in satisfaction.

"I never thought I would say this," he says out of breath, "but I think this pregnancy needs to be your last." This makes me laugh.

"I'm serious." He grabs his shirt from the floor and wipes the cum off me. "I'm getting old and can't keep up with you. I'm not sure it's normal to be this horny while you're pregnant."

I sit up, scooting off the bed, so I can get cleaned up properly. "So, what you're saying is, I need to find a younger, more—"

"Don't even think about finishing that sentence," Chase growls, pulling me into his arms. We're both naked and sweaty, and when our bodies glide against each other, my girly parts clench in need.

*Knock. Knock. Knock.*

We both freeze.

The doorknob jiggles, and I pray to the parent gods Chase locked the door because I know I didn't.

"Mom! Why is the door locked?" Hazel yells.

"Oh, thank God," I mutter, making Chase laugh.

"Mommy! I'm hungry!" Eva shouts.

"Me too!" Hazel agrees. "We want pancakes."

I roll my eyes. "Why are both of our kids calling for me and not you?"

Chase laughs. "Because we all agree you're the cook in the family."

"We'll be right out," we yell at the same time, making us both snort out a laugh.

We take a quick shower—despite me begging him for sex—and after we're dressed, head downstairs.

"About time," my dad grumbles. "You guys spend more time in your room than with us."

Chase raises his palms in a placating manner. "That's all your daughter. She's horn—"

I elbow him, making him grunt and stop talking. "Where's Mom?"

We're all staying at their house in Breckenridge for the holidays, and even though it's huge, with enough rooms for all of our families, I'm thinking it's time we get our own place.

"She's sitting on the porch having coffee with your sister and Micaela."

"Ooh! I think I'll join them."

"Mom, wait," Hazel says, her cute little hazel eyes pleading. At six years old, she looks so much like her father. She has Victoria's black hair, but her features are all Chase. "Grandpa said we have to eat cereal." Her button nose scrunches up.

My dad laughs. "There's nothing wrong with cereal. Your mother grew up on it and she survived."

Eva scoffs, her emerald green eyes that match mine glaring at my dad with her four-year-old going on fourteen attitude.

"Mommy makes us pancakes and if we're good, she puts chocolate chips and bananas in them."

"Yeah," Abigail says, joining in. "And they're so good."

"The best," Dustin, my cousin Micaela's son, agrees.

"They are," Chase adds. "Especially when she adds peanut butter chips to them."

"Did someone say peanut butter?" Lexi asks, walking into the room. Her hand goes to her protruding belly. At seven months pregnant, she's due four weeks before me. "I love peanut butter."

"Ewww." Micaela gags, waddling into the room. "No peanut butter. It makes me sick." She's due only a week after Lexi.

Ryan groans. "I can't handle this shit. Whose idea was it to let all of our wives get pregnant at the same time?"

Bella, Micaela's mom, laughs. "I think it's adorable. They'll grow up and be close just like Micaela, Lexi, and Georgia are." She glances at my dad. "Just like we were."

Chase encircles me from behind, planting a kiss on my cheek. "I'll make the pancakes. You go sit and drink your coffee."

Mason coughs, "Get a room."

"Good idea!" I grab Chase's hand, tugging him down the hall.

"Butterfly," he groans. "You can't just use me like this. I need sustenance."

"I'm hungry," several of the kids whine.

"I can make the pancakes," Lexi says.

"No!" everyone yells.

**The End.**

## ABOUT THE AUTHOR

*Reading is like breathing in, writing is like breathing out. – Pam Allyn*

Nikki Ash resides in South Florida where she is an English teacher by day and a writer by night. When she's not writing, you can find her with a book in her hand. From the Boxcar Children, to Wuthering Heights, to the latest single parent romance, she has lived and breathed every type of book. While reading and writing are her passions, her two children are her entire world. You can probably find them at a Disney park before you would find them at home on the weekends!